The
Complete
Horse Mistress
Collection

R. A. Steffan

THE HORSE MISTRESS:
BOOK 1

ONE

"Carivel! Where are you, boy? Come here at once!"

The voice of Jorun, the old Horse Master, was gruff and impatient as it rang out across the dusty horse pens. I looked up from the section of fence I was mending, quickly locating the short figure striding toward me with his distinctive, bow-legged gait.

"Here, Horse Master," I called in reply. I gathered up my tools and placed them safely outside the fence so the animals wouldn't step on them, before hurrying across to meet him halfway.

"Aren't you done with those repairs yet?" Jorun asked, his piercing, deep-set eyes raking over me from within his weathered face.

"Almost, sir," I said.

"Quick as you can, then. I want you to watch over that buckskin mare of Volya's tonight. She's finally ready to foal."

I nodded my understanding. Volya's favorite mare had delivered a creamy white colt last year—a rare prize indeed. The village chief had high hopes that she would throw a matching foal this year, so he could have a white chariot team the envy of every warrior for miles around. Mares were generally left to give birth on their own whilst out with the herd, but for this particular foal nothing would be left to chance.

"Of course, Horse Master," I said. "I'll finish up here and be back at dusk."

"Good, good," said Jorun. "Mind you eat something first, lad. Being hungry is one thing. Being tired is another. Being hungry and tired at the same time will have you falling asleep before the moon finishes rising."

"I'll get something from Gretya, sir. Thank you."

"See that you do." Jorun patted my shoulder firmly with a gnarled hand. "Maybe someday you'll actually get some meat on those bones."

I resolutely held in the sigh that wanted to escape — I wasn't *that* skinny. *Honestly.* I might not be tall or broad-shouldered, but I was certainly more than strong enough to do my job as Jorun's apprentice. However, that didn't seem to stop the man from fussing as though he were my father and not my master.

After mumbling some vague words of agreement, I returned to the final section of fence. One of the rails was rotting where it attached to the post, so I pried it free and replaced it with a new one, pausing to shoo away a curious yearling that wandered up to sniff at my close-cropped hair. Job done, I tidied everything up, wheeling the debris away in a rickety wooden pushcart.

The pens were located a short distance beyond the edges of the main part of the settlement, so that the flies and the smell of manure would not be a nuisance to the residents. The sun was already getting low in the sky when I returned to the center of the village and entered Gretya's cookhouse. The thatched, circular structure was generally a hub of activity in the evenings, and today was no exception. The late spring weather was pleasant; several men and boys were already lounging on the benches scattered around the outside of the building with their bowls of hearty stew, while Gretya's daughters flitted back and forth between the tables, filling tankards.

Gretya was a widow, and made a living serving food to those who were unable or unwilling to cook for themselves, for whatever reason. I couldn't afford to eat meals here very often with my meager apprentice's pay, but every once in a while I had reason to appreciate the availability of her hearty fare. Tonight was definitely one of those nights, since I would soon need to return to the horse pens for my watch.

"Hello, Carivel, dear," said the old woman, giving me a gap-toothed smile as she ladled meat and vegetables into a bowl. The rich aroma made my stomach rumble, causing her smile to widen. "I don't see you nearly often enough, you know. You're looking well these days."

I gave her an answering smile of my own. "Hello, Gretya. If you can convince Jorun to double my pay, I promise I'll darken your doorstep every day of the week. My own cooking always tastes like I forgot to add the salt, even when I didn't."

"Ah, you poor lad. I'll have a quiet word with the old miser one day soon and see what can be done," she said with a wink.

I laughed softly before thanking her and taking my leave. The village gossips all swore blind that Gretya was Jorun's mistress, an idea that she playfully encouraged, but which had never to my knowledge been proven one way or the other. On those rare occasions when someone was foolish enough to bring up the question within Jorun's hearing, they were treated to a stony glare and an even stonier silence. Personally, I was firmly in the "yes" camp—I found something appealing about the idea of the grizzled old grouch secretly doting on such a sweet, motherly figure.

With a quick glance around the yard outside the cookhouse, I identified several of the other boys who helped with the horses chatting amiably among themselves. More interestingly, Senovo was deep in conversation with one of the village elders on the farthest bench, his partially shaved head and the dun-colored robes of a novice priest distinctive in the early evening light. His smooth, handsome face was grim.

I dithered for a moment over asking to join them before losing my nerve and moving to a table several feet away from the pair, but still close enough that I could hear them talking.

Coward, I berated myself.

"Volya won't give in to some tin-plated Alyrion field marshal who thinks he can come in with a pack of soldiers and trample our way of life," the older man was saying. "He'll send them back where they came from with an earful."

"I do hope you're right," Senovo said mildly. "However, I fear it may not be quite that simple."

Volya, the chief of the village, had ridden out four days ago with a small party of warriors, replying to a summons from an Alyrion commander—newly arrived from the mainland—who demanded a parlay. Eburos was an island rich in resources, but it had only really gained the attention of the powerful Alyrion Empire within the last year or two. It probably helped that Eburos was protected by the sea on all sides, but it seemed that the lure of our fertile soil and productive mines had finally overcome the emperor's reluctance to send troops across the water.

Now, the collection of small, disorganized tribes and villages that called the island home found themselves facing a powerful foe. Some tribes in the south had already capitulated without even attempting to muster a defense, but as the

Alyrions moved north into areas like Draebard, they would quickly discover that not all Eburosi were so accommodating.

"I understand Volya took Andoc with him," said the elder, causing my ears to perk up even further at the mention of Senovo's close friend. "He thinks a lot of that young man, you know. Wouldn't surprise me if the Chief was grooming him as a replacement, what with Volya losing his only son last year."

"Andoc has many enviable qualities... for a warrior," Senovo replied, a wry note entering his voice. "However, I'm not certain that the patience required for leadership is among them."

I hid my derisive snort; the man across from Senovo didn't bother hiding his. Everyone in the village knew that the young priest and Andoc were virtually inseparable. Their mutual regard appeared to know no bounds despite their tendency to tease and belittle each other at every opportunity. And oh, how I envied them that easy camaraderie—the close bond between two people that I would never, ever be able to have. Instead, I was reduced to watching them both with secretive, longing glances... daydreaming about their perfect features... about Senovo's voice like melting honey, Andoc's broad shoulders and strong arms.

My wistful thoughts—not to mention my eavesdropping—were interrupted by the arrival of Gretya's youngest daughter with a pitcher of ale.

"Hello, Limdya," I said politely, forcing down a wince as she blushed and smiled at me with sparkling eyes.

"Hello, Carivel!" she replied. "Some of the others are saying that Volya's mare might have another white foal tonight. Is that true?"

"Yes, it's true. The Horse Master ordered me to keep watch over her, so he must think the foal is finally coming." I hoped that would be the end of it, but of course it wasn't.

"How exciting!" she said. "I wish I could see a new foal being born. Maybe I could come out and watch with you later?"

"I'm sorry, Limdya," I said with as much regret as I could muster. "But you know women aren't allowed to help with the horses. It's bad luck, and the gods might retaliate by making the foal stillborn."

The words seemed to stick in my throat, but at least they did the job even if they made me feel queasy. Limdya's face fell in disappointment.

"Oh. Well, I wouldn't want to risk that, of course. Perhaps you could come over to the house tomorrow morning and I'll cook breakfast for you? You could tell me all about it then. My cooking is almost as good as Mother's, you know," she added hopefully.

The queasy feeling continued to grow despite the excellent stew I'd been eating. "I'm afraid all I'll be interested in tomorrow morning is a few hours' sleep, Limdya. Perhaps another time."

The sparkle was completely gone from the girl's eyes, and she seemed to slump in on herself slightly. "Yes," she said. "Another time."

"Don't take it so personal, love," called one of the boys from the other bench. It was Dalon, of course… always a thorn in my side. "Carivel here, he never looks twice at any of the girls. Thinks himself above all of you — too good for the likes of a village lass."

"That's not true," I said quietly, trying to catch Limdya's eyes as the others at the table laughed. She wouldn't meet my gaze, and my stomach churned harder.

"He saves his lingering looks for Andoc," Dalon carried on. "He'd probably rather be taken like a maiden by a big, strong warrior than be the one doing the taking."

Oh, the irony. If he only knew.

"Who knows," said one of the others. "Andoc might even go for it. He likes eunuchs well enough, and our Carivel looks sort of like a eunuch with his smooth face and narrow shoulders. Don't you think so, Limdya?"

"Very funny, you two," I said. "You know perfectly well that I had a girl in my old village. She died of a fever, and I still miss her too much to even think about being with another woman."

The old story — the old lie — came as easily as ever. There was a bit of quiet guffawing from Dalon's table, but at least Limdya's expression transformed into one of sympathy rather than hurt before she left quietly to serve the other patrons. A cool hand closed on my shoulder a moment later, startling me. I looked up sharply at the figure behind me.

Senovo. My heart sped up.

"A very noble sentiment, Carivel," said the novice priest, and the boys at the other table suddenly found a great deal of interest in their bowls of food. "Surely, though, your lost love would not want you to be alone forever."

I forced myself to meet Senovo's green-gold eyes. To speak calmly, as if my heart were not fluttering against my ribcage like a trapped bird. "Perhaps not."

He held my gaze for a long moment, and arched one dark eyebrow. "Ah well," he said. "You are still young, after all. Barely even a man. There's plenty of time."

In truth, I was roughly the same age as Senovo. The same age as Andoc. As for the rest of it, though…

"I should get ready for my watch tonight," I said.

"Of course. May the gods smile on your endeavors," Senovo said. The hand that had been resting on my shoulder moved to touch my forehead in a brief blessing before he smiled and moved away. My skin tingled where his fingers had brushed against me.

As I rose and tidied away my half-finished bowl, I caught Dalon smirking at me out of the corner of my eye.

⋙ ♕ ⋘

In the privacy and safety of my tiny, ramshackle hut, I took a few minutes to flop down on the straw mattress in the corner and just breathe. I had maintained my secret—my ruse—for almost three years now. I wouldn't slip up now, just because Senovo was kind to me and smiled down at me with lazy green eyes.

Though it's not unheard of for a man to lie with a beautiful eunuch, said a little voice in my head, ever so unhelpfully. But… there was also Andoc.

I sighed and stripped my dusty tunic over my head, exposing the soft leather wrappings that bound my breasts to make my chest appear flat. As I unwrapped myself, pausing now and then to scrape ragged fingernails over the itchy places where the leather had chafed, I contemplated the hopelessness of my situation.

Through some cruel joke of the gods, I was born a girl. I never fit in as one, though—no matter how much my mother wished it. I was fascinated by the horse pens in my childhood village almost from the time I could walk, and railed against the restrictions prohibiting women from tending the animals.

The gods gave men and women different roles, I was told repeatedly by the village priests, after every childish infraction. *Only male spirits are strong enough to control the spirits of animals. They cannot thrive under the care of a woman. If you want to take care of living things, perhaps you should consider becoming a healer, or a grower of plants?*

I still remember the tears of frustration, carefully hidden from all who might see and judge me for them, after trying to tell the priests that my spirit was more male than female. It just happened to be hidden inside the body of a slender girl child. Watching the girls my age as I grew up was like looking at something foreign, something… *other.* Sometimes it felt as though the only thing I had inherited from my sex was a love of attractive men.

Not that it mattered much, at this point. Even had my attraction been for women, to get close to another person in such a way would be to betray my secret. A man would not want me because I dressed and acted like a boy. Even if I found someone who loved other men—a practice more or less tolerated between a man and a eunuch, but taboo between two un-castrated men—such a person would not want me because my body was still that of a woman. I was destined to be alone, and to make things even worse, my heart had fixated on two utterly unattainable people who already had each other and would certainly have no interest in me.

Perhaps it was safer that way.

Tossing the breast bindings aside, I reached for the clay pot of beeswax and tallow that I used to soothe my skin, rubbing it in and letting the pleasant sensation soothe my nerves. My breasts were thankfully small, but today they were still tender as I suffered through the tail end of my moon cycle. Pulling down my breeches, my lip curled in distaste as I pulled out the pad of rabbit fur wrapped in a linen rag that I used to staunch the flow of blood.

The bleeding had slowed since yesterday, which was good since I had no more rabbit fur and didn't have the time to go searching for moss or some other absorbent material this evening. I rinsed out the linen rag in a bucket of well water and folded it back into a square. It would have to be enough.

Dusk was fading into dark when I arrived back at the pens beyond the village outskirts. Volya's mare had been given her own small corral somewhat away from the other horses, but still within sight. A three-sided shelter stood in one corner, bedded with dried peat moss hauled in from a nearby bog. I approached the fence and held out a hand, palm-down, for the mare to sniff. Cassira was a sweet horse for the most part, but had displayed something of a fierce streak after foaling her first colt last year.

That was fine; it was a mother's job to protect her offspring, after all... something I wished my own mother had shown more of an inclination to do. After greeting the little horse and demonstrating that it wasn't my intent to sneak around and hide from her like a predator, I wandered off to find a comfortable post somewhere out of the way to lean against. With my blanket wrapped around my shoulders against the slight evening chill, and a waterskin at my side, I curled up so I could see the moonlight glinting off the horse's dappled buckskin coat. Leaning my head back against the thick, wooden post, I soaked in the faint warmth that emanated from it, left over from the day's bright sunlight.

Cassira wandered restlessly around the pen, stopping occasionally to pick up a mouthful of hay or stare across at the other horses dozing in their corral. A foal watch like this one was usually a recipe for utter boredom, and while I was aware of the level of trust Jorun was placing in me, that didn't make watching a horse walk around and eat hay over the course of several hours any more interesting. Before the full moon had reached a point halfway toward its zenith, my mind began to wander.

Because I apparently liked to torture myself, it turned fairly quickly to thoughts of Andoc and Senovo. During the summer months, Andoc had a habit of sparring with the other warriors wearing only a loincloth, which left little to the imagination when it came to his enviable physique. Senovo, though, was always clad in his robes, leaving quite a bit to the imagination. The priests—eunuchs, all of them—were softer than the warriors with their sinewy, battle-hardened bodies. Most eunuchs tended toward roundness through the belly, but not Senovo, whose features were fine and whose body was slender.

His face was nearly as smooth as my own. The front half of his head was shaved close, while the straight, black hair growing from the back of his skull was braided into the single, heavy plait that all priests possessed.

For religious ceremonies, he always lined his eyes with kohl. The sight had never failed to captivate me for some reason.

I wondered what he and Andoc did together in private. The lads in the village had plenty to say on the matter, all of it coarse and much of it rather unlikely sounding, though as someone who had never lain with another person for fear of my birth sex being discovered, I suppose I wasn't in any real position to judge.

In my mind, they kissed passionately and stroked each other with loving fingers. I had a vague idea of what being a eunuch must entail, having seen dozens of colts castrated into geldings over the years. It seemed to me to be an exceedingly cruel thing to do to a human boy. Still, the geldings recovered well enough, and some of them even continued to mount mares afterward, though of course they could not sire foals. So, in my idle daydreams and fantasies, Senovo still gave and received pleasure, writhing with Andoc in a passionate tangle of lips and hands.

The night was quiet and my solitude complete. My left hand drifted up, sliding under my tunic to brush over my raw, sensitive nipples. Leaving my breasts unbound tonight was a calculated risk—but it was dark, and if I saw anybody, it would only be Jorun as I woke him to ask for help in case there was a problem with the foal that I couldn't deal with myself. He wouldn't notice if my chest seemed slightly less flat than usual. Though my breasts were a nuisance, there was no denying that touching them like this felt good. So good, in fact, that I felt a pulse of wetness between my legs.

I sighed, irritated, letting my head fall back against the post with a soft thump. I was still bleeding a bit, and had only a linen rag to catch it. If I wasn't careful, the mess would soak through my breeches.

Mood ruined, I pulled my hand out of my tunic and returned my full focus to the mare with her swollen, heavy belly. Cassira was still restless, pacing the fence. After a few minutes, she froze, looking out into the dark at a point slightly to the east of where I was sitting. With an explosive snort, she abruptly bolted to the far side of the pen, her pendulous belly swinging with every stride. In the large communal corral, the other horses stirred nervously and started to mill around.

I rose, cautious, and followed the fence until I could get a clear look at the open space beyond. Glowing, yellow-green eyes stared at me from out of the dark, and I caught my breath in surprise.

The moonlight illuminated thick gray fur and a sharply pointed white muzzle as a large wolf crept forward silently with smooth, deliberate steps, sniffing the air. The horses were charging back and forth in their pens now, the herd forming up in a tight ring with the youngsters in the middle. Cassira squealed and cantered back and forth along the section of fence I had repaired the previous afternoon, pausing to shove against the rails with her chest as she sought escape.

The hair on the back of my neck rose and a shiver traced its way down my spine at the thought of a wolf this close to the edge of the village. Had it sensed that the mare was about to give birth to a tender, vulnerable foal? For now, at least, the creature's attention seemed more focused on me than the horses, which was... well, both good and not so good, depending on how you looked at it. I tore my eyes from its glowing gaze to cast around my immediate surroundings in the moonlight. My attention caught on a scattering of fist-sized rocks near the fence, and I dropped into a crouch, picking up as many as I could hold.

I threw the first one as hard as I could at those slanted eyes. It missed, though not by much, and the wolf skittered a step to the side. A low growl rolled across the space between us. The second stone flew true, the growl ending in a yip as the rock hit the predator just above one glowing eye. It was already turning to run as my third rock thumped into its shoulder. The rustling sound of paws running through grass faded into the darkness, and I let out a breath I hadn't even realized I'd been holding.

Clammy sweat made me shiver as I turned to check on the horses. The herd was quieting, but Cassira still stood in the far corner, head high and ears pricked as she followed the sounds made by the retreating beast. There would be no foal tonight, with the mare now on high alert after the threat. I sighed. I would have to maintain my vigil regardless, lest the wolf return.

And, of course, Jorun would have my head if I let something bad happen on my watch.

I gathered up a few more rocks, just in case, and returned to my spot against the post. While I didn't feel remotely tired just then, I knew I couldn't afford to let my guard down as the small hours of the night crept by. Resettling myself in a position that was comfortable—but not *too* comfortable—I rummaged for the worn leather satchel I'd brought with me and pulled out a damaged horsewhip, along with some leather thongs. Angling it so the moonlight hit the braided leather, I started unpicking the frayed section, pausing at intervals to check the horses and my surroundings for unwanted four-legged company.

I was just tying off the end of the intricately braided repairs to the lash some considerable time later when I heard noises coming from the far side of the village. At first the sounds made no sense. It was the middle of the night—who would be shouting and clanging around with such total disregard for people sleeping? Only when the shouting turned to screaming did my weary thoughts start to make sense of the situation, sending my heart hammering with sudden terror.

It was the sound of an attack.

TWO

This was wrong. This shouldn't be happening. Neighboring tribes and villages attacked each other sometimes; of course they did. But Draebard was not involved in any disputes at the moment. There were no blood feuds or water shortages causing friction in the area. Besides, no self-respecting Eburosi warrior would *ever* countenance such a cowardly attack on a village in the middle of the night. It was beyond dishonorable. The gods would strike down any tribe that tried such a thing with a plague of boils, or worse.

I had been frozen in place with shock, but now I clambered to my feet and silently made my way back to the edge of the village, keeping close to fences and walls. I had to see what was happening. The screams were horrible, and as I approached I saw flickering light and smelled thick, greasy smoke. Whoever it was had set fire to some of the huts on the far side of the settlement.

I made my way closer to the center of the village and peeked around the edge of the wall I was hiding behind. Moonlight and orange firelight illuminated the strange, silvery metal chest armor favored by Alyrion soldiers as the figures pressed further into the village in orderly ranks. There looked to be at least three dozen men, armed with swords, pikes and torches.

Oh, gods. They'd drawn Volya and his retinue of warriors away from the settlement, and now they were attacking. Did they mean to kill us all and burn it to the ground, or was this supposed to be some sort of lesson? A warning to other Eburosi?

The horses.

They would steal the horses, or slaughter them. I turned and ran back toward the pens as fast as I could, all thoughts of stealth abandoned. My lungs were burning — as much with fear as with exhaustion — when I reached the gate of the first pen and threw it open. Cassira snorted, trotting through the gap in the fence and making straight for the rest of the herd, which was still milling around in the largest corral. I followed her as fast as I could and opened that gate as well, entering the pen and skirting along the fence to get behind the herd so I could drive them out.

"*Hyaah!*" I shouted, herding the animals through the gate and away from the village, along the track that led north, toward the summer pastures and the foothills beyond. Within seconds, the mob of horses had accelerated into a panicked gallop, the thunder of their hooves slowly fading beneath the sounds of the battle behind me as they disappeared into the distance.

The wolf had better watch himself, I thought, slightly hysterically. *He'll be trampled in the stampede if he's not careful.*

With the horses as safe as they could be under the circumstances, I hurried back to the post I'd been resting against to grab the horsewhip, then ran toward the village, and the screaming.

In my absence, the remaining warriors who had not gone with Volya had stumbled out of their huts, with swords, spears, and axes in their hands. Their furious battle cries echoed through the village. It was strangely jarring to see Eburosi warriors fighting in whatever clothing they'd been sleeping in, without any war paint smeared across their bodies or faces. Unadorned skin made them no less fierce, however, and the Alyrions' steady progress through the village was slowed as they engaged with the defenders.

Looking around, my attention was caught by a single armor-clad soldier with a torch, moving purposefully toward the cookhouse. Without stopping to think, I ran forward and let fly with the long-tailed lash of the horsewhip, aiming for the man's eyes. When he cried out and dropped the torch in favor of clawing at his face, I bared my teeth in what might have been vicious satisfaction. It was short-lived, however, as another soldier saw me. He closed in even as I tried to back away, sword in hand and anger twisting his face.

I cracked the whip again, aiming for the sword in hopes that I could pull it out of his hand. I missed, though, wrapping the lash around his forearm instead. He hissed at the sting, but immediately used it to drag me forward, off-balance and staggering. Before I could right myself, the pommel of his sword swept up toward my face. Pain exploded in my temple where it hit me and I dropped like a stone, ears ringing. Through blurry, wavering vision, I saw the flash of the blade as he lifted it for the killing stroke.

This is it, then, I thought, feeling surprisingly calm about the whole thing as my awareness flickered in and out, in time with my pounding heart.

Just as the blade began its downward arc, a large, gray shape slammed into the soldier, knocking him to the dirt with a cry. The wolf snarled, tearing at the man's throat, scarlet liquid soaking its jaws as I struggled to make sense of the scene before me through eyes that wouldn't focus properly. The red stain seemed to spread in my vision, reaching out to meet the soft, gray fog that was swirling inward from the periphery. I slipped into darkness with every expectation that I would never wake again.

⁕

When I did wake, sunlight was stabbing into my eyes. My skull throbbed in time with my heartbeat. I tried to groan in pain, but it emerged as a dry croak. An answering whimper made me turn my head. A mistake, as my vision swam again. When it cleared, I was staring into the wide, dilated eyes of the wolf, half-hidden behind a broken cart a few feet away from me, and cowering like a guilty hunting dog expecting to be whipped by its master. Its muzzle was coated with dried gore from the fallen soldier lying in a heap across from us.

Shouting and hoof beats echoed along the central roadway, and the animal flattened itself even further against the ground, obviously terrified. I rolled painfully over to lie on my back on the packed dirt, craning my neck until I got an upside-down view of Volya's returning party. Andoc was at the front. He reined his galloping horse to an abrupt halt even as the others rode past, heading further into the village where the destruction was greatest.

Easy on that poor gelding's mouth, I thought as Andoc jumped down and raced toward me, his worried expression looking almost comical upside down. He skidded to a stop midway between my body and that of the wolf, looking back and forth between us as if torn. A moment later, he was kneeling at my side, lifting me to cradle my shoulders carefully in his arms. I smiled up at his warm, brown eyes, feeling giddy.

"Careful, there's a man-eating wolf here," I said, and promptly slipped back into unconsciousness.

The next time I awoke, I was inside a hut, lying on a straw mattress on the floor. I stared up at the golden brown thatch visible through the rafters overhead for several moments, blinking. A snug bandage circled my forehead, and I could feel the cool stickiness from some sort of poultice pressed against my throbbing temple. My vision seemed steadier, and the earth was no longer moving in stately, ponderous circles beneath me.

I wasn't alone. I could hear the sound of retching followed by ragged, unsteady breathing from across the room. Someone else was whispering a litany of soothing reassurance. I rolled gingerly onto my side, lifting my aching head with considerable effort and propping myself on one elbow so I could see. Seated on a wide, low bed frame against the far wall, Senovo was slumped sideways with his forehead resting against Andoc's shoulder, breathing heavily. Andoc's hand cradled the back of his neck, steadying him, and a chamber pot rested on the ground in front of him. The priest was naked from the waist up, a blanket thrown carelessly over his lap. His face was canted toward me. I could see dried blood coating his jaw and neck, along with a livid bruise above his left eyebrow. His eyes were tightly closed as he struggled for composure.

There was something… something about the blood and the bruise… but no. My wits were still too addled to make whatever connection it was that dangled tantalizingly just out of reach. Andoc turned slightly, and his eyes met mine. His fingers tightened around the back of the distraught priest's head for a moment, then relaxed.

"Senovo," he said softly, "she's awake."

THREE

My blood ran cold at the three simple words, even as Senovo opened anguished eyes, straightening away from his friend's support. I was suddenly, painfully aware that, like Senovo, I was naked under the rough blanket covering me.

Oh, gods. They knew. They knew my secret.

Something of my horror must have shown on my face, because Andoc raised a hand, as one might do when faced with a wild, unpredictable animal.

"I apologize," he said. "You were unconscious and there was blood soaking your breeches. I thought you'd been wounded in an exceptionally unfortunate place. I had no way of knowing it was moon blood."

"You had no right!" I said, struggling upright on the straw-stuffed palliasse with the blanket clutched around me.

Andoc raised his eyebrows. "Well, I suppose next time I'll know to leave you bleeding in the street, in that case. Live and learn." The hint of humor in his voice set my blood boiling.

"You could at least have kept it to yourself instead of spilling my secret to the very next person you saw," I snapped. "Now both of you know!"

"I knew already, Carivel," Senovo said, sounding exhausted but looking somewhat more composed than before. Andoc's attention immediately returned to the priest. He dipped a rag in the bowl of water resting on the table next to the bed, and started wiping at the blood on Senovo's face with a sure touch.

"How could you know?" I asked derisively. "No one knew!"

"The wolf smelled the blood on you earlier," said Senovo, gently moving Andoc's hand away and taking the rag to finish cleaning off his face himself.

"The... wolf?" I asked stupidly. The wolf that I had bruised over one eye with a rock. Just like the bruise now darkening

Senovo's face. The wolf that tore out a man's throat, getting blood all over its mouth and jaw. Saving my life.

"Consider it an exchange," Senovo said. "A secret for a secret."

"You're a shape-shifter?" I asked, completely taken aback. People who could transform themselves into animals were incredibly rare, and almost always rose quickly through the ranks of the priesthood to become powerful religious figures. "But… you're a priest. Why keep such a power secret?"

"Because I can't control it. Because it makes me a killer."

"Bullshit," Andoc said matter-of-factly. "*I'm* a killer. You're a mild-mannered religious man who happens to turn into a wolf sometimes."

Senovo's brows drew together, a furrow of anger forming between them. "I think there's at least one man lying in the street with his throat ripped out who would beg to differ with you… if he weren't *already dead.*"

"Pfft. He was an enemy soldier. I'd've killed him myself, if I'd been here," said Andoc in a dismissive tone.

"You aren't a priest," Senovo replied.

"I imagine Carivel here is plenty relieved that he's dead, by a priest's hand or not," Andoc countered.

"Yes and no," I said cautiously, looking between the two of them. "I'm not dead, but my life here may be as good as over, regardless. Does anybody else know? About me, I mean?"

"Not as far as I'm aware," Senovo said.

Andoc shrugged. "I certainly haven't told anyone. Who you choose to be makes no difference to me."

"Well, it makes a very big difference to me!" I flared. "The horses are my life, and women aren't allowed to work with them! Speaking of which, if I ever see you yank on your gelding's mouth again like you did this morning, I'll have Jorun confiscate your bridle and make you use a hackamore until you learn to ride properly!"

Shouting at him felt good. I resolved to do it more often. Too bad the only effect it had was to make his lips quirk as if he were holding back a smile.

"I'll keep it in mind," he said. "As for the other thing—the gods and religious law and such—that's more Senovo's area than mine."

Almost against my will, my eyes moved back to the young priest, expecting to see some form of censure for my years of heresy.

"Yes, it's all terribly shocking," he said, sounding tired but not, in point of fact, terribly shocked. "Really, it's amazing that your female presence hasn't decimated the herd over the past few years since you arrived. How odd that it is, in fact, thriving under your care—larger and of better quality than it has ever been. It's utterly inexplicable."

It was obvious that I was being teased.

"You're not a very good priest," I said, my eyes narrowed in anger.

"I know," Senovo agreed readily. "Not only am I a killer, I also question the gods' wisdom when it doesn't make logical sense. High priest Rhystel would be appalled if he found out I'd been blessed with the power to shift."

"I still say you should tell him sometime, just to see the look on his face," Andoc said.

"So, basically," I said, trying to get the conversation back on track, "if I don't tell anyone you're a shifter, you and Andoc won't tell anyone that I was born female?"

"If you want to look at it that way," Senovo said, not unkindly. "In fact, I have more sympathy and understanding than you might suspect for the disharmony between how one perceives oneself and what is hanging—or not hanging—between one's legs."

"And, as I said earlier," Andoc added, "I don't particularly care if you've got a prick or a cunt. I rather like you, regardless. You've got courage. I respect that."

Senovo sighed. "You've missed your calling as a poet, my friend. You have *such* a way with words."

Could it really be that simple? Agree to keep each other's secrets, and go on as if nothing had happened?

"You have nothing to fear from me, Senovo," I said cautiously. "If we're agreed that neither of these revelations ever took place, then I'm in your debt. You saved my life last night."

"I'm glad something good came of it, in that case," Senovo said.

"Sorry about the rock," I added, gesturing to his bruised face.

"Don't mention it," he said, and Andoc snorted.

I suddenly realized that in my horror at being discovered, I'd completely forgotten to ask about the battle. "What... happened, exactly, last night? After I lost consciousness, I mean."

The way Andoc's face went abruptly grim and angry made my heart sink in my chest. I looked to Senovo, who shook his head.

"I only shifted back a few minutes before you woke up," he said.

"I didn't want to leave you two alone for long, so I don't know details yet," Andoc said. "It's not good, though. If you're both well enough, we should probably go help outside."

Senovo nodded agreement, and gave his face a final scrub with the rag. Andoc looked at me questioningly.

"Where are my clothes?" I asked.

"On the stool," he said, indicating the rough wooden seat near the mattress where I was sitting.

Senovo stood, unbothered by his own nakedness as he reached for the robes Andoc handed him and shrugged them on. I tried not to stare, feeling a blush crawl up my face, which deepened further when I caught Andoc watching me. The two of them left the hut to give me privacy, and I dressed as quickly as I could. My breeches were still stiff with the rusty stain of dried moon blood, but in the aftermath of a battle no one would question it. I had to pause occasionally to regain my balance as my injured head swam, but I became steadier the more I moved around. The headache was phenomenal, however.

Andoc's hut was close to the north edge of the village, and when I exited the sturdy structure, things didn't seem too bad at first. Andoc and Senovo were waiting for me outside, and Andoc led the way toward the center of the settlement, where I had tried to take on armed soldiers with a horsewhip earlier. I shivered slightly. By all rights, I should be dead.

The smell of stale smoke grew more noticeable the further we went. When we turned a corner into the village green that served as a central meeting place, I stumbled to a halt, my breath catching in my throat. People were carrying bodies onto the green, laying them out in neat rows. Bodies that I *recognized*.

How utterly, utterly stupid of me not to have understood until now that people *I knew* had been killed. I thought back to the flames — to the chaos and the screaming. Of course people had died. Of *course* they had. I suddenly felt ill, and very, very young.

A hand grasped my upper arm in a steadying grip.

"Come," said Senovo, still looking pale though his voice had regained its usual even timbre. "Let us go see what we can do to help."

I nodded, a feeling of numbness washing over me. Andoc had already attracted Volya's attention and was speaking to him as we approached.

"How many dead?" Andoc asked.

"They've found two dozen so far," Volya replied, looking as if he'd aged twenty years overnight. "There are still several houses and other buildings that need to be searched, though." The chief looked to Senovo, and I felt the priest's hand tighten reflexively on my arm for an instant before he deliberately removed it. "Senovo, I'm sorry to be the bearer of bad news. They attacked the priests and acolytes in the temple barracks."

Beside me, Senovo sucked in an audible breath. Andoc looked at him with worried eyes.

"High Priest Rhystel?" Senovo asked, and I could hear the strain behind the carefully level voice.

"Gravely injured," Volya said. The anger that had been lurking behind the old chief's expression came to the forefront. "They left him for dead. Healer Sagdea is with him."

"I should go to him," Senovo said, sounding distant. He blinked, recalling himself to the present conversation. "And… the others in the barracks?"

"All killed, except for two of the younger acolytes," Volya said. "Reston hid in a storage chest during the attack, and Crenelo was visiting a friend elsewhere in the village. Those vicious Alyrion bastards think they can break us by attacking our religion. If they had their way, we'd all be worshipping their thrice-damned deity. Damick, or Damock, or whatever it is they call it."

Senovo nodded his understanding, that same look of distance returning to his eyes. I was debating internally whether to steady him with a hand on his arm as he had done for me when Volya addressed me directly.

"Carivel. Dalon reports that all of the horses are gone. I think we have to assume that they were stolen by the invaders," he said.

"No!" I said quickly, shaking my head. "No, I was watching your mare last night when I heard the fighting. Once I saw what was going on, I let the horses out of the pens and drove them toward the summer pastures and the foothills."

Volya looked surprised, but pleased. "Is that so? That's the first piece of good news I've heard today. Well done, lad. That was quick thinking."

"It was nothing," I said, uncomfortable with the praise in the midst of such terrible circumstances. "We'll have to go round them up again as soon as possible, though, and it's a large area to search. Where is Jorun?"

"I haven't seen him," Volya said.

A wave of worry washed over me. I was surprised that it had been Dalon and not the Horse Master himself who found the horses missing. Hopefully the old man hadn't been injured during the battle.

My thoughts were interrupted by a cry of grief from across the green. All four of us turned to see three of Gretya's daughters clinging to each other, huddled around the door to Jorun's sleeping hut. My heart sank.

We hurried across to the little house with its crooked doorframe and cheerful boxes of herbs hanging under the windows. The wail had come from Limdya, who was now weeping loudly into her older sister's shoulder. Volya murmured quietly to the girls, urging them away from the door so that Andoc, Senovo and I could enter.

Blood painted the walls of the small structure in ugly splashes, and I had to breathe deeply as my head started to spin again. Gretya's twisted form lay motionless on the bed, her lifeblood staining her linen nightshirt a dull brown around the wound that had pierced her heart. My gaze skittered away from the pitiful sight of the old woman's body, coming to rest instead on the second figure lying on the floor with a short sword still clasped in one gnarled hand.

FOUR

A pained, animal noise escaped my throat as I recognized Jorun, his familiar face frozen in a grimace of pain and fear. Behind me, I heard Volya groan in dismay.

I was right about him and Gretya, I thought, even as I struggled to draw breath. Jorun's eyes were open, staring at a point over my left shoulder. I found that I was backing away through the door unsteadily, my legs threatening to buckle beneath me and send me sprawling on the ground. More of the pained noises were emerging from my lips with each strangled breath—I couldn't seem to stop them.

Hands closed around my arms from either side, supporting me as I continued to stagger backwards, away from the terrible sight.

"That's right. Come away," Andoc said from my right shoulder.

"Deep breaths," Senovo said from my left. "Focus on us."

I tried, I really did—gasping for air that seemed too thick and stale with smoke from burned huts and burned bodies. I was vaguely aware of the sound of the three newly orphaned sisters weeping a short distance away. Andoc was in front of me now, taking my face in his hands as Senovo kept me upright.

"Breathe now," Andoc said, forcing me to meet his gaze eye-to-eye. "We will grieve later. You have people relying on you. Carivel, you are the Horse Master now, and Draebard's horses are running loose in the foothills."

I stared at him like some kind of simpleton. I was the *what*? Oh, gods. The old Horse Master was dead, and I was the Horse Master's assistant. I felt a jolt through my chest like I'd been kicked by a fractious yearling, and air flooded my lungs at last as I sucked in a gasping breath, and another, and another. The fog in my mind cleared slightly, and I tried to focus on the throbbing of the bruise on my temple—grasping at the dull pain like a lifeline.

"That's it," Andoc said encouragingly, as Senovo cautiously released his grip and left me to stand unaided.

"But… Jorun," I said, my eyes drifting over Andoc's shoulder and toward the crooked doorway. "I should… "

"Volya and I will take care of Jorun and Gretya," Andoc said, pulling my focus back to him. "You should go find Dalon and whoever else you need to round up the horses. Senovo, go to the temple and see if the healer needs any help with Rhystel."

I nodded, my face still framed within Andoc's callused hands, feeling the odd numbness from earlier returning. That same numbness kept me from reacting when Andoc pressed his lips briefly to my bandaged forehead before letting me go. My eyes sought Senovo, who dipped his chin in acknowledgement, his own face pale and haggard as he turned to leave for the temple barracks.

I felt strangely detached from events as I turned to Volya, who had stepped back to give the three of us some privacy.

"I will need use of the horses you and your party were riding," I said.

He nodded. "Leave one in case we have to get a message out for some reason. The rest are at your disposal."

I took my leave, barely able to feel my boots against the ground as my feet carried me toward the horse pens without any conscious direction on my part. Thinking about the details of what I would need to recapture the herd was good. It gave me something to focus on, forcing my mind into working again like a rusty wheel on a chariot axle. My own gelding, Kekenu, was loose with the herd. If I could get within whistling distance, he would come to my call, and we could let him lead us back to the others.

By the time I reached the pens, I had the bare outline of a plan. Between the wolf and the battle, the horses had been in a panic last night. They would probably have headed for the perceived safety of the foothills rather than staying in the open pastureland, though they'd likely ventured down to graze today, now that things were quiet. We would look in the valleys at the base of the hills, and work our way out from there if necessary.

Dalon and several of the other boys were clustered around the pens. Some of the younger ones were obviously fighting tears. I would have to lead them. I would have to do for them what Jorun had always done for us, before.

"Come here, all of you," I said loudly as I approached. The lads looked up in surprise, and I continued as they grudgingly gathered around. "The horses are loose somewhere in the vicinity of the foothills. We need to go get them."

"Why do you think they're in the foothills?" Dalon asked in open challenge. "I reckon the soldiers stole 'em all during the raid."

"I know they're in the foothills because I'm the one who let them out of the pens and drove them in that direction last night, so the soldiers couldn't get them," I said, and a murmur went around the group. "Now, we need to get them back before they wander too far."

"Where's Jorun?" asked a young boy named Favian.

My stomach churned, and it was as if I was listening to someone else speaking as I answered, "Jorun is dead."

There were several gasps and cries of denial. Favian burst into tears, and his friend Lundis put an awkward arm around him. Jorun had been like a father to many of these boys. I allowed the expressions of shock and grief to continue for several seconds before speaking up again.

"Jorun died bravely, with a sword in his hand," I said eventually, raising my voice enough to be heard. "We owe it to him to do our jobs and make him proud. Draebard's strength lies with its warriors and its horses. Our warriors drove off a cowardly and dishonorable attack last night, saving the village from complete destruction. It's up to us to get back our horses so those same warriors can descend on our new enemy with a swarm of battle chariots and destroy them utterly."

The boys were all quiet now—looking at me. Looking *to* me, though Dalon and a few others wore sour expressions. I wondered with an odd sort of detached panic how I was ever going to live up to Jorun's memory.

"Now," I said, "get all of the horses from Volya's riding party saddled except for the gray mare with the scar on her shoulder. We'll head out as soon as we can. Favian, I want you and Lundis to stay here in case Chief Volya needs to send out a message. Favian will ready the pens with feed and water for our return, and Lundis, you will check in periodically with Volya in case he needs you to act as a courier."

There was a split second of silence—just long enough for panic to thread through the pall of numbness hanging over me and start crawling up my spine—but then the little crowd broke up and started to carry out my instructions. Releasing a quiet breath of relief, I went to gather extra ropes, halters, and whips, along with a pocketful of dried apples.

Half an hour later, ten of us rode out along the track leading north away from the village. The chaotic hoof prints left by the herd's headlong flight were still visible on the dusty road beneath us. The foothills were more than an hour away on horseback, and our little group was largely silent at first. As our horses' hooves ate up the distance, though, Dalon could no longer contain his disagreement with my plan.

"We should have started searching close to the village and worked our way out. There's no reason to start looking so far away," he said, pitching his voice for those riding closest to him. Fortunately—or perhaps unfortunately—my hearing was excellent.

"The horses were panicked by the commotion and the smell of burning," I said evenly. "They will have sought shelter and safety in the hills."

"Maybe they did and maybe they didn't," Dalon said. "I guess we'll find out, won't we?"

It was already midday. If I was wrong and the horses were far away from the hills somewhere, we would lose the light before we could find them. It would have been all too easy to start second-guessing myself, which was exactly what Dalon wanted, I suspected. The fact remained though—I knew horses. After I fled the village of my birth and my mother's bitter anger over what she saw as my failings, I wandered the wildlands for weeks, tracking herds of native Eburosi ponies for days at a time to learn about their behavior. I had been drawn to horses my whole life—their strength, their speed and power. When I could no longer trust myself to endure the vicious words and even more vicious beatings doled out by the woman who'd given birth to me, I decided to flee my home and find out for myself if someone with the body of a woman could control the spirits of horses.

I succeeded, and it was that success which gave me the idea to start somewhere new, living as a man. My own little black and white gelding came from one of those wildland herds I'd followed. Working on foot, I had tamed him away from his herd-mates as a yearling after he'd been weakened by an ugly leg injury. Gaining his trust had taken nearly a week and was one of my proudest accomplishments, second only to attaining my position as Jorun's assistant. Thinking of Jorun made my chest start aching, so I tore my mind away from that train of thought. The point was, I knew horses. And I knew that Draebard's herd would be close to the foothills.

"Spread out," I called as we finally approached the gently sloping valleys south of the hills. "Stay within shouting distance of each other and call out if you see anything."

Clouds were moving in from the southwest, blocking out the afternoon sun. It would rain before the evening was over. I eased Andoc's gelding away from the others, silently cursing the animal's hard mouth, along with Andoc's hard hands that had made it that way. The bay gelding shook his head in annoyance, but eventually peeled away from his herd mates obediently. Keeping to the ridge tops, I stood in the stirrups, craning around to scan the waves of green grass swept by the wind.

Every few minutes, I let out a shrill whistle, in hopes that Kekenu was within hearing distance. The other boys shouted reports back and forth as they searched. For almost two hours we continued in that manner, the lads growing progressively more impatient and sullen. A brisk wind blew a handful of spattered raindrops against my face just as I heard the distant hoof beats of a single horse approaching.

FIVE

I wet my dry lips and whistled again.

A moment later, Kekenu came charging into sight, his pinto coat a bright contrast against the green grass.

"Kekenu is here! They must be close!" I shouted to the nearest boy, before dismounting and leading Andoc's horse forward to meet the little gelding.

Kekenu bounded to a stop a few feet away from me, snorting and tossing his head. When he calmed, I motioned him forward the last few steps and fed him a piece of dried apple. By this time, several of the lads had converged on us.

"Here," I said, handing Andoc's horse off to one of them. "Take Andoc's gelding. We'll let Kekenu lead us back to the rest of the herd."

I grabbed a length of thin rope from my saddlebag and tied it in a loop around the base of Kekenu's neck—since I was letting the little horse choose his own path, I didn't need anything fancier than a simple neck rope for control. Facing his flank and grabbing a hank of mane in my left hand, I bounded forward a step and vaulted up onto his low back, scooting my hips sideways with a little jerk to center myself. A quick head count showed that all of the others had joined us.

"Follow me!" I called, and urged Kekenu into motion with a squeeze of my calves.

The little horse surged forward eagerly, one ear flicked back until it became obvious that I did not have a destination in mind. He cantered around in a broad arc until we were headed back in the direction he'd come from, the others keeping pace behind us. The horse's muscles bunched and released rhythmically between my thighs as I balanced on his broad, familiar back, one hand still wrapped in the gelding's generous mane. The rain was coming down more steadily now.

After only a few minutes, we crested a small hill and there, laid out below us, was the herd. I breathed a sigh of relief. The horses—nearly a hundred of them—looked up at the disturbance as we approached. My eyes scanned them eagerly. They were moving around too much to get a proper head count, but my attention was drawn to a creamy white yearling. Cassira—the pale colt's dam—was standing nearby, keeping watch over a small, white bundle on the ground. The tiny creature stirred from its slumber and stumbled awkwardly to its feet on long, uncoordinated legs, shaking its little head in consternation before making straight for its mother's udder and drinking greedily. Another tiny piece of the tension curled inside me eased at the sight.

"Volya's mare foaled sometime earlier today," I called, pointing down at the spindly white figure. "We'll have to take it slowly on the way back. Everyone, skirt around to the north and let's drive them on to Draebard. Nice and easy, mind."

The boys ranged around the herd, giving the nervous animals a wide berth. I nodded in satisfaction as Dalon and Tenibral eased up to the front, leading the way. Both were mounted on mares that were relatively high in the herd's pecking order, and when the rest of us started putting pressure on the horses from behind, they easily followed the two mares' lead without panicking and running. I settled myself near the back, where I could watch for stragglers and keep an eye on the newborn foal trotting easily next to Cassira on its gangly legs.

The rain increased to a steady patter—not a downpour, but enough to soak through clothing and run down the backs of our necks in a chilly, unpleasant trickle. It took nearly twice as long to get back as it had to go out, and tempers were short by the time we finally reached the familiar track leading to the pens. The sky was fading from slate gray to black when the last horse trotted through the gate, eager to get to the feed Favian had laid out for them. We unsaddled the riding horses quickly and turned them loose as well.

I wavered for a moment before deciding to separate Cassira and her new foal from the others. No doubt the foal would be fine with the herd it had been born into earlier in the day, but in the small pen with the run-in shed, the pair could get out of the chilly spring rain and sleep somewhere dry.

Cassira pinned her ears and charged at me when I approached with the halter, only to come to a surprised halt as the end of the lead rope snapped stingingly across her chest.

"Yes, you're a very fierce mama," I told her, "but it's getting late, and I'm tired and cold. Now hush and come here."

The horse flung her head up and down twice, subsiding as I approached and fed her a piece of the now rather damp and spongy dried apple from my pocket. I slipped the halter on and, with a glance to ensure the foal was following, led the pair into the second pen where a pile of hay was waiting in the shed. Upon her release, Cassira went straight for her feed. I relaxed against the wall under the overhang, staying completely still as the tiny, pale foal approached and began to sniff at my wet clothing and skin.

I was losing the light, but I stayed there for a little while anyway. Eventually the young horse gained enough confidence to let me run my hands over its shoulder and back, scratching lightly until I found an itchy place that had it twisting its little head and neck into funny contortions with ecstasy. Its white coat seemed to glow with a faint, ghostly light in the encroaching darkness.

The boys had finished putting everything away and readying the pens for nighttime when I left and closed the gate behind me. They were gathered under the eaves of the storage building, talking quietly when I approached.

"Well done, all of you," I told them. "This has been a terrible day for Draebard, but each of you has done Jorun proud. Go dry off and get something to eat. Try to get some rest and I'll see you back here in the morning."

When everyone had dispersed, muttering unenthusiastically as they went, I let myself slump back against the rough wooden wall. The events of the day seemed to crash over me like a wave, leaving me exhausted and making the pounding in my already sore head even worse. A shiver wracked me, and I realized with sudden clarity that I was freezing beneath my wet clothing in the evening chill.

I knew I wouldn't feel right leaving the horses unguarded tonight, but it would be safe enough to return to my tiny hut at the edge of town for a few minutes to get some dry clothing and a rain cloak. Forcing myself upright, I trudged through the cold rain along the muddy road until my familiar door loomed out of the dark. I paused a few steps from the entrance in surprise. Candlelight was shining through the single small window.

"Who's there?" I snapped, yanking open the door.

Inside, Andoc looked up at me mildly from where he'd been lounging on the edge of my bed, eating a hunk of flatbread spread with soft cheese.

"Sorry," he said around a mouthful, pausing to swallow before he continued. "When I saw the rest of Jorun's boys were back, I thought you might want something to eat. Brought you that."

He indicated the rest of the bread and cheese with a jerk of his chin, the simple repast sitting on my rickety little table.

"Oh," I said, at a loss for anything more intelligent. "Thanks."

"You staying with the horses tonight?" he asked, taking another large bite.

"Yes," I said, and set myself to spreading cheese on my own portion of bread. "Where's Senovo?"

"Still with the high priest. Reston and Crenelo are there, as well. The poor boys are distraught, as you might imagine."

Tears threatened to rise up and choke me. I fought them down with a harsh swallow.

"How is Rhystel?" I made myself ask.

Andoc shrugged. "His wounds are serious, and he's an old man. It's not good."

"How many died, altogether?" I asked, not at all sure I wanted the answer.

"Thirty-eight, that we've been able to find," Andoc said. "Another twenty-three badly injured."

"Gods," I said faintly.

"The remaining elders are meeting in the morning to discuss our retaliation," Andoc said. "I assume you got all the horses back safe?"

"Yes," I replied. "Tell Volya that he has his white foal, if you get a chance. It seems strong and healthy. I don't know yet if it's a colt or filly."

"He'll be glad to hear that, at least."

I nodded, finishing the slab of bread. Another shiver wracked me.

"You're soaked," Andoc said with a frown. "You should change clothes and warm up before you go back. Do you want me to leave?"

"Please," I whispered, numb from more than the cold.

Andoc nodded and left, laying a hand on my shoulder briefly as he did so. I stripped out of my wet clothing and ran a threadbare towel over my body before donning a spare set of buckskin trousers and a tunic. Distantly, I noted that my moon bleeding seemed to have finally stopped. After donning a tattered rain cloak, I returned to the horse pens and curled up on a pile of hay in the storage building, where I would hear any disturbance coming from outside.

Burying my head in my arms, I let the tears come.

⤗ ⚜ ⤖

The following morning dawned gray and chill, but at least the rain had stopped during the night. My headache was duller, though still very much present. My eyes were red and swollen. With a sigh, I unwrapped the dirty bandage from my head, using the stained linen to gingerly brush off the remaining poultice, which had dried into a flaky mess over the bruise on my temple. The boys would be here soon, and I probably looked like a pile of two-day-old manure at this point.

Dragging myself outside, I walked straight to the nearest horse trough and dunked my head in the cold water, scrubbing at my face and hair until I couldn't hold my breath any longer. When I emerged, I didn't feel *better*, exactly… but I did feel more awake. The lads began to trickle in a few minutes later, most of them looking like they'd had nights not much better than my own. Dalon and two of his mates were the last to arrive.

"We need to check the horses for injuries this morning," I told them when everyone had assembled. "The herd was in a full blown stampede when I drove them off. It's likely there are some cuts and bruises."

"I still say you're not automatically the one in charge, like you seem to think you are," Dalon said from the back.

"Carivel was right about the horses being in the foothills, though, wasn't he?" young Favian piped up before I could think of a suitable response. "If we'd followed what you said, we wouldn't have got the horses back before dark yesterday."

"An' he was Jorun's assistant, everyone knows that," Lundis added. "Who else would be in charge now?"

I put up a hand to quiet them. "Regardless of who's in charge, we all know what needs to be done," I said. "The horses need to be checked over and taken out to the spring pastures — under supervision, this time. The pens need mucking out, and we need to haul the manure to the vegetable plots for fertilizer. Dalon, are we at least agreed on that?"

"'Course," Dalon said. "Everyone here knows that."

"Then it hardly matters who says it," I said. "So, we'll all go through and check for injuries. Who was slated to take the herd out today?"

"Me, Kerney, and Lundis," said Varin, one of Dalon's hangers-on.

"Fine. The rest of us will clean the pens and take a break at lunchtime," I said.

There was a bit of muttering, but no one argued. We moved through the herd, smearing salve on scrapes and cuts; checking for heat in swollen limbs. All told, the horses had fared well during their brief, unplanned foray into the wilderness. While the lads in charge of taking the horses out to graze readied their mounts, I beckoned to Favian. The boy was one of the youngest here, but he already showed a great deal of promise with the animals. When he reached me, I gestured to the pen where Cassira and the white foal were lazing in the corner.

"Come with me, Favian," I said. "We need to check the foal and work on getting it tame."

I was pleased to see his pale face light up for the first time since the attack at the prospect of getting to work with the valuable white foal. I handed him a length of soft rope and reminded him to keep an eye on the mare as we entered. The young horse was nursing when we approached. Cassira pinned her ears and pawed with one front foot, but did not move otherwise.

"Colt or filly?" I asked Favian, who worked his way around until he could get a peek under the foal's flapping tail.

"It's a colt!" he said. "Just like last year's!"

"Volya will be pleased," I said. "Looks like he's got his white chariot team after all."

Under my watchful eye, Favian approached Cassira's head and scratched it until she stopped fussing. When the mare was relaxed, he moved back to run his hands over the oblivious foal's haunches as it nursed. I directed him to stroke down the colt's legs and lift them one at a time while it continued its single-minded pursuit of milk, accustoming the youngster to having its feet handled.

When the colt's stomach was full, it craned around, startling in place comically as it truly noticed Favian for the first time. Before long, though, the boy found the same itchy spot I'd discovered last night and scratched it, sending the foal into paroxysms of pleasure.

"That's enough for this morning," I said when the little horse seemed in danger of tipping over in its attempts to lean harder against the scratching fingers. "Always leave them wanting more, Favian."

Favian grinned over at me, yesterday's trauma momentarily banished in the joy of befriending the young animal. I clapped him companionably on the shoulder as he rejoined me. The two of us left the pen to join the others, grabbing shovels and pushcarts along the way. Meanwhile, Varin, Kerney, and Lundis herded most of the rest of the horses out to graze, leaving a few behind in case anyone in the village needed transportation.

The familiar routine of cleaning the pens was soothing, and the morning passed quietly enough. It was nearing lunchtime when a boy from the village ran up, calling for me.

"I'm here," I answered, putting my shovel aside.

The child only came up to my waist, but he puffed up self-importantly as he delivered his message. "Chief Volya requests your presence in the meeting house right away, Horse Master Carivel!"

My first reaction at being addressed in such a way was shock, but I'll admit I was not above feeling a twinge of satisfaction at seeing Dalon's discomfiture. I could practically feel the disgust radiating from him.

"I'll be there momentarily," I told the boy. After a second's thought, I caught Dalon's eye. "Would you mind organizing the lads when they get back from lunch? I'm not sure what the chief needs me for, or how long I'll be."

Dalon watched me warily, but he merely said. "Yeah, all right. I'll set them to cleaning the saddles and bridles from yesterday. They need tallow rubbed on them after being in the rain."

"Good idea," I said. "Thank you."

He stared at me for a few more seconds, but didn't add anything else as I turned and headed toward the village meeting hall.

When I arrived, it appeared that the meeting was breaking up. People were leaving, but as I stuck my head inside, Andoc immediately noticed me and waved me over to where he was speaking with Volya.

"Carivel," Volya greeted. "Thank you for coming so quickly — I'm sure you must be busy. I have a task for you. I'm sending Andoc and Senovo to talk with the Mereni, in hopes of gaining their military support against those spineless Alyrion bastards who attacked us."

I blinked. That *was* an interesting bit of news. People in Draebard looked down on the Mereni to the extent that they would barely even talk about them or acknowledge their existence. But what did a potential alliance with our neighbors to the east have to do with me?

"Andoc suggested that you go with them," Volya continued. "The Mereni respect good horse trainers, and he seems to think you would be uniquely suited to dealing with them."

What?

Andoc was looking at me, one eyebrow raised slightly as if in challenge, and I felt the sudden irrational urge to wipe that cocky expression off his face with my fist. My mouth was open. I closed it, and swallowed twice.

"If you think I would be of help, I'm happy to do whatever I can," I managed.

"Good lad," said Volya. "The Mereni village is two days' ride. You'll leave in the morning. This evening, we will be holding a funeral ceremony for those who died."

Suddenly, the grief hit me afresh, like a sharp blow to the sternum, and it was all I could do to nod and say, "Of course." Volya clapped a hand on my shoulder and excused himself, leaving me alone with Andoc and my churning emotions.

"Why?" I asked cautiously, looking up at him.

His smug expression had faded at the mention of the funeral ceremony. "The Mereni really do have respect for horse tamers and trainers," he said. "As for the rest, well, you'll understand when we get there. Now, have you eaten at all since I brought you food last night?"

It took a few moments more than it should have to think back. "No," I said eventually.

"My surprise knows no bounds." Apparently, neither did his sarcasm. I frowned as he continued. "Very well, you're coming with me to deliver lunch to Senovo and help make sure he eats it. Let's go."

It had taken no time at all for Gretya's daughters to throw themselves into taking over her business with the single-mindedness of people who were trying to keep grief at bay. I watched in something of a daze as Andoc charmed an extra portion from the girls, and I returned the teary hug that Limdya offered me, patting her somewhat awkwardly on the back. Andoc and I made our way to the temple barracks, laden with fruit, cheese, and cold meat. While I was familiar with the building's location, I'd never really had cause to spend much time there. It was the largest structure in the settlement, decorated with carved stone and beaten metal representing the various deities.

Andoc stopped at the door, offering a perfunctory obeisance to the gods, and I followed suit. Inside, it seemed far too quiet and empty. An effort had been made to clean up the damage and, presumably, the blood. All of the priests' bodies had been removed to the green with the others, but the building still seemed more like a crypt than a place where people lived. I shivered, unable to help myself. Toward the end of the long, narrow structure, we heard the faint sound of voices and followed them. Andoc cleared his throat as we approached, and Senovo looked up from the chair he was occupying next to High Priest Rhystel's low pallet.

"Greetings," Andoc said, "We come bearing food, and news."

"Ah," said the High Priest in a weak voice, "Andoc. Perhaps you can convince young Senovo here to stop hovering for an hour or two and go get some rest. Oh, hello, Carivel."

"Hello," I said, trying to smile and failing miserably.

"I've given up trying to get the stubborn bastard to do anything he doesn't want to, Elder Brother. Perhaps between us, we can at least get these two to eat, though," Andoc said, shocking me a bit with his informality. *Elder Brother* and *Little Brother* were terms the priests used with each other, based on their comparative rank. I had never heard someone outside of the priesthood address any of them in such a way, much less the High Priest.

The old man huffed a soft breath of pained laughter. "Indeed, my boy. Indeed."

Rhystel was deathly pale. His upper body was swathed with bandages, soaked through with blood under his right shoulder. One of the invading soldiers must have run him through and left him, thinking him dead. The blood loss itself was bad enough for someone of the High Priest's advanced years, but if infection set in it would all be over very quickly.

Andoc set his burden of food on a low table nearby, and motioned me to do the same. "Eat," he said firmly. I picked up a slice of meat without argument and started eating. Andoc spread another slice with cheese, rolled it up, and handed it to Senovo, who had remained silent throughout.

"Are you able to eat anything, Elder Brother?" Andoc asked.

"That depends. Are those fresh lindanberries I smell?" Rhystel asked.

"They are," Andoc replied, and gathered a small handful.

"The healer said you were only to have broth," Senovo said, his voice rusty as if he had not used it for a while.

Rhystel smiled up at him kindly. "If this is to be my last season on earth, I would like to enjoy the lindanberries while I have a chance, Little Brother."

Senovo subsided, but his expression was distraught. I ached for him, and for the loss of my own mentor.

"And what brings you here, Carivel?" Rhystel asked.

I forced myself to meet his eyes, trying once again to smile. "I seem to be acting as a pack horse for the most part, High Priest. Though, speaking of horses, you might be interested to know that Volya's mare foaled a second white colt yesterday."

"Ah, that's a good omen," said the old man, pausing to let Andoc feed him a berry.

"Senovo," Andoc said, "you, Carivel, and I are to ride out to the Mereni village tomorrow morning. Volya wants to forge an alliance with them against the troops at the Alyrion outpost."

"Really?" Senovo said with a faint frown, showing the first stirrings of interest. "The Mereni? That's... unusual."

"Well, well," the High Priest said. "Extraordinary times call for extraordinary measures, I suppose. Now, if the three of you are finished eating, please go away for a while and let an old eunuch get some rest. Senovo, you have a ceremony to prepare for, I believe."

I suddenly realized that Senovo would, by necessity, be performing the funeral rites this evening. It seemed his desire to remain a figure lurking in the background was not destined to be. He looked as though the very thought made him nauseous, but he allowed Andoc to usher him away nonetheless. I set myself to tidying away the remains of the food.

"Shall I leave these for you, High Priest?" I asked, indicating the small bowl of berries.

"Please," he said, and I set them next to him, within easy reach of his good arm. "Carivel," he continued, his eyes closing and his voice sounding suddenly far away, "this is important. Don't be afraid to seize opportunity when it comes your way. The gods place doors in front of us; it is up to us to walk through them."

I stilled, trying to make sense of his words. "Thank you, High Priest Rhystel," I said eventually. "I'll try to remember."

Distracted, I left Andoc trying to get Senovo to rest, and returned to the pens. It was not yet mid-afternoon, so I busied myself with the others, oiling leather that had gotten wet in the rain the previous day to prevent it from stiffening and cracking. When the boys tending the herd drove them back to the pens at dinnertime, I gathered everyone to inform them of the funeral, and my impending absence.

"Dalon," I said, "you will be in charge while I'm gone. Favian, you will assist him. I would also like you to continue taming Cassira's foal, Favian."

Dalon appeared stuck between irritation and smug pride; Favian looked surprised, but pleased. I dismissed everyone to go about their business, and returned to my hut in hopes of girding myself for the funeral ceremony in a couple of hours.

SIX

The entire village turned out at dusk, gathering on the village green. A pyre had been laid at some point during the day. I had to suppress a shudder at the sight of the bodies wrapped in shrouds and resting on the pile of stacked wood; I'd never seen a funeral fire so large, and I never wanted to again. I had intended to find a place near the back, where I could remain inconspicuous in case my emotions overcame me, but, to my surprise, Volya caught my eye and motioned me forward to where the elders and warriors were arrayed at the front.

With another shock, I realized that I was a person of importance now. The Horse Master of Draebard. The thought circled my mind like a carrion vulture, refusing to settle. Almost against my own will, I slotted myself next to Andoc—a familiar face amongst a sea of intimidating elders. He wrapped an arm around my shoulders and squeezed for a moment before letting go; it was all I could do not to abandon my tight control and sag against him.

As twilight deepened, the eerie sound of drums broke the near-silence. From the direction of the temple, torches flared into life two at a time along the edge of the main road through the village, coming ever closer. As they approached the green, I could see the surviving acolytes, Reston and Crenelo, lighting the torches in tandem before moving on to the next pair, and the next, and the next. Behind them, Senovo followed with measured steps. Where he had been slumped and weary earlier at the temple barracks as he watched over the High Priest, he now stood straight-backed, his chin high. His eyes were lined with the kohl that had first drawn my attention and admiration when I moved to the village three years ago.

He was, in a word, beautiful.

When the last of the torches arrayed in front of the pyre were lit, sending curls of greasy smoke into the night air, Senovo raised the ceremonial bowl he was carrying high over his head.

"Mighty Deresta, She-Who-Burns," he began, his sonorous voice carrying easily across the green. "Goddess of sunlight. Goddess of immolation. Tonight your children stand before you in grief. We commend our many dead to your purifying caress, that their ashes might return to feed the earth, and their souls might return to the sky, carried upon your smoke."

"*Ever shall it be so,*" chanted the crowd, as one.

Senovo lowered the bowl, balancing it in one hand. He moved to the end of the long pyre and dipped the fingers of the other hand into the sacred oil within, flicking a few drops on the first shrouded figure.

"Wyarra," he said. "Wife of Denuto. Beloved mother and sister." He moved slowly to the next body, flicking more oil. "Cuscan. Mighty warrior. Protector of Draebard even unto death." The next shroud was heartbreakingly small. "Monis. Treasured son and source of great joy… "

Taking his time, Senovo continued around the pyre at a stately pace, his voice never faltering as he recited the names and associations of the dead. Sounds of grief and weeping swelled at some of the names, as bereaved friends and family members were embraced and comforted by those around them. Many of the names belonged to Senovo's fellow priests. Eventually, he reached the final two figures.

"Gretya. Mother and provider not only to her beloved daughters, but to all the village."

Grief swelled in my chest as I remembered a gap-toothed smile and the smell of good food, distributed with love and care. Senovo moved to the final shroud, flicking oil over it.

"Jorun," Senovo said. "Horse Master of Draebard. Caretaker of the herd. Mentor and father to his apprentices."

A choked sound forced its way up from my chest, and I felt suddenly dizzy. Before I could properly begin to panic about making a scene, a strong hand settled on the small of my back. Rested there, quietly. I glanced up through burning eyes at Andoc standing next to me, but he was facing straight ahead, his face a mask.

Senovo turned back to the crowd. "Deresta, accept your faithful children into your embrace. Return them to the earth and sky from whence they came."

"Ever shall it be so," I whispered with the rest of those present, my voice breaking.

The two acolytes circled the pyre, lighting the wood at intervals with a *whoosh* of climbing flames. Within moments, the whole thing was ablaze. It would burn all night.

"Go in peace," Senovo said. "Celebrate the lives that return to the gods this evening. Blessings be upon you all."

He swept into a low bow, rising a moment later. I was not the only one to notice the slight sway of weariness—covered quickly—as Senovo straightened. Beside me, I felt Andoc tense.

"He didn't rest at all, did he?" I asked quietly. "You should go to him."

"I will, once he gets back to the temple barracks." Andoc's hand was still resting on my back. "Will you come?"

I chewed the inside of my lip, surprised by the question, and the offer inherent in it. But... no. The horses needed watching, and I would not distract the two of them from their grief with my own.

"No, I need to return to guard the horses," I said. "I'll meet you at the pens at first light for our journey."

"Very well," he replied, his hand falling away. I tried not to miss it. "We'll see you in the morning, then." He paused. "I'll talk to Volya about setting a night guard on the pens. Should have thought of that earlier, actually."

"We've all been distracted," I said. "It's a good idea, though."

The gathering was already breaking up as people retreated to grieve in private. I lost myself in the dispersing crowd, heading back to my hut to prepare a bedroll and other supplies for the morning. A bit of stale bread and cheese still sat on my table from the supper Andoc had brought me the previous evening, and I forced myself to eat it even though my stomach felt queasy with fatigue and grief. I thought of the people gathered in groups throughout the village, toasting the dead with flagons of wine and ale. Reminiscing. Supporting each other.

Suddenly I felt very cold and alone.

You don't have to be, said a little voice in my head. It was true. I could probably go to the temple barracks right now, to join Senovo and Andoc. What was it High Priest Rhystel had told me about the gods putting doors in front of us?

I stood there for several moments staring at the wall, thinking. Eventually, I shouldered my traveling pack with a sigh and headed for the horse pens.

My tears that night burned themselves out more quickly than on the previous night, and I slept in fits and starts, waking at every tiny noise. When the first hint of dawn appeared in the east, I felt more fatigued than when I'd curled up in the hay hours ago; my eyes were red and itchy. Another dunk in the horse trough revived me somewhat, but I cringed at the thought of two full days in the saddle. It was no comfort whatsoever that Senovo was probably even worse off than I was.

The lads were staring to arrive as I straightened my rumpled clothing, cursing myself for having forgotten to remove my breast bindings last night. The leather itched horribly, but there was nothing to be done about it now. On a positive note, I was pleased to see Dalon arriving with the very first group—it seemed he was taking his role as the temporary leader seriously. We exchanged wary nods, and I left him to it.

Making my way to the large pen, I grabbed a couple of halters, catching Andoc's long-suffering gelding and a steady, reliable gray mare for Senovo to ride. Kekenu followed along behind us, chewing on a mouthful of hay as he walked. It was soothing to go through the familiar routine of grooming and saddling the horses. With a small flash of vindictive pleasure, I fastened a rope hackamore around Andoc's horse's head, rather than a bitted bridle.

After all, I was the Horse Master now.

The sun was just breaking over the horizon when Andoc and Senovo appeared. They came over and stowed their bedrolls and saddlebags, tying them into place snugly behind the horses' saddles. Andoc reached into one of his bags and handed me a parchment-wrapped pastry drizzled with honey and chopped nuts.

"Because apparently you don't eat unless I feed you," he said. As I eagerly bit into the treat, his eyes were caught by the rope hackamore on his horse's head, and he turned back to me with a raised eyebrow. "Really?"

I gave him a sharp smile in reply.

"She did warn you, you know," Senovo said, looking about as pale and exhausted as I had thought he would.

Within fifteen minutes, the three of us were riding out of town on the eastern road, heading toward the territory of our mysterious, much-reviled neighbors.

"So," I said when the silence threatened to become oppressive, "what exactly makes me so uniquely suited to negotiating with the Mereni?"

Andoc smiled across at me. "I told you. They respect horse tamers."

"*Andoc,*" Senovo said, shooting his companion a quelling look.

"What? They do." Andoc's smile gained a faintly secretive edge. "And as for the rest of it, can you blame me for wanting Carivel to see it firsthand?"

Senovo shook his head in disgust and caught my eye. "The Mereni have some fundamentally different views about things that tend not to sit well with most other Eburosi."

"Good thing Carivel's not most Eburosi," Andoc said.

"I am right here, you know," I grumbled. "Fine. Keep your secrets, both of you."

Conversation as we rode was sporadic. Both Senovo and I were still laboring under a cloud of grief, not to mention lack of sleep. I was starting to wonder if Andoc ever showed weakness, or if he always maintained such a disgustingly high level of competence and equanimity. Though, to be fair, he hadn't lost anyone as close to him as Senovo and I had. At least, I didn't think he had.

Predictably, Andoc called a halt and forced us to eat lunch as the sun reached its zenith in the sky. The chill of the past couple of days had given way to sunny warmth, and we hobbled the horses to let them graze while we sat propped up against tree trunks at the edge of a little clearing, drinking watered wine and eating dried fruit and jerky.

"You two could nap for a while if you like," Andoc said, a few minutes after we'd finished the food and drink.

I forced my eyes open, not having realized they'd closed. Across from me, Senovo rolled his head back and forth against his tree trunk, a lazy negative.

"No," he said. "It's fine."

"We should keep moving," I agreed. "We'll sleep tonight when it's too dark to travel."

Andoc shrugged, as if it was of no matter to him either way. We repacked the horses and continued on. Kekenu was a reassuring, steady presence underneath me. I gained occasional flashes of amusement as Andoc wrestled with his simple rope reins, muttering under his breath. Senovo was a pale and silent figure at my side.

The landscape changed gradually into something unfamiliar. I had never been this far east of Draebard, my own wanderings having taken place to the north of the village I now called home. The east was craggier, with exposed rocks jutting through the ochre-colored soil. Streams were plentiful and fast moving, and we crossed one river that was wider than Draebard's village green and came up to the horses' bellies at the deepest point.

Senovo was looking positively haggard and I was starting to doze off in my saddle when the sun finally slipped below the horizon.

"We should make camp," I said after jerking awake for the dozenth time in the last hour or so.

"And here I was, waiting for you to slip right off of your horse's back before you decided it was time to stop," Andoc said.

I glared at him, raising an eyebrow in my best haughty manner. "Nonsense. A Horse Master is perfectly capable of riding and sleeping at the same time." I blinked as I realized what I'd just said. "Gods. That's going to take a whole lot of getting used to."

"I know the feeling," Senovo said softly—the first words he'd uttered in hours.

We found a likely looking spot at the base of a large boulder set beside a small stream and puttered around, gathering scrub wood and caring for the horses. Senovo sprinkled some powder from a pouch on the kindling and struck a spark, which immediately set the pile to flaming brightly.

"Trade secret," he murmured in response to my impressed noise, feeding larger wood to the flames until the campfire was burning merrily in the deepening dark.

With our bedrolls arranged around the fire and our responsibilities for the day complete, we passed around food and drink, leaning against the seats of our saddles on the ground. The three of us filled our cups with a deep red vintage from a wineskin that Andoc provided. I couldn't suppress a cough as it burned down my throat, shockingly strong.

"Yup—I brought along the good stuff," he said, his smile flashing teeth. "You can thank me later."

"Pass it back," I said when I'd regained control of my voice, motioning for the skin and topping up my clay traveling cup when Senovo handed it to me.

Two cups later, I was feeling positively mellow, and maybe even a bit fuzzy around the edges. So were my companions, if their relaxed slouches were anything to go by. I frowned as my pleasant lassitude was interrupted by discomfort when I changed position. Scratching self-consciously at my midriff—trying to ease the itchiness of my bindings—I had a sudden thought.

"Hang on," I said. "I just realized that you both know my deep, dark secret already. Stay here for a minute. I'm going to go take off the wrap that I use to bind my chest."

Andoc smiled his cocky, albeit slightly drunk smile from across the fire. "Ah... don't be shy, Carivel—I've seen it all before, and Senovo here is a religious man. Not to mention a eunuch."

I ignored the little thrill that ran up my spine at his words in favor of offering him a rude hand gesture I'd learned from Dalon and his friends. When Senovo snorted softly in amusement, I counted it a victory. The firelight didn't quite extend to the creek bed, so I walked to the edge of the water to remove my tunic. The bindings had been on for far too long. Taking them off felt wonderful, even though my skin tingled and ached when the blood flow returned.

The humid evening was still warm enough that I dipped my tunic in the running water and used it to scrub at my face, arms, and torso before rinsing it out and donning it again. The damp material was clammy against my skin, raising gooseflesh and hardening my nipples to painful points before my body heat warmed it. Gathering up the discarded soft leather strips into a loose roll, I returned to the fire. I stuffed the bindings in my saddlebag with a faint flush of embarrassment, and gratefully accepted more of the strong wine.

"It's frankly rather amazing to me that you've been hiding something like this successfully for three years," Andoc said once I'd settled down again and taken a deep draught. "I mean—how did you piss?"

Senovo choked on his wine. I leaned back, giving the question all the careful consideration of the fairly drunk.

"Privately," I replied after a weighty pause.

Andoc laughed aloud, and I let myself appreciate the fine lines crinkling around the corners of his mouth and eyes in the firelight. "Yes," he said, "I imagine that would be the most prudent approach."

Senovo cleared his throat. "This is, of course, from my own personal curiosity, and not something you need to answer if you don't care to, Carivel. But, if you could wake tomorrow with the body of a young man... would you?"

I'd be lying if I said I hadn't thought about it. Some days, it seemed to be *all* I could think about, if I were being truthful. And yet...

"Maybe?" I said. "I think so. Most of the time, anyway. Even as a small child, I didn't really feel like a girl all that often."

"But you are attracted to men, yes?" Senovo probed gently.

"And eunuchs," Andoc added. I was surprised to see that his teasing smile had faded, leaving him serious.

I couldn't control the flush that stained my cheeks, but despite my drunkenness I was acutely aware that I was in the presence of the only two people in the world with whom I could discuss my life openly.

"Yes," I said. The wine gave me the courage to meet Senovo's eyes and add, "but only the beautiful ones with kind souls and eloquent eyes."

"Ah," Andoc said with a fond look at the young priest next to him, "she has the measure of you, my friend." He frowned, and looked back to me. "Oh... there's a thought. Would you rather we still referred to you as 'he,' Carivel? In private, I mean."

When I opened my mouth to reply, a choked noise that sounded suspiciously close to a sob came out instead. My right hand flew to my mouth to keep anything else from escaping.

The wine, I thought. *It's the wine, and the grief.* I forced myself to breathe deeply and slowly, not looking at the others as they straightened slightly in concern. I was more thankful than I could say that neither of them tried to approach me in that moment. I think I would have shattered and blown away like a dried puff-flower in the wind at the first kind touch.

"Sorry. I'm sorry," I said when my voice was finally back under my control. "No one has ever given me that choice before."

In twenty-three-and-a-half years, not a single person ever let me choose.

The two men across from me relaxed slightly, letting me feel out the words as I spoke them.

"In a perfect world," I started slowly, "I would have been born a boy. I would have grown up desiring girls; married and had children." Andoc and Senovo shared a look I couldn't decipher. I wasn't sure it was about me at all. "This isn't a perfect world, though. I don't know *what* I am. I desire men. My body is a woman's. My mind is mostly a man's, I think. But I still liked it when you called me 'she.' I think 'she' feels like a kind of freedom to me, after hiding the truth for so long. It will never happen of course, but ideally, I would like it if I didn't have to hide my female body from anyone. If they all knew that I was born a 'she,' but they didn't care that I dressed like a man and cared for the horses and lusted after other men."

It was the most I had ever said out loud about my unfortunate position in my entire life. I worried at my lower lip with my teeth and looked up to meet my companions' eyes.

"That seems an understandable wish," Senovo said easily.

"Very well," said Andoc. "In private, you shall be our good friend, Horse Mistress Carivel, who happens to think and act like a man most of the time, but who lusts uncontrollably after other attractive men. And eunuchs, of course. Personally, I'd love to hear more details about that last part."

The cocky smile had returned. I still wanted to punch it off his face, but between the wine and the soul baring, there was some danger that the punch would be the prelude to an attempt to jump on him and kiss him senseless.

"Too bad," I told him instead. "First, tell me more about yourselves. It's only fair. Andoc, how did you come to be a warrior of Draebard? Senovo, how did you become a priest?"

"First?" Andoc echoed. "So there's a chance we might get to hear about your uncontrollable lust afterward?" I glared at him drunkenly. "Fine, fine," he continued with a huff. "There's not much to tell, in my case. I come from Venzor, in the northeast. My father died after falling off our roof when I was thirteen. The idiot was trying to fix a leak during a thunderstorm, of all things. My mother is still alive, as far as I know. I try to visit her at least once a year."

"What brought you to Draebard?" I asked.

Andoc shrugged. "I wanted to be a warrior, but everyone in my village still saw me as the pale, sickly lad I'd been as a child. When I was sixteen, I came here for a fresh start and apprenticed myself to Volya. That's pretty much it, really. Senovo's story is far more interesting than mine, to be honest, though I'm not sure how much of it he'll care to share."

I looked to Senovo with renewed interest.

"How much do you know of initiation into the priesthood?" Senovo asked quietly, his eyes on the wine in his cup.

"Just what everyone knows, I suppose," I replied, intrigued. "You have to choose to become a eunuch, giving up your ability to sire children so that you can act as a neutral party during rites of fertility and so forth. It always seemed like a huge sacrifice to make, to me at least. Though I suppose some priests do end up becoming very powerful people."

"A slightly simplistic view, but essentially correct," Senovo allowed.

I looked at him shrewdly. "You don't want power, though. You said as much."

"Definitely not," Senovo replied.

"So why choose to become a eunuch? I've always thought that must be a horrible thing to go through."

"I didn't," he said.

"You... didn't?" Perhaps it was the wine addling my wits, but that didn't make any sense. I told him as much.

Senovo's eyes grew distant. "I was born south of here. Far to the south, in fact. Things are different there." Andoc, who had become very quiet, eased closer until his shoulder was brushing the priest's as he continued. "My family was extremely poor. My grandfather had gone deeply into debt with the moneylenders. My mother and father were still trying to escape from under it, while also feeding me and my five older brothers and sisters. I'm afraid I was a rather difficult boy. Wild. Always escaping my chores and disappearing into the woods on my own—"

"It was the wolf in you," Andoc said.

"Perhaps. Whatever the case, the year of my seventh birthday, the harvest was even worse than usual. In their desperation, my parents decided to sell me to the priest's guild."

I drew in a sharp breath. "Your parents *sold* you? A child? How was that even allowed?"

Senovo lifted one shoulder and let it fall, staring into the fire. "It's just the way things are in the south. In certain circumstances, people can become commodities. I was in service to the guild for ten years, and hated every minute of it. When I reached the age of seventeen, I received the *honor* of initiation. Even though it meant I would no longer be a slave, it was not an honor I desired *in the least*, to put it mildly. Unfortunately, my opinion in the matter was not consulted."

"That's terrible," I said, barely able to wrap my mind around such a thing. "I think that may be the most terrible thing I've ever heard."

"Four of them held me down," Senovo continued, and his eyes were very far away now. Andoc's arm came up across the priest's shoulders, gripping him lightly as Senovo continued in a flat voice. "They forced a thick leather strap into my mouth so I wouldn't bite through my own tongue. When I was completely restrained, the high priest crushed my scrotum between two lengths of oak board with a heavy mallet."

"He deserved to die for that," Andoc said, and I got the impression it wasn't the first time he'd spoken the words.

Senovo continued as if he had not heard. "The shock and pain caused me to shift into the form of the wolf for the first time in my life. I savaged the priests holding me down, ripped open the high priest's stomach, and escaped from the temple into the wildlands beyond. When I changed back, days later, I was alone and naked, in excruciating agony. I crawled to the nearest road and told the first farmer who passed that I'd been attacked and robbed by bandits. When I'd recovered enough to travel, I started walking north and didn't stop until I reached a land where they didn't buy and sell children. Somewhere no one knew me — where I could start over. Of course, my options for making a livelihood at that point were fairly, shall we say, *narrow*. You see the result before you now."

The silence stretched for several moments.

"I'm deeply sorry," I said eventually. "Perhaps I shouldn't have asked in the first place, but I'm honored that you would share something so personal with me, nonetheless. You have my word that your story will travel no further."

"A secret for a secret," Senovo said, echoing his words from yesterday. He turned to Andoc, his level voice never wavering. "Tonight will be bad, my friend. Don't let me change."

Andoc nodded and pressed a kiss to Senovo's forehead. Senovo closed his eyes and leaned into the contact for a moment before pulling back, wrapping himself in his bedroll, and turning his back to the fire. A few minutes later he was fast asleep.

"Don't be afraid of anything you see or hear tonight," Andoc said. "Senovo is far more frightened of the wolf than you or I have cause to be."

"The wolf saved my life," I said. "I don't fear it."

Andoc nodded. His faint smile was sad. "Of course you don't. Good night, Horse Mistress Carivel. Things will look better in the light of morning."

"Good night, Andoc," I replied. "Take care of him tonight."

"I always do."

SEVEN

The night was pleasant, and the wine combined with my exhaustion should have rendered me utterly insensible until morning. Instead, I jerked awake in the small hours, the dregs of a half-forgotten dream lying bitter on the back of my tongue. The fire had burned down to glowing coals, casting a faint orange light over the figures across from me. A low sound—almost a snarl—prickled the hair at the back of my neck, and I sat up slowly.

"Not tonight, my friend," Andoc said. "I do not give you leave to change."

The warrior was bare-chested, propped up on one arm so he could look down at Senovo's huddled form next to him.

"*I can't stop it,*" Senovo said, and he did, indeed, sound terrified at the prospect of freeing the animal caged within himself.

"I'm not giving you a choice in the matter, *amadi,*" Andoc said, and my chest constricted at the endearment. "You will not hunt tonight."

The rumbling growl came again. I caught my breath in shock as Senovo surged up, his hands reaching for Andoc's face and throat like claws. The warrior batted them away, seemingly without effort. There was a quick twist of bodies that I couldn't quite follow in the low light, and then he was straddling Senovo's hips, one hand pinning the priest's wrists over his head, and the other pressing against his vulnerable neck.

"Yield, my friend," Andoc said, not even out of breath as Senovo strained against him. "I told you before, you get no choice in this tonight."

After a tense moment that had me holding my breath, Senovo... *melted*; there was no other word for it. All the tension flowed from his muscles. His head tilted back, baring his throat to Andoc's callused hand like an offering.

"There you are, dear one. That's better, isn't it?" Andoc said, a soft smile crossing his face. The hands pinning Senovo loosened their grip, becoming a caress, and the priest arched into the contact with a soft noise of surrender. My eyes were drawn of their own volition to the outline of Andoc's stiff prick, tenting the soft leather of his breeches as Senovo's torso twisted beneath him restlessly. A flood of wetness pulsed between my own legs at the sight. When I dragged my eyes back up to Andoc's face, he was looking at me with one side of his mouth quirked up in half a smile.

"Carivel is awake, *amadi*," he said, leaning close to Senovo's ear. "She's watching you yield to me. I think she likes what she sees."

Senovo and I shivered in reaction to the words at the same time, and the sound that the eunuch made was almost a whine.

"Shh," Andoc said. "There's plenty of time for all that later." His eyes flicked to mine briefly as he spoke. "Tonight, we sleep."

The flesh between my thighs was throbbing as I watched Senovo nuzzle into Andoc's side, the warrior easing himself back down into his sleeping roll with an arm draped possessively around his friend. If I'd been a man in body as well as mind, my cock would have been hard enough to pound stone at the sight. I silently lowered myself back down into my own nest of blankets, unable to keep from rocking the heel of my hand against the crotch of my breeches to try to ease the pressure.

It was a testament to my own exhaustion that I fell asleep again a few minutes later, the scene between the two of them playing over in my mind, following me down into dreams.

⚜

The following morning should have been awkward. Instead, Senovo awoke with a groan, stretching — looking more rested than I'd seen him since the attack. Seeming to remember the events of the night, he froze, looking at me.

"All right?" he asked, watching me with what might have been nervousness.

I nodded. "You?" I asked.

He nodded in return.

"Of course we're all right," Andoc said in a voice far too cheerful for the early hour. "It's a beautiful morning, everyone finally got some decent sleep, and I'm possibly one step closer to hearing more details about Carivel's uncontrollable lust. What could be better?"

"I never said it was uncontrollable," I grumbled, glaring at him even as I blushed scarlet. "Senovo, is he always like this?"

"Always," Senovo replied.

By unspoken consent, we kept to neutral topics as we readied ourselves for the second day of travel. Something about daylight (or perhaps sobriety) did not lend itself as well to discussing private matters as a campfire after dark did. Instead, I attempted to pry more information from Andoc regarding the Mereni, and was once again deflected.

It was cooler than the previous day, with clouds blocking the sun most of the time. As the afternoon wore on, we were pelted with occasional fat raindrops. We'd been riding in the higher elevations for more than a day, but now we were once again descending. The fertile valleys below, while not identical to those around Draebard, were at least more familiar looking than the scrubby uplands had been.

Beneath me, Kekenu suddenly perked up with interest, lifting his head to gaze to our left with pricked ears. In the distance, I made out a herd of horses. Even from here I could see that they were taller and more slender-legged than the animals I was used to.

"The horses look different here," I said, standing in the stirrups to get a better view.

Andoc nodded. "Mereni horses have a reputation for being as fast as the wind... not to mention rank as hell."

"Perhaps that's why they respect horse tamers so much," Senovo said.

"Maybe so," Andoc agreed, turning his attention back to me. "Carivel, I know I've been playing things close to my chest, but you should know there's a chance the Leader will ask you to prove your skills on a difficult horse."

"That's fine," I said, unconcerned. A thought occurred to me. "Is he likely to ask either of you two to prove *your* skills as well?"

"It's very possible," Senovo replied.

"Hmm... this may end up being quite an interesting trip," I said.

The village of the Mereni was considerably larger than Draebard. We arrived an hour or so before dusk and entered by the main road, riding side by side. While we received a number of curious looks with our strange clothing and short, thickset riding horses, no one challenged us until Andoc dismounted outside what I assumed was the village meeting hall. He handed his horse off to me and approached the door, only to find his way barred by an extraordinarily tall man and an extraordinarily tall woman flanking the entrance.

"State your business," said the woman.

I was surprised to see that she wore loose leather trousers with a bronze short sword at her waist, and that the man with her seemed content to let her lead the discussion. The woman's long hair was an unusual shade of fiery red; her features were sharp and strong. Andoc appeared unfazed by her presence, but I couldn't help but find amusement in the fact that he had to look up slightly to meet her eyes.

"Greetings," Andoc said. "My friends and I have traveled two days from the west to meet with the esteemed Leader of the Mereni. I apologize that we were unable to send word ahead. Could you perhaps arrange for a message to be delivered?"

To my surprise, he sounded positively mature and diplomatic. I found myself strangely impressed by it.

"What's the message?" asked the woman.

"My companions and I have come at the behest of Chief Volya of Draebard to discuss an alliance against the Alyrion Empire. Alyrion troops attacked our village in the dead of night four days ago, killing and wounding dozens."

"Draebard, eh?" the woman said, looking us up and down with an expression of distaste. "I'll let Magoldis know. Can't promise much beyond that."

"That's all I ask," Andoc said, the picture of charm. "In the mean time, is there somewhere that the three of us might stay for the night? A tavern or a way-house?"

"Try Harinel's place. He lets rooms. Keep heading east, and turn right at the second road. It's the house with the yellow door. I'll send a messenger there in the morning if Magoldis agrees to see you."

Andoc bowed and offered his thanks. As I returned his horse to him, I said, "You should try employing some of that charm with your friends, you know, instead of saving it all for complete strangers."

The warrior scoffed, a twinkle in his eye. "Nonsense," he said. "It's far too much effort. With my friends, I prefer to rely on my rugged good looks for most things."

Harinel, when we found him, turned out to be a stooped old man with one eye missing. His house was ramshackle and crook-cornered, but the inside was spacious and relatively clean.

"I only have one room available tonight," he said. "Will that suit you?"

Senovo and Andoc both looked to me, and I shrugged my agreement. It wasn't appreciably different from sharing a campfire with them, and at this point I didn't have any secrets left for them to discover, to be perfectly honest.

After paying Harinel for the room, we unsaddled the horses and let them loose in the small pen behind the house, where they had access to hay and a shallow wooden trough full of water. Senovo and I were still suffering the ill effects of several nights of grief and poor sleep, so Andoc offered to venture out alone to procure food and drink for us.

When we were alone, I broached the topic that had been hanging between us all day.

"Senovo," I began, "I want to apologize for invading your privacy with Andoc last night. I hope it didn't make you terribly uncomfortable knowing that I was watching. I realize I should have left, or at least turned away. I'm sorry. I just—I wasn't expecting it, I guess, and I didn't really understand what I was seeing."

Senovo sat down on the edge of one of the low beds, giving me his full attention. I forced myself to meet his piercing green eyes and hold them.

"I didn't mind," he said. "In fact, I'm afraid to say that when I get like that, a bit of additional humiliation rather enhances the experience. Did it bother you?"

"It… probably should have?" I said, losing my battle to maintain eye contact. My hands twisted together in my lap; I looked down at them instead. "Andoc was right, though. I liked it. It was beautiful. Exciting. Even if I don't really understand why."

I darted an uncertain glance at Senovo, who appeared unperturbed. I was forcibly reminded that he was a priest, and a good one—however horrific his introduction to that life might have been. Dealing with matters related to relationships and sex was a huge part of what priests did, whether in a ceremonial context or counseling couples regarding their mutual pleasure and harmony. If the fact that the current discussion was personal bothered him, he certainly didn't show it.

"Would I be correct in assuming that your unusual circumstances mean you have not had much experience with physical love in its various forms?" he asked tactfully.

I snorted softly. "Not unless you count my own fingers in the dark." I paused for a moment, remembering. "Well. I also kissed a girl once, back in my old village. I was very young at the time. I had to see if I could want girls, like a proper boy. It didn't work."

"A reasonable experiment," Senovo replied. "In addition to the pleasure of purely physical touch, you may or may not have discovered that sexuality relies rather heavily on the mind. In the case of eunuchs, I think I can safely say that when sexuality persists at all, it becomes largely a mental exercise."

I thought of the fantasies that often played out behind my eyelids while I touched myself, and blushed faintly. It didn't help that most of those fantasies involved the very person sitting across from me.

Senovo smiled—a brief uptick of one side of his mouth. "I see the concept is not completely foreign to you."

I cleared my throat. "Not completely, no."

"Suffice to say, if you can imagine something—and even if you can't—there is probably someone who finds it arousing. What you saw last night was the way in which Andoc and I fit together. I do not feel desire in the way that undamaged men and women do; that was taken from me the day that my genitals were crushed by the men who owned me. While I can still feel physical pleasure from some forms of sexual contact, and while I happily engage in those sorts of practices with Andoc, the true gift that he gives me is control of the wolf."

"How?" I asked. "Last night, you asked him not to let you change, but surely that's something only you can control?"

"The wolf is stronger than me," Senovo said, "but Andoc is stronger than the wolf."

"I still don't understand," I said, frowning.

"Wolves in packs live within a strictly enforced hierarchy. The strongest control the pack, and the weaker wolves submit to them willingly—though a struggle for dominance may ensue at any time if a submissive wolf senses weakness in one of its superiors." Senovo paused, as if searching for the best way to put something into words. "When the wolf submits to Andoc, and Andoc forbids me to change, I don't change. It's not even a struggle. I can relax, safe in the knowledge that I will remain human. It is, perhaps, the *only* time I can truly relax, and as such, I treasure it. And him."

Something clicked within my thoughts. "The night of the attack..." I began, and he nodded.

"Andoc had been gone for days," he said, "and I was weak. I shifted."

"You saved my life," I pointed out.

"Awakening the next morning with a man's flesh in my belly, and his lifeblood smeared across my face," he added.

It was actually rather horrific when he described it that way. Not knowing what else to say, I said, "I'm sorry."

"I'm not sorry I saved you, Carivel," he said. "Never think that."

I nodded, not knowing what to do with the emotions welling up in my chest. Ever the coward, I changed the subject. "So being with Andoc lets you relax and stop fighting the wolf for awhile. I can understand the power of that, I think. And he... what? Likes controlling people? Being in charge?" I remembered the sight of Andoc straddling Senovo's hips, his erection jutting visibly within his breeches as he pinned the priest in place. Desire twisted shamefully in my belly, even now.

"He's a young, strong man, and a warrior," Senovo said. "I suppose he enjoys the struggle—the physical victory—but honestly, his pleasure seems to come mainly from meeting my needs. My need for him... for his strength and care."

"Pfft," came Andoc's familiar voice from the doorway, "Nonsense. I just like rolling around on the ground while rubbing up against a sweaty, writhing body. I mean, what's not to like?"

Mortification flooded me as he entered, swinging the door shut behind him with one foot. Still, I should have guessed that the infuriating prat would actually relish the idea of his sex life being discussed in his absence. His grin was wide as he deposited an armload of food wrapped in large, waxy green leaves on the room's rickety table. A moment later, the mouthwatering smell of roasted meat filled the room.

"So," he said as he removed the strap of a wineskin from over his shoulder and uncorked it, "we're finally discussing Carivel's uncontrollable lust, then? You two could have waited for me, you know."

He took a deep drink from the skin and passed it to Senovo, looking back and forth between us for all the world as if he were watching an archery contest or a wrestling match playing out on the village green for his entertainment. My deep-seated desire to punch him on the nose reared its ugly head once again.

Instead, somewhat surprised at my own courage, I said, "Yes, in fact I was just about to jump on Senovo and stick my tongue down his throat when you so rudely interrupted."

Senovo released a faint sound of amusement, and Andoc laughed deep and long. "Well, I'd be a hypocrite if I tried to blame you for that," said the warrior. "He is rather irresistible, isn't he?"

"Only to those with no self-control, I think you'll find," Senovo said in a wry voice. His own thirst sated, he passed the wineskin across to me.

Sensing that a certain degree of drunkenness would probably help with this conversation, I tipped it up and let the warm drink flow down my throat, enjoying its mellow taste. While Andoc might infuriate me on a regular basis, I had to admit that the man knew his wines. Corking the skin and putting it aside, I tore into one of the chunks of meat threaded onto a peeled wooden skewer. It was delicious... tender pork covered in some kind of unfamiliar spice.

"Now that we've finally gotten the 'lust' conversation out of the way," Andoc said around a mouthful of food, "you do realize it's only a matter of time until I convince you to act on it."

I... *wait, what*? I blinked, frozen in place with the meat held in front of my lips.

"You have all the subtlety of a bull in heat, Andoc," said Senovo.

"Bulls don't go into heat, *amadi*. Cows do," Andoc replied, unrepentant. "I thought you were supposed to know about these things, being a priest and all."

"Wait, *what*?" I said, my mouth finally catching up with my brain.

"I said, it's only a matter of time until I convince you to act on your uncontrollable lust," Andoc repeated slowly, as if I were hard of hearing.

"But..." I said, evidently trying to dazzle them both with my brilliance, "but, you and Senovo already have each other."

Senovo looked up from his skewer of pork. "While it's generally accepted for a young man to dally with a eunuch, the expectation is that he will eventually move on to find a woman and settle down."

I stared at him, appalled. While I knew as well as anyone that many young men and women gained their initial sexual experience from casual liaisons with acolytes and younger members of the priesthood, there was something almost... *blasphemous* about the idea of Andoc one day casting Senovo aside like some youthful folly.

Andoc rolled his eyes at both of us, and said, "However, in this case, since I have absolutely no intention of *moving on* from him, as Senovo so blithely puts it, I suppose I'll just have to find someone who lusts after both of us. Preferably uncontrollably."

I was still staring at him, relief on Senovo's behalf and irritation on my own behalf swirling together like water and wine in a cup. I think my mouth was open.

Senovo sighed. "I'd offer to hit him for you since I'm closer, but as a priest, that sort of thing is frowned upon. Also, we've already established that he's stronger than me."

"No need," I said faintly. "I think I'd rather do it myself."

Andoc lounged back, completely unconcerned. "Except you're worried you'd end up kissing me immediately afterward, am I right?"

Gods. Maybe strangling him would be more satisfying than hitting him.

"Keep telling yourself that," I managed.

"Oh, I intend to picture it quite vividly as I'm falling asleep later. As I suspect you will be," Andoc said, still smiling.

"Enough, Andoc," Senovo said. "Carivel, I should warn you that I'm going to need Andoc's help again tonight. If it bothers you, we can try to find someplace else to stay, and leave you in peace."

This was something of a moment of truth, and I was well aware of it. Andoc was looking at me with interest, though he hadn't refuted Senovo's words or offered any more infuriating comments of his own. It reinforced what I already believed—he might tease and push and prod, but Andoc had no intention of taking what was not freely offered. Helpless desire for both of them rose within me, utterly beyond my control.

Deresta's *tits.* I was so far gone for these two that it wasn't even funny.

"I already told you it didn't bother me," I said to Senovo, giving into the inevitable. "I thought it was beautiful, and that was even before I understood it. Besides, you said knowing I was watching helped."

Andoc was looking between the two of us with a speculative gaze, obviously curious about the conversation he'd missed. To his credit and my surprise, though, he didn't say a word.

Senovo nodded. "If it gives you pleasure, then I'm pleased. The gods smile on us when we utilize their gifts in such a way. As long as you know that you can leave at any time if you don't like something."

"You won't leave, though," Andoc said confidently.

Bastard. He was probably right. I ignored him, and assured Senovo that I understood. The three of us finished our meal in silence, Senovo growing visibly more distant as we did. I was beginning to understand that his distraction was the outward sign of his internal struggle for control. Andoc cleared away the remains of the meal and went to check the horses. While he was gone, I turned my back to Senovo and stripped off my tunic, unwrapping my breasts with a quiet sigh of relief. Pulling the tunic back on, I took off my boots and breeches and made myself comfortable on the smaller of the two beds, wearing only my shirt and smallclothes.

"Are you all right?" I asked Senovo, who still seemed to be off in a world of his own.

"Yes, I'm fine," he said faintly, eyes closed. "Merely very tired."

"You're stronger than you think," I told him, not entirely sure where the words were coming from. "Andoc will be back soon, though, and you can rest for awhile."

I watched in fascination as a faint tremor traveled through the priest's body, his face creasing for an instant with pain and longing.

"Yes," he agreed.

Andoc arrived a few moments later, a couple of coils of rope from the saddlebags looped over his shoulder. His smile at me was subdued, and he crossed immediately to Senovo's side, dropping the rope on the bed next to him.

"It's almost dark, *amadi*," he said, "and the candle is barely a stub. Give me a few moments to light a fire so I can watch over you properly."

"I could do that," I offered belatedly, berating myself for not having thought of it earlier.

Andoc shook his head. "No, you're already comfortable, and I don't mind. It won't take long."

I nodded, remembering what Senovo had said about Andoc wanting to care for others. Though he lacked Senovo's magic fire-starting powder, it wasn't long before he was feeding wood to a small pile of burning kindling, and soon a merry little blaze was crackling away in the hearth, lighting the room with a warm, flickering glow.

Andoc rose from the fire and returned to the bed, grazing Senovo's cheek with the backs of his fingers. "It's time, *amadi*," he said. "Take your clothes off and kneel on the bed."

I caught my breath silently. Already, this was different than the previous night. Senovo rose slowly and undid the fastenings at the front of his traveling robes. The heavy fabric slid from his shoulders, pooling on the rough wooden planks of the floor. Beneath, he wore breeches and boots for riding, but no tunic or linen undershirt. His chest was smooth and flat. Hairless.

Without hesitation, he unfastened the laces of his trousers. Sitting on the edge of the bed, he toed off his soft boots, and stood again to slide the breeches down to his ankles and off. His linen smallclothes followed a moment later, leaving him bare to my fascinated gaze as he gracefully folded himself into a kneeling position on the straw-filled mattress as if in prayer.

I had seen plenty of boys' pricks in my years working for Jorun. Most of the lads thought nothing of whipping themselves out to take a piss against the trunk of a convenient tree. And of course, I'd attended fertility ceremonies and handfastings throughout my life—though never, obviously, as a participant. I'd seen young men skinny-dipping, and warriors sparring in breechclouts—including Andoc himself—bare-skinned and sweating.

Senovo's body was the same, but different. His frame was slender, but he carried a sleek layer of fat under his smooth skin, like a river otter. Aside from his dark, perfectly arched eyebrows and the heavy plait of hair hanging from the back of his head, the only hair I could see on his body was a small patch between his legs—much finer and downier than that of the un-castrated males I'd seen.

His prick was small and limp, resting nestled between his thighs as he knelt. Where a man's balls would normally hang, there was only a flap of wrinkled skin, barely visible in the dim light.

Andoc paced slowly around the bed until he was at the priest's back, brushing his fingertips softly over Senovo's shoulders. "I'm going to tie you tonight. How do you want it?"

"Tight," Senovo said, sounding strained. "Please. Make it tight. Don't let it get free."

I caught my breath as Andoc's hand closed over the back of Senovo's neck, guiding him down until he was lying on his stomach, the side of his face pressed into the bed.

"Very well, my friend. Now. Stay there." Andoc's voice was uncompromising as he removed his hand and picked up the first coil of rope. Looping one end around Senovo's left wrist, he pulled both of the priest's arms straight down and back, binding them together behind his body tightly enough that his elbows nearly touched. Andoc quickly retrieved the second length of rope and used it to tie Senovo's knees and ankles together snugly, leaving a single long tail free.

With his grip on the rope's tail, he bent Senovo's knees and pulled his ankles up until they were even with his wrists, fastening his limbs together in a hogtie. There was still some rope left, and Andoc wove it into Senovo's single braid of hair, using the plait as a handhold to force Senovo's head up and back. He adjusted the length between the eunuch's head and ankles carefully, shortening it by increments until Senovo let out a deep groan, his spine bowed in a graceful arch. A shiver skated along my arms as Andoc tied the rope off and stepped back, raising gooseflesh in its wake.

When the warrior pulled a wicked looking dagger from his belt and set it on the table by the bed, I sucked in an audible breath, my eyes flying to his face.

"For the ropes. Just in case," he said patiently. I nodded, feeling ridiculously inexperienced and stupid.

Andoc's full attention returned immediately to the figure on the bed, as did mine. I had a fairly solid understanding of using ropes as restraint; it wasn't unusual for us to tie up a horse's leg to prevent it kicking out while an injury was treated, for instance. I could see immediately the strain Andoc's bonds put on Senovo's body, forcing it into a tense, unnatural position. I suspected it was no coincidence that it also showed off his slender lines in a most appealing manner—I could almost imagine some artist carving the elegant shape laid out before me into wood or bone.

The priest was trembling visibly with the effort of holding himself still, his eyes wide but unseeing. Andoc reached down, fisting the thick plait of hair and using it to force Senovo's head back even further with a slow, inexorable pull. He leaned over, his lips nearly touching the eunuch's ear as he growled, "*Let go.*"

I clamped my legs together around the throbbing pulse at the juncture of my thighs, trembling nearly as hard as Senovo. The priest keened; the noise tailing off to a whine, and then to harsh panting as he writhed and struggled against the rope like a wild animal. Andoc stepped back, staying within easy reach of both the knife and the bound man, his attention never wavering.

Harsh, choked growls echoed around the room, and I quailed as the firelight seemed to momentarily reflect off gray fur rather than golden skin. Andoc was intent but seemingly unconcerned, letting his captive struggle and sob and howl for what seemed like an age, until Senovo's movements eventually grew heavy and slow with exhaustion.

"Enough," Andoc said, steadying Senovo's head with one hand looped casually around his throat. "You're done now, *amadi.*"

Whether Senovo was done or not, I certainly was—shaking as hard as the priest beneath my rough blanket, and feeling as out of breath as if I'd been the one fighting the ropes. My skin felt tight and hot, as if it would combust if someone were to touch me. I was glad Andoc was completely focused on Senovo—I didn't think I could take a teasing comment right now… or even a simple question about my well-being.

Gods. Did Senovo suffer like this *every night*?

The priest was huffing little sobbing breaths, his throat moving against the gentle pressure of Andoc's hand. I watched as he slowly went limp under Andoc's care, his muscles loosening one by one; shallow panting transforming into something slower. Deeper. Andoc eased his hand away, leaving Senovo lying on his belly quietly. The eunuch gradually relaxed into the pressure of the rope, accepting it rather than fighting it.

"That's it," Andoc said softly. "You don't need to fight."

"*Please…*" Senovo whispered hoarsely.

I didn't know what he was asking for, though I doubted anyone with a heart could have denied Senovo whatever he needed at that moment. Fortunately, Andoc seemed to know exactly what was being requested.

"Of course, *amadi*," he said, and began to run one hand over Senovo's body with smooth, gentle strokes. The priest sighed and softened even further into the ropes' embrace, visibly soaking up Andoc's soothing touch. Andoc's hand roamed everywhere, giving equal attention to areas both intimate and platonic—his shoulders, his flanks, the crease of his buttocks.

My desire, which had fled completely in the face of Senovo's desperate, animal struggles, flowed back like a warm tide as I watched callused fingers running over smooth skin. It crested higher when Andoc moved his hand to caress Senovo's face and the priest rooted forward enough to pull the warrior's fingers into his mouth, heedless of the rope pulling his hair tighter against his scalp he suckled in utter contentment.

He would do that to Andoc's prick if he could only reach it, I thought, and couldn't stop the faint moan that escaped my lips.

"Touch yourself if you want to, Carivel," Andoc said, though his attention never wavered from his willing captive. "You're hardly going to offend us at this point."

I… *couldn't,* though. Andoc might tease and prod, intimating that the three of us could be together somehow. But it was all a lie. I was a pariah, and if either of them attached themselves to me, they would be as well. To pretend otherwise was simply cruel.

"What about you?" I asked, to deflect him. "Aren't you going to take your pleasure?"

Andoc shook his head, still not looking away from Senovo as he carefully pulled his fingers free. "He needs me clear-headed when it's this bad. Besides, it would be incredibly crass of me when you're still not completely committed to the idea of being with us, don't you think? You consented to stay while Senovo submitted to me—just like last night. We didn't say anything about sex."

The idea of being with us, he'd said, as if it was a real thing—a thing that could actually happen. Another little splinter of feeling pricked at my heart. *It can never be*, I told myself firmly. Aloud, I asked, "Is it always this bad for him?"

Andoc supported the priest's head with a gentle hand cupped under his chin, taking the strain out of the rope tied to his braided hair. He smoothed his other hand over Senovo's forehead, his thumb massaging slow circles against the priest's temple. "Not always," he said. "When he's tired, when he's upset. He's both right now—we all are. When he's been fighting the change for too long. I think if he ever stopped fighting the wolf and accepted it as part of himself, it wouldn't strain him so."

"Maybe someday he'll see what we do," I said quietly.

Andoc nodded. Beside him, Senovo had gone utterly slack, appearing nearly asleep within the ropes' embrace. The warrior shifted and began to untie him. I could see that he had used slipknots, and they slid free easily enough, even though Senovo had pulled them tight in his struggles. The priest slumbered on, seemingly oblivious, even as Andoc pulled the last of the rope free and eased his limbs into a more comfortable position.

"Will he be all right now?" I asked.

"Yes," said Andoc. "He'll sleep tonight. That should help with things for awhile."

"I'm glad. Goodnight, Andoc."

"Goodnight, Carivel."

My own sleep was slow to come despite my continued exhaustion. When I finally succumbed, disturbing dreams played out behind my eyelids, vivid in their detail. At one point, Jorun and Gretya rose, blood-covered, from their twisted resting places in Jorun's hut and pointed at me accusingly, staring with empty eye sockets.

Your fault, they seemed to say. *You lied to us. You brought this curse down upon us... the gods' punishment for your unnatural inclinations.*

I shuddered awake with a cry of fear on my lips and tears on my face as I sat up and struggled for breath.

The embers of the fire cast a faint glow in the darkness, and a figure shifted in the bed across from me.

"Carivel?" Andoc's voice was groggy—newly awakened. He rose, his silhouette crossing the room. The bed creaked as his weight settled on the edge. He reached toward me as if to place a hand on my shoulder, but I knocked it away in a near panic, still gasping out sobs.

"Don't—" I croaked, unsure what exactly I was warning him against. *Don't make me show more weakness in front of you. Don't make me need you more than I already do.*

Andoc froze, and slowly pulled his hand back. Instead, he eased himself off of the bed to sit beside it, leaning back against the wooden frame. "Very well," he said. "I'll just sit here for awhile, shall I?"

I couldn't answer; it needed all of my focus to stay silent as I cried. True to his word, Andoc said nothing, remaining a solid but unobtrusive presence nearby. Eventually, the tears subsided, leaving me with a throbbing headache. It was not enough to prevent me from sliding back into sleep, though, clogged nose and all.

It was Senovo who woke me many hours later with a light shake of my shoulder. I grunted and rolled up on an elbow, disoriented in the gray morning light. The feeling of red, swollen eyes and phlegm clogging my throat was becoming depressingly familiar after days of grief, but my surroundings were not.

"We're in Meren," Senovo reminded me, correctly interpreting my confused expression.

Meren. Yes. Right. I nodded understanding, and the rest of it came flooding back as I awoke more fully. I cast an assessing gaze over Senovo's form. He looked considerably better than I felt, except for the faint red rope mark barely visible on his wrist, below the sleeve of his robe. I hoped that meant he'd slept soundly through the night.

"Where's Andoc?" I asked, looking around the room.

"Three guesses," Senovo said, a wry note entering his voice.

I let out a little huff of what might have been laughter. "Getting food?"

"Of course. Where else?" Senovo said. He indicated a large wooden bowl sitting on a table next to the room's single window. "There's water if you want to wash."

He made no other mention of my obviously tear-stained face, for which I was very grateful.

"Thanks," I said, rising. The water was cool and helped clear my head. I pulled on my breeches and took my leave to check the horses and relieve myself in a private corner of the pen, away from prying eyes.

When I returned, I was feeling considerably more like a human being except for the low, throbbing headache that had plagued me since my injury during the battle. A young girl was just leaving the room as I re-entered, and I twisted to the side to let her past through the narrow doorway. Inside, Andoc handed me a chunk of coarse, dark bread with dried fruit baked into it.

"Who was that?" I asked.

"Messenger from Magoldis," Andoc said around his own mouthful of food. "We're to present ourselves at the meeting hall in half an hour. Apparently we merit an audience after all."

>

The three of us walked back to the meeting hall a few minutes later rather than take the time to groom and saddle the horses. The tall woman from the previous evening was once again guarding the entrance, though the man across from her was a different one.

"Good morning," Andoc greeted her. "Thank you for passing on our message."

The woman eyed him up and down. "Don't mention it," she said, her stony expression never flickering. "Go inside. Magoldis is waiting in the first room."

Andoc sketched a shallow bow and led the way through the door, into the large building. Senovo and I followed, tipping our heads to the guards as we passed. The entryway was at one end of a low-ceilinged hallway, which opened out into a spacious room with a large table surrounded by heavy chairs. Another large, muscular woman sat in one of them, facing the doorway. She was older than the female guard outside, but they shared the same shade of striking red hair and there was a similarity to their features, which made me think that they were probably related. She was also alone in the room.

It was odd seeing women in and around a meeting hall. I wondered if this was the Leader's wife, sent to entertain us until the Leader himself arrived.

"Magoldis," Andoc said next to me, bowing low. "It is our honor to meet with you. Thank you for agreeing to see us on such short notice."

I stared at him for a blank second or two. *This* was Magoldis? Magoldis, leader of the Mereni, was… a woman?

EIGHT

The woman in question rose from her chair and circled the table to stand before us. I felt Senovo's hand touch my elbow, the faint brush of fingers breaking me free of my shocked immobility. Senovo bowed as Magoldis' eyes moved over him, and I quickly followed suit.

"Varanis said you'd come from Draebard, at old Volya's request," Magoldis said, her attention returning to Andoc. Her voice was low and pleasant, but with an underlying steel.

"That is correct," Andoc said. "Our village was attacked in the dead of night a few days ago. The Alyrion commander who took over an abandoned hill-fort west of Draebard drew the Chief and half of the warriors away from the settlement on the pretense of a parlay, only to send soldiers in to attack while the villagers were vulnerable."

"A cowardly act," Magoldis agreed, though her tone gave away nothing. "I notice that Volya did not think meeting with me was important enough for him to come in person."

Senovo stepped forward. "Leader Magoldis, Chief Volya could not allow the village to appear vulnerable again so soon after the last attack. We have many seriously injured, including the High Priest. Most of the temple priests and acolytes are dead. Our Chief meant no disrespect to you, Leader. However, he had to put the people of Draebard first."

Magoldis raised an eyebrow. "Very pretty words, priest. So, who has Volya sent to speak to me in his stead? A warrior, a priest, and… ?"

The Leader's eyes raked over me, and I froze again, my thoughts still spinning in rapid circles. Andoc rescued me by beginning the introductions.

"I am Andoc, First Among Warriors in Draebard," he said. "This is Senovo, the most senior of the surviving priests excepting the High Priest himself."

"And you said the High Priest was injured?" Magoldis asked.

"Gravely," Senovo answered in a soft voice.

I knew next to nothing of the politics between tribes, beyond the obvious—who was feuding with who, who was allied with who. Nonetheless, I could begin to understand what Volya had done. In his own absence, he had sent his most powerful warrior and likely replacement, the soon-to-be High Priest of the village, and the Horse Master. While two of the three of us might not have come to terms with our new status yet, it was undeniably a dramatic gesture.

Still, the bad blood between Volya and Magoldis—whose society dared to put women in power—was obvious. Looking at Magoldis' stony mien, I wasn't at all sure it would be enough to sway her after years of disagreement and distrust.

The Leader's eyes returned to me. "And this is?" she asked.

The question was directed to Andoc, but before he could answer, I straightened proudly and uttered the nine most reckless words I had ever said in my life.

"Leader Magoldis, I am Carivel, Horse Mistress of Draebard."

The silence on either side of me spoke volumes, and I did not dare look at either of my companions. I could imagine their expressions of shock all too clearly as it was. Indeed, even Magoldis' impassive expression finally slipped, revealing keen interest.

I knew my features were plain and my body, angular and boyish. It was what had allowed me to pass for male these last three years. Still, I could tell from the Leader's face that she was looking past all that and seeing the feminine attributes underneath. It was all I could do not to tremble as the unimaginable consequences of what I had just done began to clamor for my attention.

"Well. That is certainly unexpected," Magoldis said. "I've never met a female Horse Master before. To find one from Draebard, of all places, is a surprise indeed. I can't help noticing that you have taken pains to look like a man, though."

"Skirts are impractical for starting colts and mucking out pens," I said, forcing my voice to stay matter-of-fact, almost dismissive. "And braiding up long hair takes time that can better be spent doing my job."

Magoldis let out a startled bark of laughter at the last part, and I couldn't help noticing her own waist-length, intricately braided red hair. Sensing I had gained something of an advantage, I pressed on before she could remember that she didn't like us.

"I understand it's traditional for visiting horse tamers to demonstrate their skills," I said. "If you have a suitable horse on hand, I would be happy to do so."

The Leader looked at us speculatively. "I'm sure something can be arranged. Why don't the three of you relax for a few hours? I'll send for you after lunch."

Andoc had apparently found his voice again. "Whatever suits you, Leader. We are, of course, at your disposal."

All three of us bowed and took our leave, passing the dour guards on the way out and heading back in the general direction of Harinel's rooming house. The silence between us was complete, and—to me, at least—more than a little disconcerting. Of *course*, the one time I could have actually used some of Andoc's shallow banter and teasing, the man had absolutely nothing to say.

That changed as soon as the door to our rented room closed behind us and he rounded on me.

"That was simultaneously the most brilliant and idiotic thing I've ever witnessed in my life," he said. I couldn't read his expression as he stared at me, but his eyes were wide and a bit manic.

"Thanks…?" I offered in a small voice, my own mind whirling like a tempest as the full realization of what I'd just done began to truly sink in.

Perhaps sensing that I was frozen in place like a statue, Senovo took me by the elbow and steered me toward the bed I had used last night, urging me to sit. He then sat across from me on the edge of the other bed, dipping his head until I was compelled to meet his eyes.

"Carivel," he said, "I know you didn't think it through completely before you spoke, but it's quite possible that you have played the one card that will soften Magoldis toward our cause."

"My name is Cara," I said, apropos of pretty much nothing.

Senovo frowned. "I beg your pardon?"

"My name," I repeated. "My mother didn't name me Carivel. I chose that later because it could be a name for a boy or a girl. She named me Cara."

The priest was still frowning. "Would you… like us to start calling you Cara?" he asked.

"No," I replied, feeling blood buzzing strangely beneath the skin of my fingers and toes. The edges of the room were starting to take on a grayish tinge. "Not really. I'm sorry—I don't even know why I said that."

"She's in shock," Andoc said from somewhere behind me. There was a sound of footsteps on the flagstone floor and a bit of rummaging. A wineskin appeared in my field of vision. Andoc handed it to me and said, "Drink."

I did. The burn of strong alcohol made me cough, and my vision cleared a little.

"Shit," I said, letting him take the skin away. "What have I done? I just—*shit*."

I looked up at Andoc with a panicked expression, and he could only shrug his agreement. "That's pretty much the size of it, yes."

"I think there's a way this could be turned to all of our advantages," Senovo said from his perch on the other bed. "I need a little time to think about how it could work, though. Right now, I'm more concerned about whether you are in any condition to tame a Mereni horse in a few hours, Carivel."

What? Oh, yes. I'd told Magoldis that I'd do that, hadn't I?

"I'm not sure I want to know what qualifies as a problem horse among the Mereni," Andoc said, oh-so-helpfully. "From what I've heard, even the good ones will take your face off if you look at them the wrong way."

"A horse is a horse," I said, still focused on how badly I'd just sabotaged my life. "All of their problems come from people. It'll be fine."

"Even so," Senovo said, "you should probably rest first."

I almost laughed out loud at him, but stifled it at the last moment so it came out as more of a choking noise. "Sure," I said. "Rest. I'll get right on that."

"Hey," Andoc said. I felt a jolt of surprise when his callused fingers framed my chin and tilted my face up until I was forced to look at him. "If Senovo says there's a way for this to work out, then you can believe him. We just need to keep you from getting eaten by a fire-breathing Mereni dragon-horse before then. I need to know that you're taking this demonstration seriously, and can handle it."

A small thread of anger pierced the gray blanket of despair cloaking my thoughts, which was perhaps the best thing the irritating sod could possibly have done for me at that moment.

"Of course I can handle it," I snapped, jerking my chin free. "Do you think I got my position as Jorun's assistant on the basis of my fine singing voice, Andoc? Or perhaps my talent as a dancer? Don't you dare patronize me!"

Andoc let out a breath, as if with relief. "That's better," he said nonsensically.

"Who's the First Warrior of the Mereni these days?" Senovo asked. "Because you'll probably be fighting him later this afternoon, Andoc."

"I have no idea," said the warrior. "I'm sure I can give him a run for his money, though. Do you know the High Priest here?"

"Only by reputation," Senovo said. "They say he has the second sight. I think he and Rhystel know each other personally."

The mention of the injured High Priest dampened our already strained spirits further. After a moment, Andoc sighed gustily and said, "Come on, both of you. I'm tired of playing fetch and carry with your food. Let's go take a look around the village. We'll get something to eat before people start throwing man-eating horses at you, Carivel, and trying to poke me with sharp objects. And... well... whatever it is they're likely to do to you, Senovo."

"I shudder to think," Senovo said. "It will probably involve mind-altering substances and copious amounts of chanting, though."

"I think you're getting the best end of this deal, my friend," Andoc said, and I couldn't help but agree. Something a bit more strongly mind-altering than the wine Andoc had given me earlier sounded absolutely wonderful right about now.

⤚✦⤙

Andoc chivvied us out of our rented room and toward the nearest stall selling food. Once we'd secured our meals and found a pleasant, shady place to sit and eat, I turned to him, scowling.

"You should have warned me ahead of time that the Mereni Leader was a woman," I said.

"Yes. Sorry about that," he said. "It seemed like quite a witty joke on my part at the time. Not so much, now."

Andoc was extremely lucky that my shock was stronger than my anger at this particular moment. Rather than waste breath berating him, I focused on trying to understand the circumstances we were dealing with.

"So, I gather that's why no one in Draebard even wants to talk about the Mereni?" I asked.

"Partly," Senovo said. "Magoldis was the wife of the last Leader. When he died during a raid on the village, they say she picked up his sword and hacked the attacking Chief to pieces. Afterward, she just sort of... took things over, and the Mereni followed her. That's why she calls herself a Leader instead of a Chief—she claims she'll only hold the position as long as the Mereni choose to follow her."

Andoc took up the thread of the story. "When Volya heard she'd taken over the leadership, he immediately made overtures of marriage, even though the two of them barely knew each other. He'd lost his wife a few years before, and he probably saw it as a way to consolidate power in the region. Magoldis apparently *didn't* see it that way, however. She not only refused him; she basically laughed in his face. It insulted Volya badly enough that he started flying off the handle if he so much as overheard someone discussing it. Before long, the whole thing just sort of became *that incident with the Mereni of which we do not speak.*"

"When did all this happen, anyway?" I asked. "It must have been before I came to Draebard."

"It was," Senovo said. "I believe it was almost five years ago, now."

We ate in silence after that, as I digested what I'd learned and tried not to panic over what I'd done. Afterward, we took in the sights, wandering aimlessly through the unfamiliar village. When we returned, the little messenger girl was waiting for us at the entrance to our room.

"Come to the horse pens," she said in a high, piping voice. "Leader Magoldis says they're ready for you."

I nodded my understanding and the girl hurried off to her next errand. Andoc and Senovo were looking at me with matching worried expressions, and my irritation flared once more.

"I need a straight tree branch roughly the span of my outstretched arms," I told them. "Something strong and flexible, but light enough that I can hold it in one hand. There's probably a suitable one near the pen out back; there are several trees there."

Senovo nodded and left to get a branch for me, leaving Andoc watching as I rummaged through our saddlebags for a piece of cloth. I couldn't find anything light enough for my purpose, so I un-tucked my linen undershirt and ripped a strip from the bottom edge.

"What are you doing?" Andoc asked, still looking at me like he was concerned I'd gone mad.

"You just worry about poking people with swords," I growled, "and leave the horse stuff to me."

When Senovo returned with a sturdy branch a little shorter than I was tall, I nodded my thanks and tied the strip of linen to the narrow end, anchoring it by twisting and knotting it around a fork in the wood where a twig had snapped off. I grabbed a spare halter and lead line made of light rope from my bag and gestured for the others to follow me. They did, throwing each other a look I couldn't interpret.

The horse pens were at the south edge of the village. We'd passed by them earlier when we were exploring the place. I was somewhat surprised to see the size of the crowd that had gathered there, but I suppose something like this would be a rather unusual occurrence in Meren. Apparently, we were to be entertainment for the town folk as well as emissaries to the Leader.

Magoldis herself was already present. She gestured us forward when she saw us.

"Is there anything in particular you need, Horse Mistress of Draebard?" she asked.

I looked around. "I would like to use that pen, Leader Magoldis," I said, pointing toward a training ring with a high, sturdy fence, about twenty-five or thirty strides across at its widest point.

"Very well," she said. "I will have the stallion brought there and released."

"What's wrong with this horse, exactly?" Andoc asked. "What problem does he have that needs fixing?"

"He maims people," Magoldis said matter-of-factly. "Sometimes he kills them. A pity, since he is otherwise an exceptional specimen."

Before Andoc could do more than go pale and open his mouth to protest, there was a loud squeal from the direction of the other pens. Two men appeared, each holding tightly to a thick rope attached to the tall, muscular black stallion between them. The horse shook its head angrily, trying to lunge for first one man, then the other, only to be yanked back at every attempt. He was easily the tallest horse I had ever seen, towering over little Kekenu by four hands or more.

Magoldis was right—he was utterly stunning. Already, I was plotting to trade for Mereni horses to interbreed with our own stocky mares.

My thoughts were interrupted by Magoldis shouting instructions to the burly handlers, who guided the frustrated, furious animal to the pen I had indicated, fighting for every step of progress. Grabbing the rope halter and my tree branch with its little cloth flag flapping from the end, I hurried away from my appalled companions, wanting to be inside the pen myself before the stallion was released.

"Carivel!" Andoc called after me, and I might have been touched by the worry in his voice if I weren't so irked by it.

I slipped through the rails of the fence on the opposite side of the circular pen from the gate and draped the rope halter over the nearest post for later. Around me, I was aware of the crowd gathering outside the fence, with Magoldis, Senovo, and Andoc right at the front. A nervous-looking boy opened the gate, and the handlers dragged the stallion into the pen. The two men wrestled the animal around to face the gate again. The lad swung it closed until there was only enough space for a man to slip out. The first handler unhooked his rope from the stallion's halter and darted through the opening. The second handler blocked the horse's attempt to bite him with a vicious punch to the animal's tender muzzle and ducked out as well, leaving the remaining lead rope hanging free from the halter. The boy slammed the gate shut and latched it closed, scurrying back out of range.

There was a moment of complete silence as the stallion paced back and forth in front of the gate, the loose length of rope dragging on the ground. I leaned against the fence on the opposite side of the pen, watching from the corner of my eye, my stick held loosely in my right hand, the cloth flag resting on the ground. I had been aware of Andoc's gritted teeth as he stood a few feet away on the outside of the pen... of Senovo's hand on his forearm, holding him back from doing or saying anything rash, but now everything outside of the fence fell away.

The horse shoved at the wooden gate with his nose, making the wood creak, but the latch didn't give. Frustrated, he reared and stomped down with his forefeet, shaking his head and making the loose rope flap around his legs. The stallion turned, acknowledging me for the first time with an explosive snort. Most horses would have threatened and bluffed first before truly coming after a human with the intent to injure, but given this stallion's description, I was not particularly surprised when he pinned his ears and lunged across the pen toward me almost immediately.

I could hear the collective intake of breath from the crowd as he covered the distance in three strides and reared, hooves flailing toward my head. Without moving from my position leaning against the fence, I whipped the branch up and shook the linen cloth in the horse's face, letting it flap against his eyes and ears. Taken completely by surprise, the black horse twisted in midair and nearly fell as he tried to scramble away. Ears flat against his head, he ran back to the gate and shoved at it again, half-rearing this time to crash against it with his shoulder.

I hoped for the sake of the people milling around outside that the Mereni constructed strong gate latches.

After a few moments of ignoring me in favor of testing the strength of the fence, the stallion turned and lunged for me a second time, only to pull up short when I casually raised the cloth flag toward his head and shook it. Rather than rear and strike, he whirled and kicked out at the flapping rag, raising another gasp from the crowd even though his heels didn't come within an arm-span of my body.

This time, rather than return straight to the gate, the stallion galloped along the fence, circling the pen with the loose rope dragging and flopping along beside him. As he approached the spot where I was lounging against a post, I pushed myself upright and took a step away from the fence, claiming a slightly larger area of the pen as my own. The flapping cloth flag forced the animal to skid to a halt and pivot over his haunches, running back in the direction he came. We repeated the same dance a few more times until the stallion no longer gave the impression that he would prefer to trample straight over the top of me as he approached the little patch of fence I had staked out as my territory, instead turning smoothly to run in the other direction.

Once I was confident that we both understood and accepted the basic rules of the game—don't barge into my space or I'll shake a scary flapping thing at your head—I walked to the center of the circular pen, keeping the cloth flag low and unthreatening. Without my presence blocking his way, the horse cantered along the fence in a continuous circle, tossing his head occasionally and striking out with his front feet in mid-stride to express his frustration.

Without letting my attention waver from the large animal circling me, I addressed the crowd, trying to pitch my voice so as many as possible of them could hear. "Basically, between the two of us inside this pen, the one who moves their feet the most loses the game. It's how horses interact with each other, and it's how I'm going to interact with him. The dominant horse—me, in this case—stands by her pile of feed, and if another horse tries to come up and displace her, she just pins her ears back and snaps her teeth, or maybe cocks a hind leg as if to kick. The other horse skitters away, out of reach, and the dominant horse keeps her pile of hay."

I lifted the stick I was holding ever so slightly. "This stick is how I pin my ears back and threaten to kick. It doesn't hurt him, but he doesn't want it flapping near his face because it's unfamiliar and frightening. As long as I only use it to give clear and reasonable instructions about how he should act around me, it can be the key to letting us build a rapport without anyone getting hurt."

I could hear some muttering from the crowd in response to my words, but my eyes were only for the animal circling me. As he passed the gate, I smoothly moved forward toward the fence at an angle, once again blocking his progress, forcing him to turn into the fence and change directions.

Every second or third time the stallion circled past the gate, I repeated the exercise. Gradually, the horse slowed to a trot, the turns becoming smoother and his expression calmer. In addition to turning into the fence to change direction, I coaxed him into turning toward me before swerving back out to go the opposite way, flapping the cloth at him whenever he laid his ears back or tried to crowd in toward the center where I was standing. When I could reliably turn him inward and outward, speed him up with a flick of the flag toward his haunches, and slow him down with a flick toward his nose, I took a deep breath and let it out, lowering the stick and fading backward a few steps.

The black horse turned in toward me in anticipation of another change of direction, but slowed to a stop when I did not raise the flag or step toward him to push him back out toward the fence. We watched each other for a long moment before old habits returned, the stallion pinning his ears and pressing forward. Rather than allow him to build up to a full-blown charge, I stepped forward as well, the flag raised slightly in warning. Instead of turning tail this time, he scrambled backward a couple of steps and stopped, still facing me. I relaxed, letting him know that was all I wanted, and he blew out a soft breath, licking and chewing thoughtfully as he pondered this strange new development in his life.

"Now that he respects my little cloth flag and stick, it's time to teach him to accept it without fear," I told the crowd. "Fear of the flapping cloth kept him at a safe distance from me in the beginning, but fear will be dangerous now that I'm ready to approach him. Trust will serve me better for that."

Keeping my body language friendly and relaxed, I began to lift the flag smoothly toward the horse's body, withdrawing it and taking the pressure off whenever he showed signs of acceptance. Any hint of aggression was met with a quick flap as a reminder of who was in charge of our nascent partnership.

Within half an hour, I was able to run the cloth softly over the stallion's neck and shoulders, using the stick as an extension of my arm. When he stood quietly with his head lowered and his eyes soft, I untied the cloth from the stick and laid the stick aside. With the cloth in my hand, I continued to stroke it over the front half of his body, letting my fingers brush against his sleek coat occasionally. Before long, I was running my right hand over him directly, the cloth wadded up in my left in case he decided to revert to aggressive behavior.

He didn't.

Moving slowly and deliberately, I unfastened the stiff, heavy leather halter from the stallion's head. Gods knew the last time it had been taken off — the hair underneath was worn away and the exposed skin was rough and scabby. The horse closed his eyes and released a quiet sigh, as if of relief. I let my fingers rub delicately over the damaged flesh, scratching lightly when he pressed against me, rubbing to relieve an itch. We stayed like that for several minutes.

With a final stroke, I straightened his forelock and took a step back. The stallion raised his head, watching me with pricked ears. I turned my back on him and calmly walked toward the far side of the pen, where my soft rope halter was still hanging from a post. Behind me, I heard the horse follow quietly, his hoof beats muffled by the sandy soil of the pen. There was yet another noise of surprise from the crowd, followed by excited murmuring as I picked up my light rope halter and let the stallion sniff at it curiously. When he was satisfied, I placed it around his head and adjusted the knots until it wasn't resting over any of the sores left by his old halter.

Using the cloth flag to communicate and reinforce my requests, I ran through some simple exercises to get him yielding to the rope, pleasantly surprised to find that when he wasn't being dragged around by two burly men, he was actually fairly light and responsive. Once I was satisfied with my ability to lead him safely, I approached the place where Magoldis was standing, flanked by Andoc and Senovo, both of whom looked like a stiff wind might blow them over at any moment.

"Leader Magoldis," I said, "if you are satisfied, I feel this is a good place to end the day's session. Where is the horse normally penned? I'll take him there and save his regular handlers the bother."

Magoldis had a smile playing around her lips that looked like it wanted to be a full-blown grin. She turned to a middle-aged man standing a short distance away, raising an eyebrow in question. By the man's sour expression, I guessed him to be the Mereni Horse Master. Going on what I had seen so far, I couldn't say that I was particularly impressed.

"We keep him in the southernmost corral," the man said gruffly. "Best wait until the crowd leaves, though. He'll start acting up again once he's out of that training pen."

Magoldis looked to me, one eyebrow quirked and amusement still written on her face.

"He's fine," I said in response to the unspoken query. "If he decides to test the boundaries, I've still got this." I flashed the little cloth rag, still crumpled in my hand. Beside me, the black horse shook his head and sneezed, spraying everyone around with a fine mist of snot.

The Leader laughed aloud, obviously delighted with the afternoon's entertainment. "Off with you then, Horse Mistress Carivel of Draebard. I think you've taught us all a thing or two today, not just the horse."

Upon hearing the title of *Horse Mistress*, pleasure and panic washed over me in roughly equal measure. Beside me, the black horse stepped sideways, tossing his head nervously, and I forced myself to let the conflicted feelings slide away for the time being. "It was my pleasure," I said. "I should warn you, though, if this horse continues to get the same sort of treatment he's always gotten, he will revert to his old ways in no time at all."

The Mereni Horse Master's sardonic snort did not escape me, but Magoldis only said, "That would be true of any living creature, I think. Not to worry, I've had a thought on that subject. We'll discuss it later."

She gestured for me to take the horse back to its pen, so I gave a short bow and did so. The stallion fussed a bit once we were in the open, but subsided quickly enough when I backed him up several paces, flicking the cloth back and forth toward his chest until his attention was firmly focused on me once more. I released him into his corral, daring anyone to comment as I removed the light rope halter, leaving him free and bare headed for the first time in who-knew-how-long.

Nobody said a word.

The crowd was dispersing, sensing that the afternoon's drama had drawn to a close. When I returned to the training pen to retrieve my stick, however, Senovo and Andoc were waiting for me. Andoc, still looking a bit wide-eyed, hustled me away to a private spot around the corner from one of the horse sheds.

"What—?" I began, only to be wrapped in an enthusiastic embrace strong enough to lift my feet off the ground and drive an undignified squeak from my lips.

"That was amazing," Andoc said in my ear. "You were amazing. Why didn't you tell us earlier how amazing you are?"

The blush that reddened my skin was from more than just embarrassment as Andoc's scent of musk and sweat surrounded me, his breath tickling my neck. Flustered, I pushed him back to arm's length and said, "Andoc, this is just what I *do*. It's my job!"

Senovo's voice came from behind me, and I twisted until I could see him. "Nonetheless, it *was* a rather extraordinary spectacle," he said.

I shook my head, bewildered. "Not really. The horses with the most extreme behavior problems are generally the ones that are most desperate for someone to trust."

Senovo's lazy green eyes crinkled at the corners in the most genuine smile I had seen from him since before the attack on Draebard. "Who knew there was such wisdom to be found in the horse pens?" he asked. "Happily, as payment for that bit of insight into the soul of man and beast, I believe I can offer you a workable plan for your present precarious situation, along with a backup plan, should that fail."

I stared, looking back and forth between Senovo and Andoc.

"Really?" I asked, feeling the first stirrings of hope.

"The first plan is entirely dependent upon Leader Magoldis' willingness to throw in her lot with ours against the Alyrions," Senovo cautioned. "If she does, however—and she appears to be particularly well inclined toward you at the moment—Volya may be desperate enough for her help that he would be forced to acknowledge you as a female, and Draebard's Horse Mistress. It would need to be implied that Magoldis' willingness to offer her troops hinged upon his acceptance of a female into a male role, as proof that he has changed in the years since his ill-received marriage proposal and attempt to usurp her position. Besides, Volya is a practical man. After three years, he can hardly argue that your presence in the horse pens constitutes any real threat to the herd, can he?"

I was struck speechless at the audacity of the suggestion. What Senovo was describing was essentially blackmail. Blackmail *of the most powerful man in the village.*

"And if it doesn't work," Andoc added, "I think I can safely say that you could find a place here in Meren if you had to. Although it doesn't look like you'd be too popular with the current Horse Master, unfortunately."

It was almost too much for me to take in. "I don't know what to say," I whispered faintly. "I'll... I'll have to think about it. But, Senovo? Andoc? *Thank you.*"

Senovo shrugged it off. "As I said, much of it depends upon Magoldis. You mustn't think your situation hopeless, though. It's not."

I nodded, still stuck for words.

"Now," Senovo continued, "we should probably head back to the central square. I believe it's Andoc's turn to attempt to curry favor."

"You'll be fighting?" I asked, turning back to the warrior.

Andoc cleared his throat, looking strangely discomfited. "Yes, that's right."

I frowned, looking to Senovo for answers. The look of sly amusement had returned to the eunuch's face.

"Indeed. Andoc will be facing Varanis, First Warrior of the Mereni," he said.

NINE

My mind was blank for a moment. When the name finally registered, a ridiculous smile spread slowly across my face. "Varanis? As in, the guard outside the meeting hall? Andoc, you're fighting a woman?"

"More specifically, I'll be fighting Magoldis' firstborn daughter," Andoc said, looking like he'd eaten something sour. "If I accidentally hurt her, they'll probably have me publicly flogged. This is going to be a nightmare."

I couldn't help it. I collapsed into laughter as Andoc glared at me, his offended expression sending me into further uncontrollable fits that had as much to do with a release of the day's tension as it did with Andoc's situation.

"If you're *quite* finished," he grumbled when I had finally wrested myself back under control, wiping tears from my eyes as Senovo looked on tolerantly.

"Oh, yes," I said. "I'm definitely finished. Come on; let's hurry back to the village center. This is going to be the highlight of the entire journey for me."

Andoc merely growled something unintelligible in response.

⤙ ♔ ⤚

The crowd in the village square was even larger than the one at the horse pens had been. Apparently, word had spread that the visitors from Draebard brought good entertainment value with them. Andoc retired briefly to our room to prepare himself for the fight, which Senovo reassured me was not actually intended to result in death or serious injury. Or in public flogging, for that matter.

Still, I could see that it was a bit of a delicate situation. Andoc obviously thought that his victory was a foregone conclusion. And, indeed, he was a highly respected warrior for a reason—he was good. *Very* good. If the fight were completely one-sided, Magoldis might be offended at seeing her daughter humiliated. However, to be seen to purposely fight with less than one's full skill would be dishonorable in the extreme, and also highly insulting.

By comparison, I'd had it easy — no one was rooting openly for the horse. Well… except, possibly, for the Mereni Horse Master. Senovo gained my attention with a touch to my elbow and indicated that we should join Magoldis at the front of the gathering spectators.

"We'll be expected to attend the Leader during the contest," he explained, and I nodded my understanding.

A platform had been erected at one end of the square, with three heavy wooden chairs placed atop it. Magoldis sat in the middle chair, looking down over an empty stretch of packed dirt where the fight would presumably take place. When she noticed us, the Leader beckoned us forward and onto the platform.

"Sit," she said, indicating the other two chairs with a flick of her hand. Senovo bowed and lowered himself into the chair at Magoldis' left with a graceful swish of robes. I quickly followed suit, sitting on her right.

A chalk circle perhaps half the size of the training pen I'd used earlier had been laid out before us on the hard ground. I was familiar with this sort of contest — it was a common enough occurrence both in Draebard and the village where I'd grown up whenever the warriors got too bored between skirmishes. The opponents would battle either to first blood, capitulation, or until one of them was driven out of the circle. Such competitions were generally friendly enough within the ranks of a village's warriors; I had a sneaking suspicion they would be less so between warriors from different tribes. Especially tribes with as much bad blood between them as the Mereni and Draebardi.

In contrast to the hush that had characterized the spectators around the horse pens, the crowd around the village square was raucous and celebratory. Mereni warriors were making their way toward the front, forming the first rank around the fighting circle. I had no doubt they would provide as much distraction for Andoc as possible during the contest.

I fidgeted slightly in my seat, resisting the urge to look to Senovo for… what? Reassurance? Calm? Cheers erupted from the far end of the square, spreading among the crowd until the noise became nearly deafening. The spectators parted, opening a path for Varanis to approach. Magoldis' daughter wore leather armor over her shoulders, forearms, and torso. Her bronze shortsword hung at her waist, and in her left hand, she carried a leather-covered wooden shield bearing the Mereni crest of a horse head and a lion head painted back to back. Her fiery hair was plaited tightly against her head and secured with a leather headband.

She entered the chalk ring to chants of "Varanis, Varanis!" and stopped before the platform we were sitting on, saluting the three of us with her sword. Watching Senovo from the corner of my eye, I copied him as he rose and bowed deeply to the First Warrior. When we had seated ourselves once more, Magoldis spoke loudly to the assembled crowd, who quieted immediately.

"Who challenges Varanis, First Warrior of the Mereni, to single combat this day?" she called, her voice carrying across the square.

"I do!" called a voice in response.

The crowd parted once more, this time with jeers and catcalls, though they seemed relatively good-natured to my ear. I couldn't help but catch my breath at the first sight of Andoc as he stalked toward the circle. He was wearing only soft leather boots and the loincloth he used for sparring, but he had tied back his hair and painted his face and body with swirls of red and yellow ochre war paint, as if for a true battle — Volya's colors, and now his as well. In addition to his bronze sword, which was longer and heavier than Varanis', he grasped a cone-shaped bronze buckler in his left hand rather than a full shield. The buckler was smaller and lighter than a shield — maybe half again as wide in diameter as Andoc's spread hand — though it performed roughly the same function. He would use it to protect his hand and arm while blocking blows from Varanis' sword, and perhaps to try to trap her blade during an attack.

It was a surprisingly nuanced approach. In a contest that ended with first blood, showing that much exposed skin was a rather blatant expression of confidence... and yet, the full war paint was a sign of deference and respect to one's opponent. Andoc was armed and dressed for speed and maneuverability over strength, implying that he did not assume he could simply overpower his female opponent. Given that she was taller than him by perhaps half a head, I figured that was probably a wise assumption.

Andoc entered the circle and came to a halt next to Varanis, bowing to Magoldis before raising his sword in salute.

"Andoc, First Warrior of Draebard, challenges Varanis of the Mereni," Magoldis called to the crowd, and was rewarded with a response of hoots and derisive catcalling. When it quieted, she continued, "Andoc. Varanis. Face each other. You will fight until first blood, capitulation, or expulsion from the circle."

The two fighters faced each other, Andoc with a sunny smile and Varanis with a sneer. When they had bowed to each other, Magoldis raised her hands and clapped once, sharply.

The two immediately fell into fighting stances, circling each other warily. Varanis was the first to lunge, her sword knocked to the side by Andoc's buckler even as her shield impacted his shoulder with an audible thump. Andoc twisted, not giving ground, and tried to trip her with an ankle behind her right leg. Varanis staggered back a step but kept her balance, and the two resumed their wary dance near the center of the chalk circle.

Andoc feinted left and pressed right, letting Varanis' blade slide along the buckler until he could trap her sword arm, tangling it with his. Her heavy shield protected her from his longer blade as they grappled. Andoc briefly gained enough leverage to spin them close to the chalk edge of the fighting ring, only to have it nearly come back on him when she threw her weight sideways, forcing him even closer to the edge than she was. He broke free at the last instant, dancing sideways away from both her blade and the chalk line.

Moving faster than I expected, he whirled past, trying to flank her on the right so he could get around her shield. Varanis' sword clanged against his buckler hard enough to make me wince in sympathy, but he wrenched her blade to the outside and swung low with his own sword. In a move so impressive that it made me catch my breath, Varanis leapt over the sweeping cut, Andoc's blade swishing through air where her lower legs had been an instant before. She came down swinging, the shield in her left hand slamming into Andoc's unprotected right side and sending him to the ground.

The crowd roared and my fingers clenched the edge of the chair convulsively, but Andoc rolled to his feet in a single smooth movement, weapons still in hand. He shot Varanis a terse nod of respect, and her responding grin was predatory. The tip of her shortsword described a looping figure of eight as she spun the blade with a loose, easy motion of her wrist.

The pair stepped forward in unison, clashing once more, but rather than parry with the buckler, Andoc met her blade with his own heavier one. Both swords would show dents in the blades from the impact, I was sure, but the tactic left Andoc's metal buckler free to deliver a solid punch to Varanis' left temple. She staggered back from the blow to the sound of the crowd's vocal displeasure, dropping to one knee before quickly righting herself and shaking off the hit.

Andoc didn't allow her time to recover, lunging under her guard and attempting to force her out of the circle. Varanis shouted in surprise, losing her grip on the shield, which fell to the ground and rolled just past the edge of the chalk, out of reach of either fighter. Both warriors wrapped each others' sword arms with their free arms, trapping the blades as Varanis set herself against Andoc's charge. It was a contest of brute strength now, and I looked on avidly as the pair wrestled for the upper hand.

Varanis had the advantage of height, while Andoc had the advantage of muscle. Completely against my will, I found myself thinking about what it would feel like to be trapped in those sinewy arms, wrestled to the ground and pinned there beneath Andoc's hard body. I shifted uncomfortably in my seat, suddenly feeling warm and jittery.

It was obvious that Varanis shared none of my interest in ending up beneath Andoc at the moment, and would probably sympathize more with my frequent desire to do him bodily injury. To that end, she took advantage of the close quarters to head-butt him in the face. Andoc went down with a grunt, but managed to pull the Mereni warrior down with him, their arms and legs tangled together. He used their momentum to roll them over, and had almost succeeded in pinning Varanis, when she kneed him directly in the groin.

There was a collective wince from the male warriors gathered around the circle, who up until that point had been cheering and calling out taunts at the visiting fighter. Andoc curled to the side in reaction, and Varanis wrenched herself free and rolled to her feet. She'd kept hold of her blade as they grappled, and smoothly brought the tip down to rest above Andoc's heart.

For a moment, the only sound was Andoc's harsh breathing as he tried to wrest the sudden agony under control. When he spoke, it still came through in his hoarse voice, if not in his actual words.

"So," he said, grinning up at Varanis through the pain. "We'll call it a draw, then?"

Senovo's huff of amusement was nearly silent, and was quickly swallowed by less restrained laughter from the crowd. Varanis stared down at him, a bruise blossoming on the side of her face from Andoc's metal buckler. Without speaking a word or breaking expression, she flicked her wrist and the tip of her sword drew a thin red line across Andoc's left pectoral. Andoc sighed, and let his head fall back against the packed dirt. Varanis stepped back, and beside me, Magoldis rose from her seat.

"The victory goes to Varanis, First Warrior of the Mereni!" she called, and the crowd erupted into cheers. "A good fight, well matched."

Below us, Varanis sheathed her sword and offered a hand to Andoc, pulling him to his feet when he accepted it. Her tone was arch when she spoke, but the words were accompanied by the first hint of a smile I had seen from the woman. "Hmm... I begin to see why old Volya thought he needed our help."

Andoc's answering smile was wry. "One battle with you at our side, and the Alyrion troops will start wearing codpieces along with the rest of their strange silver armor," he said.

"I trust I haven't permanently deprived the world of offspring from Draebard's First Warrior," Varanis said, speaking under the cover of the crowd's celebration.

"I daresay the likelihood remains as great as it ever was," Andoc replied, and I frowned at his careful wording. "I trust that I, in turn, have not deprived the world of your beauty."

Varanis snorted and prodded gingerly at the bruise on her temple. "I'll probably gain a slew of new suitors based on the story alone," she said.

"In that case," Andoc said with a bow made stiff by the bruising on his side and the pain that was doubtless still plaguing him, "I thank you for a challenging fight. You are a talented warrior, Varanis of Meren."

"And you, a worthy opponent, Andoc of Draebard," Varanis replied, bowing in turn.

Pleasantries completed, Varanis allowed herself to be pulled away by her compatriots, who were evidently intent on celebrating their First's victory by drinking all the wine and ale in the village. Andoc came over to the base of the platform, looking up at Magoldis. A thin trickle of blood trailed down the left side of his chest through the war paint, drawing my eyes.

"Your daughter is fierce and strong, Leader Magoldis," he said. "I would be honored to fight at her side, should the opportunity arise."

"And that opportunity will be discussed in due course, First Warrior," Magoldis said. "You acquitted yourself well despite your defeat. Now, though, you should clean yourself up and present yourselves at the temple in an hour. There is to be a handfasting ceremony tonight, followed by a feast." She turned her attention to Senovo. "The High Priest has requested that you join him in officiating the ceremony, which will be public."

"Of course, Leader," Senovo said. "I will be pleased to assist in any way I can."

⚜

After irritably waving off our questions about his health, Andoc looked down at himself—streaked war paint, blood, and all—and decreed that he would clean up in the river. Like most villages, Meren was built on the banks of a waterway and, like most villages, there was an area on the upstream side where people went to wash.

As the three of us made our way there, we were alternately applauded and jeered by small groups of Mereni going past who recognized us from the day's events. The attention made me blush, but Andoc made a point of saluting or bowing mockingly as the situation demanded. Senovo, unsurprisingly, appeared completely unaffected.

The washing area was fairly empty, since most people were attending the impromptu festival that seemed to have sprung up around our visit. Without ceremony, Andoc shed his boots, weapons, and loincloth before wading in, giving me a shameless view of his well-muscled backside for a few seconds until the water closed over it. When he was chest deep, he ducked under the surface and rose a moment later, scrubbing at his face and hair. He turned back to the shore, wiping water from his eyes.

"Senovo?" he asked. "You need to purify yourself before the ceremony, don't you? Might as well do it here. And Carivel? If you want a dip, it's safe enough. Senovo's distracted by important priestly ponderings right now, and frankly, my balls still hurt like a bastard."

Senovo sighed and threw me a glance that might have contained the barest hint of an eye-roll. Turning away, he unfastened his robes, stripping and wading in after Andoc. Still a coward—always a coward—I called, "I'm good, thanks." Screwing up one tiny iota of courage from someplace deep inside, I added, "I'll just stay here and enjoy the view."

Andoc barked out a laugh, and started scrubbing at his chest. "So, blood and smeared ochre paste get you going, then, Horse Mistress? Good to know."

"What makes you think I wasn't talking about Senovo?" I called back.

"Leave me out of this," Senovo said to both of us, and dove under the water even as Andoc groaned dramatically, clutching the uninjured side of his chest.

"Another wound!" said Andoc, his eyes twinkling. "First the balls, then the breast, and now the heart. What a cruel day to be a warrior!"

I grabbed a pebble from the bank and chucked it at him, successfully bouncing it off his shoulder. Pretending to wince, he laughed again and went back to washing as Senovo surfaced near the center of the river. Keeping half an eye on the two of them, I crouched down by the shallows and rinsed the dust from the training ring off of my face and arms. When the others emerged a few minutes later, clean and glistening, I forced myself to watch openly as they climbed up the sloping bank toward their piles of clothing. I even managed to answer Andoc's challenging leer with a smirk of my own.

We returned to our room long enough for Andoc to change into regular clothes, leaving just enough time to grab some food from one of the many stalls that had been erected around the square before we were due to arrive at the temple. Senovo turned down the skewer of roasted vegetables and chunks of fowl, preferring to fast ahead of the ceremony. He seemed increasingly distant as we approached the ornate temple with its generous courtyard, and I hoped the wolf was not beginning to trouble him as the daylight slanted toward evening.

As we neared the entrance, Senovo took his leave, accompanying two acolytes who appeared to escort him inside to the High Priest. Left alone with Andoc for the moment, I looked up at him, unable to hide the slight twinge of worry plaguing me.

"He'll be all right, won't he?" I asked. "He seems a bit... I don't know..." I trailed off, unsure how to end the sentence.

Andoc smiled. "He's fine. He just takes it very seriously, that's all."

I nodded, reassured. A public handfasting was a fairly significant event, true enough. High Priest Rhystel would have said that to have one on the day of our arrival at Meren was a good omen for the negotiations between our two tribes. In a village this size, there would be many handfastings throughout the spring and summer, but if things were the same here as in Draebard, only a handful would be public.

The priests were always very careful to ensure that both parties were completely comfortable with the idea of coming before the village and sharing their vows and first official coupling with any who wished to attend. Public handfastings were said to bestow luck and fertility on the couple, so it was all too easy for the family of one or the other to put pressure on them to have one. It was the priests' job to be sure it was the couple's own choice, and to guide the ceremony so that both participants found comfort and completion with each other despite the presence of an audience.

I had attended a few such ceremonies over the years for friends or acquaintances. All had been happy events, if somewhat bittersweet for me personally. Such a union had always been out of my reach—or so it had seemed. After Senovo's words this afternoon, though, it was becoming harder and harder not to wonder if such a thing might, after all, be possible some day.

"Come," Andoc said. "We should find Magoldis and join her before the ceremony starts."

With a light touch to the small of my back that was simultaneously settling and unsettling, he guided me into the courtyard. We skirted the stone walls of the temple, keeping to the outer edges of the open area until we saw the Leader's distinctive red hair. She was talking with several elders when we approached, including a short woman with a plait of long, white hair and a face full of laugh lines.

Introducing them to us as the other members of the village's ruling council, Magoldis indicated that they wished to speak with Andoc after the handfasting ceremony about the details of the Alyrion attack on Draebard, and Volya's intended response. Andoc agreed readily, throwing me a look which clearly communicated his relief that we were finally getting someplace with the negotiations.

We were interrupted by the sound of drums and the lighting of torches around the courtyard—clear signals that the ceremony was about to begin. Magoldis led all of us to a set of stone benches with a clear view of the low altar in the center of the open space. We had scarcely seated ourselves when a tall, immensely fat priest appeared from within the shadows of the temple door, followed by the happy couple, naked except for the flowers braided into the girl's hair. Behind them, Senovo followed like a shadow, his hands folded into the wide sleeves of his dun-colored robe.

The little procession emerged fully into the torchlight in the deepening dusk of the cloistered square. I was surprised to see that the man's right arm ended in an ugly stump below the elbow, the flesh red and puckered, but obviously long healed. He was tall and broad, well muscled except for a bit of flabbiness around the belly. A handful of battle scars across his chest and shoulders marked him as a warrior, at least at one time.

"Keenan and Ciero," Magoldis said quietly. "Ciero lost his hand in battle. Now he is an artist of some repute."

I nodded. Beside me, I felt Andoc shudder faintly, and wondered at his reaction.

The young woman—Keenan—was Ciero's opposite in practically every way. She was tiny where he was large, dark where he was pale, and fine-boned where he was broad-featured. She looked up at him with adoration as they approached the altar, and he clutched her right hand in his left as if she were his most precious treasure in all the world.

Meren's High Priest turned to address the onlookers with upraised hands.

"Mighty Naloth, He Who Seeds the Earth and Brings the Rain," he began in a powerful, booming voice. "Bountiful Utarr, She Who Bears Fruit. Bless, tonight, this union between Keenan and Ciero, two of your children. They come before you as they came into this world—naked in the eyes of gods and men."

"*Ever shall it be so,*" answered the onlookers in turn.

The High Priest turned his attention to the couple. "Ciero. Keenan. Tonight you tie your destinies together under the gods' watchful gaze. To symbolize this union, Priest Senovo will bind your hands, teaching you to work together as one, relying on each other as you have previously relied only on yourselves. Do you both agree to this public handfasting, freely and joyfully?"

"We do," the pair said in unison, still with eyes only for each other.

Senovo moved from his unobtrusive position behind the altar to face the couple, his back to us. He held out the leather thongs that would seal the handfasting. Keenan and Ciero raised their clasped hands, and Senovo skillfully bound them together palm to palm, weaving the thongs around their fingers so that the ties would last for a night and a day—the prescribed length of time before they could be untied.

When he was finished, he laid a hand on each of their foreheads, murmuring a quiet blessing, and faded back into the shadows once more.

"You are now joined—one heart, one soul," The High Priest intoned. "Celebrate your union before the gods and the people of Meren. Find your joy within each other, that new life may grow from the fertile field of your love."

"Ever shall it be so," intoned the crowd once more.

Keenan's smile was radiant in the firelight as she surged up, standing on tiptoe even as Ciero bent down to kiss her, his abbreviated right arm circling her waist to pull her closer. There was polite applause as the onlookers slapped their thighs lightly, and the drumbeat, which had faded to the background, grew in intensity and complexity—a primal rhythm.

Keenan backed up step by step until the backs of her legs pressed against the edge of the altar, pulling Ciero with her by their bound hands. In Draebard, the altar was covered with the hide of a cow or deer for handfastings, worked into soft suede and used to catch virgin blood, if there was any. Of course, many girls weren't virgins at their handfastings, or were, but didn't bleed. There was nothing wrong with that, but sometimes there was a bit of blood, and in those cases the stained leather was used by the priests in powerful ceremonies.

In Meren, the altar was covered with some sort of soft, woven cloth that appeared to be quilted—stuffed, perhaps, with dried moss or eiderdown. To my eye, it looked considerably more comfortable to lie on than a simple leather hide. Keenan reclined on the stone slab, Ciero following her down as they continued to kiss. Normally, the man would caress his new bride with his free hand until she was near completion before entering her, but Ciero had no free hand and I hoped that Keenan would still be able to find her pleasure without his fingers.

I needn't have worried; pulling back slightly from the kiss, Ciero moved his lips to Keenan's jaw and throat, nibbling his way down to suck at her breasts until she was moaning softly in counterpoint to the drums. He continued down her body, nudging her legs apart to lap at her sex even as her free hand tangled in his sandy hair, stroking and tugging gently in time with her breathy cries. His care and desire for her were obvious, and I felt warmth growing low in my own belly as I watched them. Eventually, Keenan pulled him away, urging him back up the length of her body.

As he loomed over her, I couldn't help noticing how large he was, his erect prick seeming huge in comparison to her tiny body. My mind always seemed to shy away from thinking about how it would feel to be penetrated by a man for the first time, lingering instead on thoughts of what it would be like to have a cock of my own—to thrust into a slick, welcoming space. Now, I winced uncomfortably at the thought of such a large man taking such a small woman, thinking of tender flesh stretching... tearing.

I startled slightly when Andoc's hand rested discreetly on my forearm. "It's all right, Carivel," he said, his voice pitched for my ears only. "Watch."

Indeed, at that moment Senovo moved forward just enough to murmur a few words to the couple on the altar. Without taking his eyes from Keenan, Ciero nodded and the pair smoothly switched places so that Ciero was the one reclining on his back on the quilted cloth, while Keenan clambered up to straddle his hips. She leaned down, pressing their bound hands over his head as she kissed him and rutted slowly against his hard flesh. When they were both gasping with need against each other's lips, she straightened and guided Ciero's erection into place with her free hand, lowering herself slowly onto it with a cry.

Ciero was trembling, beads of sweat glimmering on his face in the torchlight, but he stayed utterly still as Keenan rocked up and down, taking him a bit deeper each time until he was finally buried to the hilt. They looked at each other in wonder for a long moment before Keenan began to roll her hips, her free hand delving between her own legs to rub in time with the slow thrusts. As she gained confidence, I could see Ciero start pressing up to meet her as she rocked up and down, the two of them moving faster and faster until she tensed with a cry, back arched, eyes clenched shut in ecstasy. Ciero followed a moment later, curling up into her with a hoarse shout, hips losing rhythm.

They collapsed together, breathing hard. Keenan's face was tilted toward us, and I could see her blissful smile as she rested on top of her new husband. His damaged arm came up to cradle her shoulders. I tried to release my emotions with a slow breath through my nose, painfully aware of Andoc's fingers still resting on my forearm. His touch was like a brand. When he removed his hand a moment later, the skin tingled and burned where it had been.

Acolytes appeared at the altar to help the couple unsteadily to their feet and lead them to the room inside the temple where they would spend the remainder of their handfasting together before the bindings were untied. The altar cloth was cleared away and taken inside. In the shadows, I could see the High Priest speaking quietly with Senovo.

Magoldis spoke over the murmuring of the onlookers. "A propitious event, I should say. High Priest Jyrrel is planning a short ceremony next to honor your compatriot, I believe, but if you've no objection, Andoc, the council would like to begin negotiations with you as soon as possible."

Andoc looked surprised, then pleased, before a faint furrow appeared at his brow and he looked at me. Guessing his concern, I nodded and said, "Don't worry, I'll stay here until they're finished. We'll join you as soon as we can."

The furrow smoothed, and he smiled at me. He turned to the others and said, "Thank you, Leader. Elders. I would be honored to accompany you."

Magoldis caught my eye. "We will be at the meeting hall, Horse Mistress Carivel. You and Senovo are, of course, welcome to join us as soon as the ceremony is finished."

"We will come immediately afterward, Leader Magoldis," I assured her. "Thank you for your continued hospitality."

A corner of Magoldis' mouth twitched up in a brief half-smile. "You have proven yourselves to be most diverting guests," she said.

I bowed as the elders filed away behind Andoc and the Mereni leader. When they had departed, I resumed my seat on the bench and looked around. Many people had made their way out of the courtyard at the conclusion of the handfasting, but a surprising number had stayed. Presumably, they hoped to see a bit more of Senovo, who had been largely in the background so far. The drums started up in a new rhythm, and the remaining spectators settled down, their attention returning to the altar, bare now except for two stone goblets.

"Priest Senovo of Draebard," began the Mereni High Priest, "you honor us with your presence and your assistance in the joining of Keenan and Ciero. In return, please accept the honor of our sacred drink, an elixir from the gods which brings truth and clarity to the mind."

I raised an eyebrow. While chanting had been in short supply so far, it looked like the mind-altering substances were finally arriving front and center. I wondered with mild amusement if Senovo was going to be in any condition to attend negotiations tonight.

Senovo went smoothly to his knees in front of the onlookers, bowing his head before looking up at the corpulent High Priest. "I humbly accept the honor of the gods' gift."

Jyrrel lifted both goblets and handed one to Senovo. "Drink with me, then, Senovo of Draebard, that we may both see the truth clearly."

The priests lifted the cups to their lips in unison, Jyrrel standing and Senovo still on his knees before him. For a moment, nothing happened, but then Senovo tensed, scrambling inelegantly to his feet as I frowned in sudden concern.

"No!" cried the slender eunuch, sending my heart pounding against my ribcage as I half rose to my own feet. "What have you — ?"

The heavy goblet fell to the ground as Senovo clawed at his throat and chest. I was frozen in place, unable to even breathe as he writhed with panicked eyes, bone and sinew popping and twisting impossibly in the flickering torchlight. A moment later, the light reflected off gray fur and yellow eyes as a large wolf crouched where Senovo had been, snarling with fear and rage as it struggled free of Senovo's robes.

TEN

"Shit!" I choked out as screams and panic erupted around me. "Shit... *shit!*"

High Priest Jyrrel had dropped his own goblet in shock, backing away as the wolf seemed to focus its terror and fury on him. Without conscious thought, I shoved through the bodies running past me and charged forward, sliding to my knees next to the snarling animal and wrapping my arms around its shoulders, heedless of the razor sharp teeth bared inches from my face.

"Senovo!" I said. "You're safe! It's all right, I promise! I won't let anything happen."

The rough-coated, sinewy body in my arms was shaking like a leaf in a storm, so great was the animal's fear. I tugged the wolf backward a bit until our backs were at the altar, feeling it hunker further into the space between my body and the unyielding stone, still growling. New chaos erupted as guards charged into the courtyard armed with swords and javelins, no doubt drawn by the screaming onlookers who had fled moments ago.

The wolf stiffened as the guards' attention honed in on us, its hackles rising under my hands. I tried to press the animal more fully behind my body, but now it was struggling, fighting to free itself from my hold and reach the new threat. I could feel the situation spiraling out of control as the guards raised their weapons. Oh, gods, *where was Andoc?*

As if my thoughts had conjured him, Andoc ran full speed into the courtyard and slid to a halt, taking in the scene with wild eyes.

"*Stop!*" he roared, and shoved past the line of guards to stand between us and them. "Varanis! Have your guards lower their weapons! It's not a real wolf, it's Senovo—he's a shape-shifter!"

I hadn't even realized Varanis was among the guards, so focused had I been on keeping Senovo behind me. Now, though, I recognized the tall, red-haired form as she straightened from her defensive crouch, the bruises from her earlier fight with Andoc livid on the side of her face.

"Will he attack?" Varanis called warily.

"Not if you *lower your damn weapons*," Andoc snapped, still standing squarely between us and the raised javelins.

"Do it," said High Priest Jyrrel, who had retreated to the space in front of the benches. His voice was breathless, but he seemed steadier than he had before as he continued. "This is my fault. I didn't realize… but yes, lower your weapons. Clear the courtyard, calmly and quietly as you can. The situation is under control."

He was looking at me — no, at Senovo — with wonder in his eyes. After a moment's hesitation, Varanis said, "You heard the High Priest. Stand down, and get the remaining people out of here, as quickly and quietly as you can. And Andoc? You *might have mentioned this ahead of time*, for Deresta's sake."

"Not my secret to tell," Andoc said grimly.

Varanis made a noise of disgust, but her guards were already following orders, escorting the remaining handful of frightened spectators away and giving the three of us at the altar a wide berth. I loosened my hold on the wolf's shaggy neck slightly, as it once again tried to cower back behind the protection of my body. When we were alone except for the High Priest, Andoc turned to Jyrrel and said, "We need a room in the temple where we won't be disturbed tonight."

"Of course," Jyrrel said. "Anything you need. There is an empty guest room at the end of the hallway on the left, through that door." He indicated an open doorway off to our right. "I will precede you and make sure the way is clear."

Andoc nodded tightly and crossed the final few steps to us as Jyrrel went to clear the hallway. He fell to his knees and took both of us in his arms, the wolf squirming forward with a whimper to nuzzle between us.

"I shouldn't have left," Andoc said, as I let myself lean on him. "I'm sorry. I should never have left you alone."

At first, I thought he was trembling, but after a moment I realized that it was me. "You couldn't have known," I said into the skin at the juncture of his neck and shoulder, the wolf's fur tickling my left cheek. "It's all right, though. We're all right."

"Thanks to you," Andoc said, kissing first the top of my head, then the top of the wolf's. "*Gods.* They could have killed him."

I shuddered again, and allowed Andoc to help me to my feet. Holding me tight against his left side, with the wolf pressed close against his leg on the right side, he led us into the temple and down the hallway to the room Jyrrel had described. The door had been left invitingly open for us. Inside, there was a low bed with a rough, woven blanket, a table with a couple of candles burning on it, and a chair. There was only a single small window set high in the wall, and once Andoc had closed the door behind us, I finally felt myself start to relax.

The wolf remained glued to Andoc's side as I peeled away and sank into the chair, exhausted beyond measure. Man and beast crossed to the bed together, and I watched as Andoc lifted one edge of the blanket, patting the straw mattress beneath. The wolf jumped up and nosed his way under the rough cloth, circling a couple of times before curling into a miserable ball, completely hidden by the blanket. Andoc sighed and flopped down next to the large lump, which immediately shuffled over a bit to press against his thigh.

Andoc looked up and saw me watching. He shrugged. "It seems to help him," he said. "I think maybe it feels like a den or something. What happened out there?"

I scrubbed a hand over my face, trying to clear the cobwebs. "There were two goblets. Jyrrel and Senovo both drank from them. Jyrrel said the drink was an elixir from the gods. It was supposed to bring truth and… what was it? Clarity, I think. Truth and clarity. A few seconds after he drank it, Senovo started to panic. Scrambled to his feet, dropped the goblet, and then he just… changed."

"Truth and clarity? *Fuck.* I guess it worked," Andoc said, his face grim. "I imagine Jyrrel is running to report to Magoldis even as we speak. There will be no hiding this—not now. He'll have to deal with it whether he wants to or not."

"At least nobody was injured," I said. "Will this hurt the negotiations, do you think?"

Andoc shook his head, smoothing a hand over the tense curve of the wolf's spine through the blanket. "It'll probably help them, ironically enough. Not only did Volya send the likely replacement for the injured High Priest, but oh, by the way, he's a shifter. Even if he never wanted to be one."

"It must be incredibly rare," I said. "It was pretty obvious that no one at the ceremony had ever seen one, and I know I certainly never have."

"It's rare enough," Andoc confirmed, still stroking the tightly curled body beside him. "The High Priest in Draebard before Rhystel was a shifter—he could turn into a ram. And I heard that there was one down south who took the form of a fox. Those are the only two I know of, though."

He looked at the form on the bed, and then to the door.

"You need to get back to the meeting hall, don't you," I said. "Explain about Senovo, and continue with the talks."

"I should, but…" Andoc looked at the wolf again.

"I'll stay with him," I said. "I'm sure he'd rather have you, but we'll be all right. This is too important to risk everything now."

Reluctantly, he nodded and got to his feet. I rose as well. Andoc crossed the small room and pulled me into an embrace. With no defenses left after the day's events, I leaned against his strength and let my own arms close around him in return. I could feel his words rumble through his chest as he spoke.

"I should have been able to prevent all this somehow."

I pulled back enough that I could look up at his face. "Need I remind you that it was my own stupid decision to blab my secret in front of the Leader of the Mereni? I don't recall asking you first. And as for Senovo… well. We'll just have to do whatever we can to support him. Right now, that means you going back there and giving his side of the story, since he can't do it himself. I'll watch over him until you're done."

Andoc nodded, pulling me close again for a moment before letting me go. The wolf had nosed forward until its face was peeking out from under the edge of the blanket. When Andoc walked to the door, it let out a piteous whine.

"It's all right," I said to both of them, crossing to sit on the bed. Andoc, who had paused with his hand on the door handle, nodded again and quickly slipped out. The whine grew into a full-throated howl, and I wondered what the people nearby would make of it.

"Quiet, you poor, pitiful beast," I said over the noise. "He'll be back soon, and until then you'll just have to put up with me.

Now shove over—you're taking up the entire bed and I can barely keep my eyes open."

Suiting word to deed, I shoved the animal closer to the wall, the howl tailing off into a surprised yip. Mission accomplished, I reached over and blew out the candles, plunging the room into darkness. After a moment's hesitation, I left all of my clothes on and lay down on top of the blanket. The wolf disappeared back underneath the rough wool, curling up again with a huff. When it had settled, I rolled onto my side, spooning around the shapeless lump and resting my arm across it in a loose embrace. It huffed again and went quiet against me, a warm weight breathing in quiet counterpoint to my own heartbeat.

Within minutes, exhaustion won out over the novelty of the situation, and sleep claimed me.

Light was slanting in through the small window when I was awakened the following morning by thrashing in the bed next to me. The form I was curled around twisted improbably in my arms, and suddenly I was holding Senovo tangled up in the blanket instead of the wolf. The priest struggled free, sucking in great, panicked breaths, and lunged across me to the side of the bed where he heaved and retched, bringing up only a thin stream of bile.

I disentangled us and braced his shoulders before he could slide off the bed completely and land face-first in the mess on the floor. Senovo curled forward, his hands coming up to grasp at his face like claws.

"Senovo," I said sharply. "*Senovo*! It's all right!"

"Oh, gods," he choked. "Gods have mercy on me. Did I—?"

Immediately guessing what he was asking, I shook my head sharply from side to side. "No! It's all right, Senovo. You didn't hurt anyone. Everyone is fine."

He shuddered under my hands, the tremor seeming to rise up from the depths of his body, and his noise of relief was nearly a sob.

"What do you need?" I asked, wishing now that I'd talked to Andoc last night about what to expect. Honestly, I'd assumed he would return before Senovo changed back. Had the negotiations really run all night?

Senovo just shook his head in lieu of an answer, his face still buried in his hands. "Where's Andoc?"

"I sent him back to the meeting hall to continue the talks," I said, adding, "He wanted to stay here."

"You did the right thing," said Senovo, letting his hands slide down to rest limply in his lap. "The elders. Do they... know? About the wolf?"

"I'm afraid the whole village knows by now, Senovo," I said. "I'm truly sorry."

"I'll have to tell Rhystel when we get back," he said in a distant, listless voice. "If he still lives."

"Rhystel loves you like a son," I said. "He'll understand."

It was the wrong thing to say, or maybe the right thing. Senovo curled forward, shoulders shaking as he began to weep silently. I thought of all the tears I had shed for Jorun and the others over the last few days, and wondered if this was the first time Senovo had truly succumbed to his grief.

Unsure what to do, I settled on reaching for the hand nearest to me and twining my fingers with his, squeezing tightly. That was how Andoc found us some time later, when he entered bearing a pitcher of water and a pile of neatly folded clothing and clean rags for washing. His brow furrowed as he took in the scene. He set the items he was carrying on the table and detoured around the small puddle of sick on the floor to sit at Senovo's other side, shoulder to shoulder.

Seeming to draw strength from Andoc's touch, the priest took a deep breath and straightened, staring vacantly across the room.

"I'm deeply sorry, *amadi*," Andoc said. "I betrayed your trust and told the elders parts of your story. It was either that, or let them start speculating wildly about why you hid your ability, and why the wolf was so threatening."

Senovo nodded, eyes still focused on something distant. "It doesn't matter. None of it matters now."

"Are they inclined to help us?" I asked.

"They haven't turned us down outright," Andoc said. "They questioned me all night and into the morning before finally taking a break for food and rest. They'll reconvene this evening to discuss the matter privately between themselves, and then we'll see, I suppose."

"Is anything expected of us today?" I asked.

Andoc shook his head, and I noticed for the first time how tired he looked. "Not as far as I know. I think Magoldis realizes that we need some time to regroup after yesterday."

We were interrupted by a soft tap at the door. "It's Jyrrel," came a muffled voice. "May I enter?"

Andoc and I looked to Senovo, who nodded absently.

"A moment, High Priest," Andoc called. To Senovo, he indicated the pile of clothing on the table and added, "Do you want your robes?"

"It's of no import," Senovo said. "The High Priest has already seen everything of me that there is to see."

Andoc nodded. "Come in," he said, loud enough to be heard through the door.

Jyrrel entered quietly, closing the door behind him. He was silent for a moment as he took in Senovo, still half-tangled in the wool blanket, with Andoc flanking him protectively on one side and me, on the other.

"I had a vision," the High Priest began without preamble, "on the night of your arrival. A vision of a young priest, slender and unassuming, wielding power greater than anyone has seen in a generation. When I met you the following day, I could sense none of that power—only a desire to remain in the shadows, and an undertone of fear... almost dread. I resolved to see if I could learn the truth behind the veil. It was self-serving of me, but I promise you that it was not my intention to harm you or cause you pain."

"There was panic. Chaos," Andoc ground out. "People could have been killed. *He* could have been killed."

"Enough, Andoc," Senovo said quietly, straightening his spine and meeting Jyrrel's eyes. "High Priest Jyrrel, I understand why you did what you did, and hold no grudge against you. I must return to Draebard and confess to my lies of omission, but understand this. I wield no power, nor shall I wield power in the future. What you consider power is in fact a weakness of the highest order, which I must strive every day to overcome."

Jyrrel held Senovo's eyes for a long moment, before looking over all three of us with an assessing gaze. "You are mistaken," he said mildly, "but being mistaken is, of course, your prerogative. You have my deepest apologies for causing you pain."

"It would be best if you left now," Andoc said, his anger under control again, but no less obvious for it.

"As you wish," Jyrrel said. "The room is yours to use as long as you need it. I'm afraid that you will attract a fair amount of attention if you go out into the village right now, Senovo."

Senovo only nodded silently, and Jyrrel let himself out, closing the door behind him. The young priest rose and tugged on his smallclothes, which had been cleaned and neatly folded along with his robes — presumably by the temple acolytes. He was wetting a rag to clean up the congealed puddle by the bed when I shook off my reverie and took it from him.

"Let me," I said. "Rest some more. You still look shattered. Andoc? You, too. You've been up all night. Have you eaten?"

Andoc attempted a smile, but it came out forced. "Isn't that supposed to be my line? But, to answer your question, yes, they fed me."

"I'll go back to Harinel's place and check the horses. I can get us some food for later while I'm out."

Andoc nodded. "Hurry back, Carivel," he said.

I swiped up the mess on the floor and accepted the silver coins Andoc handed me for the food. To my surprise, he did not immediately let go of my hand, but instead used it to draw me into another embrace. Tired of resisting my attraction to him, I returned it, holding tight for a long moment. When we released each other, I sought out Senovo's eyes and he dipped his head briefly in acknowledgement.

Leaving the soiled rag on the floor outside the door for the acolytes to take away, I headed down the hallway to the door that led into the courtyard. It looked completely different in the daylight — innocent and commonplace. Priests and acolytes were scattered around the space, engaged in menial tasks. Several looked up as I passed through, staring until I met their eyes with a challenging glare of my own that sent them scurrying back to their work.

Outside, in the village proper, I kept my head down and walked purposely down the street to the lodging house. I ignored, as best I could, the whispered conversations that seemed to spring up around me. As I approached the corral behind Harinel's ramshackle house, Kekenu nickered softly, and the other two horses looked up from their piles of hay.

I checked the feed and water, pleased that the boy who worked for Harinel seemed to have taken good care of the animals in our absence. Entering the small pen, I checked them over carefully for injuries or swelling after the long journey here, and took a few minutes to scratch under Kekenu's heavy mane while he rubbed his muzzle against my hip in return.

Our saddlebags were still inside our rented room, where we had left them the previous day. I wasn't keen on dragging all three of the heavy bags back across the village with me, so I dug through them and stuffed a few essentials into one, leaving the others behind for now. Errand completed, I decided to stop by the horse pens before returning to the temple and see how the black stallion was doing. As I walked to the edge of town, I wondered idly how long it took a person to become accustomed to people pointing and talking about you as you passed.

When I reached the horse pens, someone finally plucked up the courage to approach me directly.

"Horse Mistress Carivel?" said a boy, whom I recognized as being the one that had manned the gate of the training pen yesterday when the stallion was first brought in.

"Hello, again," I replied. "I'm sorry, I don't know your name…"

"It's Previn," said the lad eagerly. "I just wanted to say how amazing it was to watch you with Nietre yesterday—that's what we call the stallion. This morning I was putting out his hay and he let me scratch his forehead. He just stood there, calm as you please, and let me do it. Before it was always a race for me to get in and out before he charged me. He tore a chunk out of the last boy's arm, you know. It never did heal right."

I let the flood of words trail off and smiled at the boy. "I'm glad it made a difference for you. A horse like that—he needs to know that you've got a plan, and that you'll treat him fairly and look after him. Otherwise, he thinks he has to look after himself, and he'll do it with teeth and hooves before you can even blink. As soon as you let anger or fear guide your dealings with him, you'll lose his respect."

"I'll remember," Previn said, looking at me with something uncomfortably close to hero worship.

"May I go in and see him?" I asked, wanting to follow up with the stallion as much as possible while I was here.

Previn nodded enthusiastically and led the way over to the pen. The Horse Master wasn't around as far as I could see, but several other people looked up in interest as we passed. The crumpled strip torn from my shirt the previous day was still hanging from the waistband of my leather breeches where I had stuffed it when I left the horse pens. Odd to think of how much had happened since then.

I pulled it free and held it in my closed hand as I entered the stallion's pen. Rather than stalking straight up to him like a predator would, I wandered toward him in a gentle arc. The horse looked up from his pile of hay and snorted. As I approached him from the side, I was pleased to see that he moved his hindquarters away, squaring up to face me. As a further test, I motioned him to back a step or two away from his feed, flashing the cloth rag when he hesitated.

The stallion shook his head and pawed, but gave way, allowing me to step up to the hay and claim it. After giving him a moment to think about things, I invited him forward to join me. He sniffed at my tunic curiously for a few seconds and returned to eating, keeping an eye and an ear cocked in my direction. I ran my hands over him as he ate, keeping the strokes rhythmic and sure. After a few minutes, I again asked him to back away from the hay so I could leave without him getting the idea that he'd run me off somehow.

I was pleased that he seemed to have accepted the idea of ceding power to a human, even if I was skeptical of the Merenis' ability to keep him sweet on the idea after I'd gone. Still, the naked admiration in Previn's eyes as I took my leave and returned to the center of the village gave me hope that he, at least, would take my words to heart.

Not wanting to leave Andoc and Senovo waiting too long, I wasted no time in procuring some food and returning to the temple. I opened the door to the room quietly, not wanting to disturb the pair if they were asleep. The light from the window illuminated the bed, where Andoc was indeed sleeping, curled into Senovo with an arm thrown across his hips. Senovo, however, was awake, sitting propped up against the wall at the head of the bed and running one hand slowly through Andoc's tousled brown hair.

"You should be sleeping, too," I said quietly.

"I'm just thinking," Senovo said, the back of his head resting against the rough wattle and daub of the wall.

"Well, stop thinking for a few minutes and eat something instead," I told him, handing him one of the savory, leaf-wrapped cakes I'd purchased. "You and I both have far too much to think about right now. The reality is, though, that all we can do is go home, confess our sins, and hope for the best. Beyond that, dwelling on things is just a waste of energy."

"More wisdom from the horse pens," Senovo teased quietly, and I was pleased to see the hint of a smile playing around his mouth.

"You'd better believe it," I said.

We ate in comfortable silence, Senovo continuing to soothe Andoc with his free hand as the warrior twisted and muttered in his sleep.

"Is he all right?" I asked finally, putting aside the remains of my meal.

"Just restless," Senovo said. "I think we scared him half to death last night."

I nodded, remembering Andoc's expression when he'd charged into the courtyard to find us surrounded by guards with raised weapons. I also remembered the way he'd stepped in front of those weapons without a second thought, and felt a warm shiver ripple through my chest and down into my belly.

"How much do you remember about what happens when you change?" I asked to distract myself. "You must retain some of it—you knew that I was female because the wolf smelled my moon blood."

"I get flashes," said Senovo. "I remember wanting to attack Jyrrel right after I changed last night. I remember you grabbing me—which was incredibly foolish, by the way. I could have killed you." He cleared his throat and his voice, which had grown soft and faint on the final sentence, strengthened again. "I remember Andoc arriving, and the relief of knowing that he would protect us so I didn't have to."

I nodded. "I felt pretty much the same thing when he showed up, to be honest," I confessed.

Senovo stretched across to place his partially eaten meal on the table near the bed. Andoc moaned as he leaned away, momentarily breaking contact. Straightening and resuming his slow caress across Andoc's scalp, Senovo looked at me frankly.

"You should join us, Carivel," he said, sending my heart into a short, staccato rhythm of surprise. "Just to sleep," he clarified. "You're still exhausted as well. He'll sleep sounder with both of us in his arms."

"I don't want to intrude," I whispered. A bald-faced lie — I wanted few things in life more than to worm my way into their partnership.

Senovo shook his head. "It's obvious to all but the blind that he adores you, and you yearn for him. It serves no one for you to continue to deny yourself."

I pulled my eyes away from Andoc's sleeping face to meet Senovo's gaze. "You must realize by now that it's not only him I want."

Senovo made a small, self-deprecating gesture. "You'll do yourself no favors by becoming romantically entangled with a disgraced eunuch," he said.

An unexpected flash of anger tightened my chest. "And neither of you will do yourselves any favors by becoming entangled with a woman who dresses and acts like a man!" I snapped. "Which is why I've been resisting this all along. If we're going to ride roughshod over convention, we might as well trample it in more than one way."

Senovo let out a long, slightly unsteady breath. "Between the three of us, we're likely to end up being run out of town and forced to wander the wildlands," he said, trying for humor but sounding, in the end, as though he fully expected such a thing to happen.

"Then we end up wandering the wildlands," I said. "I did that for weeks after I ran away from the village where I grew up… did you know that? There are worse things."

"In which case, we have come full circle, and I ask you again to join us on the bed and rest."

Senovo was a stubborn bastard; you had to give him that. Suddenly, I felt exhausted — despite having gotten a surprising amount of sleep last night while curled around the wolf. I was tired of running. Tired of fighting my feelings and desires. Honestly, I could think of nothing I wanted more in that moment than to be in bed with the two of them, huddled close together so no one would fall off. For the life of me, I couldn't remember at this particular point in time why I'd been resisting so hard.

"Fuck this," I said out of nowhere and started pulling off my boots and outer clothes almost angrily. "Fuck every last fucked up part of it."

"Perhaps not until Andoc wakes up and we've had a word with him," Senovo said mildly, but the hint of amusement had returned to his eyes.

I let out an indelicate snort and crawled under the blanket, clad in my smallclothes and linen shirt. Any question about whether Andoc wanted me there was answered immediately… as soon as he felt the mattress dip, he muttered, "Car'vel?" and pulled me into his arms with sleepy, uncoordinated movements. I ended up with my head pillowed on his broad chest, one arm and leg thrown over him. *"Finally,"* he breathed, and dropped into a deeper sleep with a contented murmur.

I glanced up at Senovo, still sitting propped against the wall, and received an arched eyebrow that very clearly said 'I told you so' in return. With a deep sigh that felt like it cleared all of the dust and cobwebs from the last few days out of my body, I let my outstretched hand inch closer to the eunuch until my fingers rested on his blanket-covered thigh, just above his knee. I was rewarded a moment later when the hand that had been combing through Andoc's hair moved to stroke my own closely shorn head, sending delicious shivers down the length of my spine.

I drifted like that for a long time, feeling safer and more relaxed than I could remember feeling since childhood, before my father had died and left me to my mother's bitterness and anger. I didn't want to miss a moment of that bone-deep contentment by sleeping. Eventually, though, the soothing movement of fingers trailing over my scalp pulled me down into a sort of peaceful doze where everything was warm and wonderful, and the cares of the wider world beyond our closed door were unimportant.

⤜ ⚜ ⤛

When I regained awareness of my surroundings, it was to the rumble of low voices nearby. My cheek was still resting on the warm skin of Andoc's chest, but my neck had developed an uncomfortable kink.

"Mmph," I groaned as I tried to get my leaden limbs to cooperate.

"Well, hello there," Andoc said, looking up at me with a quiet smile as I struggled upright.

"Hello," I replied, my voice soft and raspy with sleep.

"Senovo says you and he had a talk earlier," he said.

I looked across at Senovo, who was still sitting in much the same position as he had been. His expression was calm and gently encouraging.

"Yes," I said, after a moment's hesitation. "We came to the conclusion that we're both going to ruin your life with our various secrets and problems, but since you apparently don't care, there's not much we can do about it and we might as well stop pretending."

Andoc's smile grew wider.

"That might be a *slight* oversimplification..." Senovo said.

"Nonsense," Andoc said. "I think that sums things up quite nicely. Perhaps I'll even forgive you for somehow neglecting to ravish me in my sleep once you finally came to your senses, Carivel. I suppose even uncontrollable lust can be pushed to the wayside after what we've been through in the last couple of days."

"My lust is *not uncontrollable*," I groused, somehow oddly delighted that being in Andoc's bed did not erase his ability to get my back up with a few simple words.

"No?" he asked, and pulled me down for a kiss.

The noise that was startled out of me when our lips touched was completely undignified and embarrassing... and I didn't care one whit. Every ounce of my attention was focused on the sensation of Andoc's cool, chapped lips sliding against my own, growing warm and wet as he deepened the kiss. It was *nothing* like the innocent kiss I'd shared with a hapless young girl when I was thirteen and trying desperately to understand myself.

This—*this*—was every passionate kiss I'd ever seen newly handfasted couples share at the altar... every warmly welcoming kiss I'd seen a returning warrior share with his lover upon being reunited after a battle. Andoc's tongue slid across the seam of my lips, teasing them open and licking deep inside. Desire pooled in my belly, hot and heavy and more urgent than

I'd ever felt in my life. When we parted, my gasp was as desperate as if I'd been drowning.

My eyes flickered up to meet Senovo's, unsure what I would find in his expression. His face was hard to read, but I had the sense that he still half-expected the two of us to drop him like a hot stone and run off into the sunset together. Apparently, I wasn't far off the mark, because Andoc followed my gaze and frowned, immediately reaching up to drag Senovo down to his level with a hand on the back of his neck.

"You're being an idiot," he growled when they were forehead to forehead. "I can practically *hear* you thinking ridiculous things. Stop it."

With that, he pulled Senovo down the last inch and sealed their lips together in a biting kiss that made me catch my breath as my cunt throbbed in reaction. Senovo made a noise not markedly different than the one I'd made a few moments ago, and Andoc rolled them both over until he was poised above the eunuch, pressing him down into the bed. I sat up to get a better view as Senovo melted under Andoc's lips and hands, closing his eyes in blissful, heartfelt surrender.

When they parted, Andoc looked over his shoulder at me. "I think you'd better come down here and show Senovo that he's stuck with both of us," he said.

I swallowed, and Andoc relinquished his position as I moved to replace him. Looking down at Senovo, still lying on his back with his eyes closed and his head tipped back trustingly, I felt a sudden nervousness. Andoc had made no secret of his desire for me—for all that I couldn't understand what he saw in my angular, coltish body and plain features. We had bantered about uncontrollable lust, and I hadn't outright denied it; he knew full well of my feelings. Similarly, I'd told Senovo straight out of my desire for him earlier while Andoc was sleeping. Even though—as a eunuch—Senovo did not feel the same sort of physical lust that Andoc or I did, it was obvious that he desired intimacy with Andoc, and gained pleasure from being with him.

But did he really want *my* touch as well?

He was so naturally reserved that I wasn't sure. He hadn't mentioned any objections to the idea, but he hadn't encouraged it either. Before I did anything to the priest lying so vulnerable beneath me, I had to know.

"Senovo," I said softly, letting my fingertips ghost over his cheek. "Look at me."

Those extraordinary gold-green eyes blinked open, gazing up at me.

"Just because you and I both care for Andoc doesn't mean that you automatically want my advances as well," I said, trying to shape my misgivings into words. Andoc rested his hand between my shoulder blades, radiating approval, and I relaxed minutely. "I very much want to kiss you right now, but only if you want to be kissed."

Senovo's face softened to fond affection, making something in my chest swell and break open in response. "Carivel," he said, "you've already seen how Andoc and I fit together. I don't know how you and I will fit together—we'll find that out as we go along. For now, though… yes. Kiss me. It pleases me to hear Andoc bid you to do so, and it pleases me even more that you would stop to ask first."

I was smiling broadly as I closed the distance and touched my lips to Senovo's, trying to take possession of him the way Andoc had done, but painfully aware of my own inexperience. Kissing Senovo was completely different than kissing Andoc. Where Andoc had dominated the kiss from the first instant, Senovo yielded beneath my lips. His hand came up to my touch my face, mirroring the way I cradled his cheek. Before long, I realized that he was quietly and tactfully guiding my movements—not controlling, but suggesting different angles, different techniques.

We explored each other slowly, the kiss gentling until it was almost chaste… or would have been if my breasts hadn't been tingling and my smallclothes damp between my legs. Almost without realizing it, I started to catalog the things that made Senovo relax further into the mattress, or puff out a little breath of appreciation. He liked it when I nipped his bottom lip and worried at it; I loved it when he nuzzled up against the corner of my mouth as if begging for more contact. When we finally parted, I was light-headed with desire and the moisture leaking from between my legs was beginning to drip down my thighs.

"Beautiful," Andoc breathed. His hand, which had remained resting between my shoulder blades, slid down to the small of my back.

Suddenly, all I could focus on was *too many clothes — gods, why are we wearing all these clothes*, but before I could begin to remedy the situation, a knock at the door shattered the moment.

ELEVEN

Andoc growled, and flopped over onto his back. "Who is it?" he called.

"Messenger from the Council of Elders," said a young voice.

"Hang on a minute," Andoc said. "I'll be right there."

I couldn't help my own groan of disappointment.

"*Fuck*," he added, quietly enough not to be heard in the hallway.

"Apparently not," Senovo said, and I could tell that the smug bastard was *laughing* at the two of us—on the inside, at least.

Andoc kissed us both quickly and fiercely. He rolled out of the overcrowded bed and pulled on a shirt and breeches. I followed suit and tossed Senovo his robes. Within moments, we were decent, and Andoc opened the door to the hapless messenger boy.

"What is it?" Andoc asked.

"Your pardon, sir," the boy said. "The council asks that all three of you come to the meeting hall."

"We'll be right there," Andoc said.

⟵ 👑 ⟶

The transition from animal lust to fidgety nervousness was abrupt and unsettling. As we walked to the meeting hall, I was uncomfortably aware of the way my thighs slid against each other with every step, gradually becoming sticky as the evidence of my earlier desire slowly dried up.

The people watching us didn't help. If I'd thought I was getting a lot of attention when I'd gone out to get food and check the horses earlier, it was nothing to the excited chattering and looks of fear that Senovo garnered as we made our way into the village square. Andoc and I flanked him protectively, but Senovo's face might as well have been made of stone. He looked neither right nor left, and I cursed the circumstances that had transformed him from the relaxed and trusting lover of a few minutes ago to this stiff, defensive figure.

It was almost a relief to escape the curious, excited villagers by entering the meeting hall — right up until I remembered why we were there. Unlike our first visit, the heavy table in the large meeting room was completely surrounded by men and women, with Magoldis at the head. We entered at the guard's behest and bowed before the assembled Mereni elders.

"Thank you for coming," the Leader said. "We have been discussing your proposal, Andoc, and we have a few more questions for the three of you before we reach a final decision."

"Of course, Leader Magoldis," Andoc replied. "Please ask your questions."

A wizened little man spoke up. "Horse Mistress Carivel. We were quite impressed by your demonstration yesterday. If the council agrees to an alliance with the Draebardi, we would like to foster an exchange of both breeding animals and methods of horse training. Would this be acceptable to you?"

"Sir," I said, "I've been plotting to trade for some of your horses pretty much since I arrived." There was a quiet smattering of laughter around the table. "I'd say that's a more than acceptable provision."

"Very well," Magoldis said. "Priest Senovo. I have been speaking to our High Priest about you, and First Warrior Andoc was also kind enough to fill us in on some details of your background."

Senovo stood tall and stony-faced, not quite looking at the men and women around the table. I saw his throat bob up and down once in a nearly undetectable show of nerves, and ached to be able to somehow go back and undo the previous evening's events.

"We would like assurance that you will, in fact, be returning to Draebard to assume your position as High Priest upon Rhystel's death," Magoldis continued.

"Should High Priest Rhystel succumb to his injuries," Senovo said stiffly, "and should the people of Draebard accept my continued presence after learning of my secret, then I will do my duty. There is, to put it bluntly, no one else left. The only other survivors of the temple massacre are mere boys."

Magoldis tipped her head to the side to confer quietly with a silver-haired woman sitting next to her. After a moment, she straightened. "That is acceptable," she said. "Finally, First Warrior Andoc. The Mereni are involved in a disagreement with the Rhytheeri tribe to the south. Can Meren count on the support of Draebard in the event of an out-and-out conflict?"

"An alliance goes both ways, Leader Magoldis," Andoc said. "Should Meren agree to help Draebard, we would be honor-bound to help Meren in turn."

Magoldis nodded. "Very well. Please wait outside while we make our decision. The guard will show you to a room with refreshments where you may relax."

Relax? Seriously? I did my best not to gape at Magoldis in open-mouthed disbelief, instead following the others' example as they bowed and backed out of the room.

As promised, the silent guard showed us to a small room further inside the building, where a bowl of fruit and a flagon of wine sat on a small table with three cups. Andoc immediately picked up a crisp piece of fruit from the bowl and bit into it, crossing to fall into one of the chairs arrayed around the edges of the room.

"Hmm," he said, looking at the fruit. "That's really good. You should have one."

"I think anything I tried to eat now would come right back up," I said, though I did pour two cups of wine, one of which I pushed into Senovo's unresisting hands. "Drink," I told him.

Taking my own advice, I downed half the cup in one go and flopped down into my own chair. "How long do you think it will take?" I asked.

"Put that many elders in a single room together and they could talk all night," Andoc said. "Hopefully, they got most of that out of their systems earlier, though."

"It sounded as though they were close to a decision," Senovo said, and I was relieved that he was still engaged enough to talk with us given the pressure he must be feeling.

"You're not drinking," I pointed out, and he gave me an ironic little salute with his cup before raising it to his lips.

The silence stretched out for several minutes before Andoc broke it.

"If the Mereni agree to ally with us, I want to ride ahead to Draebard and talk to Chief Volya before you two arrive," he said. "Once I know whether he's going to see sense or not, I can leave you some sort of a signal outside of the village to let you know whether it's safe to come back."

I had successfully taken my own advice about not obsessing over my fate for the better part of a day, but now a sense of deep foreboding reared its head once more.

"Volya won't risk the Mereni alliance over your secret, Carivel," Senovo said, sounding very sure. "Once he hears that Magoldis only agreed because she thought the attitudes toward women were changing in Draebard, he'll have to accept you."

"I agree," Andoc said. "Nor will he turn you away, Senovo, when he finds out you've been a shape-shifter all this time. Still, it makes me feel better to have a plan in place."

"What if Magoldis *doesn't* agree to the treaty?" I asked.

"That's a little more complicated," Andoc said. "On the one hand, there's no reason anyone in Draebard needs to hear about either of your secrets if the Mereni aren't coming back with us. On the other hand, all it would take is one traveler or trader coming in and saying the wrong thing to the wrong person, and you'd be exposed, but without the leverage of the treaty to protect you."

"I'm not sure I could go back to hiding my secret," I said, feeling miserable at the prospect. "Particularly if it also meant having to sneak around in order to be with you two. I think they'll have to be told."

"Well," Andoc said, "in that case, let's hope that the council chooses in our favor. We should know for certain before long."

It had been early evening when we were summoned to the meeting hall. As we waited, dusk descended outside the room's single window, followed by full dark. After lighting the candles on the table, Andoc began to pace while Senovo sat pale and distant in his chair, and I fidgeted. We were unable to keep up even a desultory conversation, each wrapped up in our own worries.

When the guard finally entered and bade us to follow him back to the council room, it was both a relief and the pinnacle of all our concerns, both public and private. Magoldis rose to meet us as we entered, her face giving away nothing.

"After lengthy discussion," she said, "the ruling council of the Mereni have decided to ally themselves with the Draebardi against the incursion of the Alyrion Empire. While our two peoples have had their differences over the years, we are all

Eburosi, and it is Eburos itself that is under threat—not merely a single tribe."

It was over. All of the tension bled out of me in a single instant, leaving me light-headed. Senovo was cool and composed beside me, but I did hear Andoc's faint sigh of relief.

"Thank you, Leader Magoldis. Thank you, Elders," he said with heartfelt gratitude. "Like you, I fear the attack on Draebard was only the beginning of something much larger, but perhaps if we work together, we can still prevail." He took a deep breath, and continued. "I would like to propose that I leave for Draebard with a representative from Meren as soon as possible, leaving Senovo and Carivel behind to finalize the details. They can follow on with more comprehensive information about weaponry, numbers, and the timeline for troop movements."

"That seems reasonable," Magoldis agreed, and just like that, Andoc's plan to go ahead and speak with Volya on our behalf was in place. "Now, though, it is late and there is nothing more to be done regarding this matter tonight."

We bowed, and Andoc thanked the council once more.

"Wait," Magoldis said, as we were turning to leave. "I nearly forgot. There is one more thing. I wish to make a personal gift of the black stallion to you, Horse Mistress Carivel. You spoke earlier of your desire to open a horse trade between our tribes, and from what I've seen, you are perhaps the best person available to take on that particular horse."

I was struck dumb until Andoc nudged me unobtrusively. "Thank you," I stammered. "That is an unexpected and most welcome gift. I don't really know what to say."

"*Thank you* will be perfectly adequate, Horse Mistress," Magoldis said with a faint smile tugging up one corner of her mouth for an instant. "We'll discuss more details of our future horse trading agreement tomorrow."

We took our leave again and let the guard escort us to the door of the meeting hall. Outside, it was late enough that the streets were mercifully free of curious onlookers.

"Where do you want to go?" Andoc asked us. "Back to the temple, or to our room at Harinel's place?"

Senovo shrugged his indifference, and I said, "They'll probably expect us to be at the temple. If we go to Harinel's, it might take them a bit longer to find us in the morning."

Andoc raised an eyebrow, the light from the torches flanking the meeting hall door illuminating his predatory smile. "Well, well. I do like the way you think, Horse Mistress Carivel."

"We should go back to the temple first, though," I added. "Some of our things are still there, and there's food left over from what I bought earlier today."

"A reasonable plan," Senovo agreed, and we turned down the road to the temple. Andoc's hand settled at the small of my back, in the same place it had been when the messenger knocked on the door and interrupted us. Desire flared low in my belly, making my breath hitch.

Arriving at the temple, we made quick work of packing our meager belongings and quietly slipping back out. The three of us split the remaining food left over from lunch evenly and ate it as we walked across town to Harinel's ramshackle boarding house. I sent the other two inside, wanting to check the horses again. The two geldings were dozing, lying down on the ground, Kekenu snoring comically with his muzzle mashed into the dirt of the corral. The mare was awake, standing watch between them, and pricked her ears as I approached but did not react otherwise. I checked the water trough and reassured myself that all was well before letting myself into the boarding house and entering our room at the end of the hallway.

The door had been left invitingly open. I closed it behind me, took a deep breath, and let it out slowly. Inside, Senovo was seated on the edge of the bed with one leg tucked underneath himself, while Andoc was sprawled on the floor, lounging against the bed frame with his shoulder pressed up against Senovo's inner thigh.

I stared at them both, so beautiful together in the light from the hearth. "We did it," I breathed, the realization washing over me like a warm wave.

Andoc smiled at me, a slow grin lighting up his face.

"I know," he teased. "I was there, remember?"

"No, but—*we did it*," I reiterated, trying to get the weight of it across.

Andoc laughed aloud. "Are you sure that stallion didn't kick you in the head while our backs were turned?"

"Oh, shut up," I told him, grinning like a loon.

Andoc rose to his feet, smooth as a panther. "Why don't you make me?" he said, still smiling and with a gleam in his eye.

I lunged forward, tackling him to the bed and startling a surprised *oof* from him as Senovo scrambled out of the way.

When I was straddling Andoc's hips, my hands braced on his shoulders, I looked down at him with an insolent tilt of my head.

"So sorry," I apologized. "I guess I just couldn't control myself."

Behind me, Senovo snorted his amusement, making my heart swell even further.

"A regrettable character flaw, if you ask me," Andoc opined from his position on his back. "We'll have to work on that."

Before I could come up with a reply, Andoc was twisting underneath me, rolling us both over with an easy strength that made my heart flutter. Two seconds later, I was the one pinned to the bed, Andoc straddling my waist and holding both my wrists over my head with one large hand. I lay on my back, panting as the glow of affection lighting my chest from within was replaced in an instant with a surge of raw, base need.

Andoc tilted his head up to look at Senovo, who had returned to stand at the edge of the bed and was looking down at both of us with a tolerant gaze. "*Amadi,*" Andoc said in a conversational tone, "I believe our Horse Mistress is in need of a lesson. Do you want in on this?"

Senovo tipped his chin down as if considering the matter, and I felt a new flare of arousal at the thought of the two of them discussing me casually while I lay pinned under Andoc's bulk.

"Honestly," Senovo said, "I can think of few distractions more attractive right now than beginning Carivel's remedial education in matters of physical love. Besides—I am, after all, still a priest."

Andoc nodded thoughtfully, not budging an inch as I squirmed beneath him. "That's very true. I mean, you're practically duty-bound at this point."

"Indeed," Senovo agreed.

I bucked my hips, gaining myself precisely nothing. "Stop talking about it and start *doing* it, then!" I growled.

Andoc laughed down at me and rolled off the bed. "Very well, Horse Mistress," he said with a mocking half-bow. "Senovo and I are going to move these two beds together so we've got a bit more room to work. Be naked by the time we're done."

TWELVE

My hands were scrabbling at the ties of my tunic almost before he'd finished speaking. The two each took an end of the other bed, Senovo struggling a bit with his end as they half-carried, half-scooted the heavy mattress and frame across the room. My nervous fingers fumbled with the knot holding my breeches laced shut even as I toed off my soft boots. I was shoving my breeches and smallclothes down my hips as they pushed the second bed up against the one I was currently occupying, and by the time Andoc finished rolling up the spare blanket and jamming it into the space between the two mattresses to close the gap, I had flopped back down, completely naked in the firelight.

"Mmm… yes," Andoc said as he rose and began to remove his own clothing. "Very nice. Senovo, I believe I'd like both of you naked for this."

Senovo immediately started unfastening his robes. The priest ran a critical gaze over Andoc's body as he worked and said, "Before we start, are you fully recovered from your… ahem… *unfortunate injury* during the contest against Varanis?"

My own hands, which had been wandering lazily up and down my body as I watched the two of them, stilled. I had all but forgotten the rather vicious blow that Varanis used to end her fight with Andoc.

"Still a bit tender," Andoc said in reply, not sounding overly concerned. "I probably won't be fucking anyone in the traditional sense tonight, but I'm stiff as a board right now and it doesn't hurt… so I'm going to call it good enough for our purposes."

"Perhaps it's just as well. Traditional intercourse brings with it some complications that we could probably do without for now," Senovo said.

I rolled onto one elbow as Senovo's words penetrated my desire-muddled thoughts. "You mean pregnancy?" I asked, the possibility literally not having crossed my mind until Senovo said something. The idea was a daunting one.

"Yes," Senovo said, as he continued to disrobe. "That's a discussion we will need to have at some point, but perhaps not at this exact moment."

It was a relief not to have to worry about it immediately, so I just nodded my understanding and left the question for another day. Stripped down to his smallclothes, Andoc joined me on the bed and let his hand trail down the side of my neck and over my collarbone, raising gooseflesh in its wake despite the warmth of the fire.

"Still doing all right?" he asked, and I smiled, letting my own fingers trace over the hard muscles of Andoc's chest and stomach, as I had dreamed of doing for so long.

"More than all right," I told him.

Senovo joined us on the bed a moment later, as naked as I was. Andoc leaned over to capture my lips in a brief kiss that left me wanting more, before leaning back against the wall at the head of the bed and easing me against him to rest between his spread legs. I reclined against his body, resting my head on the uninjured side of his chest. I could feel his hot, hard length pressing against my spine through his smallclothes. Senovo crawled across the newly enlarged expanse of mattress on his hands and knees, settling next to my hip. His hand came to rest on my lower leg, sliding slowly up to the top of my thigh and sending pleasant shivers through me.

"Every person is different," he said, "but there are a few things that most people tend to enjoy. The most important thing is to be able to communicate with your lover—"

"Or lovers," Andoc interrupted.

"—or *lovers*," Senovo continued, throwing Andoc a long-suffering look, "about your preferences, and know that they will stop immediately if you don't like something."

I frowned. "But… you and Andoc…?"

"I need to feel as if I'm being overpowered," Senovo said, "for reasons that you and I have already discussed. However, if I were in physical pain or needed to end things for some other reason, I would only have to say *stop* and Andoc would stop instantly."

"That kind of sex is a serious responsibility for the one taking control," Andoc added. "I enjoy it—quite a bit, actually—

but it means you can't ever lose yourself completely in the moment, because someone you love is counting on you for their safety."

I lay quietly between them for a moment, relishing the feeling of being protected and watched over as I considered their words.

"The first time I saw you together like that, I thought it was beautiful. Now I think I understand *why* it was beautiful," I said finally.

"All such expressions of love have a beauty to them," Senovo agreed. "The pleasure people can give each other is one of the gods' greatest gifts."

A feeling of sadness washed over me. "One that was stolen from you," I pointed out.

"Not at all," said Andoc. "It might take a bit of a different approach, but later I'll show you how to help me break through our mutual friend's cool reserve."

"Oh, yes?" I said, intrigued. "I look forward to it."

"As do I," Senovo said easily. "Now, though, let us return the focus to you. You told me that you had touched yourself, and once kissed a girl but found the experience lacking. Yes?"

"That's right," I said, feeling a faint blush crawl up my neck.

"So you've never lain with anyone, then? Man or woman?" Andoc asked, his curiosity plain.

I shook my head. "I couldn't. I was a social outcast in the village where I grew up—the girl who wanted to be a boy. And I certainly didn't dare get that close to anyone in Draebard. They would have learned my secret. What about you, though? Have you ever been with a woman before?" I asked.

"A handful, over the years," he said. "Also a handful of men."

That surprised me, although maybe it shouldn't have. Andoc had already proven that he was not particularly concerned about taboo and convention.

"Well... it sounds like I'm in capable hands, then," I said, giving them both a smile and relaxing back in Andoc's arms.

Andoc huffed out a breath of laughter. "I do believe that was a hint, *amadi*. Perhaps it's time for you to put that eloquent tongue of yours to a different use."

"As you wish," Senovo said, sending my desire spiraling to the fore again.

Andoc's hand slid down to cup my breast, testing its weight. I moaned and pushed into the touch, seeking more contact. Meanwhile, Senovo was rearranging himself to lie between my legs, easing them apart to make room. A moment later, I felt the same soft, meticulously thorough lips I had so enjoyed kissing earlier close over a patch of skin on my inner thigh, tongue flicking out to tease the soft flesh. I choked back the cry that wanted to escape, a new pulse of wetness dripping down from between my thighs.

Senovo's mouth moved higher, suckling at a new patch of skin while Andoc let his callused palm slide over my erect nipple, sending another rush of sensation through me. Senovo continued his slow ascent up my inner thigh until I was shaking with desire, squirming against the arm Andoc wrapped around my stomach to hold me in place, trying to get Senovo to move that last… little… bit… higher…

The flat of Senovo's tongue slid along the seam of my cunt at the same instant Andoc's fingers pinched my aching nipple and rolled it slowly back and forth. I arched from the bed, crying out in shock at the jolt of pleasure that raced between the two points. Senovo's long fingers closed over my hipbones, pressing me back down and holding me in place. His tongue continued to lap at me, slipping a bit deeper inside each time. Writhing against Andoc's lap, I felt him thrust his hips up against me, humming approval as he tweaked and worried at the pebbled tip of my breast.

"Gorgeous," he murmured, as I threw my head back and panted with need.

Senovo was methodical and relentless, driving me higher and higher toward my peak before pulling me away from the cliff, only to press me even closer to the edge moments later. Between them, they pinned me in place, unable to twist either toward or away from the delicious torture of hand and mouth. Dragging his fingers away from my nipple with a final sharp tug, Andoc raised his hand to trace over my throat… my chin. When the rough pads of his fingertips brushed across my lips, I stretched up to draw them into my mouth as I had seen Senovo do when he was bound and helpless two nights ago on this very bed.

With the weight of Andoc's fingers pressing on my tongue, and Senovo's lips wrapped around the little bud of flesh between my legs that made sparks tingle behind my closed eyelids, I finally sobbed my release, hips jerking against Senovo's restraining hands as my pleasure crested in a powerful wave and slowly ebbed.

Senovo gentled his movements, drawing trembling aftershocks from my body, and I continued to suck and lick lazily at Andoc's fingers as he pressed them deep into my mouth and slid them back, over and over in an easy rhythm that made me feel like I was floating. Senovo eased himself away, replacing his mouth with his smooth, soft hands.

My thighs and cunt were drenched after my climax. He dragged his fingertips back and forth through the slippery moisture, avoiding the place where I was still painfully oversensitive. After a few moments, one finger pressed smoothly into my slick passage. I grunted around Andoc's fingers and stiffened in surprise. Both men froze. Andoc slid his fingers out of my mouth, and Senovo remained very still.

"No?" asked the priest.

"Sorry," I said, trying to relax around the intrusion. "I've tried that a few times, but I've never liked it."

The finger slipped out immediately, Senovo's hand moving to rest on my thigh instead. I breathed a sigh of relief and tried to explain.

"It doesn't hurt, really… it's just… I don't know. It's not how I see myself, does that make sense?"

"Ah," Senovo said. "I think I understand. You think of yourself more as a man in this respect, too?"

I nodded. "I suppose that's it. When I daydream about sex, I always picture what it would be like to have a prick. To fuck like men do."

"I can understand that well enough," Andoc put in. "I mean, it *is* pretty amazing."

I reached back and smacked him on the thigh—the only place I could easily reach right now—even as I thanked him silently for his unerring ability to cut through the tension.

"In that case," Senovo said, "let us try something slightly different. Andoc, did you bring grease to mix your war paint?"

"As it happens, I did," Andoc replied. "Saddlebag. Left pocket."

Senovo rose and returned with a small clay jar, which he uncorked and set within easy reach. "I'm going to raise your hips up a bit," he told me.

Andoc eased me down to lie flat on the mattress while Senovo pulled the remaining blanket free from the end of the bed, where I'd shoved it out of the way earlier while getting undressed. He folded it up and rolled it into a tight cylinder, urging me to lift my hips up so he could slide it underneath me.

The new position left me feeling wanton and exposed as Senovo resettled himself between my thighs and Andoc half-reclined onto an elbow next to me so he could watch. His free hand roamed up and down my body, sliding over my breasts and belly.

"The little bud at the front of a woman's slit isn't so different from a man's penis," Senovo said, sliding two slick fingers gently on either side of the delicate flesh, up and down, making me gasp and throw my head back—the sensation just on the right side of too much. "It's very sensitive; it becomes erect when you're excited. The closer you are to release, the more stimulation it can take, but once you climax, all but the lightest hint of a touch becomes too much until you've had time to recover."

"Yours is large for a woman's, Carivel," Andoc said, peering between my legs with obvious curiosity. "It really is like a little cock."

"I thought so, too," Senovo said. "I believe it's the largest I've seen."

"*Gods*," I said, the combination of their words and the slow, delicious drag of Senovo's fingers over my flesh driving me to fresh heights.

"However, there's something else that men do with other men—and with eunuchs—that I'd like to try," Senovo said. "Have you ever touched yourself here?"

Without varying the rhythm of his fingers over my deliciously engorged flesh, he slid a knuckle on his free hand down and back, rubbing it over my rear passage and making me see sparks.

"No," I replied, and it came out as an undignified squeak. I cleared my throat, trying to regain control of my voice. "It never—ah! Never even occurred to me."

"But you sort of wish it had, now?" Andoc teased, tweaking a nipple.

I nodded frantically as Senovo twisted the knuckle and pressed more firmly, merciless in his ministrations. "Uh-*huh*," I said, my voice going up another octave. A trickle of sweat trailed down between my breasts; Andoc twisted around and leaned over me to lap it up, pressing a kiss to each pebbled nipple before he straightened.

With almost no warning, I was teetering on the edge again. Senovo—sadistic bastard that he was—must have sensed it, because he eased off, slowing his movements. I couldn't stop the whine of protest that escaped my throat.

"More," I begged. "*Please*, Senovo…"

"Patience," he said. "This will feel a bit odd. Give yourself a some time to adjust before you decide if you like it or not."

I nodded frantically, desperate for more of his touch. There was a slick smear of cool grease over my opening, warming quickly with my body heat. Senovo began to press with a single finger, moving around the rim of my tightly puckered entrance with small, circular motions. The flesh gave way with a flutter of tense muscles and the tip of his finger slipped inside, meeting a second point of resistance. I held my breath as he continued to rub tiny circles, and eventually his finger slid deeper, disappearing into my body all the way to the third knuckle.

"Breathe," Andoc reminded me, stroking my head, and I emptied my lungs with a gasp. "Try to relax."

I forced myself to breathe, trying not to fight against the intrusion inside my body, but painfully aware of the way my muscles cramped and clenched around it. I was just about to beg Senovo to stop when the priest resumed the slow drag of his fingers across the erect nub of flesh at the top of my slit. Suddenly, the sensation that had been uncomfortable a moment before was the single most amazing thing I had ever felt.

"Mmnh!" I said, grabbing the nearest part of Andoc I could reach, which happened to be his bicep.

"Better now?" he asked.

For some reason, there didn't seem to be enough air in the room for me to answer aloud, but I nodded, my eyes clenched tightly shut. Senovo continued to work me open at the same time he drove me closer and closer to my release.

"*Fuck!*" The curse was punched from my chest when he slipped in a second finger, stretching me even wider. Andoc, who had been teasing my breasts as Senovo slowly drove me mad, leaned down and muffled my moans with a searing kiss, taking effortless possession of my mouth. I gasped for air and he thrust his tongue inside, mimicking the rhythm of Senovo's fingers. Andoc swallowed my sobbing scream as I came, straining up off the bed and clenching around Senovo's fingers, completely overwhelmed by sensation.

It went on long enough that my vision dimmed, leaving me shrouded in shadowy warmth. When I came back to myself, Andoc was still kissing me, gentler now, while Senovo carefully pulled his fingers free. I moaned softly against Andoc's lips, feeling empty where I'd been full a moment before. He reluctantly broke the kiss, running his fingers through my short hair, and Senovo pressed his lips to my inner thigh in wordless apology before rising from the bed. The priest returned a moment later with a damp rag. I was vaguely aware that I'd squirted a truly embarrassing amount of release onto the bed during my climax, and I blushed as Senovo gently cleaned me up with the cool cloth.

Once he'd cleaned his hand as well, he discarded the rag and retuned to the bed, pulling the folded blanket out from under my hips and reclining next to me so that I was bracketed on both sides.

"I think we can call that a successful first lesson," he said.

"I'd say so," said Andoc.

"Mm-hmm," I agreed, still floating.

"In fact, I believe we may have broken her," Andoc said.

I smacked him on the thigh again, though the movement was uncoordinated and weak.

"Shut up," I mumbled. "Lemme rest a minute and then I want to see you two together."

THIRTEEN

"That can be arranged," Senovo said, visibly amused.

"Indeed it can," Andoc agreed. "*Amadi*, how are you tonight? What do you need from us?"

"I am well enough," Senovo said. "The wolf is quiet now, watching things from the background. I would enjoy being of use. Or simply being used, in whatever way the two of you desire. As I said earlier, it sounds like a most agreeable distraction from my worries."

Impossibly, the words stirred a new flutter of desire in my sated, boneless body. With difficulty, I rolled onto an elbow. "I want to see you tied again," I told him. "But not fighting and straining — just quiet, submitting to the ropes while he uses you for his pleasure. Is that… all right? Would you like that?"

Senovo guided me forward with a touch to the cheek and kissed me softly. "I would like that very much."

"Told you she'd have good ideas," Andoc said from my other side, letting his fingers trail down my spine. "In fact, I've got an idea of my own that involves you on your knees in front of me, with your arms tied behind your back while you swallow my cock right down to the root."

I was still facing Senovo, so I saw the nearly imperceptible shiver that worked its way through his body, and the way his eyes darkened, the pupils blown wide. Andoc pressed his lips briefly to the juncture of my neck and shoulder before pushing upright and sliding off the mattress. After tossing the folded blanket onto the floor near the edge of the bed, he cupped a hand under Senovo's chin, guiding the priest off the bed. With an uncompromising hand on his shoulder, Andoc positioned him as promised on his knees, cushioned by the blanket.

Senovo knelt quietly as Andoc went to retrieve some rope. I shifted closer to the edge of the bed, unable to resist the temptation to reach out and stroke Senovo's face and lips. Senovo nipped at my fingertip, his amusement once again shining through the reserved mask.

"Hmm... do I need to muzzle you as well?" Andoc teased, returning with the coils of rope.

Senovo released my finger and looked up at him. "That would make it rather difficult for me to choke myself on your cock, don't you think?" he said, perfectly deadpan.

I couldn't stop a bark of surprised laughter at seeing this new side of the quiet, serious man. Andoc snorted his amusement and knelt behind him, pulling Senovo's arms behind his back and positioning them wrist-to-opposite-elbow. When he had tied them firmly in place, he reached around, pulled Senovo's head to one side, and bit down on the long, elegant line of muscle running from the priest's neck to his shoulder.

Senovo's sharp, indrawn breath of surprise stoked the low burn of desire that had been smoldering in my stomach. He held himself stiffly as Andoc worried and sucked at the skin, as if trying not to react visibly to the assault. When Andoc pulled away, there was a livid mark where his mouth had been, and Senovo sagged for a moment before dragging himself upright once more. I stared at the fresh bruise, feeling the sudden urge to fit my fingers to it and press until Senovo cried out.

Andoc grabbed the second coil of rope while Senovo breathed unsteadily through his nose. He eased Senovo back to sit on his heels, and bound him ankle to thigh on both sides to keep him that way. When Andoc stood and backed away to check his work, the priest was left kneeling with his knees spread, the ropes binding his arms behind him forcing his spine straight.

"This what you had in mind?" Andoc asked me.

I nodded appreciatively, unable to tear my gaze away. "He looks amazing. If I were you, I'd be tempted to keep him tied up like this all the time."

Senovo shivered, and Andoc chuckled. "Hear that, *amadi*? Our Carivel has plans to hide you away as her personal concubine."

"It sounds a much more appealing lifestyle than the one that actually awaits me back in Draebard," Senovo said, evidently having regained his composure. "I can't honestly say I'm averse to the proposal."

"Well, it's always good to have a back-up plan," Andoc said, seating himself on the edge of the bed so that Senovo was positioned between his legs. "Here, come and watch, Carivel. If you're up for it, you can do this to him in a bit, so you'll want to see what's involved."

I wasn't about to miss it—the image of the priest using his mouth on Andoc had been popping up randomly in my thoughts during idle moments ever since I watched Senovo fellating his lover's fingers two nights ago, his face a picture of bliss. I knelt on the bed behind Andoc and rested my chin on his shoulder, wrapping my arms across his chest and looking down at the bound man. Senovo gazed up at us through dark eyelashes, and I couldn't stop the little rumble of appreciation that escaped my throat.

"He is good, isn't he?" Andoc agreed.

"Years of practice," Senovo said, leaning forward to rub his cheek over the tent in Andoc's smallclothes like a cat, never breaking eye contact.

Andoc growled low and grabbed the heavy braid of hair at the back of Senovo's head, using it to force him back. "Enough talk," he said, and began unlacing his smalls with his free hand.

Senovo's eyes glazed over at the manhandling and a small huff of breath escaped his lungs. He licked his lips, completely powerless in Andoc's grasp with his arms and legs bound. I was torn between watching Senovo's face and watching Andoc pull his generous cock free of his smallclothes, my eyes flickering back and forth between the two.

Andoc was not as large as Ciero had been, a fact for which I was frankly rather grateful. Nonetheless, his prick was thick and hard, and I could hardly wait for a chance to explore it. Now, though, Senovo was straining forward against the grip on his hair, reaching out to lap at the angry red tip. I plastered myself a bit tighter against Andoc's back, watching avidly.

"As long as you keep your teeth covered and aren't too shy about it, sucking cock is almost guaranteed to please a man," Andoc said in a rough voice. "Senovo takes a certain pride in his technique, though…"

Andoc was slowly feeding his cock to the priest, who closed his eyes with evident enjoyment. Senovo choked a bit when he was about two-thirds of the way down the shaft, and I realized with a shiver that the head of Andoc's prick must have hit the back of his throat. I watched in awe when, rather than pull back, Senovo swallowed around the intrusion a couple of times, relaxing his neck and jaw before sliding forward the last few inches until his nose was buried in Andoc's dark pubic hair.

All of the tension seemed to bleed from Senovo's muscles. Only the slight jerk of his chest as his lungs tried to drag air past the cock lodged in his throat marred his perfect stillness. By contrast, I could feel Andoc's muscles quivering under my arms as he fought to stay still. His hand held Senovo in position as the priest worked his tongue against the underside of Andoc's prick, his jaw muscles rippling.

The flesh between my legs throbbed hot and insistent at the sight. Finally, Andoc pulled Senovo back by the hair, and the priest's wet gasp was followed immediately by a muffled groan of disappointment. Senovo sucked hard on the tip of Andoc's shaft, his tongue curling around the hard flesh as he bobbed his head in shallow movements, guided by the hand controlling him.

Letting my own hands and lips wander, I ran my fingers lightly over Andoc's chest, feathering across the bruises left by Varanis' shield and skirting the edges of the shallow cut from her sword. I let my palms slide over his nipples as Senovo worshipped his cock, feeling them pebble underneath my touch. Experimentally, I scraped one lightly with a ragged fingernail. Immediately, I was rewarded with Andoc's choked curse and Senovo's pleased moan as Andoc's hips snapped forward, driving him further into Senovo's willing mouth.

"He wants you deeper," I whispered into Andoc's ear. Senovo's dark, dilated eyes met mine, giving me the courage to keep talking. "He wants you to fuck his mouth properly until he forgets everything except the smell and taste of you."

"*Carivel.* Gods above," Andoc groaned. I scratched across his other nipple, lowering my head to nip my way down the side of his neck, and was rewarded with another jerk of his hips as Andoc whispered, "*Caradi...*"

I froze; my breath caught in my lungs at the unexpected endearment.

Amadi. Worthy of love.

Caradi. Worthy of care and respect. A variant of my name... my *real* name.

I couldn't breathe for a moment. As I forced myself back under control, I was aware of Senovo looking up at me with perfect understanding.

"Say it again," I said, tightening my arms even as Senovo took advantage of Andoc's distraction to swallow him to the root once more. "Then give your *amadi* what he needs."

"*Caradi!*" Andoc gasped, and pulled Senovo back by the hair only to fuck into his throat again, and again, and again. Senovo gave himself over with utter abandon, his expression as serene as if he were gazing upon the faces of all the gods and goddesses. I clung to Andoc, lost in a heady mix of desire and burgeoning love as I kissed every bit of him that I could reach, running my hands over the tense muscles of his stomach.

Before long, his hips stuttered, losing their rhythm. With a groan, Andoc's spine arched like a bow and he came, spurting his release into Senovo's mouth until he couldn't swallow any more and it dribbled down his chin in pearly globs.

Andoc shuddered in my arms, breathing as hard as if he'd just run a footrace. He curled further forward, the hand holding Senovo in place gentling to a caress. Senovo rested his cheek on Andoc's thigh, eyes closed, suckling gently even as Andoc's flesh softened in his mouth. Eventually, he pulled off with a faint pop, drawing a final shiver from the spent man.

"Dear *gods*," Andoc said faintly, and I squeezed my arms tighter around him in response. "Sorry… *sorry*. I need to—"

He made to rise and move toward Senovo, who was sitting back on his heels looking soft and relaxed. Andoc reeled a bit when his muscles didn't cooperate as he expected.

"Sit for a minute," I told him firmly. "Just tell me what I need to do for him."

Andoc blinked, obviously struggling to drag his thoughts back into focus. "Untie his legs. Check his arms to make sure the blood is flowing all right. If it is, leave them tied and help him up onto the bed."

"Got it," I said, pressing a final kiss to his shoulder.

Senovo was a subdued, pliant figure as I knelt next to him. He leaned into me trustingly, and remembering the way Andoc had reassured him the other night after he'd stopped fighting the ropes, I took a few moments to run my hands over his soft skin with firm, even strokes. I traced the lines of his shoulders and arms, checking the color of his hands in the flickering firelight to make sure the ropes weren't too tight.

Sliding my hands down his chest and over his stomach, I traced one of the ropes binding his ankles to his upper thighs, following it inward, close to where his small prick still hung limp, despite the evident pleasure he'd experienced while sucking Andoc off.

"Don't touch his sac," Andoc said quietly from the bed. "It still pains him sometimes, and the associations aren't good, as you can imagine. The prick is all right, though."

I nodded, once again feeling a surge of deep, burning anger at the people who had done this to Senovo against his will. Pushing it down, I focused instead on the feeling of having him here, now, so relaxed and unguarded under my hands. Avoiding the flap of wrinkled skin where his stones should have hung, I traced his cock with the tip of my finger, fascinated by the way it twitched faintly under my touch. I cupped it in my palm, and Senovo sighed out in contentment. The column of flesh stiffened a bit under my tentative ministrations, only to soften again almost immediately.

Mindful of Andoc's instructions, I moved my attention back to the rope, untying the knots that held Senovo in a kneeling position. When he was free, I tossed it aside and guided him into a loose sprawl against me. Unable to resist, I lapped up the dribble of Andoc's release that trailed down Senovo's chin, rolling it around on my tongue to explore the bitter saltiness of it. Senovo nuzzled closer, seeking a kiss, and I licked into his mouth, chasing more of the salt-sea flavor.

Kissing Senovo lost none of its allure when he was in this soft, submissive place, and I had to force myself to pull away. When I did, my eyes were drawn to Andoc's love bite on his shoulder. My desire surged, and I indulged my earlier fantasy of fitting my fingers to the livid bruise and pressing down. Instead of crying out, though, Senovo went limp against me — all except his prick, which twitched and filled slightly.

With a growl of lust, I shifted him in my arms until I could bite down on his other shoulder, sucking my own mark to the surface while I wrapped a hand around his half-hard cock. At that, Senovo did groan — his voice roughened by the throat fucking he'd received earlier.

"You two are going to kill me," Andoc said from the bed. "Get him up here now, before I'm forced to come down there and make you."

The prospect of Andoc *making me* was enough to have me breathless and — impossibly — even wetter than before. I worried at Senovo's shoulder, dragging a final shudder from him as another pulse of moisture dribbled down my thigh. Guiding him into a more upright position, I levered myself to my feet and helped him stand on unsteady legs. Fortunately, the bed was right in front of us, and it was mostly a matter of spilling him into it. Andoc had roused himself enough to drag Senovo closer to the center and position him on his side, facing me. Once Senovo was safely spooned against him, eyes closed in contentment, Andoc reached over and picked up the little jar of grease Senovo had used earlier.

"I told you earlier that I'd show you how to help me take him apart," he said. "He's ready for it now, I think. With eunuchs, it's not so much that they can't feel sexual pleasure. More that they don't miss it when they don't have it, and tend not to think about it when they aren't actually in bed with someone."

"I felt him start to get stiff in my hand just now," I said, intrigued.

Andoc nodded. "You and I can get excited just by seeing someone we'd like to fuck, or thinking about sex. He needs our hands and mouths on him before he can really get going."

"You said earlier that I could suck him?" I asked eagerly, stroking my fingers over Senovo's scalp as he lay cradled between us.

"You suck, I'll fuck," Andoc said, a smile tugging at his lips as he waggled greasy fingers at me.

Senovo groaned against my shoulder, evidently back from wherever he'd been floating earlier. "*Really*, Andoc?" he said, his voice still gravelly. "I'm going to pretend I didn't hear that."

"Hush, you," I told him, affection threatening to bubble over inside my chest once more. "This is all part of my education. And, as you reminded us earlier, you're a priest."

"But just for that, you're not to come until I give you permission," Andoc added. He pulled Senovo's head back into an uncomfortable arch. "Understood?"

As quickly as that, Senovo's eyes glazed over, and he was back in the quiet place that only Andoc seemed to be able to send him.

"I could watch that all day," I said.

"Oh, it gets better, believe me," Andoc said. He arranged himself at Senovo's hips and lifted the priest's top leg, resting the ankle on his shoulder to keep him spread open. "Here, Carivel—lie on your side facing his feet. You can use his thigh for a pillow while you suck him."

I eagerly shuffled into position, scooting Senovo's bottom leg forward until I could get a good angle at his cock while resting my head on the smooth skin of his inner thigh. At first I was unsure quite what to do with my legs, but then it occurred to me to return the favor, and I rearranged us until we were mirroring each other, Senovo resting his head on my leg and nuzzling eagerly against my damp curls.

"Very nice," Andoc approved. "Now… let me just—"

With Senovo's upper leg raised and resting on Andoc's shoulder, I had a pretty clear view of things if I craned my neck a bit. From my vantage point only a few inches away, I watched Andoc press a greased finger into Senovo's tight opening. The priest moaned against my cunt as his small cock filled, growing until the head poked out of the foreskin and nudged against my lips. I kissed the tip, darting my tongue out to taste.

"Remember," Andoc said, "no teeth, and don't try to take more than you can manage. All good?"

"Mmm… very," I replied, as Senovo nuzzled between my legs again.

Andoc twisted his wrist and Senovo grunted, his prick twitching hard. I kissed it again and slid my lips over the tip, exploring the shape with my tongue and breathing in the smell of musk. Already, I was beginning to understand what Senovo saw in this. As Andoc worked him slowly open, I concentrated on taking more, letting Senovo slide deeper and breathing through my nose. I still had a decent view of what Andoc was doing and I watched, fascinated. After a few minutes, Andoc added a second finger and scissored them back and forth, stretching Senovo's fluttering opening while I hollowed my cheeks to suck as I'd seen him do to Andoc earlier.

Senovo's breath was coming in shallow pants that huffed against my own dripping flesh, making me shiver. Every once in awhile he would lap at me or slide his nose along my inner lips, making me hum around him in pleasure.

"Here's the really good part," Andoc said, scooping up more grease and pressing a third finger alongside the other two. "Brace yourself, now—"

He changed the angle of his wrist, the muscles of his forearm working as he moved his fingers inside Senovo's body as if searching for something. The result was dramatic—the priest stiffened and *keened*, writhing around the fingers penetrating him and jerking his arms against the bonds trapping them behind his back. Andoc clamped his free arm around the thigh of Senovo's raised leg to keep him in place and I grabbed his hip, further restraining him.

Andoc set up an unforgiving rhythm, never letting up as he slid his fingers across whatever it was inside Senovo that made him jerk his hips against our hold, trying to drive himself alternately back onto the invading fingers and forward into my mouth. I worked at letting him in deeper until I was taking all but the final inch or so, keeping my lips carefully over my teeth. My jaw and neck were starting to ache, but it was worth that and more to watch Senovo mindlessly chase after the pleasure we were bringing him.

"Do you need to come, *amadi*?" Andoc asked solicitously, when Senovo's gasps started sounding suspiciously like sobs.

The priest nodded urgently, apparently beyond words—I could feel the motion where his head was still pillowed on my thigh.

"Hmm. Such a pity you don't have permission yet," said Andoc, and added a fourth finger.

Senovo jerked in my mouth and cried out, but miraculously did not come. I gave him an extra-hard suck just to see what would happen, and, yes, that time the noise was *definitely* a sob.

"Tell you what," Andoc said. "You make Carivel come with your hard prick stuffed in her mouth, and maybe we'll let you have your release after she's done."

Senovo's lips were clamped around my aching nub before I could even think about bracing for it. All of his earlier methodical technique was completely gone—he sucked and laved at the tender flesh desperately, nipping and licking for all he was worth. I cried out around the cock in my mouth, completely unprepared for the landslide of pleasure crashing over me. In retaliation, I sucked Senovo down to the root, trying to drag him with me as I plummeted headfirst over the edge.

I was vaguely aware of Andoc twisting his fingers and saying, "That's it, *amadi*. Come for us now."

Senovo shouted something wordless against my oversensitive flesh, drawing a final shudder from me as he swelled and pulsed against my tongue. A tiny spurt of fluid squirted onto the back of my tongue and I swallowed it—nothing compared to the load that Andoc had choked him with earlier. I continued to suck Senovo's softening cock lazily as Andoc's fingers milked a few more tremors of pleasure from his body. His breath was hot against me as he gradually subsided into a limp, shivering mess between us. Though, to be fair to him, I wasn't doing much better.

I gave him a last, lingering lick and let his soft flesh slide out of my mouth, the thought of moving any further completely laughable at the moment. Andoc carefully pulled his fingers out and wiped his greasy hand on the rag—somewhat awkwardly since he was still holding Senovo's top leg up to keep it from crushing my head.

"Roll over," he said, giving my shoulder a nudge until I rolled onto my back with a heartfelt groan. He lowered Senovo's leg and reached up to untie his arms; the priest remained completely oblivious, still lost in the afterglow. Apparently unconcerned, Andoc rose to set the rope aside and retrieve the blanket from the floor. He urged me to scoot around until I was facing the right direction on the bed. Senovo immediately burrowed into my arms, and Andoc looked down at us both with an expression of proprietary pleasure.

"Gorgeous, the pair of you," he said, stroking my hair.

"I want to suck you off next," I murmured, already half-asleep.

"Soon, but not tonight," he said with a hint of amusement. "Even if I weren't too sore to go again, I think both of you are pretty much done at the moment. Here—budge over."

Crowding me even closer to Senovo, Andoc crawled in behind me and curled his body around mine, pulling a blanket over all three of us. He threw an arm over me to rest his hand on Senovo's shoulder protectively, and let out a deep sigh of contentment.

Tomorrow, Andoc would ride home to Draebard. His meeting with Chief Volya would determine our future—and possibly the future of Eburos, as the Alyrion Empire stood poised at our borders. Now, though, I was safe in the arms of the two men who had become more important to me than anything else. With Andoc guarding my back, and Senovo curled trustingly in my arms, I slid down into a deep, untroubled sleep.

end of Book 1

THE HORSE MISTRESS:
BOOK 2

ONE

It was still dark when I woke, feeling pleasantly safe and relaxed. After an enjoyable few moments of drowsy lassitude, the events of the previous few days played across my mind's eye. We were in the village of Meren. Andoc, Senovo, and I had successfully managed to negotiate a defense treaty with Magoldis, the female Leader of the Mereni tribe. In doing so, both Senovo and I had revealed long-held secrets that would drastically change our lives upon our return to Draebard. However, we had also gained... *this.*

It took some time to convince myself that I truly was awake, and that the two warm bodies curled up on either side of me were not, in fact, figments of a dream. For one thing, the Andoc that lived in my dreams did not snore and drool in his sleep, and for another, the strangely pleasant ache between my legs was an inescapable reminder of what the three of us had gotten up to a scant few hours ago. The hearth fire in the rented room had burned down to glowing embers as the night passed, signifying that dawn would soon be upon us. Soon, but not quite yet. For now, I could still hoard a few more precious moments of peace before we would rise and part ways to face an uncertain future.

I stretched, feeling my joints pop and crackle. Andoc slept on, oblivious to the disturbance. When I rolled onto my back to check on Senovo, however, it was to find him already awake, propped up on an elbow. His eyes were dark and deep in the warm glow of the burning coals as he looked down at the two of us pensively.

"Good morning, Carivel," he said, pitching his voice low.

"Good morning," I murmured. "You know, by rights, I should probably be uncomfortable about the idea of you watching me sleep."

"And are you?" he asked, his tone genuinely curious.

"That depends on whether you're going to keep staring at me now that I'm awake, or come here and kiss me."

He smiled, but the low light made it impossible to tell if the expression reached his eyes. Nevertheless, he leaned down to press his mouth to mine, one hand coming up to cradle my jaw as our lips slid sensuously together. Desire rose, warm and insistent in my belly. The ache where I had been teased and stretched open last night sharpened for a moment before melting into a deeper pleasure. A groan escaped my lips, only to be swallowed by the mouth and tongue dancing against my own.

I caught my breath when Senovo eased away, straightening to look down at me once more. On my other side, Andoc slumbered on, mouth hanging open, one leg half off the edge of the bed. I smiled at the sight.

"Does he always sleep like that?" I asked, amusement lacing my tone.

Senovo reached across me to smooth the backs of his fingers over the warrior's stubbled cheek. "He is tired. The last few days have been difficult for all of us."

I sobered at the reminder of our troubles. Since the Alyrion attack on Draebard, the death of so many of our fellow villagers and the tense negotiations with the Mereni, Andoc had been our rock. Both Senovo and I were brittle with grief and worry for the future, but he had never faltered. Little wonder if events were finally catching up with him.

"That being said," Senovo continued, his tone growing lighter, "a pitcher of water to the face is often one of the few effective methods to rouse him before mid-morning."

I snorted, my somber mood broken as quickly as it had come over me. "Is that the voice of experience speaking?"

"It is," Senovo replied. "Although, to be fair, there are a couple of less drastic and more enjoyable approaches to try first."

Turning my attention back to Senovo, I let my eyes trace his finely chiseled features, trying to gauge his well-being. "And what about you?" I asked. "How are you this morning?"

He met my gaze squarely, one sculpted eyebrow quirking. "In a similar state to yourself, I should imagine," he said.

"So… wishing you could hide away here longer before the sun comes up and brings with it the pressures of the outside world?" I hazarded.

"Concisely put," he agreed, a wry note entering his voice.

"The sun's not up yet," I pointed out.

"Indeed, it is not."

"We could distract ourselves until it is," I said hesitantly, unsure, in the newness of our union, what I was allowed to ask for.

"We could."

"But I don't know what you would enjoy," I said, deciding that honesty was the best policy despite my discomfort with speaking so plainly. "I sort of got the impression that a scene like last night's isn't an everyday thing for you."

He smiled, looking suddenly younger—a bit pleased, a bit shy. "No, you're right. It isn't," he confirmed.

"So… what *would* you enjoy?" I asked, genuinely curious.

Curious, and in no way expecting the answer I got.

"I would enjoy watching you wake Andoc with your mouth on his cock."

I was not prepared to take ownership of the undignified, high-pitched noise of surprise that escaped me, even as fresh desire slammed into me with all the subtlety of a runaway chariot team.

"That being one of the less drastic and more enjoyable methods I alluded to earlier," Senovo added helpfully. "Though the pitcher of cold water does bring along its own amusement value at times."

My mouth opened and closed a couple of times before I finally managed to get words out. "You are *evil*," I said, somewhat in awe. "You walk around all prim and proper, and underneath is this secret *evil* streak that hardly anyone gets to see."

"I'm sure I have no idea what you mean," he said, the innocent words belied by a humorous glint in his eyes that was positively wicked. I wondered if I was seeing a glimpse of the man Senovo might have been, had he not been sold into slavery as a child and castrated so cruelly by the men who owned him.

A feeling that I was resolutely not labeling *love* swelled in my chest. Rather than say something that would just embarrass both of us, I reached up and pulled him down to kiss him again. He submitted easily, a faint smile lingering on his lips as we parted.

"So," I said, somewhat breathless, "you think I should… suck him awake? He wouldn't mind?"

The eyebrow quirked again, higher this time. Amusement was writ large on Senovo's face as he answered, "You have actually *met* Andoc, yes?"

I grimaced and shoved an elbow into him playfully. "Hey, you were the one lecturing me about the importance of communication with your lovers..."

"He already gave you his consent, as I recall."

I frowned for a moment before my brow cleared with understanding. We'd been resting together after Andoc's all-night meeting with the Mereni ruling council. Senovo and I talked about our unconventional three-way relationship while Andoc slept... gods, was it *really* only yesterday? When I awoke later, it was to find Andoc smiling down at me.

"Perhaps I'll even forgive you for somehow neglecting to ravish me in my sleep once you finally came to your senses, Carivel," he'd said. *"I suppose even uncontrollable lust can be pushed to the wayside after what we've been through in the last couple of days."*

"Right, I suppose he did, at that," I said, excitement and nervousness twisting in my stomach. "So... do I just—?"

I gestured toward Andoc's blanket-covered hips, at a bit of a loss. Senovo smiled and stroked soft fingers across my cheek.

"Help yourself," he said. "You may lack experience, but I, for one, have no complaints about your technique."

I blushed, remembering the feeling of Senovo's stiff flesh pulsing in my mouth as he lost control.

"Andoc is more generously endowed, of course," the priest continued. "You won't be able to swallow him all the way. You can use your hand on him as well, though."

I nodded, not bothering to point out that Senovo had been able to swallow him down to the root well enough. There would be plenty of time for that later—or so I hoped. Now, my mouth was watering at the thought of tasting Andoc... comparing him to Senovo and making him lose control. I turned my attention to the sleeping man and eased the blanket down the length of his body until his cock was exposed.

He was half hard already, and I looked at Senovo with a question in my eyes.

"Morning erection," he explained. "It's not unusual for men."

I scooted down until my head was level with Andoc's hips. I'd gotten a pretty good look at him last night, but it was too dim to see details right now without candles and with the fire burning so low. Instead, I nuzzled forward and brushed my cheek against the tender skin of his cock, feeling it twitch in response. Burying my nose in the wiry curls at the base, I breathed in his scent, which was muskier and more complex than Senovo's. It seemed to go straight to my head, faster than smoke from the High Priest's ceremonial herbs.

I moaned, wanting to wallow in the scent of *contented, sleeping man* until everything else in the world fell away. A smooth hand rested between my shoulder blades from behind and stroked down the length of my spine, making my senses tingle — Senovo.

"He is intoxicating, is he not?" he asked.

I nodded agreement and reached out my tongue to taste, licking up the length of the heavy shaft, feeling it fill and thicken further. Andoc mumbled in his sleep and shifted under me, chasing the sensation.

He was *big*.

Last night, it was the feeling of power at being able to reduce Senovo — a eunuch — to a shaking, begging mess that made my blood sing. Now, though, it was Andoc's overpowering *maleness* that had me rubbing my thighs together to ease the ache building there. Unable to ignore the temptation for a moment longer, I scooted up to get a better angle and let my lips stretch over the head of his cock, now peeking out of its wrinkled foreskin as he came to full hardness under my tentative touches.

Andoc groaned, thrusting into the welcoming warmth, still more asleep than awake. Taken by surprise, I gagged a bit as the thick shaft slid deeper than I expected. Remembering Senovo's advice, I grasped the base of his cock with one hand to keep him from accidentally choking me.

"Sen'vo?" Andoc mumbled, hovering on the edge between sleep and wakefulness.

The hand resting at the base of my spine slid away, and I was vaguely aware of Senovo repositioning himself on the bed to look down at Andoc's face.

"Guess again," said the priest, that same hint of devilish humor still audible in his voice. I smiled around the flesh filling my mouth for a moment, then closed my lips and sucked.

"Wha—? Oh, *fuck*," Andoc moaned, and bucked up again. This time, I followed the movement without mishap, still licking and sucking.

"He'll get it in a minute," Senovo said, no longer even trying to hide his amusement, and I sniggered around Andoc's prick.

"… Carivel?" Andoc asked a moment later, and I flushed at his tone of awe-filled surprise. "*Gods…*"

Pressing my cunt against a ridge of the rumpled blanket beneath me to ease the throbbing there, I hummed an acknowledgement against his sensitive skin. Whether it was the low vibration from my throat, the knowledge that it was me, or his return to full consciousness, Andoc's cock swelled even further in my mouth, pulsing in time with his heartbeat. I continued my inexpert but enthusiastic movements, feeling the veins and ridges throb against my tongue.

"Move your hand up and down in time with your mouth," Senovo counseled. "He's getting close; you can pull off when he starts to come, if you'd rather."

I nodded my understanding around the cock in my mouth, though I had no intention of pulling off.

"Gods!" Andoc cursed. "You two are going to kill me with your… *mmph*—"

His words were muffled without warning, and I could just about make out Senovo bending down to kiss him deeply. A strong, callused hand came to rest on the back of my head—a heavy and grounding weight. I shivered with excitement at the thought of being held in place, my sex growing wet and swollen.

With a series of rhythmic grunts stifled by the lips covering his, Andoc came in my mouth with bitter, salty spurts. Taken by surprise at the volume and odd texture spurting over the back of my tongue, I choked a bit and pulled back. The rope of sticky white that splashed across my lips and cheek should in no way have been exciting, but that didn't stop my cunt from twitching and releasing a pulse of its own moisture onto the blanket beneath me.

I swallowed the mouthful of thick fluid as best I could, relieved that neither of the others immediately asked after my well-being or made a fuss about it. It might not have been the smoothest performance, but Andoc had obviously enjoyed it, which was the important part. I hoped that I would have plenty more chances to practice in the future.

The hand on my head gentled, caressing the soft stubble of my short hair against the grain. I shivered with pleasure. Beneath me, Andoc's muscles went soft and lax. I rested my cheek against his inner thigh and ran my tongue over my lips, chasing the saltiness there as I listened to the soft, wet sounds coming from the head of the bed. A few moments later, the mattress shifted slightly as Senovo straightened.

"That's a wake-up call I could get used to very easily," Andoc said, his voice gravelly with sleep.

"Better than a face full of cold water, then?" I asked, craning to look up the length of his body.

"Cheeky…" he observed. "Has someone been telling stories about me while I was asleep?"

"They're not stories when they're true," Senovo observed, all bland innocence.

I snorted, and the hand cradling the base of my skull urged me up the length of Andoc's body. I followed willingly, amused and turned on in equal measure.

"Sounds like someone needs teaching a lesson," Andoc said, rolling us over so I lay on my back, half under him.

"Me?" I groused, trying to hide the way the manhandling affected me. "What did I do?"

"Oh, *caradi*," he growled, the endearment making me shudder. "*So* many things…"

He gathered my wrists together over my head, pressing them into the straw filled mattress. "Hold her for me, Senovo. You might also see about muzzling that cheeky mouth."

Senovo's smooth, long-fingered hand replaced Andoc's work-roughened one around my wrists, and I arched with a groan, testing the strength of the restraint. A fine tremor of anticipation worked its way down the length of my body, and then Senovo was lapping at my cheek, gathering the sticky residue of Andoc's release from my face with his tongue before feeding it back to me in a deep, penetrating kiss.

I exhaled shakily, only to suck in a surprised breath when Senovo's free hand cupped my breast, thumbing the nipple. Meanwhile, Andoc positioned himself between my thighs, trapping my lower legs with his muscular arms. Dragging his fingers through the moisture dripping from me and soaking the thatch of hair around my sex, he slid back to spread the slickness around my puckered rear entrance, still tender and sensitive from the previous evening.

Where Senovo had teased and massaged my untried flesh extensively before penetrating me, Andoc took immediate possession, swirling around the rim with slow, insistent pressure… circling the edges once, twice, before sliding into the center. I cried out into Senovo's kiss as the blunt finger pressed into me, my muscles clenching and fluttering around the intrusion. Andoc twisted and wormed his way deeper until his finger was completely inside, before leaning down to run the flat of his tongue up the lips of my sex and over the sensitive bud at the front in a broad swipe. At the same time, Senovo pinched my nipple between the pads of his fingers and plucked at it, stretching the tight bud straight up until it slipped free.

I bucked against them, causing Senovo to hastily tighten his grip on my wrists before I could get loose. The two men pinned me a bit tighter and continued their joint assault on my mouth, breasts, sex, and ass. Within moments my release rose and crashed over me, dragging a sob from my lips as I gushed over Andoc's face and hand. They nursed me through it, drawing shuddering little after-shocks as they teased at my oversensitive flesh until I lay spent beneath them, completely limp.

"She may have woken me up just now," Andoc observed, grabbing a rag from the nearby table to clean us up, "but it looks like we put her right back to sleep."

"Mmhmm," I mumbled as Senovo rearranged my arms into a more comfortable position.

"Perhaps a pitcher of water…?" the priest offered, his wicked streak now aimed my way, apparently.

"Shuddup," I grumbled. "I'm awake."

"Actually, a dip in the river before the rest of the village wakes up does hold a certain appeal," Andoc said, stretching and yawning widely.

"I wouldn't say no," Senovo conceded.

"Nngh," I said, more in response to the idea of moving than the idea of bathing. Bathing was probably a good idea, given how sticky and sweaty I was.

"You're outvoted," said Andoc. "Come on… up with you."

He chivvied me, grumbling, to my feet. We dressed to the minimum degree that we could get away with on the off chance that we were to meet anyone, and quietly left the rented room. The streets were nearly deserted, only a few merchants carrying their wares for the day sharing the grey predawn with us. It was humid and a touch cool outside, a layer of thick mist clinging to the slow-moving water of the river.

Working as I did with the horses, I was often out and about at this time of day. However, I rarely took the chance to appreciate it for what it was—quiet time, when nature lay largely undisturbed by people. I came to a halt on the pebbled beach by the washing area and took a deep breath, holding it for a long moment before letting it out.

We were silent, as befitted our serene surroundings. Rather than undress ourselves, we undressed each other in wordless accord, pausing to kiss and stroke newly exposed skin tenderly. Naked, the three of us waded into the dark, mist-shrouded waters. The river was cold and exhilarating, waking me better than any cockerel's crow.

"How are your injuries today?" Senovo asked Andoc, and I was sharply reminded of the bruises and shallow sword wound the warrior had suffered in his recent contest against Mereni's female First Warrior.

"I'm perfectly fine, mother hen," Andoc said, somewhat irritably, as he ducked down to scrub at his chest and shoulders. "Just a bit stiff."

"Well, you were certainly a bit stiff earlier," I pointed out, unable to keep my stupid grin completely hidden. A moment later, I squealed as a wave of chilly water splashed me in the face. "All right! Mercy! *Mercy*! Gah, it's too cold for that…"

We washed quickly, and emerged to rub at our gooseflesh-covered skin with whatever piece of clothing was to hand. I bound my breasts—partly out of habit and partly because the idea of having them bounce around all day sounded terribly un-comfortable. My worn boy's breeches and tunic were reassuring in their familiarity, a less than subtle declaration to all who saw me that I would not suddenly change who I was inside just because my birth sex had been revealed to all and sundry.

The sun was just beginning to breach the horizon, turning the misty late-spring surroundings into a palette of orange and lavender. The Mereni townsfolk were beginning to make an appearance as well, and I felt my good humor and relaxation start to drain away as some of them pointed and whispered, no doubt sharing the latest wild rumors about our motley delegation.

Beside me, I could feel Senovo closing off as well. Only Andoc seemed unaffected. He looked us both over with an expression of regret that quickly hardened into determination.

"I fear you're both going to have to get used to this," he said, not without sympathy. "Here and in Draebard."

It was true. Senovo was getting the bulk of the attention here in Meren, after the dramatic and unforeseen revelation of his shape-shifting abilities. When I returned home, though… *if* I was able to return home, I would be a pariah of the highest order. The woman who had pretended to be a man.

The thought made me nauseous. It made me angry as well.

I must not have been very good at hiding the direction my thoughts had taken, because Andoc sighed and clapped a gentle hand on each of our shoulders.

"Come on," he said. "No point in worrying about it yet. Back to Harinel's place."

We trudged back to the boarding house, shivering slightly in the rising breeze. The sun was fully up by the time we reached the center of the town, and Andoc, true to form, stopped to buy us some breakfast to eat along the way. Rather than subject the other two to my increasingly foul mood, I excused myself and went to care for the horses, penned behind the ramshackle inn.

Kekenu, my stout little pinto gelding, whickered insistently at my approach, eager for his own breakfast. I grabbed a pitchfork and threw forkfuls of sweet hay over the fence—a separate pile for each of our three mounts. The water trough was still more than half full, so I left it to drag a shovel and a large wooden tub into the pen. Proceeding to muck out the accumulated manure, I stopped to scratch under Kekenu's mane as I passed his solid form.

The familiar activity soothed me, and when I was done, I felt up to facing the others again. I was in no way ready for us to be parted, though at least Senovo and I would remain together. The two men looked up as I entered the room, and I forced a smile, weak though it probably was.

"A messenger came while you were out with the horses," Andoc said. "The Second Warrior of the Mereni will be traveling with me back to Draebard. He wishes to leave as soon as possible. Also, Varanis would like to meet with you two at your earliest convenience, to discuss details of the larger delegation that will follow."

Even though I'd known it was coming, it still hurt. I looked at Senovo, but his face had transformed into the impassive facade he often wore to hide his thoughts. I looked back to Andoc and nodded my understanding.

He frowned. "I've been thinking more about your arrival back at Draebard, Carivel. I thought if everything works out all right with Volya, I could leave a strip of white leather tied to a branch of the tree at the edge of town where Senovo and I first met. He knows the one."

I glanced at Senovo, who nodded, still not breaking expression.

"If there's a problem," Andoc continued, "if Volya refuses to accept you back, I'll leave a strip of black leather instead. Turn right back around and return here to Meren. I'll join you as soon as I'm able, so we can decide what to do next."

"All right," I said in a faint voice. I could hardly bring myself to contemplate it. Such an outcome would put the entire treaty with the Mereni at risk. Almost as bad was the idea of Andoc or Senovo ripping up their roots in Draebard on the strength of what the three of us had built together over the course of a handful of days… I simply couldn't bear it.

Andoc looked at me with concern, but moved on to the next point rather than make a fuss about it—for which I was grateful.

"Senovo," he said, "I'll eat my boots if anyone makes an issue of your return. That said, if they do, I'll put brown leather in the tree. Same plan—come back here and wait for me. High Priest Jyrrel will offer you safe harbor until then."

Senovo nodded, looking grim.

Suddenly, I couldn't stand to be there a moment longer. "I'll get your horse ready, Andoc," I said, and all but rushed from the room. The others let me go.

The animals were still eating quietly. I grabbed a brush and entered the pen, moving to Andoc's bay gelding and scratching his withers in greeting. The horse snorted and went back to his feed, ignoring me for the most part as I groomed him. I swallowed convulsively against the burning sensation in my throat and at the back of my eyes, tamping everything down. No matter what happened back in Draebard, Senovo would need my support over the coming few days. I concentrated on that, and tried not to think about the rest.

When I led Andoc's long-suffering mount around to the front entrance of the boarding house a few minutes later, saddled and ready, the others were waiting for me. Andoc had his saddlebags thrown over his shoulder, and he moved to secure them behind the saddle before coming up and taking the reins attached to the simple rope hackamore from me.

"Still?" he said ruefully, eyeing the bitless bridle with a mixture of humor and irritation.

"I told you," I said, striving for the same light tone, "Horse Mistress's prerogative. Learn to ride properly with your seat and legs, and I'll give you your bitted bridle back."

"Hmph. Perhaps I should arrange for some private lessons with the Horse Mistress in question."

My hesitation was too noticeable before I finally managed to reply, "Maybe so."

"Hey," he said, cradling my cheek with his hand. "None of that, now. Whatever else you may think about him, Volya is a practical man. And I will fight for you, whatever it takes." His gaze flicked over to include Senovo as well. "That goes for both of you."

I steeled myself not to show weakness—not to collapse against him like some fainting, lovelorn maiden. He eased me forward into an embrace, and it was all I could do to stay strong as I squeezed him back and nodded against his broad chest. He released me and extended his hand to Senovo, who stepped forward. Rather than embrace the eunuch, he drew close and pressed their foreheads together. Senovo closed his eyes and leaned into the contact, though the rest of his face remained carved in marble.

"Look after each other," Andoc said. "I'll see you both soon."

"Safe journey, Andoc," Senovo said, lifting a hand to grip the warrior's forearm for a moment. "May the gods smile on your endeavors."

Andoc straightened and smiled before mounting his horse and settling himself into the saddle. A moment later, he turned and was gone, riding around the corner with a final wave.

"Well," I said, feeling strangely adrift.

"Come," Senovo said after a moment of contemplative silence. "We should ready ourselves and join Varanis at the meeting hall."

TWO

The First Warrior of the Mereni was waiting for us when we arrived, along with the High Priest, Jyrrel. I glanced at Senovo, unsure how he would react to the old man's presence after Jyrrel had unknowingly triggered Senovo's shape-shifting ability with a mysterious elixir two nights ago, setting a terrified wolf amongst the guests at a handfasting. The slender eunuch's face was still a mask, but he did not hesitate as we entered the room.

"Good morning," Varanis greeted. "I take it Andoc has already left?"

"He has," Senovo replied, his voice level and pleasant.

Varanis nodded. "I've asked the High Priest to join us so we could discuss a proposal of his."

She gestured for us to join her at the heavy table dominating the room. When we were seated, it was Jyrrel who spoke first.

"I know our two tribes have a long and storied history of conflict," he began, "but, given we are about to join together against a common enemy, it occurred to me that I might be able to help you in a different capacity."

"How so?" I asked before Senovo could respond, my wariness not completely hidden. For all that Senovo had expressed his forgiveness for Jyrrel's unwitting exposure of his transformative ability, I could not help but blame the man for turning Senovo's life upside down in the space of a moment.

Unfazed by my poorly disguised hostility, Jyrrel merely leaned back in the chair and laced his hands together over his generous stomach. "The ranks of the priesthood have swelled in Meren in recent years," he said. "Many of the novices have ambition, but they are unlikely to be able to move up the hierarchy with any sort of speed... there are too many others in front of them."

"And?" I prompted.

"Well," said the old eunuch, "at the risk of being unforgivably indelicate, Draebard needs new priests. It seems like a situation which could provide mutual benefits to both tribes."

It was on the tip of my tongue to berate Jyrrel for his gross insensitivity — High Priest or no. Before I could, though, Senovo sent me a quelling glance. His expression was thoughtful, possibilities turning behind his eyes.

"That is indeed an interesting proposal, High Priest Jyrrel," he said mildly. "How many individuals are we talking about?"

"Half a dozen or so, including two who are willing to leave immediately with the initial delegation. The first two are novice priests, and the others are acolytes."

I forced myself to put aside my emotions and think about it logically. The ranks of Draebard's priesthood had gone from almost two dozen to a mere four in the space of one night... soon to be three, if High Priest Rhystel died. Senovo could not hope to perform all the necessary religious duties in the village with only two young and grief-stricken acolytes to help him.

"I would like to speak with them later today," Senovo said, "but I am certain that Draebard would welcome them, as would I."

I envied Senovo his ability to compartmentalize his grief. Aware that I'd sounded churlish earlier, I said, "Of course we would. Please forgive my hasty words. Our village suffered a traumatic loss, and I let it affect my judgment."

Jyrrel met my eyes, his expression one of understanding. Even that was enough to make me bristle, but I reminded myself that this man was a friend of our own injured High Priest. No doubt the news of the attack had affected him as well.

"Horse Mistress Carivel," he said, "you have no reason to trust me and every reason not to. But — though it may be hard to remember at times — we are all on the same side here. Rhystel is my brother in the eyes of the gods, and I am pleased to help his people in any way I can."

I nodded, unsure of what I could say that would be appropriate.

"We are pleased to help each other," Senovo said, rescuing me from committing any more diplomatic blunders. "If I can help these young priests and acolytes to reach their potential, it is my honor to do so."

The talk moved on to the rest of the delegation. Varanis informed us that her mother, Leader Magoldis, would be traveling to Draebard along with the acolytes and a small escort of warriors—no doubt intending to make a statement about Volya's failure to appear before her in person to discuss the treaty. Varanis herself would remain behind to organize the larger military force for the planned attack on the Alyrion outpost.

The first delegation would be ready to depart two days hence. Varanis urged us to stay an extra day and travel with the group, but we declined. The Mereni could not know about the fact that everyone in Draebard still thought me a man—Senovo and I would have to travel ahead of them to face the potential repercussions before Magoldis arrived.

With the details more or less arranged, the meeting ended. Varanis and Jyrrel left to deal with their various responsibilities. It was nearly midday, so I suggested Senovo and I get something to eat. "… in Andoc's honor," I added with a wan smile, feeling somehow as if the responsibility for such necessary tasks had fallen to me in his absence.

Senovo quirked a half-smile in response. We left the meeting hall, braving the stares and whispers once again. The first market stall we came to was run by an elderly woman, and my thoughts turned instantly to old Gretya, killed in the attack on Draebard. I swallowed, dragging myself back to the present only to find that the woman in the food stall was bowing deeply—nearly abasing herself to us. Well, to *Senovo*, to be more precise.

"Please don't do that," Senovo said, his tone mostly level, though I could tell that underneath, he was stricken.

"Ma'am," I added quickly, "it's all right. We only want to buy some food."

The woman straightened, but kept her eyes averted. "Holy One," she said in a quavering voice, "please—I saw you after the handfasting. I saw you change. My son is ill. He has the paralyzing sickness. Please, I beg of you… will you come and bless him? The Healers say they can do nothing."

I was close enough to Senovo to sense the fine tremor that ran through him, but his mask was firmly back in place when he replied. "I have no additional sway with the gods because of my ability. Please understand that I cannot magically heal your son.

However, if you wish me to visit him and perform a blessing, I will do so, as would any priest."

"Oh, thank you! *Thank you!*" said the stall-keeper, looking up at him finally with tears in her eyes, and patently oblivious to the parts of Senovo's response that she did not wish to hear. "Here, please — take some food in return for your generosity, Holy One..."

She eagerly served up generous helpings of spiced meat and vegetables for us. I glanced at Senovo again; his face was pale. I took the wrapped portions she offered us and placed a handful of coins firmly on the counter of the stall.

"No, really. I insist," I told her when she tried to demur.

"Where is your son staying?" Senovo asked, and nodded his understanding as the woman gave him directions. When she was done, he assured her that he would visit shortly, and we took our leave.

"I will visit the sick man as soon as we're finished eating," Senovo said as we stood in the shadow of a building, hiding away from prying eyes while we picked at our meal. "Afterward, I should go to the temple and meet with the acolytes and novice priests who wish to come to Draebard."

"I could come with you," I offered.

Senovo shook his head, leaning against the wall with one shoulder. Despite the fact that the day was barely half over, he looked exhausted.

"It's not necessary," he replied. "I understand what you're trying to do, and I do appreciate it, but this is my life now. You cannot protect me from it, much as you might wish to do so. I will see the woman's son, and speak to the novices, and afterwards I will return to our room and meet you there, probably around dusk. If you wish to help, perhaps you'd be willing to purchase our dinner, so that I won't have to face a repeat of this experience at the end of a long day." His eyes flickered down to the food in his hand, clearly recalling the stall-keeper's bowing and scraping.

I nodded, chastened, and pasted on a smile. "Of course. I should visit the horse pens and make plans for taking the black stallion when we leave in the morning." I swallowed the last of my meal and threw the leaf wrapping away. "I'll see you this evening."

Senovo squeezed my shoulder, and I briefly covered his hand with my own. He stepped back as I moved to leave the shadowed alleyway where we had retreated to eat in relative privacy. With a final glance behind me, I made myself stride confidently toward the edge of town where the horses were kept, my head held high.

The horse pens were a hive of activity at midday, with people coming and going on various errands. I looked around and was pleased to find Previn, the young apprentice who had taken something of a shine to me after my horse-taming demonstration two days ago, hand-walking a sweaty, blowing mare around the perimeter of the pens to cool her down.

"Hullo, Previn," I called, lifting a hand to catch his attention. His face immediately lit up in a grin.

"Horse Mistress Carivel!" he greeted, leading the mare toward me eagerly. "How are you today?"

"I'm well, thank you," I said, not completely truthfully. Still, I had to admit that I was better for being near the horses.

"What can I do for you?" Previn asked, quieting the mare when she began to fuss.

I indicated that we should walk together, not wanting to interfere in the boy's duties. "I was hoping you could answer a couple of questions for me."

"About Nietre?" he said.

"Just so," I replied, nodding. "I'm mostly curious if he's ever been ridden, or harnessed."

"Oh, yes," Previn said, as if it were a foregone conclusion. "He was started in the fall of his two-year-old year, just like all of them are. Harnessed with an experienced horse first, pulling a chariot, and then under saddle a month or two later."

I perked up visibly at that piece of information. "Really? Did they have any problems with him back then?"

"Nah, not that I can remember," said Previn. "He was pretty normal until he was about four. Started really noticing the mares that spring and it all kind of went downhill from there." He looked at me with a sly gaze. "You gonna ride him, then?"

I smiled. "I'm seriously considering it."

"You should! I heard the Leader gave him to you. Made me grin from ear to ear, hearing that." The same grin split Previn's features as he spoke, making him look even younger than he was. "Can I watch?"

"Tell you what," I said. "Finish cooling out this mare, and I'll let them know I need to borrow you for a bit. Is the Horse Master here? Or is someone else in charge this afternoon?"

Previn pointed at a tall, broad-shouldered young man some distance away. "Logan is looking after things for a few hours. You can talk to him."

"Very well," I told him, feeling secretly relieved not to have to talk to the Horse Master of Meren, who had seemed rather hostile to me on first acquaintance. "Meet me at Nietre's pen when you're done. Mind you take good care of this mare first, though."

Previn nodded enthusiastically and led the mare off for a few sips of water from one of the troughs scattered around the area. I walked over to Logan, who eyed me somewhat warily.

"Can I help you, Horse Mistress?" he asked, shooing away the apprentices he'd been speaking to before I arrived.

"Yes, thank you," I replied. "I was hoping to borrow Previn for a little while, once he's done with the mare he's cooling off. I'm to take the black stallion, Nietre, with me when I leave for Draebard in the morning, and I'd prefer to throw a leg over him inside a pen before I try to do it in the middle of the wildlands."

Logan eyed me skeptically. "You know that horse hasn't been ridden in years, right?"

"I'd gathered, yes."

After a second or two more of staring at me, Logan shrugged. "It's your neck, Horse Mistress. Tell Previn to go polish the saddles in the north tack shed when you're done with him."

"Will do," I said agreeably. "Thank you."

I was leaning against the fence of the stallion's pen with my chin resting on my hands when Previn jogged up a few minutes later. "I brought you this," he said, handing me a rope halter with a long lead rope attached. "I saw you didn't have one with you today."

"Thanks," I said, flashing him a genuine smile. It was true; I hadn't gone back to Harinel's boarding house before coming, so I didn't have any of my own equipment with me... well, unless you counted the grubby strip of linen cloth still jammed in the pocket of my breeches. Which, now that I thought about it, might come in handy today. "Could you find me a straight, sturdy stick a little longer than your forearm?" I asked Previn.

"Sure," he said. "You want me to get a saddle and bridle, too?"

I shook my head. "Not today. Accepting the rider is a different thing than accepting the saddle. I don't want to deal with both today, but I really *do* want to ride him."

Previn was staring at me with an expression somewhere between worry and awe—apparently they didn't do much bareback riding in Meren. I cleared my throat, and the lad seemed to come back to himself. He flushed slightly in embarrassment and hurried off to find my stick.

In the pen, Nietre looked up from his hay and pricked an ear after the boy. I made a clucking sound with my tongue, and the stallion's attention turned to me. Gods above, he was a beautiful animal—so different from the horses of Draebard, with their stout, feathered legs and barrel-shaped bodies. I was *desperate* to take him out to a stretch of flat road and give him his head. Long-legged and muscled as he was, the horse's speed had to be breathtaking.

When Previn returned, I took the stick he'd found and tied the piece of cloth to the end. When I entered the pen, the stallion lifted his head high and snorted. As I had done when I visited the previous day, I approached him from the side and moved him a few steps away from the pile of hay, claiming it for myself. This time, though, instead of inviting him back to join me, I used the stick and cloth flag to move him around me in a wide circle.

After a few moments of fussing and bucking, he settled into a steady trot. I revisited the lesson we'd done on the first day, turning him toward me and away from me to change directions, slowing and speeding his gait using my body position and the cloth flag. This time, when I invited him to approach me, I backed up several steps so that he had to pass by the pile of hay to reach me. I was pleased to see that he ignored it completely, walking up to me confidently, but without aggression.

I let him sniff the flag, and then my hand, before scratching and rubbing at the scabs from the heavy halter that had been left on the unruly horse for months before I'd removed it during the demonstration. As he had before, Nietre leaned into the touch, bobbing his head up and down to get friction where the itching was worst. After two days, some of the crusty scabs were already starting to fall off, revealing tender new skin underneath.

When the horse's expression was soft and relaxed, I put the rope halter on, adjusting the knots to avoid any tender places. I rubbed him all over with the stick and cloth, noting any spots that made him defensive and spending extra time there until he calmed. Once he accepted both the stick and my hand all over his body, I ran through a series of yielding exercises, moving his forequarters and hindquarters in both directions, backing him up and drawing him forward with the halter and rope.

It was still a bit surprising to me that the horse was as responsive as he was, given the years of rough treatment he'd received. I hoped that was a sign that his early training—including his training under saddle and harness—had been skillful. Leading him over to the fence, I climbed up to perch on the top rail. Nietre raised his head to stare at me and released an explosive snort as he backed up a few steps.

"Oh, I see how it is," I told him. "You're happy enough to rear up and loom over me with your hooves flailing all over the place, but as soon as I'm taller than you, you turn into a scared little bunny rabbit."

Previn snickered from his spot a few paces away, outside the fence. "I always thought he was really just frightened, underneath it all," said the boy. "Didn't make him any less dangerous though."

"Most of the aggressive ones are only trying to protect themselves," I said, pleased at Previn's insight. "You get the very rare one who isn't afraid of people at all and just wants to dominate them. Those are the ones you can't do much with, if they're bad enough. The scared ones, though—the scared ones can become some of the very best horses if they decide to trust you. Once they finally trust, they trust completely. They'd give their lives for you."

While I was speaking, Nietre crept forward again to sniff at me as I sat on the fence. I was ready to correct him with the stick and flapping cloth if he forgot himself and showed teeth, but it was important that I trust him to snuffle and nudge at my clothing as he investigated this new development. After all, I was about to ask him to trust me to sit on his back, in the same place a cougar or lion would try to latch on in order to bring him down and eat him.

When he seemed satisfied that it was still me, even though I was suddenly taller, I went back to scratching his head until he was happy and relaxed again. I repeated the routine of rubbing him all over with the stick and flag, urging him to line himself up parallel to the fence with gentle taps of the stick against his opposite hip. I reached over his muscled back to rub the flag along his far side, and waved it smoothly back and forth above his head and neck to see how he would react to something moving around in his peripheral vision where a rider's torso—*my torso*—would be.

He lifted his head in mild alarm, ears swept back to listen, but soon calmed again. I wasn't surprised. He'd been ridden for more than a year with no issues when he was younger. All of his problems originated between his ears, not on his back. I stretched my hand forward, grasping his bony withers and rocking his weight from side to side. The stallion rolled his nearside eye around to stare at me, but obligingly set himself square over all four feet, ready to accept a rider without losing his balance. I leaned down to hook my arm across his back, letting the weight of my upper body settle onto him. His attention was still focused on me intently, but he did not shift an inch.

Straightening, I gathered the lead rope and stick into my left hand and slipped lightly from the fence onto his back.

THREE

The powerful back beneath me bunched up, tensing at the unfamiliar weight. I breathed deeply and slowly, scratching Nietre's withers with my free hand. After a span of thirty heartbeats or so, he blew out a long breath and relaxed. I continued to scratch his shoulders and neck for a bit, before drawing myself up straight—a warning that I was about to ask something of him. His ears remained fixed towards me as I suggested that he swing his hindquarters away from the fence in a broad arc, using the same yielding cues I'd taught him from the ground.

I eased him around until he was facing the other direction and urged him forward with my seat muscles. His walk was free and swinging, hinting at the speed and grace I knew he must have. I couldn't help the grin that stretched across my face as everything else fell away, leaving only the present moment— the delicate new line of communication and trust between myself and this dangerous animal carrying me around on his back.

We wove around the pen, practicing turns and yields as I flipped the lead rope smoothly over his head to change direction. As he gained confidence, he slipped into a loose, ground-eating trot, so different than the flat, slightly jarring gait of Draebard's chunky, heavy-bodied horses. I longed to urge him into a lope, but the pen was really too small for it. *Soon*, I promised him silently.

After a quarter of an hour or so, I spiraled him down to a halt with my single rope rein, describing decreasing circles until he was reduced to pivoting in place for a few steps. He relaxed to a stop with a soft-blown sigh. The blood was singing through my veins as I stretched forward to scratch between his ears for a few moments before sliding my right leg across his back and slipping to the ground. It was farther away than I was used to; I had never ridden a horse so tall before.

The stallion reached around to nudge against my hip, almost playfully. I rubbed under the halter, and led him to his water trough for a drink, then back to his pile of hay, where I untied the halter and let him go with a final pat. He watched me leave before returning to his interrupted meal.

Outside the pen, Previn looked like he was about to burst from excitement.

"You did it! You rode him!" he said. "I can hardly even believe it's the same horse!"

I smiled at his enthusiasm. "He's been ridden plenty of times, Previn, even if it has been a while."

"Yeah, maybe, but he's also killed a person and maimed two others since then," Previn said, his eyes still wide. "Can I ask a question, though?"

"Always," I told him, meaning it. Again, it struck me that this was my job now. Training and caring for a tribe's horses fell to a large group of men and boys. The training of those men and boys, however, fell to the Horse Master... or, now, to the Horse Mistress. If I was lucky.

"Why didn't you tie the lead rope in a loop to make some proper reins?" Previn asked, his brow furrowing. "Seems like it'd be easier and safer than having to throw the rope over 'is head every time you wanted to change direction. If he'd taken off, you'd've gone *splat*."

I laughed. "Eh, if he wanted rid of me, he'd have got rid of me regardless. I would have bailed if he'd started getting out of control," I told him. "As far as the single rein, it's habit, mostly. You can use two reins when starting a horse, but you'd better be sure that you've got enough self-control not to grab at him if you get flustered. With a single rein, I'm forced to give clear cues, one at a time. Getting his face yanked on doesn't mean anything to a colt; it just scares him. But he already knows how to follow the feel of a lead rope leading his head to one side or the other. If he runs off, my best bet is always to spiral down to a stop, nice and easy."

Previn looked thoughtful. "I've never seen anyone do it that way. Kinda makes sense, though. It worked well enough with Nietre, that's for sure!"

I smiled at the lad's enthusiasm. "Well," I told him, "I think that's enough for now. Logan asked me to tell you that the saddles in the north tack shed need polishing next."

Previn's expression soured immediately.

"Surely it can't be that bad," I teased. Glancing at the position of the sun, I made a quick decision. "Come on. I'll help you for a couple of hours before I have to get back."

"Really?" he asked, stunned that a Horse Mistress would offer to help him oil saddle leather.

"Why not? You can tell me more about how colts are started in Meren." Also, it was better than worrying about Senovo. Worrying about Andoc. Worrying about… *everything*. I clapped a hand on Previn's shoulder, and followed him to the lean-to where the saddles were kept.

⁎⁂⁎

When the sun started to disappear behind the buildings, I took my leave of Previn and headed back into the center of town. Remembering Senovo's request from earlier, I picked up some food and drink on my way, making sure to go to a different stall than the one we'd visited for lunch. Thinking about that uncomfortable encounter made everything else come flooding back after my peaceful few hours with Previn and the horses. I hoped that Senovo was all right. The slight twinge of guilt at not having worried more about him was irrational, I knew. In fact, I could practically picture Andoc rolling his eyes at me and telling me not to be ridiculous.

Still, when I arrived back at our room in the boarding house to find Senovo absent, I felt tension knot in my shoulders. To distract myself, I left the food on the table and went out to care for our own horses before complete darkness fell. When I returned, he was waiting for me.

He'd started a small fire burning in the hearth pit, more for light than heat since it was a warm evening. Now, he was sitting in one of the chairs, one elbow resting on the table, his normally straight back bowed with fatigue.

"I brought food," I blurted stupidly, feeling suddenly and unaccountably awkward now that we were alone together in the room.

Senovo raised his head, the firelight playing on his golden skin and fine features. He smiled, though it only lasted a moment. "Yes," he said in a faintly teasing tone. "I noticed."

Of course he'd noticed. The food was sitting on the table right in front of him. I blushed, wondering why this suddenly seemed so difficult.

It's because Andoc isn't here, a voice in my head answered. *We're no longer in balance.*

"Of course you noticed," I said with a sigh, and sat in the other chair. "Sorry, I'm being stupid tonight. How are you?"

"Tired and worried," he said, "as I imagine you are as well."

"Yep. Pretty much," I agreed. "Although I did pass a pleasant few hours down at the horse pens. I rode that black stallion for a few minutes, to see how he'd be on the trip home. I think he's going to make a really nice horse, to be honest."

Senovo stared at me with that slightly odd expression he sometimes seemed to get. "Is everyone who works around the horses reckless, then? Not just you?"

I raised an eyebrow at him. "The horse has been ridden before, you know. They rode and drove him for almost two years before the trouble started." Senovo just continued to stare at me, and I eventually conceded, "Although in fairness, Jorun did used to say that it took a special kind of crazy to work in the horse pens."

Senovo's eyes softened. "Forgive me. Only a few hours after I ask you to let me do my job, here I am questioning yours. I'm pleased the horse will work out. He is a very impressive animal."

I tried to smile, but thoughts of my fallen mentor had made me melancholy. To distract myself, I changed the subject. "How is the sick boy?"

"The paralysis is taking hold of his lungs, and I fear he will not survive much longer. I offered my blessing, for whatever it is worth."

A wash of sadness came over me as I thought of the boy's desperate mother. "I'm sorry to hear that. Did you speak with the novices?"

"I did. They seem quite sincere in their desire to relocate to Draebard."

"I have to admit, I'm surprised you agreed so easily," I said, frowning a bit. "I mean, I know you'll need help, but it just seems so... I don't know... *intrusive,* I guess."

"If you'll forgive my presumption, I believe you may be allowing anger at High Priest Jyrrel to blind you to the larger picture," Senovo said mildly.

"What larger picture is that?"

"You can see no benefit to populating the Priests' Guild in Draebard with acolytes and novices from a village that accepts women in traditionally male positions?" Senovo asked pointedly.

I blinked, the implications hitting me all at once.

"Gods above," I said. "Look at you. You're *plotting*."

Senovo shrugged. "It's in the job description, I'm afraid. Right after the part about being sanctimonious and an insufferable meddler."

I laughed, and shoved half of the food toward him. "I'm sorry I ever said that you weren't a very good priest. I was wrong. You're *terrifying*. Now, stop plotting and eat something."

We ate in relative silence, and planned our departure for the following morning after we were finished. I would need to rise early to make sure that Nietre would accept a saddle and bridle, since I intended to ride him, at least on the first day. Better that than trying to lead him from another horse — it had been too long since he'd had any interactions with his own kind that didn't involve fighting or breeding. Kekenu could carry our provisions and Senovo could lead the little gelding while riding the gray mare.

As we cleaned up the remains of the meal and readied ourselves for sleep, I felt the tinge of awkwardness creep over me again. It was hard to describe — Senovo had never been anything but kind and accepting toward me. I had seen him at his most vulnerable, as he had seen me at mine. Now, though, in the absence of both Andoc and any immediate crisis, with an uncertain future ahead of me, I didn't quite know how to act. What did he need from me? What — if anything — did he even *want* from me?

I knew exactly what Andoc wanted from me. It was the same thing I wanted from him, more or less. Affection. Sex. Maybe a deeper love, as time went on. I knew what Senovo needed from Andoc — strength, support, control of the wolf. But... I wasn't at all sure I could give him those things in

Andoc's absence. Worse, I didn't even know if I was supposed to try.

"You look like a wide-eyed stag cornered by hunters in the forest," Senovo said, startling me from my thoughts and making me flush with embarrassment. He sounded tired.

As I had this morning, I reminded myself that Senovo was a priest and honesty was the best policy. "I'm sorry," I said. "I don't really know how to... be... with you like this. What's *appropriate*, I mean. What you need from me. You seem tired. How is the wolf tonight?"

"Carivel, you've never been in a relationship with another person before," Senovo said. "Much less two people at once. No one expects you to have everything worked out in the first two days. Least of all me."

I ran my hand over my face and let it fall. "I know. Sorry. Though I notice you didn't answer my question."

Senovo sat on the bed. "Restless. The wolf is restless tonight."

"I wish I could be Andoc for you, but I don't think I'd know how." I sat next to him, our arms barely brushing.

"I don't need another Andoc," Senovo said, nudging my shoulder with his. "One Andoc is enough for anyone, would you not agree?" I snorted out a weak breath of laughter, and he continued, "You needn't worry, though. You won't wake up in the middle of the night tonight and find a wolf in your bed. My word on it."

I looked up at him. "Would that really be so bad, if I did? It's only us in here. What would be the harm?"

Senovo appeared taken aback, his green eyes searching my face in the dim firelight. "I... can't allow myself to give into it so easily. What if I lost even the small amount of control over it that I have now?"

His voice sounded younger. Unsure.

I thought about my words carefully before speaking them. "It's your choice, of course. I just want you to know that I don't fear the wolf. Why would I? It's only ever tried to protect me."

Senovo was silent for a long time. "I wish I could say the same," he said eventually.

Feeling more certain of myself, I did not reply with words, but instead drew him down to lie on the bed, facing away from me. When he was settled, I fitted myself to his back, curling an arm around his middle and pressing my forehead between his shoulder blades. I was gratified when one of his arms settled over mine, as if to hold it in place. Pressing a kiss to Senovo's spine, I sighed and slipped quickly into sleep.

Senovo slept restlessly through the night. I awoke several times to find him dreaming in the way that animals dream—running, fighting, eating. Chasing, and being chased. Each time, I woke him, not sure what else to do. We were both weary and red-eyed when we rose, but neither of us spoke of it. I sent Senovo to purchase dried rations for us and say our farewells to Leader Magoldis before we left. Meanwhile, I went out to ready our horses and meet him at the horse pens, after which we would depart.

When I arrived at the pens with Kekenu and Senovo's mare, it was light enough to see, but the sun had not yet slipped above the horizon. It looked to be a cloudy, dreary day, and I hoped it would not rain heavily. At least it was warm.

I tied our horses out of the way and took Kekenu's saddle and bridle to Nietre's pen. The stallion raised his head as I approached and snorted at the scent of the unfamiliar horses. I entered and greeted him before setting the tack down on the ground for him to investigate. It took about twenty minutes to get him calm and quiet while I saddled him and snugged up the cinch. When I stepped back and drove him out to circle around me, he took one stride and drew in a deep breath, exploding into a series of bucks as the unfamiliar equipment creaked and swung on his back.

I let him get it out of his system for a few minutes before gaining his attention and redirecting him into the familiar yielding exercises we'd been doing for the past few days. When he was once again paying more attention to me than to the saddle, I brought him to a halt and readjusted everything. I would have to talk to our saddler about having a special saddle made when we got back; his back was a completely different shape than those of the barrel-chested Draebardi horses.

For now, though, I padded and shimmed up Kekenu's saddle so it wouldn't rub or irritate the slender stallion's spine.

When I looked over to where I'd hung the bridle on the fence, it was to find Senovo watching us.

"*A special kind of crazy*, I believe you said?" he said, wearing a slightly pinched expression.

I grinned. "What… you're worried about this little spate of bucking? This is pretty normal. It's been awhile since he's been saddled, is all. You're a priest, Senovo. Have a little faith."

I threw in a wink for good measure and took up the bridle.

"Hey," I added, as a thought struck me. "Did you get any dried fruit? If so, bring me a couple pieces, please."

Senovo shook his head in apparent despair, but went and got me a couple of bits of dried apple from the saddlebags. I pocketed one and held the other in the palm of my hand, trapped under the mouthpiece of the metal snaffle bit as I positioned my other hand over the stallion's head, holding the leather straps of the headpiece. Nietre sniffed at my palm for a few moments, and delicately opened his mouth for both bit and treat. He chewed in quiet contemplation as I adjusted the straps to fit him.

When I took up the reins to repeat the yielding exercises with the bridle instead of the halter, he shook his head and pulled up in surprise when the metal bit clanked against his teeth. He mouthed at it for a moment, and responded more quietly when I asked him a second time. After turning him in both directions a few times, I stopped him and checked his response to having the stirrup leathers flapped and popped against his side. When it appeared he wouldn't panic at the movement of the saddle on his back, I gathered the reins and put a foot in the stirrup, lightly mounting.

As he had yesterday, he flicked both ears back to me, listening hard. I rubbed his withers until he blew out a breath and relaxed, then took up the reins in my left hand and my little stick and flag in my right. We trotted off and wove around the pen, turning this way and that until his back no longer felt tense and humped under my weight. When he was moving freely with long, sweeping strides, I returned to where Senovo stood by the fence and pulled up.

"Open the gate for me, if you would. Then get mounted and grab Kekenu," I told him. "We're ready to leave."

He nodded and went to the gate, unlatching it and swinging it wide. I went back to riding circles and snaking curves until Senovo was settled in his own saddle with Kekenu's lead rope held in one hand.

I exited the pen and led the way out past the other corrals, into the open country beyond. As the road stretched out in front of him, Nietre arched his neck, getting increasingly excited until he was dancing almost sideways along the rutted track. I wasn't surprised; this was the first time he'd been in the open in who-knew-how-long. I could only imagine how he felt.

"Senovo, I need to let this horse work off some of his energy," I called back. "I promised him a good run today. We'll stick to the road—just follow on behind us at a nice steady canter and we'll meet up a little way ahead, all right?"

"Whatever you think best," he said. "Don't get killed, please—it would be a bit awkward to explain."

"Nonsense," I called in reply. "I imagine Volya would be relieved beyond measure not to have to deal with me except for a quick funeral."

With that, I turned Nietre straight on the road and gave him his head.

FOUR

The stallion's powerful hindquarters launched us forward, and we were at a full gallop in three strides. His speed was like nothing I had ever experienced. The wind whipped my face, threatening to take my breath away as I let out an excited whoop and crouched forward, close to his neck.

It was like flying. I urged him faster, and he stretched out, his ears flat back against his head, breath coming in rhythmic snorts as his pounding hooves ate up the road. I was going to feel the strain in my back and thighs tomorrow. I'd never ridden a horse with such a large, rolling stride before. I vowed to do so as often as possible from now on.

I risked a quick glance behind us, where Senovo was a rapidly diminishing speck in the distance. A laugh bubbled up in my chest. Volya had been a fool to cut off ties with the Mereni. How much could Draebard's warriors accomplish with horses like these? If the gods smiled on me and I was allowed back into the village as Horse Mistress, I would make it my life's work to make sure that we got more of them.

We galloped until my eyes were blurred with tears from the wind and sweat was lathering Nietre's neck beneath the reins. When he began to slow of his own accord, I straightened in the saddle and eased him back to a rocking lope. The stallion blew softly with each stride. After another couple of minutes, I relaxed my seat and breathed out, long and deep. The horse melted down to a walk, and I stroked his steaming neck.

"Better now?" I asked, thinking that even if he wasn't, I most certainly was. With an animal like this, wandering the wildlands as an outcast suddenly didn't sound quite so bad.

I let him amble on down the road on a loose rein, his breathing slowing by degrees as the sweat dried on his coat. It was a good quarter of an hour before the sound of steady hoof beats approaching behind us heralded Senovo's reappearance. Nietre flicked his ears back and tried to crane his neck around to look, but he was too exhausted to do more than snort a weak challenge at Kekenu as the two horses approached... just as I had planned. For his part, Kekenu ignored the stallion completely, though the gray mare tossed her head flirtatiously as Senovo reined her in.

"Don't let your mare get too close," I warned him. "I do believe she's a bit smitten."

"I'm no expert," Senovo said, slightly out of breath from his own brisk ride, "but that appears to be one exceptionally fast horse."

"It does appear so," I agreed with a grin.

"You're *glowing*," Senovo accused.

"Special kind of crazy, remember?" I said, and made a concerted attempt to control my glee. "Sorry. Giving a horseman a new horse is like giving a toddler a new toy."

"Between the horses and the acolytes, it appears the Mereni bring far more to the table than we originally hoped."

I nodded in complete agreement. "It was shortsighted of Volya to alienate them, especially on the strength of his own bruised pride."

"It was," he agreed. "Though it may not be politic to say so directly, once we return."

I sighed, my momentary elation dulling. "I doubt I'll be able to get any further on Volya's bad side than I already am. But don't worry—I'm not planning on engaging in debates with the man. I'd be happy not to engage with him at all, though that's probably unrealistic."

"Probably so," Senovo agreed, not without sympathy.

We traveled on through the day, the gray clouds dripping a slow drizzle onto us for a couple of hours before giving way to patchy, late-spring sunshine. Nietre was obviously tired after his initial, exuberant gallop—not surprising for a horse that had been confined to a small pen for much of his adult life. I could not fault his spirit, though. He never balked or fussed, just trudged along with his head level with his knees.

The green valleys of the Mereni lands changed gradually to rockier, elevated plateaus, and I judged we were in roughly the same area where we'd camped overnight on the way here a few days ago. It was here that I'd first seen for myself the true depth and shape of the bond between Andoc and Senovo. Where I'd first dared to dream—as we'd passed around a skin of strong wine—of having something like that for myself.

I stood up in my stirrups, pointing at a familiar rock formation. "Look! Isn't that our campsite?"

Senovo peered into the deepening dusk. "I think it might be," he agreed. "I'm sorry to say that I wasn't paying all that much attention that night."

I remembered how shattered he'd been at the time—exhausted after the recent attack and mass funeral in Draebard, sick with grief over Rhystel and the other slain priests. I remembered how shattered we'd *both* been. But whereas I was only fighting grief, he was also fighting the wolf inside him. I looked closer at him in the gray evening light. Even now, his green-gold eyes were sunken and red-rimmed. His shoulders, slumped under the weight of the worry he was carrying.

I should have been watching more closely today.

"I think it's the same place," I told him. "Regardless, it's a good spot to stop for the night."

Senovo nodded, and dismounted. I followed suit and found a sturdy scrub tree to tie the stallion. The other horses could graze through the night, wearing hobbles, but I would have to hand-graze Nietre for a couple of hours this evening, and again in the morning unless I wanted him trying to fight with Kekenu and breed the gray mare while we slept.

"I'll tend to the horses if you'll get a fire going with your magic powder," I said.

We each took care of our various responsibilities, and when I plonked my saddle on the ground near the merrily blazing little fire and sat down against it, Senovo handed me some dried meat and fruit from the saddlebags, along with a water skin.

"My apologies—I didn't think to buy any wine," he said.

I took the rations and settled back. "I guess that's why you keep Andoc around, eh?" I teased. "He is good with the wine."

"One of the reasons, certainly."

Studying Senovo surreptitiously, I decided that I really didn't like what I saw. "Don't take this the wrong way," I said, my tone tentative, "but you really look terrible. Are you going to be able to keep control tonight?"

Senovo shrugged a shoulder. "I don't really have a choice."

I sat forward, staring at him openly, and crossed my arms. "Well, yeah… you really kind of *do*."

"Don't mince words, please, Carivel," he said, sounding tired.

"You *do* have a choice. You could wait until you can't hang on a moment longer and change form in agony, fighting it every step of the way, or you could just fucking *change*, out here where it's only you and me and the crickets. The wolf can go for a nice stroll with me for a couple of hours and hunt rabbits, or mice, or whatever wolves do, while I let Nietre graze. Then we can both curl up by the fire and get some decent sleep."

Senovo opened his mouth to argue, and I cut him off. "The wolf isn't going to hurt me, Senovo. If the wolf wanted to hurt me, it would've done so when I was dragging it around by the scruff of the neck to try and keep it from charging into the point of a javelin at the temple in Meren the other night."

"What about the horses?" Senovo asked, almost defiantly. Almost as if he was desperate to prove to me how dangerous his inner animal was.

"I don't consider you a stupid man," I replied, unable to keep a faint tone of irritation from creeping into my voice. "I'm going to assume that means the wolf isn't stupid either. It might have a chance with a newborn foal or a sick, lame animal, but no lone wolf is going to try taking down a healthy, adult horse. Kekenu and the gray mare would kick you in the teeth if you tried anything. Nietre would probably pound you into a greasy little puddle with bits of fur sticking out of it. We're in the middle of nowhere, Senovo. *There's no one here for you to hurt.*"

"You don't understand," the priest said weakly.

"No, I don't!" I shot back. "So please, explain it to me. You're going to change eventually, either way. We both know that! What's so much worse about changing voluntarily?"

"It's a form of weakness!" Senovo retorted. "The wolf preys on weakness."

I set aside the uneaten food and crawled over to kneel in front of him, taking his hands in mine. He looked up in surprise, only to quickly look away again.

"It's not, you know," I said, purposely gentling my voice. "It's control. Somewhere along the way, you got it into your head that 'control' means hanging on until you can't any more. That would have been like me trying to keep Nietre at a slow walk this morning when he wanted to run, and fighting with him until he finally bolted or bucked me off out of frustration. How is that control?"

I dipped my head, trying to catch his eye again. He met my gaze reluctantly. "You saw what I did instead," I told him.

"You let him run," Senovo said softly.

"No, I *told* him to run," I clarified. "In fact, I told him to keep going for a couple of minutes even after he was tired, because I'm the one in charge of the partnership. But I knew he needed to run, and since I'm the leader, it's my responsibility to make sure he has what he needs. That's what leaders *do*, Senovo. Otherwise, why would this horse ever trust me enough to want to follow me?"

Senovo's expression crumpled, and he leaned forward until his forehead was resting against our joined hands, hiding his face. I squeezed his fingers and disentangled long enough to draw him into an embrace.

"The wolf needs to get out and hunt rabbits for a few hours," I whispered against his ear, as sure about this as I'd ever been about anything in my life. "Where is the harm in that?"

He shuddered against me and went still, barely even breathing. A few moments later, the body in my arms warped and changed, doubling over, a rough gray coat erupting under my hands. The wolf whined and wriggled in my grip, half knocking me over onto an elbow before licking enthusiastically at my neck and face. The sound I made as I struggled upright and fended him off was half-laugh, half-sob. I cradled the large head between my hands, fingers curling into the ruff of longer fur framing the animal's cheeks.

"Look at you," I told him approvingly, pressing our foreheads together and closing my eyes. "Look how brave you are."

The wolf panted and nudged me with his wet nose. When I straightened and released him, he yipped once and leapt away, leaving Senovo's robes puddled on the ground next to me. He turned back and dropped his front end to the ground in a play-bow, tongue hanging out in the firelight.

"Gods, Senovo," I told him, "Andoc would give his left eyetooth to see you like this."

It was true. The wolf, like all animals, lived totally in the moment. Right now the night was pleasant and free of threats.

Interesting smells wafted from the tufts of grass and enticing crags in the rocks, and all was right in his world. I envied him for a moment until I remembered my early morning gallop on Nietre—the way everything else had fallen away into unimportance. I blushed a little. Perhaps I was not so far removed from the wolf as I thought.

The shaggy creature yipped again, and flopped down on his belly to stare at me with golden eyes.

"All right, all right," I said. "Let me get Nietre and we can go explore a bit."

I had hobbled the other two horses earlier and let them out to graze on the other side of the rocks, with access to the small stream and a broken field of scrubby grass. Nietre, though, was watching the scene intently from where he was tied nearby. When I rose, he let loose an explosive snort, pawing at the tree trunk with one front foot.

"Yes, I know," I said, and made sure to grab my stick and flag before I approached him. "It's a bit much to ask of you on the strength of such short acquaintance. Just pretend he's a really large dog, all right?" I turned back to the wolf. "And you—remember what I said about furry grease puddles, eh?"

The wolf continued to stare at me, tongue lolling as he panted.

I asked Nietre to yield a step or two away from me as I untied him, and made a point of keeping my body between him and the large predator. "Come on, both of you," I called, and led the horse out into the deeper darkness away from the fire. The wolf leapt to his feet and trotted off to explore his surroundings. Before long, he was happily digging away at the underground burrow of some unfortunate small creature.

I led Nietre a little distance away to a patch of dry upland grass. He stared at the wolf for some considerable time before blowing out a breath and lowering his head to graze. We wandered slowly from tussock to tussock while the wolf amused himself chasing after smells and sticking his nose into whatever he could reach.

After a couple of pleasant hours, a soft whine came from a short distance behind me. Nietre's head shot up, and I turned to find the wolf regarding us with shining eyes.

"Had enough already?" I asked, keeping my body language focused but relaxed, to reassure the stallion that I was aware of the wolf but did not consider him a threat.

The big predator whined again and crept forward on his belly, pausing to flop over on his side and hitch himself comically along with his hind legs. He rolled to and fro, scratching his flanks and back on the pebbled ground with obvious enjoyment. Nietre lowered his head and snorted loudly at the unusual performance, neck arched and ears pricked. I watched the two animals closely, intrigued by the interaction but unwilling to risk Senovo getting hurt. The stallion spooked in place, jumping slightly but not backing away as the wolf righted himself and continued forward on his belly, tail flopping rhythmically against the ground. He stopped about three arm-lengths away, looking up at both of us with a hopeful gaze.

"I can't help wondering how much of you crosses over," I said, fascinated by the idea of dignified, reserved Senovo stretched out in front of me begging for ear scratches. I thought about the eunuch arching into Andoc's touch in bed, and smiled.

Keeping a close eye on Nietre and with my stick and flag ready, just in case, I closed the distance between us and crouched down. The wolf immediately nosed into me with a whimper of pleasure as I reached out to rub at the shaggy head. He twisted his neck this way and that, positioning my fingernails where he wanted and closing his eyes in apparent bliss. Nietre stared with rapt attention, frozen in place for several moments. Then, he began to inch forward, one tiny step at a time, his neck stretched out to its utmost.

The wolf sneezed and looked up with wide eyes when the stallion's breath wafted across his face from a few inches away. I watched carefully, poised to intervene as the black horse snorted softly through flared nostrils, ruffling the wolf's fur once more. Nietre jerked back when the wolf reached out and licked at his muzzle, but returned seconds later to resume his tentative exploration.

"All right, you two, break it up," I said, after a minute or two of this. I reached into my pocket, suddenly remembering the second piece of dried apple still buried there. I had to shove the wolf away as he tried to sniff at the treat, so I could feed it to Nietre instead. "Rude," I chastened.

I stood up, spilling the furry creature off my lap. He huffed and shook himself, causing the stallion to scramble back a step. "Come on," I said to them both. "Let's get back to the camp."

I allowed Nietre to drink his fill from the stream and tied him to the tree again to keep him out of trouble. After checking that the other horses were all right, I flopped down next to the fire and picked up the remains of my rations, tearing into them hungrily. The wolf trotted up and sniffed around the area, quickly locating Senovo's own discarded dinner and gulping it down without ceremony.

"You've certainly got more of an appetite than human Senovo does," I told him. "Maybe I should have had you bring me your rabbits so I could cook them first." The animal canted his head, watching me intently. "I draw the line at cooking mice, though. Sorry."

I looked at the night sky. The clouds were breaking up, patches of starlight visible overhead. I decided to take a chance on the rain being finished for now, and forego the tent. It was still warm and muggy, but I dragged the blankets from both of our bedrolls anyway and set them out by the fire. The wolf wandered over to sniff at my boots once I'd removed them, and watched as I arranged the blankets into a sort of rough nest.

Resting my head on the seat of my saddle for a pillow, I scooted around until I'd managed to find a relatively comfortable, rock-free spot to lie on. Once I'd settled, the wolf slunk over and pawed a few times at a corner of one of the blankets, dragging it partially free of my legs.

"Blanket thief," I accused. Ignoring my words, he continued to scratch and nose at the rough woolen cloth until it was arranged just so. When it was finally to his satisfaction, he circled twice and curled up in the space in front of my stomach and thighs with a big sigh. Staring out into the darkness beyond the campsite, he rested his head on my hip—a warm and grounding weight.

I reached out and stroked the thick fur, listening to the gentle night sounds—insects, the occasional rustle as Nietre changed position by the tree where he was tied, our soft breathing. After a while, my hand grew heavy, sliding down to rest on the wolf's lean, sinewy shoulders and staying there as my eyes slipped closed.

The sun was just rising over the horizon when I woke. Sometime during the night, the wolf had stretched out in front of me, and I now lay with one arm thrown carelessly over his torso. Roused, perhaps, by my own return to consciousness, the animal yawned and stretched luxuriously, muscles bunching and rippling under my touch.

I was shocked to have slept so soundly, given what awaited the two of us later today. I hoped that Senovo had found the wolf's sleep as restful. Knowing we had to face the day, but not wanting to break the moment, I ran my hand over the thick fur with slow, even strokes.

"Senovo," I said softly. "It's time to come back now. Can you come back for me?"

The wolf whimpered. I shushed him, and continued to stroke my hand over his warm flank. A few moments later, the unnatural twisting, writhing *change* heralded Senovo's reappearance in my arms. The eunuch froze, holding his breath, muscles trembling, and I resumed my rhythmic caress over the naked skin of his side and hip.

"Everything is fine," I said, pitching my voice low. "We're fine, there's no danger. Just breathe. It's all right. Breathe now."

The trapped breath exited Senovo's lungs in a great *whoosh*, and he sucked in a gulp of air, and then another. I continued to speak to him softly and run my hand up and down his side, reading the gradual ebb of his panic in the ever-slowing thump of his heartbeat.

"Carivel?" he asked eventually, still frozen in place.

"That's right, it's me," I said. "We're camped between Meren and Draebard. Do you remember?"

There was a tiny hesitation.

"Yes, I… yes."

"Are you in pain? Do you feel like you need to be sick?" I asked, remembering the two other times I had seen Senovo change back from the wolf.

"… no."

"That's good, isn't it?" He shivered again, this time from the slight chill of the morning air, and I flipped the edge of my blanket over him. "Here, just stay put for a few minutes."

I was already pressed up against him from shoulder to ankle, but I tugged him a bit tighter against me under the blanket and resumed running my hand over every part of him I could reach. We were silent for some time, watching the sun rise slowly over the rocks. Small tremors wracked Senovo's body, growing farther apart and of shorter duration as I continued to hold him.

"How do you feel?" I asked, when he lay quiet against me at last.

He was still a bit slow to respond, as if he was lost inside his own head. "Strange," he said.

"Good strange or bad strange?" I pressed.

"Just strange," he replied. "That was..."

"Yes?"

"That was... the easiest transformation I've ever experienced."

A wave of sadness washed over me for the man in my arms. Shaking and gasping, muscles frozen in fear for long minutes—and that was the easiest it had ever been for him. All I said, though, was, "I'm glad."

He nodded, and stretched tentatively against me, unlocking stiff joints with a series of crackling pops. I followed suit, a huge yawn splitting my face.

"Are you all right on your own for a bit?" I asked. "You can stay here. Get a bit more rest while I take the stallion out to graze again."

Senovo hummed an affirmative noise, so I crawled out from under the blanket and tucked it around him once I was free. I was still dressed except for my boots, so it was the work of a moment to pull them on. After relieving myself behind the rocks and splashing water from the stream onto my face and arms, I took Nietre out to graze for a while and check the other horses.

The stallion was a bit stiff after a long gallop followed by a full day of work and a night of inactivity. I decided to ride Kekenu today, judging that Nietre would be too sore and tired to pose much of a problem as the packhorse. I would just have to keep a close eye on him as I led him to make sure he stayed out of biting or striking range of Kekenu.

I returned after a little more than an hour and put the packsaddle on the stallion, aware that I was in danger at this point of dallying merely to put off our arrival in Draebard. By the time I led the other horses back to the campsite and saddled them, Senovo was up and dressed, looking steady enough, but still quiet.

We ate a bit of dried meat and washed it down with fresh water, but I could already feel my stomach growing queasy as I thought more about the day ahead. The two of us packed up the rest of the camp and headed out. My attention was taken up by Nietre for the first few leagues, as he danced and postured and tried to threaten poor Kekenu, only to run into my stick and flapping cloth flag with each attempt.

Eventually, he subsided, and the two horses trudged side-by-side, eyeing each other with matching sour expressions. Without the constant distraction of their fussing, my mind slid back to what we would find at the edge of the village — a strip of leather tied to a tree limb, but what color? Time seemed to drag, while paradoxically also passing too quickly. We rode straight through, stopping only to water the horses at convenient rivers and streams without dismounting. The terrain became more familiar as we descended from the uplands to the rolling hills and rain soaked valleys of western Eburos. The rough trail flattened and widened out into a road, and before I was remotely ready for it, Senovo was pointing to a large tree with twisting, knobby branches, just becoming visible in the distance.

"Can you see it?" I asked, hating the breathless quality of my voice.

"Not yet," he said.

We cantered forward, closing the last stretch separating us from answers. The breeze picked up, and something white flapped in a branch. I let out all of my breath at once.

FIVE

"Andoc succeeded," Senovo said, pulling up next to me. "Volya has accepted you as Horse Mistress."

I nodded and urged the horses forward again. It should have been a great relief. Instead, I could only think that now I would have to confront the consequences of my deception.

"Maybe it would have been easier to run," I muttered, not sure if I wanted Senovo to hear the words or not.

But hear them he did. "You still could," he said.

I couldn't, though. "No. The treaty depends on me. I have to be Draebard's Horse Mistress or Magoldis will never believe that Volya has changed."

I only wished my voice wasn't quavering.

"We both have hard realities to confront," Senovo said.

Feeling suddenly churlish as I remembered High Priest Rhystel, I nodded agreement. Senovo would soon discover whether his mentor still lived or not. If Rhystel had survived, Senovo would have to confess his own lie of omission. Neither of us was destined for an easy time of it this evening.

The priest swerved off the road to retrieve the strip of leather and stuff it into one of his saddlebags. I looked at the bent old tree.

"So, this is where you and Andoc first met?" I asked, desperate for distraction.

The priest's face softened for a moment in the golden light of early evening. "It is," he confirmed. "Remind us to tell you about it sometime. It's quite a story in its own right."

"I will," I promised. "Now, let's go to the horse pens to drop off the horses with Dalon. Then I'll go with you to the temple."

Somewhat to my surprise, Senovo nodded and didn't protest. He must truly be dreading what he would find there. The frozen, lifeless features of Jorun, my own mentor, danced briefly across my memory and I shivered.

We skirted around the edge of the village, heading to the north side, where the horse pens were located. Afternoon chores were in full swing, the young men readying the pens with feed and water for the night. Several familiar faces looked up as we approached, and awareness seemed to travel across the area in a slow wave. The usual bustle stilled until the pens were completely quiet except for the snorts and hoofbeats of the milling animals.

Confronted with dozens of unfamiliar horses, Nietre arched his neck and trumpeted a challenge into the silence. As if called by the stallion's cry, Dalon—my longtime rival and, more recently, my reluctant ally—separated from a group of yearlings and approached us.

"You're back, then," he said, looking from me to the black Mereni horse and back again.

"I am," I replied, unsure what else to say, really. "Did Volya tell you…"

"Yeah," Dalon said when I trailed off. "He did. Lotta stuff makes more sense now, to be honest." His eyes strayed back to Nietre, and he indicated the stallion with a flick of his chin. "Nice horse you got there."

"A gift from the Mereni Leader," I said. "We really need to negotiate a proper horse trading agreement with these people."

Dalon nodded thoughtfully. "Can't disagree if all their animals look like that," he said. He motioned to Lundis and Varin to come forward, which they did, glancing warily at both me and Senovo. "Here, let us take your horses. I imagine you'll be wanted at the meeting hall right away."

We dismounted and handed the horses over, though neither of the younger boys seemed willing to meet my eyes. Even so… could it really be this easy? I could hardly credit Dalon's reaction, or, rather, his *lack* of reaction.

Before I could press further, Senovo spoke up. "Dalon, what news of the High Priest. Is he—?"

"He still lives," Dalon said. "As of midday, at least. I haven't heard any different since then."

Senovo nodded tightly.

"Thank you, Dalon," I told him as he took Nietre. "We'll… talk later?"

"Yeah, I expect we will," Dalon said, and headed away with the Mereni horse.

I hefted our saddlebags over my shoulder and let out a slow breath.

"Come," Senovo said. "I… feel that we should not tarry."

"Of course," I said immediately, and followed him toward the village. Around us, the apprentices continued to regard us in silence. Most of them glanced away when I looked at them, but I caught Favian staring at me from the shelter of one of the lean-to sheds, anger and betrayal shining in his eyes.

Ignoring the pang in my chest as best I could, I hurried after Senovo, whose long legs carried him toward the temple — and High Priest Rhystel — with purposeful strides. As we entered the main part of the settlement, the whispers and stares that eddied around us were reminiscent of our final days in Meren. Only these faces were familiar to me — people I had known for years.

Senovo's fixed expression and obvious purpose seemed to keep anyone from actually approaching… or perhaps I had become untouchable now that my secret was common knowledge, a virtual outcast in all but name. My stomach churned, but I reminded myself forcefully that *Dalon*, of all people, had still seemed willing enough to speak to me in a civil manner. We walked past the meeting house without slowing. No doubt I, at least, should have stopped there to announce our return, but I was more than willing to put off the inevitable confrontation with Chief Volya as long as possible.

We crossed the village green and approached the long, low building that housed the temple and the priests' quarters. The burned-out huts scattered on the south end of the village were a stark reminder of the massacre that had occurred little more than a week ago, and my stomach grew even queasier. Senovo stopped at the main door and offered a deep obeisance to the gods, which I copied hastily.

Straightening, we entered and moved quickly through the long, deserted hallway toward the room near the back where the injured High Priest lay bedridden. Crenelo, one of the two surviving acolytes, looked up from the bedside at the sounds of our footsteps. With a cry, he leapt up from the chair he'd been sitting in and rushed forward, practically flinging himself into Senovo's arms.

I was shocked for a moment, but as Senovo pressed the boy close and murmured words of comfort to him, I stopped to think about it. Crenelo and the other acolyte, Reston, were barely more than children. The High Priest was like a father to them, and except for Senovo, all of their other comrades had been killed in the attack. Of *course* they would turn to him for comfort and strength. How alone they must have felt these past few days, keeping vigil over Rhystel and knowing nothing of what the future might hold.

Senovo held the overwrought boy patiently until he regained control of his emotions. When the hitch in Crenelo's breathing finally quieted, Senovo eased him back to arm's length and crouched to meet his eyes.

"Where is Reston?" he asked.

"He's sleeping now," Crenelo replied, wiping his eyes surreptitiously. "He was keeping watch over the High Priest last night and this morning."

Senovo nodded. "Why don't you go get some food and rest as well?" He placed a hand on the side of Crenelo's face, cupping his cheek. "You've done well under terrible circumstances, Little Brother. I'm so proud of you, and grateful to you both."

Crenelo's eyes welled up again, but the tears did not fall. "Thank you, Elder Brother," he said. "I'm... I'm really glad you're back now."

Senovo smiled, though it was a sad expression, not a happy one. "Rest, Crenelo. I will watch over High Priest Rhystel tonight."

Crenelo dipped his head and ducked out from under Senovo's hands—making his escape before he lost his composure again, I suspected. Only when the young acolyte was out of sight did Senovo sag, his eyes taking in Rhystel's appearance with dismay. I laid a hand on Senovo's upper arm, trying to offer support despite the tightness in my own throat.

The High Priest looked positively deathly. I could hardly credit that he still drew breath. His skin, which had been pale from blood loss the last time I'd seen him, was now yellowed and dry. His sunken cheeks and the deep hollows under his eyes added to the ghastly effect. The smell of festering flesh filled the room, emanating from the pus-soaked bandages swathing Rhystel's upper body. Only the slow rise and fall of his chest indicated that the old eunuch's spirit had not yet fled his failing body.

"… Senovo?" The weak whisper barely carried across the small room. "Is that you?"

Senovo shuddered under my hand before locking his muscles and straightening away from my gesture of support. He crossed to the low pallet in three strides and fell to his knees, gathering one of Rhystel's hands in both of his. Lowering his forehead to rest on their joined fingers, he said, "I am here, Elder Brother. Please, I must… make a confession to you."

I stood back, feeling like an intruder as the High Priest blinked open rheumy, unfocused eyes.

"Let me see your face, Little Brother," Rhystel said, pausing for breath between the words, "and tell me what troubles you so."

Senovo lifted his head, still grasping the High Priest's wrinkled hand like a lifeline. "Has Chief Volya told you about… about what happened in Meren?" he asked, stumbling uncharacteristically over the words.

Rhystel moved his head back and forth weakly against the pillows supporting him. "I fear Healer Sagdea has barred the Chief from my sickroom. Some rot about not wanting him to tire me out. It is… rather vexing, if I am to be perfectly honest."

Senovo swallowed, his throat bobbing. "I—" he began, only to hesitate before starting again. "I have lied to you about something important in the years since I first came to Draebard, Elder Brother."

"Oh?" Rhystel asked mildly. "Have you?"

Just tell him, I urged Senovo silently, holding my breath.

Senovo closed his eyes. "I am a shape-shifter. Ever since the Rhytheeri priests castrated me at the age of seventeen, I turn into a wolf in times of overwhelming stress."

Rhystel didn't even blink. He merely nodded and said, "Yes, Senovo. I am aware."

"I… you… *what?*" Senovo said, his usual eloquence deserting him completely.

"I love you like my own flesh and blood, Little Brother," the priest rasped, "but you are not nearly as subtle as you believe yourself to be."

When Senovo merely continued to stare at him, open-mouthed, Rhystel added, "However, I am sorry that you are now forced to confront the true implications of your gift before you are ready to do so."

"It isn't a gift, Elder Brother," Senovo said, regaining the use of his tongue. "It's a curse. The wolf is a killer."

"The wolf is a wolf," Rhystel corrected, his voice gentle.

"The wolf saved my life," I added, feeling the need to continue pointing this out to Senovo until it finally stuck.

"There you have it," Rhystel said, as if the matter was settled. His voice was growing even weaker than before, his strength nearly gone after only a few minutes awake.

"I don't know what to do now, Elder Brother," Senovo admitted, sounding utterly miserable.

Rhystel raised the ghost of a smile. "Some food and wine, I should think, followed by a few hours resting in that chair next to my bed... since I'm sure it's useless to try to get you to spend the night in your own bed. Then, tomorrow or perhaps the next day, a brief funeral service to perform. After that, I'm afraid it's rather up to you..."

His voice trailed off, drifting into sleep, or perhaps unconsciousness. My throat felt thick and clogged as Senovo let his head dip again to rest on the edge of the bed.

"Carivel," he said without moving or looking up, "forgive me, but could you give me some time alone with him?"

I had to clear my throat twice before I could answer. "Of course. I'll... um... go to the meeting house for a bit. Andoc is probably there. I'll bring him back with me when we're done."

Senovo nodded against the straw mattress, but did not reply. I stood, frozen, unable to think of a single word or gesture that would help, and eventually slunk from the room feeling utterly useless. I had to pause for several moments at the outer door of the temple before I was ready to face what lay beyond it. Finally, with a deep breath, I exited, bowed to the gods, and turned toward the meeting hall to find out what awaited me there.

The sun was disappearing below the rooflines of the village when I arrived. One wall of the sturdy building had been damaged by fire during the Alyrion attack; someone had patched it in our absence. I swallowed hard and entered, feeling an unwelcome sense of wrongdoing. Women were not often allowed in the hall, the rule of the tribe being the province of men. Resentment rose a moment later—had I not sufficiently proved myself as a man in the years I had lived here?

I followed the sound of people talking. As I grew closer, the indistinct murmur grew into intelligible conversation. My heart leapt a little when I recognized Andoc's familiar voice.

"They probably went straight to the temple barracks to check on High Priest Rhystel. I could go and check."

"No need," I said, poking my head in the open door. "I'm here."

Andoc's gaze flew to me, a brief smile breaking across his face that did not completely erase the lines of stress around his eyes. He was seated around a table with Volya, an elder named Tolmac, and Jacun, a friend and fellow warrior of Andoc's, who I did not know well.

Volya's expression was cold. "We expected you to come here immediately upon your arrival."

My lips pressed together in a thin, tense line. "I needed to accompany Senovo to the temple first, to check on High Priest Rhystel. My apologies for the delay."

Volya sat back in his chair, looking me up and down. "So," he said, "It's true, then? What Andoc said? I'll admit, I could hardly credit such a thing."

Tolmac was also staring at me, the two of them making the back of my neck prickle with their searching eyes. "No, Volya," said the old man, "I can see it now, can't you? In fact, it seems odd that no one noticed before, now that I think of it."

I bristled. Three long years I had lived as a man in this village, and now, suddenly, it was *obvious* that I was a woman? Andoc was looking at me sympathetically, his eyes urging caution. I ignored him, my temper rising.

"I am as I have always been, Elder Tolmac," I said, biting the words off with precision. "My body may be a woman's, but I have lived as a man and proven my ability to do a job the people of Draebard insist can only be done by a man."

"And violated our religion and our trust by doing so," Volya said flatly. "For you are *not* a man. You are a woman."

My heart was beginning to pound now. It was difficult to keep my fists from clenching at my sides. "The Mereni follow the same religion we do. Yet they have women as leaders and warriors. You obviously value them enough to seek them out as allies in our time of need. Perhaps it is time to reconsider Draebard's position on such matters."

My words were on the cusp of what was acceptable for a man addressing the village Chief, and far over the line for a woman. Andoc was watching Volya warily, saying nothing to discourage me, yet obviously concerned. Tolmac looked rather taken aback at my audacity. Jacun appeared to be somewhere on the spectrum between entertained and impressed.

"Whether Draebard will accept you as some sort of female *Horse Mistress* remains to be seen," Volya said, and the trickle of ice in his voice sent a faint shiver up my spine. "However, there is one thing you must do first if you wish to stay here."

In the corner of my eye, I saw Andoc stiffen. The cold feeling inside me spread a little further, despite the warmth of the evening outside. "What is that?" I asked.

"When he first approached me to tell me about your deception, Andoc made it clear that he considered you to be under his protection," Volya said, his frosty gaze now including the First Warrior as well. "Given that claim, I think it would be best if you two were handfasted as soon as is practical, given the current upheaval at the temple. A public handfasting would be best, to show the village your willingness to acknowledge the truth and put your history of lies behind you. Once Rhystel's funeral has taken place, Senovo can do it."

"*What?*" I asked, not sure I'd heard correctly. Across the table, Andoc was looking slightly pale, but not nearly as gobsmacked as I was feeling right now.

"Yes," said the Elder thoughtfully. "That should help to calm some of the confusion and outrage over such a scandalous deception. An excellent idea, Volya."

I opened my mouth to say something—I wasn't sure what—but another glance at Andoc showed him shaking his head at me, almost imperceptibly. I nearly ignored him, but Andoc had done much to earn my trust in the last few days and I knew, intellectually, that he had far more experience dealing with Chief Volya than I did. Clamping my jaw shut, I allowed him to take the lead.

He cleared his throat. "Carivel and I will need to discuss the details with Senovo, Chief Volya. As you know, he is somewhat overwhelmed with responsibilities right now, as the last remaining senior priest."

Volya waved the words away irritably. "Yes, yes. Of course," he said. "The sooner, the better, though."

Jacun was still watching the whole exchange the same way one might watch an interesting sporting contest. He did, however, speak up for the first time at that point. "Perhaps we could adjourn for the evening, then? Everything is in readiness for the arrival of Leader Magoldis and her delegation tomorrow. I need to speak to Andoc for a few minutes about the plans for integrating our warriors with the Mereni, though."

"Very well," Volya said, his expression turning sour. "If I'm to face *that woman* tomorrow, I'm going to need a flagon of good wine and a full night's rest first."

The meeting adjourned in awkward silence shortly thereafter. Andoc ushered me outside into the deepening dusk, with Jacun tagging along behind us. Once Tolmac was out of hearing range, heading off toward his own bed after a final long, searching look at me, Jacun spoke up.

"You really are constitutionally incapable of doing anything the easy way, Andoc," he observed casually.

"What can I say? I get bored easily," Andoc growled back, his heart obviously not in the banter.

"And *you*," Jacun said, his attention turning to me. "I have to say, I did *not* see this coming. I have absolutely no clue how you managed to pull it off for so long, but—well played, Carivel. I'm impressed."

My nerves were still on edge, as was my temper. "Is that all?" I snapped. "You're not going to berate me for putting Draebard's horses at risk and trampling our culture and religion?"

Jacun shrugged. "Seems kind of pointless, don't you think? Especially since I'm going to be fighting alongside women warriors in a few days. If anything, I should probably offer you condolences on your upcoming handfasting to this lout." He jerked his chin toward Andoc.

My heart was pounding double time again, making me feel dizzy and short of breath.

"About that—" I began.

"Not here," Andoc said. "Soon, though. Jacun, did you really need to talk to me?"

"Nothing that won't keep," Jacun said. "Go speak with Senovo. And Rhystel, too, if he's awake."

Andoc nodded and clapped him on the shoulder. "Thanks, old friend. Bet you didn't expect anything like this when I rode back into town yesterday."

Jacun grinned at him. "Eh, it keeps life interesting, that's for certain. And I can hardly wait to meet this Varanis who rubbed your face in the dirt of the combat ring." Jacun flashed me a quick smile as well. "See you around, Carivel. Try not to let things get to you too much. You've still got plenty of friends in Draebard, I'm sure."

Jacun's words lightened my mood slightly, and I tried to smile back at him in the late evening gloom. "Thanks, Jacun," I said. "Really. That means a lot."

Once we were alone, I turned to Andoc and practically fell into his arms.

"I keep thinking it would have been easier to run," I said into his shoulder.

"Yeah," he agreed, "it probably would have been. I'm sorry—I couldn't think of any way to warn you ahead of time about the handfasting thing."

"Not your fault," I said, and made myself pull back. "Jacun was right. We need to get back to Senovo. I'm worried about him, Andoc."

"Did he talk to Rhystel?" Andoc asked as we separated and started the trek back to the temple barracks.

"Yes," I said. "The High Priest said he'd known about Senovo's shifting for a long time."

Andoc came to an abrupt halt. "*Seriously*?" He shook his head. "That sneaky old bastard. He never said a thing."

"I don't think I've ever seen Senovo lost for words like that before," I added.

"I can imagine," Andoc said as he started walking again. "I'm just glad Rhystel hung on long enough for Senovo to get back and speak with him. I think it would have eaten him up inside not to have had the chance to get absolution from the old man."

I nodded agreement. "There's something else you should probably know," I said, after a slight hesitation. "Senovo was struggling on the ride back—with the wolf, I mean. I don't think I can really do what you do for him, when he gets like that. So… I… talked him into changing voluntarily last night, while we were alone in the middle of nowhere and he couldn't hurt anybody."

Andoc's eyes bit into me, sharp as an arrow. "And he *agreed*?"

"Well, to be honest, I don't think he would have been able to hold on much longer regardless. But, yes, he let the change happen without fighting it, and he spent a few hours hunting rabbits before we curled up in front of the fire to sleep. In the morning, he shifted back when I asked him to, and while it wasn't *pleasant*, it also wasn't nearly as bad as the two times I saw before. So… I guess that's good… right?"

The more I talked, the less certain I became. Last night, it had been such an obvious decision. Now, as I listened to the words coming out of my mouth, it sounded an awful lot like I'd taken advantage of Senovo's weakness to get him to do something he didn't want to do. As the silence dragged on, worry began to squeeze my chest, making it hard to breathe.

When Andoc spoke, though, there was wonder in his voice, not censure. "Gods, Carivel. What I would have given to see that for myself."

All at once, I could breathe again. "You think it was the right thing to do, then?" I couldn't help asking.

"I have no idea," Andoc said, still sounding faintly stunned. "But if he seemed all right afterward, surely it was better than letting him fight against the wolf and lose."

Relieved, I let the last of the panic ebb away, only for it to slam right back into me when I realized we'd reached the back door of the temple. The temple, where we would now have to tell Senovo that Volya intended me to be handfasted to Andoc. To the man he loved.

SIX

I could still run, I told myself. If I had to, I could still leave before I destroyed everything.

Coward that I was, though, I let myself be led inside. The temple was designed to house a score of priests and acolytes. The unnatural silence of the place since the attack seemed more upsetting each time I came here. It should be filled with the bustle of devotions and lit with flickering lamplight long into the night, not dark and quiet, its handful of occupants holding their breath in anticipation of yet another death.

I followed Andoc to the High Priest's sick room, where he knocked lightly on the rough wood of the doorframe. Rather than finding Senovo watching over an unconscious Rhystel, though, we entered to find Rhystel awake, looking down at Senovo's bowed head lying on the mattress beside him, his hand resting on the back of the younger man's neck as if in benediction.

"Good evening, Elder Brother," Andoc said quietly as we slipped into the room.

Rhystel looked up, but seemed to have difficulty seeing us in the candlelight. "Who's there?" he asked.

Andoc crossed to the side of the bed, and I followed, standing at his shoulder. "It's Andoc and Carivel."

"Oh, good. Good," said the old priest absently.

Senovo blinked his eyes open, raising his head to look up at us. Rhystel's hand slid away from its position at his neck. Senovo caught it and lowered the old man's arm gently to the bed.

"Hello, *amadi*," Andoc said, gripping Senovo's shoulder. "We've just come from meeting with Chief Volya. I'm afraid there's been a development I didn't foresee."

I chewed at my lower lip, not understanding how Andoc could sound so calm about the whole thing.

"What's this?" Rhystel asked, sounding more coherent than when we'd first come in. "Come now, Andoc, you know I'm starving for village gossip since the Healer stopped allowing members of the council to visit me."

Andoc sighed, and looked at me, a question in his eyes. I nodded. It wasn't as though the High Priest could do much to me at this point, and both Andoc and Senovo trusted the old man's counsel.

"As gossip goes, I suppose this is about as juicy as it gets," Andoc said. "Our friend Carivel has been living as a man, but she was born with a woman's body. Leader Magoldis agreed to the treaty with Draebard at least partly because she assumed that having a female Horse Mistress meant Volya had softened his stance on women doing men's jobs. We've backed the Chief into a corner—he has to accept Carivel or risk the treaty with the Mereni—but now he's decided that Carivel will be less of a threat to the status quo if she and I are handfasted as soon as possible. Preferably publicly."

Senovo looked taken aback, but within seconds the impassive mask he used to hide his thoughts slid over his face.

The High Priest lifted an eyebrow. "How extraordinary," he said. "Nevertheless, Chief or not, no one can compel two people to enter into a handfasting if they do not desire to do so."

"I don't believe that is truly an issue," Senovo said, in a detached tone of voice that I didn't like *at all*. "Andoc and Carivel have recently entered into a romantic relationship. They are a compatible couple, and obviously deeply in love."

My mouth had fallen open. I shut it and crowded forward. "I entered into a romantic relationship with *both of you!*" I snapped. "Don't you dare act like you're not a part of it!"

Senovo's expression did not change. "Eburosi culture does not place the same importance on relationships with eunuchs as relationships between men and women. At best, such a relationship is a stage in one's sexual education. At worst, it is light entertainment."

"Oh, *Senovo*," Rhystel said softly, even as I cried, "No—you do *not* get to belittle what we have— what you and Andoc have had for years!"

Andoc cleared his throat. "Could we maybe talk about this calmly instead of shouting about it?"

"I'm not feeling particularly calm right now," I said angrily, "and I'm not sure why you are."

"Because I know that being handfasted to you, Carivel—or not—does nothing to change my feelings for either of you," he said, adding, "No offense meant to the institution, Elder Brother."

"The heart wants what it wants," Rhystel said, his voice growing weaker again as his strength ebbed. "I wish I could solve this for the three you, but I fear such matters are out of my hands now. Carivel... know that I absolve you of your deception and wish you well, no matter your choices in the coming days. Perhaps we in Draebard have not understood... all the gods have tried to tell us... about men and women..."

His words trailed off, his eyes closing in sleep once again. Senovo gripped the old man's hand loosely in his own, not looking up at us.

"Senovo," Andoc said. "You can say no to this. Either of you can, and it won't happen."

"On the contrary, you should both agree to it," Senovo said, still not making eye contact. "It makes sense. Volya is trying to place you in a context that is more understandable to the people of Draebard, Carivel. It costs you nothing to go along with it. However, you must refuse the public handfasting. Such a thing would be intended for the curious and the gawkers, as a way to put you in your place, so to speak. Not for your own happiness and well-being. As your priest, I will not allow it."

I bit back the angry words that wanted to come, and made myself breathe deeply for a moment or two. As the presiding priest, it was, in fact, Senovo's prerogative to prevent a public handfasting if he suspected that the parties involved were being coerced. And, in fact, a public handfasting was just about the last thing I wanted. I was simply angry, and lashing out at whoever was available.

"I can't make this decision right now," I said eventually. "I need some space to think about it. I'm still not convinced that the best thing I could do for you wouldn't be to saddle up Kekenu and leave town."

"And what about the treaty with the Mereni?" Andoc asked, not unkindly.

I gripped my forehead with one hand, fingertips digging into my temples, where an incipient headache was beginning to erupt. "I don't know," I said, feeling nausea swirl in my stomach as the true weight of my decision settled onto my shoulders. "I have to think about things."

"Go to the horse pens," Senovo suggested. "That is where you feel most comfortable, I think. Just know that you will not be harming me in any way by agreeing to this."

It bothered me a great deal that I couldn't tell if he was lying or not. Suddenly, the need to be near my horses was nearly overwhelming. Still, though...

"Will you two be all right here?" I knew Andoc would not leave Senovo's side with Rhystel hovering near death, but I could not abandon them without asking the question.

"I won't leave him," Andoc said, and leaned down to kiss my forehead.

"Senovo?" I asked.

"He will not leave me," Senovo echoed, the ghost of a smile lifting one corner of his lips, though it came nowhere near his eyes.

"Send for me if you need me," I told them, and pressed my own kiss to Senovo's temple. "You know where to find me."

⤙ ♕ ⤚

The pens were quiet, with most of the lads gone home for the evening now that darkness had nearly fallen. The smell, along with the sounds of horses moving about in their pens and the occasional snort or nicker—all these things combined to soothe my troubled thoughts to a degree. I wandered among the corrals, taking advantage of the last hint of gray evening light to check on Kekenu... on Andoc's bay gelding... on Volya's buckskin mare and her creamy white foal.

When I approached the pen where Dalon had put Nietre earlier, I was surprised to hear a human voice speaking in low tones. As I reached the fence, I recognized Dalon himself, standing next to the stallion's neck. The black horse was only visible as a darker shadow in the failing light, but I could hear the rhythmic *huff, huff, huff* of his breath as he sniffed at Dalon's arms and torso.

I whistled low and soft, wanting to get their attention without startling them. The stallion looked up, ears pricked, and Dalon called, "Who's there?"

"It's me," I replied, and Nietre stepped forward, crossing the distance to where I stood outside the pen and shoving his nose in my face. I motioned him back to a more polite distance before reaching out to scratch the itchy places on his head. Dalon joined us at the fence a moment later.

"Bit of an attitude on this one," Dalon said, cocking a thumb toward the stallion. "Bet he could be a nightmare in the wrong hands."

I nodded. "You bet right. They say he killed one person and maimed a couple of others back in Meren."

Dalon blew out a breath. "And he was a gift, you say? Did you piss someone off while you were there, or what?"

That startled a laugh out of me. "I think it was just a clever way for them to be rid of him and make it look like they were being generous," I said. "Seriously, though—he rides all right, and allegedly drives. I rode him day before yesterday and I've never galloped so fast in my life. He's fine. He just needs consistent work and a fair hand. Besides, can you imagine the kind of foals he'll sire for us? I think we came out on the better end of the deal."

Dalon snorted agreement before changing the subject. "You get all squared away with Volya and the rest of them?" he asked.

The momentary calm and relief that came from talking horses with a fellow horseman fled.

"Not yet," I said.

"Yeah... I didn't get the impression that old Volya was too pleased with you," Dalon said.

"I don't think anyone's too pleased with me right now," I pointed out warily. "Which makes me wonder, why are *you* being so chatty and, well, *civil*? You already hated my guts, even before this."

Dalon shrugged. "Thought you were a queer before, didn't I? Turns out you're a girl. No wonder you were always mooning after the warriors when they practiced, and putting off poor little Limdya all the time."

I paused, trying to wrap my mind around this logic. "So... you'd rather answer to a female boss than a male one who likes men instead of women?"

"Eh, I've seen you with the horses for years. You're good with 'em, and if anything bad were going to happen because you're a girl, it probably would have already, right? 'Sides, we've got all these Mereni coming in a few days. Guess we have to get used to it." He paused, and snickered a bit. "They're saying a Mereni girl beat Andoc in single combat. That true?"

"It is," I replied, unable to stop the hint of amusement from entering my voice. "She kicked him in the balls. Felled him like a tree in a windstorm. Though I wouldn't let her hear you call her a girl—she was a full head taller than Andoc, and almost as broad."

Dalon winced in sympathy. "That must have been a sight to behold," he said. "S'pose things are gonna start changing around here from now on."

"I imagine so," I said, suddenly struck by the surrealism of having a pleasant evening chat with *Dalon*, of all people. How was this my life now?

"I should warn you, though," Dalon continued. "Some of the boys aren't gonna be so quick to accept you. I know Favian's pretty upset, for one."

I remembered the angry look the lad thrown me when Senovo and I first arrived, and felt a pang of regret. Favian was the youngest apprentice at the horse pens, and had an unusual talent with the animals. He'd looked up to me… before all this.

"I'll try to talk to him," I promised. "Make him understand."

"You'll not have an easy time of it here," said Dalon. "But you won't get any lip from me, not as long as you keep doing right by the horses, and by the lads."

"Thank you, Dalon," I said, meaning it quite sincerely. "I couldn't ask for a better second-in-command. You've carried more of the responsibility of Horse Master than I have, since Jorun was killed."

Dalon's grin was lopsided. "Well… if you want to step down and give me the job, you just have to say so…"

"Not on your life," I replied, and suddenly became aware that I had made my decision without even realizing it. "I'm afraid Draebard is stuck with me for the time being."

⤙ ♕ ⤚

I stayed at the pens long after Dalon left for his bed, leaning against the very same post where I had spent the night waiting for Cassira to foal. Where I had first seen the wolf, and heard the distant sounds of the Alyrions' night attack on the village. I dozed for a bit, waking intermittently to turn my situation over in my mind.

I would not be driven from Draebard, leaving Andoc and Senovo behind or forcing them to flee in order to stay with me. If Volya said I had to be handfasted to Andoc, I would be handfasted to Andoc. We would simply have to convince Senovo of our sincerity when it came to our continued desire for him as well.

After drowsing for longer than I had intended, I roused myself and headed back to the temple. It was well into the depths of the night, easily past midnight. The village was silent and dark except for the occasional hearth throwing weak, flickering light through the windows of a hut. The sense of solitude was reassuring after being the focus of so much attention over the past several days. I strolled past the familiar landmarks, so well known to me that the darkness was barely a hindrance.

When I arrived at the temple, I realized that I was unsure of the protocol this late at night. Should I knock? After a moment's contemplation, I opened the door quietly, and entered unannounced. If anyone was sleeping, I had no desire to wake them.

No one was sleeping.

As I approached the open door leading to Rhystel's room, it was to find the small space filled with people. The stench of decay and sickness had grown worse in the hours I'd been gone, but Senovo and Andoc still hovered at the sides of the bed. Each of them had an arm wrapped around the shoulders of one of the two young acolytes. The boys were trembling, obviously trying to hide their distress, but betrayed by an occasional sniffle and hitched breath.

In one corner, Healer Sagdea stood leaning against the wall, her arms folded, watching over the scene silently. Wisps of white hair escaped the messy braid that hung down her back, and she was dressed in a tatty robe thrown over sleeping clothes, as if she had been roused in a hurry. The old woman glanced up at my arrival and tipped her chin in acknowledgement, but did not speak or do anything to draw the others' attention to me.

My eyes drifted to the High Priest, drawn by the sound of his wet, wheezing breath. Andoc and Senovo each held one of the old eunuch's hands in one of theirs, but Rhystel showed no sign of awareness. As another labored, bubbling gasp squeezed free of his chest, I decided that was probably just as well. I stood framed in the doorway in silent vigil as the High Priest's dying body continued to struggle for life.

The minutes crawled by, with the pauses between Rhystel's rasping inhalations growing longer and longer, until he finally exhaled quietly... and breathed no more. Next to Senovo, Reston began to sob as the reality hit, burying his face in the older priest's shoulder.

Across from him, Crenelo ducked out from under Andoc's arm and fled the room, pushing past me in his haste. Andoc looked up, and though his expression was calm, I could see the redness ringing his shining eyes. It hit me all at once that Andoc must have been close to the High Priest for nearly as long as he'd been close to Senovo. His grief was personal, and obviously profound. I stepped into the room and came to a stop behind him, wrapping my arms loosely around his chest, feeling the faint tremor of suppressed emotion there.

The corpse on the pallet was a pitiful sight as Healer Sagdea stepped forward to confirm Rhystel's passing with a wrinkled hand held just above his nose and mouth. She nodded, her own complexion pale. I expected her to reach down and lift the sheet up to cover the old man's face, but I realized a moment later that Senovo was still holding Rhystel's fingers loosely entwined in his right hand, even as he pressed Reston against his shoulder in a one-armed embrace with his left.

I was the only person here who did not have a long-standing personal connection to the High Priest. It made me feel like something of an outsider, at least until Andoc covered my hands with his own and squeezed. I let my chin rest lightly on the top of his head, holding him from behind as he regained his composure.

On the other side of the low bed, Senovo looked utterly blank. *Lost.* His eyes traveled slowly from the dead man's face to the hand he still held in his own. As if moving underwater, he laid the claw-like appendage down on the High Priest's bandaged chest.

"Reston," he said, pausing to swallow hard when the word emerged as a barely audible croak. "Please go and find Crenelo. Gather the funerary herbs and bring them here to me."

Reston stayed pressed to Senovo's side for a long moment, silent sobs wracking his young body. Eventually, he nodded agreement against the dampened robes at Senovo's shoulder and pushed away, not meeting any of our eyes as he left the room in search of his friend.

"Thank you for your attendance, Healer Sagdea," Senovo continued in the same distant, dazed tone. "Please, return to your bed and get some rest. I will attend to the body."

The Healer placed a hand on Senovo's shoulder. "There is no shame in asking for help, High Priest Senovo," she said.

Senovo flinched slightly at the title, but did not react otherwise. "Your concern does you credit, Healer, but it is unnecessary. The funeral ceremony will take place tomorrow evening, once the sun is down. Thank you again."

Sagdea offered a shallow bow and saw herself out of the room. Her eyes dragged over me briefly as she left, but I could not read her impassive expression. Andoc gave my hands a final squeeze, and I let my arms fall away as he rose to cross to where Senovo was seated. To my surprise, Senovo half-raised an arm in a fending-off gesture while he was still two steps away.

"Not yet," he said, still sounding far away. "Please, my friend."

Andoc blew out a breath and turned to the bed. "Very well," he said. "I'll stay to help you and the boys prepare the body, if you don't mind. Least I can do for the old rogue. Carivel, you don't have to—"

"I'll stay," I said quickly. "Though you'll have to show me what to do."

Reston and Crenelo returned a few moments later bearing baskets of fragrant herbs, along with a large mortar and pestle. The process of stripping and washing the body, pounding the herbs to paste and smearing them over the old man's wounds was strangely intimate... heartbreakingly so. The young acolytes wept silently through most of it, obviously kept from total collapse only by Senovo's quiet strength. I suspected that strength only held because of the boys' desperate need for it, and I grieved more for Senovo than I did for Rhystel.

When the body was neatly wrapped in a clean shroud, we carried it to the dark, silent village green and deposited it in a bed of fresh conifer boughs to await the funeral ceremony and pyre the following evening. Senovo led us to bathe in the river afterward, cleansing ourselves of death both literally and symbolically. Back at the temple, Senovo went to the refectory and heated cups of mead. Into the boys' cups, he crumbled a mixture of dried herbs and brown powder before commanding them to drink and return to their rooms.

Reston and Crenelo took the mixture eagerly, practically swilling it in their haste. When they had left, Senovo's knees buckled and he sat down heavily at one of the large trestle tables. "They will sleep dreamlessly for a few hours now," he said in a flat voice.

Andoc and I moved to bracket him on the low bench seat. I half-expected him to break down, but he only stared across the room, his empty gaze leagues away.

"I can't feel anything," he said, in the tone one might use when discussing the weather.

"*Amadi…*" Andoc began, only to trail off.

Suddenly, I knew what to do—what needed to happen now. I stood up and faced the other two. "Can the village spare both of you until morning?"

"There is nothing more to be done this night," Senovo said, still distant.

"Yes, it can. Why?" Andoc asked.

"Come with me, both of you," I said in lieu of answering. Taking Senovo by the arm, I urged him up. He followed meekly enough, though he seemed slightly unsteady on his feet.

I led them out of the suffocating atmosphere of the temple, still thick with the smell of death and pungent herbs. Outside, the night was cool and misty. I skirted around the village green with its sad, sheet-wrapped bundle, heading south. The waning moon was up now, visible through shreds of drifting clouds as we reached the edge of the village. Unlike the rolling pastures to the north and the craggy plateaus to the east, the land south of Draebard was thick forest. It was here that we harvested firewood and timber for building, using teams of horses to drag felled logs down the series of rough tracks that wended through the woods.

It was along one of those tracks that I now led Senovo and Andoc, away from the buildings and sleeping townsfolk. Senovo moved like a man in a dream, allowing me to guide his footsteps along the packed dirt of the logging road without protest. Andoc's silence as he moved to flank Senovo on the other side made me think he had divined my purpose. And, indeed, after a few more minutes of walking, he indicated a clearing off to the side, soft spring grass illuminated by the moonlight.

"What about here?" he asked.

"Perfect," I said, and between us we led Senovo into the center of the secluded forest glade.

When we stopped, he seemed to jolt into sudden awareness. "Where are we?" he asked. "I don't—"

I faced him and grasped his shoulders. "We're in the middle of nowhere in the woods. Away from people. It's just us. You can let go now."

Senovo shuddered under my hands. "Andoc…?" he asked in a small voice, his eyes seeking the other man's.

Andoc placed a strong hand on the nape of Senovo's neck, grounding him. "It's all right," he said. "I'm here. We both are. We won't let anything happen."

Senovo's breath hitched. He lowered his chin to his chest for a long moment. Then, without looking up, he raised his hands to unfasten the ties on his robes and let the heavy material slide off his shoulders to land on the ground. I stepped back, giving him space. He removed his sandals, naked now in the weak silver light of the crescent moon.

Turning away from us as if ashamed, he dropped to his hands and knees with a sharp cry. A moment later, the wolf bounded a few steps away and turned, a whine rising from his throat. Andoc put an arm around my shoulders, pulling me close to his side as we watched. I went willingly.

The whining continued, heart-wrenching in its bereft sadness. After a few moments, the wolf raised his voice in a full-throated howl that resonated in my own chest and prickled the hair at the back of my neck. Throwing back his head and pointing his muzzle toward the moon, the animal bayed out its loss to the night sky. The chilling noise rose and fell, echoing off of the trees and ridges surrounding us until it seemed all-pervasive.

SEVEN

Andoc sucked in a breath next to me. It took me a few moments to realize that other voices had joined Senovo's, the howls of wild wolves intertwining with his own in an unearthly chorus of grief. They were *close*, too. I shivered, overcome by a sense of the surreal. The feeling of wonder grew as the howls trailed off, replaced by the sound of panting and rustling in the undergrowth at the edge of the clearing. Gray shapes began to appear from out of the trees. First, a single scar-faced old veteran, then other wolves in twos and threes, until there were almost a dozen.

I should have been scared. I *know* I should have. I felt Andoc tense beside me, but a moment later he relaxed with an audible breath and shook his head. I looked up at him with a question in my expression, and he shrugged.

"Yeah, I know," he said, as if I'd spoken aloud. "It's crazy, but what the hell. If they decide to turn on us, at least it'll have been an interesting way to go."

The wolves were ignoring us for the most part, milling around Senovo instead. I felt a brief pang of worry, but the sleek, silver-gray animals showed no aggression toward him. Quite the opposite, in fact—the strange wolves crowded close, jostling for position to rub their bodies along his and nuzzle at his jaw as if offering comfort.

"By all the gods..." Andoc breathed in awe.

Within the ever-moving swarm of furry bodies, it would have been easy to lose track of Senovo, were he not at the center of the mob—the fixed point around which the rest rotated. As Andoc and I continued to watch, I began to get more of a sense of the dynamics... at first, the pack leaders kept the others at bay so they could pay their respects. The senior wolves were followed by those lower in the pecking order, ducking in to lick at Senovo's throat and rub up against his shoulders. Finally, the young wolves—gangly adolescents—slunk in, many rolling onto their backs, offering their vulnerable necks and bellies, paws waving in the air and tails wagging when he deigned to drape a paw over them and greet them with a sniff and a lick.

With the single exception of Senovo's own transformation, it was the most extraordinary thing I'd ever seen in my twenty-three years of life.

Eventually, the frenzy of lupine affection and comfort subsided, the strange wolves settling down near Senovo in pairs and trios, watching him with lolling tongues. Senovo whined again, his attention turning back to the two of us. Andoc released his grip on my shoulder and went down on one knee, showing no surprise when the wolf sidled forward to lap at his throat and jaw in much the same way the other wolves had greeted Senovo earlier.

I fell to my knees next to them, receiving the same treatment, even as the other wolves looked on curiously. The large animal shoved at us until we both toppled into an inelegant sprawl, his whines subsiding into plaintive whimpers. Eventually, we ended up tangled together, the wolf half in our laps with his head burrowing into the space under Andoc's left arm. I dragged my fingers rhythmically through the thick undercoat along the wolf's flank, curling my upper body along the length of his back to rest my head and shoulder against Andoc's side.

The animal continued to whimper out his distress, hitching himself even closer against our bodies. My own eyes burned and my nose started to run at the display of primal grief, so raw and immediate. The wolf hurt; it sought comfort and received it. If only human interactions could all be so straightforward.

The three of us huddled in the middle of the clearing, wrapped around each other, surrounded by a pack of wild wolves watching us with interest as the night wore on. Eventually, the darkness began to give way to predawn, and finally true dawn as the sun peeked over the barren ridge running above the tree line in the east. The wolf moaned low in its throat, writhing against us. Suddenly, we were holding Senovo's naked body, his chest hitching as he pressed his face into the juncture of Andoc's neck and shoulder.

I scooted around until I could embrace him fully from behind, wrapping him up between us. A few moments later, I heard a snuffling noise next to me, and something wet and cold fluttered against my arm where it lay half-entwined with one of

Senovo's. I opened my eyes, finding myself face-to-face with the scarred pack leader, its gray fur backlit by the golden light of the rising sun. We regarded each other steadily for the space of several heartbeats before the yellow eyes blinked, and the animal turned to leave.

Around us, the wolves melted away, returning to the depths of the forest as if they had never been there at all. Distant movement caught my eye and I looked up to the ridge top above us. Three riders on horseback stood silhouetted by the morning light, looking down at us. One of them extended an arm, as if pointing. I straightened away from Senovo, blinking, and ran a hand over my face to clear the cobwebs left by a largely sleepless night.

"Carivel?" Andoc asked, drawing my attention. When I looked back at the ridge, the riders had gone.

"Nothing," I said after a moment, and ran a quick gaze around the clearing. "Looks like our furry friends have all left."

Andoc craned around to confirm it as best he could without dislodging Senovo. "Huh. Looks like it," was all he said.

In his arms, Senovo's breathing had finally quieted. The eunuch twisted until he could see a little bit of our surroundings.

"What... just... happened, exactly?" he asked after a short stretch of silence.

I opened my mouth to explain, only to close it again when I couldn't think of any words.

Andoc cleared his throat and stepped in. "You turned into a wolf and somehow called a pack of wild wolves to us. They stayed with us until the sun came up and you changed back, at which point they all wandered back into the woods."

Senovo blinked. "... oh," he said eventually, still not moving from Andoc's embrace.

I rose on uncertain legs, the tingle of returning blood flow making my flesh prickle. Senovo's discarded robes and sandals were a few steps away; I picked them up and brought them back to him.

"We have to get back, don't we," I said, knowing it was true. By rights, I should have been at the horse pens by first light, but I was confident that Dalon would have things well in hand. No doubt Senovo and Andoc both had things to do in preparation for the arrival of the Mereni delegation later. Not to mention for the funeral tonight.

"Yes, we do," Senovo agreed, although he stayed where he was for a moment longer before reluctantly pushing away from Andoc and dressing himself.

The three of us were quiet and thoughtful on the walk back. The other two, I suspected, were still too raw from High Priest Rhystel's passing to give much thought to the implications of what we'd just experienced. I, however, found it fascinating. Why would strange wolves comfort an unfamiliar lone wolf? And, perhaps even odder, why would grizzled pack leaders defer to a strange, castrated male who displayed no dominant characteristics? There had been no snarling or snapping or wrestling for position—the other wolves had simply accepted Senovo among them without fuss.

I had no idea what that could mean, but it seemed, well, *important* somehow.

Before I was really ready, we reached the edge of the settlement. The smell of delicious food wafted to us from the direction of the cookhouse, and my stomach rumbled. I suddenly realized that I hadn't eaten a thing since midday yesterday, which meant that Senovo probably hadn't either. I snuck a glance at Andoc, who was, as expected, regarding me with a raised eyebrow.

"Let me guess," he said. "In the absence of my constant reminders, you both have skipped one or more meals and only just noticed the fact."

"I'll get food and bring it to the temple," I said meekly.

It was more than a bit embarrassing, to be honest. I was an adult, and had successfully been taking care of myself even when I was still a child. Admittedly, the amount of stress I'd been under lately was considerable, but there was some secret part of me that simply loved the idea of someone caring enough to look after me. To provide for my needs. I flushed, and ducked away toward the cookhouse.

Unfortunately, the big round hut in the center of the village was an unavoidable reminder of Gretya, its longtime proprietress, who was killed during the attack. Gretya, in turn, was an unavoidable reminder of Jorun, my mentor. I wondered how he would have reacted upon discovering my birth sex. Perhaps it was better this way—I could never know the truth of it now, so it was easy to pretend he would have judged me on my merits over the years he'd known me, and welcomed me back to Draebard with open arms.

Thinking about it so soon after seeing Senovo lose Rhystel was making me teary-eyed again. I blinked rapidly, forcing the feelings down into the cavity of my chest.

Gretya's three daughters had immediately taken over running the cookhouse after her tragic death. The youngest daughter, Limdya, was behind the counter this morning when I entered, and I winced a bit. Limdya had demonstrated a stubbornly single-minded crush on me, when everyone still thought me a man. I had tried to put her off as gently as I could, but—

"Carivel." Limdya's voice was flat and angry. She stared at me with the same searching look that most people seemed to have since I returned—looking for evidence, looking for something that gave me away as female.

I was growing to hate that stare.

"Limdya," I said.

Limdya slapped her hands down on the counter top. "You've got a lot of nerve coming in here. I should throw you out on your ear."

I bristled. "I came to buy food. The High Priest passed away early this morning. Senovo and Andoc were up all night with him, and none of us have eaten."

"If you think I'm cooking for you, Carivel, you're a fool as well as a liar," Limdya snapped.

"Oh?" I said, my own temper barely reined in after a night of grief and little sleep. "Has my being born female harmed you in some way, Limdya? Because I can't really see that it has."

When I'd walked in, I'd been one of the first customers of the morning, but as others drifted in, we were quickly drawing an audience. Somehow, it wasn't enough to stop me.

"You know, I *never* encouraged your advances," I continued, anger at the unfairness of it all driving me on. "I tried to be gentle about it, but I never said or did *one single thing* to lead you on!"

"You… conceited *bitch*!" Limdya gasped. "That has nothing to do with it! '*Oh, Limdya, women aren't allowed to work with the horses!*' '*Oh, Limdya, I'm sorry you can't come with me to see the foal being born, but if a woman was nearby it might cause the foal to be stillborn!'* You're a filthy *hypocrite!*"

I felt increasingly sick as she parroted my own words back to me in a singsong voice. Some of my anger drained away as the reality of my behavior hit me.

"I worked hard to get where I am," I said, my voice growing quiet. A defensive note crept in that I couldn't seem to help. "I risked everything to become Jorun's apprentice."

"How nice for you," Limdya spat. "Too bad you didn't stop to think about the rest of us."

Gods. It was far too true for comfort. I'd been focused on living *my* life. Keeping *my* secret. I'd known for a long time that Limdya was also fascinated by the horses. Aside from feeling vaguely bad about it, though, I hadn't hesitated to use the old line about only men caring for the animals whenever she seemed in danger of getting too close to me.

And yet, why was it *my* job to change things? If Limdya was serious enough about it, she could bloody well have done the same thing I did.

Maybe she didn't want to run away to a new village and live as a boy, said a voice in the back of my head. *Maybe she wanted to work with animals and still live with her family. Still be a woman.*

"Fine," I told her, just wanting the conversation to be over. "You know what? You're absolutely right. I'm a weak and terrible person. I won't darken your doorway again, and I won't ask for food for myself. That said, Draebard's First Warrior and the new High Priest are still hungry. Don't take your anger at me out on them."

Limdya glared daggers at me and slapped two portions down on the counter. She swept the coins I laid down into the wooden till box without even looking at them. I gathered up the food and headed to the door, only to stop a few steps away.

"The Mereni think very differently about men and women," I said without turning around. "Things are going to change, from here on out."

"And to think," came Limdya's bitter voice in reply, "it only took the death of dozens of people, including my mother."

I cringed, and walked out without saying another word. Outside, the town was waking up as the sun crept higher in the sky. Perhaps it was just as well Limdya had refused to serve me;

I was so nauseated by what had just transpired that even the smell of the food I was carrying made my stomach churn.

My dark thoughts at least kept me from paying too much attention to any gawkers who might be pointing and whispering as I hurried back to the temple. The long, low building was still eerily quiet. I bowed perfunctorily to the gods and let myself in, relieved that the smell of illness and putrefaction was starting to dissipate somewhat. Someone—probably Senovo—had also lit some incense in an attempt to cover the stench. Even so, the lingering smell of death made my already sour stomach worse.

I wasn't quite sure where the other two were likely to be… probably not Rhystel's sick room, but other than that, they could be anywhere. It seemed odd that I knew how Senovo liked best to be kissed, and could picture exactly what he looked like when he closed his eyes in ecstasy, but had no idea where his sleeping room was located. I tried the refectory first, to no avail. Not sure what else to do, I entered the long hallway filled with sleeping cells and called, "Hello?" in a voice that was hopefully loud enough to be heard by anyone still awake, but not so loud as to wake the acolytes from their peaceful, drugged slumber.

A moment later, Andoc poked his head out of an open door about a third of the way down the hall, and beckoned me in. Relieved, I entered the tiny room to find Senovo seated in the narrow bed, his back braced against the wall and legs curled beneath him. He looked up listlessly at my entrance, only to do a double take at whatever he saw in my expression.

"Has something happened?" he asked. "Something *else*, I mean."

I shook my head and handed out the food. "It's nothing."

"Doesn't look like nothing," Andoc said, accepting his portion. "And where's *your* breakfast, by the way?"

"Ate it on the way over," I lied. "Seriously, it's not something either of you need to worry about. It's just—not everyone is thrilled to have me back, under the circumstances. No surprise there."

Part of me *did* want to talk about it—to have them tell me I'd done nothing wrong and Limdya was over-reacting. The larger part of me, however, didn't. Mostly because there was merit in the things she had said, about hypocrisy and dishonesty. Not to mention the fact that both Senovo and Andoc had other, more important things to worry about right now.

Senovo studied me a moment longer before nodding and leaning back against the wall again to pick at his food. Andoc continued to watch me as he flopped down onto the floor next to the bed and tore into his own breakfast.

"Well… just let me know if anyone needs their heads banged together," he said around a mouthful of meat roll.

"Honestly, the person in question had a pretty good point," I replied, and immediately changed the subject. "I should go to the horse pens now, and I'm sure you both have a lot to do before Leader Magoldis and her delegation arrive. I wanted to tell you both, though, that I decided last night to agree to the handfasting, if that's what it takes for me to stay here. I don't like it, Senovo, and I don't agree with what it says about our relationship with you, but when it comes down to it, it's just a length of cord and some words, really."

Senovo exchanged a look with Andoc before turning to me and raising an eyebrow. "There's a bit more to it than that," he said. "We still need to talk more. But you're right, we're all exhausted right now, and it's going to be a long day. Perhaps now is not the time."

It was true; both of them looked terrible, with dark circles under their sunken, red-rimmed eyes. The last thing they needed was to be worrying about me.

"Of course," I said, and forced a small smile that was probably not very convincing. In desperate need of some sort of reassurance, I moved forward and knelt on the bed, placing a kiss on Senovo's forehead and, when he lifted his face to mine, his lips. Andoc's hand wrapped around the calf of my right boot, tugging me back to the edge of the mattress and down to where he was leaning up against the bed frame.

I joined him on the floor, sprawling half in his lap and closing my eyes in relief as he manhandled me into position and kissed me deeply. I sighed as—for a moment or two—my worries receded in favor of the feeling of his lips moving against mine. How much trouble would we get into, I wondered, if I just crawled back up on the bed and pulled them down with me to sleep in each others' arms for a couple of hours?

It wasn't practical, of course. In fact, it was a bit surprising that no one had been sent to track us down yet. The trip to

Meren had kept me away from the horse pen in the first days of my promotion to Horse Mistress, but now that I was here I had no excuse for neglecting my duties. I pulled back from Andoc after a final nip at his lower lip and looked at them both regretfully.

"I have to leave now," I told them, "but the two of you will be in my thoughts all day."

"One of us will send for you when the Mereni delegation arrives," Senovo said. "I'm sure the Leader will want to see you again."

"You can help us act as a buffer between her and Volya," Andoc added ruefully. "I suspect it's going to be at least a three-person job."

"Sounds lovely," I replied in a tart voice, though I was actually rather curious to see the two tribal leaders interact.

It promised to be entertaining, if nothing else.

⤛ ⚜ ⤜

As I expected, Dalon was directing the others to ready everything for the day when I arrived.

"Well, well," he called upon noticing me, "look who decided to show up."

I thought I detected a note of teasing, and I wasn't about to make a fuss with one of the few people who seemed to be largely on my side. Not to mention the fact that I absolutely should have been here on time, regardless of what else was going on in my life.

With that in mind, I smiled and said, "Consider it a mark of my trust in you. Though I won't make a habit of it, I promise."

He snorted, then sobered. "Heard the High Priest died in the night. I hope someone's gonna make those Alyrion bastards pay."

"That seems to be the plan," I said.

"When's the funeral?" Dalon asked.

"This evening, after the sun goes down. We should arrange the schedules so everyone can attend, though I don't want to leave the pens completely unguarded," I said. "Has Volya been posting night guards while I've been away?"

"Yeah, they take it in shifts."

"Maybe a couple of the apprentice warriors can watch the horses during the ceremony. Have those two chestnut mares foaled yet?" I asked.

"One did—a filly. The other one looks like she'll go soon," Dalon said, and proceeded to give me a detailed report of all that had happened while I was in Meren. When he was finished, I nodded in appreciation. Things had been largely uneventful, which was usually good news when it came to livestock.

"Who's taking the herd out to graze today?" I asked.

"Tenibral, Kerney, and Favian," he said.

"Good," I replied. "Dalon, I'd love to give you the day off in exchange for all the hard work you've done for me this last week or so, but unfortunately they're going to call me back into town once the Mereni delegation arrives. That said, if you want to take the rest of the morning for yourself, you're more than welcome."

Dalon shrugged. "Yeah, I'll do that. Mind you, I'll still take your job if you decide to chuck it all in and go become a seamstress or something, but I can't deny it's a hell of a hard slog."

It was my turn to snort. "You have obviously never seen my attempts at sewing," I told him. "Go on, off with you. Come back after lunch."

Once Dalon had gone, I went to find Favian, figuring that I might as well try to take the bull by the horns. I wondered how many of the apprentices would accept me, and how many would actively fight my presence here. With Dalon gone, I was about to find out.

Favian was saddling his mount for the day, getting ready to ride out to the spring pastures with Kerney and Tenibral. The dun gelding he was readying stood half-asleep, resting one hind foot as the young boy dragged his saddle to the downed tree trunk lying next to the animal and used it as a step so he could reach the horse's back. I waited until he'd settled the saddle in place and leapt nimbly from the top of the log to the ground before getting his attention.

"Favian?"

I could see the boy's shoulders stiffen, but he did, at least, turn around to face me.

"What do you want?" he asked, his blue eyes flat and hard.

It was not the most encouraging start, but I vowed to let the interaction go wherever it needed to, and merely said, "Let Kerney finish saddling your gelding. I'd like you to show me what you've done with the white colt while I was away."

Kerney looked up at the sound of his name and nodded, his expression wary but not openly hostile. He moved to take over from Favian, who pivoted on his heel and stalked off toward the corral where Cassira was penned with her creamy white foal, born the morning after the Alyrion attack. Favian veered off to grab a length of soft rope from the line of pegs nearby, still not acknowledging me.

I let him go, watching as he entered the pen through the gate, not—*quite*—slamming it closed behind himself. Anger and upset were still visible in every line of his small body, and I could already guess how this was going to go. Indeed, as he strode stiffly through the herd of horses to get to the mare and foal, several of the animals darted out of the way nervously, turning to snort at him from a safe distance away.

Cassira, on the other hand, puffed herself up and moved to stand protectively between Favian and the foal, which huddled behind her and peered at the boy mistrustfully. I let myself into the pen after him, not willing to risk seeing the lad injured just to make a point.

Favian circled around the mare, trying to get to the colt, but the colt circled around the other side, always keeping its mother between them. At the instant I saw Cassira's patience with Favian come to an end, I stepped forward and blocked her charge with a sharp smack to the side of the muzzle. The mare shook her head in irritation, but backed off.

"Turn your back and take a few steps away," I told Favian sternly.

The boy looked shocked as well as angry now. "But... they've been *fine*," he protested. "I've been working with the foal every day, he comes right up to me!"

"Do as I said," I snapped, still standing between the mare and the boy.

Something in my tone made Favian comply, moving a little way away from the two horses. Cassira relaxed immediately, and the foal poked its head out from behind her a moment later, sneaking forward until it could nuzzle at my hip curiously.

"You're letting your anger with me affect your interaction with the horses," I said in a slightly gentler tone. "They're two separate things. Don't mix them up. Now, can you let it go for a few minutes so you can show me how the colt is doing?"

Favian was silent for several seconds. "I don't think I know how to do that," he said finally.

"Then get out of the pen before you get hurt and the colt gets traumatized," I told him bluntly.

I followed him out and latched the gate. He stopped and stood a few steps away from me, fidgeting a bit.

I sighed. "Is there anything you'd like to say to me?" I asked, trying to keep my tone neutral.

"Not really," Favian mumbled, and clamped his jaw shut tightly.

"I'm still exactly the same person I was a week ago, Favian," I tried, feeling completely at sea.

"Sure doesn't seem like it from where I'm standing," the boy said.

I tried another tack. "Are you going to be able to follow my orders, do you think?"

"Don't seem like I've got much choice in the matter," Favian said, staring at my chin instead of meeting my eyes directly.

I felt myself deflate a bit, defeated, at least for the moment. "No," I said, a bit sadly. "I suppose you don't. Not if you want to continue as an apprentice."

Favian shrugged, a sort of *there you have it, then* gesture.

At the far end of the pens, the others were ready to take the herd out for the day to graze. I let out a slow breath and said, "All right. Off you go. The others are waiting. Make sure to be back well before dark tonight; the High Priest's funeral is this evening."

Nodding tightly, Favian made his escape back to the others. He mounted, not looking back in my direction. I went to open the gates and let the herd out. Rather than focus on my problems, I watched the horses as they trotted through the gate by twos and threes, looking them over for any illness or injury. By the time the last mare had passed through the opening and headed north down the track to the grazing lands, I had regained some of my equilibrium.

I resolved not to waste any more of my energy today trying to make friends with those who were resentful or angry at my presence. If there was outright mutiny I would deal with it. Otherwise, let them be angry, so long as it didn't interfere with their work.

As the morning wore on, I discovered that most of Dalon's hangers-on seemed to have absorbed his viewpoint on the current situation, as they did on so many things. Several of the others were wary, but not openly hostile. The ones who definitely opposed my presence appeared to be content with ignoring me rather than being blatantly insubordinate. Operating, as I currently was, on far too much stress and far too little sleep, that was fine by me for the moment.

Dalon arrived back at midday, right about the time my body decided to remind me that I hadn't eaten in almost a day. Fighting a wave of mild dizziness, I excused myself to go get something. With the cookhouse no longer an option, I went instead to the market stalls. I didn't have the time, let alone the inclination to cook, so I merely bought some dried meat and fresh fruit from the first vendor who didn't appear to be openly hostile to me. I thought briefly about stopping in at the temple before I went back to the pens, but Senovo was likely to be busy, and frankly so was I.

I had no desire at all to go to the meeting hall, where Andoc was likely to be, since that would mean facing Volya again. I'd be seeing him soon enough, but I preferred to do so after the Mereni Leader arrived, when he would have other things to worry about.

I returned to the pens. The afternoon passed more quickly than I expected. Dalon had done an admirable job in my absence, but there were still a lot of things that needed attention. I was quickly gaining a real appreciation of the smooth and effortless way Jorun had seemed to run the place. I wondered how many years of practice it had taken him to make it look so easy.

A runner from the meeting hall interrupted my ruminations.

"The Mereni delegation has arrived," the child reported breathlessly. "The First Warrior requests your presence at the meeting hall, Horse Mas—" he paused, eyes wide, hastily correcting himself. "Horse *Mistress*."

"Very well," I replied. "I'll go there directly."

The boy nodded and jogged back toward the village. Looking around, I spied Dalon overseeing the repair of a damaged storage building and crossed to speak with him.

"You get called away?" he asked, and I nodded.

"I gather the excitement is about to begin," I said tartly.

"Maybe they should just lay out a chalk circle and let Volya and whassername fight it out that way," Dalon suggested impertinently.

I tried to stifle the wholly inappropriate laugh that bubbled up, with mixed success. "I imagine it would draw quite a crowd at that."

"Just think of the wagering," Dalon added. "You could make a small fortune on that alone."

"From what I've heard about them, it may yet come down to a brawl," I said, shaking my head and trying not to let my amusement show. "I'd better go. Don't want to miss anything."

"I'll take care of things here and let everyone know about the funeral. At least they'll have to stop fighting long enough for that."

"Yeah," I agreed, the inappropriate humor draining away at the reminder of Rhystel's death. "Let's hope."

EIGHT

The village green in front of the meeting hall was bustling with townsfolk, milling around the small contingent of Mereni warriors and acolytes who had accompanied Leader Magoldis. I pressed my way through the crowd, relieved that I was no longer the most interesting source of gossip in the village.

The warriors were split roughly evenly between men and women, a fact that appeared to be a source of fascination to the inhabitants of Draebard. Embarrassingly, no one seemed to have made the group welcome yet—they stood holding their horses, looking vaguely uncomfortable at all the attention.

"You, there!" I called to a gaggle of village lads standing at the edge of the green. "Take our guests' horses to the pens to be cared for."

The boys looked startled at the snapped command. They glanced at each other hesitantly, but a couple of them stepped forward to take some of the animals, and the others soon followed.

When the horses were gone, I turned my attention to the Mereni. "Has anyone offered you food or drink?"

"Not yet," said a petite warrior with dark hair, a bow and quiver slung over her shoulder. With a brief shock, I recognized Keenan, the young woman who had been handfasted to the artist, Ciero, while we were visiting Meren.

"My apologies for the oversight," I said. "Can we bring you anything while you wait?"

Another of the warriors answered. "We ate on the way, but some wine or ale would not go amiss."

"Of course," I said. I turned to find some more people to get drinks for the visitors, only to be interrupted by a male voice calling from somewhere in the middle of the crowd.

"You gonna run and fetch some wine for your new friends, Horse *Mistress*?" the voice jeered.

Heat flooded my face, but I forced myself to call back, "No, I'm going to tell some of you to go fetch it so I can join Chief Volya and Leader Magoldis in the meeting house, as they requested."

"I'll do it," said someone nearby, even as the voice scoffed loudly. I turned, discovering to my surprise that the speaker was one of Limdya's sisters— Gretya's oldest daughter, Charyal.

"Thank you," I said, wondering if it was just a matter of pride for the girl that Draebard not be seen as inhospitable. When I returned my attention to the Mereni group, it was to find Keenan watching me closely. My cheeks reddened once more, and I cleared my throat. "You'll, er, have to forgive us for the disorganized welcome. Things have been in upheaval here recently. If you need anything further, just ask."

I fled into the meeting hall before anyone else in the crowd could jeer me, wondering how in the world we could expect to keep the village's disapproval of me a secret. When I followed the sound of voices to a room near the far end of the hall, it was to find Volya and Magoldis glaring daggers at each other across the length of a large table, with Andoc, Senovo, the two novice Mereni priests, and an unfamiliar man—possibly the Second Warrior of the Mereni—arrayed uncomfortably between them.

Trying to ignore the feeling of intimidation that crept over me at the presence of so many important people, I knocked lightly on the doorframe. Magoldis and Volya both looked up at me—Magoldis with a half-smile and Volya with a sour expression that communicated his feelings in no uncertain terms.

"Oh," said Volya, "it's you. I suppose you'd better come in."

Magoldis frowned, her gaze jerking back to Volya. "Is that any way to address your Horse Mistress, *Chief?*" she asked pointedly.

Volya clenched his jaw. "How I address someone in this village is no concern of yours, woman."

From the corner of my eye, I caught Andoc blowing out a slow breath, and I wondered how close our Chief was to unraveling all the work Andoc and Senovo had put into the formation of this unlikely alliance.

Magoldis raised an eyebrow and directed her next words to me. "Dear me, Horse Mistress Carivel. Do you often have to put up with this sort of behavior?"

I cast about for some sort of response that wasn't, *Well, you see, Chief Volya only found out I was female a couple of days ago,* and came up with, "You'll have to forgive our Chief, Leader Magoldis. He and the old Horse Master were very close. We are all still grieving our losses, and everyone is on edge right now."

Magoldis gave me a shrewd look that said she was fully aware of my verbal deflection. "I see," she replied. "Tell me, then. How fares the black stallion? I heard a rumor that you rode him out of town when you left."

"No rumor," I said, on firmer ground here. "He is an outstanding horse. I couldn't resist a hard gallop that morning, and I have never ridden his equal. I have a feeling he will sire many wonderful foals for Draebard."

The man I presumed to be the Second Warrior spoke up. "Mereni horses are fast, but I'll wager Draebardi horses can out-pull them. We'd be interested in one of your heavier colts for our own crossbreeding, if you're willing to part with one."

"Of course," I said immediately, already running through a mental list of suitable animals. "I look forward to what our two tribes can accomplish together when it comes to horse breeding."

"Yes," Volya said grudgingly, having apparently remembered some of the reasons why this alliance was important. "From what I hear, that stallion you gave us is a rather nice one. That was generous of you."

Magoldis sat back in her chair and folded her arms across her chest. "I didn't give him to Draebard," she said placidly. "I gave him to Carivel."

"Nevertheless," Volya replied, "I'm certain our Horse… Mistress… will use him for Draebard's betterment."

It was the closest to a nice thing that Volya had said about me since my return, grudging though it was. With luck, things would go more smoothly now, without the continuing open expression of his hostility.

"Hmm," Magoldis said. "Well, perhaps we should move on to the details of your planned attack on the Alyrion outpost…"

The discussion moved on to the logistics of combining Meren's and Draebard's forces, and while it was never what one would call *friendly*, it was at least not openly hostile. I answered questions about Draebard's chariots and the number of teams available; Andoc answered questions about weaponry and the production capacity of the village's metalsmiths.

As the late afternoon sun slanted lower through the room's single window, Senovo rose and quietly took his leave to prepare for the upcoming funeral service. The young Mereni priests mirrored him, bowing to the two leaders and following him out. I watched surreptitiously, not liking Senovo's pale complexion or the lines of exhaustion at the corners of his eyes. Though, honestly, Andoc didn't look much better. Nor, I suspected, did I—but at least I had dozed for a couple of hours last night before returning to the temple.

Not long after the priests' departure, Magoldis shifted in her chair. "Perhaps we should adjourn for some food before the ceremony," she said. "The ride here from Meren was a long one."

Volya replied with a curt nod. Andoc roused himself and gracefully took things over, arranging to have the Mereni delegates shown to their temporary lodgings and asking whether they would prefer to have food brought to them, or to explore the village and eat with the townsfolk.

I let the words wash over me, and felt a fond smile tug at my lips. Of *course* Andoc would have the provision of food well in hand. I wondered if he'd personally chosen the wine to go with it. Magoldis pushed back from the table and we all rose, standing respectfully—or, in Volya's case—somewhat reluctantly—as the Mereni Leader and Second Warrior left to rejoin the rest of their contingent. Once the great and the good had all exited the room, Andoc's eyes sought mine, a faint grin lightening his haggard features in response to the one I was giving him.

"Perhaps Gretya's daughters would be willing to hire you on if you decide to give up soldiering," I teased lightly, and his smile grew wider for a moment before fading back to austerity.

"While both jobs are worthy pursuits, I'm afraid warriors are currently in higher demand," he replied, and we both sobered. He cleared his throat, becoming strangely awkward. "This hardly seems the place, but with so much going on right now... we really *do* need to talk more about the handfasting."

I nodded, feeling my stomach tighten. "We do. Not without Senovo, though. I won't place that burden on him until after the funeral ceremony, *and* after he's had a decent night's sleep."

The fond look was back in Andoc's eyes. "So you're not worried about me getting a decent night's sleep first, then? Now I see the lie of the land..."

I scoffed, but gently. "Come, now. Big, strong warrior like you? You probably miss one night's sleep out of every three, carousing until the wee hours."

"It has been known," Andoc admitted. "Though the older I get, the longer the next day seems to grow. Strange how that works." He gestured toward the door. "We should go. Volya was supposed to meet with the village elders over supper, and I'm not sure I trust them to keep him in check if Magoldis is nearby."

⥌ ♕ ⥍

Afternoon gave way to evening without any major diplomatic incidents, though the visitors were still the subject of much attention and discussion. Andoc and I were both picking at our food, distracted—our worry for Senovo keeping us from enjoying the rich roast meat and vegetables. I looked up as a slender figure dropped down on the bench next to me, and found Keenan watching me with interest.

"Mind if I join you?" she asked belatedly.

"Of course not," I said, and turned to Andoc. "You remember Keenan."

Andoc nodded, swallowing his mouthful of food. "Yes, indeed. Forgive me, I hadn't realized you were a warrior."

Keenan smiled an impish smile. "Never seen one as small as me, I'll wager," she said. "That's all right. I'm actually an archer. I leave the close combat to those with bigger muscles and thicker skulls."

I snorted, and Andoc laughed. "Probably a wise tactic," he said. "So, how's bonded life treating you so far?"

Keenan's reply was dry. "Well, it's not as though we've had much time to enjoy it since the handfasting. Between the... excitement... at the end of the ceremony and planning for this trip, Ciero and I might as well be illicit lovers stealing the occasional moment together at the end of the day."

Andoc winced a bit, no doubt remembering the chaos that had erupted after the bonding when Senovo turned unexpectedly into a wolf. "Indeed. I'm sorry we didn't get a chance to apologize for ruining your ceremony."

"Are you joking?" Keenan asked, her expression incredulous. "People will still be talking about our handfasting generations from now. Ha—they'll probably compose songs about it. How many girls can say that, eh?"

"Well, I'm… glad you see it that way," said Andoc.

I changed the subject before the ensuing silence could get too awkward. "So, you're an archer? Archery used to fascinate me when I was young. How long did it take you to learn?"

Keenan shrugged. "I'm still learning. I first picked up my father's bow when I was about ten, though. The stupid thing was taller than I was."

"Have you ever shot from horseback?" I asked, curious.

"Not really," Keenan said, looking suddenly very interested. "I've shot from chariots of course, but from horseback—well, you'd need a way to control the horse without reins, for a start. And you'd have to use a much smaller bow, I'd imagine."

"You two should experiment with it," Andoc said, sounding intrigued. "That could be a real tactical advantage."

I nodded, already thinking about letting Keenan use Kekenu to try some bridleless riding. Our conversation was interrupted by the sound of drums from the direction of the temple, and I realized with a start that darkness had fallen while we talked.

"Sounds like they're starting," Keenan said. "I'll let you return to your duties. My condolences on Draebard's loss, by the way."

"Thanks," I said with a tentative smile, sensing that Andoc was momentarily overcome. "If you don't have other responsibilities, come to the horse pens at mid-morning tomorrow and we can discuss mounted archery some more."

Keenan smiled back, bright and easy. "I'd like that."

By this time, the acolytes were lighting the line of torches mounted along the path between the temple and the village green, two by two. Andoc and I rose, heading to the cleared area around the funeral pyre. The pyre had been laid sometime during the afternoon; it was an impressive structure, but thankfully nothing like the one that had been required in the immediate aftermath of the Alyrion attack, when shroud-wrapped bodies had lain side by side like cordwood.

As we joined the two tribal leaders and the surviving elders, a hush fell over the assembled crowd. I craned around, stretching to see over the shoulders of the taller people surrounding me. Behind the two acolytes strode Senovo, pausing every few steps as two more torches flared to life in front of him. The novice priests from Meren flanked him, following a couple paces behind, and it made something relax slightly in my chest to see that he was no longer quite so desperately alone in his responsibilities.

Even so, exhaustion and mourning had leached all the color from Senovo's normally golden skin. Even in the warm, flickering light of the torches, he resembled nothing so much as a wandering wraith. It was disrespectful, but I longed for the funeral and the evening's duties to be over, so I could drag Andoc and Senovo someplace quiet and shove them into each other's arms.

I liked to think that, far from being offended, Rhystel would have agreed with me.

The procession from the temple entered the space surrounding the pyre, close enough to where I stood that I could make out a faint smudge at one corner of the heavy kohl Senovo wore around his eyes for important ceremonies. I had always admired the way it enhanced his already considerable natural beauty, but tonight it only made him look young and lost. The desire to hustle him away to some safe, quiet place surged again, and I chewed the inside of my cheek to hold myself in check.

Standing in profile to us, facing the pyre, Senovo closed his eyes for a moment as if gathering his strength. When he opened them, his spine straightened, and he wrapped authority around himself like a cloak. Rather than his usual dun robes, he now wore robes of pure white, and I realized with a jolt that I was truly seeing *High Priest Senovo* for the first time.

He turned smoothly to face the row of high-ranking officials around me, and accepted the ceremonial bowl of oil from one of the Mereni novices. He lifted the wooden vessel over his head, and his voice rose strong and sure.

"Mighty Deresta, She-Who-Purifies. Goddess of light. Goddess of flame. Tonight your children stand before you in grief. We commend unto your cleansing caress your humblest and most devoted servant, Rhystel of Draebard, Priest of Priests. May his ashes return to feed the earth, and his soul return to the endless sky above, carried upon your smoke."

"Ever shall it be so," I whispered in unison with the crowd around me.

Senovo lowered the bowl, balancing it in the palm of one hand and dipping the fingers of his other hand in the sacred oil. He flicked oil over the white-wrapped figured lying atop the stacked wood and, in a gesture that was not part of the funerary rites, dropped to one knee in front of it, head bowed.

"By convention," he began in a softer tone, "Rhystel was Elder Brother to everyone in the temple. In practice, however, he was father to all who had need of him, no matter their background… or their worthiness. Rhystel—father of my spirit, if not of my flesh—I commend you to your rest."

Beside me, I felt Andoc shudder where our arms brushed. Echoing the way that he had supported me at my own mentor's funeral, not so very long ago, I placed my hand firmly in the center of his back and held it there. His breath hitched out sharply under my touch, once, before he dragged his tattered composure back together.

Senovo rose and turned back to us. "Deresta, accept your faithful servant into your embrace. Return him to the earth and sky from whence he came."

"Ever shall it be so."

The novices and acolytes lit the pyre from all four sides simultaneously. Flames licked toward the night sky, quickly overpowering the flickering torches and throwing light across the whole of the village green.

"Blessings be upon you," said Senovo. "Celebrate the life—" His voice broke, and he had to pause for a moment. "The life that returns to the gods this evening. Go in peace."

He bowed low. Rising, he swept out of the central clearing in such a way that his face was kept averted from the majority of the crowd. I watched as the acolytes and novice priests surrounded him and headed back toward the temple. They were soon out of sight, swallowed up by the milling crowd. When I looked away, it was to find Leader Magoldis approaching us. I gave Andoc's back a firm rub and let my hand drop a moment before she arrived.

"My condolences on your loss," said the tall, red-haired woman. Her formal words were for both of us, but her eyes rested on Andoc. "Our own High Priest always spoke highly of Rhystel. I gather they had been close friends when they were younger. Jyrrel sends his regrets that he could not attend in person."

"Thank you, Leader," Andoc said, his voice steady. I admired his control.

"Yes," I echoed, "thank you. He was an extraordinary man. I'm only now learning how extraordinary. He will be missed."

"Indeed." Magoldis paused, as if slightly unsure of her next words. "Notwithstanding this tragic event, however, I understand… that congratulations are in order?"

I stared blankly for a beat before realization hit me. The handfasting. She meant the handfasting. Beside me, Andoc was standing with his mouth slightly open, uncharacteristically lost for words.

You've already decided to go through with this, I chastised myself. *Now act like it.*

I took a deep breath and summoned confidence that I did not feel. "Yes," I said, too brightly. "That's right. We, erm, haven't decided on a date yet, but it will probably be soon. What with, uh, the planned attack on the Alyrion outpost, and all."

The looks that both Andoc and the Mereni leader were giving me said quite clearly that I wasn't as smooth as I'd hoped to be. I pasted on a smile and threaded my arm through Andoc's, brazening it out.

The awkward silence was broken in the worst possible way a moment later when Crenelo hurried up to us, looking right and left as if to make sure no one else was watching. His young face was pale and drawn; his eyes, red-rimmed.

Andoc tensed. "Crenelo?" he asked. "What is it? Is something wrong?"

The acolyte's eyes flickered to Magoldis and away again. The Leader stared at the frightened boy for a moment and tactfully excused herself. Once she was gone, he let out a relieved breath and looked up at Andoc pleadingly.

"Please, First Warrior," he said breathlessly. "Can you come right away? Senovo collapsed right after we got back to the barracks—I don't know what's wrong with him!"

My stomach dropped as abruptly as if I had just taken an unexpected tumble off of a galloping horse. The blood left Andoc's face, and he growled, "Come on," taking me by the hand.

We hurried toward the temple as fast as we could without openly running, garnering a few strange looks as we pushed past knots of people. When we arrived at the front door, Reston was there, pushing it open and beckoning us inside with wide, worried eyes.

"He's in the bathing room," said the second acolyte. "That new priest, Eiridan, is with him."

I followed Andoc and the boys, not knowing the layout of the temple well enough to navigate on my own. We ended up in the wing that backed up close to the edge of the river, which made sense since it meant water buckets wouldn't have to be hauled very far for indoor bathing. The room was generously sized, with a large hearth for heating the buckets. It reeked of that peculiar, mildewed smell that seemed to permeate anyplace where water and steam were common over long periods of time.

A wave of relief swept over me upon finding Senovo within, standing under his own power and irritably waving off the novice priest who was apparently named Eiridan. Andoc sighed out some of his own tension next to me.

"What's this I hear about you collapsing?" he asked, his voice admirably calm.

Senovo looked back in surprise, evidently not having noticed our arrival. That was a bit worrisome in itself, since we hadn't exactly been quiet. The eunuch frowned, directing a glare at Crenelo, who cringed and backed away until he was partly hidden behind me.

"I *stumbled slightly*," Senovo said with great dignity. "I did not *collapse*, as you so dramatically put it."

His declaration might have been more convincing if he didn't look like a stiff breeze would blow him over. Eiridan crossed his arms, unimpressed.

"You fell over for no obvious reason and caught yourself on one knee," said the novice—a pleasant-featured young man who was already sporting the fat belly and double chin that seemed so common among members of the priesthood.

"Yes, well, please do feel free to recount my episode of clumsiness… *again*," Senovo snapped in a fit of pique that was badly out of character for the man I knew. "By all means, don't spare the detail."

Eiridan only shook his head and turned his attention to us. "Crenelo said he was going to get help. I assumed he meant a healer, but…?"

"We'll take care of things," Andoc assured him. "No need for the rest of you to stay around and act as targets for his foul temper."

"As you wish," Eiridan said, and motioned to the two acolytes to precede him out of the room. "The rest of us will purify ourselves in the river, rather than the bath. It's warm enough this evening that it will be no hardship. After that, we will retire to the refectory, and then to our rooms, where you may find us if you need help with anything."

"Thank you," I said, impressed with the young priest's efficiency.

"We are all here to serve, Horse Mistress. First Warrior," he said with a shallow bow to each of us. "Now, please do get him to rest."

"We will, Novice Eiridan," Andoc vowed, "even if I have to knock him out to do it."

Eiridan tipped his head in acknowledgement and herded the boys out of the room before closing the door to give us privacy. Senovo, in the mean time, had turned his back on us and was now leaning with a hand against the rim of the large copper tub to steady himself. He lifted his other hand to cover his eyes, finger and thumb squeezing at his temples as if to combat a headache.

"I'm fine," he said without turning around.

"Uh-huh," Andoc said, crossing his arms in unconscious imitation of Eiridan's pose earlier. "We can see that."

"We need to talk about the handfasting," Senovo said, still looking like he was one breath away from tumbling over into the empty tub against which he was currently leaning.

"Shut up, Senovo," I said. "Yes, we do need to talk about the handfasting. We need to talk about it *in the morning*, after we've all gotten a decent night's sleep."

Senovo slumped a bit further in reaction to my words. I sighed and crossed the room to grab a wooden chair that was sitting against the wall. After dragging it over and placing it behind Senovo, I peeled his hand from its death grip on the edge of the metal bath and basically shoved him into the seat. He looked up at me, surprise flashing across his ashen features.

"Sit," I said firmly, pointing my finger in his face to keep him there. When I moved toward the line of buckets standing at the edge of the hearth, Andoc seemed to rouse himself.

"Let me—" he started, but I cut him off with a dismissive gesture.

"Hauling buckets of water around is something of an area of expertise for me, you might say," I said, picking up the first two and carrying them over to dump in the bath.

Andoc huffed a breath of surprised laughter. "Right. I suppose it would be, at that."

He left me to it and moved to stand behind the chair, placing his hands on Senovo's shoulders and kneading the tense muscles. Senovo made a noise like a rusty gate hinge and curled forward, bracing his elbows on his knees and burying his face in one hand.

I hauled the last pair of buckets from the hearth to the tub and dumped them in. After a quick test with one finger, I added two buckets of cold water from the collection lined up against the far wall and stirred it a bit. Judging that it was warm enough, but not *too* warm, I turned to Senovo.

"Robes off," I said firmly. Andoc removed his hands from Senovo's shoulders and straightened. Senovo stayed frozen in place for the space of a few heartbeats, but then he sat up and began to untie the fastenings of the unfamiliar white robes, his movements as slow and labored as those of an old man. When his clothing lay draped over the chair, he got up and climbed into the large metal bath with something less than his usual grace, a low hiss escaping from between his teeth as he slid down to sit on the bottom. He leaned his head back against the rim, the warm water lapping at his chest, and closed his eyes wearily.

Andoc grabbed a rag and a sliver of hard lye soap from a table nearby. He pulled the chair around until it was positioned near Senovo's head and sat down in it.

"Why don't you get in there with him?" he said, as he urged Senovo to sit forward so he could pull the priest's heavy, shoulder-length plait of black hair free and unravel it.

I frowned. "Me? What about you?"

Andoc flashed a brief smile, though it didn't ease the weariness around his eyes. "Not enough room left in there for a big, beefy warrior like me," he teased. "And frankly, I've never seen the appeal of simmering in a giant kettle of hot water like a hunk of mutton. But if you're inclined to parboil yourself, I think a skinny eunuch and a slip of a Horse Mistress could probably squeeze into the stew pot together."

I snorted, but really, the idea was more than a little appealing. I'd had a total of three hot baths in a tub as grand as this one during my lifetime—all of them on various travels to neighboring towns with my father before he died. Staying at an inn or boarding house had seemed a great adventure when I was a little child, and he was prone to indulge me with small extras like sweetmeats or use of the inn's bathhouse, if they had one. It had been many years since I last had the opportunity.

"Senovo?" I asked.

"Yes, please do," he replied, not opening his eyes.

I shrugged at Andoc and stripped out of my worn and travel-stained clothing. I would have to see about purchasing some new shirts and breeches soon, now that my meager apprentice's salary would be supplemented by both my new position and my upcoming handfasting to Draebard's First Warrior. The thought was sobering, but I put it aside for now.

I had forgotten the singular sensation of sinking into warm water up to my collarbones. Gooseflesh prickled over my skin and disappeared almost instantly as I eased into the space in front of Senovo, unsure how I was supposed to fit, exactly. The eunuch roused himself enough to spread his legs apart and open his arms to me. I curled up so I could rest my cheek on his chest, with my legs bent at the knee and draped over one of his thighs. The warm water lapped at my chin and I sighed deeply, feeling a fraction of the day's tension drain from my body.

This close, I could still smell the smoke of Rhystel's funeral pyre clinging to Senovo. I gestured to Andoc for the soap, and poked Senovo in the ribs until he opened bloodshot eyes.

"Hair," I told him, holding up the soap and lifting myself away from him enough that he could slide further down into the tub. He groaned and dunked himself completely, emerging a moment later in a plume of bubbles and scrubbing his hands over his face as the water ran down. I shoved and scooted us around awkwardly until we had switched places, his back to me and my legs framing his. Scrubbing up a lather between my hands, I worked it into the heavy waves of black hair in front of me.

"I thought you had no patience for long hair," came an amused voice from behind me.

"I don't," I growled, tugging at a tangle.

"Here, lean your head back," Andoc said, guiding me with a hand on my forehead.

"What—?" I asked, just as a pitcher of warm water emptied slowly over my scalp. A pleasant, tingling shiver skittered down my spine. The tingle spread through my body as strong fingers massaged soap into my short, closely cropped hair, and... well... I might have moaned, just a little.

"Focus," Andoc said, drawing my attention back to my own fingers, which were still buried in Senovo's hair. I started scrubbing again, working the soap right down to his scalp to get every last hint of smoke out of it—aware that Senovo was on the verge of falling asleep under my touch.

Andoc finished with my own hair—such as it was—and moved on to my neck, back, and shoulders, scrubbing away with the soapy rag. Meanwhile, I gave Senovo's hopelessly tangled locks a final tug and urged him down to rinse. He leaned back and slid toward the far end of the tub until the water closed over his ears, leaving only his face above the surface, his head floating a few inches above my lap.

I let my hands run over his forehead and the front half of his skull, kept shaved as was the custom for all priests. He shivered a little as the pads of my fingers slid over the hint of soft stubble there, and into the long hair in back. I rinsed out the soap as best I could, grumbling at the ever-growing nest of tangles. When I was done, I tapped him lightly and helped him sit upright again.

"How in the gods' names do you deal with this mess *every day*?" I asked once he'd shaken the water from his ears, lack of sleep robbing me of whatever minimal amount of tact I might ordinarily possess.

"It comes with the job," he mumbled, still sounding more than half asleep.

Andoc's hands left me for a few seconds, and I heard the legs of the chair scrape as it was pushed back. His footsteps crossed the room and returned, out of my line of sight.

"Here," he said, handing me a small vial with a wooden stopper.

"What is it?" I asked, looking at the small, cunningly carved stone bottle in confusion.

"Hair oil," said Andoc, as if it should be obvious.

Of course, it probably *was* obvious to anyone who had to maintain long hair. I nodded and unstoppered it so I could pour a little into my palm. The smell was familiar—part of the myriad of smells that, together, smelled like *Senovo*.

The soap had made Senovo's hair squeaky and prone to knot. The oil smoothed it, untangling the wet strands so I could comb them out with my fingers. Meanwhile, Andoc picked up the rag again and finished scrubbing every part of me he could reach. Desire sparked weakly in my belly as the rough cloth slid over my breasts, but exhaustion won out in short order. Tonight was for sleep. Tomorrow was for talking. Already, I was longing to return somehow to that one lovely, perfect night and morning the three of us had shared in Meren.

Maybe you shouldn't have fallen for a First Warrior and a High Priest, if you wanted a life of leisure, said the little nagging voice that lived in the back of my head. *Maybe you shouldn't have become Horse Mistress.*

It was true enough, I supposed, as Andoc handed me the soapy rag so I could scrub my legs and feet. Still, none of us could have predicted the extraordinary series of events that had befallen us. Maybe it was just the gods' will.

When I was clean all over, I moved to Senovo, giving him a quick but thorough wash. Sleep was what he needed, but I wanted every trace of the funeral fire gone from his skin first. Andoc helped me rinse my hair with the pitcher, before giving it to me so I could rinse Senovo off. When we were finished, my hands and feet were starting to turn soft and wrinkly, and the water was growing lukewarm.

I handed Senovo up to Andoc, who helped him out of the tub onto shaky legs and dried him off with a square of burlap toweling.

"Are we going to need to bail this thing out with the buckets?" I asked as I climbed out after him, eyeing the cloudy water and feeling less than enthusiastic about the prospect.

Senovo shook his head and gestured to a stone-lined trench running from under the metal tub and disappearing under the wall that faced the river. "The trench runs right out to the edge of the river," he said. "There's a wooden plug at one end of the bath to let the water drain out."

I hadn't felt anything in the bottom of the tub at my end, so I reached into the murky bathwater at the other end and felt around until my fingers caught the edge of the soft, waterlogged cylinder of wood. I pried it out, letting the water drain away and taking a moment to admire the ingenuity of the system.

When I turned back, Senovo had slumped forward in Andoc's arms, and I stifled an audible sigh of satisfaction. Not even bothering to dry off first, I walked over to them and plastered myself over Senovo's back. One of Andoc's hands immediately stretched forward to rest on my bare hip, and I buried my nose in Senovo's clean, freshly oiled hair, breathing in.

"I don't know how to do this with him gone," Senovo said into the skin of Andoc's neck, sounding calm but utterly exhausted.

NINE

I wormed my hands in between the two of them to circle Senovo's waist and rest on his stomach. "All you have to do tonight is sleep, Senovo. That's all."

After a moment of hesitation, he nodded.

"Where do you want to go?" Andoc asked. "I don't think your bed is big enough for all of us."

"Definitely not," Senovo murmured. "Not Rhystel's room, though."

I shuddered a bit at the thought. Of course, Senovo would now have use of the High Priest's rooms, but I could think of few worse places for him to be right now. After a moment of introspection, though, a thought occurred to me.

"What about one of the rooms used to counsel couples on lovemaking?" I asked. "I presume the beds are bigger."

"That'll work," Andoc agreed. "Given the, um, handfasting… you could even say it's pretty legitimate." He nudged Senovo upright. "Come on, then. Let's go. I can barely keep my eyes open."

Senovo and I donned the bare minimum amount of clothing necessary to get from one end of the nearly deserted temple to the other. The hint of smoke tickled my nose again and I frowned, having completely forgotten that the stench would also permeate Senovo's robes. I should have thrown our clothes into the bathwater and scrubbed them before I drained the tub, but it was too late now. My spirits sank at the realization that I had not succeeded in my self-appointed quest to cleanse Senovo of all reminders of the evening's ceremony.

He and Andoc led the way through darkened hallways to a wing of the temple with which I was unfamiliar—never having been in a relationship before, and therefore having no cause to seek intimate counseling from the priests. Indeed, I'd had every reason not to, since it would have risked revealing my birth sex. We turned into a side corridor and Senovo opened the first doorway on the left.

The room was faintly illuminated by torchlight from the village green, filtering in through a small, high window. It was a reminder that, outside, the villagers were still drinking, eating, and socializing after the funeral—celebrating the life of the departed. However, the reflected light also allowed us to navigate the cozy room without the need for lighting candles or starting a fire in the hearth, and, even damp as Senovo and I were, it was a sufficiently pleasant evening that we would not need the hearth for warmth.

A low bed big enough for two people to fuck in, while a third watched and assisted, dominated the shadowy room. It would offer plenty of space for three exhausted people to huddle together in a tangled pile and sleep. As soon as the thought entered my mind, my body *ached* for rest. Andoc was way ahead of me; he was already stripping Senovo of his robe and pulling the blankets back.

The bed had a faintly musty smell, as if it had sat for some time, gathering dust with the mattress unaired—one of many small tasks that had fallen by the wayside after the slaughter of most of the priesthood. With more acolytes from Meren coming to Draebard soon, perhaps the temple would once again become a bright and welcoming place.

Movement next to the bed snapped me from my idle thoughts. While I was engaged in woolgathering, Andoc had undressed, leaving me the last one still clothed.

With a start, I roused myself long enough to pull off my linen shirt and smallclothes while Andoc climbed into bed and dragged Senovo down after him. With a deep sigh of relief at finally getting the eunuch where he truly needed to be, I followed suit and scooted close, bracketing Senovo's body between mine and Andoc's.

The priest lay on his back, his face close to mine. The faint glow from outside reflected in his damp eyes as he stared at the nearly invisible rafters above us. His breath hitched unevenly in and out. I reached out a hand under the blankets, covering Andoc's where it lay low on Senovo's stomach.

"The gods will surely not begrudge you a night's rest," I told Senovo. "And I *know* that Rhystel wouldn't."

Senovo's eyes closed and his chest convulsed a few times in the unmistakable rhythm of silent weeping before he sucked in a long inhalation and gradually relaxed in our arms. Sooner than I would have expected, he was asleep, with Andoc's even breaths descending into light snoring soon afterward. I lay awake for a little while longer, wishing that life could just be as simple as this—as the three of us, together. Eventually, though, fatigue from the long day and the longer night that had preceded it pulled me down to join the others in darkness and dreams.

⤙ ♕ ⤚

When I woke, it was still dark. The stiffness of my muscles and the welcome feeling of being reasonably well rested made me think it must be almost morning. I wrinkled my nose, fighting the urge to sneeze, and swiped at a strand of Senovo's long, unbound hair which was tickling my right nostril.

The movement roused him, and he stretched against me—the slide of skin on skin doing all sorts of interesting things to my groggy, early morning thoughts. Before I could act on my baser impulses, however, reality intruded in a thoroughly jarring manner.

The handfasting.

We were supposed to discuss the handfasting this morning, before I was due back at the horse pens to oversee the apprentices and meet with Keenan about mounted archery.

"We need to talk now, Carivel," Senovo said, a slight rasp of sleep still roughening his voice. His words echoed my own thoughts eerily.

"Yes," I said.

"Is there anything you'd like to speak about before we wake Andoc?" asked Senovo.

"No," I said, already starting to feel strangely numb.

I felt Senovo nod as he replied, more than I saw him… it was very dark in the room now. "Very well, then."

A moment later, there was the sound of someone being slapped lightly on the cheek, followed by Andoc's sleepy groan. The slapping grew brisker and Andoc flailed a bit, coming awake all at once.

"Wha—?" he said. The mattress shifted as he sat up abruptly and looked around in confusion. "Where are we?"

"It's almost morning," I told him. "We're in one of the rooms at the temple, remember?"

He paused for a moment. "Oh. Right. Almost morning, you say? So, time to talk, then."

"Yes," Senovo agreed.

Andoc settled himself back on the bed. Outside the window, the faintest hint of gray was creeping into the sky as he spoke. "You're absolutely certain you want to do this, Carivel? You've thought about what it'll mean?"

For now, I could still convince myself that it was too dark to meet his eyes as I replied, "I've thought about what it will mean if we don't. Volya will try to make me leave, even if he has to wait until after the Mereni go home to do it. So… I'm willing if you two are."

"You're thinking about the broader implications," said Senovo, sounding bone-weary despite having slept through the night. "I don't think you're considering the more immediate practicalities of the ceremony itself."

"What do you—" I began, only to cut myself off as comprehension dawned. "Oh."

"Yes," Senovo agreed. "The ceremony assumes a union between a man and a woman. A physical union, as well as a spiritual one."

I would have to let Andoc fuck me. Like a woman.

"In addition to the act itself," Senovo continued, "there is also the possibility of pregnancy."

My circling thoughts froze solid and crashed to the ground like falling icicles. Gods—I hadn't even thought… how could I not have *thought* about that?

Because you did not want to think about it, said the snide voice in my head.

"Carivel," Andoc said, "say something, please."

My eyes flew up, locking with his in the gradually lightening predawn. Another moment of truth. This was what I'd agreed to… I had to go through with it. It would be fine. Women did it all the time—how bad could it be?

I cleared my throat. "Yes, sorry. It's fine. It won't be a problem. And… as far as pregnancy, well, we usually have to breed mares several times during their cycles before they fall pregnant. I assume it's the same way with people."

My stomach was twisting in unpleasant ways as I pictured myself growing round and heavy with child. My breasts swelling; my ankles filling with fluid. Becoming the perfect, fecund woman that my mother always tried to shape me into with her harsh words and harsher blows.

Senovo's next words made my gut churn a little harder. "There is no way to know. The timing after your last moon cycle is right for conception, I fear. We could perhaps reduce the possibility by waiting until you start bleeding again in a couple of weeks..."

"The Chief will never let you postpone the ceremony that long," I said.

"He wants it to be today," Andoc said heavily.

My heart stuttered and thudded hard against the wall of my chest.

"No," said Senovo in a flat voice. "Absolutely not."

Almost defiantly, I said, "What does it matter? If we're going to do it, who cares if it's today, or tomorrow, or next week? I *might* get pregnant. I *might* not be able to reach completion like a woman is supposed to during the ceremony. Fuck, I should probably just agree to a public handfasting so that at least one aspect of the damn thing will be a good omen!" My voice rose toward the end despite my best efforts, and I hated the slightly hysterical edge I could hear in it.

"*I forbid it*," Senovo snapped immediately, sounding as angry as I had ever heard him. "Whatever else I may be to the two of you, right now I am your priest. You have both been... *coerced* into this ceremony. By Volya... by the elders... even by me!"

"By you!" I snapped back. "How do you figure *that*?"

"I told you to do it," Senovo practically growled. Amber light flared in his eyes, glowing softly in the predawn for an instant before it receded. "I told you it was a good idea, and you listened to me. But I will *not* see you become some kind of public spectacle on the flimsy excuse of it being a *good omen!*"

I opened my mouth to say something unwise—anything, rather than make it apparent that I was close to angry tears over the unfairness of the whole situation.

"Shut up, both of you," Andoc said, his voice level, but demanding instant obedience from us both. Complying was an honest relief; I clamped my jaw shut, breathing slowly through my nose as he continued. "We're going to discuss this now like reasonable human beings, so listen closely. There is not going to be any public handfasting. A *private* handfasting still seems like the easiest way to appease Volya and the elders so we can secure Carivel's position in Draebard, however. Are we agreed?"

"Yes," I said, albeit in a slightly sullen tone.

"Agreed," Senovo replied cautiously.

"So, the question comes down to whether Carivel is willing to accept having sex like a woman during the ceremony—"

"I already said I would," I interrupted.

"—and whether the three of us are willing to accept the possibility that she might become pregnant," Andoc finished.

Silence filled the room for the space of several heartbeats.

"There are… steps which can be taken," Senovo said tentatively, "if a woman with a baby has other responsibilities that keep her from the normal demands of motherhood. Wet nurses, that sort of thing. Healer Sagdea used a wet nurse for both her son and daughter, many years ago now, of course. It was considered somewhat scandalous at the time, according to the High Prie—" He corrected himself quickly. "—to… Rhystel."

"Yes," I said tartly. " Because gods forbid I should do something scandalous."

"*Carivel*," Andoc chided.

"The point is," Senovo said, "there are things that could be done, to reduce the burden of having a child."

"And I would like to make it clear, too, that I would not consider any child we had to be a *burden*," Andoc said.

I wrapped my arms around my knees, and was relieved when the other two gave me a few moments to think. I was probably the least maternal person I knew. To me, motherhood was hopelessly tangled up with memories of my own mother: controlling, abusive, and hateful. I would have to be mad to wish myself as a parent on any unsuspecting child.

But… still. I thought again of the mares—how the stallions bred them several times to make a foal. With the ceremony, it would only be once. It would be all right, surely. And if the worst happened, well, Senovo knew ways to help, apparently. Or maybe I could just give it away to another family. It wasn't as if most of the villagers could feel any more disdain for me than they already did.

"It's fine," I said. "It will be fine—it's not a problem. We need to do this."

Andoc and Senovo watched me closely for a moment in the dim light.

"Very well," Senovo said, not sounding at all sure. "Though you may change your mind at any time. The handfasting will not happen today, however. Tomorrow, Andoc. Tell Chief Volya that the ceremony will be tomorrow afternoon. And it will be *private.*"

"Agreed," Andoc said. "Carivel?"

"Agreed," I echoed, carefully keeping all traces of uncertainty from my tone.

It was a relief to have the discussion over. I rose from the bed and dressed quickly, excusing myself to the horse pens while Senovo was occupied in braiding his hair into its customary plait, and Andoc was still hunting around for his clothes. It did not occur to me until I was halfway to my destination that, in my eagerness to escape, I had not offered to kiss or embrace either of them.

⁕

The day dragged slowly by, my meeting with Keenan the only bright spot. The young archer was not only talented with a bow; she was also a natural with horses. After her first, rather unexpected bout of giggles over Kekenu's jouncing, jarring trot had subsided, she quickly gained confidence in directing the little gelding using only her seat and legs. We could not devise any practical way to use her Mereni longbow from horseback, so she had to content herself with drawing back an imaginary bowstring as she galloped past the series of targets we'd set up in one of the alleys between the pens.

"I'll speak with our bowsmith about designing some sort of small compound bow for use from horseback," she promised. "Perhaps one of the new recurve bows she's been experimenting with."

I had no idea what a recurve bow was, and told her so, but she only laughed and promised to show me next time. Feeling a bit lighter after the promising session, I threw myself into the work that seemed to have piled up for me overnight. It was difficult to ignore the sullen looks and words from many of the lads, but, sullen or not, they did what was required of them, and by the time the sun was falling behind the western hills, everything was caught up.

I jumped a bit when a hand settled on my shoulder as I was standing by the fence of the large holding pen for a final evening headcount—since my return, the apprentices avoided any sort of physical contact with me like the plague.

"Done for the day?" Andoc asked.

I nodded, relaxing under his fingers. "Just finishing up. Did you and what's-his-name—the Mereni Second Warrior—manage to keep Volya and Magoldis from killing each other?"

Andoc snorted in amusement. "His name is Wynethal, and there were a few tense moments, to be honest. The pair of them disappeared into another room to shout at each other for a bit after lunch. We weren't sure if they'd both make it back out or not, but it actually seems to have helped. They were almost civil this afternoon."

"That's good, I suppose," I said. "Look, I need to apologize for running out on you and Senovo this morning—"

"You really don't," Andoc said, letting his hand fall away. The skin of my shoulder felt cold where it had been.

"Well, then," I said with some asperity, "I *want* to apologize for running out on you. It's not as if either of you are responsible for this mess."

"Fine, you're forgiven. Not that there's really anything to forgive." Andoc stepped around so he could look me up and down critically. "You can make it up to me by letting me feed you."

"Hey," I protested, to hide the little trickle of warmth that snaked up my spine, "I'll have you know that I ate a handful of dried apples and some of the flatbread that Dalon brought for lunch."

"Oh, yes—sounds delicious," Andoc teased. "Maybe something a bit more substantial for dinner, though?"

"As long as it's not from the cookhouse," I said sourly. "I've been banned for life on pain of Limdya scratching my eyes out."

"Not the cookhouse," Andoc agreed, "though I'm sure she'll soften as time goes on. We can eat at the temple, after which I believe we're both due for a little more *counseling*."

My heart and stomach did something complicated at the prospect, but I swallowed it down and simply nodded. With a final look around to make sure all was well for the evening, I followed him back into the village, past the whispers and the unfriendly expressions, to the somewhat melancholy and grief-tinged sanctuary of the temple. It occurred to me as I offered my obeisance to the gods that I had hardly been back to my own hut since my return—only to duck in and unload my saddlebags or get fresh clothing. The place was a hovel, to be sure, but it was *my* hovel, and it seemed odd that I barely missed it.

I was getting handfasted tomorrow, and I hadn't even discussed living arrangements. I shook my head in faint disbelief at the turn my life had taken.

Inside the temple, someone had gone to the effort of lighting all the torches, bathing the interior in warm light. It went some way toward combating the sense of death and abandonment that had permeated the building after the Alyrion attack, and I hoped it boded well for the well being of the priests and acolytes who still resided here. I breathed in cautiously, pleased to discover that the smell of illness and decay was almost completely gone as well, replaced with a slightly heady scent of smoke and herbs.

"Someone's been busy," I whispered to Andoc.

"Several someones, I'm sure," he replied. "Eiridan and Feldes have already proven their worth several times over. Their presence may be one of the best things to have come out of this treaty."

I nodded agreement. Feldes was presumably the second novice priest from Meren. I had not met him properly yet, though it appeared that might change tonight. As we approached the refectory, I could hear the sound of low voices from within, and smell simple, hearty food. We came to the low, wide entryway and Andoc rapped his knuckles against the doorframe.

Crenelo looked up at the noise and smiled, his face less pale and drawn than it had been the last time I'd seen him. I smiled back, pleased to see him in better spirits, and was somewhat surprised when he and all of the others at the table except Senovo rose to their feet as Andoc and I entered.

"Horse Mistress. First Warrior," Eiridan greeted, and I was once again forced to grapple with the jarring realization that I was senior in status to everyone here except Andoc and Senovo—if I succeeded in keeping my position intact, of course.

Senovo waved us over to join them. Reston ran out of the room to get more bowls and eating implements while the rest of us sat down around the heavy trestle table.

"Good evening, everyone," Andoc said, genial as ever. "What's for dinner tonight?"

"Crenelo and Feldes have prepared a stew for us," Senovo said, and Crenelo blushed happily. "It seems our new arrivals have many valuable talents to offer, cooking being one of them."

"One cannot properly nourish the spirit without also nourishing the body," Feldes replied primly. I couldn't help noticing that Feldes was apparently quite serious about nourishing his own body—the young novice was already fantastically fat.

"Well stated, Novice Feldes," Andoc replied amiably. "I've spent considerable time and energy trying to convince *certain people* of that for years now."

His brief glances at Senovo and me were not remotely subtle, and I rolled my eyes at him. Before either of us could take the bait, though, Reston returned and set bowls, knives and spoons in front of us. Senovo reached forward and served us from the large pot himself, while Eiridan passed a board with chunks of coarse brown bread. My earlier nerves dissipated in the face of hunger as the fragrant steam from the bowl tickled my nose. I touched my forehead, lips, and heart, giving thanks to Naloth and Utarr for the food as I had been taught to do when in polite company, and dug in.

The seven of us ate in silence for a few minutes, enjoying the well-prepared meal. When Eiridan and Senovo had finished their modest portions, Eiridan looked at me with interest, threading his fingers together and resting his chin on his knuckles. I sopped up the last of my broth with a bit of bread and pushed my own bowl out of the way, even as Andoc helped himself to seconds.

"I understand you are to be handfasted tomorrow, Horse Mistress?" Eiridan asked.

My stomach clenched despite the pleasant meal. I forced a happy expression onto my face and replied, "Yes, that's correct. We're here for some final counseling before the ceremony."

Before I could decide if taking Andoc's hand at the table would be overkill or not, the sound of heavy footsteps approaching from the hallway interrupted us. We all looked at the refectory entrance, wondering who it could be, only to find Chief Volya standing in the door, flanked by a slightly sheepish looking Jacun. Except for Senovo, all of the others rose in deference to the new arrivals, and I quickly followed suit.

"Senovo, I need to have a word with you, son," Volya said, before seeming to register my presence, and Andoc's. "Oh — I didn't realize these two would be here. So you're having the ceremony tonight after all, then? That's as well. Glad to hear calmer heads are prevailing, lad."

I raised both eyebrows, my hackles rising on Senovo's behalf. Volya may have been Senovo's senior in age, but to refer to a High Priest — even a young one — as *son* or *lad* was… beyond disrespectful. There was a reason Senovo hadn't risen from the table with the rest of us. His position was equal to Volya's, though the Chief and the High Priest generally moved in different spheres within village life. Volya's behavior could only mean he was making a grab for power, trying to dominate an inexperienced High Priest who was, furthermore, crippled by fresh grief at the recent loss of his beloved mentor.

My pulse pounded, and I started to draw in breath to speak, but Andoc's fingers brushed mine in a quelling gesture. My trust in his judgment held me back, but only by a thread.

Senovo arched one perfect brow in response to Volya's words, and still did not rise. "Good evening, Chief," he said, ignoring the nervous glances from the Mereni novices, not to mention Andoc's tension and my own simmering anger. "Would you and Jacun care to join us for a meal? The stew tonight is excellent."

Volya frowned, and stepped forward to stand at the end of the table opposite Senovo. "I didn't come here to talk about stew, son." The grizzled Chief leaned forward, pressing the fingers of one hand against the scarred wood of the tabletop. "I came here to find out why you're dragging your feet on a simple handfasting ceremony. They're both here. Let's get it done and over with so the village can try to move on from the disgraceful deception perpetrated on all of us by this… *girl*." His eyes flicked to me briefly, and I nearly choked.

TEN

Senovo wove his fingers together and gazed steadily over them at the man glaring down the length of the table. "Andoc and Carivel are here tonight, at my behest, to complete some final counseling before the ceremony... which, as I explained in my message to you earlier, will take place privately, tomorrow afternoon."

"You are presuming quite a lot on the strength of a position you've held for barely a day, Senovo," Volya said.

Without changing expression, Senovo rose from his seat and mirrored the other man, leaning forward slightly over the table with his weight resting lightly on his fingertips. His voice was like forged iron as he said, "I presume nothing. The position of High Priest exists independently of the individual who inhabits it. It is you, Chief Volya, who are overstepping your bounds by attempting to interfere in matters that do not concern you. I am the first shape-shifter to hold the position of High Priest on the island of Eburos in a generation. *Do not* set yourself against me over such a meaningless trifle. The ceremony will take place tomorrow. It will be private. Now, unless you have legitimate business at the temple, please remove yourself so that we may finish our meal and I may attend my duties to the betrothed couple."

Volya continued to stare, unblinking, at Senovo, who returned his hard look impassively. I don't think anyone else was even breathing. Just when I feared that the tension in the air might somehow manifest to crumble the wattle-and-daub walls around us, Volya straightened and swept from the room without another word. Jacun scurried after him, throwing us a wide-eyed look as he left.

"Well," Andoc said, breaking the silence that had lingered after the Chief's abrupt departure. "That was certainly interesting."

His words were apparently enough to break Feldes free from his immobility. "Of all the presumptuous... how *dare* he try to interfere in such a way!" said the fat novice, his face a parody of offense.

Senovo still had not moved from his slightly predatory stance at the head of the table, and I felt a sudden and completely inappropriate desire to throw him down on the conveniently flat surface and ravish him. He gradually relaxed, blinking as if coming back to himself.

"One does not become the Chief of a tribe without daring much," he said, his voice as calm and level as if he was speaking of the weather. "Now, perhaps Andoc, Carivel, and I should retire someplace quiet so we may see to that counseling. Feldes, Crenelo, thank you for a lovely meal. Reston and Eiridan, please see to the dishes and stand watch in case anyone has need of the temple this evening. Good night to you all."

The others, still somewhat in shock by the looks of it, murmured polite responses as Senovo gathered us up with his eyes and shepherded us out of the refectory, toward the wing where we had spent the previous night. Though my feet moved along the corridors as if by their own volition, my mind was still stuck fast, mired somewhere in the vicinity of *retiring somewhere quiet* where I could hopefully rip Senovo's robes off and do unspeakably wicked things to him. So distracted was I, that it was a complete surprise when a door shut behind us and I found that we were in the same room as last night.

"Fuck, *Senovo*," said Andoc, flopping down on the bed and sounding as stunned as I felt.

Since actions spoke louder than words, I contented myself with grabbing Senovo by the front of his robes and whirling him around, thumping his back against the closed door to hold him in place while I tried to get my tongue down his throat. He made a surprised *oof* noise at the impact, followed by a soft whine that sent the blood pulsing thickly between my legs. When I let him up for breath, he was shaking a bit, and I pulled back in concern.

"As much as I'm enjoying the view, maybe you two had better sit down," Andoc said from the bed.

Using my grip on the flowing white linen twisted around my fingers, I tugged Senovo across the room and deposited him next to Andoc, who looked at him closely.

"All right?" Andoc asked, and Senovo nodded.

"Just… give me a minute," said the priest, still sounding a bit breathless.

I sank down to the floor in front of him, curling my legs beneath me and looking up at him with what was no doubt an idiotically adoring expression.

"That was… " I began, only to trail off when I couldn't find adequate words.

"Ridiculously arousing?" Andoc offered, breaking the tension somewhat.

Senovo eyed him sideways. "You are as predictable as you are steadfast, my friend," he said, in a tone more like himself. "Please never change."

I swallowed, laying a hand on Senovo's knee to draw his attention. "Senovo, I'm… no good at putting things like this into words, but, well, I'm not used to people speaking up for me like that. I… I just… thank you."

Senovo shook his head, deflecting my words. "Any priest would have stood up for your rights in the temple. It was merely Volya's attempt to extend his power and influence in Draebard by out-maneuvering a weak High Priest."

"You are *not* weak," Andoc said.

"Not remotely," I added emphatically.

"My *position* is weak, for now, at least," Senovo insisted. "Though perhaps slightly less so at the present moment than it was half an hour ago."

Andoc snorted. "I should say so."

Senovo closed his eyes and breathed in and out deeply, once, as if centering himself. When he opened them again and spoke, his tone was brisk. "Now, let us move on to other things. You are not here to speak of our esteemed Chief and his machinations. You are here so we may prepare for tomorrow."

"Does preparation for tomorrow include me getting your robes off?" I asked, unable to help myself. I was rewarded by a snicker from Andoc and a faint blush that rose up Senovo's neck to color his cheeks in the candlelight.

"That can perhaps be arranged," Senovo said. "First, though, I've been thinking about some things. I can see no way to avoid having Andoc penetrate you like a woman. Not if the handfasting is to be properly completed."

I sat back, regarding him. "I didn't expect you to."

He shook his head. "Let me finish. I do wonder, however, if there might not be a way to alter your perception of the act, somewhat."

"What are you saying?" Andoc asked, curious.

"Andoc, you are obviously aware of the place inside a man or a eunuch's passage that causes pleasure," Senovo said. "Though Carivel may not be."

"Yes, of course," Andoc said, "but I'm still not sure what you're getting at."

"Carivel doesn't have one," Senovo said, and Andoc's expression turned considering.

I frowned. "What do you mean? I got quite a bit of pleasure that way, in case you didn't notice."

"You did, from the combination of that, along with other stimulation," Senovo said. "We are speaking of something slightly different. There is a small, round node—a sort of firm nodule about the size of a shagbark nut—located under the front wall of a man's passage. Rubbing against it can bring many men to completion without a single touch to their shafts. I could not find it inside of you."

"I don't understand," I said, still frowning. "You couldn't find it? You think it's—what? Because I have a female body?"

"I suspect that may be the case. I have never had occasion to explore a woman in precisely that way before. Andoc?"

Andoc shook his head. "Sorry, I'm afraid I'm no help in that regard. I've been with a few women, but we never did anything like that together."

"It's of no consequence," Senovo said. "The point is, it started me thinking about a similar place on the front wall of the passage to a woman's womb."

Andoc's brows drew together. "You think it's the same thing, but in a different place? I must confess I've never found anything like that inside a woman."

Senovo shrugged a shoulder. "The area is softer than in a man, and seems to require a firmer touch to produce results. But, yes, after pondering it I am of the opinion that it is basically the same thing."

I was following the conversation closely, trying to quell the nervousness I felt at the prospect of what was almost certainly coming. "I'm still not sure I understand what you're getting at. I already know that most women get pleasure from being penetrated. I've tried it—with fingers, at least. I don't. But I *do* get pleasure from the... other passage. Even though you say I don't have the thing inside that makes it feel good for men. What's your point?"

"The point is, you have probably never felt what it's like to receive pleasure from this place inside you. It's unlikely you would have found it during your own tentative explorations," Senovo said patiently. "If you would allow me, I will attempt to show you using my fingers, and I thought you might find it more palatable if you think of it as experiencing penetration more like a man does."

The other two let the silence settle around us as I considered this idea. It was a bit of a relief that no one was talking about fucking me tonight. After all, while I didn't enjoy it, I'd at least had fingers inside me before—my own and, once, Senovo's. It wasn't like it was the worst thing I've ever experienced. I tried to relax a bit, and made myself say what I was thinking, knowing that Senovo couldn't do his job properly if I didn't.

"All right," I said, "I think we should try it. I was a bit worried that you'd want Andoc to try to fuck me tonight, but I think I can handle fingers."

"If either of us could think of a way around this, *caradi*, you'd never have to do anything you didn't want to," Andoc said, sounding troubled.

I smiled up at him from my position on the floor, and brought his hand to my lips, kissing the knuckles tenderly. "I know. I keep telling you it's fine."

"It is not *fine*," Senovo said, "but it's a strategic decision designed to achieve a particular goal—namely, your acceptance within the village and the security of your position as Horse Mistress. That said, I see nothing to be gained from subjecting you to it more than once."

"Well," I said, making an effort to lighten the mood, "I *am* a virgin, you know. It doesn't seem like there's going to be much about this ceremony that's propitious, so let's not go messing up the one thing I've got going for me."

"Neither of us give a tinker's bollocks about how propitious the ceremony is," Andoc said. "We just don't want you hurt."

I clambered to my feet and leaned over to kiss him softly on the lips. "Don't be dramatic. You're not going to hurt me—men have been fucking women since forever. I may not feel like a woman in my mind, but unfortunately my body disagrees." I straightened and started pulling off my clothes. "Now, get undressed, both of you, and let Senovo show me this amazing thing that's supposedly inside me."

Senovo nodded agreement and shed his robes, fussing around with arranging me on a pile of pillows while Andoc finished unlacing his breeches and smallclothes so he could pull them off. My earlier ardor had cooled at the prospect of the ceremony tomorrow, but as I lay looking up at my two beautiful lovers, who looked down at me with such tender devotion and care, I could hardly help the way my pulse began to race once more.

"Kiss each other for me," I said. "I don't get to see you kiss nearly enough."

Andoc smiled roguishly, and reached across me for Senovo. Senovo came willingly enough, but paused halfway, placing a finger on Andoc's lips.

"Don't let me go under for you tonight," said the priest. "Not now, at any rate. I need to be able to concentrate."

With a nod of understanding, Andoc kissed the finger resting against his mouth. Senovo lowered his hand to rest on the swell of my breast and allowed Andoc to close the remaining distance between them. They explored each other with lips and tongues, leaning over my body to meet in the middle. Warmth bubbled up in my chest as if from an underground spring as I watched the way they cared for each other, and I felt the warmth overflow at the knowledge that they wanted to care for me, too.

Senovo's hand slipped gradually lower in what I suspected was a calculated move, until the pads of his fingers trailed over my pebbled nipple and dragged a hiss from me. At the noise, Andoc broke the kiss and looked down, one corner of his mouth quirking in amusement. He lowered himself to lie next to me so he could lean forward and take my other nipple in his mouth, drawing it in with firm suction and flicking the aching point with the tip of his tongue until I cried out with need.

Leaving my breasts to Andoc's tender mercies, Senovo scooted down to sit even with my hip and ran his hand up the length of my inner thigh. I tensed in anticipation, and he shushed me. "Shh… easy. It's not happening yet. I'll warn you before I do it."

Andoc pulled off my nipple with a soft *pop*. "Touch her cock," he said. "You know how much she likes that."

I couldn't help the desperate groan that forced its way past my lips. On the night we'd first become lovers, Senovo and Andoc had both commented on the unusually large size of the bud of flesh at the apex of my cunt. Andoc had called it a little cock, and the very idea had nearly made me come on the spot.

Senovo hummed agreement and slid a finger up the seam between my inner lips, dragging moisture to the front. He circled the small column of flesh, which swelled and hardened under his light, maddening touch. Andoc swooped down to cover my mouth in a searing kiss, muffling my gasps and moans as Senovo slowly tortured me below.

I was coming to understand that there were advantages and disadvantages to having a priest as a lover — one of the disadvantages being that he knew my body better than I did and was a master of taking me to the brink and easing me back, again and again until I finally tore my lips away from Andoc's, cursing and begging.

"*Fuck*! Please, gods — Senovo, please, please *let me come*!"

Andoc eased himself around so he could lift my head and shoulders into his lap. I rooted blindly until my cheek brushed his hard cock and rubbed my face against it like a cat, still groaning and cursing Senovo's name.

"Easy," Senovo said again. "You're almost there. I'm going to slip one finger in, and then I'll help you come."

I sobbed with need — I just wanted him to keep touching me the way he had been, but at this point I was willing to do whatever he wanted if it led to release. He slowly slid a finger back until the tip, following the contour of my body, disappeared inside. I tensed as the intrusion slid deeper, stretching me unpleasantly, and Andoc smoothed a hand over my cheek.

"Breathe for me," he said, and I let out an explosive breath so I could draw fresh air into my lungs.

Senovo's thumb teased the erect flesh at the apex of my cunt, even as his finger slid inside to the hilt, sending confusing jolts of sensation barreling through my body. "You're doing well," said the priest. "I know it's strange — give it a minute."

I nodded, my eyes tightly closed, and burrowed further into Andoc's lap while he stroked a hand through my short hair. Senovo's long finger pressed a tiny bit deeper and curled to rub against my front wall. I grunted in surprise and clenched around the intrusion.

He repeated the motion, setting up a slow but firm rhythm. I writhed against the strange pressure.

"All right?" he asked.

"Feels like… feels like I have to piss," I gasped.

"I promise that you don't, and it will pass soon," he said. "Can you hold on for me a little while longer?"

I nodded tightly, not opening my eyes. I had to do this. I didn't want to. I wanted to tell him to stop, but I'd gone too far to back out now. The pressure grew, changing gradually from the feeling of a full bladder to… something else. Senovo sped up his movements and let his thumb brush over my… my *cock* even as his finger rubbed back and forth over the place inside me. My breath jerked in and out in quick, shallow almost-sobs. I didn't want this strange and disconcerting feeling, and I hated the way my body was betraying me with its response. Its instinctive, female response. Andoc continued to soothe me, sliding his hand over my forehead… my cheek.

When the pressure was almost too much to bear, Senovo placed his free hand low on my abdomen and pressed down, which increased the force of his movements within. With no warning, I convulsed and squirted fluid over his hand and forearm in strong spurts, contracting rhythmically around his finger until I collapsed back, spent and shaky and over-stimulated. Fighting tears.

I shuddered as Senovo withdrew, fighting the urge to roll away from them both and curl up in the corner. Even Andoc's slow stroking of my cheek was too much right now, but I didn't want to worry them.

Of course, I wasn't taking into account Senovo's preternatural empathy.

"Do you need a moment?" he asked, his voice pitched low and even.

I nodded, keeping my eyes closed so I wouldn't have to see them yet. Andoc's hand disappeared, and then I was being lowered back to rest against the pile of pillows once more.

When my breathing had quieted, Andoc cleared his throat uncertainly. "I… couldn't tell if that was good or bad," he said.

I opened my eyes, but did not meet either of their gazes. "I don't ever want to do that again," I said.

"Then we never will," Senovo said, his voice troubled. "Please forgive me, Carivel—I truly thought it might help."

"It's not your fault, Senovo. None of this is your fault." I covered my face with one hand. "If I weren't such a fucked-up—"

"Stop," Andoc said. "Don't finish that sentence."

I huffed out a frustrated breath. "I'm not going to be able to come during the ceremony. Not with you inside me."

"Is there still going to be a ceremony?" Andoc asked cautiously.

"Yes, there's going to be a fucking ceremony!" I scrubbed at my eyes and forehead. "Nothing has changed since Volya came charging in here an hour ago."

"Carivel," Senovo said, urging me to look at him with a gentle touch to my chin, "If you think that no participant in a handfasting has ever been too nervous or tense to achieve release during the ceremony, you are very much mistaken. There is a degree of polite fiction involved in such things. I have faith that the gods take intention into account, and do not begrudge their children the worries and insecurities that make us human."

I looked into his solemn, green-gold eyes and felt tears pressing at the back of my throat. Swallowing them down, I replied, "Since our *intention* is to undergo a sham handfasting to keep Volya happy, I'm not sure that really helps."

"You love each other," Senovo said, as if it was an answer.

"And both of us love you," Andoc said. I felt the mattress dip as he settled on my other side. "Carivel, can I hold you now, or do you need some more time?"

In lieu of an answer, I half-crawled and half-scooted into his arms, where I could bury my face in the crook of his shoulder and breathe in his scent. Since I was basically sprawled in his lap, it didn't take me long to notice his cock, barely stiff now where it rested against my thigh. I nudged against it, drawing his attention.

"You all right?" I asked. "Do you want me or Senovo to—"

"I want you to stay right where you are," he said. "What about you, Senovo?"

"There are still one or two things I need to check on before I retire for the evening," Senovo said, sounding weary.

"You'll come back, though?" I asked quickly, raising my head to find him shrugging into his white robes.

"I will," he assured, and reached down to kiss me on the forehead. He let his own forehead rest against Andoc's for a moment, and then he was gone, closing the door behind him quietly.

"This is all so incredibly screwed up," I said, and flopped back against Andoc's chest. "I realized earlier that we're getting handfasted tomorrow and we haven't even talked about where we'll live."

Andoc was silent for a beat before answering, "Well, I imagine you'll continue to more or less live at the horse pens, and me, at the training yard and the meeting hall. No doubt we'll both require *extensive* counseling from Senovo in the evenings, since we're such a pair of bull-headed rogues."

A puff of laughter escaped my lips. "Life really is that simple for you, huh?"

Andoc tightened his arms around me. "It's been my experience that if you try to control and struggle against every little thing, you have no energy left for the important fights... the ones that really matter. I honestly don't care about our living arrangements, *caradi*. If you want to move into my hut because it's bigger, go ahead. If you want to keep yours so you'll have a place to yourself, do that. Personally, I'm fond of the temple. I managed to squeeze into the tiny bed in Senovo's sleeping cell on many a night over the past few years. I'm sure the High Priest's rooms are spacious enough for three."

"People will talk," I said.

"People are already talking. If you're going to let that bother you, I'm afraid you've got a difficult life ahead."

I was quiet for a long time after that.

"Try to get some sleep," Andoc said eventually. "Things'll probably look worse in the morning... but they should start looking up again by the morning after that."

I snorted in bleak amusement and let him rearrange us in the bed so he was lying down with me curled up against his side. I was still awake when Senovo came in some time later on silent feet, snuffed the candles, and slipped into the bed on Andoc's other side. Indeed, I was still awake hours later, listening to the reassuring sound of their breathing as they slept.

Eventually, I sank into a world of tangled dreams that left me groggy and disoriented when Senovo woke me just before dawn, the backs of his fingers ghosting over my cheek.

"Go," he told me. "Do your job; clear your mind. Eat something, bathe yourself in the river, and return to us here before the sun reaches the top of the old sentinel tree at the edge of the village green. We will be waiting for you."

I nodded up at him and searched for the words I wanted to say.

"Senovo… I just want you to know. I'm glad it's going to be you. Today, I mean. I don't think I could do this, if it was someone else."

The priest gave me a quick, faint smile that was gone almost as soon as it appeared. "I will help in any way I can, Carivel. Now, go on, and let me deal with this lump." He indicated Andoc's oblivious form in the light of the room's single candle. "Judging by the level of snoring, I fear it will not be pretty. Pitchers and cold water may be involved."

The fond smile that tugged at the corner of my lips was heartfelt. I rolled out of bed and pulled on my clothes in the flickering light, glancing at the high window to judge the time.

"I'll leave you to it, then," I said, and darted in for a brief kiss.

"There should be some bread left from last night in the refectory," Senovo added as I turned to leave. "Help yourself, lest I be subjected to a lecture on the importance of making sure you get breakfast."

"Gods forbid," I agreed, still smiling a bit, and took my leave.

The butterflies were already stirring in my stomach as I ducked into the refectory and sheepishly greeted Reston, who was starting a pot of gruel to simmer. I left the temple, eating the coarse bread as I made my way to the horse pens. For once in recent days, I was the first person to arrive, so I excused the night guard and started organizing things for the day.

The apprentices trickled in as the sun came up. I watched Favian working with the white foal from a distance, pleased at his progress, and wondered again if there was anything I could do to salvage that particular relationship. When the early morning chores were complete, I caught Dalon's attention and motioned him to one side.

"Which horse would you say is our fastest in a straight gallop?" I asked.

Dalon considered the question for a moment. "I'd say it's that tall chestnut colt with two front socks and the knot on his shoulder."

"Agreed," I said. "Catch him and saddle him up before the lads take the rest of the herd out to graze. You and I are going out to the summer pastures for a little race later this morning."

Dalon made an interested noise and headed into the large corral to get the colt. I puttered around, taking care of odds and ends until mid-morning, when things tended to naturally slow down. Nietre nickered to me as I approached, clearly pleased to see me. I saddled him and ran through an abbreviated series of yielding exercises while we waited for Dalon to show up with the chestnut colt.

The colt was tall and lanky for a Draebardi horse, but still more than a hand shorter than the black stallion. Nietre snorted a challenge, puffing himself up and arching his neck until I flashed my trusty flag-on-a-stick and backed him up several steps.

"That colt's no threat to you, Fidget-Brain," I chided. "He's not going to be taking away any of the lovely mares I've got lined up for you."

Nietre shook his head and blew out an explosive snort. I gathered up the reins and mounted, still not used to feeling so incredibly tall once I was seated in the saddle. Dalon and I headed out on the northern road, drawing a small crowd of onlookers as we trotted away. Nietre continued to try to fuss with the poor colt, which looked ready to flee if the older, larger stallion so much as breathed on him wrong.

Once we'd reached a flat stretch of land with no obstacles ahead, I pulled up and grinned across at Dalon. "What do you think?" I asked.

"I think I'm about to get my arse handed to me," Dalon replied, but his grin was every bit as wide and predatory as mine. "You call it."

We pointed our mounts toward the open road ahead. Both animals danced in place, champing at their bits.

"Three... two... one..." I counted. "*Go!*"

The chestnut colt was quicker off the mark than Nietre, his shorter legs and more powerful hindquarters giving him more thrust during the first few strides. Nietre half-reared and flung himself in pursuit, flattening out into a ground-eating gallop as I leaned into the wind and gave him his head. I could just make out Dalon whooping with excitement a couple lengths ahead of us, his shouts nearly swallowed up by the mad pace of the two running animals.

The rush of exhilaration at the speed and danger welled up in me as well, crowding out everything else as I crouched in the saddle and let Nietre hurtle us forward, gaining ground on the chestnut colt. I could barely breathe as the wind whipped past my face, but I would not have traded that feeling for anything in the world. At that moment, if Nietre had been capable of running forever, I'd probably have let him.

We were coming even with the colt's haunches now, and the black stallion was so focused on the race that he didn't even try to pin his ears back or snap at the horse next to him. I let out my own whoop as we drew even with Dalon's saddle... then the colt's shoulder... then his neck, until the two animals were running as if in tandem.

The chestnut was outclassed, though, and he knew it. The colt's neck was already lathered and his nostrils wide open, blowing hard with every stride. Nietre put on a fresh burst of speed and the other horse fell back, back, back, until we were running clear. My heart pounded with excitement and joy as Nietre flattened his ears and swept forward toward the horizon, carrying me along as if I weighed nothing.

When I finally straightened my upper body and settled deeper in the saddle to slow the stallion to an easy canter, and from there to a walk, I looked back to see Dalon far behind us, reining in his own mount and giving me a cheery wave.

"Naloth's balls," he called when I had wandered back close enough for him to be heard. "That's the most amazing thing I've ever seen! I thought he'd keep going all day!"

"Too bad he'd try to kill any other horse he was hitched with," I answered. "I bet he could pull the axle right off a chariot."

"We don't have any horses big and fast enough to hitch him with, anyway," Dalon pointed out. "Guess we'll just have to breed our own."

I grinned, thinking of the plans I had for Draebard's herd. "Guess so." I glanced skyward, and the position of the sun drained some of my good humor. "I suppose we should get back."

"S'pose so. You're getting hitched yourself this afternoon, aren't you?" Dalon asked, ever tactful.

"So they tell me," I replied, letting some of the sourness in my thoughts filter into my voice.

"Ah... you netted yourself a First Warrior, though, yeah? Can't be as bad as all that," Dalon said, utterly guileless.

"Yes—I guess I did, didn't I?" I said, wishing that life could be as simple for me as it seemed to be for other people. "Come on. It wouldn't do to keep him waiting."

We headed back to the village at an easy trot, letting the horses slow to a walk at intervals to cool them out. By the time we'd gotten back and unsaddled our mounts, the sun was right overhead. I hurried back to my hut for clean clothes—not that I'd be wearing them for very long—and gave up on the idea of trying to put anything in my roiling stomach. Instead, I headed to a secluded spot upriver and stripped off my dusty work clothes before plunging into the chilly water and scrubbing away the day's grime.

When I presented myself at the temple, dressed in fresh linen and shivering slightly since I'd forgotten to bring anything clean to use as a towel, the sun was just dipping toward the upper branches of the sentinel tree at the edge of the green. I bowed low at the wide-open entrance, trying not to wonder about what the gods might think of this charade. I was probably happier not knowing—I just hoped that any potential bad fortune would be confined to me... or maybe Volya, who certainly deserved it.

Scarcely had I straightened and stepped through the door when I was met by Eiridan, who dipped his upper body in acknowledgement before speaking. "Welcome, Horse Mistress Carivel. Your beloved awaits you at the altar. Please follow me."

I nodded, and let him lead me deeper into the temple. It wasn't surprising that Senovo had chosen Eiridan to assist him in the ceremony—of the two Mereni novices, he seemed the least likely to be shocked or offended by any potential... irregularities. And, though I hardly knew Eiridan at all, after witnessing his concern for Senovo following the funeral two nights ago, I already felt the beginnings of affection for him.

Eiridan brought me to a small room just off the large space that housed the altar and helped me remove my clothes. I couldn't stop the faint blush that climbed up my chest to heat my face. Even though Eiridan showed no interest whatsoever in my nakedness, I had bared my body to so few people in my lifetime that I couldn't help some embarrassment over the soft, coltish curves of my breasts and hips, where there should have been hard angles and muscles.

And yet, if I'd had the body of a man, I wouldn't be joining publicly with Andoc. Of course, I also wouldn't have to submit to being taken by him in a way I didn't want to be. It was all so confusing. While it was possible that Andoc and Senovo would still have wanted me if I were fully male, at least now, our relationship would not have to be hidden. Well... not *completely* hidden, at any rate.

I wondered what the response from the village would be if it became common knowledge that we were both still involved with a eunuch despite being handfasted. Would it spawn outrage, or simply give people another thing to gossip about? And, more importantly, would it endanger Senovo's position as High Priest?

There was so much to worry about that it was overwhelming. Sometimes I really did envy the apparent simplicity of Andoc's worldview. This was definitely one of those times.

Now, though, I was using worry about the future as an excuse not to think about the present. Eiridan was peering at me closely, so I must have tarried too long, lost in thought.

"Sorry," I said, "I guess I'm a little more nervous than I thought."

The young priest's expression softened. "It is a major step in one's life," he said kindly, "but you and the First Warrior appear to be admirably matched, and our High Priest is clearly very fond of both of you. All will be well, Horse Mistress."

"Thanks," I said, relaxing slightly almost in spite of myself. "If you don't mind me saying so, I think you've got a great future ahead of you here. You're really good at this."

Eiridan smiled, looking genuinely pleased. "You are too kind. Now, however, let us not keep the others waiting."

ELEVEN

The novice led me from the small changing room to the huge central space dotted by wooden support pillars and dominated by a low altar, where Andoc stood tall and proud in his nakedness. I flushed again, for a slightly different reason this time, before my eyes were drawn to Senovo, clad in white, standing behind the flat stone with his hands folded into the sleeves of his robes. As I got closer, I could see the ceremonial kohl lining his eyes, making them appear even deeper and more striking than usual.

My heart was racing by the time Eiridan delivered me into Andoc's arms. I was somewhat surprised to discover that Andoc's was beating nearly as fast, thrumming between us where our skin touched. Eiridan moved smoothly into an unobtrusive position behind the altar, which was draped with a soft suede deer hide to catch my virgin blood, if there was any. I shivered a bit at the thought.

Senovo met our eyes in turn and raised his hands, palm up.

"Mighty Naloth, He Who Seeds the Earth and Brings the Rain," he said in a clear tone that echoed around the space but was still, somehow, quite intimate. "Bountiful Utarr, She Who Bears Fruit. Bless, tonight, this union between Andoc and Carivel, two of your children. They come before you as they came into this world, naked in the eyes of gods and men.

"Carivel. Andoc. Tonight you tie your destinies together under the gods' watchful gaze. To symbolize this union, Novice Eiridan will bind your hands, teaching you to work together as one, relying on each other as you have previously relied only on yourselves. Do you both agree to this handfasting, freely and joyfully?"

"We do," I lied smoothly, Andoc's voice echoing mine a breath later.

Eiridan circled around the altar to face us, and I got my first glimpse of the thongs that would tie our hands together for a night and a day. Andoc held out his right hand and I grasped it with my left, feeling lightheaded as the novice wove the soft leather bindings around our fingers and palms in a complicated web that was both effective and beautiful to look upon. When he was satisfied that the tie would hold, Eiridan reached up and pressed his cool hand to my forehead in a blessing.

"May the gods smile upon your future together, Horse Mistress," he said, and moved his hand to Andoc's head. "Peace and prosperity be upon your union, First Warrior."

Once the novice priest returned to his position in the background, Senovo lowered his hands to rest lightly on the altar. "You are now joined—one heart, one soul," he said. "Celebrate your union before the gods. Find your joy within each other, that new life... may... grow from the fertile field of your love."

The pause was tiny, but noticeable, and my stomach clenched. *Actually,* I thought to the unseen presences who were presumably hovering around us in the temple, *if we could avoid that part for the time being, that would be great. Please?*

Andoc's kiss dragged my attention back to the here-and-now. I pulled him to me almost desperately, alarmed to find that I was about as far from aroused as I had ever been in my life.

"Easy," he said between kisses. "Easy, now, *caradi...* I've got you... it will be all right..."

I tugged him back toward the altar, just wanting it to be over. When the backs of my knees hit the hard stone, Andoc steadied me using our bound hands, and I flinched at the reminder that I was trapped in this way as well.

"Senovo," Andoc said under his breath, and suddenly Senovo was there as well, with a hand under the elbow of my free arm. The two of them eased me down to sit on the edge of the stone slab and I concentrated on breathing for a bit. When I came back to myself, Andoc was running the fingers of his left hand through my short hair and Senovo was crouched in front of me at eye level.

"Carivel," he said, speaking very slowly and clearly, "talk to us. Do you still wish to complete the handfasting?"

"Yes!" I gasped, even more panicked than I was before at the thought of all this having been for nothing.

"Very well," Senovo soothed, while Andoc continued his slow caresses, never breaking the rhythm.

Through an effort of will, I swallowed down all the worry and fear inside me until I could meet his eyes and speak more calmly. "I'm sorry. Don't mind me, it's only nerves. It's fine."

Senovo looked like he was fighting his own demons, but his voice was level as he replied. "I understand completely. We both do." His eyes flicked up to Andoc, who looked unusually pale as he nodded. I wondered idly what Eiridan was making of all this, but I was afraid to look and find out.

"Carivel," Andoc said, drawing my attention back to him, "do you want to be on top for this? Would that be easier?"

I thought about it for a moment, or tried to—my mind still shied away from speculating about the act directly. I didn't want to think about Andoc's prick shooting seed into my womb. About falling pregnant. About being a mother. Having a child I didn't want... just like my mother hadn't wanted *me*.

"I don't want to have to move or do anything... you know—*during*," I managed eventually.

After a moment, Senovo said, "Hands and knees at the edge of the altar, then, while you take her from behind, standing up, I think. Andoc?"

"Whatever you think would be best," Andoc said, still watching me closely. "Carivel... *caradi*? Did you hear that?"

I nodded, not caring about the details, just that it would be over soon. To that end, I twisted around so that our bound hands wouldn't get tangled and knelt on the edge of the stone, the thick hide covering it barely sufficient to protect my knees. I balanced my upper body over my right forearm, my left arm stretched awkwardly across the small of my back, to join with Andoc's right as he stood behind me.

"Carivel, *wait*," Andoc said, sounding more at sea than I'd ever heard him as his free hand steadied my hip. "At least let me prepare you first. We can pleasure each other in some other way..."

I shook my head, almost frantically. "It won't work right now... I can't. Please, Andoc, I just want it *over*!"

"You're not even wet!" Andoc shot back. "And I'm certainly not hard!"

"Andoc," Senovo said, his voice injecting a welcome calm, "I have oil. Under the circumstances, this may be the best way... and it is what Carivel wants."

"High Priest," Eiridan interjected, "Forgive me, but I am not at all comfortable with what is happening here."

I clenched my eyes shut, sensing yet more obstacles in the offing. Senovo's voice showed strain for the first time as he replied, "Eiridan, you are correct to offer an objection, of course. There are circumstances involved in this handfasting of which you are unaware. My failure to explain them to you ahead of time was probably poor judgment on my part, and my only excuse is that I am tasked with protecting a number of conflicting confidences related to this matter."

I flopped over, boneless, and buried my face in the crook of my free arm. "It's all right," I said into the hide beneath me. "I'll tell him. I... I trust him."

"Horse Mistress?" Eiridan asked, sounding completely lost.

"You call me Horse Mistress, Eiridan," I said, "but up until a few days ago, the people of Draebard knew me only as a man. I'd been living as one since I moved here three years ago and apprenticed myself to the old Horse Master. Volya was furious when he found out I was female, but he needs the treaty with the Mereni, and Magoldis only agreed to the treaty because she thought Volya had softened toward letting women hold positions of power."

Eiridan was silent for a moment, digesting this new information. "And... this handfasting?"

I rolled my head to the side so I could see him properly, aware of the ridiculous figure I must have cut, curled naked on the altar. "The handfasting was Volya's price for my position in Draebard. As First Warrior, Andoc is under his control, and now I will be under Andoc's."

"But you do love each other," Eiridan said, watching my face intently even though he'd presented it as a statement rather than a question.

"Yes," I said without hesitation. "And that's why we've agreed to do it."

"And yet, you fear coupling with him."

I steeled myself to reply honestly. "Yes. When I said I'd been living as a man since I came here, I didn't just mean I'd been cutting my hair short and wearing trousers."

Eiridan looked taken aback. "So you do not desire men?"

"No, I *do* desire men. I just don't desire to be taken like a woman. However, thanks to Volya, that's the price of my acceptance here, as Horse Mistress in Draebard."

Eiridan blinked. "I see." His gaze turned inward for a moment before he looked back at Senovo. "High Priest... my loyalty to you, and to the temple is absolute, and I want you to know that nothing said here will go beyond these walls."

"Thank you, Little Brother," Senovo said. "You have behaved honorably. I unwittingly trapped you in a difficult position, for which I am sorry."

"I understand why you did it, Elder Brother. However, there are many things here that I find unacceptable. I think it might be preferable if I were not present for the remainder of the ceremony in case there are any further... unusual occurrences that people might later ask me about—if you take my meaning." He turned his attention back to me. "Unless, of course, either the Horse Mistress or the First Warrior would prefer me to stay?"

I shook my head almost immediately, relieved at the idea of having one less person witness what was likely to be an unpleasant few minutes for everyone involved. Beside me, Andoc said, "No, Eiridan, you don't need to stay. And I'm sorry you were put in this situation in the first place."

"And I am sorry that the two of you were placed in this position by circumstances you could not control," Eiridan replied. "If asked, I will say that High Priest Senovo sent me for some tea to help the couple relax during the ceremony. Unfortunately, as I am still unfamiliar with the temple, it took me longer than it should have, and the coupling was complete when I returned."

"You're a good man, Eiridan," Andoc said.

Eiridan flickered an eyebrow. "I can see now why the High Priest chose me instead of Feldes to assist, despite the fact that he has almost a year's seniority over me. I think Brother Feldes might have suffered an apoplectic fit after hearing this tale."

"It is true that I've sensed a certain... flexibility in you that Novice Feldes does not possess," Senovo allowed. "Thank you again, Little Brother. If you could... go get that tea, it would be greatly appreciated."

Eiridan bowed to all of us and left the room, his sandals clacking softly against the stone floor until the sound faded away into the depths of the temple. When we were alone, Andoc turned to Senovo.

"Novice Eiridan has just given me an idea," he said, "and I need both of you to trust me. Senovo, hand me that oil, and then sit down in front of Carivel and let her rest her head in your lap while I take her from behind. Just... focus on *her*, please, *amadi*."

Senovo gave Andoc a long, speculative look, but he unstoppered the oil and handed it to Andoc without further comment. My heart resumed its frantic pace — this was it, it was really going to happen now. I swallowed against the strange obstruction blocking my throat and resumed my position at the edge of the altar, presenting my cunt in the air like a bitch in heat. *Though the bitch actually wants to be fucked*, my inner voice added, snide and unhelpful as always.

This time, Senovo sat down in front of me, and I buried my face in his flowing white robes. Rather than stroke my head as Andoc had done, he looped an arm across my back and cupped my left shoulder in a gesture of support.

"Hurry, please," I begged, the words muffled in soft linen. Tears were pricking at my eyes, and I didn't know how much longer I could maintain my composure.

"Just a moment more, *caradi*," Andoc said. I could hear the sound of flesh slapping against oiled flesh, and I pictured him oiling up his cock, bringing it to full hardness. Clammy sweat broke out across my face and chest despite the pleasantly cool air inside the temple.

I jerked in surprise and clenched my eyes shut when his free hand touched my left buttock, pressing my face harder against Senovo's thigh. Fingers trailed down and I held my breath, but rather than pressing inside me, they slid, slick and oily, into the space between the top of my thighs. Andoc spread oil generously over my slit and around the skin of my inner thighs.

"There," he said, pulling his fingers away. A strong, slippery hand repositioned my legs slightly, urging me to kneel with my knees pressed tightly together. "Perfect. Trust me now, *caradi*. I promise not to hurt you."

Andoc's large, blunt cock pressed at the apex of my thighs, but instead of invading me painfully, it slid home into the soft, tight space framed by my mons and the top of my legs.

"Wha—" I gasped in surprise, as pleasant tingles skittered up my spine. Andoc pulled back and slid home again, taking up a smooth rhythm that rubbed back and forth over my sensitive inner lips rather than penetrating me.

I clutched convulsively at Senovo's robes, a few of the tears that had threatened earlier squeezing out past my tightly closed eyelids as gratitude overcame me. Andoc was going to fake our coupling, right here on the altar. I wasn't sure if his attempt to protect Senovo from complicity in the deception had any merit in the gods' eyes or not. If the gods were just, I suspected we were going to end up paying for this duplicity sooner or later... but right now I didn't care one whit.

"That's it," Andoc soothed as I gradually wrestled my ragged breathing back under control. "You're all right now, *caradi*. So slick and tight for me... you feel so good."

I couldn't help it... I *whimpered*, and Senovo smoothed his hand down the length of my back, playing the pads of his fingers over the dimples at the base of my spine. Andoc's thrusts grew faster and stronger, his balls slapping against my skin as he drove home again and again. The slip and slide of sensitive, oiled flesh grew more and more enjoyable as my earlier panic receded into the background. I thought that I might like to try this sometime when I wasn't quite so busy committing blasphemy with one arm twisted uncomfortably behind me. Perhaps Senovo would let me suck him some day while Andoc took me like this...

My thoughts were interrupted when Andoc grunted, his smooth thrusts becoming erratic. He buried the head of his cock in the soft skin of my thighs and growled, his warm spend dripping down my legs onto the deer hide beneath me. His heavy body draped over mine, taking the pressure off our bound wrists and trapping Senovo's hand between us.

"It is done," said the priest, both sadness and resolve audible in his voice. A new wave of guilt swept over me as I realized that this had been Senovo's first handfasting ceremony as High Priest, and, thanks to me, it was a fraudulent joke from start to finish. When he laid his hand on first my head, and then Andoc's in a heartfelt blessing for our happiness, it somehow made things even worse.

Andoc roused himself enough to untangle us and get us into a more comfortable position on the low block of stone. I made a surreptitious move to wipe the back of my free hand across my eyes.

"All right?" he asked, studying my face. I gazed into his deep-set brown eyes, searching for a reason why he would continue to risk himself and break rules for someone like me, but all I saw was concern mirrored back at me. I nodded, feeling a sudden wave of utter exhaustion sweep over me.

"Tired," I said.

"If you have both recovered sufficiently, I will take you to your room," Senovo offered, his mask firmly back in place.

Andoc was slightly unsteady as he rose, urging me up with him, and we braced each other as Senovo gathered up the hide—covered with Andoc's spilled seed rather than my virgin blood. Without once looking down at the soft brown leather folded neatly in his hands—or the substance staining it—he led us slowly down the hallway to the same room where we had spent the previous two nights. Now, though, it was filled with platters of fresh food cut into pieces that would be easy to eat one-handed, along with pitchers of wine and mead, clusters of lit candles, and clean blankets and pillows on the large bed.

"Rest," said the priest. "I will inform the Chief that everything in the ceremony went as it should, and return to check on you this evening."

Senovo left before either of us could offer any gesture of thanks or affection. I was so tired that it took several long moments before the sense of his words percolated through my mind.

"Everything 'went as it should'..." I echoed, collapsing onto the edge of the bed.

"As I feared, he's far too intelligent to fall for such a transparent ruse," Andoc said. "Still, our dear and devious Senovo has a bright future ahead of him as High Priest. I don't think Volya stands a chance in this particular battle of wits."

"He's upset, though," I said quietly as Andoc sat down next to me on the bed. "Even if he hides it, lying to the gods doesn't sit well with him."

Silence reigned for a long moment.

"Come on," Andoc said in lieu of a reply, "rest with me awhile. You're knackered, and I usually fall asleep after sex anyway. I'll even refrain from asking if you ate before the ceremony like Senovo told you to."

"Just as well," I muttered under my breath, as we clumsily rearranged ourselves around our bound hands and curled together on the thick, straw-stuffed mattress.

"As I suspected," Andoc said, sounding resigned. "Sleep first, then food."

I hummed agreement, already drifting off despite the drama of the last hour. Andoc cuddled me closer, our joined hands resting on his hard-muscled stomach as I slipped into a deep sleep.

When I awoke, it was dark outside the small window.

"Thank the gods," Andoc said. "I'm about to burst if I don't get to the chamber pot."

"You are *such* a romantic," I grumbled, right before I became aware that I was in roughly the same predicament.

The next few minutes fluctuated somewhere between awkward and amusing, and I began to understand what the Ancestors were getting at when it came to this part of the handfasting ceremony. It was eye-opening to have to rely on someone else's assistance for things that I normally did without thought.

Andoc and I washed up a bit, cleaning the oil and dried spend from my legs before we descended into childish attempts to flick water on each others' faces. When a knock came on the door a few minutes later, we were curled up on the bed with platters of food, while I alternated feeding myself and Andoc, much to his apparent amusement.

"Come in!" he called, and the door opened to admit Senovo, carrying a small, wrapped parcel in one hand.

"Oh good," said the priest. "I wasn't honestly sure what I'd find when I returned."

A few hours of sound sleep had done wonders for my mood, and I tossed a piece of spiced ground tuber at Senovo's chest good-naturedly. He ignored it beyond the raised eyebrow he shot in my direction, and placed the mysterious package on the corner of the table.

"Join us, *amadi*," Andoc said, his voice warm and deep enough to send a pleasant shiver up my spine. "Things aren't complete without you here."

"No," I agreed. "It's much harder to keep from smacking him when you're not around."

"In that case, my congratulations on your self-control," Senovo replied. I was pleased to see a twinkle of amusement in his eyes, though he seemed unremittingly weary these days. He came to Andoc's outstretched hand and allowed himself to be guided down for a kiss, first from Andoc and then from me.

When he pulled back, I noticed something and frowned, lifting my free hand to trace the thin skin under his left eye with a light touch.

"What is it?" asked the priest, his brow furrowing slightly.

A faint blush heated my cheeks. "Sorry," I apologized, "it's nothing. I just noticed that you've removed your kohl, is all."

He still looked faintly confused when he answered. "I... only wear it for ceremonies, Carivel."

Andoc laughed softly, his eyes catching mine. "He honestly has no idea."

"I honestly don't," Senovo agreed, his look of confusion growing deeper. "Perhaps someone would care to enlighten me?"

"Whenever you line your eyes with kohl, Carivel stares at you like she wants to devour you whole, you fool," Andoc said, amusement coloring his tone. "She has for years now."

Senovo blinked, his face going blank. "Oh," he said. "I... see. A moment, then. Excuse me..."

He left the room, and I fought a losing battle not to collapse into undignified giggles. When I flopped back, spent, I shook my head in amazement. "He really doesn't get it at all, does he?"

"Nope," Andoc said. "Perhaps you'll have better luck getting through to him than I've had over the years."

"Maybe it's a two-person job," I countered.

"I suppose it might be, at that."

When Senovo returned a few minutes later, his striking amber-green eyes were once again lined with black, ending with a stylized curl at the corners. He wore a sleeveless jerkin of gray animal fur over tan breeches and soft boots. I let out a soft gasp, leaning forward for a better look at the sleek, newly exposed lines of his body, even as Andoc gave a low rumble of approval beside me. His cock twitched against my hip.

"Better?" Senovo asked, a faintly tentative note in his voice.

"In three-and-a-bit years, I don't think I've ever seen you in clothing other than priests' robes," I said, still drinking in the sight. "I wasn't even aware that you owned other clothing…"

"The jerkin is Andoc's," Senovo said, causing hot desire to flood my belly at the thought. He paused for a beat before adding, "It seemed appropriate. I am not here right now in my capacity as priest. At least, not unless you wish me to be." The last sentence was hesitant… almost shy, and my heart melted anew.

"We just want you, *amadi*," Andoc said. "Whether you are a priest or a flea-bitten wolf or the scared and angry kid you were when you and I first met. Just be *you*."

"I want to know every part of you that you're willing to show me," I added. "You've given me so much already, Senovo."

Senovo looked away, as if he could not quite meet our eyes after such declarations. When he looked back up, faint color tinged his cheeks in the candlelight. "Well, I have one more thing to give you tonight. Or, I suppose, three things, to be more accurate."

He crossed to the table and picked up the package he'd brought earlier, handing it to me. Andoc's blatant curiosity made it obvious that he was none the wiser regarding the contents. "Open it," he urged, giving me a nudge.

TWELVE

"Give me back my other hand and I will," I huffed, tugging at our bound wrists. When Andoc scoffed and let me drag his hand over so I could get both of mine on the cord holding the covering closed, I unwrapped the parcel with awkward movements, revealing two intricately carved wooden phalluses resting on a bundle of soft leather strapping.

I stared for a moment before lifting one and examining it closely. This one was slightly curved, where the other one was straight. Both were life-sized, slightly shorter than Andoc's generous prick and not quite as thick, with wide, flat bases—so they could stand on a table or shelf, I supposed. I ran my finger over the lifelike veins. The wood had been polished until it was as smooth as silk, and rubbed with oil until it gleamed.

"They're beautiful," I breathed.

Senovo stood looking down at us, a faint uptick at one corner of his mouth. "One of the woodcarvers in the village makes these for the priests. We give them to men who can't get hard for one reason or another, but who still desire intimacy with their partners. I'm told they can be quite effective."

I looked down at the smooth wooden cock in my hand. "Wait, you mean people actually *use* these?"

"They do indeed."

An odd frisson went through me as I pictured it. But... "Don't we have enough real cocks here? I mean, they're lovely and I appreciate the gift, but I think on balance, I prefer the real thing."

Senovo only smiled, as if at some secret joke. "If I could give you one of those, I surely would, Carivel. Unfortunately, that is beyond even a High Priest."

Andoc sucked in a surprised breath, and I looked over at him. For his part, he was staring up at Senovo with an expression of shock. I glanced back and forth between them, aware that I was missing something important.

"There's another thing that old men do," Andoc said slowly, "if the stories in the training yard are to be believed, that is."

"Oh, yes?" Senovo prompted, all innocence.

"Apparently you can get a hollow tube made out of stiff leather, shaped like a cock. You stick your own prick in the tube, and attach it to a harness around your hips. Then you can fuck your partner with the fake leather cock, even if you can't get your real one to stay up."

My brow furrowed in confusion. Even though he was a eunuch, I had already seen that Senovo could get a perfectly decent erection with the right help. The priest reached down and pulled the leather straps out of the parcel, letting them dangle over his fingers as he raised both eyebrows in a teasing expression. "A harness like this one, you mean?"

I stared at the collection of straps and buckles, similar to something you might find as part of the harness for a chariot team. A beaten bronze ring lay in Senovo's palm, forming the center point of the contraption. A ring that was slightly smaller than the flared bases of the carved phalluses. Something slipped into place in my head with a nearly audible click, and my eyes flew back to Senovo's.

"You… had this made… for *me*?" I asked, trying to wrap my mind around what Senovo was offering.

"I thought it was the least I could do, under the circumstances," he demurred. "Would you like to try it on?"

My mouth opened, but no words came out.

"She means *yes*," Andoc said, and gestured for Senovo to move the platters of food off the bed so he could more or less drag me to my feet.

I stood and watched in a daze while Senovo slipped the curved phallus through the bronze ring of the harness. He buckled it around my hips and the tops of my thighs, adjusting the straps until the whole thing fit snugly. When he finally pulled away, I looked down to see a pale brown cock jutting proudly from the thatch of curly hair between my legs. The base rested low on my pubic bone, promising a delicious grind against my own small and useless nub when I pressed the sleek wood deep into a willing body. My skin flared hot, and immediately cold again.

"Why did you give me two?" I asked, my voice emerging breathy and high-pitched.

Senovo stepped into my space and smiled down at me, his beautiful eyes wavering in and out of my vision as all the blood in my body rushed downwards. Beside me, Andoc steadied me with our joined hands and an arm around my waist. His fingers played with the edge of the strap at the small of my back.

"I would imagine it's so you can use one for fucking," Andoc said.

"Precisely," the priest agreed. "Which leaves the other one available... for this."

Senovo dropped smoothly to his knees in front of me, grasping my hips in his hands and sliding his lips over the flared head of the carved cock. I gasped, my knees turning instantly to water as I watched the hard column disappear, inch by inch, into that talented mouth. Only Andoc's grip kept me from dropping as if pole-axed.

Senovo looked up at me with kohl-lined eyes, holding my gaze as he worked his way down the unforgiving length. I tried not to hyperventilate or faint on the spot. Wetness flooded my throbbing cunt and immediately started to drip down my thighs.

"I think she likes it," Andoc said smugly, still more or less holding me up. "I know I certainly do."

Senovo started to nod agreement, only to choke on the hard wood brushing the back of his throat and pull back.

"Bit harder to swallow than flesh, eh?" Andoc asked.

"Evidently," Senovo said in a slightly hoarse voice, before clearing his throat. "The straight one would be easier."

"Good thing you like a challenge," Andoc said.

"*Guh*," I said, brilliantly.

"You still with us, there, *caradi*?" Andoc asked, managing to somehow cram both amusement and concern into the simple question.

My mouth worked for a moment before anything came out. "I... Senovo, Andoc, I... I need—"

I looked down at my hand, bound to Andoc's, then up at Andoc's face, and down at Senovo, still kneeling in front of me. Andoc followed my gaze, and after a moment his face cleared.

"Yes," he said. "You know, I think you're absolutely right."

He attacked the complicated web of thongs binding us together with his free hand, and I followed with mine.

"What are you doing?" Senovo asked, sounding utterly taken aback. "You mustn't—"

"*Senovo*," Andoc said, cutting him off. "This handfasting has been a fraud from the beginning. We don't want to be bonded as a couple. We want to be bonded with *you*."

Senovo dropped back to sit abruptly and un-gracefully on the flagstone floor. "There's no such thing as a three-way handfasting," he whispered.

The blasted thongs finally came loose and I fell forward, heedless of my bare knees hitting the hard stone as I straddled Senovo's lap and hugged him close, the wooden cock trapped between our bodies.

"I don't care... it's not fair; none of this is *fair*!" I said.

Senovo's arms came up to close around my shoulders reflexively. "It's just a ruse. It doesn't matter, Carivel. Nothing has changed."

"We're making it so that you have to lie to everyone, though," I said miserably. "The gods—"

"I haven't said a word so far that wasn't the truth," Senovo interrupted, "I've merely let people make their own assumptions. And besides..." He looked down and to the side. "You should already know that I am a past master when it comes to lies of omission."

Unable to hold back, I surged up and kissed him, pressing in, deep and urgent, when he opened for me. "Want you both," I gasped between kisses, "Need you both so badly..."

"Good gods, you two," Andoc said, "you really are trying to kill me, aren't you?" Strong hands pulled me off Senovo's lap, and Andoc growled, "Clothes *off*, Senovo..."

The priest's eyes darkened, the pupils dilating in the light of the flickering candles. He moved to unfasten his borrowed jerkin while Andoc kissed me, our stiff cocks pressed together between us like crossed swords. When Andoc turned me in his arms so we could both look down and watch Senovo undressing, my hand wandered to the smooth wood between my legs as if of its own volition. I cupped the curved phallus gently for a moment before gripping it in loose fingers and fisting it, up and down. The flat base pressed against my mons, rubbing my inner lips over sensitive flesh. I hummed out in pleasure, leaning back against Andoc and feeling his own hot prick nestle into the crease between my buttocks.

Senovo's hands had fallen still as he looked up, watching me.

"The faster you get naked, the faster Carivel can put that cock you're staring at to proper use," Andoc said over my shoulder.

I was nearly panting now, overcome by the way Senovo stared at my pumping fist with open want. And I was going to give it to him… *oh*, was I ever. But first…

"I want you to swallow it all the way down while Andoc opens you up for me," I said, my cunt growing heavy and full as I shaped the words. "Can you do that for me, Senovo?"

He stared at me like a man dying of thirst in the scrublands stares at water.

"Yes, Carivel, I will do that for you," he said eventually, sounding half-gone already. A shiver went through me at the realization that he was sliding into that soft and quiet place already, and he was doing it for *me*.

Andoc's arms tightened around me, and he tweaked a nipple between his finger and thumb. "I do believe you're speaking his language, *caradi*. We've corrupted you already."

He sounded unaccountably pleased by the idea.

Senovo, meanwhile, resumed his slightly clumsy attempts to untie his laces and strip off breeches, boots, and smallclothes. Andoc urged me onto the bed and directed me to lie back, my upper body resting on the rather decadent pile of pillows we'd been leaning against when Senovo first arrived. No sooner was I arranged comfortably than Senovo crawled up onto the bed as well, stalking forward on hands and knees. He shoved my legs apart to make room for himself and settled in between them. The bed creaked as Andoc lowered himself to sit near Senovo's hips, jar of oil in hand.

Senovo wasted no time, pressing biting kisses up my left thigh and making me squirm. When he reached the top, he ran his tongue along the edge of the strap that looped around my leg, following it down and darting across to lick a broad stripe along the seam of my cunt. He worried the sensitive nub at the top until I moaned with pleasure, and then kissed his way up the stiff wood rising from my dark curls.

After regarding the curved length for a moment, he braced himself on an elbow and gently twisted the fake phallus around until the curve was pointing down toward my feet instead of up toward the rafters. Comprehension dawned as he smiled up at me and swallowed the head, sliding his lips down to encompass more and more of it. Now, the curve would follow the contour of his mouth and—I swallowed hard—his throat.

Senovo was going to choke himself on my cock.

Fuck. Fuck. Oh, *fuck.*

"Such a pretty picture, isn't it?" Andoc said. I could see his own cock, red and weeping, as he dribbled oil over his fingers and down the crease of Senovo's arse. I watched, enraptured—jealous even as I appreciated the astonishing sight of Senovo working his way down the unforgiving length of wood between my legs. Wanting it all. Wanting everything *right now.*

I couldn't see exactly what Andoc was doing as his hand slipped between Senovo's legs, but I could see the results. Senovo keened around my cock and swallowed another fraction. The muscles of Andoc's forearm flexed and he shuddered, one hand gripping my hip like a lifeline.

"Yes. So beautiful," I murmured, love bubbling up and mixing with the lust that was already threatening to consume me. I lifted a hand, tangling my fingers in the thick black hair at the back of Senovo's head and letting it rest there, heavy and grounding.

Andoc removed his fingers to pour more oil over them. Senovo groaned in disappointment, only to writhe and arch as he was abruptly filled again, fuller than before.

"That's it, almost there, *amadi,*" Andoc said. "Is this what you need, to be stretched open and filled at both ends?"

On a hunch, I urged Senovo farther down onto my cock—not hard enough that he couldn't push back against it, but enough for him to feel it. Without warning, his body went soft and pliant, the last inch of the wooden prick sliding home past the ring of his throat.

I held my breath and kept my hips absolutely still as I stroked the back of his head, feeling small movements transmitted through his body as Andoc continued to stretch and work him open. I couldn't see Senovo's face, but the normally tense line of his back was relaxed into a gentle curve. His nose nuzzled into my wiry curls.

Andoc ran his free hand over a smooth flank. "There now; all ready for us."

Senovo's chest began to hitch against my thigh, marring his perfect stillness and serenity. I immediately pulled him up and off, despite his low moan of protest. Andoc eased his hand free soon after, and Senovo hid his face in the juncture of my hip and thigh.

"It's just for a moment, love," I told him, stroking a hand over his scalp, scratching lightly.

"It'll be so worth it, *amadi*," Andoc added. "You realize, don't you—it won't matter how hard you come or how perfectly you milk her cock with that gorgeous ass." He got up and cleaned his hand with a wet rag, then sat on the edge of the bed next to me and stroked over the faint bumps of Senovo's spine. "She'll stay hard no matter what you do—she could plow you into this mattress all night long, until Eiridan or one of the others comes looking for you in the morning and finds you melted into a puddle, still getting fucked while you beg us for mercy."

Senovo's shoulders trembled. An explosive puff of breath tickled the sensitive skin in the crease of my hip.

"Do you want that?" I asked, feeling shaky and overheated.

"… yes," came the weak answer, murmured into my skin. "Yes, please. I want that."

"We'll give you all that and more," Andoc said. "There's just one more thing we need to do for you first."

I looked at him and he held up the discarded thongs from our handfasting, raising an eyebrow and throwing a significant look down at Senovo, buried in my lap.

"Oh!" I exclaimed, the word wrenched from me. "Oh, yes, that's *perfect*."

Andoc grinned at me before turning his attention to Senovo. "Come on, *amadi*. Let Carivel up and give me your hands. We need to make sure that you can't possibly get away from us before she's done with you."

Senovo made a small, desperate noise of want and allowed himself to be lifted so I could shuffle out from beneath him. Andoc bound his wrists together with the thong and tied them to a sturdy slat on the headboard. He positioned Senovo on his knees with his upper body resting on his elbows, bound arms stretched out in front of him as I watched avidly.

"There," Andoc said when he was satisfied. "Perfect."

"Can I—?" I asked not sure quite how to proceed. It occurred to me that, with everything we'd done since that night in Meren, I'd still never even seen a man getting fucked.

Andoc knelt on the bed and gestured me to join him. "Bring the oil," he added.

I grabbed it and slotted myself in behind Senovo's legs, in front of Andoc's reassuring bulk. He took the little jar, slippery now from being handled with oily fingers. With a secret little thrill of acknowledgement that I was allowed to do this now, I ran one hand over the smooth globe of flesh in front of me, making Senovo shiver.

Andoc reached around me to dribble more oil down the crease of Senovo's buttocks. "First, make sure he's still loose and ready for you," he instructed, and poured oil over my fingers when I held them out.

I slid slippery fingers over the delicate skin in front of me, letting my fingertips explore the soft pucker hidden there. My only experience with this was when Senovo, and later Andoc, had penetrated me. Compared to the tense resistance that I remembered, Senovo's hole accepted my own fingertip almost greedily. I pulled out and ran two fingers around the rim, fascinated by the feeling, and by the way the loose muscles fluttered and yielded to this second, larger assault. Senovo was warm, and welcoming, his tender flesh one of the softest things I had ever felt. I immediately wanted more.

Andoc rested his chin on my shoulder, watching. "Slide your fingers in all the way. Keep your palm pointed down and curl them forward a bit. See if you can find that place on the front wall that makes him lose control."

I bit my lower lip in concentration and pushed deeper, reveling in the feeling as Senovo rocked back at the same time, seeking *more* until his bound hands brought him up short. I wasn't sure what I was searching for, but I tried to explore the front of his passage with my fingertips, feeling for anything different than the smooth, soft flesh that pulsed and gripped around my gentle intrusion.

At the very deepest point I could reach, my middle finger brushed against something firmer than its surroundings, and with a slightly different texture. Instantly, Senovo gasped and clenched around me.

"Found it," Andoc said, and I could hear the grin in his voice.

I had seen Andoc take Senovo to pieces, using his fingers on this spot once before. I tried to rub over it again, but with my smaller hands, I could only reach the very bottom edge of it. Senovo pressed back again, reflexively, but I couldn't go any deeper.

"I can't quite reach it properly," I said.

"Hmm," Andoc practically purred in my ear. "Too bad you don't have something a little longer. Oh, wait..."

For once, I couldn't really fault him for being a smug bastard. With a wide grin of my own and a racing heart, I carefully pulled my fingers out, steadying Senovo's hip when he groaned at the loss. I immediately grabbed the wooden prick, angling my body so Andoc could pour oil over it. While smearing it around to cover the hard length thoroughly, I understood for the first time the reason for the gentle curve. With Senovo on his knees and the curve pointing down, the flared head would rub over that spot I'd just found with every thrust. If I wanted to take him while he lay on his back, I could flip it around until the head pointed up, and it would do the same thing.

"Oh, Senovo," I vowed, "I am going to make this so good for you..."

Senovo panted as I lined up the head with his entrance, straining back against his bonds as he tried to impale himself in a single movement. I smacked a smooth buttock firmly in warning and earned a startled yelp—a wonderfully undignified noise from such a normally dignified man. "Oi, you! Give me a minute," I ordered, not willing to risk hurting him with the hard wood.

"I believe you may have met your match, my friend," Andoc said, reaching past me to rub a hand over the reddened flesh. "Come now, don't torture the poor man, Carivel—just press in nice and easy."

A strong hand rested on my hip, guiding me gently forward. I felt a moment of resistance; a moment of surrender. The head of the cock—*my* cock—slipped past the ring guarding Senovo's passage and disappeared inside. He moaned, long and low, and I stopped, needing to make sure I wasn't hurting the beautiful man beneath me.

"More," he begged hoarsely, and I echoed his moan with one of my own. My hips pressed forward of their own accord, and I watched in fascination as my cock disappeared inside the warm, tight passage. Just before I bottomed out, Senovo shuddered and stifled a cry against the mattress. I realized I must have hit that place where my fingers couldn't quite reach.

I closed the final inch between us, my hips resting snug against Senovo's welcoming arse. The surreal nature of the moment overcame me—*I was fucking a man*. My cunt pulsed, soaked and dripping. A needy noise from beneath me on the bed brought me back to myself. I draped my upper body over Senovo's back, bracing one hand on the mattress and wrapping the other arm around his sweat-dampened chest.

"This is amazing," I whispered. "You are amazing."

"You both are," Andoc said behind me. "Touch his cock, *caradi*. I bet he's hard and aching for you already."

I moaned and slid my hand down Senovo's smooth belly until I encountered his thatch of downy hair and the small but very erect prick emerging from it. "He is," I said with wonder. "He's so hard for us, Andoc."

Senovo made a small noise and arched into my loose fist. Andoc spread his hand intimately over my arse and urged me to move, rolling my hips back and forward in an easy motion. I rested my forehead on Senovo's trembling back and fucked into him with a rhythm that seemed as primal and natural as anything I'd ever done. Trapped between my fist around his cock and my cock buried in his arse, Senovo jerked and shook beneath me, his breathing growing ragged.

I felt like I could have gone on forever. Sweat had broken out over Senovo's body, slicking our skin where we slid together. I rubbed my face over the damp flesh of his shoulder blades like a cat, and licked a stripe up his spine even as I snapped my hips forward sharply.

Senovo gasped as if taken by surprise and came abruptly, his prick pulsing in my hand and dribbling a small spurt of fluid over my fingertips. I ground my mons against the base of the wooden cock buried inside him and followed, my pleasure cresting and slowly ebbing. We both sagged a bit, the weight of my body bearing him down.

I milked Senovo's softening cock with slow movements, dragging a final shudder from the sweaty body underneath mine. Though this was not the hardest or longest climax I'd ever experienced, it was by far the sweetest, I decided with a smile.

After a moment, Andoc's hand, which had been caressing my buttocks and thighs as I fucked Senovo to completion, moved to trail over my own tightly puckered opening. Sparks scattered across my vision and I jerked into Senovo without meaning to, dragging my cock roughly over that sweet spot inside him.

Senovo cried out sharply, his knees scrabbling for purchase on the mattress, and I froze.

"Sorry, was that too much?" I asked, worried.

"*Yes,*" he gasped.

Andoc leaned around me until he could see Senovo's face, half-pressed into the bed. "Do you want to stop?" he asked.

"N-no."

Andoc must have been satisfied with what he saw, because he nodded and gave me a quick, reassuring smile. "I did warn you," he told Senovo, running a hand possessively over the eunuch's side. "Our Carivel is barely getting started. And now, I'm going to open her up and fuck her while she fucks you."

My self-control must have been in tatters, because I gasped at the picture Andoc had just painted and jerked into poor Senovo *again.* He made a sound as if he'd been punched, and clenched hard around the shaft of wood impaling him.

Andoc turned his attention from Senovo to me, leaning down so he could whisper in my ear. "I may not want to fuck you like a woman, but I *will* fuck you like a man tonight."

Fresh desire flooded my belly. "What are you waiting for?" I growled, and ground into Senovo again—with intent, this time—reveling in the feeling of power as he bucked helplessly beneath me.

Andoc chuckled and reached for the oil. "Nothing at all, *caradi.* Nothing at all."

Oil dribbled down my crack; Andoc's insistent fingers followed. My head swam as first one finger, and then more pressed into my tight opening. The feeling of unbelievable fullness made me squirm, drawing more gasps and cries from Senovo as the movement continued to torture his deliciously oversensitive flesh.

I nipped and worried at the skin of his shoulder, digging my teeth in properly when Andoc added a third finger. Senovo collapsed beneath me by slow degrees, even as my own body melted into bonelessness from the firm, relentless stimulation of Andoc's probing fingers.

Eventually, the fingers slipped out, leaving me with a horrible feeling of emptiness. I burrowed my cock deeper inside Senovo to escape it and he moaned, pressing back in return.

"Are you two going to make me do all the work here?" Andoc said, not sounding too put out about it, really. "Come on—no lying down on the job."

There was a wet sound that I took to mean that Andoc was oiling up his cock. I shivered in anticipation; Senovo shivered in reaction beneath me. A moment later, strong hands reached past my hips to grab Senovo's, dragging us both back into a kneeling position using brute force.

Something large and blunt pressed at my entrance. "Are you ready?" Andoc asked.

"Oh gods yes please," I answered in a rush, drawing partway out of Senovo as I attempted to push back onto Andoc.

Andoc steadied my hips and pressed forward, his cock feeling impossibly large as it pushed against my untried flesh. Just when I started to worry that it wouldn't work, the head popped past the outer ring of muscle, only to hit a second obstruction.

"Breathe out slowly and bear down for me, *caradi*," Andoc said, his voice slightly strained. "Let me in now."

My heart was thudding with excitement and nervousness, but I wrapped one arm around Senovo's stomach, took a deep breath, and focused on pushing out. Andoc's cock immediately slipped inside, stretching me until it felt I would surely burst. Hot tingles ran up my spine to my scalp, and down my legs to my toes. Large, proprietary hands slid over my back as I was immediately and utterly *possessed*.

"Move when you're ready, beloved," Andoc said on a hoarse whisper. "We'll make Senovo feel both of us."

I buried my face in the space between Senovo's shoulder blades and nodded, even as I focused on breathing in and out, trying to relax around the huge cock buried inside me. When the feeling of being overwhelmed finally started to fade a little, I tentatively slid forward to bury myself fully in Senovo once more, feeling Andoc retreat until the flared head of his prick caught against my rim. I pressed back, taking more of Andoc and pulling partway out of Senovo.

With small, experimental movements, I gradually took Andoc deeper until finally, I felt his balls slap against me as he bottomed out.

"So good," he murmured.

Bracing himself on his knees behind me, he grasped my shoulders and lifted my upper body, pulling me up to rest with my back against his broad chest. The new position changed the angle of his cock inside me, and I hummed approval, feeling limp and dizzy with desire. He thumbed my nipples, sending little shocks throughout my body.

"We're going to fuck Senovo now, until he comes again," he said into my ear, his breath tickling at the sensitive skin. I could only moan and nod as Senovo writhed on the end of my cock.

Andoc took my hips and drove into me over and over, burying me to the hilt inside Senovo with every thrust. I let myself be used, a willing puppet under his control. Beneath me, Senovo had retreated completely into the place he went whenever Andoc took command, mindless with pleasure and oblivious to everything but the overwhelming ecstasy Andoc was forcing on him… using my body as a conduit.

Time was meaningless, but my knees were beginning to ache distantly when Senovo keened and clenched his second release around the wooden phallus buried inside him. Andoc followed a moment later, and the feeling of his warm seed bathing the inside of my passage dragged me over the edge as well.

When the wash of blinding white faded from my vision, I discovered that we had collapsed into a tangle of arms and legs on the bed. Andoc was half-braced with one hand to keep his weight from crushing us fully, though I could see a faint tremor in the corded muscles of his forearm.

"I'm going to pull out now, *caradi*," he said, his voice warm and deep. "Bear down again."

I resisted the urge to whimper like a child, knowing that we couldn't stay like this for any real length of time. Holding my breath against the strangeness of it, I bore down and helped Andoc slide out, hating the bereft feeling that overcame me when he was gone. He dragged his fingers down my spine in wordless apology as he rolled off us, leaving me still buried in Senovo, sprawled across the eunuch like a beached starfish.

I started to lift myself enough to pull out, but a hand on my back stopped me.

"Stay put for a minute," Andoc said. "No reason we have to drag him back up from the depths quite yet."

I paused, confused until I felt Andoc fumbling with the buckles that held my harness in place. After a few moments, the straps slid away, and I eased myself off of Senovo's body, leaving the wooden cock still buried inside him. He started to murmur a muffled protest at the loss of my weight against his back, but Andoc palmed the base of the carved phallus and pulled a groan from him instead.

"None of that," Andoc warned. "No one said we were done with you yet, *amadi*. Carivel, could you reach up and untie him for me, please?"

I hummed agreement and crawled up until I could fumble with the slipknots binding Senovo's hands to the headboard. They came loose easily, and I tossed the thong onto the table next to the bed. Andoc urged Senovo onto his back, with his shoulders in my lap and his head resting on my belly. He was completely pliant, relaxing into my body with a deep sigh of contentment.

I split my attention between Senovo—the smudged kohl around his right eye doing nothing to detract from his ethereal beauty—and Andoc, puttering around the room in search of rags and water, the candlelight reflecting off hard muscle and sinew. Andoc returned to the bed to clean me up, and Senovo started to stir.

"Ah, *ah*," Andoc warned. "I already told you we're not finished with you."

Feeling warm and sated, I took the hint and ran my hand over Senovo's collarbone, dragging it up his exposed throat and sliding two fingers over his slightly parted lips until he opened for me and pulled them into his mouth. He laved the pads with his tongue and suckled at them. I was beyond desire, but the soft, insistent suction tugged at something deep inside my chest nonetheless.

When Andoc was satisfied with his cleanup efforts, he settled at Senovo's hip and lifted the leg that was closest to him, bracing it against his shoulder. I watched as he drew the wooden cock partway out and poured another generous measure of oil over it before sliding it home once more. Senovo's eyes flew open, glassy and pleasure-drugged as he stared sightlessly at the rafters.

I continued to offer him my fingers, letting him suck them and teasing his nipples with my other hand. Meanwhile, Andoc fucked him with small, slow movements using the carved phallus. No doubt he was stroking it back and forth over Senovo's oversensitive sweet spot with merciless, unerring precision.

There was absolutely no urgency… we must have kept Senovo under for an hour or more, until he finally fell asleep to the tantalizing, continuous brushes of pleasure from our hands and the wooden cock. When Andoc finally slid it out of him, a slow fraction at a time, he didn't even stir. I traced one perfect brow with my thumb, watching the priest's serene face with fascination.

When Andoc finished tidying things up, he snuffed the candles that hadn't already gone out and climbed in behind Senovo, pulling the blanket over all three of us. I shuffled down until Senovo's head was resting on my shoulder instead of my stomach, marveling that he didn't wake during the jostling.

"Where does he go, when he gets like this?" I asked, the words disappearing into the darkness.

"I'm not sure," Andoc said, thoughtful. "But it seems like a very nice place, don't you think?"

⪼ ⬥ ⪻

I woke early the following morning, as was my habit. The sky outside the small window showed the first hint of gray as the sun prepared to rise on what appeared to be a cloudy day. Normally, I would be up and about immediately, getting ready to head to the horse pens.

This morning, however, was the morning after my handfasting. Or at least, it would be if my handfasting hadn't been an utter sham. Nonetheless, nothing was expected of me this morning other than lounging naked with my new "husband," while partaking of good food and wine between rounds of enthusiastic sex.

I shifted position slightly, and the ache between my legs immediately reminded me why any sex this morning might, in fact, need to be of the slightly subdued variety while my arse recovered from playing host to Andoc's generous cock for the first time. I wondered if Senovo was in similar straits after being plowed into the mattress for well over an hour.

The man in question was fast asleep on his back next to me, with Andoc's arm thrown across his chest and their legs tangled together. Senovo's face was tipped toward me, the ruined kohl smudged around his eyes completely failing to detract from his elegant features. A thin line of drool trailed from the corner of his slightly open mouth to a small wet spot on the pillow. I could not have stopped the helplessly fond smile that stretched my lips had my life depended on it.

Next to him, Andoc lay on his front, his face mashed into the bed and his body curled around Senovo protectively. For once, he wasn't even snoring.

Senovo—also a habitually early riser—blinked awake in the uncertain light of morning. He stared up at the thatched roof for what seemed an unusually long time, as if disoriented. I propped myself up on an elbow so I could watch him, unsure if I should be doing anything for him. Eventually, the faint line between his brows smoothed, and his eyes flickered over to meet mine. The unguarded gaze made him look very young.

"Good morning," I said softly, and traced his cheek with my fingertips. His eyes slipped closed as he pressed into the contact. I cradled the side of his face, and stretched down to place a kiss on his forehead, then his lips.

"'Morning," he rasped, his voice sleep-heavy.

The fact that he did not immediately enquire after my wellbeing was a telltale sign that he was not quite back from last night's travels. Trusting my instincts, I smiled at him and settled back down on the bed, mirroring Andoc with an arm and a leg thrown across him, wrapping him up between us and anchoring him in place. He breathed out—a slow exhalation—and went back to staring at the rafters, blinking every few seconds.

The room gradually lightened. After several minutes of relaxed silence, Senovo cleared his throat and rolled his head to look first at Andoc, and then at me.

"Good morning," he said again, sounding more like himself this time. "Are you well?"

I hid my grin against his shoulder for a moment until I could shape my expression into something a bit more neutral. "I feel like I've been nearly split in two, actually. You?"

"Same," he answered after a faint, embarrassed pause. "It's just possible that I didn't fully think through the ramifications before giving you that gift in Andoc's presence."

I couldn't hold back a snort of amusement. "Yeah, you may have been asking for it just a *tiny* bit. You're all right, though?"

"Of course," he said dismissively. "It can sometimes be a bit difficult to… come back… after going so deep for him. For both of you, in this case. That's all."

I propped myself up again and traced his collarbone absently. "I wish I understood it all a bit better," I said slowly. "Where are you, when you disappear like that?"
His eyes were heartbreakingly wistful and unguarded as he looked up at me.

"Safe," was all he said.

THIRTEEN

As the only one of us who was expected to perform his normal duties this morning, Senovo rose soon afterward, extricating himself from the oblivious Andoc and dressing quietly as I watched.

"I will have one of the boys draw a warm bath for you in a bit," he said. "It will help with the discomfort—which, I should add, will become less as you gain more experience."

"You could join me?" I added hopefully, but he smiled and shook his head.

"Unfortunately, I have a full day ahead of me. The new Mereni contingent will be arriving by this evening. With Andoc otherwise engaged this morning, I will need to attend the meetings with Volya and Magoldis."

I frowned, remembering the confrontation in the refectory. "Do you think Volya will try to do anything to you?"

Senovo shrugged. "It seems unlikely that he will attempt anything untoward in the presence of the village elders. Whether they approve of me personally or not, most of them are so rooted in tradition that they would protest any ill treatment merely on the grounds of my position as High Priest."

I relaxed back, mollified. "If you're sure. Though, if he does try anything, I expect you to glare him into submission again, and I want to hear about it in painstaking detail afterward. Andoc wasn't lying when he said that was ridiculously arousing."

Senovo blushed, but his voice was dry when he replied, "You'll forgive me if I'd prefer not to have to make a habit of it, merely for your titillation."

I grinned. "Of course not. Perish the thought."

He scowled at me, not terribly convincingly, and searched until he found the thongs from the handfasting on the low bedside table.

"I'll need to bind you together again. If you are to maintain the ruse of your handfasting, it would be best if you allowed yourself to be seen together this morning." He sat down on the bed and gestured for my hand, placing it in Andoc's limp one and starting the complicated web that would tie us together until early afternoon. "I would strongly suggest having the bindings unwrapped in public to encourage the right kind of gossip and silence any naysayers. You could use the excuse of coming to find me at the meeting hall so I could do it personally — perhaps at Andoc's request. People will believe that story readily enough, I should think." He paused, meeting my eyes. "It will, of course, mean that you'll be the center of quite a bit of attention — some of which may be negative."

It was fairly common for newly handfasted couples to have their bindings removed in the village green, if the weather was not too bad. As in the rest of the day-long ceremony, they did so unclothed. *Naked in the eyes of gods and man.*

I sighed.

"I can't say I'm thrilled with the idea of the whole village coming out to gawp at the fact that I have tits," I said, "but it's not as if they don't stare at me already. At least this way, they'll have a reason."

"In that case, send Crenelo or Reston to fetch me to the green at the appointed time. In the mean time," he said, tying off the bindings with a slight flourish, "I'll leave you to deal with returning Andoc to the world of the living. There's clean water in the bucket by the bed, though I don't know how cold it is."

This startled a laugh from me, after which Senovo took his leave and left me alone with my sleeping so-called husband. Tempting as it was to douse him with a ewer of water just to see what would happen, I decided that it would be the better part of valor to wait until I wasn't tied to him by the wrist before trying out that method. Looking over the expanse of muscle and tanned skin laid out before me, I went back to something that had yielded success before, and started kissing my way down his torso with slow deliberation.

After a lazy and decadent half hour of teasing each other with our mouths and fingers, a tentative knock on the door heralded the readiness of the promised warm bath. Andoc grumbled about sitting around while I parboiled myself *yet again*, but once we got there he seemed happy enough to run the soapy rag over me while I lay back, letting the water soak away some of the ache from the night before.

Wandering through the temple together had the added benefit of letting the acolytes and novices—not to mention a pair from the village who had come to talk to a priest about their own upcoming handfasting—see us playing the part of the happy couple.

Not that it was truly an act. For all our grousing, Andoc and I were good together. In another life, perhaps we could have been a typical couple, pledging our commitment and going on to raise a family, as was expected of a man and a woman. *This* life, of course, was considerably more complicated.

Still, after a night of amazing sex and a morning of lazy, sensual indulgence, I was feeling considerably better about things in general. Senovo did not seem to be angry or upset about our disregard for the ceremony. Andoc was, as he had always been, the epitome of equanimity. The village—and Chief Volya, in particular—had no reason to suspect that anything untoward was going on, and with any luck at all, we would be able to go forward with as much normalcy as might be expected while the village was getting ready for a major battle.

I refused to think too closely about that battle. Whenever thoughts of it tried to intrude, I told myself firmly that both Draebard's and Meren's warriors were exceptional, and with our forces combined, the troops stationed at the Alyrion outpost in the hill fort wouldn't stand a chance. We Eburosi would triumph, sending a message to the Emperor of Alyrios that the island was not worth the bloodshed that would surely ensue should he try to take it. Afterward, things would go back to normal.

Of course they would.

My musings were interrupted by a kiss on the top of my head, and I looked up from where I was resting against Andoc's shoulder in the rumpled bed, a platter of fruit sitting forgotten next to us.

"Deep thoughts?" he asked.

"Empty head, more like," I said with a wry half-smile. "I think you fucked my brains right out of my skull last night."

"Hmm. Imagine how Senovo must be feeling, in that case," he replied with a crooked grin of his own. "Just think—going from that to sitting through endless meetings while Volya and Magoldis glare across the table at each other."

"Poor man," I said, meaning it.

Andoc's broad chest expanded with a deep breath, and relaxed as he sighed. "Well. It looks like midday has come and gone. We should send for Senovo and head to the village green. Then you can finally be free of me." He jiggled our bound wrists lightly.

I snorted. "Oh, yes. I'll be free of you until you show up this evening to berate me for not eating enough to suit you."

"Actually, I'm afraid you'll have to fend for yourself this evening," he said. "The rest of the Mereni will be arriving in a little while, and I suspect battle planning will run long into the night."

"Hmm," I said, a bit disappointed that the three of us would not be able to spend the night together. "I guess it's a good thing you slept half the day today, in that case."

He flicked my nipple lightly and I smacked his arse in retaliation.

"Must've been your stimulating company that sent me to sleep," he quipped.

"It seemed plenty *stimulating* for you when I woke you up this morning with my mouth... and when I brought you off with my hand while I was in the bath... *and* when you spilled mayapple sauce all down your front a few minutes ago and I licked it off..."

He groaned. "Yes, yes, all right. Come on—get up. I've no desire to meet the Mereni forces with my bare ass on display for all to see. Much less with my cock bobbing out in front of me like a lance because you can't stop driving me crazy with your filthy mouth."

"*My* filthy mouth!" I gasped, pretending offense.

"Yes," he said, and dragged me up until he could press a searing kiss to my lips. "*Your filthy mouth.* Now, come on. Let's get these bindings off so you can get back to your horses, and I can get back to trying to stop our fearless leaders from eviscerating each other."

As Senovo had warned, our appearance outside of the temple quickly drew a crowd of slack-jawed onlookers. Dalon even made a brief appearance as we were waiting for Senovo to arrive at the green.

"Don't you have other things to be doing right now?" I asked, feeling the tips of my ears heat. "Yes. I have breasts. Get over it."

"Pfft. Had to come and see for myself, didn't I?" Dalon said with a grin. "Congratulations and all that, by the way."

"Fuck you," I said, in a more-or-less good-natured tone. "Just remember who has the power to make sure you spend the next week polishing bits and harness buckles."

"Right you are, boss," he said, still grinning. "I'd best get back to it, then."

He left with a jaunty salute, conversation buzzing in his wake. I sighed. Perhaps seeing that my second-in-command accepted me as Horse Mistress would help sway opinion in my favor.

"All right," Andoc murmured in my ear. "I have to admit, that surprised me a little bit."

"He thought I was queer before," I muttered back. "Apparently finding out that I was actually a girl is quite a relief to him."

Andoc stifled a guffaw. "I guess if it works…"

"My thoughts exactly."

Senovo arrived a few moments later, looking harried. His eyes softened when he saw us, but I wondered what had been happening in our absence.

"First Warrior," he said, loud enough for the onlookers to hear. "Horse Mistress. Thank you for allowing me the honor of completing the final act of your handfasting ceremony. Kneel, please."

I hoped I was as successful as Andoc at keeping my face composed as we knelt in the soft grass at Senovo's feet and lifted our joined hands to him. His movements were gentle and precise as he unpicked the knot in the thongs and unwrapped them with slow deliberation, the picture of priestly detachment. His fingers did not so much as brush ours unnecessarily.

"The bindings are whole and unbroken," he told the crowd, lifting the intact thongs so those nearest could see the truth of the words. "The ceremony is finished. All those who complete such an undertaking are bonded as husband and wife before the gods."

There was a smattering of rather hesitant sounding applause—people slapping their thighs as Andoc bent to capture my lips in a kiss. I returned it, trying to ignore the ache at not being able to pull Senovo down to join us.

Andoc lifted his head from mine and helped me to my feet before turning to the crowd. "All right, you lot—stop staring at my wife's perfect ass and get back to work!" he called, throwing the onlookers a broad wink.

The laughter was more widespread than the applause had been, and amazingly, many people did wander off, back to whatever had been occupying them before our arrival. I shook out my wrist, rubbing my right hand over the indented red marks left by the thongs. Meanwhile, Andoc turned to Senovo under the guise of thanking him for officiating the ceremony with a handshake.

"How bad are things?" he asked under his breath, flicking his eyes toward the meeting hall.

Senovo shook his head minutely. "The hand-fasting appears to have eased tensions somewhat, thankfully."

"Oh, good. So I have time to get dressed before I show up, then?"

"You're asking *my* opinion?" Senovo said with complete innocence, and I had to swallow the laughter that wanted to bubble up. Were things really going to be all right now?

"Yeah, on second thought, don't answer that," Andoc said. "Carivel, I hate to talk shop while we're still standing here naked, but how is the maintenance on the chariots coming?"

"I've had Dalon liaising with the carpenters and wheelwrights since we got back. They should have finished work on about three-quarters of the chariots and wagons by now," I said, sobering at the reminder of what still lay ahead of us. "I'll get a more detailed report as soon as I get back to the pens, and send it to you via runner."

"Perfect," Andoc said. "Senovo, why don't you go take a break for a bit. I'll take over diplomatic duty until you get back."

"Trousers first," I reminded him, stretching up for a final, brief kiss. "Then diplomacy."

"Ever practical," Senovo murmured, and we took our leave.

It was a relief to don my familiar, worn clothing and return to the horse pens, even if it did mean facing a new round of teasing from Dalon, asking me when I was planning on having my skirts and dresses made.

"All of those bits and buckles are looking pretty dull right now," I reminded him.

I spent an hour collecting updates on the state of the chariot teams, particularly the half dozen that included young horses as yet unused to battle. Dalon and I spoke with the lads responsible for training the green animals, getting a feel for which colts would pair best with which experienced horses.

Even with the new colts, we would still be two teams short for the number of chariots we had. It was regrettable, but sending a chariot into battle with two completely untried horses was worse than not sending it at all. I resolved to track down Keenan and see if she'd heard back from the bow-maker yet. If it was at all possible, perhaps we could bolster the ranks with a couple of archers on horseback, using animals that did not tolerate being harnessed in a team.

I sent Favian with the detailed report for Andoc and the tribal leaders. I trusted his quick mind not to garble it, for one thing, but I was also hoping to soften his sullen anger with a gesture of my continued trust. He listened to the message, stone-faced, and repeated it back to me word for word before running off toward the meeting hall.

I spent the rest of the day overseeing an inventory of supplies needed to manage dozens of horses on a multi-day campaign—halters, hobbles, picket ropes, feed wagons, water barrels, and a dozen other miscellaneous things that were now my responsibility. Once again, I marveled at Jorun's ability to run everything so effortlessly. It certainly didn't help that I'd spent more time off doing other things since his death than I had actually *being* the Horse Mistress.

Still, with any luck at all, my focus could now stay where it was supposed to be… with my apprentices, and with Draebard's fine herd of horses.

An afternoon shower gave way to drizzle, and then to a fine, clear evening. Lundis came by to inform me that the Mereni had arrived, and their horses were pasturing temporarily in the small fields west of the village. The lads on duty for the day brought Draebard's horses back in from the northern pastures, penning them up for the night. I made a final round of the corrals, counting heads and checking legs as the sun slipped below the horizon in a blaze of orange and violet.

The night guard arrived soon after. With nothing left at the pens that needed my attention, I screwed up my courage and headed for the meeting hall. No matter Volya's disdain for me, I *was* Horse Mistress and he would have to deal with me in matters concerning the herd.

In a moment of inspiration, I stopped at the tent of a street vendor who was just closing up for the evening and purchased some simple food, in case Andoc had been unable to get away long enough to eat.

The meeting hall was lit brightly from within, those inside obviously settling in for a long night. I made myself stride in confidently, nodding to the guards, who either nodded back or merely stared at me impassively. I'd noticed that none of the warriors had done anything that could be construed as openly hostile toward me since my return, and wondered if I had Andoc's influence to thank for that.

Voices were coming from the large meeting space that took up most of the back half of the hall. I followed them to find the room full of faces both familiar and unfamiliar. A flash of red hair caught my eye, and I nodded at Varanis, who lifted her chin in return. Her expression was pinched, and I wondered how things were going.

Andoc noticed me a moment later and bent to speak to the Mereni warrior next to him before rising to cross to me.

"Hey," he said.

I smiled, though I'm sure it didn't reach my eyes. "Hey. I just wanted to stop by and see if you needed any more information from me. It looks like all the chariots will be ready by noon tomorrow. Other than that, there's nothing new beyond what I sent in the message earlier."

"Good news about the chariots—thanks for that. I think Varanis wanted to talk to you and Keenan about the idea of mounted archers." Andoc lifted an arm to get the attention of the small, dark-haired woman, who smiled and waved when she recognized me.

The three of us converged on Varanis. To my surprise, Keenan immediately drew me into a brief embrace, murmuring congratulations in my ear.

"Andoc and Carivel were just handfasted," she explained to Varanis when the Mereni First Warrior raised an eyebrow at the display.

"Brave woman," Varanis said to me, in lieu of anything more sentimental. "Now, what's this about archers on horseback?"

Keenan and I explained what we'd done and talked about, while Varanis nodded thoughtfully.

"You've spoken to the bowsmith?" Varanis asked Keenan.

The archer nodded. "She says she can have something made up by the end of next week for us to try."

"That's too late," Varanis said. "The attack on the hill fort will take place late next week. There's no way to use a regular longbow?"

"I don't see how," I said. "We never found a way to keep the saddle and the rider's leg from interfering with the draw."

"In that case, we'll abandon it for now," Varanis said firmly. "It's a good idea for the future, but the weapon-makers need to concentrate on things we can use for the current conflict."

I nodded, disappointed, but seeing the sense of it. Keenan caught my eye. "We'll talk about it more after the battle," she said.

"Of course. I look forward to it," I replied, not allowing myself to speculate on the likelihood that some of us would not be around after the battle. "Thank you for taking it under consideration, First Warrior Varanis."

Varanis waved off my words. "I told you, it's a good idea—just not a timely one. Talk to me again when you can stage a proper demonstration for me. I think quite a few people will be interested."

Andoc and I excused ourselves and retreated to a relatively quiet corner. "Have you eaten?" I asked, lifting the package of food I was holding.

"I have, thanks," he said, the corners of his eyes crinkling a bit. "You don't put this many warriors in one place for hours at a time without plenty of food being involved, believe me. Tell you what—do me a favor and take it to Senovo at the temple. He only headed out a few minutes before you got here. We're getting down to the details of battle planning now... not really something that requires priestly input. He left to get the new acolytes from Meren settled in, I think. I didn't really like the look of him; I'd feel better if you could check on him for me."

"Absolutely," I said. "Has Volya been after him again?"

"Not that he mentioned to me," Andoc said, grim, "but you know how much that means."

"I'll go there right now."

Andoc lifted my hand to his lips and kissed my knuckles, sending a faint flush to my face. "Thank you, *caradi*," he said. "I won't be back tonight, but I'll try to see you for a bit tomorrow morning."

"I don't envy you in the least," I told him, giving his hand a squeeze before letting it go. "Have fun playing diplomat."

"Thanks," Andoc said wryly. "Have fun prying answers about his well-being out of a tight-lipped, stubborn-ass priest."

"Ha," I said, and left him to it.

The village seemed unusually crowded for the time of night, between the visiting Mereni and locals trying to get any new information or gossip about either the visitors or the upcoming battle. There were many unfamiliar faces, and, in a refreshing change from recent days, most people ignored me.

The crowds thinned as I neared the temple, though a group of men wearing a style of clothing I'd never seen before were loitering in the courtyard across from the entrance. Their eyes followed my progress as I disappeared inside, making the short hair at the base of my skull stand on end. I let out a breath as the door closed behind me, shaking off the odd moment.

Inside, the temple was well lit and the sound of voices carried from other parts of the building. I remembered that in addition to Feldes and Eiridan, High Priest Jyrrel had promised to send four acolytes to Draebard. With their arrival, the priesthood was approaching half of its original numbers before the devastation of the Alyrion attack.

I had scarcely gone halfway down the length of the hall leading from the entrance when Eiridan intercepted me. "Can I help you?" asked the pleasant-faced novice. "Ah! Good evening, Horse Mistress Carivel. Are you here to see the High Priest?"

"Yes," I said, trying to raise a smile. "I know he's busy, but I'd hoped to offer him a meal as thanks for performing our ceremony. I also need to have a brief word with him, if he has a few moments."

If anything, Eiridan looked a little bit relieved. "I am sure that between us, we can convince him to spare the time," he said.

I frowned a bit, not happy about Eiridan's apparent worry on top of Andoc's. "Is the High Priest not well?"

"Not that he has indicated to me," Eiridan said carefully. "Though certainly some good food and a few minutes' quiet conversation is always beneficial to the spirit. Why don't you wait in the room off the main sanctuary, and I will send him to you?"

"Thanks, Eiridan," I said. "I'd appreciate it."

Eiridan tipped his upper body in a shallow bow. "Give me a few minutes," he said.

I wandered down the main hallway toward the sanctuary containing the altar where our botched ceremony had taken place only yesterday. The little room off to the side was commonly used for counseling. It was surprisingly cozy, and had apparently received the benefit of the new arrivals' recent efforts to breathe life back into the grieving temple. Fresh fruit lay piled in a bowl on the low table; clean cushions and furs padded the comfortable looking low-backed bench and chairs. A brace of lit candles set off to the side bathed the small room in a soft, warm glow. Almost immediately, the homey, intimate surroundings unknotted something in my chest that had been tight and sore since the meeting hall.

I placed my slightly mashed package of food next to the fruit bowl and picked up a bunch of plump wineberries to snack on as I curled on the bench, waiting for Senovo. He did not keep me waiting long, sweeping in silently and closing the door behind him. The backrest of the bench faced the entryway, and I craned around as his slightly raspy voice asked, "What seems to be the problem — ?"

Our eyes met, and he froze for a moment. "Ah," he said. "I appear to have been tricked. Eiridan said only that someone from the village needed to speak with me, and that it seemed urgent. Hello, Carivel."

FOURTEEN

$\mathcal{S}$enovo was pale—his eyes sunken, with dark circles underneath. His shoulders were tense, as if it took considerable effort for him to stand straight rather than hunching. I raised an eyebrow.

"I guess that means he thought you'd wriggle out of it if he told you I'd come to see how you were and make sure you ate something," I said.

Senovo huffed out a breath and dropped down gracelessly on the other end of the bench. "Probably."

I got up and poured two goblets of wine from the pitcher sitting on the shelf by the candles. After shoving one of them unceremoniously into Senovo's hands, I put the other one down on the table and unwrapped the food, such as it was.

"Eat," I said, before taking my own advice and scooping up one of the slightly mashed meat-and-ground-tuber patties.

Senovo eyed the abused and vaguely pathetic-looking meal over his wine. "When it comes to a fine meal, presentation is everything, they say."

I glowered at him, even though I was secretly relieved he felt well enough to tease. "Yes, yes. Normally we have Andoc for this, but I'm doing my best, all right? Now shut up and eat your starchy meat... thing." I tossed a piece of fruit onto the wrapping. "There. Dessert."

Senovo's shoulders seemed to relax a bit, and he picked delicately at the food as I worked my way through my own portion. When we were finished, I turned to him.

"Now. Spill. Something's obviously wrong—what is it?"

Twirling the stem of his metal goblet between his fingers, the priest shook his head as if to minimize the importance of his ghastly appearance. "It's nothing out of the ordinary or particularly unexpected," he said. "Being in such a contentious atmosphere, crowded, with so much poorly disguised hostility—it makes the wolf... *restless.*"

"Ah," I said on a breath. "I guess it would at that."

Senovo shrugged. "There is little to be done, but I do appreciate your concern."

I stared into my own wine for a few moments, deep in thought.

"Ride out with me to the woods tonight," I said on impulse, lifting my eyes to meet his. "Come out where it's quiet, and let the wolf run."

Senovo's expression immediately closed off. "I don't think it's wise to indulge in such a way. Not on a regular basis. I have responsibilities now."

I stifled the urge to growl at him in frustration, knowing it wouldn't help. "We've talked about this before. One of your responsibilities is to stay healthy so you can do your job without falling to pieces."

The slender eunuch placed his wine on the table with a careful, deliberate movement and scrubbed a hand over his face, not looking at me. "I'm not falling to pieces, Carivel."

I gritted my teeth. "Glad to hear it. And what about tomorrow night? Or the night after that? Or the night after *that*? Andoc will be neck-deep in planning and carrying out the battle, and to a great extent, so will I... if that part even matters. We'll be *gone*, while you'll be here, trying to look after things in the village. And probably sick with worry the whole time. I know I will be."

Senovo let his hand fall to his knee with a faint slap. "Yes," he said sharply, "Well. I am High Priest. You are Horse Mistress and he is First Warrior. That is to be the way of things now. What of it?"

Resisting the urge to grab him by the shoulders and shake him until he stopped being stupid was more difficult than I expected. "*I'm here now*," I said, as patiently as I could manage. "I want to help you. Look me in the eye right this second and tell me that letting the change happen without a fight didn't make things better for you."

Green-gold eyes snapped with frustration in the glow of the candlelight. I forced myself to ignore the little jolt that ran through my chest at being on the other end of that intense gaze, and focused on returning it impassively.

"*I can't* tell you that, as you know perfectly well," Senovo said. "But what would you have me do? Abandon the temple on the eve of battle without explanation so I can go chase rabbits in the forest?"

"For the gods' *sake*, Senovo!" I flared. "*You're. A. Shape-shifter.* In case you've forgotten, everyone here knows that now! You might have missed this part somehow, but apparently it's considered to be a pretty big deal—the mere mention of it certainly helped bring Volya to heel the other day. So go finish up whatever else you legitimately need to do this evening, and then tell the others that you have to go—I don't know—commune with the wolf before the warriors start preparing for the battle, or something. Do you *honestly* think that Feldes or Eiridan are going to raise a protest?"

I let out a huff and unclenched my hands, which had somehow worked themselves into fists during my little rant.

"You understand why this is difficult for me, surely," Senovo said, not quite posing it as a question.

"I don't understand a damn thing about your ability," I replied, feeling a bit calmer than I had been. "I only know that you persist in fighting against a part of yourself. A part that is important, and powerful, and would make an amazing ally if you'd only let it."

"And if the wolf is more powerful than I am? What then? Shall we put white robes on it and let it perform handfastings and funeral ceremonies?"

Just like that, I understood.

"You think you'll disappear. As a person, I mean," I said, shaping the sudden revelation into words.

"It does seem somewhat inevitable, when faced with a stronger opponent who fights relentlessly for control of my body and mind," he replied in a quiet, hoarse voice.

I stared at him, open-mouthed for a moment, and scrambled forward to wrap my arms around him. "Oh, *Senovo*," I breathed. "All these years, you've believed that the wolf seeks your destruction?"

"Do you disagree?" Senovo asked, the words muffled against my shoulder. My chest hitched, and I swallowed it down.

"Here's what I think," I said roughly. "I think the wolf saved you from a life of cruel slavery. It helped you escape to find freedom, and people who love you. It protects those you care about fiercely, and mourns your losses deeply. It's affectionate with the ones close to you; it trusts the people that you trust." Senovo pressed his face harder against the juncture of my chest and shoulder, and I tightened my arms. "You promised me a while ago that you'd tell me how you met Andoc. How did he first find out about your shape-shifting?"

"He was lost in a blizzard. The wolf found him and led him to shelter. It saved him." The words emerged slowly, as if pulled free one by one. Senovo was trembling now, one hand fisting in my shirt.

"*You* saved him," I said, trying to make him understand. "Senovo, *you are the wolf.* You're fighting *yourself.*"

The man in my arms let out a harsh, choked noise. His trembling had grown more pronounced as I spoke, until he was shuddering against me almost violently. I clung to him, not sure what else to do. A moment later something shifted and I had an armful of warm, furry canine pressing against me and lapping with frantic, jerky movements at the bottom of my jaw.

"All right," I said, sliding my fingers into the rough coat and holding tight. "There, now — you're all right."

The wolf whined and tried to burrow between my body and the back of the bench, its tail thwacking back and forth rhythmically.

"How did two people as messed up as us end up with someone as normal as Andoc?" I wondered aloud, and the wolf whined again. I shook my head in dismay at the picture we must present and dragged the animal's head up so I could see his luminous eyes. "I still want to get you out to run around for a bit," I told him, "but first, I think it's time that everyone here in the temple met you properly, don't you?"

The wolf blinked up at me slowly, its tongue lolling out as it panted.

⚜

I kept one hand buried in the thick fur at the nape of Senovo's neck as I led him toward the sound of low voices in the refectory. The wolf seemed relatively at ease in the familiar surroundings, and I was careful to keep my own body language open and relaxed. The novices and acolytes were seated together at one of the heavy trestle tables. I smiled a bit to see both Reston and Crenelo chattering away excitedly with the four young newcomers, glad that they would have new friends their own age to support them after their terrible loss.

My light knocking on the heavy beam supporting the entryway drew Eiridan's attention. He stilled, staring with wide eyes for a moment before gesturing to the others for quiet.

"Hello," I said. "The High Priest will be going out to the forest this evening to, umm, to commune with the spirit of the wolf before the battle preparations. Before he goes, though, he thought this would be a good time for you all to meet him in his animal form."

It was not the most inspiring of speeches. Particularly since, in actuality, the wolf was plastered nervously to my leg, his entire demeanor indicating that he might flee back to the sanctuary of the counseling room at any moment. I scratched my blunt fingernails soothingly over his shoulder blades.

Crenelo's eyes were the size of dinner plates. "Is that really Senovo?" he asked. The wolf perked up and yipped at the sound of the familiar voice. Everyone at the table jumped a bit.

"It is," I told him calmly.

"Can we come closer and see?" Reston asked, his eyes also wide with wonder.

Beside me, Senovo was sniffing the air, his head cocked in interest.

"You and Crenelo can come over to us," I decided. "I think it would be best if the rest of you stayed back for now. Let him come to you if he wants to."

"Very sensible, Horse Mistress," Eiridan said. "Everyone, please remember that while this extraordinary animal is indeed our High Priest, he is also a wolf. Allow him to greet his familiar pack-mates first, with no distractions."

The others at the table nodded agreement, though Feldes, in particular, seemed awestruck by Senovo's very presence. *Oh, how Senovo in his human form would hate that*, I thought with a flash of humor.

Reston led Crenelo over to us and dropped to his knees a few steps away. Crenelo hung back, obviously torn between nervousness and fascination. I let my hand trail over the wolf's furry back and fall to hang at my side as he stepped away from me. He padded up to Reston and snuffled over his face and hair as the boy grinned widely. After a moment, Crenelo gained courage and knelt beside him as well, only to be subjected to the same treatment, followed by a paw on his shoulder and a lick to the face that nearly sent him sprawling.

"He does seem to lack just a touch of his usual dignity when he's in this state," I observed dryly.

The three figures in front of me were quickly descending into a tangle on the floor, with the wolf on top, dispensing licks and nuzzles with abandon. Reston laughed in delight.

"This is amazing!" he said, grabbing the wolf's face gently between his hands. "Elder Brother, why ever did you hide this for so long?"

Senovo whined, and I said, "I'm sure there were some good reasons." I nudged the wolf's haunches with my toe to get his attention. "Senovo, are you all right staying here while I go saddle Kekenu and bring him back? That way you can go for a run in the woods and I'll be able to keep up with you."

The wolf looked back at me with his tongue hanging out of the side of his mouth and thumped his tail against Crenelo's leg.

"We'll be fine, Horse Mistress," Novice Feldes said from the table, where he was still gazing at his new High Priest with wonder. "Our esteemed Elder Brother is among friends here."

Eiridan nodded agreement, and flashed me a quick smile.

"I'll only be a few minutes," I said, and left to the sounds of Crenelo urging the wolf to come and say hello to the others.

When I exited the temple, I noticed that all but one of the strangely dressed group from earlier had gone. The remaining man was still leaning against the low wall of the courtyard, and he touched one of his fingers to his forehead in a cheeky salute when he noticed me staring. I frowned slightly and headed for the horse pens, putting it from my mind.

After a quick visit with the guard to alert him to my presence, I went to the tack shed to grab a saddle and bridle. Kekenu nickered in response to my low whistle and wandered over to the gate, leaning his head over the top to nudge my shoulder and sniff at the scent of wolf.

I saddled him up and hopped on for the quick ride back to the temple. The little gelding snorted at the darkness beyond the courtyard as I dismounted and tied him to a post, but I couldn't see anything—the area appeared to be completely deserted now.

Inside, I found Senovo lounging on the refectory floor like a favored hunting dog, his tail wagging lazily as the acolytes fed him bits of food left over from dinner. As soon as he saw me, he bounded up and placed his paws on my shoulders, nearly sending me tumbling to the ground with his enthusiasm.

"What was that I said about dignity?" I muttered as I shoved the huge animal off.

Senovo panted up at me with a wolfish grin.

"A fair evening to you both, Horse Mistress," Eiridan said, and rose to hand me a cloth bag with a shoulder strap. "I sent one of the boys for this—it seemed as though it might come in handy at some point."

A look inside revealed one of Senovo's old brown priest's robes and a pair of sandals. My expression cleared with understanding. "Thank you," I said. "That was thoughtful. I'm not quite sure when we'll be back, but I don't think it will be terribly late."

Eiridan and Feldes both bowed to me, and the younger acolytes continued to stare after us as the wolf trotted out the doorway at my side. When we reached the temple's exit, I motioned for Senovo to stay put for a moment while I went and untied Kekenu. As expected, the little black and white horse spooked violently when the wolf appeared at the door.

"Easy now," I said. "You smelled him on me earlier, and he was around when we camped overnight on the way back from Meren. If Nietre can cope with him, I'm sure you can too, old friend."

Kekenu and the wolf eyed each other with distrust for a few moments, before the gelding let out a loud snort and shook his head, sending the buckles of the bridle jingling.

"All good now?" I asked, as Kekenu champed at the bit, still keeping one eye and one ear pinned on Senovo. "Right. Same rules as before, with Nietre. You—" I pointed a finger at Senovo, "—don't do anything stupid, and you—" My finger migrated to point at Kekenu's broad forehead, "—don't be a coward. Now, we're all going for a nice run."

I swung up onto Kekenu's back, tutting when the little horse danced sideways. Things had quieted down somewhat as the hour grew later, but to be safe, rather than skirt the village green and head south, I headed straight out of town behind the temple and made a wide loop around the perimeter of the village before rejoining the logging roads.

At first, Kekenu pranced nervously, his ears flicking to and fro. His mood appeared to communicate itself to the wolf, who paused a few times to growl, seemingly at nothing. When we reached a clear stretch of road and broke into a run, however, both animals quickly calmed, and I drew in a deep breath, enjoying the starlit gallop with the wolf loping along at my side.

We ran until Kekenu was blowing hard and slowed of his own accord. The wolf was panting lightly, not seeming over-tired from the exertion. Nonetheless I turned back toward the village, not wanting to get too far into unfamiliar territory. We took our time heading back, as I allowed Kekenu to plod along on a loose rein while Senovo trotted here and there, sniffing at whatever caught his interest.

We were about two-thirds of the way home when Kekenu pricked his ears and the wolf darted purposefully toward a side trail. Despite the near-darkness, I recognized the trailhead leading to the beautiful clearing where Andoc and I had taken Senovo on the night of Rhystel's death.

"You know where we are, Senovo?" I asked. "Do you want to go see the clearing again?"

Senovo was still sniffing around, but without warning, he growled, a low and dangerous sound, before charging into the trees and disappearing.

"Senovo!" I called, suddenly and unaccountably afraid. "What are you doing? Come back!"

The sound of snarling and the rustle of running paws on leaf litter grew fainter as the wolf put more distance between us. "*Senovo!*" I yelled again, as Kekenu pawed restlessly beneath me, tossing his head.

In the distance, I heard a loud yelp of surprise or pain. With my heart in my throat, I spurred Kekenu forward into the trees, urging him into a fast canter. Low branches slapped at my face in the near-total darkness, so I bent low over Kekenu's neck as he crashed down the trail. The little horse's ears were flat back, his neck stretched out as he negotiated obstacles in the narrow path.

Senovo's growls of fear and anger were growing louder as we rounded a bend in the path, only to run straight into a group of men waving torches. Kekenu tried to slide to a stop as the flaming branches flashed in front of him, but one leg caught on a root or some other obstruction and he stumbled. I felt his shoulder dip sickeningly beneath me, my hunched position leaving me unable to compensate. The force of my shifting weight pulled the saddle sideways and suddenly I was falling.

The ground was hard and uneven, driving the breath from my lungs and sending the left side of my body numb. I rolled over twice, feeling my shoulder wrench painfully as I came to a stop against the base of a tree, dizzy and disoriented. At the edge of the flickering torchlight, the wolf was trapped under a heavy net, biting and clawing at the ropes as it tried to tear itself free.

"Over here!" called a gruff male voice, just as a smear of black and white slid across my wavering vision.

I grabbed a handful of loose soil with my right hand and tried to cry, "*Hyah!*" as I threw it at Kekenu's side. I didn't have breath for a proper yell, but some of the clods of soil thumped against the gelding's flank. That, combined with the shouting men and waving torches, was enough to send the little horse galloping back the way he'd come.

Back to Draebard, I hoped… and help.

Hands grabbed at me. I kicked and fought, but I couldn't even breathe properly. My movements were weak. Uncoordinated. Somewhere nearby, I could hear the wolf struggling frantically. Fighting for its life.

"Yeah… I thought you and your pet wolf might come back here, when I saw you was both heading south together," said the gruff voice. "Looks like I was right."

No, I thought. *No, no, no…*

The dizziness grew worse. Someone forced a coarse burlap bag over my head and fastened it around my neck with rough hands. The damp, rank cloth settled over my mouth and nose, nearly smothering me. The pounding of my heart seemed to grow all consuming, drowning out everything else. I tried to focus on the rhythmic thud, but soon even my frantic pulse faded away, out of reach as darkness slipped over my awareness and suffocated me.

FIFTEEN

I awoke with a jerk, lying on my side on a flat, hard surface that rocked and juddered unevenly, sending jolts of pain along my bruised and battered body. *Wagon*, I thought groggily, having been in enough of the things over the years to recognize the motion even with a bag over my head.

My mind cleared by degrees, and I gasped. *Senovo!* I tried to scramble upright, but my arms and legs were trapped — bound tightly at the wrists and ankles. Panic flooded me. I thrashed and tried to call out for Senovo, but it emerged from my dry throat as an unintelligible croak.

"Carivel! Thank the gods… can you hear me?"

The voice, muffled by the cloth over my ears, was nearly as hoarse as mine, but it was unmistakably Senovo's. Relief nearly made me pass out again.

I tried to clear my throat, and descended into a coughing fit that brought the extent of my bruised ribs into painfully sharp focus. When I finally regained control, I rasped, "Where are we? Are you hurt?"

At first, I thought it wasn't loud enough for him to hear me over the creaking of the wagon. After a short pause, though, he replied, "I don't know, and not badly. South, somewhere, I think."

Wriggling toward the sound of his voice as best I could, my knees encountered something softer than the wood of the wagon.

"Yes, that's me," Senovo said. "I'm tied as well — I'm sorry."

"Shut up back there!" shouted an unfamiliar voice from the front of the wagon. "Unless you want a bag of your own, freak!" Something impacted sharply with the wooden slats near my head, and I flinched, heart pounding.

No, I thought, *this is my fault. I'm the one who's sorry. Oh, gods, Senovo — I'm so sorry.*

The next several hours were some of the worst of my life. I must have been unconscious through most of the night, because soon after I awoke again, I could feel sunlight warming my clothing and see it lightening the world beyond the mildewed bag over my head. The wagon bumped and jolted endlessly down whatever road or track our captors were following. I was desperately thirsty, and any attempt to communicate with either Senovo or the men holding us was met with harsh words and blows.

There was nothing to do except wallow in my own misery and think about everything bad that could be happening, or about to happen. I pictured Kekenu, lying somewhere on the road with a broken leg, or tangled in the stirrups of the saddle hanging off his side where it had slipped. I pictured Eiridan, frowning as he discovered that the High Priest and Horse Mistress had not returned by morning. I pictured Andoc, wondering if Senovo and I had decided to run away from Draebard after all, leaving him behind without a word. And Senovo... *oh, Senovo.* I pictured him, changing back to human form in the depths of terror, under the uncaring eyes of strangers who intended who-knew-what for him.

Because there was no doubt that it was Senovo they'd been after. I suddenly remembered the riders on the ridge, looking down on us in the clearing on the morning after Rhystel's death. What a fool I had been, to ignore them. To ignore the men — no doubt the *same* men — as they loitered around the temple. To ignore Kekenu's uncharacteristic nervousness as we left the village, heading for the forest.

This was my doing... perhaps it was the gods' punishment for lying about my sex and trying to cheat my way out of the handfasting. I clenched my eyes shut under the hood and tried to keep the tears from squeezing out. If I could only go back somehow, I'd let Andoc fuck me and put a dozen babies in my womb if it meant that Senovo would be safe.

How could either of them ever bear to so much as look at me again?

Throughout the endless journey, Senovo was a silent but steadfast presence. I couldn't even tell what part of his body my knees were jammed up against, but he never shifted or moved away from that single point of reassuring contact. It was once more growing dark beyond the suffocating barrier of my hood when the wagon rattled up an extended incline and came to a halt.

"Fucking *finally*," growled the driver from somewhere in front of us. "This had better damn well be worth it."

"Quit your moaning, Gerty," said another voice from close enough to me that I flinched with surprise. "You know he'll pay well for the wolf-man."

Hands grabbed my bound ankles and dragged them to the edge of the wagon—I could feel empty air under my feet. I tried to struggle, but there was no leverage.

"Easy, lad," Senovo said hoarsely. "He's just cutting you loose."

I froze in surprise. *Lad*? But as Senovo had said, a blade rasped through the strands of rope, parting them and freeing my legs. Blood rushed back to my feet in a torrent of pins and needles.

More hands dragged me upright, or tried to—my knees wobbled and refused to hold me. Our captors let me slither to the ground, where I landed on my bruised hip and hissed in pain. Someone jerked the bag off of my head and I was momentarily dazzled by torches flanking a rough double gate. I blinked rapidly, scanning my surroundings as best I could from the ground.

Merciful Utarr. They'd brought us to the hill fort. They'd brought us to the *Alyrions*. I began to shake, my eyes seeking out Senovo like a lifeline. Other men were pulling him, naked, from the back of the wagon and slicing through the ropes binding his ankles. Like me, his wrists were tied tightly behind him. Unlike me, there was a loop of rope tied around his neck with a length hanging from it, almost as long as he was tall. One of the men grabbed it and dragged him forward, using it like one might use a hunting dog's leash. Nausea flooded my aching stomach.

Senovo stumbled, but regained his equilibrium and did not fall.

"Come on, freak," growled his captor, before turning to the men standing over me. "You two—bring the boy."

I was grabbed from either side, hands lifting me onto my feet again as my injured shoulder screamed in protest. Dizziness washed over me, but gradually subsided as the men hustled me toward the gates.

The huge portals swung open on creaking hinges to reveal two guards wearing shining silvery chest plates. Alyrions. Our attackers. The savages who had killed Jorun. Gretya. Rhystel. So many others. If I'd had a drop of saliva left in my body, I'd have spit on the one closest to me as I was dragged inside.

The man holding Senovo like a collared hound spoke in an unfamiliar language to the second guard, gesturing animatedly toward the two of us. After a moment, the guard nodded and waved at us, indicating that we should follow. Senovo and I were dragged after him. Behind us, I heard the gates swing shut, one at a time.

I had never been to the hill fort before, but I knew of it. It was a ruin, left over from a time of greater prosperity a few generations ago, when the most powerful tribes maintained it as a sort of combination trading post and statement of wealth. The entire thing had been ringed with huge posts hewn from tall, straight trees and buried side-by-side—packed so tightly together that they formed an impenetrable wall twenty feet high.

Time had taken its toll even on so mighty a structure, travelers reported, and parts of it had rotted into ruin over the years. I couldn't help thinking that the gate we'd just come through seemed sturdy enough, but perhaps if Senovo and I could get free, we could escape through some other gap in the fortifications.

Inside, what had once been a warren of halls, alleyways, and buildings with wood-shingled roofs was now a tangle of half-collapsed walls and bare rafters. The guard led our little procession toward a structure that was in better condition, with solid walls and most of its roof intact. He motioned us to stay where we were and disappeared through a heavy door, leaving it open behind him.

A few moments later, he reappeared and gestured for our captors to bring us inside. Something deep in my brain balked at going into the dark building, but the men holding me dragged me forward easily. Inside, the cramped hallway opened out into a large room lit by a hearth fire and several oil lamps. A silver-haired man with sharp features and a prominent nose sat at a heavy table, staring down at a rectangular piece of thin, flat hide or cloth with colorful drawings marked on it.

He looked up as we entered, his eyes raking over Senovo's naked body with interest before flicking quickly over me.

"Is this the one you claim is a shape-changer?" he asked in passable but heavily accented Eburosi.

"It is," said the leader of the men holding us. "He was in the form of a wolf when we netted him last night. They say he's the new High Priest of the Draebardi tribe, after you killed the last one."

"Ha! *Barbarians*," said the silver-haired man with a sneer. "What a load of superstitious nonsense." His eyes, pale in the firelight, moved back to me. "And this one?"

Senovo cleared his throat softly. "This is Carivel, my servant. He rode out with me last night to assist me with a religious ceremony that can only take place on the night of the new moon. We were accosted by these men on our way back to the village."

"You lying piece of shit—" said the man holding Senovo's rope. He wrapped it around his fist as if in preparation for a vicious tug, but the Alyrion leader held up a hand to stop him.

"So you admit to being a priest, then?" asked the man.

"Of course," Senovo said, as if there was never any doubt. "I am, in fact, the new High Priest of Draebard."

"And a shape-changer?" the Alyrion prodded.

Senovo quirked an eyebrow. "There, I'm afraid, I cannot help you. It's true that there are stories of people changing into the form of animals in Eburosi culture, but they are stories. I suspect that the tale of me turning into a wolf is one designed to gain a larger bounty from you... assuming that bounty is, in fact, what we're discussing."

The Alyrion watched with something like amusement as the men holding us gaped at Senovo's blatant lie. "And do Eburosi priests often wander around naked in the forest at night with their young male servants?"

"Not generally," Senovo said. "As it happens, our captors took my robes and threw them away right after they overpowered us, presumably to bolster their claims about my so-called ability."

"You empty-sacked *fucker*," snarled Senovo's captor, driving a fist into his ribs with no warning. Senovo collapsed to the ground with a grunt, choking as the rope collar jerked tight.

I lunged forward with a cry, only to have my injured shoulder nearly yanked from its socket as my captors pulled me up short.

"Enough!" snapped the Alyrion commander. Everyone froze, and Senovo rolled up on a shoulder to get the pressure off his windpipe. "Let the eunuch go. Wolf or not, he is a valuable hostage, and I will pay you eighty silver pieces for the pair of them. Take it or leave it."

"Eighty!" said the leader. "He's worth a hundred at least!"

"Come on, Seb," whined the one called Gerty from my right side. "Just take the damn money and let's get out of here. I told you from the start this was nothin' but trouble!"

The leader—Seb—ground his teeth in frustration. "Fine," he said eventually. "But the difference is coming out of your cut, not mine."

The Alyrion commander counted out silver from a wooden box and swept it into a cloth bag with a drawstring. He threw the bulging purse down on the table, and Seb quickly snatched it up. As soon as he had it, my captors shoved me forward to land on the ground in a sprawl, unable to catch myself with my hands bound behind my back. I started to shuffle toward Senovo, but he shook his head minutely, holding my eyes with his. His mouth was a grim line.

"Get out of my sight, the lot of you," said the commander. The men filed out with the guard following behind, watching them closely as they muttered.

The three of us who remained behind regarded each other, points in a silent triangle. After a moment, the commander turned his back on Senovo and me dismissively. He sat down at the table again to pore over the mysterious markings on the thin hide, ignoring us completely. I shifted, drawing breath to say something, but again Senovo's sharp shake of the head stopped me. So I lay there, unable to get myself upright with my bruised side and bound hands, letting the packed dirt floor slowly leach the heat from my body. I wondered what it was doing to Senovo's bare skin.

A few long, tense minutes later, the guard returned. The commander looked up again, addressing us as if we hadn't lain ignored in the dirt at his feet for the last quarter hour.

"Did your captors offer you food and water?" he asked, directing the query to Senovo.

"They did not," replied the priest.

The commander nodded to the guard. "Water for the boy," he said. "Nothing for the eunuch."

I swallowed my protest, suspecting that, were I to voice it, the offer of water would be withdrawn as quickly as it had come. At least this way, maybe one of us could keep our strength up. The guard slopped water from a bucket in the corner into a cup. I swallowed as much of the stale, lukewarm liquid as I could when he poured it over the lower half of my face and tried not to worry about how sick it was likely to make me later. There was a good reason people mostly drank wine or ale instead of water.

"My servant was injured during our abduction last night," Senovo said evenly, once the guard had removed the empty cup.

"He walked in here well enough earlier," The commander said, dismissing the claim. "It can't be as bad as all that, can it?"

"I'm fine," I muttered, forcing my voice to work now that there was some moisture in my mouth and throat.

"There you are, then," said the commander. "Guard, take our guests and shackle them in the old larder. We will talk later, eunuch."

The guard leaned down to grab the end of Senovo's rope before dragging me upright... by my uninjured right arm, thankfully. The fact that this was probably going to be our best chance for escape was not lost on me, but in reality it was no chance at all. I was so weak I could barely walk, and the guard need only pull the rope in his hand to choke Senovo into submission.

As it was, the man grabbed a torch and marched us down a series of alleys. We went past groups of tents where Alyrion soldiers cooked food and sharpened weapons, looking up curiously to watch as we passed by. Eventually, we came to a room with thick walls made of stacked stone blocks, and a roof with huge holes in it. It was cool inside. *A larder*, I reminded myself. *Of course it's chilly.*

The guard pushed me down by one wall and put the torch in a sconce before taking Senovo across to another wall. Iron bands hung from both walls on strange lengths of interlinked metal rings, flexible like rope, but heavy and unbreakable. The man pulled a dagger from his belt and used it to cut Senovo's hands free, only to lock first one wrist and then the other within the heavy shackles. I got the same treatment a moment later, the metal weighing my wrists down so much it felt as though I could hardly lift them.

When he was done, the guard kicked an empty wooden bucket toward me. It fetched up against my hip, smelling of piss and vomit. Then he left without another word, taking the torch with him and plunging the room into darkness as the door slammed closed with finality behind him.

"Senovo—" I began, on the verge of tears.

"Wait," Senovo ordered, and I swallowed whatever I might have said next.

I held my breath, waiting for the guard's footsteps to disappear.

"Quickly, now," Senovo said. "They may yet post a guard outside, even though we are shackled. You must not let them know that you are female, Carivel, and you must *not* show any unusual degree of affection for me. You are a servant, nothing more. Do you understand?"

"You're afraid they'll rape me," I whispered.

"*Carivel*," Senovo said sharply. "Say it back to me. *You are my servant, and beyond that we mean nothing to each other.*"

"I am your servant, and we mean nothing to each other," I echoed in a faint voice.

I heard Senovo sigh as if in relief. "That's right. Do nothing to draw attention to yourself. *Promise me*, Carivel."

The words tasted like bile as I choked them out. "I promise."

A pall fell over the dark, chill room. I shivered, half in response to the cold stone at my back, and half in response to my troubling thoughts. Again, I wondered how much worse it must be for Senovo, in his nakedness. I remembered the robe Eiridan had so thoughtfully sent, lost now during my fall from Kekenu and the scuffle that followed. Silence reigned, inside the room and out... either we did not merit a guard or they were being slow about it.

"How can you be so calm?" I asked when I couldn't stand it anymore, hating the slightly hysterical pitch of my voice.

Senovo shifted in the darkness. "They will do nothing more tonight. Why should they, when hunger, thirst and cold stone will do their work for them?"

"But..." I began.

"You forget, Carivel," Senovo continued, his raspy voice sounding far away. "I was raised a slave, amidst such cruelty as this. These vicious games of power and control are imprinted far more deeply on my spirit than the subtle posturing of Volya or the politics of the temple."

I swallowed hard, and whispered, "I'm sorry."

"Don't be," Senovo said, still sounding far removed. "We may have cause to be grateful for my experience in such matters over the coming days. Now, though, please forgive me. Thirst is making it difficult for me to speak."

I bit back another apology and nodded instead, only to realize that he couldn't see me in the dark. "All right," I said, clamping down on the quaver that wanted come out with the words.

We sat in the dark through the long night. It rained for a while, sometime after midnight, pouring through the gaps in the roof above us. I tried to shuffle away from the chilly deluge, but could only get far enough to keep half of my body dry. A few flashes of lightning illuminated the room with a flickering silver glow and my eyes instinctively sought Senovo's form across from me. He was shivering, positioned under one of the gaps with his head thrown back to capture as much of the water dripping down as possible in his open mouth.

When the lightning passed, I hunched against the cold, damp wall and cried silently, making sure that my face was turned away from Senovo and my breathing did not hitch enough for him to hear. My head and throat ached terribly from the strain, but eventually exhaustion took over and I slipped into a sort of strange fugue state—not truly sleep, but not exactly wakefulness either.

The next time I opened my eyes, morning light was streaming through the holes in the roof. I gasped and jerked upright, metal dragging against metal as my arms flailed. I was freezing cold, and my stomach felt like an empty pit beneath my lungs. It took several tries to un-stick my tongue from the top of my dry, fuzzy mouth.

When my blurry vision cleared, it was to the sight of Senovo seated a few inches away from the wall. His arms and legs were curled into as much of a ball as the shackles would allow. He was shivering noticeably; his skin was pale as marble, covered with grime and raw scrapes. He looked up at my movement.

"T-they will be h-here soon," he said without preamble, his voice weaker than the evening before. "Remember your promise."

I nodded reluctantly, not trusting my voice.

In truth, it was perhaps half an hour before the sound of someone lifting the bar on the outside of the door heralded the return of a guard—a different one from last night, I was pretty sure. He spoke sharply in the unfamiliar tongue of the Alyrions, pointing at Senovo, who sat motionless but for the tremors wracking his body.

The guard unfastened the shackles and dragged Senovo to his feet. I tensed, but Senovo's eyes pinned mine for a bare instant, silently reproving. Biting the inside of my cheek until the blood flowed, I stayed quiet and meek as he was led away.

It was worse once he was gone. I lost all sense of time. The heavy clouds above made it impossible to track the progress of the sun through the gaps in the shingles. I tried to distract myself by using the disgusting bucket, my efforts made more difficult by the shackles and my stiff, bruised body. I catalogued every nook and cranny in the abandoned larder. I examined the strange metal links that ran from my shackles to the wall. They were ingenious, but must have been incredibly time-consuming to make—each small iron loop presumably being forged individually around the one preceding it.

I stared at the heavy iron links and cried some more, keeping silent out of long habit as the tears ran.

When the sound of footsteps approached the heavy door, I quickly wiped the evidence from my face and hunched back against the wall, waiting. A guard came in and tossed a bit of bread onto the filthy floor at my feet, following it up with a wooden cup. Water slopped over the edge as he thunked it down without finesse. He sneered at me for a moment and left without a word.

I reached for the pathetic meal, but my hand stopped inches shy of the cup, caught by the shackles. The urge to weep again washed over me, but I fought it. After a few moments' thought, I scooted around and nudged the bread closer to the wall with the heel of my boot, until I could finally reach it. The water was more difficult, some of the precious liquid spilling over the edge as I slowly eased it close enough to pick up and drink greedily.

The manacles chafed at my raw, bruised wrists as I shoved the stale brown bread into my mouth, ignoring the muddy grit that clung to it as I ate with ravenous haste. I had to keep my strength up—one of us *had* to escape and get back to Draebard.

And assuming someone deigns to unshackle you, would you even know the way back to the front gate? Much less back to Draebard. The insidious voice in my head was snide.

I would follow the outer wall until I found a break, and then I would head north, of course. There were roads; I could find people and ask. Or maybe Senovo would escape. At least he wasn't manacled right now. I passed a few minutes fantasizing about Senovo turning into a wolf… attacking his guard and running away. I had almost convinced myself that it might have happened when the guard brought him back in and chained him up once more.

The first thing I noticed was that he now wore a simple tunic in the Alyrion style. The second thing was that, while he was still frightfully pale, he actually looked a bit better than when he'd left. I stared, drinking him in as the guard tugged on the shackles to make sure they were secure and left the room. The bar dropped against the outside of the door and I held my breath, but the man's footsteps did not recede. I took that to mean he was staying to guard the room.

"Don't worry," Senovo said in a tired voice. "That one doesn't speak Eburosi. Just keep your voice quiet and conversational. Did they feed you?"

"Sort of," I said, and he nodded in satisfaction. "Senovo, what happened? Are you all right?"

Senovo leaned back against the rough stone wall and closed his eyes. "Broadly, what I have just experienced was the carrot before the stick. This afternoon will not go as well for me."

This afternoon? I blinked in surprise. Was it really only midday? I had convinced myself that it must be nearly evening already.

"And… less broadly?" I asked, trying to draw Senovo out.

"The Field Marshal desires information about Draebard's military plans and alliances. I negotiated for what concessions I could, and gave him information that was incorrect or unimportant. Unfortunately, he is well aware of the inadequacy of my response."

"You got me the food," I said, not making it a question.

"Food, water, clothing." He gestured at the over-large tunic, which hung awkwardly on his slender frame. "It was a tactic on his part as much as mine, but no matter."

"Why you?" I asked. "They targeted *you*."

Senovo shrugged a shoulder. "The bandits wanted money. The Alyrions are notoriously intolerant of religions other than their own... those that they consider *barbarians*. They believe that the spirits of non-believers will reside in a pit of fire for eternity after they die, but they help matters along by burning alive anyone who shows evidence of magic. Or *witchcraft*, as they insist on calling it." He opened his eyes, staring at the wrecked ceiling. "It is a deeply vicious and unforgiving faith."

I wrapped my arms around myself, holding tightly as he continued.

"I was treated to a genial, but rather pointed description of the fiery fate that might await a confirmed shape-shifter," he said, still sounding as if he were discussing the weather or plans for a casual meal. "I'm afraid there was no mention of what would be done to the servant of a shape-shifter." Senovo paused and looked down. "I... didn't ask."

It was my turn to close my eyes, trying to blot out the image of fire. "Does he even believe in such things, though?" I asked.

"Unclear," Senovo said. "The Field Marshal appears to be a practical man for the most part. He is most interested in what he may face from Draebard, but there is still little doubt that the first flash of fang and fur would seal both our deaths."

"How long can you hold out?" I asked hesitantly, taking in the dark circles under Senovo's eyes and the faint sheen of clammy sweat on his brow.

"Until I can't anymore," he answered simply.

Silence fell for long moments.

"I'm so sorry I got you into this," I forced out, past the lump in my throat. Senovo's eyes leapt to mine.

"Carivel," he began, but I shook my head sharply and hid my face in the space between my arms and knees as I curled up. Curled away from him.

We sat quietly, separated by my guilt as much as by our shackles. I obsessively ran through increasingly desperate and unlikely scenarios inside my mind, where I leapt up when the guard returned and proclaimed myself to be a more valuable hostage… or pretended to be sick and overpowered the guard somehow when he came to check on me… or ripped open my tunic to expose my breasts, proclaiming that I was a woman and would service everyone in the fort in exchange for Senovo's peaceful release.

"*Carivel.*" Senovo's voice was more insistent this time. "*Stop.* This is a game of waiting. A mental game, though it will no doubt grow physical as well. Your own mind can too easily become the enemy."

My ragged breathing as I grew more and more panicked must have given me away, but I could not control it any more than I could look at Senovo right now. I hugged my knees tighter, ignoring the stab of discomfort from my ribs. Before he could make another attempt to engage me, a guard stormed into the room, unshackled him, and dragged him roughly away. The sound of the bar dropping across the door behind them was like a wordless accusation.

"I'm sorry," I whimpered into my knees. "Oh, gods. I'm sorry, I'm sorry, *I'm so sorry…*"

SIXTEEN

It was nearly dark when they brought Senovo back. I could only see the dim outline of his body, but it was enough to tell that he wasn't moving right. Once manacled, he rolled awkwardly to the side to lean one shoulder against the wall. I bit my lip—*hard*—until the door closed behind the guard, muffling his boot steps.

"Senovo!" I whispered, urgent with fear. "What did they do to you? Where are you hurt? Senovo, *please*! Talk to me."

"I'm sorry, Carivel… I can't… right now," Senovo said faintly. "It's all right. Try not to be afraid…"

His head lolled to rest against the wall, and my increasingly desperate cries could not rouse him. I called his name until my voice grew hoarse and painful. Tears tracked steadily down my cheeks. My guts churned—fear for Senovo or a result of the bad water, it was all the same. In desperation, I tried to jerk and twist my hands out of the manacles, succeeding only in tearing my wrists up even more badly than they had been before.

The night crawled by in sluggish misery… possibly the longest night I had ever experienced. Utter relief flooded me when Senovo finally blinked awake in the morning light, only to flee immediately when two guards showed up moments later and hauled him away again.

This must be what it's like to go mad, I thought some time later.

I had explored the place where the shackles attached to the unforgiving stone walls with my fingernails, stretching up on my toes to reach until dizziness and cramps sent me back to the floor in a heap. Now I was staring at my left hand, wondering if it would fit through the manacle if my thumb was broken… and if I'd be able to stay conscious long enough to somehow break the other one afterward.

But how would I get past a heavy, barred door with two broken hands?

I jerked upright with a gasp as the door in question opened. The two guards from earlier half-dragged Senovo in and chained him up. Without their support, he slid down the wall immediately and curled up on his side, hissing in pain.

"Oh, gods," I moaned as the guards turned, uncaring, and left. "Oh, gods, *Senovo*..."

Senovo shook his head and gritted his teeth, pulling himself into a more upright position. "It was only foot-caning," he grated out, his voice sounding like a rusty hinge. "Somewhat... effective in the moment... but the effects fade quickly."

"I can't do this," I said in a rush, "I can't watch this any more, I *can't!*"

"Carivel," he said. "Stop, *please.*" He let his head roll back to rest on the wall and let out a huff of humorless laughter that nearly broke me. "It appears the Field Marshal's methods are more effective than he realizes. Just not with... the person he expects."

"*Please*... I don't know what to do, Senovo! What do I do?" I implored.

Senovo's brows twitched together in confusion. "Nothing," he said after a moment, as if it was obvious. "You do nothing."

A few minutes later, he slipped into a doze, or possibly a faint. I watched him for as long as I could bear before burying my face in my hands, ignoring the feel of rough metal scraping along damaged skin.

I couldn't do this.

I couldn't do this.

The words repeated over and over inside my head as I rocked back and forth endlessly. Pressure grew within my chest, pushing against my heart and lungs until it seemed I must burst with it. I had to stop this. I *had* to stop it somehow.

Time passed. The guards came back. Senovo startled awake as the door slammed open. I scrambled to my feet on shaking legs. "Stop!" I screamed at them, beyond thought. "I won't let you take him! Leave him *alone!*"

"Carivel, *no!*" Senovo cried hoarsely.

"Shut up! *Shut up!*" I shouted, the words tearing at my sore, dry throat. "You mustn't take him, *take me!*"

The guards looked from one of us to the other in confusion. I groaned and stumbled to my knees, realizing that they hadn't understood a word I'd said. "Please, take me…" I begged in a raspy voice.

The two of them conferred in low voices for a moment, gesturing at Senovo. To my shock, after a brief conversation they turned and left the room, closing the door behind them.

My mouth was hanging open. I flopped to the floor in a boneless heap. "Why did that work?" I asked, feeling faint as the buzz of raw terror subsided. I turned bleary eyes on Senovo.

"You *promised*, Carivel," whispered the priest, stricken. "Gods have mercy on us both. You promised, and now I've failed."

A few minutes later, the door opened again, admitting the guards, along with the Field Marshal himself. Unease pooled heavily in the pit of my churning stomach.

"Well, well," said the Alyrion commander pleasantly. "I've just heard a most interesting report from my men."

He drew a short, wicked looking dagger from his belt and examined the blade closely.

"It can't have been that interesting, since these guards don't speak a word of Eburosi," I said, surprised by how strong my voice sounded. I dragged myself straighter to glare at the man who had hurt Senovo.

The Field Marshal's pale eyes flicked toward me, as if surprised that I'd spoken. "No, no," he said. "It was actually most informative. It seems I've been directing my attentions toward the wrong person."

"Go fuck yourself," I growled, bravado rising to the fore as our situation grew more hopeless. Senovo flinched at my words, but remained stubbornly silent.

One of the guards stepped toward me aggressively after my outburst, his hand on the hilt of his sword. The Field Marshal laughed. "There! You see? One need not understand the words of a language to learn all sorts of interesting information from the person speaking it. All this time and effort I've spent on the half-man, when I should have focused on his sweet, beardless boy instead. Perhaps our High Priest *does* make a habit of cavorting naked in the woods with his young, fresh-faced servants."

Again, I wished longingly for enough saliva to spit in this butcher's face. He hauled me up by the shirt front, twisting me around to slam me face first into the wall, heedless of the shackles as they tangled around my bruised torso.

"Is this the motivation you need, eunuch?" he asked, angling himself to give Senovo a clear view.

"I have no wish to see anyone harmed," Senovo said, the undercurrent of strain in his voice painfully, blatantly obvious. Iron links clinked against each other as he pulled himself to his feet, breathing hard. "But Carivel is merely... merely a... servant..."

The bright blade of the dagger appeared in my peripheral vision. "Oh, yes? So his fate is of no personal interest to you whatsoever, then?" asked the commander.

Distantly, the sound of clattering and shouting filtered through the open doorway to us. The guard who was still in my field of vision turned as if startled, and the Field Marshal stilled at my back. After a moment, he barked an order and I heard the second guard leave the room through the open door—presumably to see what was causing the disturbance.

"Maybe you should go see to that personally," I gasped, jerking weakly against the man's hold.

"If it is important, the lieutenant will report back," said the commander, unconcerned. "I'm much more interested in our current little drama at the moment. Aren't you, High Priest?" The blade flicked toward my cheek, and I cried out at the bright line of pain as the Field Marshal added, "After all, I would *so* like to hear your *honest* answers to my questions..."

I could hear Senovo heaving air past his raspy throat. The blade flicked again, drawing a shallow, burning line across the thin skin of my throat. I froze, terror sending a fog of red floating across my vision. Behind me, Senovo's cry of rage transformed into the feral snarl of a wolf. The guard shouted in fear, and I heard the rasp of his sword being drawn from its scabbard even as the Field Marshal shoved himself away from me and turned to face Senovo fully.

I pushed away from the wall, dizzy at the sudden loss of support. A warm trail of blood dribbled down my face and neck. Senovo was loose. The wolf's slender legs and paws had slipped out of the manacles as soon as the change started. The animal struggled free from the material of the loose tunic. He was hunched with pain from whatever had been done earlier to his human body, lips drawn back in a deadly snarl, ears flattened.

"It's true, then?" the Field Marshal said in shock, staggering back a few steps and falling into a defensive crouch.

The guard stood stunned and unmoving as Senovo leapt forward toward his commander. The massive wolf plowed into our tormenter with his full weight, and I cried out as the dagger flashed. Senovo yipped in surprise, but the pair crashed to the ground and in an instant, powerful jaws latched onto a vulnerable throat, ripping and tearing. The guard began screaming for help as his commander jerked and flopped, heels scrabbling against the filthy floor with frantic movements that slowly grew weaker and more disjointed until his body finally went limp.

Giving the corpse a final, vicious shake, the wolf lifted his bloody face from the ruin of gore and gristle, fixing narrow yellow eyes on the remaining man. The guard had backed slowly around the perimeter of the wall during the attack, trying, I gathered, to get to the door. He stopped instantly when the wolf's eyes pinned him, his calls for help growing higher pitched. He was only a step in front of me and a step to the side, his back turned to me — obviously discounting me as a threat.

Boots pounded toward the open door of our prison and I took advantage of the distraction to throw a loop of the heavy chain attached to my right wrist around the man's throat. The sword dropped from his hand in surprise as he scrabbled at the metal links with both hands. I was too weak to jump on his back, but I pulled as hard as I could, letting my body weight drag against the makeshift garrote.

Two more guards ran through the door, swords drawn, and slid to a stop as they were confronted with a slavering wolf standing over the bloody remains of their commander. I clung to the guard in front of me as he bucked and seized under my grip, the pair of us sliding down the wall in a tangle as his legs gave out.

Outside, the sounds of chaos and confusion had grown exponentially louder — shouts, screams, the clanging of metal. My sluggish brain struggled to make sense of it. The attack was not supposed to take place for a week yet. Had I somehow lost an entire week in this horrible place? Was someone *else* attacking the hill fort?

The guard's flailing elbow crashed into my bruised side, driving the breath from me and dragging my wandering mind back to the present.

"Senovo, don't!" I cried as the injured wolf charged one of the newly arrived guards. Blood stained one furry flank where the Field Marshal's dagger had hit home, and his gait was uneven. The man cried out and lifted his sword to strike, but powerful jaws clamped his arm and dragged him down to his knees.

"*No!*" I screamed as the second guard raised his weapon, poised to bring it down on the back of the wolf's neck in a killing blow.

Without warning, the man jerked sideways and collapsed to the ground with a horrible gurgle, the shaft of an arrow emerging grotesquely from his neck. I watched, trapped by my shackles and the dead weight of the guard I'd just strangled—my heart in my throat. The man Senovo was fighting twisted free and staggered to his feet, blood dripping from his arm, only to fall an instant later to a second arrow.

I shoved weakly at the heavy corpse lying half on top of me, trying to get free. The wolf grabbed his downed opponent under the jaw and shook him, as if checking for signs of life. When there were none, he backed away, slinking into the corner with his belly close to the ground and growling at the open door.

"Who's in there?" called a familiar female voice. "Identify yourselves!"

"K-Keenan?" I choked, not truly believing it.

"Carivel, is that you?" Keenan asked. Her dark head appeared in the doorway, scanning the room cautiously. The wolf snarled and backed further into the corner.

"Don't come in!" I exclaimed. "Just stay outside for a moment."

Keenan's eyes had fixed on the wolf, shock giving way to wonder in her expression. "Is that—?"

"Yes, it's him," I said. "Just… just give us a minute. It's not safe."

"It's not all that safe out here, either," called a second, male voice that I didn't recognize.

"He's not wrong," Keenan told me. "Things are a bit crazy right now. Be quick, yeah?"

With that, she withdrew and closed the door, the heavy wood muffling her companion's voice mid-protest. I was shaking violently from head to foot, but I clenched my eyes shut and forced composure. *Just hold it together for a few minutes more,* I told myself.

"Senovo," I said aloud. "I—I need you to come back now. I know your instincts are probably screaming at you not to do it, but it's really, *really* important. Please come back for me. *Please,* Senovo…"

The wolf stared at me from the corner, its eyes hugely dilated above its gory muzzle, trembling nearly as hard as I was. Those eyes stayed glued to mine as Senovo shifted into human form and promptly collapsed onto his side with a cry of pain.

"It's all right," I babbled, "it's all right, our friends are here. Keenan's going to come in now and she'll help you… Andoc's out there somewhere, too, I know he is…"

I was interrupted when Keenan cautiously opened the door again. Her eyes fell on Senovo, and she quickly gestured her companion to come inside and close the door behind them.

"Gods above, what a mess," she said, as her fellow warrior knelt to check the two guards near the door for signs of life.

"Dead," he reported.

There was no question of the Field Marshal being alive. The two of them crossed to me, and I shook my head. "No, Senovo's hurt, you've got to help him…"

"You're both hurt," Keenan observed. "First things first, though."

Her companion unwrapped the metal chain from my guard's neck and pressed fingers under his jaw. "Heart's still beating… barely. He'll die in a minute—his windpipe is completely fucked. Well done on that, by the way, Horse Mistress."

For some unfathomable reason, knowing that the man sprawled across me was still sort of alive sent me into a panic. I shoved at him with renewed energy, trying to scrabble backward even though I had nowhere to go.

"Get him off, get him *off!*" I cried, and the two Mereni each grabbed an arm to pull the dying man away.

"All right Carivel, he's gone," Keenan said when they'd deposited him next to the commander's corpse. "Stay with her for a minute, Nereth—see if you can get those manacles off."

The man—Nereth—crouched next to me. "Let me see one of your hands," he said, and examined the catch on the heavy metal shackle, twisting it this way and that as he tried to figure out the trick to it.

In the meantime, Keenan approached Senovo slowly. "Hey, now," she said. "First you go and disrupt my handfasting, and now you've stolen my thunder during a perfectly good rescue mission, as well. If I didn't know better, I'd think you had it in for me personally."

Senovo did not raise his head or open his eyes. "C-Carivel," he choked out. "Is she—?"

"Couple of shallow cuts and her wrists are pretty torn up," Keenan said. "I think she's more worried about you."

The first shackle fell away from my wrists as Senovo shook his head. "I'm all right."

"You're bleeding," Keenan pointed out, peering at the flesh over Senovo's hip.

"Am I?" Senovo asked blankly.

The second shackle fell away and I immediately crawled toward the pair in the corner, every joint protesting the movement.

"These two are in no shape to walk through the middle of a battle, Nereth," Keenan said.

"This isn't a good place to stay," Nereth replied in a grim tone. "Only one entrance, and too easy for someone to drop the bar across the door on us if we keep it closed."

"Agreed," Keenan said. "Can you go and get us some reinforcements? I'll stay here to defend them, just in case."

"Right," Nereth said. "Try not to get killed, yeah? Ciero would come out of retirement just to string me up by my big toes."

"Don't be such a baby, Nereth," Keenan said. "He's only got one arm. You could take him, surely."

I let the teasing wash over me as I approached the corner where Senovo lay curled on his side, facing away from me. The Field Marshal's dagger had slashed a neat line over his hipbone and haunch, from which blood welled sluggishly. It was his back, though, which made my breath catch. It was crisscrossed with welts from a vicious beating, easily a hundred or more bruises extending from his shoulders to his tailbone and the tops of his buttocks.

I collapsed forward and retched, bitter bile scorching its way up my parched throat to splatter onto the floor as I heaved.

"Nereth, just *go*," Keenan said, moving to support my shoulders. "Hurry."

"Going," Nereth said. "I'll close the door, but I won't bar it."

Keenan nodded, still focused on keeping me from collapsing face first in my own filth. The door opened and closed softly, signaling his departure.

"Are you done?" she asked when I stopped heaving and hung limply in her grasp. "Only you're heavier than you look."

"Sorry," I rasped, and let her help me back to sit propped against the wall.

She looked around the room and went to retrieve the Alyrion tunic Senovo had been wearing before he shifted. "Let me have your jerkin, too, Carivel," she said as she ripped a strip from the cleanest looking part and wadded it up.

I removed the jerkin with difficulty, my injured shoulder flaring as I dragged my arms free. Giving it to Keenan, I allowed her to guide my hand down and press the torn cloth over Senovo's wound, staunching the slow drip of blood. I echoed his hard flinch at the first touch, sitting tense and guilty by his side as he gradually relaxed a bit.

Keenan helped him get the remains of the tunic arranged over his upper body, and placed my jerkin beneath him to keep his lower body slightly insulated from the damp chill of the floor. She had no way to know that cold was only part of the reason he was shaking like a leaf in the wind. He had killed again—ripped tender human flesh between his teeth until the blood stopped pulsing—and again, it was all my fault.

"I'm sorry I don't have anything to drink, or to use to clean you up," Keenan said.

My entire body yearned for a cool draft of ale, but there was nothing to be done for it right now. "What's happening out there?" I asked instead, shaping the words around the sour taste of bile on my tongue. Behind that question, several others jostled for attention. *Why did you attack early? Did Kekenu reach*

Draebard safely? Is Andoc out there? Is he injured? Will he ever be able to forgive me for what happened to Senovo?

"When that little horse of yours showed up alone a couple of days ago with his saddle hanging under his belly, Andoc nearly went through the roof," Keenan said, and I swallowed a sob of relief at the knowledge that Kekenu had survived. "He badgered Volya until the old man finally caved and agreed to attack immediately, even though we were nowhere near ready. Volya kept arguing that there was no proof the Alyrions had taken you in the first place, and all Andoc would say was that he had a feeling about it. We had bets going on the Mereni side over whether they'd come to blows over the whole thing."

"And... Magoldis?" I asked. Surely the aloof Mereni leader would not have been swayed by emotional arguments.

Keenan shrugged. "I gather Varanis talked to her. No idea what was said, but when Volya finally gave in, she went along with it. And here we are—Andoc was right. I'm just sorry we couldn't get to you sooner."

"I'd say... that your timing was... impeccable," Senovo offered in a weak voice, pausing for breath every few words.

"Could've been worse, I suppose; definitely could've been better," Keenan said. "Now we just need to get you both out of here safely. The Alyrions must have deployed more men here since the meeting with Volya took place. Things were supposed to be a *lot* more one-sided than this."

There was noise beyond the door, and Keenan leapt to her feet with bow and arrow in hand, only to relax a moment later as a complex series of knocks sounded against the wood.

"That's Nereth," she said, before calling, "Don't take all day about it!" in a voice loud enough to carry outside.

The door open, and several people piled in with Nereth in the lead.

"Things are still chaotic on the far side of the compound," he reported, "but the only organized resistance seems to be on the hillside beyond the missing wall. We think something must've happened to their command structure—there's no coordination inside the fort at all."

I realized that I'd neglected something important. "That's the Field Marshal," I said, pointing to the bloody corpse across the room. "He didn't even know there was an attack."

Nereth blinked. "Fuck. Seriously?"

"Well, that certainly explains quite a lot," said one of the newcomers.

"Can we get these two out of here safely?" Keenan asked. "The First Warriors need to know what's happening in here."

"Can they walk?" one of the others asked skeptically.

"Yes," Senovo rasped from the floor.

"… maybe?" I said hoarsely from my spot propped against the wall.

"Great," Nereth said without enthusiasm.

SEVENTEEN

"Well, we can't stay here forever," Keenan pointed out. "Wendes, you help the High Priest. Bornik, you help the Horse Mistress. I'll take point. Nereth, you and Delia can cover our rear."

The muscular woman named Delia prodded the skinniest of the dead guards with the toe of her boot. "Here, hang on. I think these trousers and boots will fit you, High Priest. Better than walking out barefoot."

She efficiently stripped off the clothing and helped Wendes get them on Senovo, belting the trousers in place to help hold the bandage steady over his wound. The two of them levered him to his feet and Wendes steadied him. I shuddered at the sight of the blood staining the priest's lips and chin, and Senovo himself looked rather green for a few moments after the abrupt change in elevation.

I was distracted when Bornik—a wide, burly man with a shock of curly red hair—reached down to help me up. He grasped my left arm and I could not choke back my gasp of pain as the shoulder screamed in protest. Bornik immediately froze, looking worried.

"Other side," Senovo said, leaning heavily against his own escort.

"Right. Sorry, ma'am," Bornik said in a sheepish voice, and reached for my right arm instead.

"It's fine," I grated, letting him pull me up and sling my good arm over his shoulder so he could brace me.

My knees were as wobbly as a newborn foal's and my gut sloshed back and forth worryingly, but I leaned on Bornik's sturdy bulk and put one foot in front of the other as he led me forward.

"This should be fun," I heard Nereth mutter from behind us as we trailed out into the open, Keenan peeking around corners to check that the way was clear, holding an arrow nocked and ready to let fly at a moment's notice.

Twice we were surprised by lone soldiers running toward us, apparently fleeing the fighting further ahead. Keenan shot one through a gap in his armor, and Nereth hacked another to death, nearly separating the man's head from his shoulders. At one point, he and Delia fell behind for a few moments, trading blows with a pair of Alyrions who came at us from a side alley. It was just about all I could manage to keep up with the brisk pace Keenan set for us, but I still spared a moment for a short prayer of relief when they caught up, Delia bleeding freely from a gash on her shoulder.

Ahead, I could make out a gap in the outer fortifications. Several of the giant posts had essentially crumbled to nothingness, and others leaned into the empty space like drunkards after a night at the tavern.

"We need to get outside and see where the battle lines are," Keenan said. "The terrain is rough here — the fighting should all be around the corner on the east side where the chariots can maneuver."

We snuck through the gap in the timbers, on to the rocky scree beyond. The steep slope played havoc with my already questionable balance. I stumbled repeatedly into poor Bornik, who wobbled but never lost his footing as we crept toward the southeast corner of the hill fort.

Still taking point, Keenan was the one to stick her head around the edge and survey the scene beyond. "It looks like we're taking them," she said a moment later, relief thick in her voice.

"Thank Deresta for that," Bornik said.

"Keenan," Nereth said, "can you and Delia guard these two while Bornik, Wendes, and I go back to help clean up inside the fort?"

"I think so," Keenan said. "Delia, how's the shoulder?"

"It'll keep for a while longer," said the taller woman, craning to check the wound.

"Right. High Priest, Horse Mistress, why don't you two try to rest for a bit while our side finishes things up," said Keenan. "No point in trying to get across the battlefield when the battle will likely be over within the hour anyway."

"Thank you," Senovo said weakly, and allowed Wendes to ease him down against the smooth base of a timber. Bornik helped me down as well, but I scooted forward until I could peek out beyond the corner of the wall and see the field of battle for myself.

The village where I had grown up was a tiny one, not prone to fighting with its neighbors. The three years I had spent in Draebard had been relatively peaceful ones, as well. While I had seen a few skirmishes over water rights during the drought, I had never seen anything on this scale. My bleary eyes could make little sense of the overall scene, though I trusted Keenan's assessment.

Instead, I sought out familiar figures, chief among them, Kekenu's familiar black and white splotches. The little gelding was harnessed with a chunky bay, charging hard into a knot of Alyrion soldiers who were attempting to draw bowstrings before the chariot was upon them. A jolt shuddered through my chest as I recognized the bay horse as Andoc's, and the figures in the chariot as Dalon, driving, while Andoc readied his sword behind him.

"Mind your flank, you great fool," Keenan muttered above me, also peeking out to watch the action.

More soldiers bearing swords were approaching from the side, and I held my breath. One of the archers managed to let off a shot in the instant before the two geldings plowed into them, and the arrow buried itself in the wood of the chariot in front of Dalon. A few inches higher…

The bowmen scattered, a couple of them falling under the churning hooves of the chariot team. The wheels jerked and bounced over their bodies. Andoc slashed at another soldier as they went past, and leapt out of the back of the chariot to engage the ones still standing as Dalon pulled up.

Meanwhile, a band of Eburosi warriors had converged on the Alyrion swordsmen approaching from the flank. I recognized Varanis' fiery red hair, leading the charge, keeping the Alyrions from reaching Andoc and Dalon. Even from here, I could see that Andoc fought as one possessed, hacking and punching without mercy, his bared teeth a white slash against yellow and ochre-red war paint.

I watched as the remaining Alyrion resistance crumbled over the next half hour or so. As soon as it was safe to do so, Keenan turned to Delia and ordered her to report to Varanis and Andoc. It seemed to take forever for the injured woman to cross the battlefield. My eyes flickered over the forms of downed fighters and... downed horses... but everything seemed increasingly distant, as if my emotions were simply shutting down in the face of yet more horror.

I felt truly awful—my stomach threatened to turn on me once more despite being completely empty, and cramps clawed at my guts. Sweat had broken out on my forehead at some point, and stung sharply as it dripped into the shallow cuts on my face and neck.

Delia finished her report to Varanis—of course she would speak with her own First Warrior before anything else—and the two of them crossed to where Andoc was crouched over an injured Alyrion wearing fancier armor than the others. Andoc looked up as the two women approached, and they spoke together for a moment. Delia pointed back to where we were huddled at the corner of the fort. Andoc followed with his eyes, and his sword slipped from slack fingers to clatter to the ground.

A moment later, he was running.

I closed my eyes, caught between my desperate need for him to be here and my dread at what would happen once he found out that I'd dragged Senovo into the forest, exposing him to capture and days of torment. The sound of boots pounding on thin dirt and rock made me look up again, just as he crossed the final distance and slid to a stop, falling to his knees halfway between the two of us.

"Oh, thank the gods," he whispered. "Thank the gods."

He looked awful. His leather armor was slashed in several places, blood staining some of the pieces rusty. The side of his face was swollen, the beginnings of a spectacular bruise visible where the war paint had smeared. Furthermore, he had the appearance of someone who hadn't slept properly in days—not a look I'd ever seen on him before.

Senovo's green eyes were soft despite his pain and the blood coating his face. "If you're done bashing heads for the day, my friend, Carivel and I would appreciate some weak wine to drink and a bucket of water to wash in," he said, voice hoarse.

Andoc surged forward to kiss first his forehead, and then mine, as Keenan looked on curiously. "Of course," he said. "Anything you need, *amadi*. Let me help you back to the wagons..."

He looked between us as if torn.

"Help Senovo," I said quickly. "Be careful of his back and his left side."

It only made sense, really. I was lighter, and it would be easier for Keenan to support me, petite as she was. It had nothing at all to do with the fact that I was likely to shatter into a thousand pieces if Andoc put his arms around me.

The dizziness was much worse this time when Keenan helped me upright. I had to breathe deeply for a moment to keep the swirling gray at the edge of my vision from closing in. Thankfully it receded, and I was able to stumble along beside the shorter woman toward the line of carts and wagons at the edge of the woods east of the hill fort.

While we made our painfully slow and awkward way across the battlefield, Varanis had ordered the wounded Alyrion in the fancy armor brought over to the wagons on a makeshift stretcher. She, Magoldis, and Volya were arrayed around him in a menacing half circle, and he glared up at them with glassy, bloodshot eyes as we arrived.

"You take outpost," he said with a sneer in broken, deeply accented Eburosi, "but Empire come soon and take island. Kill you all."

The last was delivered on a slow exhale, and the soldier's face went slack and still. He did not inhale again.

Another wave of weakness hit me, making the scene spin in slow circles as I swayed. Andoc helped Senovo to an area nearby where Healer Sagdea and her two apprentices were looking after the wounded. When Senovo was settled, Andoc returned to help Keenan support me.

The gray fog was back. As Andoc took my arm, I looked up and tried to focus on his pale, worried face.

"I'm so sorry," I said very carefully and distinctly, before falling into a dead faint.

Things were strange for a long time after that. I was weak and feverish as my body fought the effects of the contaminated food and water I'd consumed. I vaguely recall various people trying to wake me and make me drink foul-tasting tea and plain broth, most of which came right back up. I was too weak to sit up or even raise my head on my own, and my whole left side hurt terribly at the slightest movement.

I think I woke several times calling Senovo's name, worried that everyone was so focused on me that they were neglecting him. Andoc was there some of the time, too. I worried that Senovo might be hurt too badly to have told him about what happened, because surely if he knew, Andoc would not waste his time sitting by my pallet in the tent where I was being tended, along with some of the other injured.

My most vivid recollection, however, was of waking in the back of a wagon. Panic took me momentarily as my mind was thrust back to the night of our capture, but my wrists and ankles weren't tied. There was no hood smothering me. And, most importantly, the wolf was curled up next to me, relaxed and quiet, watching me from between its front paws with serene yellow-green eyes. My hand was tangled in the ruff of fur at his neck, like a child gripping a beloved blanket or straw dolly.

I stared back at the canine gaze with something like wonder as the wagon rocked gently back and forth. No one else seemed to have noticed my waking, and we were left alone in the warm spring sunshine. I was still feverish and wrung out, too weak to do more than lie there with my fingers buried in the thick pelt. I would have thought it a dream were it not for the hot, slightly rank breath puffing against my face.

There was some reason why I should not be able to have this, I thought, but I could not recall what it was. So I watched those beautiful, deep eyes until my own eyelids became too heavy to hold open, at which point I slid back down into sleep or unconsciousness, feeling more at peace than I had since the abduction.

When I truly came back to myself, I was lying on a bed inside the temple in Draebard.

"Senovo?" I gasped on the tail end of a dream, trying to scramble upright and falling back, still too weak to support my own weight.

"Carivel? Are you awake?"

I blinked dry, sticky eyes, trying to clear my vision. Senovo sat in a chair next to my bed, leaning forward to place a hand on my forehead.

"I think so?" I hazarded in a dry whisper that immediately descended into coughing. Senovo moved to sit on the edge of the bed and lifted my head enough to raise a cup of sweet, cool tea to my lips. I drank greedily, and blushed a bit when my stomach rumbled.

"It appears that your fever has finally broken," Senovo said as he eased me back down onto the pillow. "Do you think you could eat something?"

My belly growled a second time, and I was suddenly overcome by desperate hunger. "I'm starving," I said, and tried to reposition myself on the bed only to gasp in pain as my left side flared. "Ah!" I gasped. "What's wrong with my ribs?"

Senovo's expression went grim and he peeled back the light blanket that covered me. I was naked underneath.

"What—?" I began, only to go silent as I looked down at my body. My entire left side was black and blue, fading to ugly yellow and brown at the edges. "Oh," I said.

"How much do you remember?" Senovo asked as he replaced the blanket over my bruised body.

Frowning, I cast my mind back until—

The last several days filtered into my memory, backward. My eyes flew to Senovo's, and I tried to scrabble upright again until his hand on my uninjured shoulder halted my progress.

"Easy," he said. "We're safe now."

I stared at him, seeing him properly for the first time since I'd awoken. He was pale and tired, hunched a little to one side as if to favor his back, or perhaps his wounded hip.

"What..." I began tremulously, "what are you *doing* here, Senovo?"

Senovo's finely arched brows drew together in confusion. "Andoc and I have been taking it in turns to sit with you. We didn't want you to wake up alone. With any luck, Andoc is sleeping right now."

"But you're injured!" I blurted.

The confused frown deepened. "Not seriously. Certainly not enough to keep me from sitting in a chair."

"I don't understand," I said miserably. Why would Senovo waste his time at my bedside? Did he feel it was somehow his duty as a priest? And what about Andoc? Had Senovo *still* not explained to him about what I had done? What was he waiting for?

"Carivel, I think perhaps you are still disoriented after your fever. You were desperately ill—you've hardly managed any food or drink for days," Senovo said. "Let me go get you something to eat. I'll inform Andoc and Healer Sagdea that you are awake and feeling better."

"Don't wake Andoc," I begged, desperate to put off the inevitable talk for as long as possible.

"If that is what you wish," Senovo allowed, still looking troubled. "I will be back shortly. Try to rest while I'm gone."

His slow, careful gait as he rose and crossed to the door of the small room was like a knife to my heart. *You did that to him,* the voice in my head reminded helpfully, as if it really needed to be said. I looked around the small room. It was familiar. It was Senovo's. Not the High Priest's generous suite, but Senovo's old sleeping cell. I was resting in the bed Senovo — and often Andoc — had slept in for years. The knife twisted deeper.

The room's owner returned a few minutes later with a bowl of weak soup balanced in one hand and the Healer in tow. Unimpressed by my mind's distraction, my body immediately focused on the food with the single-mindedness of survival. My mouth watered, and I found the strength to sit up for the first time, leaning toward the enticing smell.

"Hmm," said the elderly Healer, "yes. You're looking decidedly better, Horse Mistress."

I dragged my attention away from the food by force of will. "How is Senovo? He won't tell me how badly he's hurt." The priest huffed in annoyance as he settled himself on the edge of the bed and helped me cradle the bowl in my lap. The spoon trembled faintly in my right hand, but it still got the soup from the bowl to my mouth, so I was going to count it as a win.

Sagdea raised a silver eyebrow. "You'd do better to worry about yourself, young... woman," she said. "The High Priest is recovering, and his condition was certainly a lot less precarious than yours."

I frowned around a mouthful of fowl. That didn't really tell me anything. "He'll be all right, though?" I prodded.

"Of course I'll be *all right,*" Senovo said with a faint touch of asperity. "You make a mountain of a trifle, Carivel."

"There will be some scarring, no doubt," the Healer said, reaching forward to feel my forehead and examine my eyes as I scraped up the last of the soup. "He may have a few new aches when the weather changes, but don't we all."

I tried to keep my expression neutral, since Senovo obviously did not wish to speak of it. So, he would be scarred for life, then. And every time Andoc saw his back or hip, he would be reminded of my culpability. My stomach gave a little heave of complaint.

"I think that's enough food for now," the Healer said, watching me closely. "Keep drinking the tea—as much as you can until your urine is clear and pale." She shook her head. "I must say, a lot of things make sense now. For years, I thought you were terrified of healers for some reason, the way you avoided me."

"I was terrified of healers," I said absently. "One good fall from a horse and everything would have come crashing down around me as soon as you removed my shirt."

"Hmm. Well, it looks like you've had *one good fall* now, so mind you don't strain those ribs, and give the shoulder another week before you try to use it too much," Sagdea said, her tone tart. "I'm sure I've never heard of such a thing... and yet, now we suddenly have female leaders and female warriors and Horse Mistresses running all over the place. It's too much for this old woman to take in, I'll tell you that."

"I didn't ask to have the spirit of a man trapped inside a woman's body," I said. "It's not like I chose to be this way."

"Well, lass," Sagdea said, "I'm relieved to tell you that your spirit's not my concern—that's what the priests are for. All I know is that your body has had a rough time, and you need to go easy for a while unless you want to end up right back in this bed. Eat small amounts of bland food as often as you can, drink as much as you can manage, and call for me if you start to feel worse again."

"Yes, Healer," I said obediently, feeling exhausted already after only a few minutes of activity.

"*Humph.*" Sagdea frowned at me for a moment, and left us to our own devices.

When the door had closed behind her, Senovo looked down at me intently. "I believe we need to talk," he said, "though I would prefer Andoc to be present as well."

A pit opened in my stomach that had nothing to do with lack of food. I swallowed hard. "Yes, I'm sure you're right," I said, proud of how steady my voice sounded. "Only... I'm feeling really tired and weak right now. Can… can we wait a bit until I'm feeling more myself?"

Coward.

Senovo's expression softened, though he still looked troubled. "Of course—forgive me. Sleep now. You've had a very difficult few days. Someone will be here with you when you wake."

⟿ ⚜ ⟾

Someone turned out to be—of all people—Dalon.

"Hey, boss," he said quietly when I rolled onto my uninjured side and blinked awake.

"Whu—?" I mumbled, pithy as ever.

"And here I thought they were exaggerating when they said the fever nearly took your wits."

I scowled at him.

"Bits. Buckles. Polishing," I managed, quickly checking to make sure that my blanket was covering everything it was supposed to.

Instead of laughing or even smiling at the running joke, though, Dalon's face fell and he looked off to the side, not meeting my eyes.

"Sorry," he said. "I'm sure I'm not who you were expecting. That new priest—what's his name, Feldes? Anyway, he bullied the High Priest into resting, and Andoc is in meetings with the Chief all morning, so they asked if I'd come sit with you for a while." He gestured to the small table next to the bed, still not looking at me directly. "There's, um, some food here. And some tea I'm supposed to get you to drink."

My stomach immediately made its enthusiasm known for this plan, so I sat up against the headboard and reached for the bowl with one hand while holding the blanket up with the other.

"What's wrong, Dalon?" I asked between spoonfuls of bland porridge. "Talk to me."

Dalon reached up, rubbing at his forehead with the fingers of one hand. When he finally met my eyes, his own were red-rimmed and bloodshot. "You need to come back, Carivel. As soon as you can. I… we… lost eight horses during the battle. I had to slit the throats of five of 'em myself, on the battlefield.

And... Favian got hurt. Took an arrow to the shoulder while he was driving a chariot. Then they said you might die of your fever, or the stomach sickness. I can't do this alone. I... we... need you back."

"Oh, gods. Dalon," I said, stricken, the spoon falling from my limp fingers to clatter in the bowl. I set the remains of the porridge aside and leaned forward to cover his hands with mine, where they lay twisted on the edge of the mattress. He looked away again, and I felt a sense of numbness come over me—a strange but welcome form of detachment stemming from my mind's inability to take in any more horror and tragedy right now.

"Look," Dalon said, sliding his hands out from under mine slowly. "I'm really sorry to lay this on you when you're still in your sick bed. I shouldn't have—"

"No," I cut him off. "If you need anything, you *always* come to me. All right? I'm your Horse Mistress, and you're my assistant. My assistant, who has been forced to take on far more than he ever should have had to, since Jorun died." I looked around the room, spying a pile of clothing in the corner. "Now, bring me those clothes and give me and my inconvenient tits a few minutes to get dressed in private. We're going to let Feldes or Eiridan know that I'm leaving. Then we're going to go see Favian, and go to the horse pens together for a bit."

"Yes, boss," Dalon said, relief heavy in his tone.

He handed me my clothes and left the room, closing the door behind him. Dressing was more difficult than I'd expected, but I managed it. Standing was less difficult than I'd expected, though I did have to keep a hand on the wall or a piece of furniture to maintain my balance. Once outside, I used Dalon as a slightly awkward, too-tall crutch, and we headed toward the main part of the temple.

We found Feldes in the refectory, doling out more of the bland porridge from a large, steaming pot.

"Horse Mistress!" he exclaimed. "We did not expect you out of bed so soon."

"I'm feeling much better this morning, Novice Feldes, thank you," I told him. "There are several things which require my attention now that I'm no longer ill. I was hoping you could give the High Priest my thanks for looking after me, and let him know that I will be staying in my own hut for now. There are still many here who need care more than I do, I'm sure."

Feldes nodded eagerly. "I will tell him, certainly. I'm very glad to see you so much improved. For a while, we all feared the worst."

"Oh—one more thing," I said. "I've just learned that one of my apprentices was injured. Do you know where I might find him, and how he's doing?"

"You speak of young Favian?" Feldes asked, and I nodded. "He is just down the hall. Fourth door on the left. My understanding is that he will recover, though he may lose some flexibility in the arm."

I thanked Feldes again and let Dalon lead me out of the refectory. I should have felt more emotion after hearing the news about Favian, probably, but at least now I was *doing* something. My personal life might lie in tatters around me, but I would bloody well be Draebard's Horse Mistress, regardless.

There was no answer when Dalon knocked softly on Favian's door. When we entered, we found him awake but listless, staring at the rafters.

"Favian," I said softly, bracing myself on the bed while Dalon pulled a chair over for me to sit on. Favian's eyes flicked to me, then to Dalon, and back to the ceiling.

"You're still alive, then," he said in a flat voice.

"Seems so." I settled down next to the bed.

"I've decided I'm going to join the priesthood," Favian said without preamble. "I need you to release me from my apprenticeship with you."

It was as well that I was already sitting down. "Favian," I said carefully, "You are one of the most talented young horsemen Draebard has. I know I've disappointed you, but I don't want you to let this injury ruin a promising future. You're young, and you will heal."

"It's not because of my shoulder."

"If it's not your shoulder, then what would possess you to leave the animals you love so much?" I asked, thinking of the close bond that the boy shared with Cassira's white foal.

"Not to mention agreeing to have your balls cut out," Dalon added in faint disgust. "Because—I'm sorry, kid—but that's just sick."

"*Dalon*," I chided.

"'S my choice," Favian muttered.

"Maybe so, but it's a *crazy* choice," Dalon countered—ever the soul of tact.

I sighed in frustration. "Look, Dalon," I said, "could you give us a minute?"

"As long as you talk some sense into the pipsqueak, fine. I think he must've got knocked on the head as well as getting skewered."

Dalon left, shaking his head, and I turned back to the slip of a boy lying bandaged on the bed. "Please, Favian, I need you to help me understand. I know Jorun was like a father to you. He was like a father to me, too. But do you really find it so intolerable to work for a woman that you would give up your passion for the horses to avoid it?"

Favian's face twisted in anger, a flush of red staining his pale cheeks. "You *lied*! I thought you were like me!"

"Like you?" I echoed, completely confused.

"I thought you liked Andoc!"

"I *do* like Andoc," I said, still utterly wrong-footed. "We're handfasted, after all."

"You just don't *get it*!" he snarled. "*You* can get handfasted to Andoc *because you're really a girl*!"

Realization hit me all at once.

"You're angry because I was Jorun's assistant, and people thought I was a man who liked men."

"Like me," Favian said, deflating miserably. "I thought you were like me."

"Oh, Favian."

"But it turns out you're just a normal girl, and except for everyone getting all excited about it because you can ride a horse, nobody *cares*."

It probably wouldn't help to point out that he was the first person to refer to me as *normal* in... well... my entire life, actually. I took a deep breath and let it out slowly.

"Favian," I said, "you were right, though. I was the Horse Master's assistant, and apparently a bunch of people thought I was queer. It would be no different for you."

Favian finally met my eyes. "Not if I ever acted on it. Not if I got caught. People didn't think you were really *doing* anything—just that you *wanted* to. You really think they'd've shrugged it off if someone caught you taking it up the ass?"

Well. That was a bit awkward, actually.

"I don't know what to say to that," I said truthfully. "Though I do know a man—a very successful man—who has had male lovers. People sometimes do, even though it's supposedly forbidden."

"And this happened in Draebard, did it?" Favian asked, sounding skeptical.

"Well... no," I said. Andoc had loved a few men in his so-called misspent youth in Venzor, but he had stopped the practice after moving here, not wanting to risk his apprenticeship with Volya. "Still, it *did* happen, and he never got caught."

"Am I supposed to spend my whole life hiding because I don't fancy girls, then?"

It all made a twisted sort of sense, and my heart ached for the sweet and talented boy in front of me.

"That's why you want to join the priesthood," I said slowly, thinking of Andoc and Senovo—their well-known love for each other, politely ignored for years by those in power, who found it a minor embarrassment at best. "*That's* why you want to become a eunuch. It's not encouraged, but it's tolerated."

"Why else do you think young men agree to get castrated?" Favian spat. "You think people like Dalon are lining up to join the temple?"

It was incredibly embarrassing to realize that I'd never really thought much about it before.

"Very well, Favian," I said quietly. "I want you to speak with High Priest Senovo about this—or Novice Eiridan, in case Senovo isn't well enough. If you still wish it, afterward, I will absolve you of your apprentice's vows, and wish you well. You will be extraordinary at whatever you decide to do in life. I'm only sorry that my secret hurt you so."

"It's not you that hurt me," Favian said in a quiet voice. "Not really. Only, I thought maybe some day, when you were Horse Master, you'd... change things, somehow. I don't know. You gave me hope, for a while. Sort of, anyway."

"And then I took it away," I finished. "I understand."

Favian picked at the corner of his blanket with the hand that wasn't strapped to his chest. "I know you didn't mean to."

"I didn't mean to do a lot of things," I told him, "but that hasn't kept people from getting hurt anyway."

I leaned forward and kissed Favian on the forehead, smoothing some of the too-long blond hair away from his eyes. With only a bit of wobbling, I managed to leave the room under my own power and rejoin Dalon outside.

"Did you talk him out of it?" he asked.

"I told him to speak with the priests about it," I said. "It's his decision, though."

"He's a good kid, really," Dalon said. "It'd suck if we lost him."

"Yeah. It would."

⤛ 🜲 ⤜

The trip to the horse pens was a slow one, and I was more than a little surprised when we were waylaid by a handful of well-wishers along the way. By the time we arrived, it was obvious that I should have let myself recover longer before trying to do so much at once, but it was too late to make a fuss about it.

I let Dalon drape me over the rails of the biggest pen's fence, and within moments Kekenu was trotting over to me. The little gelding shoved his nose in my face and snuffled, while I rubbed his jaw with a shaky hand. A quick once-over showed a long scrape on his flank where the hair had come off, either during his flight through the forest or the battle. Otherwise, he seemed fine.

Nietre was penned nearby with some mares that were coming into heat and ready to be bred. He snorted as I hobbled over on Dalon's arm and walked toward the fence hesitantly, only to shy away before quite coming within reach.

"Stupid horse," Dalon said fondly.

After watching the animals for a few minutes, Dalon deposited me on a comfortable pile of hay in the largest building. Most of the apprentices poked their heads in at some point, either to say a few mumbled words about how well I was looking—*ha*—or just for a quick gawp confirming that I was not, in fact, dead, and they would, in fact, still have to put up with my presence.

I took reports about the aftermath of the battle—which horses we'd lost, and what equipment had been destroyed. Apparently, seventeen warriors had died: ten Mereni and seven Draebardi. I'd known four of them well enough to exchange more than a casual hello. The funerals had already taken place while I lay insensible with fever.

I… still didn't really feel anything.

When I once again thought that I had a handle on what was going on at the pens, and the sun was beginning to sink down behind the buildings, I flagged down Tenibral and asked him to help me back to my hut. Dalon's friend had also been driving a chariot team in the battle, and he sported an ugly graze on one cheek but no other obvious injuries. He was silent for most of the slow walk back to the edge of the village where my tiny hovel sat. As he dropped me off at the door, though, he muttered, "Glad you're back."

"I'm just sorry I've been gone so much," I told him. "You've all done an amazing job under really tough conditions. It would have made Jorun proud, and it means a lot to me, too."

Tenibral blushed a bit in the fading light. "We're just doing our jobs, Horse Mistress," he said, and headed back toward his own home.

I turned to face my own door, bracing myself against the frame and taking a deep breath. I had not failed to notice the candlelight that shone faintly from within, so it was no great shock to find Andoc and Senovo seated inside at my rickety table, three bowls of something hot arrayed in front of them.

"Sit," Andoc said, and the tightly controlled anger in his voice finally succeeded in penetrating the shroud of numbness that had cloaked my mind for most of the day.

EIGHTEEN

Since both of my chairs were occupied, I had little choice but to make my way carefully to the bed and drop down onto the edge. Senovo handed me a cup and said, "Drink."

I looked down at the rapidly cooling herbal tea, my stomach knotting in anticipation of what was to come.

"I'm not really thirsty right now," I said.

"*Drink*," Andoc snapped. I flushed and raised the cup to my lips, aware as soon as the liquid slid across my tongue that I was, in fact, quite thirsty after the afternoon at the pens.

When the cup was empty, I set it down on the floor. "Look, I know pretty much what you're here to say, Andoc. We can get Senovo to cut the thongs whenever you want... I'll leave it up to you whether you want to do it publicly or privately and—"

"Gods *damn* it, Carivel, will you just shut up and *listen!*" Andoc interrupted, bringing a fist down on my table hard enough to make it shake.

My jaw snapped shut, and I looked down. I owed it to them both to take whatever verbal reaming they wanted to dish out.

It was Senovo who spoke first. "I assume that since you've seen fit to spend the day completely ignoring Healer Sagdea's instructions, it means you are now feeling well enough to speak with us," he began. "We are both worried about you. I have seen several things—both during our incarceration at the hill fort and afterward—that concern me."

"What?" I asked, looking up again in confusion. "I don't—"

He continued without letting me finish. "I was unsure exactly how best to address these concerns, and I fear my hesitation has caused me to leave things too long."

"None of this is your fucking fault, Carivel," Andoc said, each word like a hammer blow. "So stop acting like it is."

"Succinct," Senovo said.

I stared at them for a minute.

"Did you both miss the part where I dragged Senovo out into the woods in the middle of the night, right into the hands of the people who wanted to abduct him?" I asked. "Or the part later, where I did exactly what he made me promise not to do, and nearly got both of us killed?"

"Gods, give me patience," Andoc muttered, before continuing in a stronger voice. "And did you know that anyone was after Senovo? No, of course you didn't. Were you trying to stop him from being taken out and beaten again when you finally lost your composure *after two days of torture* and yelled at the guards? Yes, of course you were!"

"I wasn't being tortured," I said blankly, uncomprehending. "He was."

"Carivel," Senovo said, and where Andoc's anger had punched a hole through my defenses, the priest's soft tone wormed its way inside to prod painfully at what lay within. "You were shackled to a stone wall at the mercy of the elements for two days, injured, with almost no food or water, while someone you cared about was periodically taken away for hours at a time to be interrogated. *You were tortured.*"

I opened and closed my mouth a couple of times, silently. When I finally gathered the coherence to speak, it was to ask in a horrifyingly young and quavering voice, "You're… not angry with me, then?"

"Yes, I am fucking angry with you!" Andoc nearly yelled. "Less than a day after waking from a fever that nearly killed you and you're running off without telling anyone where you were going! I haven't even seen you since the fever broke!"

"I told Feldes!" I said defensively.

"You told Feldes that you were leaving, and had, I quote, *things to do*," Senovo pointed out, calm as ever. "Things which, I gather, did not include drinking, eating, and resting as the Healer told you to do."

"I told him I'd be in my hut," I mumbled.

"And here we are, hours later, waiting for you," Andoc grumbled. "Personally, I wanted to go to the pens and carry you back here over my shoulder, but Senovo wouldn't let me."

"I was sure you'd be furious with me for letting Senovo get hurt," I admitted in defeat. "I was trying to put it off as long as possible."

"That's because you're an idiot!" Andoc flared, and leaned forward to run his hands over his face, gingerly. I took a moment to really look at him. He was bruised and battered.

Exhausted. Maybe... frightened. All three of us had been through the wars in these last several days.

"I'm sorry I ran," I said in a quiet voice.

"I doubt any running was involved," Senovo said dryly.

"I'm sorry I hobbled."

Andoc groaned and put his head on his forearm, resting on the table for a moment. "And I'm sorry for yelling," he said. "Mostly, though, I'm sorry for whatever I did that made you think I would immediately throw you over the first time something bad happened."

"Senovo got hurt," I whispered, "and I couldn't stop it."

"You were hurt as well," Senovo said, "and I couldn't stop it."

"It's not the same." I still couldn't look at him.

"Just... please don't hide from us again, Carivel. Agreed?" Andoc asked.

It was terrifyingly difficult not to burst into sobs and fling myself into their arms, bruised ribs and all. Only my long years of practice at keeping my tears hidden from everyone around me allowed me to simply nod and say, "I'll try. I'm sorry, I'm not good at this."

"You merely lack practice," Senovo said, ever patient. "Now, however, you need to eat and drink, lest you end up subject to the Healer's tender mercies once more. Soup?"

We ate in glum, but comfortable silence, and the others acquiesced without too much fuss when I pled sore ribs and a tiny bed, kissing me goodnight and heading back toward the temple at an easy pace in deference to Senovo's injuries.

That, it seemed, should have been that. I threw myself back into my duties as much as my weakened condition would allow—this time, taking care to also eat, drink, and rest frequently in order to avoid Sagdea's—or Andoc's—wrath.

I released Favian from his apprenticeship. In a stroke of inspiration, I spoke to Limdya afterward about becoming an apprentice in his stead, and weathered the short but ugly shit storm that followed when she accepted and it became public knowledge. After officially becoming an acolyte, Favian visited the pens one last time and wept into the white colt's shoulder while the young animal nuzzled curiously at his hip. He accepted my embrace as we carefully avoided each other's injuries, along with the well-wishes of the other apprentices who came along to symbolically see him off.

For several days after the confrontation in my hut, I continued to plead soreness in the evenings. Eventually, though, I found myself back in bed with Andoc and Senovo, who was somewhat further along in his recovery than I was in mine. I watched, touching myself at first, as Andoc tenderly prepared and fucked Senovo, opening the priest with his fingers while simultaneously tracing his lips over each and every one of the slowly fading welts on his back. After the first few minutes, my hand fell away from my aching flesh. A pit seemed to open up in the depths of my chest where my heart should have been, threatening to swallow me whole.

Because there was still something wrong with me. Badly wrong. There had been, ever since the hill fort. I should have been *ecstatic* when Andoc made it clear that neither he nor Senovo blamed me for anything that had happened... but instead, I just felt a sort of dull relief. I should have been *gutted* at the deaths of humans and horses alike during the battle... but instead, I felt only a sense of ambiguous regret.

My sleep was plagued with half-remembered dreams that left me nauseated, my heart pounding a staccato rhythm against my ribcage. It was a relief to rise in the early morning darkness so I could head to the horse pens, and I often stayed there late into the evening doing silly tasks that were either wholly unnecessary, or better done by the apprentices.

Most telling, though, was Nietre.

It was as if, in the stallion's eyes, I was a completely different person from the one who had worked so hard to gain first his respect, and then his trust. He avoided me, darting away whenever I tried to engage with him. The first time I attempted to push the issue, he came disturbingly close to tearing off part of my arm with his teeth. It was a good thing he'd accepted Dalon and a couple of the other boys fairly well, or we might have had a nightmare of a time dealing with him during the busy breeding season.

On several occasions, I caught Senovo watching me with an expression I couldn't quite parse. Andoc mostly seemed worried, like he thought there was something he should be doing, but didn't know what it was. We all just sort of trudged forward together, regardless, our bodies healing even as my spirit retreated into a form of hibernation, or perhaps outright atrophy. The only emotion I could feel was a kind of ongoing, vague dread.

It was the lack of decent sleep that was really killing me, though. I felt *old*, as though I'd gone from a youth to a creaky, wrinkled elder in the space of weeks. I toyed with the idea of asking Senovo for some of the special drink that he'd once used to help his grieving acolytes rest peacefully for a few hours after Rhystel's tragic death. I knew, though, that he would first demand the details of why I wanted it, and I wasn't quite sure what to tell him.

Because every night, I'm still shackled in that larder, seemed stupidly melodramatic, and *because I think I'm going insane* was even worse.

As it happened, the night things finally came to a head was the night when I woke up with my arms wrapped tightly around Senovo's body, one leg thrown carelessly over his scarred hip.

"*Shit!*" I gasped, scrabbling backward with such force that I knocked Andoc off the side of the bed.

This, it turned out, was another highly effective way to rouse him, because he abruptly came awake with a shout, flailing in surprise. Senovo, also rudely startled into wakefulness, jerked bolt upright.

"Carivel!" he gasped. "What is it, what's wrong?"

"I'm sorry," I babbled, only halfway free of the dream, "I'm sorry, I'm sorry, I didn't mean to—"

"*Easy.* What just happened?" Andoc said as he climbed back up on the bed and held my shoulders from behind to steady me. I flinched hard, expecting pain in the left one that did not come.

"What are you sorry for, Carivel?" Senovo asked. "Tell me what you didn't mean to do."

I couldn't see him in the pitch darkness... couldn't tell if Keenan had managed to stop the bleeding...

"I hurt you!" I cried. "I didn't mean to!"

"Carivel, he's *fine*," Andoc said at my back. "Try to calm down..."

"Right," Senovo said. "A moment, both of you. I'm not having this conversation in the dark."

The mattress shifted, and sparks flew as he struck a flint. A moment later, the candle by the bed sputtered into life. He turned back in the flickering light, looking slightly sleep-rumpled, but nothing like the pale, hunched figure in my mind's eye. The dichotomy was jarring. Lifting his hands, he framed my face and forced me to maintain eye contact.

"Now," he said, "Look at me. You didn't hurt me. I'm perfectly well."

"No," I said, trembling now under the hands on my face and shoulders. "You were hurt! I *saw*! They *hurt* you! And I just—"

"We were both hurt, Carivel," he said slowly, "but that was weeks ago, now. We're almost completely healed. Look down. Look at your side." I tilted my head down. The candle illuminated pale skin, with only a couple of small, discolored spots where the worst of the bruising had been. "See? Would you like to check my back?"

I clenched my eyes shut and shook my head in a violent negative. I was back in the present, more or less. I knew he still had a few scars, though, and I could hardly bear to look at them. He stilled my frantic movement, and ran a thumb over my cheekbone, soothing.

"Very well," he said, "but I need you to listen to me now. *Really* listen. After what was done to me by the men who owned me when I was younger, physical pain holds little fear for me. What the Alyrions did was cruel. It was torture. But it was not the worst thing that's ever happened to me. Sadly, it was not even *close* to the worst thing that's ever happened to me. Do you understand?"

I looked into his eyes, desperate for *him* to understand. *It was the worst thing that's ever happened to me*, I tried to say, but when I opened my mouth, what came out was, "I think I'm going mad. Please help me. *Please!*"

"Anything, *caradi*," Andoc said from behind me, his hands squeezing tighter. "*Anything*. Tell us how we can help you, and we will."

My mind flashed back to this very bed, not so terribly long ago. In my memory, I was propped up on an elbow, looking down at Senovo as he lay there, relaxed and content.

"I wish I understood it all a bit better," I said slowly. "Where are you, when you disappear like that?"

He looked up at me with a trusting, unguarded gaze. "Safe," he said.

Recalling myself to the present, I lifted a hand to clasp it over one of Andoc's on my shoulder. "I need to go to the place where Senovo goes sometimes." I met the priest's eyes, begging him to understand. "I just… I just need everything to feel safe again. Even if it's only for a little while."

He stared deeply into my eyes, and then met Andoc's gaze over my shoulder, communicating silently with him. After a moment, Senovo leaned forward to brush a kiss over my forehead.

"Of course. We will do our best to give that to you, if that is what you desire."

"We will always try to provide whatever you need from us, *caradi*," Andoc added.

"Not tonight, though," Senovo said. "Tomorrow, perhaps. Right now, I'm going to go make you a drink that will help you sleep without nightmares. When you are more rested, we can discuss the details of what, exactly, you need from us."

My chest hitched silently and I nodded, my face still framed between Senovo's smooth hands. A sense of relief so profound that it nearly made me dizzy settled over me.

"Thank you," I whispered.

⋟⋔⋞

I slept more soundly for the rest of that night than I had in weeks. I was groggy and fuzzy-mouthed when Andoc shook me awake the following morning, the drug still draped across my mind like a warm blanket. The cool, slightly misty morning air soon cleared my head as I walked out to the horse pens, however, leaving me feeling better and more centered than I had in some time.

The day slid by in a haze of busywork and vague, nervous anticipation. It was punctuated by Andoc's appearance at lunchtime to deliver a meal and a scorching kiss that drew a mocking wolf whistle from Varin, along with jeers of disgust from several of the younger boys. Andoc only grinned and waggled his eyebrows at them before leaning down and whispering, "Temple. Sundown. Eat something before you come," in my ear.

"Back to work, the lot of you!" I called, once he'd gone. "Have you never seen a handfasted couple kissing before?"

I ate half of the food he'd brought, and saved the other half to eat on the walk back to the temple that evening, so I wouldn't need to stop on the way. It seemed likely that Andoc had anticipated this—there was a *lot* of food in the package.

At odd moments, my mind drifted toward speculation about what, exactly, Andoc and Senovo would do to me tonight. Part of me still wanted to be… *punished*, somehow, in hopes that it might take away the guilt that lingered on, despite everything. Part of me was terrified of what I might expose to them, if I broke down completely. What if, instead of traveling to Senovo's peaceful haven, I simply shattered?

That fear was, I think, the clearest and most straightforward emotion I'd felt outside of my nightmares since all this had started.

I decided, toward sundown, that I would simply accept whatever they did to me tonight. If it ended up being horrible, then it would fulfill my desire for punishment. If, instead, it ended up having the same effect on me as it had on Senovo, then I would get a few moments of peace. Either way, I could not continue as I had been doing—that much had been made painfully obvious last night.

By the time I knocked on the temple door a handful of minutes after sunset, I had retreated back into my familiar state of detached numbness. Favian opened the door, and I blinked in faint surprise. It would be years yet until he ascended to the position of novice priest and underwent castration, but in all other ways, the blond-haired, blue-eyed boy had been transformed. His patched and stained clothing had been replaced by clean, dark brown acolyte's robes; his unruly hair was slicked back into a short plait at the base of his skull. Most notably, though, his flat, angry gaze had been replaced by a look of profound serenity.

"You made the right choice," I blurted, in lieu of a greeting.

Favian smiled up at me. "Yes," he said simply. He opened the door wider and waved me in. "Follow me, please, Horse Mistress. The High Priest and First Warrior are waiting for you."

A little wave of vertigo passed over me as I entered— perhaps I was not so numb to what was about to happen tonight as I'd thought. I only nodded, though, and let Favian lead me down the familiar route to the room where we'd spent so much time receiving Senovo's *counseling* since the handfasting ceremony. I wondered what the village gossipmongers had to say about my ongoing conjugal difficulties. Whatever it was, it probably made for entertaining storytelling, if nothing else.

Favian knocked on the door to the room, and a voice inside said, "Come."

Before Favian could open the door, I placed a hand on his shoulder. "I wish things could be different, but if you're happy here, I'm happy for you," I told him when he looked up at me.

Favian's eyes flicked to the entrance of the room containing the two people who meant more to me than anything else in the world. "I'm happy for you, too," he said.

I wondered if he only meant Andoc, or if he had somehow understood what was between the two of us and Senovo. It didn't matter, really. If Senovo had felt it important to give a young boy hope that he might find lasting love even as a eunuch priest, I certainly would not begrudge him.

Favian opened the door so I could enter. Inside, Andoc was seated on the bed, leaning back on his hands with his legs stretched out in front of him, crossed at the ankles. Senovo leaned casually against the far wall.

"Thank you, Favian," the High Priest said, his tone warm, and the adoration in Favian's eyes as he looked at Senovo was impossible to miss.

"Good evening, High Priest. First Warrior. Horse Mistress." Favian bowed and took his leave, closing the door behind him.

"You've gained another devotee, *amadi*," Andoc observed.

"There is something liberating about being in a place where others can see you as you truly are, without censure." Senovo's eyes met mine.

"Yes," I agreed. "There is."

"How are you tonight, *caradi*?" Andoc asked, still leaning back on the bed.

"Strange," I answered, watching myself as if from outside my own body. "I can't feel things properly. I haven't been able to for a while now. It scares me."

"Do you still wish to explore the kind of surrender that you have seen me experience?" Senovo asked. "You can change your mind at any time, Carivel, or decide to wait until you've had a few more nights of proper sleep before we discuss it."

"No!" I was strangely panicked by the idea of putting it off.

"That suggestion upsets you," Senovo observed.

I stood there, still hovering just inside the door, and tried to form words. Nothing came out.

Andoc rose and crossed to take my elbow, leading me over to sit in the place he'd just vacated, still warm from his body heat. He dropped down to sit on the floor nearby, one arm propped on the bed as he looked up at me.

I swallowed. "I can't... I can't keep going the way I have been, and I don't know what else to do besides this," I said. "The drug last night helped, but I can't drug myself to sleep forever."

"True enough," Senovo said. "The drug loses its effectiveness before long, for one thing."

"You told us last night that you wanted to feel safe," Andoc said.

"Based on something I said once, during a morning of particularly languid afterglow, I believe," Senovo explained, saving me from having to try. "It was the morning after the handfasting, as I recall. Carivel asked me where I'd been, during the time I seemed to be... absent."

Andoc's eyes flickered away from me to land on Senovo instead. "And you said that you had been... safe?" he asked, in a tone I couldn't readily identify.

"I told her the truth," Senovo replied, and the look in Andoc's eyes spread a small thread of warmth through the cold emptiness that had been my constant companion for so long now.

"You've never described it that way to me before."

Senovo shrugged a shoulder, an attractive look of shyness crossing his features. "I would have if you'd asked," he said.

Andoc turned his attention back to me, the soft expression lingering. "And that's what you want from this, *caradi*?"

I nodded. "I need it, Andoc. I *really* need it. Every time I let my guard down, I'm back at the hill fort, or tied up in a wagon with a bag over my head. They're hurting Senovo, and I can't stop it. So... I never let my guard down, except in dreams. I don't dare."

"That's no way to live," Senovo agreed. "Now, though, we need to talk about *how*."

I steeled myself. "Just… do whatever you want to me. I won't try to stop you."

Andoc raised an eyebrow. "Yeah… *no*. That's not how this is going to work," he said flatly.

"Isn't that what it means to submit?" I asked, confused. "That's what I'm trying to do, isn't it?"

"Would you have Andoc take you like a woman, then?" Senovo asked in a gentle tone. "Put his seed in your womb?"

I tensed.

"No, I didn't think so," said the priest. "Let's try it this way instead. Has there been anything that we have done to you in the past that you did not enjoy, other than what we already know regarding your female passage?"

"No," I said. "I've loved all of it."

"I'm pleased to hear it," Senovo said. "Now, has Andoc ever done anything to me that you did not enjoy watching, or think that you would not like to experience?"

I thought back over the weeks since our trip to Meren. "It upset me when Andoc tied you up tightly and you fought against the ropes until you were exhausted."

"You should have said," Andoc told me.

"Senovo needed it," I said.

"I did," Senovo confirmed, "but we will all agree that nothing like that will happen tonight."

"What about being tied in general?" Andoc asked. "After being chained in manacles, I mean. Would you be all right with it?"

I thought of the times I'd seen Senovo resting soft and trusting in Andoc's bonds. "If it's you," I said.

"And a blindfold?" he asked. "After the hood they put on you?"

A blindfold could hide part of my expression from them. Could soak up errant tears. "If it's you," I repeated.

"Your wrists are completely healed from the shackles?" Senovo asked. "There's no pain or soreness?"

"None," I assured him. "They're fine." They hadn't even scarred.

"Very well," Senovo said with a note of finality. "I have an idea of what it is you need tonight, to find the peace you seek.

Within the bounds of what we've just discussed, do you trust us to try and provide what you require?"

I realized that they must have been talking about me before I arrived. I prodded at the idea, testing it out, but it still didn't provoke any particular feelings inside me.

"Yes," I told Senovo. "Can we start now, please?"

"Of course, *caradi*," Andoc said. "Take off your clothes for us and lie back on the bed.

A little shiver of… something… passed through me, and I stood up so that I could remove my clothing, a piece at a time.

"You, too, Senovo," Andoc added. "As we discussed, I think."

"Indeed," Senovo said, and unfastened the closures on his white robes, letting them drop to the floor.

I was naked by the time he reached me. I accepted the brief, almost chaste kiss that he bestowed on my lips, and allowed him to guide me back, until I was sprawled against a pile of pillows resting against the headboard. Andoc, still dressed, handed him coils of soft rope, similar to the type we used to make halters for the youngest foals. Senovo took first my right hand, and then my left, guiding them up to the top rail of the headboard, where he bound them to the sturdy wood with a complex tie that reminded me of the handfasting weave in both its beauty and its sturdiness. When he was finished, I twisted my wrist and tugged against the binding. There was no give.

I wriggled, getting used to the position. My heart started to beat a little faster, waking up from its long nap.

Senovo moved next to my legs, bending them double at the knee and running a web of binding from my ankle to my thigh, weaving up the length of each calf until both legs were encased, held in place like a frog's legs as it readied for a jump. I was powerless to straighten them, left spread open and exposed. The faint pulse of excitement trickled lower, from my heart into my belly. My breath came faster as I looked up at the gentle priest and the fierce warrior who now had me under their complete control.

"There is one more thing," Senovo said, reaching across me to pick something up from the bedside table. He held it up so I could see—it was a molded bronze cylinder of the type that artists used to imprint a repeating pattern on clay. Heavy, but easily held in one hand.

"What's that for?" I asked.

Senovo placed the cylinder in my right hand and closed my fist around it. I gripped it and looked at him questioningly.

"If at any time you need to stop, for *any* reason, no matter how large or small, you are to drop this object. Just open your hand, and let it fall out."

I craned my neck around to look at the unprepossessing metal cylinder. With my wrist bound to the headboard, as soon as I let the thing go, it would clatter loudly onto the flagstones behind the bed. I nodded my understanding.

"Just to be clear," Senovo said, "dropping the cylinder is the *only* thing that will cause us to stop. You may beg us, scream, curse our names, bargain anything you can conceive of for an instant of respite… and we will ignore your pleas."

I stared at Senovo, my jaw going slack.

"Oh, I *want* her begging. I'll have her begging before the candles have burned down halfway." Andoc put in, drawing my open-mouthed attention away from the wolf in priest's clothing who had just tied me to the bed and then metaphorically yanked the mattress out from under me. Andoc looked back at me intently. "I'm more interested in what's going to happen after the begging stops."

"Carivel," Senovo said, his serious tone drawing my eyes back to his, "tell me what you are to do if you need to stop."

I closed my mouth and swallowed a couple of times so I could get words out. My heart was thudding against my chest now in earnest, as if trying to escape the cage of my ribs. "I let the cylinder fall."

"Correct," Andoc said. "Senovo, why don't you start getting her ready, while I get you ready."

"Gladly," Senovo said, and reached for a length of clean, soft woven cloth.

The blindfold closed over my eyes, cutting off my vision except for the vague, flickering glow of the candles scattered throughout the room. Senovo lifted my head and tied it snugly in place before settling me back.

The mattress shifted, and I heard a clink that I tentatively identified as a jar of oil being picked up. I gasped in surprise when warm liquid dribbled into the hollow at the base of my throat a moment later, trickling down between my breasts in a thin stream, over my ribcage and stomach to pool in my navel, before finally soaking the patch of fur between my forcibly spread legs.

"What are you doing?" I asked in a breathy voice.

Senovo shifted, perhaps handing the jar to Andoc. "Getting you ready," he said, and dragged a flat palm through the mess, spreading it across my skin and awakening every nerve as he went.

"Oh, yes," Andoc said, from where he was seated behind Senovo. "Didn't we mention? Senovo's going to fuck you in a minute. We just need to get him hard first, and bind the base of his cock so he can keep going for a nice, long time."

Senovo shuddered at the same time I did, hissing out a heavy breath. I imagined Andoc's fingers breaching him—seeking the place inside him that would make his limp, eunuch's cock fill and lengthen. Meanwhile, Senovo's hand continued to slide over my oiled flesh, palming first one nipple and then the other until both were pebbled and aching. I gripped the metal cylinder with white knuckles, tension coiling between my bound legs, my cunt already yearning for release even though no one had touched me there yet.

I could follow Andoc's progress in the way Senovo groaned in pleasure as his own hand dipped teasingly lower along my belly, never quite reaching the place where I so desperately wanted it.

"Is this working for you, *amadi?*" Andoc asked in an innocent voice.

"Mmm," Senovo hummed, his sonorous voice lower than usual. "'S good. I think I might need a *little* something more tonight, though."

Two oil-covered fingers trailed up my neck and over my chin to tease at my lips. I moaned as Senovo's meaning became clear, and he pressed into my mouth, plunging deep. My sex pulsed, still untouched but growing heavy and swollen with desire.

"What a good idea," Andoc said. "Since she can't have you where she really wants you yet, I'm sure she'd be happy to show you how well she can swallow you down in the mean time."

I nodded frantically around the fingers in my mouth.

"So it appears," Senovo said, sounding faintly breathless. The fingers pressed down on my tongue and stroked their way out. A moment later, he swung a leg over me — like mounting a horse — and straddled my torso. I smelled his clean, faintly musky smell an instant before tender, soft skin brushed at my lips. I opened for him immediately, sucking him in. He was half hard, his small cock twitching and filling further as I tongued it.

I knew from previous experience that I could take him all the way, but there was admittedly something new and exciting about the realization that, tied as I was, if he desired it, I *would* take him all the way, ready or not. I squirmed against the bindings, thinking about it. Maybe he could tell, because he pulled out a bit and pressed in deeper, growing fully hard as I sucked and laved. With the next stroke, he pressed in all the way, tickling the back of my throat. Tears prickled at my eyes behind the blindfold and saliva flooded my mouth. I swallowed convulsively, drawing a shudder from him.

He pulled back to let me breathe and set up a slow rhythm. I concentrated on relaxing, letting him all the way in and swirling my tongue over the vein on the underside every time he slid out. I felt Andoc settle down next to me to watch, and I hummed around Senovo in pleasure.

"So good for us, *caradi*," Andoc said, and a hand smoothed over my temple, steadying me so Senovo could press a fraction deeper. "Before long you'll be taking me down to the root, just like this."

I shivered, picturing it.

"I'm ready," Senovo interrupted in a slightly strained voice, pulling back until only the head of his cock rested on my tongue.

"Suck him hard for me, *caradi*," Andoc ordered. "I'm going to bind his cock for you now, so he'll stay nice and stiff inside you."

I moaned and sucked, tonguing at the slit as Senovo's thighs trembled around me, slippery with oil. I smelled leather, and the end of a thong briefly tickled my lips and chin. Senovo grunted, and for the first time I regretted the blindfold. I had never seen Andoc tie Senovo's cock, and had no idea if it was something they had done in the past.

"There we go," Andoc said. "All right?"

I gave a final suck and Senovo jerked, slipping out of my mouth. I missed him immediately.

"Sensitive," he said tightly.

"Hmm," Andoc said. "Just think what it'll feel like, buried inside Carivel's tight ass.

"Believe me, I am."

So was I, and my moan probably conveyed that fact quite clearly. Senovo dismounted, and a strong hand—Andoc's, I thought—lifted my hips long enough to stuff more cushions beneath them, raising my arse and exposing me even further as my knees curled up against my chest. The same hand brushed across my puckered opening, setting off sparks behind the blindfold.

"Thought you were supposed to be getting her ready, *amadi*," Andoc said, sounding amused.

"I might have become somewhat distracted," Senovo answered, his voice still tightly controlled.

Oil poured over me, and the sensation as it dribbled across my inner lips was nearly enough to make me come on the spot, I was so tightly wound. A blunt finger screwed its way inside my tight opening without mercy, and red washed across my filtered vision at the delicious burn of it.

"Please," I gasped.

"Yes?" Andoc replied in a tone of casual interest. The finger swirled, sliding and stretching. It pulled out, and returned with a second one.

"*Ah!* Please, Andoc, I'm so close… I need to come!"

"Well, you should have said something sooner, *caradi*. I am more than happy to make you come." The heel of Andoc's other hand dragged over my sensitive bud and I cried out, convulsing around his fingers as my release tore through me. "I intend to make you come until you will offer me anything in your power, if I'll only stop."

He rocked the heel of his hand again, forcing a shuddering aftershock as he spread and twisted the fingers inside me. For the first time, I started to understand what I had gotten myself into.

"Your turn, Senovo," Andoc said. "I have to say, I'm quite looking forward to watching this."

Andoc's fingers slipped free, and the bed shifted. Smooth hands grasped my bound ankles, using my legs as leverage to tilt my pelvis further forward.

"To say that I'm out of practice with this is a considerable understatement," Senovo said hoarsely.

"Oh gods," I moaned as the head of his stiff, bound cock pressed against me.

"I'm sure it will come back to you. It's just like riding a horse, I imagine," Andoc observed. "Push out against him, *caradi.*"

I bore down, biting my lip against the mental picture I had of Senovo looming over me, ready to fuck me. Both of us gasped in surprise when he slipped past my ring of muscle and sank inside. I fluttered around the intrusion, much smaller than Andoc's unforgiving girth, but every bit as sweet.

"Take me," I moaned. "Senovo, *please*! I *need* you..."

Senovo pressed in slowly, and leaned down to brace one hand against the mattress as if steadying himself. "S-sorry," he said. "A moment, Carivel. It's been a very long time... I didn't know if I would ever get to have this again."

"You only ever had to ask, love." Andoc's voice was quiet.

"It was not what we... needed from each other..." Senovo said between pauses for breath.

"Perhaps not," Andoc said. "It's what Carivel needs from you now, though."

Senovo's hips stuttered, drawing a wavering moan from me. I wondered if Andoc was touching him, slipping fingers back inside to stroke at his sweet spot as he fucked into me. Senovo bent down, lowering himself into the cradle between my bound legs, his smooth, hairless chest sliding against my oiled breasts as he stretched forward so that he could kiss me deeply. His hips flexed, and I strained against my bonds, trying to meet him.

There was no friction anywhere except at the place where he pierced me. Our tongues slid together in a languid dance; our oiled bodies slid wetly against each other, pebbled nipples occasionally dragging as he moved and making us both shudder.

Already, my second release was trying to rise up and break free. The angle was not *quite* right... Senovo's pelvis brushed mine with every slow thrust, but didn't provide the pressure I needed. I groaned into the kiss, wriggling underneath him as I tried to get *more... harder... faster.*

Senovo nipped my bottom lip and pulled back, tugging it with him until it popped free, as sensitive and swollen as my sex. I whimpered as he interrupted the sensuous slide of our slick bodies, rearing up to put space between us as he continued the slow, measured roll of his hips. Without warning, callused fingers wormed their way between us to slide up and down the tiny column of sensitive flesh that Andoc called my *little cock*.

I stiffened and threw my head back as the perfect, wonderful combination of fingers and prick dragged me *up... up... up* the slope and pushed me over the edge to fall *down, down* into ecstasy. Senovo grunted in surprise and stilled as I clenched hard around him, milking him mindlessly in the throes of my second release.

Before I had even finished, he started moving again in the same slow rhythm as before. Andoc's fingers stroked me with a butterfly touch that was still far too much, and I cried out. I couldn't wriggle away, though — Andoc and Senovo easily held me in place by my tightly bound legs.

The sudden reminder that *I couldn't stop them* sent a new jolt of excitement through me, shifting everything back from *too much* to *just right* in the space of an instant. Twice more, they pushed me slowly to my limits and past them, leaving my body singing and wracked with tremors, unraveling beneath them.

"Andoc," Senovo gasped, after the third time I clamped down helplessly around his cock. "Unbind me — I need to come."

"I'd let you stew a little longer first, my friend," Andoc said, "only I can see the way she's been milking that poor prick of yours."

Senovo pulled out, and I choked on a plea, not sure if I was begging them to stop or keep going. A moment later, the decision was taken out of my hands when Senovo pushed back in, meeting no resistance from my loose, relaxed opening. He snapped his hips forward over and over, perhaps, I thought with a shiver, driven by Andoc pressing insistent fingers into his own arse.

Before long, his hips lost rhythm and he groaned, pulsing into me with the little spurt of hot, clear fluid that was all his eunuch's body could produce. I relaxed with a sigh, going limp in the ropes as he carefully pulled out.

"Good, *amadi*?" Andoc asked, as Senovo crawled up to flop down next to me on the bed and trail a hand over my throat and breasts.

"I'd forgotten," he said, sounding thoroughly shattered.

"It looked gorgeous," Andoc said, shifting around to kneel between my bent legs and manhandle my lower body into his lap. "Good enough that I'm thoroughly looking forward to this."

I could feel the buckskin of his breeches against my naked flesh. Gods—he was still almost completely dressed. He must have just unlaced his breeches and smallclothes enough to let his prick out, while Senovo and I rutted naked on the bed. I felt him line himself up, the blunt head of his large, thick cock pressing intimately into the space that Senovo had opened for him.

"No, wait!" I gasped as he thrust in, stretching me wide. "I can't—"

"Can't you?" he asked, pressing in steadily until I thought I would split in half. "Feels to me like you can."

My cunt pulsed in reaction to the words. Beside me, Senovo gently drew his fingers up my right arm, stroking over my fist and the heavy bronze cylinder clenched within, warm now from my body heat. My head spun. I gripped the metal tighter.

"That's it," Andoc soothed, the wrinkled skin of his sac nestling against my buttocks as he bottomed out.

Beads of sweat broke out on my forehead, soaking into the cloth of the blindfold. *"Please..."* I moaned, not even knowing what I was asking for.

What I got was Senovo's fingernail dragging over an oiled nipple at the same time Andoc plucked my little cock between the pads of two slick fingers, working it from base to tip as if it really was an erect prick. Each slow pull was the most delicious torture, lighting every nerve even as his solid length filled me from behind—unmoving except for the occasional twitch and pulse.

I screamed when I came, and thrashed when the fingers continued to torment my cock and nipples without pausing even for a moment.

"Please, no..." I moaned, my voice growing hoarse. "I can't any more, I *can't*, don't make me!"

"You keep using that word," Andoc said, rolling his hips and making me feel his cock. "And yet, you keep coming for us."

I keened, feeling like the room was spinning around me. Andoc fucked into me, still working my tiny cock without mercy while Senovo pinched and twisted my nipples. My next climax was silent, my eyes rolling back beneath the muffling cloth of the blindfold as I jerked and shook.

I surfaced some time later as if from drowning. "Please, no more," I gasped, "No more! I can't—I'll do anything!"

Andoc's fingers slowed their movements against my oversensitive flesh, but did not stop. "Anything, you say? And what do you think you could offer me that I'd prefer to this? Making you lose yourself over and over, gripping my cock like a fist while you beg me for mercy?"

He thrust into me sharply, driving another cry from my raw throat. I cast around for something. Anything. "I'll... I'll suck you off. I'll take you all the way down... choke myself on your cock until you come down my throat."

"Hmm..." The fingers paused, as if Andoc was considering. I let out a sort of choked sob, and the maddening, unendurable stimulation started up again. "No, actually, I think I prefer this. In fact... Senovo? If you wouldn't mind?"

Senovo's fingers once again brushed my fist, drawing my fractured attention back to the cylinder in my hand.

"No, please, I'll... I'll..." I cast around for something else to offer them. Before I could come up with anything, one warm, soft hand settled over my throat, holding but not squeezing. A second settled firmly over my mouth, muffling my words, smelling of scented oil.

"Mmph! Mmph... *mmph!*" I tried to force words out. My breath whistled through my nose in the small gap above Senovo's hand.

"Shh," he said. "You're close now, Carivel. Let it happen. We've got you—just let yourself fall."

The realization that I had *no control* over the situation hit me like a runaway wagon. I could *stop* it, true—I only had to drop the cylinder—but I couldn't *control* it. My chest hitched in a sob, even as Andoc inched me closer to yet another climax with his fingers and cock. I stared with wide eyes at the back of the blindfold, sightless, physically trapped, and now, without even a voice. Completely at the mercy of these two men.

These men, who wanted nothing more than to bring me pleasure until I was drunk with it, and keep me safe, even if it cost their own lives to do so.

Suddenly, I understood.

I didn't have to worry about anything right now.

I didn't have to make choices.

I didn't have to do *a single thing* except lie here and let Andoc make me come, over and over.

My exhausted muscles trembled, and began to loosen one by one.

"That's better, beloved," Senovo soothed, and his lips pressed against my forehead above the blindfold.

"It's all right now, *caradi*," Andoc said, sounding almost relieved as I went limp and heavy under their hands. "We have you. We won't let you go."

His fingers still teased at my oversensitive flesh. His hips still rolled against mine in a slow grind. And that was all right. That was *fine*. If this was what they wanted me to feel right now, then feel it I would. In the absence of physical tension and nervous worry, it was only pleasure. I floated along on the feelings, growing looser and more relaxed as waves of sensation crested and ebbed, over and over.

Some indeterminate amount of time later, Andoc groaned low and pulsed into me with hot spurts. I quivered with a final euphoric release of my own, and the warm metal in my hand slipped out of my slackening grasp to clatter on the floor below.

"Stay where you are for a minute, old friend," Senovo said softly. "Let me get her untied first."

I frowned when Senovo slid his hands away from my face and neck, rooting toward him as best I could with my wrists still bound to the headboard.

"Shh," he said, and dropped a chaste kiss on my lips. "I'm right here. I'm not going anywhere."

He freed my hands, pausing to rub at them and raise each one to press against his lips. My legs were next—a bit stiff where the joints had been bent double for so long. Andoc's softening cock slid out of me as Senovo helped me lower them to the bed, and I whimpered a protest.

"Greedy," Andoc teased in a fond tone, sliding three fingers in to fill up the emptiness. I shivered happily as he stroked around the rim, gathering up the oil and seed I could feel dripping out and pushing it back inside, where it belonged.

I was half-dozing by the time he finally slid his fingers free. Senovo had pulled me into his arms and was stroking my short hair, the blindfold still holding the outside world at bay. Andoc left the bed and returned a moment later to clean me up. Then there was the rustle of clothing being removed, and the bed dipped as he got in.

I lay cradled between them for a long time, all the sharp edges of my mind smoothed down like pebbles in a river, until there was nothing to poke or rub against. It was utterly blissful… the most peaceful I've felt since childhood.

Safe.

There was no one particular thing that made me start to come back… just a sort of vague curiosity about what was happening in the world beyond my blindfold, and the hands stroking gently over my skin.

I stretched, and made a quiet humming noise as my muscles tingled pleasantly.

"I think our traveler is returning," Andoc rumbled against my back. "Let me take off your blindfold, all right, *caradi*? Most of the candles have gone out, but you might want to close your eyes at first."

I made a noise of agreement, and blinked my eyes open cautiously a few moments later in the dim light. Around me, all the little details of the room came back into focus as I rolled onto my back. On my other side, Senovo propped himself up on an elbow so both he and Andoc were looking down at me.

"Back with us, then?" he asked, cupping my cheek and tracing his thumb over the sensitive skin under my eye.

I looked up at the two men who had taken care of me in ways I didn't even know I needed. They were beautiful. Strong. Equally devoted to each other, and to me. I opened my mouth to say *yes, I think so,* and a hiccupping sob emerged instead. My eyes welled up and overflowed as I burst into helpless tears.

Senovo said nothing, but immediately sat up and pulled me into his arms, tucking my head into the crook of his shoulder.

"Oh, *caradi*…" Andoc said, and draped himself over my back, his strong arms coming around both of us. "There you are, finally. Let it out, beloved. You're safe here."

I wept ugly tears into Senovo's neck—utterly powerless to stop them. I had not cried openly in the presence of another person since my mother screamed at me and slapped me for weeping during my father's funeral. I was six years old at the time.

Now, I sobbed out my fear and anger over what the Alyrions had done to our village... to Senovo... to me. I cried tears of guilt and frustration over my inability to protect someone who meant everything for me, and over the immediate and inexplicable forgiveness for my failings that I'd received from these two.

Warm, solid bodies cradled me in front and behind, holding me up when I sagged and demanding nothing more than that I trust them with this part of myself. Eventually, the sobbing subsided, leaving my chest feeling empty and light. The warm skin under my cheek was wet and sticky with salt water and snot. I burrowed further into it anyway.

"What will we do when the Empire comes?" I asked them both, once I could breathe past the tears.

Andoc's arms tightened around us. "We'll fight," he said.

"Survive," Senovo added.

"Together," said Andoc, in a tone of finality.

end of Book 2

THE HORSE MISTRESS:
BOOK 3

ONE

The door to Favian's small sleeping cell in the temple was open when I approached. Flickering candlelight came from within, pushing back the deepening gloom of evening. I paused in the entryway to take in the scene inside. Renthro, Favian's father, sat in the room's single chair with his back to me as he blotted the boy's sweaty forehead with a damp rag.

Favian had been one of many injured during the battle at the hill fort. He'd been driving a chariot team for one of the warriors when an Alyrion arrow struck his left shoulder and lodged there. That was weeks ago, though, and the wound had appeared to be healing well. I knocked on the doorframe, not wanting to startle either the boy or his father. Renthro turned at the noise.

"Hi," I said, hovering in the doorway. "Lundis told me Favian was ill—I just wanted to stop by and see how he was doing."

Renthro looked flustered for a moment, eying me with the slightly uncertain look that people generally gave me when they weren't openly hostile, but didn't really know how to deal with me either.

He cleared his throat, shaking himself free of his momentary reverie. "Oh. Yes, of course. That's kind of you… Horse Mistress Carivel. Please, come in."

"Just plain *Carivel* is fine, Renthro," I told him. "No need to stand on ceremony. How is he? His shoulder seemed to be doing so much better."

His father frowned and turned back to dab at Favian's forehead again. "Healer Sagdea doesn't think that it's wound sickness, thank the gods. She says that the energy necessary to heal his shoulder drained his spirit and left it vulnerable to a simple fever and cough. She's fairly confident he'll recover in a couple of days."

I let out a quiet breath of relief. "Well, that's good news," I said.

"It is. It's just hard seeing him like this again, so soon after being shot. I know a father can't always protect his children, but that doesn't stop me wanting to, you know? Especially after losing his mother when he was still so young."

I nodded sympathetically. Though I didn't have a parental bone in my body, I could easily understand the depth of Renthro's worry for his son's safety. His wife had died during the birth of Favian's little sister, Frella, leaving Renthro alone with two young children and no other family in the area to help him.

"At least Favian is safe in the priesthood, now," I said. "No more chariots or battles in his future."

The tension did not leave Renthro's shoulders. "That may have been true at one time, but the temple wasn't exactly a safe place to be when the Alyrions attacked Draebard."

I cringed at my gaffe. "Forgive me. Of course it wasn't. That was a stupid thing for me to say. Even after everything, I find it far too easy to slide into the desire for things to be as simple as they once were, before all of this upheaval began."

Renthro glanced up and smiled at me, though it was strained. "I think we all find it so." He ran the backs of his fingers over Favian's forehead, and the boy sighed, settling deeper into the pillow. "He has always been a sensitive child, but I know I shouldn't worry so. It lies in the gods' hands—what will be, will be."

"Favian has a rare talent for dealing with animals. I am confident that talent will extend to dealing with people as well. I think he will excel in the priesthood, or whatever he puts his mind to, Renthro."

Renthro continued to stroke his son's feverish skin, but his worried expression smoothed out. "You are right, Carivel. I know you are. He already looks up to the High Priest, I can tell." He shook his head in mild wonderment. "I remember when Senovo first came to Draebard, years ago now. Whoever would have thought that such a quiet boy would end up with so much power? We're lucky to have him. Especially after... well. After what happened."

The look of fondness that slid over my face was completely involuntary. "I couldn't agree more," I said, when a sudden thought hit me. "Who's watching Frella for you tonight?"

"I left her with the neighbors," replied Renthro. "I didn't want to risk bringing her here and ending up with a sick toddler as well as a sick son."

I nodded. "I can't blame you for that, certainly. Look, if you need to get home to her, I'll be happy to stay with Favian this evening."

He looked up at me, surprised. "You don't mind? You don't have other things to do?"

"Of course I don't mind," I told him, "and I'm done for the day unless there's some sort of emergency at the horse pens overnight. If that happens, I'll get one of the acolytes to come sit with him. He has brothers here now, Renthro. He's not alone."

Renthro's eyes grew shiny. "Thank you, Carivel. Sometimes it's hard to let go. Especially knowing that I left him so often to his own devices as a young boy, when time and money were short and his sister required most of my attention. But you're correct, of course. He has other people to help look after him now."

I held out my hand for the damp cloth Renthro was still holding, and stood out of the way while he leaned over to kiss Favian's forehead before gathering his things and giving me a final, grateful look.

"Thank you. Tell him I'll come back in the morning," he said.

"I will," I promised, and took over the vacated seat.

Once the sound of Renthro's boots had faded, I sat in silence except for the faintly congested breathing of the boy in the bed. Beads of clammy sweat dotted Favian's face and chest, so I resumed swabbing at his exposed skin every few minutes with the cool rag, feeling a strange peace descend over the room as dusk deepened into full darkness beyond the small, high window.

Before too much time had passed, new footsteps entered the room. A familiar and welcome presence warmed the skin at the back of my neck.

"I expected to find Renthro here, not you," Senovo said softly, so as not to disturb his sleeping acolyte. The scent of sandalwood and musk surrounded me as a smooth hand rested on my shoulder. I breathed out, feeling more of the day's tension drain away.

"I sent him home to Frella," I replied, and Senovo made a noise of understanding.

He leaned past me to rest his other hand briefly on Favian's forehead. "It feels like the fever is starting to go down," he observed. "Good."

"Can you stay a while?" I asked.

"Yes, of course. I've nothing pressing at the moment. Let me go get another chair." Senovo slipped from the room silently. He returned a minute later to maneuver the second seat into the narrow space beside mine, and closed the door so we could have a semblance of privacy.

Once he was settled, I let my shoulder press against his as we sat side by side. "How was your day?" I asked. "It feels like I've barely seen you since the festival two nights ago."

"A High Priest's work is never done, it seems. Nor, I suspect, a Horse Mistress's," he teased. "I must admit, I am beginning to understand why Rhystel was such an inveterate meddler. It's a distinct temptation in a job where people constantly come to you with their problems, the solutions to which seem obvious to you but completely impenetrable to them."

"So, in other words, Charyal and her intended are fighting again and they want you to fix it?"

"The code of the priesthood prevents me from commenting on private matters of the townsfolk, obviously," Senovo said, though his dry tone told its own story.

"Don't you ever wish you could just turn into the wolf and snarl at them until they both stop being stupid?" I asked.

"You shouldn't even joke about such things, Carivel."

Still, he sounded far less appalled than he would have mere weeks ago, and his upper arm continued to press companionably against mine. I nudged him with my shoulder. "Come on. You can't tell me it's never even crossed your mind. Jeppel is a self-centered prat, and Charyal deserves better."

Whatever Senovo would have said in response was cut off by a low moan from the bed. We both frowned, our attention turning immediately back to Favian. The boy's head thrashed back and forth restlessly against the pillow.

"Is it the fever?" I asked, my breath catching in my throat.

Senovo reached out to feel the boy's face again before shaking his head. "No, he still feels cooler. I think he's just dreaming."

Indeed, Favian's eyes were flickering back and forth rapidly beneath their lids. His limbs jerked with small, abortive movements that hitched the blanket lower around his chest, and he cried out in a strange, strangled voice. I sat frozen in place, unsure what to do—the lack of any siblings and my relatively solitary existence up until the last couple of months leaving me ill-prepared to deal with a sick child's nightmares.

Fortunately, Senovo had no such limitations. He leaned forward, clasping a gentle hand around Favian's uninjured shoulder. "Come now, Little Brother. Easy, it's only a fever dream."

Favian tried to twist away from the contact, but did not awaken. Senovo frowned as the boy's congested breathing grew fast and labored. "Favian. Wake up, now. Come back to us."

But Favian only flailed and cried out again. Senovo gave his shoulder a single, firm shake. "*Favian.*"

Finally, Favian woke, jerking upright in the bed, his blue eyes open wide and unseeing. He was breathing hard, as if he'd just run a footrace, and immediately fell into a bout of wet coughing. Senovo moved from his chair to sit on the edge of the bed, where he could support the boy with a hand splayed between his shoulder blades.

"Get him something to drink, please," he ordered quietly, breaking me free from my paralysis.

I looked around the small room, quickly locating the flagon of medicinal tea sitting on the table, next to a wooden cup. I poured him some, noting the smell of honey and spices mixed into the concoction. Rather than crowd in next to Senovo, I sat on the other side of the bed, waiting for Favian to get his coughing under control.

"Here," I said, and steadied the boy's shaking hand as he lifted the cup to his lips.

When he was done, I set the cup aside. "All right now?" I asked.

Favian seemed to crumple in upon himself, Senovo's hand on his back the only thing keeping him from collapsing.

"It was terrible," he whispered, not looking at either of us.

Senovo stuffed a couple of pillows against the headboard. He urged Favian to lie back with his upper body slightly elevated, to help ease his chest. "It was only a dream, Little Brother," Senovo said again. "All is well."

"No, I—" Favian paused to clear his raspy throat. "I've *never* had a dream like that before, Elder Brother. It was as if I was right there, seeing…" He trailed off, his breathing growing ragged once more with fear or some other emotion.

I glanced at Senovo, who was watching the boy closely, a slight furrow forming between his finely drawn brows. "It's all right, Favian," he said. "There's no reason to be afraid. Can you tell us what you saw?"

Favian squeezed his eyes shut, his right hand clutching the edge of the blanket until the knuckles turned white. "I s-saw mountains."

"The southern mountains?" Senovo asked.

"I don't know," Favian said. "I've only ever seen the northern mountains. These were bigger, though."

Senovo nodded his understanding. "What else?"

"There was… fire. Like… the whole mountain range was on fire. I didn't know a fire could *get* that big. And… people were screaming. Dying, in the flames." Favian was shaking now. Still feeling out of my depth, I reached over and tucked the blanket in around him.

Senovo laid a hand on the boy's shoulder again. "That does sound horrible," he said, still using the soothing cadence that I myself had found much reason to appreciate in recent weeks. "However, you're awake now. The nearest mountains are almost three days' ride from here, but even in Draebard we would surely see the smoke from such a fire as you describe. No one has reported such a thing. And no one from Draebard is traveling that far away at the moment, so everyone you know is safe. Do you understand?"

"I know it's not real," Favian muttered, still wracked by little bouts of shivering. "It just felt real, is all. More real than this, almost." He gestured around the room with a small wave of his hand.

Senovo patted his shoulder and sat back. "Dreams during an illness can be odd," he offered. "Still, I think your fever is breaking, so hopefully you won't have any more like that tonight."

"S'pose so," Favian said, not looking at us, embarrassment starting to war visibly with his upset.

"Can you rest some more, do you think?" Senovo asked. "I don't want to give you anything to help you sleep without speaking to the healer first, but I can call for her if I need to."

Favian shook his head. "No, I'll try. Only…"

"What is it, Favian?" I prompted when he trailed off into silence.

Favian wrestled with himself for a long moment. "Could you both stay here for a while?" he blurted eventually.

I hid my smile. "Sure," I said, not making a big deal of it. "We were going to anyway." I reached out to ruffle a hand through his blonde hair, and he ducked away, blushing. "By the way, I spoke with your father earlier. He said to tell you he'd be by again in the morning to see you. He'll be pleased that your fever has broken."

Favian nodded—a small movement. "He worries," he said.

Senovo settled back in his chair with a faint huff of amusement. "You're his son, Favian. It's his job to worry."

I paused in my own journey back to my seat, caught unawares by a surge of bitterness. Neither Senovo nor I had seen much in the way of protective worry when we were children, though at least *his* parents had the excuse of looming starvation when they'd agreed to sell their seven-year-old son to slavers. When it came to me, however, the only thing my own mother seemed to worry about were my *unnatural inclinations*, as she had been prone to calling them—usually right before she raised her hand or a leather strap to me.

Returning to the present, I took a careful breath and sat down next to Senovo again. Perhaps sensing that I was not going to be a fount of helpfulness just now, the priest leaned forward, resting his elbows on his knees.

"Well, Little Brother," he said, "since we've nothing better to do right now, this seems like as good a time as any to go over the religious histories again. You will, after all, be required to recite them correctly before you ascend to the rank of novice priest."

"Yes, High Priest," Favian replied dutifully, relaxing a bit when it became obvious that there would be no more talk of either his dream or his father.

"Remind me how far you had progressed with the story of Naloth and Utarr in your studies with Novice Feldes?"

"To, umm, the part where Naloth pursues Utarr into the desert and gains her love by bringing the rains," Favian said. *"Upon the sand, warm rain did fall; the grass sprung up and covered all.* That bit."

"Very good," Senovo replied. "In that case, let us continue…"

I closed my eyes and leaned back in the chair, letting the low, sonorous drone of Senovo's voice roll over me as he recounted the courtship of the two gods in the most boring and sleep-inducing manner imaginable. My knee pressed companionably against his, out of Favian's line of sight. When, a rather short time later, the sound of Favian snoring through his partially blocked nose grew louder than the sound of Senovo's recitation, he trailed off at the end of a stanza.

"You are surprisingly good at that," I told him, not bothering to open my eyes.

"I wasn't the only frightened slave-child in the southern Priests' Guild," he said, his voice wistful. "As I grew older, soothing the young ones from their night terrors became a useful skill to have, particularly if I wished to have any undisturbed sleep myself."

And who comforted you after your nightmares, I wonder? Rather than say it aloud, I let my head roll to the side and rest against his shoulder as Favian snored on. Senovo's body expanded and contracted in a deep sigh under my cheek.

"This concerns me," he said in a quiet tone. "Favian is a deeply empathic boy."

I opened my eyes and straightened so I could look at him. "The dream, you mean? It was only a nightmare, surely."

"I certainly hope that's the case," he said.

"What else would it be?" I asked, my brow furrowing in confusion.

Senovo drew breath as if to reply, but we were interrupted by a soft knock at the door. Since I was closer, I rose and opened it, revealing Andoc standing in the hallway. He smiled and leaned down to press a kiss to my forehead.

"Thought I might find you here," he said. Despite his brief grin, his eyes were troubled. "Come out for a minute, both of you. There's news."

Senovo joined us in the hall and closed the door silently behind him. "What is it?" he asked.

"I've just come from the meeting hall," Andoc said. "We have visitors. They arrived just as night was falling."

"What kind of visitors?" I asked.

"A group of ambassadors have come to talk about the attack on the hill fort."

My blood ran cold. "Alyrions?" I asked.

"No, they're Eburosi," Andoc said. "From, uh... down south somewhere."

"You might as well come out and say it," Senovo said, sounding tired. "You're being cagey, and it's not difficult to guess why."

"Sorry. They're Rhytheeri," Andoc said after a slight pause, as if it was an admission of some sort.

"Who are the Rhytheeri?" I asked. "Hang on. Isn't that the tribe who had some kind of conflict going with Meren?"

"It is," Andoc said. "The Rhytheeri come from the southern coast, but their influence extends as far north as the mountains. They more or less rolled over for the Alyrions as soon as the Empire came knocking at their doorstep a couple of years ago. Started paying the Emperor tribute; let him install a puppet king to rule in Rhyth. That kind of thing." He paused, a muscle working in his jaw. "We also think that the bounty hunters who captured you two in the forest were Rhytheeri."

Senovo leaned backward a couple of inches until he was braced against the wall. His voice was completely flat when he added, "And, of course, what Andoc is so tactfully refraining from saying is that the Rhytheeri are my own people—the people who made me a slave and castrated me against my will. The ones I escaped six years ago."

TWO

I stared at him. "The men who captured us were your own people? You never said."

Senovo continued to let the wall take his weight. His eyes stared through the opposite side of the hallway, focused somewhere far away as he shrugged a shoulder. "It hardly seemed relevant at the time. There were more pressing concerns."

"Do you think they knew who you were?" I asked. "That you had escaped from the Rhytheeri, I mean."

"I hope not," Senovo said.

"No reason they would," Andoc added. "People move around to different parts of Eburos all the time. Lots of Rhytheeri come north."

I wondered how many freshly castrated shape-shifting slaves who had just savaged and killed their owners came north from Rhytheeri, but wisely refrained from asking aloud.

"Is Volya meeting with them now?" I said instead, changing the subject.

"No," Andoc replied. "Not until mid-morning tomorrow. They pled weariness after the long journey. It's six days' ride to get here from Rhyth. We put them up at Threstal's place for the night."

"Does the Chief want me to attend tomorrow?" I asked, not wishing to take anything for granted. That Andoc and Senovo would attend such an important meeting was a given. My own welcome was still something of an open question.

"It's well within your rights as Mistress of the Horses to attend meetings that might affect Draebard's future," Senovo said.

"That's not quite what I asked," I pointed out in a wry tone.

"Come, by all means," said Andoc. "I'm sorry to say that if you don't want to lose your power, you're going to have to exercise it. Otherwise, Volya will squeeze you out. You already saw what he tried to do to Senovo."

I nodded. "I'll be there, in that case. I'm supposed to meet with Keenan first thing in the morning to work on the mounted archery project. I'll bring her with me—she can act as an observer for Meren."

"There, see? Now you're getting it," Andoc said, letting a faint smile briefly chase the worry lines from his face. "So, are we all staying here tonight?"

"Someone needs to watch over Favian," I told him, jerking my chin toward the closed door. "His fever's broken, but he's having nightmares and I don't want to leave him alone. His father will be back in the morning, but if you're willing to take a shift, we could split up the vigil three ways and two could rest while one of us stays with him."

"Of course," Andoc said. "Poor kid… I thought he was doing better."

"It's merely a case of the coughing sickness," Senovo said, rallying enough to push away from the wall. "Nothing to do with his wound, which is nearly healed. Why don't you take the first watch, old friend?"

"That way we won't have to try to wake you up later," I added, unable to help myself.

"Ha, yes, very funny," Andoc said. "You've just guaranteed yourself an interesting method of being awoken for your own shift. You do realize that, right?"

"As long as it doesn't involve cold water in the same bed where I, too, am trying to sleep," said Senovo, raising an eyebrow pointedly.

"No promises," Andoc replied. "Now, go get some rest, both of you. I'll sit with the boy and Carivel can relieve me around midnight."

⚜

My *interesting method of being awoken* turned out to consist of a large hand closing over my mouth and a rough whisper in my ear. "Not a sound, now. Don't wake Senovo."

After the initial startle, I relaxed into the grip, shivering a bit as Andoc's breath tickled the shell of my ear. I'd gone to sleep curled around Senovo's back, one arm thrown over him in a protective embrace, but we'd separated as the night wore on and I now lay on my back, a short distance away on the bed.

Andoc's other hand trailed possessively over my naked skin, and the breath left my lungs in a long, shaky exhalation. As the flat, callused palm slid across my stomach, then lower, I hitched my leg to the side to give him better access, careful not to make the mattress shift. A pulse of wetness flooded my cunt. Andoc did not keep me waiting, but pressed his hand a bit tighter over the lower half of my face to enforce my silence even as he trailed fingers over my inner lips, gathering the slickness there and dragging it forward to slide across my painfully erect nub.

The barest hint of a stifled whimper escaped from behind his hand, and he whispered, "Shh... don't move. Don't make a sound."

I locked the breath in my chest, staring sightlessly into the darkness as talented fingers pushed me inexorably toward release. The blood was singing in my veins. My muscles kept getting tighter and tighter, but I forced myself not to move beyond the involuntary quivering of my thighs. In no time at all, I squeezed my eyes shut and huffed out my climax silently through my nose, as tingles raced through my body and red flashes flared behind my eyelids.

"Well done, you," Andoc whispered, sounding amused and affectionate in equal measure.

I relaxed back, dizzy. The hand over my mouth was replaced by chapped lips that grew slick and warm as we kissed. Eventually, Andoc pulled back and pinched my hip to get me up and moving. My hideously embarrassing squeak of surprise immediately woke Senovo, who muttered something uncomplimentary and rolled over with his pillow pulled over his head while Andoc and I tried to stifle our guilty amusement.

"I think we've irritated him," Andoc whispered when he had himself under control again, nearly sending me straight back into undignified giggles.

I dragged myself out of bed on weak knees and stumbled around getting dressed in the darkness. Meanwhile, Andoc took over my place in the bed. A smile tugged at my lips as Senovo's mumbled protests at the jostling melted into a contented hum, presumably when Andoc pulled the other man into his arms.

Favian was quiet through all three of our watches, sleeping peacefully. When Senovo returned just before dawn to report that Renthro was with him once more, I returned Andoc's favor from earlier by drizzling oil over his cock and pumping him lazily in my fist until he spilled, still only half-awake, but with my name on his lips.

I kissed them both and slipped out of the temple to get some breakfast. After smoothing things over with Limdya and inviting her to become an apprentice with the horses, I was once again welcome in her sisters' cookhouse—a fact about which my stomach was quite relieved. Hearty brown flatbread topped with melting butter and dotted with sweet berries made a pleasant accompaniment to my morning walk to the pens, and I arrived just as the first few boys showed up.

Limdya arrived soon after, and I set her to work with Lundis, learning how to trim ragged hooves. Favian's young friend had been quiet after the revelations about my birth sex—neither openly supportive nor openly hostile—and I trusted him not to make Limdya's life a misery simply because she'd had the temerity to be born female. It probably helped, too, that Lundis was obviously terrified of her blunt, bossy manner.

When Keenan arrived with Ciero in tow, I had already met with Dalon, my second-in-command, both to let him know about the meeting with the Rhytheeri and to get the day's activities planned. The sun was up, promising another dry, hot day. It was good that the wet spring had raised a healthy crop of grass in the pasturelands—otherwise the drought that seemed to be setting in might have become a real worry. As it was, there was still plenty of fodder for the animals. And, unless the wind came up and made the dust a problem, today would be a perfect day for practicing archery.

"Good morning," Keenan said cheerfully, dropping her gear on a convenient table.

"Hello, Keenan. Hello, Ciero," I greeted.

Ciero, who had traveled to be with Keenan when she decided to stay in Draebard for a while, smiled and nodded. I liked them both immensely, though they were a study in opposites—Keenan, blunt and outgoing; Ciero, quiet and shy.

"Hope you don't mind if I camp at one of your tables while you two practice your archery," Ciero said in his soft, self-deprecating voice.

I smiled. "Of course not. What are you working on?"

Ciero lowered a satchel to the table, the strap looped over the stump of his right forearm. He deftly opened the drawstring left-handed and pulled out a large burl of ebony. I caught my breath upon seeing the carving that emerged from it, half-finished.

"Is that Nietre?" I asked in awe, reaching out to touch the chiseled head and neck of a horse.

He grinned, pleased. "It is indeed. I figured I had a perfectly good subject for a carving right here under my nose and might as well take advantage of it."

"It's beautiful," I said, meaning it.

"Hopefully the wood will continue to cooperate," he joked. "I thought there was a horse trapped inside it somewhere when I first saw the piece, but one never knows for certain until it's finished."

Keenan wrapped an arm around her husband's chest from behind and kissed the top of his head as she caught my eye. "Don't get him started talking about art," she said with a wink. "We'll be here all day."

Ciero blushed. "Yes, yes. Go play with your bow and arrows, dearest. Leave a starving, unappreciated artist to his work."

She snorted and gave his slightly rounded stomach a firm pat. "I'll do that, dearest."

I grinned at their playfulness, but sobered a moment later. "By the way," I told Keenan as she readied the latest bow that the bowsmith had sent her to test, "We only have a couple of hours to work. There's a meeting in the village at mid-morning."

Keenan grew serious as well. "So I've heard. They're saying the visitors traveled up from Rhyth."

"That's what Andoc tells me. Apparently the Empire didn't take kindly to reports of its garrison of soldiers being slaughtered." I shivered, and blinked to dispel the momentary image of an Alyrion dying on top of me, the chains of my shackles wrapped around his neck. Keenan squeezed my shoulder, a brief and grounding gesture.

"Maybe they should have thought of that before they attacked your village in the dead of night," she said, voice grim. "Fucking Alyrions. They and the Rhytheeri deserve each other."

"I'd never even heard of the Rhytheeri until Leader Magoldis mentioned that Meren had some kind of dispute with them," I said. "Now I can't seem to get away from them."

"They're far enough away that they have no business anywhere near Mereni territory," Keenan said. "But they've somehow diverted most of the water from one of the rivers we use for livestock, until it's nearly running dry. It's probably something the Alyrions taught them how to do. Those spineless southern bastards sold their souls for whatever trade agreements and technological advancements the Emperor was willing to give them."

"I don't think anyone realized at first how much of a foothold the Alyrions had gained in Rhyth," Ciero added.

"It's like the Empire quietly took over the entire southern third of Eburos and nobody even noticed," Keenan said. "I mean, I know the mountains kind of limit travel between the north and south, but you'd think someone would have raised more of a fuss."

"And now by attacking the hill fort, we've basically gone and poked the hornets' nest with a stick," I said, feeling the full weight of understanding settling on my stomach, perhaps for the first time.

"Pretty much," Keenan said, sounding unaccountably cheerful all of the sudden. "Still, the Emperor will find the northern tribes a little more challenging to deal with than a bunch of soft southerners."

I couldn't help wondering how many northerners would have to die in order to prove that point. Shaking off the thought, I remembered our discussion about the meeting last night. "You two should come to the meeting hall as observers from Meren. I'm sure Magoldis would appreciate a first-hand report of what goes on."

"I'll pass," Ciero said, his voice wry. "I've already given part of an arm to Meren. I'd prefer not to have my ears talked off as well."

"I'll go," said Keenan. "In the mean time, though, I want to try out this new bow. Is that little horse of yours done with his breakfast yet?"

I smiled, relieved to be getting back to more comfortable territory. "You've seen the size of his belly. If he's not, I think he can live without it for a couple of hours."

Kekenu was easily distracted from his feed by Keenan's approach. I might have taken his apparent fascination with the Mereni archer more personally, had I not suspected her of gaining his affection mostly through the liberal application of dried apples. While Keenan readied the little black and white gelding, I caught and saddled another horse from the group Dalon and I had chosen as archery prospects.

Several of the apprentices were working on getting the animals in question solid with bridleless riding, but I'd recently had an idea that I wanted to try out. The big problem was, what we were currently doing required not only a highly trained horse that would be reliable without reins in a chaotic battle situation, but also a rider who was unusually skilled in both horsemanship and archery.

I'd gotten lucky in that Keenan was both of those things, though much of her talent with Kekenu came down to a combination of superb balance, athleticism, and complete fearlessness on horseback. Finding an entire contingent of such individuals and providing reliable mounts for them seemed decidedly unlikely.

With this in mind, I bridled the gray colt I had picked out and mounted him. My jerkin was held closed at the waist with a wide leather belt. To this, I tied a very thin leather thong—one that would break with only a few pounds of pressure. Gathering up the reins, I rode out to the space between the pens and warmed up the horse until he was supple and responsive. For what I had in mind, the trick was going to be getting the length of the reins correct. I experimented a bit, making them shorter and longer until I could change the colt's speed from a walk to a canter and back again without having to change the length of the reins. When I was satisfied, I marked them with a fingernail and tied a knot in the reins at exactly that spot. Then, I attached the knot to my belt with the thong.

By leaning my upper body forward a bit, I could give the colt enough room to move out without feeling trapped by the bridle. By straightening up and sucking my stomach in—which incidentally deepened my seat, reinforcing the aid—I could bring him back down to a halt. We cantered around the pens, slowing and speeding up by turns as I shot an imaginary bow and arrow with my newly freed hands.

It was not a perfect system—the thong attaching the reins to the rider's belt *had* to break easily, or risk bringing a horse down on top of a falling rider and possibly breaking its jaw. But in a battle, there was also the very real concern that the flimsy connection would snap at an inopportune moment during an abrupt maneuver. Still, it seemed a safer system than relying on the rider's ability to control a horse in battle with *no* reins. Assuming, of course, that the riders could learn enough self-discipline not to give unintentional and conflicting signals with the movements of their upper bodies.

Leaving the reins as they were, I rode over to where Keenan was shooting the bulls eyes out of targets as she cantered past on Kekenu.

"Let me see the new bow and a couple of arrows for a minute," I said when she trotted over to me.

"I think the bowsmith has really got it right this time," she said as she handed it across and removed a couple of arrows from the quiver behind the saddle. "Hey! That's clever."

She motioned toward the rein arrangement and I shrugged. "I thought this might be easier for most riders. Got to make sure you can fire an arrow without accidentally yanking on the horse's mouth first, though."

Ever since my ribs had healed enough for it not to be painful, I'd been learning archery from Keenan. I absolutely loved it. Which was not to say I was particularly *good* at it yet, but I was certainly better than I had been when I started. From the ground, I could usually hit somewhere on the target while standing a reasonable distance away. From horseback—not so much, though I was determined to master the skill eventually.

Fortunately, accuracy wasn't necessary for this experiment, so I pointed the gray colt down the alley studded with straw targets and urged him into an easy lope. It was simpler than I'd thought to move my arms and shoulders independently of my torso, nocking an arrow and letting fly, then repeating the process for a shot to the other side. Both arrows sailed past their targets and flew harmlessly into the empty pens beyond, but, more importantly, the colt cantered smoothly on, not slowing or faltering as I shot from his back.

I pulled up at the end of the alley and wheeled around. "I like the new bow!" I called once I was in shouting distance. "Much easier to use!"

Keenan met me halfway and took the gracefully curved object from me. "I agree," she said. "I think she finally got the right balance between size and draw weight. The recurve helps. You should see this thing when it's not strung—it's crazy looking. I'll show you some time."

I nodded and glanced at the sun, climbing steadily in the sky.

"Time to go?" Keenan asked.

"Looks like it," I said.

We unsaddled the horses and cooled them out in companionable silence. When we returned to the table where Ciero was working, it was to find that more of the black stallion's sleek body had emerged from the twisted burl of wood.

"Good session?" he asked.

"I think so," I said, and Keenan made a noise of agreement.

After offering Ciero the use of the table for as long as he wanted it, the two of us headed for the meeting house. I couldn't help noticing the vague aura of tension in the village, and wondered what sort of rumors and gossip were making the rounds. For once, the unembellished truth was probably more than enough to fuel legitimate nervousness among the people of Draebard. The Empire was powerful. *Very* powerful. Battling an isolated garrison of Alyrion soldiers was one thing, but if the Empire decided to descend on the north in force... well. Despite Keenan's dismissal of *soft southerners* earlier that morning, it wouldn't be pretty. In fact, it would be utterly devastating.

Not for the first time in recent weeks, I was overcome by the feeling that everything was poised to change around us in ways none of us could foresee.

When Keenan and I reached the meeting hall, the entrance was flanked by a warrior named Balzoc who I knew to be a friend of Andoc's, along with a young apprentice warrior whose face was vaguely familiar but whose name I could not recall.

"Well, well!" said the young guard, eyeing Keenan's tight breeches and sleeveless leather vest with blatant appreciation. "Looks like the entertainment has arrived! You gonna dance for our guests, love? Because I'd sure like to get an eyeful of that..."

I stopped in my tracks, appalled. Keenan raised an eyebrow, and turned to Balzoc.

"New boy?" she asked in a bland voice.

"Yup," Balzoc replied, caught somewhere between irritation and embarrassment at the apprentice's impropriety.

"Huh," Keenan said. She returned her attention to the lad, whose features were hardening into anger at her casual dismissal. "You'll get your private dance tonight, New Boy. Training yard. One hour before sunset. Short blades — first blood or capitulation. I'll see you there."

With that, she strode through the door Balzoc opened for us, not looking back. Unable to think of anything more constructive to do, I followed her. Behind us, I could here the apprentice say, "What — ?" and Balzoc start to berate him in hissed tones, his words cut off as the door closed.

"No offense, Carivel," Keenan said from in front of me, "but a lot of Draebardi men are assholes."

"Gods, Keenan," I blurted, my tongue coming unstuck as I hurried to draw even with her, "I am *so sorry* about that. I'll talk to Andoc. He'll take care of it. There's no need for you to fight that little prick — "

"Pfft. Don't be ridiculous." Keenan turned to meet my gaze as we walked. "I enjoy a good spar now and then, especially when it lets me put a clueless whelp like that in his place."

"I thought you didn't like close combat?" I asked.

"Eh, it's not my favorite, but it's still important to keep my hand in. I'm pretty decent with a dagger, and that kid is obviously as wet behind the ears as a newborn calf. It'll be good for him." A rather alarming smile slid onto Keenan's features as I watched. "I promise not to break him. *Much.*"

I could only shake my head. "Apparently being plain-looking has its benefits," I said. "I've dealt with some steaming horse shit around here, for sure, but never anything quite like that."

My companion gave me an odd look that I couldn't quite decipher. "I expect it's got more to do with Andoc and you being together, to be perfectly honest, Carivel. If Ciero had come with us, I can guarantee New Boy would have kept his mouth shut." She grinned again. "But then I would have missed out on tonight's entertainment. So there's that."

I shook my head. "Senovo is always going on about the people who work at the horse pens being a little bit crazy. I still maintain we've got nothing on warriors. No offense, but you lot aren't quite right in the head."

"Comes with the territory, I expect. At least it's never boring," Keenan said, unconsciously echoing a sentiment that Andoc regularly expressed.

I snorted in amusement.

Ahead of us, the door to the largest meeting room was open. Jacun stood guard outside, and flashed us a friendly smile as we approached. Muted voices drifted out from inside.

"Have they started?" I asked.

"They're just about to, I think," he said. "Best go on in."

The room was not completely packed, but it was still obvious that pretty much everyone with any sort of legitimate excuse for being here had made a point of attending. White-haired elders wandered the room, mingling with warriors and merchants. In one corner, Volya was talking to a knot of strangers, dressed similarly to—if more richly than—the group of men who had followed Senovo and me from the temple a few weeks ago and abducted us in the forest.

Andoc and Senovo stood nearby, flanking the Draebardi Chief, who looked as if he'd just eaten something sour. Senovo caught my eye and flickered an eyebrow in subtle greeting. Andoc looked over a moment later and gestured us toward the group with a jerk of his chin. I touched Keenan's elbow to get her attention and led her through the crowd, feeling the looks of surprise and disapproval at our feminine presence follow us across the room.

None of the looks were more blatant than those of the visiting ambassadors, however. The one speaking with Volya frowned as he noticed us. Before anyone could introduce us, he said, "What is this, Chief Volya? You allow a *woman* in the meeting hall?"

The irritation that had been simmering under my skin since the apprentice outside ogled Keenan like a piece of meat flared into anger. I drew breath to say something unwise, only to be shocked into silence as Volya spoke first.

"Should I worry for your eyesight, Ambassador Derenza?" he asked, still looking as though he'd rather be strangling the man in front of him than talking to him. "There are two women here. One is our esteemed Horse Mistress, Carivel of Draebard, and the other is Keenan, Fourth Warrior of the Mereni."

I blinked. Esteemed? *Really?* Since when?

The ambassador's disdainful gaze raked over my body, searching, as so many seemed to feel the need to do, for my alleged femininity. "I... see," he said. "Forgive me. Your northern ways are very different to what is considered acceptable in the south. I intended no disrespect."

Volya pressed his lips together in a thin line, a muscle in his jaw working visibly. "Of course not," he ground out. "Perhaps we should all take our seats and begin."

The group broke up and headed toward the large table that dominated the room. I hung back, stopping Andoc with a hand on his arm. "What just happened?" I asked, trying to speak without moving my lips or otherwise drawing anyone's attention.

The corners of Andoc's mouth turned down, and he kept his voice low as he answered. "Our Chief may resent you, *caradi*, but that situation is on a whole different level from what the Rhytheeri represent. You're a scandal as far as he's concerned, true. But you're *Draebard's* scandal."

I pondered that as I allowed Andoc to usher me toward the meeting table, where everyone was already taking their places. In matters of tribal negotiation, the elders took precedence over those who might have higher rank in day-to-day life. For this reason, Keenan, Andoc and I found ourselves standing behind Senovo and Volya, where they sat together at the head of the table as equals — High Priest and Tribal Chieftain.

The half-dozen ambassadors were grouped at the far end, with their backs to the door. Ambassador Derenza cleared his throat and addressed the room.

"Good people of Draebard," he began. "Those of us in Rhyth were extremely troubled by recent reports of conflict between your village and a nearby outpost under the control of the Alyrion Empire. We are here to discuss ways to repair the relationship between Emperor Constanzus and the peoples of northern Eburos, lest everyone in the north suffer unnecessarily."

"Quite a bit of *suffering* could have been avoided had the Alyrions not launched an unprovoked attack on Draebard, killing dozens," Senovo said. His voice, though calm, carried clearly throughout the room.

"A cowardly night attack, I might add, after drawing our Chief and several of our warriors away on the false pretense of negotiations," put in Elder Tolmac, and several voices around him rose in agreement.

"I'm afraid I have no information about such an occurrence," the ambassador replied, "but surely the complete destruction of the Empire's garrison constitutes adequate revenge for whatever came before. The focus, going forward, must be on peace."

"You call our actions *revenge*?" Volya echoed in disbelief. "You make it sound like the Field Marshal cuckolded me, or stole some of my cattle. When a foreign power attacks and kills civilians with no provocation, it is *war*, not some petty tit-for-tat as you seem to imply!"

"It's also worth mentioning," said Keenan from beside me, "that the Field Marshal had kidnapped—and was torturing— high ranking members of the Draebardi tribe at the time of the attack. Hardly the actions of someone seeking peace."

A faint wave of dizziness swept over me at the unexpected reminder of our captivity, and I was relieved that Keenan had not identified either Senovo or myself by name.

Derenza looked down his hooked nose at Keenan as if she were a smear of dirt on his boot. "Indeed. And you are... a representative of the Mereni tribe, is that correct?"

"I am. Though an unofficial one."

"The Mereni tribe has some stake in Draebard's conflict with the Empire, then?"

Keenan raised an eyebrow. "I'm sure I wouldn't know about such things. I was merely enjoying a visit when you arrived, and it seemed prudent to attend what is obviously an important meeting when the opportunity arose."

One of the other Rhytheeri visitors leaned forward to whisper something in Derenza's ear. He tilted his head, listening intently, and straightened a moment later.

"Of course it did, my dear. That was very clever of you," he said in a condescending tone, and my temper flared once more on Keenan's behalf. "Now, though, if we could return to the matter at hand. The Empire has some diplomatic ties with Rhyth, and they have empowered me to offer terms. They are willing to broker peace in exchange for tribute from Draebard in the amount of ten thousand gold pieces per year, or the equivalent in cattle, horses, or metal ore. In addition, they require Draebard to peacefully house one hundred Alyrion soldiers under the command of a centurion, providing food, shelter, and a salary of two silver pieces per soldier, per week."

The room erupted into shouts and shocked conversation. After a moment, Derenza raised his hand and spoke over the noise. "Otherwise, you risk the destruction of your tribe. Should the Empire choose to descend on Draebard in force... well. When they were finished, there would be nothing left but bare ground and ashes. That would be intensely regrettable, and I urge you to treat this prospect with all the seriousness that it deserves. If the Emperor cannot have your loyalty, he might well decide to have your lives instead."

Volya rose slowly to his feet. "The Emperor," he said very clearly, "can go fuck himself up the ass with a rusty gate hinge."

Silence fell over the room. All eyes looked from the Draebardi Chief to the Rhytheeri ambassador across from him. Derenza stared at Volya for a long moment, and made a self-deprecating gesture with one hand, deflecting a bit of the tension that filled the room. "Obviously, sir, I am a mere messenger. Such decisions are for you and your elders to make, but I would implore you to consider them carefully." He turned his attention to Senovo, who had remained silent through the commotion. "High Priest, I cannot help noticing that your features and coloring have the look of the Rhytheeri tribe about them. I appeal to you as a fellow southerner to employ reason in this matter. No good can come of continued conflict with so powerful a foe."

I could not see Senovo's face, standing behind him as I was, but there was tension in his shoulders. Volya, still standing, spoke before Senovo could.

"If you wish to speak of power, you need look no further than Draebard's High Priest. He may not have been born here, but he is loyal to his northern home. Senovo has more power than the Emperor can ever dream of," the Chief boasted. "He is the first shape-shifter in more than a generation to hold the position of High Priest on Eburos. To set yourself against Draebard is to set yourself against such power as that."

I cringed internally and held my breath. Several of the Rhytheeri visitors started murmuring to each other in the background. Derenza stared at Senovo with renewed interest.

"That is fascinating indeed, Chief Volya," he said when the conversation behind him died down. "Shape-shifters are vanishingly rare these days. Though, as it happens, they are not unheard of in the south. For instance, many people around Rhyth tell the story of a young wolf-shifter who murdered a group of Rhytheeri Priests on the day of his castration and ran away. An interesting coincidence, would you not agree?"

THREE

I was frozen, and Senovo might as well have been carved from stone. Beside me, Andoc was practically vibrating with tension. Not surprisingly, he erupted a moment later.

"Considering the fact that the Rhytheeri *force* castration on their acolytes," Andoc said, "I'd imagine it's not too unusual for the victims to fight their way free by whatever means are necessary."

Derenza's eyes flicked to him, and he raised a dark eyebrow. "The practice of initiation into the priesthood is distressing, I grant you, but as the Alyrions' religion gains more of a foothold across Eburos, the old ways will doubtless fade into unpleasant memory. Until they do, however, the people require priests, and—no offense to present company, High Priest Senovo—but I'm sure most of you here would agree that no sane man would voluntarily submit to such a thing."

I thought of Favian and the other acolytes, my heart pounding with rage. Beside me, Andoc tensed, a low, almost inaudible growl rumbling in his throat. Senovo rose smoothly from his chair, cutting Andoc and the ambassador off from each other's view. I nearly took a step back, unprepared as I was for the aura of power radiating from him. Next to me, Andoc sucked in a sharp breath.

"*Enough.* Such matters have no bearing on the present discussion," Senovo said in a voice like forged iron. "The Chief of the Draebardi has informed you that his people will not pay tribute or house foreign troops. What is your response?"

Derenza's assessing gaze rested on Senovo for the space of two breaths before the ambassador dipped his head in a shallow bow. "Forgive me," he said, his voice oily with sudden deference. "As you say, such distractions are a waste of everyone's time. Your Chief's response was quite clear, but I would nonetheless offer him and his advisors an invitation to travel to Rhyth for a meeting with delegations from the other northern powers in three weeks' time. Our King will be hosting this meeting personally. He conveys his most sincere desire that Draebard will attend, so that we Eburosi may come together to decide the future of the island we call home."

"The King of Rhyth is an Alyrion puppet ruler," Volya said, still standing shoulder to shoulder with Senovo.

"I will... ignore that remark, and merely say that this is a rare opportunity for cooperation among the leaders of Eburos," Derenza said. "If the other northern leaders feel the same way you do, surely uniting as one voice will send a stronger message to the Empire than many whispers with no organization among them. I invite you to take some time to discuss it with your council before making a final decision."

"We will consider it," Senovo said.

"This audience is ended, Ambassador," said Volya. "Second Warrior Jacun will escort you and your compatriots back to your rooms."

"Of course, Chief Volya," Derenza said. He and the other Rhytheeri bowed low, and allowed Jacun to lead them from the room. Once the door closed behind them, conversation swelled as those in the room began discussing what they had just heard in worried tones.

"I need to get out of here," I muttered. The nearly unbearable tension and heavy atmosphere around me was making it hard for me to breathe.

"I think I'd better stay and find out what they decide," Keenan said. "Then Ciero and I will ride back to Meren immediately and talk to Leader Magoldis."

"Will Volya attend the meeting, do you think?" I asked Andoc, keeping my voice low.

"Probably," he replied in the same tone. "I imagine the elders will insist on it."

His eyes were locked on Senovo, who had reseated himself as smoothly as if the worst moment of his life hadn't just been dragged out into the light and thrown at his feet in front of half the village. My own gaze followed.

"You'll watch over him?" I asked. Senovo's entire demeanor screamed *danger — stay away*, and I had to fight the urge to physically drag him out of here to someplace small and dark and private where Andoc and I could wrap him up between us and make everything else disappear.

"Yeah, of course I will. Just try and stop me," said Andoc, and I pitied anyone stupid enough to take him up on that challenge.

I leaned into Andoc for a brief embrace. "Tell him I'll come to the temple at dusk."

"We'll be waiting," he said, and dipped his head to kiss my hair.

I... *escaped.* There was really no other word for it. Perhaps I should have stayed, for Senovo or for Draebard, but I honestly had no idea if the tribe should send a delegation to Rhyth or not. Even if I did, it was unlikely that my opinion would sway Volya, much less the elders. The past and the future were converging on us, and I feared that when they collided we must surely be crushed between them.

It was a relief to return to the pens where I could pick up a bucket and shovel like the lowliest apprentice. Dalon immediately sidled up to me for details, and I summarized things as best I could — leaving out the part about Senovo's ugly past. No doubt he would hear about it later, probably in lurid and thoroughly embellished detail, but it certainly wouldn't be coming from me.

For the first time in over a week, I found myself at odd moments getting sucked into memories of the abduction. Our captivity. Senovo's torture. The battle. I made myself breathe slowly and recited Utarr's prayers of solace until the past fell away and released me back into the present, just as Eiridan had taught me. When the pens were nearly ready for the horses' return from the pastures that evening, I went to visit Nietre.

The stallion had been an interesting measure of my recovery after our return. When my mind was mired in trauma, my connection with the dangerous black horse slipped away as if it had never been. When I finally let go of some of the guilt and accepted help from the people around me, he returned to me with such enthusiasm that it almost appeared to be relief. As time passed, I grew to understand that the stallion was not only an indicator of my progress, but also a touchstone of sorts. When I was struggling, I could slip back into a better state of mind by working with him, because to do otherwise was to risk a deadly attack of teeth and hooves.

It was to this purpose that I turned myself now. Nietre snorted at me as I approached, his head jerking up in alarm. I took a deep breath and let everything fall away, until it was just me, the stallion, and the pen. After a moment, he blew out and shook his head, licking and chewing thoughtfully as he wandered over to greet me.

I saddled him and did a quick warm-up on the ground, eager to get out into the open with him. With my mind effortlessly tethered to the present moment and the powerful animal standing next to me, I mounted and headed out along the northern road. When we were in open country, I let the stallion surge forward, running toward the horizon like wind blowing over the western plains. We must have galloped a full two leagues when he finally slowed, sweat lathering his neck where the reins had whipped it up.

On our way back, we came across the herd being driven back in from the summer pastures. I hailed the lads who were riding point, and joined the rear of the group. Nietre pranced, his neck arched as he postured for the mares. I effortlessly shaped the display with rein and leg, guiding him in dancing, controlled steps that moved lightly sideways, forward, or backward at my slightest touch. We floated along together until his energy for showing off was exhausted, at which point I let him trot along behind the herd on a loose rein, as calm as any other working horse at the end of the day.

After we arrived back at the pens and I had finished up the last few tasks of the evening, I took a deep breath and stretched, feeling centered and fully present once more. Now, I thought, I was in a position to be there for Senovo and—should he need me—for Andoc. Not to mention for poor Favian.

On the way through the village, I stopped at the cookhouse and purchased four sweet pastries filled with mince. It was still something of an adjustment not to have to worry about the weight of my purse at the end of the week, but it was definitely the sort of adjustment I could get behind.

The temple was well lit and cheery despite the tension in the village. The influx of new acolytes, along with the two transplanted Mereni novices, had seemingly returned the building to life, making it once again a pleasant place to come in the evenings. I bowed to the gods and made my way inside. My presence had become common enough that it was hardly remarked upon—at least, not by members of the priesthood. No doubt the rumors and gossip outside the temple walls were rife with tales of scandal and my troubled handfasting with Andoc, based on the amount of *counseling* we had sought since the ceremony.

Inside, several villagers were engaged in various activities—some tending small memorials to lost friends or family members, others praying at the large altar after hearing the day's alarming news. The sound of coupling filtered out from one of the rooms dedicated to those receiving help with such things from the priests.

I wended my way through the halls to the temple barracks and poked my head into Favian's open door, only to find the room empty. Pleased that my former apprentice was apparently well enough to be up and about, I left one of the wrapped pastries on the table by his bed and made my way to the refectory.

"Good evening, Horse Mistress," Novice Feldes greeted. He was stirring a large pot of something hot and fragrant—not surprising, since he seemed to have appointed himself the temple's provider of nourishment. A couple of the new apprentices from Meren were eating at another table, their heads bent together in low conversation.

"Hello, Novice Feldes," I greeted. "I don't suppose you've seen either Andoc or the High Priest this evening?"

"I believe High Priest Senovo is counseling a couple this evening," Feldes said primly. "I'm afraid I have not seen the First Warrior."

I nodded. "Thanks. Could I prevail on you for a bowl of whatever that is? It smells delicious."

A wide smile graced the novice's broad features—it had taken me no time at all to discover that complimenting Feldes' cooking was a sure way to keep him well disposed toward me.

"Of course, Horse Mistress! Let me just ladle you up a nice helping."

I tucked my package of pastries under one arm and accepted the warm bowl of vegetable stew. "Much appreciated. I'll be sure to bring the bowl and spoon back later and clean them."

"See that you do!" he called after me.

On a hunch, I headed toward the High Priest's personal quarters, tucked away in a part of the temple where lay people did not normally go. Senovo had resisted moving from his small sleeping cell to Rhystel's suite of rooms for some time after the old High Priest's tragic death, but practicality finally forced his hand. He and Andoc had somehow managed to cram themselves onto the tiny bed in Senovo's old sleeping cell during the many nights they had spent together over the last several years, but fitting all three of us into it was an impossibility.

Using one of the rooms set aside for intimate counseling had worked for a while, and even gave us a more or less legitimate reason to be together, but creeping out the next morning was *awkward*, to say the least. My hut was… well… *not great*, and while Andoc's was perfectly adequate, it was usually much easier for the two of us to get to the temple after our duties were done than for Senovo to leave the temple, where his duties were essentially ongoing, should anyone have need of him.

The High Priest's quarters, however, were spacious, private, and had, quite frankly, an amazing bed.

"Did you know this was in here?" Andoc had asked Senovo upon seeing the feather-stuffed monstrosity for the first time.

Senovo shrugged. "Despite his rather advanced age, I gather Rhystel still entertained lovers on a fairly regular basis. Evidently, he was not averse to taking advantage of some of the trappings that came along with his elevated position."

"That old rogue," Andoc said, wonder in his voice.

"Right," I said, not about to let this opportunity pass. "I saw the way he was with you two, you know. There's no way he wouldn't want you to have this, Senovo."

And so it was that, on nights when Senovo's duties permitted and all of us could get away, we had the use of a huge bed with the most luxurious down-filled mattress on which I had ever slept. Those nights did not come nearly as often as I wished, but this evening, as I had half expected, I arrived to find Andoc already waiting for me, slouched in a heavy chair padded with furs.

I set the stew on a nearby table, leaned down to give him a kiss, and shoved a mince pastry at his chest.

"Hello to you, too," he said, fumbling the faintly squished pastry for a moment before righting it and taking a bite.

"Senovo's with a couple right now," I said, flopping down on the edge of the bed and biting into my own treat.

He smirked a bit, though it didn't erase the worry lines around his eyes. "I know," he said around a mouthful of mince filling. "Heard 'em on the way in. They were a bit hard to miss."

"Did you see Favian at all?" I asked. "He wasn't in his room. I assume that means he's feeling more like himself again."

Andoc nodded. "He and Reston were lighting the lamps and candles in the altar room. I didn't talk to them, but he looked fine. Heard him coughing a bit—nothing too bad, though. He even had his arm out of the sling."

"Good," I said, relieved. "He's had a rough time of it recently."

The door creaked open and we both looked up as Senovo entered. Light from the oil lamp illuminated his pale complexion and sunken eyes. Without a word, I rose from the bed, set the remains of my food on the table, and crossed to wrap him in my arms. He returned the embrace, and I felt a modicum of his tension drain away under my hands.

"Sit," I said when he eased back. "Eat. There's vegetable stew from Feldes, and pastries."

Andoc stretched a foot out and hooked a second chair closer to him, next to the table. I looked around and grabbed a wineskin from a peg on the wall, along with three goblets from the sideboard. When we were all settled with food and drink, I asked, "So, what was decided today?"

"We will attend the meeting in Rhyth," Senovo said. "There was little question about it, to be honest. Volya may posture and rattle his sword, but the elders know that Draebard faces potential destruction. The Chief, meanwhile, is content to view the meeting as fertile ground for warmongering."

"He worries me lately," Andoc said quietly. "There's no strategy, no planning. Only bloodlust. The attack on Draebard changed him."

We were quiet after this, sipping wine and digesting Andoc's words as Senovo ate his stew. When he was finished, I set my goblet down decisively.

"Answer me one question," I said. "Is there anything that either of you can do tonight to influence the situation?"

Andoc smiled, and Senovo put his bowl aside with the little puff of exhaled air that was as close to laughter as he ever seemed to come. "No," Senovo said. "There is not. However, I sense that we are about to be treated to more wisdom from the horse pens."

"That's because you know me too well. So. If there's nothing either of you can do right now, then I want you to put it all aside for tonight and just... be here. With me. With each other. All right?"

"Good advice, *caradi*. Not always easy to follow, but definitely good." Andoc set his empty goblet aside, as I had.

"In that case," I told him as I settled on his lap in the heavy chair, straddling his thighs with my own, "I will make it my goal to be as distracting as possible."

I kissed him, tasting wine and spicy mince. His prick stirred against me with interest.

"Well done. I'm distracted already," he said when I pulled back.

"So I gather," I said with a smile, and rocked against the hardness underneath me with lazy movements.

Andoc wrapped his arms around my back and leaned forward, rising from the chair as though my added weight was nothing to him. I scrambled to wrap my legs around his hips as he carried me across the short distance to the bed and spilled me backwards into it. As always, the manhandling secretly delighted me.

"*Amadi*," he asked Senovo, "are you thoroughly sick of sweaty bodies grinding together tonight, or do you want in on this?"

The legs of Senovo's chair scraped over the floor, and a moment later he was standing by the bed next to Andoc. "I am too weary for any real exertion, but you are deeply mistaken if you believe that an evening—or a lifetime—spent counseling shy, fumbling lovers could ever dampen my taste for your touch, or Carivel's."

It was suddenly difficult to swallow past the mysterious lump in my throat. Rather than answer with words, Andoc pulled Senovo into his arms. The priest's eyes fluttered closed, more of the tension flowing from his muscles as he rested against his lover's strength. Andoc eased him back to kiss his forehead, his eyelids, and finally, his mouth.

Watching them, the lump lodged in my throat grew bigger, but my chest felt light. Open. My heart expanded unhampered to fill the space inside. I still had no idea why I was allowed to be part of this, but if the Empire descended on us tomorrow and burned everything to the ground, I would count myself as having lived well because I'd somehow been gifted with this measure of incredible love.

"Let me take off your robes," I said to Senovo when they parted. I rolled up to sit on the edge of the bed, looking up at them both. "Let the High Priest have a few hours' rest, and just be our Senovo for tonight."

Senovo smiled his shy smile, Andoc's kiss having stripped away the barriers with which he guarded himself by day. He knelt next to the bed, in the space between my legs. I stretched forward to kiss him as I ran my hand under white linen and untied the fastenings inside.

A moment later I slid the material over his shoulders and let it fall to puddle around him on the floor, baring smooth, golden skin to my eager gaze. Behind him, Andoc was also disrobing. Senovo lifted one of my legs and pulled off the soft boot before repeating the action with the other. I unbelted my summer jerkin and shrugged it off. Senovo's deft fingers unpicked the laces holding my breeches closed, the brush of his fingers igniting a smolder of desire in my belly.

I lifted my hips so he could pull breeches and smallclothes down together. A moment later, Andoc shucked my sleeveless linen undershirt over my head, leaving all of us bare to each other's gazes in the humid summer night.

"Up," Andoc urged, guiding Senovo into the bed as I scooted out of the way to make room.

I wrapped myself around Senovo from one side, while Andoc did the same from the other. "It's a bit warm for this tonight, is it not?" Senovo asked, while making absolutely no move to free himself from our arms.

"Probably," Andoc agreed, running a large hand slowly up and down Senovo's chest and stomach. His palm skimmed over my arm where it draped across Senovo's body, and continued down into the crease of his hip, brushing past his soft cock and over the top of his thigh before repeating the journey back up. I followed Andoc's lead, stroking over whatever skin I could reach, our hands tangling briefly whenever they encountered each other.

Senovo shivered under our combined touches and went lax, his body growing heavy and soft between us. This, I knew, was what he craved on nights when he did not desire to lose himself completely—our love, our touch, our reassurance that he was desired and desirable despite the cruel, horrific thing that had been done to him.

I pressed my lips to his cheek and the side of his neck, smiling against the warm skin as he rolled his head to give me better access. My own desire was a pleasant buzz beneath my skin—nothing urgent about it as I nuzzled at the sensitive place behind Senovo's ear. Andoc rolled up on an elbow to get a better view. He loved to watch, always wanting to see everything. I looked up at him, maintaining eye contact as I nipped an earlobe, drawing it between my teeth and tugging slowly until it popped free.

"Minx," Andoc said, approval tingeing his voice as Senovo arched and exhaled a shuddering sigh.

I rolled up on an elbow, mirroring Andoc across Senovo's body.

"Can I ask you a question?" I said, letting my hand continue to roam over Senovo's smooth skin.

Andoc raised an eyebrow. "Is it a distracting one?"

"Oh, yes," I answered with a smile. "Most definitely."

"Go ahead then. I'm intrigued."

I licked my lips. "Have you ever been fucked?"

The second eyebrow rose to join the first, and he laughed. "Have you not been paying attention, or…?"

I scowled in mock annoyance. Senovo stretched under our hands and opened his eyes. "Don't be dense, Andoc," he said, one corner of his lip twitching in amusement. "You know perfectly well what she's asking."

Andoc tweaked his nipple. "Not my fault if she's fun to tease," he said, all innocence. "Yes, *caradi*, I have been fucked on a few occasions during my misspent youth."

"What didn't you like about it?" I asked, truly curious.

Andoc appeared taken aback by the question. "Well, I… wouldn't say I *disliked* it, exactly. It was sort of uncomfortable at the beginning, and I'm not particularly sensitive back there. Not like Senovo is, certainly. It was all right, I suppose. Not nearly as enjoyable as the other way 'round." He shrugged. "The issue hasn't really come up since I was a horny adolescent back in Venzor. When I moved here to Draebard, I gave up my wicked ways and became the fine, upstanding member of society that you see before you today."

Senovo snorted, and Andoc grinned. "Yes, all right. I gave up *most* of my wicked ways."

I chewed at my bottom lip as I digested his words. "What would you say if I asked you to let me fuck you with my wooden cock?" I asked.

Andoc looked surprised. Senovo looked suddenly very interested. I held my breath and waited nervously.

"You didn't see that one coming, apparently?" Senovo said, amused.

Andoc laughed, and I breathed. "I should have, of course," he said, regarding me across the arm's length that separated us. "Hmm. What would I say to that?" His smile grew wicked. "I'd say that would be something you'd have to earn."

"And how would I go about doing that?" I asked with a slightly breathless edge.

"Well," he said, "I think I'd need you to best me in some sort of a contest first. That seems fair, doesn't it, Senovo?"

"Don't drag me into this," Senovo said.

"What kind of contest?" I asked. "Horseback riding? Chariot driving?" I paused, grinning. "Shit shoveling?"

"No, no," he said. "Something martial, I think."

"Chariot driving is a martial pursuit," Senovo pointed out.

"I thought you were staying out of this," Andoc said, and Senovo shrugged, all innocence.

"Fine," I said, thoroughly amused. "So, sword-fighting, daggers, that kind of thing?"

"That sounds about right," Andoc said, the smirk still firmly on his face. At Senovo's look of alarm, he hastily added, "with practice weapons, of course."

"Wrestling?" I asked, smiling sweetly.

"Oh, *definitely* wrestling," he said, his voice slipping into a lower register that made me shiver.

Without warning, I scrambled across Senovo, who yelped and rolled out of our way with a huff. Tackling Andoc to the bed, I wrapped my arms and legs around him to try to pin him in place. He laughed at me and grabbed my arse, using his grip to thrust his hardening cock against the crease of my hip even as he flipped us over. I managed to wriggle part way free — enough to sling an arm across his lower back and grab the meat of his flank.

Unfortunately, I had no idea what I was doing. The sum total of my wrestling experience consisted of five scuffles with other children in the village where I'd grown up... four of which I'd lost.

Andoc, on the other hand, knew exactly what he was doing—namely, toying with me. I suspect that whenever I was able to squirm free for a moment, it was because he was letting me. It certainly didn't help that desire was pooling between my legs, growing hotter and heavier every time his hand *accidentally* grabbed my breast, or his cock *accidentally* dragged along my inner lips as we grappled.

In less than two minutes, I lay splayed out beneath him, covered in sweat and gasping for breath, my wrists trapped above my head by one strong hand and one of my legs caught in the crook of his elbow. The position left me spread open, my sex gaping and wet as he rutted his erect prick against it with small movements.

"So," I said, my voice emerging as a croak, "we'll call this one a draw, then?"

FOUR

Andoc laughed, deep and hearty. When he bent down to kiss me, it stole all the remaining breath from my lungs.

"She has your bravado, my friend, if not necessarily your skill in wrestling," Senovo said from the far edge of the bed. I shivered and thrust up against Andoc's cock—there was something about being calmly discussed while I was helplessly pinned to the bed that got me *every single time*. They both knew it, too—curse the pair of them.

"She does at that," Andoc agreed. "Of course, now that I've got her, I suppose we need to figure out what to do with her."

Whatever you want, I urged silently. *Do whatever you want with me.*

I wriggled against Andoc's cock again, and he pressed me deeper into the soft, down-filled bed.

"Would you like her mouth, *amadi*? And I'll have her from behind while she sucks you?"

I moaned as my cunt throbbed, fully in support of this idea.

The mattress dipped as Senovo crawled back to the center from his safe haven out of our way. "That sounds like a plan everyone can agree with," he said, settling against the headboard next to us.

Andoc gave another little jerk of his hips against mine and rolled off me. Before I had time to miss his weight, he was urging me up on hands and knees. I crawled between Senovo's legs. My mouth was already watering, and I pressed my cheek into Senovo's palm like a cat when he raised it to caress the side of my face. His thumb brushed across the sensitive skin of my lips.

Behind me, Andoc smoothed a hand over the flesh of my arse. "Beautiful," he said. "Not too great at wrestling, mind you—but nonetheless, that was definitely the most fun I've ever had winning a match."

"I'm up for... *ah*! Up for a rematch any time." My voice caught when his thumb slid down the crease of my buttocks, followed by a drizzle of oil.

"Tempting," Andoc said, a slick finger toying with my puckered opening. "For now, though, less talking. More sucking."

A haze of lust settled over my mind and I nuzzled forward, placing kisses along the tops of Senovo's thighs. He was still soft—no reflection on me, I knew, just the reality of being a eunuch. His smooth fingertips played with my short hair, slipping through the strands and sending delicious tingles down my spine. Meanwhile, Andoc's finger breached me, but only to the first knuckle. Teasing.

I licked at the tip of Senovo's prick, feeling it twitch. The temptation to push back on the finger playing with my rim was strong, but that would take me away from Senovo. Instead, I pulled his soft cock into my mouth, and was immediately rewarded with the slow, delicious burn as Andoc pressed into me from behind. I groaned around my mouthful, and felt Senovo begin to fill and grow heavier on my tongue. His hand rested on the crown of my head, grounding me while Andoc slowly stretched me open.

I laved the underside of the small prick hardening in my mouth. When Senovo was stiff enough, I sucked on him and slid my lips up his length until only the head was inside, then plunged back down until my nose was buried in the downy hair at the base. A second finger pressed into my arse, stretching me wider and making me moan. Senovo swelled to his full length and girth for a moment, the tip of his shaft nudging the top of my mouth, almost far enough back to make me choke, but not quite.

"Is she taking you down all the way, *amadi*?" Andoc asked.

The hand resting on my head stroked through my hair and settled, a bit heavier than before. "She is," Senovo said. His voice was low. Relaxed. Almost dreamy.

A third finger pressed into me, the burn growing sharper for a moment before subsiding back into the indescribable pleasure of being taken. I pulled back partway along Senovo's length, pressing further onto the fingers, then forward, swallowing him deep again. The haze grew thicker as I pictured how it must look as I fucked myself back and forth between them.

The vibrations of my muffled protest when Andoc's fingers pulled out drew a shiver from Senovo. I dragged my thoughts back into some semblance of order, and lifted my head.

"Do you need more?" I asked, aware that I had never seen Senovo achieve release without some kind of stimulation of that place inside him that was so sensitive.

He smiled down at me and his thumb stroked my temple, soothing. "No, beloved. This is perfect. I have no desire for more tonight."

It must be an odd thing to be a eunuch, I thought, even as I smiled my understanding and wrapped my lips around his softening prick once more. My own body was heavy. Aching. Almost desperate for Andoc to fill me and take me over the edge.

"Every time I think I couldn't possibly love the two of you any more," Andoc said softly from behind me.

More oil poured over my sensitive flesh. Fingers played with my opening—loose and ready, now. The mattress shifted; blunt pressure replaced the teasing touches. I took a deep breath through my nose and exhaled, pushing with my internal muscles. The now-familiar feeling of being breached and filled completely slithered up my spine to lodge in my ribcage. All three of us stayed motionless for a minute, adjusting.

When the sensation of being overwhelmed receded to manageable levels, I hummed encouragement and pressed back a bit. Andoc's hands gripped my hips.

"That's it, *caradi*," he said. "I'm going to move now. Just let me do everything."

I moaned again as Andoc slid deeper, filling me to bursting even as the motion pressed me forward, forcing me to take Senovo to the root. Raw desire crashed over me as the reality of being used and filled at both ends filled my senses. Andoc fucked into me, and fucked me onto Senovo, who steadied me in turn, encouraging me with soft words and softer touches.

Visions of what I must look like, buffeted back and forth between them like this, alternated with visions of Senovo throating Andoc's large cock while I plowed my curved wooden prick across the place inside him that made him unravel, over and over. My excitement swelled impossibly higher as I imagined it.

"Touch yourself, beloved," Senovo said, still stroking his hand over my hair and face. "Let us watch you come apart between us."

The words ignited a deeper flare of heat in my belly and I sucked hard on Senovo's cock, drawing a moan from him. I widened my knees for stability and braced myself with my left arm across Senovo's thighs, freeing my right hand to delve between my legs.

My cunt was soaked, my own fluids mixing with the oil and dripping down my thighs. I trailed my fingertips through the slickness, rubbing back and forth in time with the sharp thrusts that drove Andoc and Senovo deep inside me. My climax was upon me in seconds. I hovered on the threshold, perfectly balanced, buoyed up by the inevitability of my coming release. Nothing existed except the hands touching me, the cocks filling me. Everything was pleasure, and suddenly I was there—clenching around Andoc, straining to get Senovo just a fraction deeper. Andoc groaned and followed me over the edge, spilling his hot seed inside me.

The world beyond the boundary of my heavy, sated body was fuzzy and distant. I was dimly aware of Andoc directing us into a sort of controlled sprawl that would not crush Senovo beneath us... of Senovo easing me away from his prick and soothing me when I whimpered at the loss. It was even worse when Andoc pulled out. I shivered, feeling cold and empty despite the warmth of the summer night.

The bed shifted. Water splashed elsewhere in the room; Andoc was cleaning himself up. Senovo scooted down so he could hold me. A few moments later a damp cloth moved tenderly over my skin, washing away the oil and seed that had leaked down my legs. When he was satisfied, Andoc settled on Senovo's other side.

"I'm perfectly fine, my friend," the priest said when he was once again bracketed between us. "You needn't worry so."

"Humor me," Andoc replied.

"But what of you, Carivel?" Senovo asked, continuing to stroke my head as he had done while I pleasured him. "We were both reminded of things today which we would prefer to leave forgotten, I think."

I burrowed a little closer. "Hearing people talk about the abduction brought everything back at first. But I went out and rode Nietre, and that made things better again."

"Are you still making time to meet with Eiridan?" Andoc asked, and I nodded.

After my breakdown in the weeks following our capture, Senovo asked me to seek counseling at the temple with Eiridan. It made sense, he'd said, since the novice priest already knew most of my secrets, and had proven himself both trustworthy and empathetic.

"Can't I just talk to you?" I'd asked Senovo, still raw from my tears and the release of emotion.

Senovo caressed my cheek, thumbing away the tear tracks that were starting to dry on my skin. "You may speak to me at any time about any subject, beloved," he'd said, "but I cannot promise that I will be able to answer as your priest, and not your lover."

Back in the present, I shifted a bit so I could rest my head on Senovo's shoulder and meet Andoc's eyes. "I don't see him as often as I did at first," I told him, "but we still talk every week or two."

"And you still feel he is helping?" Senovo asked.

"I do. We've actually been talking about my mother lately, rather than what happened at the hill fort."

Andoc looked interested, even drunk on the afterglow of sex as he currently was. "Your mother? You hardly ever mention her," he said.

"And you need feel no obligation to discuss her now," Senovo said firmly.

"No, it's all right," I said, feeling safe and warm and thoroughly protected, here in bed with the two people I loved. "I just... never really realized how much influence she still has on me, even though I'm miles away and haven't seen her in years."

Senovo held me a little tighter. "The past and the present are inextricably linked. Only by shining light on the invisible bonds holding us mired in our own history can we begin to cut through them and free ourselves."

I nodded, and a little self-deprecating laugh slipped past my lips. "Well, I certainly plowed through the one about not crying or showing weakness in front of other people in fairly spectacular fashion."

"And yet, it still bothers you, even now," Andoc said with uncharacteristic insight.

I looked down, studying Senovo's hairless chest. "It just feels selfish, to dump something like that on other people. Like I should be stronger than that, you know?"

"Huh. Well, Senovo," Andoc said, "I hope you weren't ever planning on asking for help from us again when you have problems with the wolf. Looks like Carivel will think you're weak if you do."

My eyes flew to Senovo's face. He was looking at Andoc with an expression that was simultaneously tolerant and gently chiding. "Tactful as ever, Andoc," he said.

"What? No!" I said. "I don't think that at all!"

"We know you don't, *caradi*," Andoc said, his voice gentle now. "But you can't have it both ways. Either you and Senovo are both weak, or neither of you are."

I subsided, but only for a moment. "And what about you?" I asked. "I don't see you needing help from either of us."

Andoc stretched across Senovo until he could kiss my forehead. "Then you're not looking hard enough."

I frowned, but there was no point in arguing, particularly when I was cozy and sated, and sleep felt like something that would make an already pleasant evening even better. Instead, I burrowed a little closer against Senovo and let my eyes slip shut as Andoc extinguished the lamp.

Bad dreams still plagued me occasionally, but tonight it was as though I closed my eyes for only a few moments, and when I opened them again it was morning. That wasn't the surprising part, though. The surprising part was that when I awoke, it was to find the wolf curled in the space between my body and Andoc's.

"*Oh*. Hello, you," I said softly, and was rewarded by a slow blink of the animal's beautiful amber-green eyes.

Senovo did not seem upset or fearful; indeed, now that I was awake his jaw opened in a massive yawn, wolfish breath wafting past my face. He stretched luxuriously, making my own muscles tingle in sympathy.

"Andoc," I said, wanting him to see this. "Hey, *Andoc*."

Andoc, of course, slept on, oblivious—at least, until the wolf craned around and licked a broad stripe up his neck and over his ear.

"Whu—?" he said, and flailed upright in the bed, blinking.

"Effective," I told Senovo, and scratched him behind the ears. "I like it."

Senovo shook himself and flopped back down on the bed, panting lightly as he regarded us.

"Uh," Andoc said, as the reality of the situation percolated through his half-awake mind. "Did something happen while I was asleep?"

I shrugged. "Not that I know of. He was like this when I woke up."

"Well." Andoc reached over and ran hand down the length of Senovo's furry spine. "That's new. Good morning, Fur Ball."

The wolf arched into the contact and squirmed, rolling over to expose its neck and belly. Andoc obligingly scratched the finer hair growing there, and was rewarded by one hind leg circling madly in the air with small, involuntary movements.

"With everything I've seen in the past few months, I *still* have to convince myself it's not a dream sometimes," I said.

"It's been years for me, but I know exactly what you mean," Andoc said. "You know, he shifted a couple of times during the journey back to Draebard when we were transporting the two of you from the hill fort."

I looked down at the predator lying on its back between us, paws waving in the air like a puppy. "I thought maybe I'd dreamt that part."

Andoc shook his head. "At the time, I put it down to him being injured, and more than a little frantic over you."

The wolf's body twisted, and suddenly Andoc's hand was resting on Senovo's hairless human ribcage, over his heart. I covered it with mine, my attention immediately focused on the man lying between us. Senovo held his breath, his eyes staring at the rafters as the gray of predawn filtered into the room. I could feel his heart racing beneath our joined hands, but he exhaled in a drawn out sigh, and the frantic fluttering began to slow.

Senovo swallowed, his throat bobbing up and down before he spoke. "Complex emotions are… *simpler*, for the wolf. He cares only for what is, in the moment, not for what was or what might be." Andoc and I moved in tandem to wrap him in our arms. He shivered once, and relaxed into the embrace. "The more often I change, the easier it becomes. Last night, I woke, plagued with worries about the future, and could not return to sleep. You were here, and it was safe, so I shifted."

"You understood what we were talking about," I said with wonder. "Just now, I mean."

Senovo nodded hesitantly. "When the wolf is calm, I can understand more."

"And you're all right?" Andoc said. "Changing back hasn't made you sick?"

"Not sick, no. Merely a bit disoriented, but it's fading quickly." Senovo cleared his throat. "However, I am sorry if I startled either of you. I shouldn't have changed like that without warning you both first."

"Don't be stupid," Andoc said. "The wolf has been my friend for as long as you have."

"Same," I said. "Besides, now we have another way to wake Andoc up. That was even more entertaining to watch than the cold water."

Andoc reached across Senovo's body to shove me, and things quickly devolved into poking and tickling until Senovo groaned in disgust and kicked us both out of bed. We both made a point of watching him carefully as we readied ourselves for the day, but he honestly did seem to be all right—more rested and centered than he had been since before the meeting the previous morning.

I had scarcely arrived at the pens when the Rhytheeri ambassadors called for their horses and headed out, shortly after the sun rose. No doubt they were eager to get to their next port of call, and perhaps they were also smart enough to know that they had gained no friends in Draebard during their brief visit.

The next few days were quiet, though the mood in the village was subdued. I split my time between my regular duties and working on archery, missing Keenan's vibrant presence whenever I had a question about technique or theory. Eventually, I sent a request into town for Balzoc to come join me. Andoc had mentioned that he was Draebard's most talented archer, though I knew him to be something less than a competent horseman.

Not for the first time, I thought it might be beneficial to arrange more structured horsemanship training for some of the warriors. Draebard's reliance on chariots for battle meant that those, like Andoc, who hadn't grown up riding saw no real need to gain more than a basic proficiency at it—and that was a weakness that could use correcting.

To my surprise, when Balzoc arrived the morning after my message, he had New Boy in tow. New Boy—who now sported a nasty, half-healed cut on his left cheek, and whose name was apparently Zolis—was allegedly good with a bow and had grown up around horses.

"Balzoc told me what you and that Mereni hell-cat were doing over here," he said, a sullen note in his voice. "He thought maybe I could help."

I shrugged and showed him the recurve bow as I explained the different possibilities we'd been exploring. His eyes lit up as he examined the graceful composite shape, pulling back the bowstring to test the draw weight. Balzoc looked on, nodding and offering suggestions at intervals as we talked. An hour later, Zolis was mounted on the gray colt, trotting back and forth down the alleyway we'd designated for archery practice and testing out different techniques for shooting.

"Looks like your mounted archery team just grew by one," Balzoc observed.

"So it seems," I agreed. "I don't suppose you've got any more like him hidden away?"

Balzoc laughed. "I'll ask around," he said.

⤚ 🐚 ⤙

Keenan returned six days after she and Ciero had left, along with Leader Magoldis, a couple of gray-haired elders, and a small contingent of warriors. I was just finishing up for the day when the group rode in and dismounted, handing their horses off to the apprentices who came hurrying forward to take them.

"Horse Mistress," the Mereni Leader greeted as I strode up to the visitors.

"Hi, Carivel," Keenan said. "We figured we'd drop the horses off with you and make our way into town on foot."

"Of course," I said. "Welcome, all of you. I'll be happy to escort you." I turned to see who was still around, and gestured to Lundis. "Lundis, run into the village and see if you can find the Chief, or, failing that, Andoc or Senovo. Tell them I'm bringing Leader Magoldis and her party to the meeting hall."

Lundis nodded, wide-eyed, and hared off.

The rest of us followed at a more sedate pace. "Have you eaten?" I asked, feeling a flash of humor at the thought that Andoc must be rubbing off on me. "I can have something brought over for you."

"We stopped earlier for a meal on the road," said a short, elderly woman with deep laugh lines wrinkling her face. I recognized her vaguely from our visit to Meren. "However, if there is any possibility of a hot bath to soak the travel stiffness out of my back, it would be much appreciated."

"I'll ask at the temple," I told her. "I'm sure something can be arranged."

"Not sure what you were thinking, Briethe," Magoldis said under her breath. "Rhyth is still six days' hard ride from here."

"I was thinking I'd ask for a hot bath when we got to Rhyth, as well," Briethe replied with a twinkle in her eye. I hid my smile, liking her immediately.

I glanced back to Magoldis. "You're attending the King's meeting, then?" I asked.

"Well," said the red-haired Leader, "we didn't stage this visit solely so I could have another joyful reunion with old Volya."

As we approached the meeting hall, we met the Chief coming from the direction of the cookhouse.

"And so, my night is complete," he said by way of greeting.

"Good to see you, too," Magoldis said in a dry voice.

"Where are Andoc and Senovo?" I asked, and Volya turned an irritated eye my way. "Well," he said slowly, as if I was a simpleton, "seeing as how Senovo is the High Priest, I would imagine he's in the temple. And as Andoc is your husband, I'm sure that if you don't know where he is, I certainly have no idea."

I gritted my teeth, a muscle working at the corner of my jaw as I pasted on a smile. "Of course," I said. "How foolish of me. I'll just go and get them for you."

Pivoting, I headed off toward the temple under the sharp gazes of Keenan and Magoldis, both of whom looked deeply unimpressed by the entire exchange. When I arrived, I waylaid Crenelo and asked if he could prepare a hot bath for any in the Mereni delegation who had need of it later. I ran Senovo to ground in the altar room, where he was comforting a distraught woman who I'd heard had recently had a miscarriage.

I silently backed out, and stood waiting around the corner from the entrance until he was through.

"Magoldis and a contingent from Meren are here," I told him when he came out a few minutes later and greeted me with a questioning gaze. "They're alone with Volya at the meeting hall."

"Where is Andoc?" Senovo asked, as we both headed toward the entrance, intent on getting back to the visitors before any blood was shed.

"I'd hoped he was here," I said, "but apparently not."

As luck would have it, we ran into Andoc as we were going and turned him around, hustling him along with us.

"What's going on?" he asked, allowing himself to be hustled.

"Volya is in the meeting hall with Magoldis," I said succinctly.

"Right," Andoc replied, and lengthened his stride.

When we arrived, it was to find an uneasy detente.

"Magoldis here was just suggesting that we all travel to Rhyth together," the Draebardi Chief said. "It makes a kind of sense, I suppose."

All three of us relaxed minutely.

"Hope you left Meren under tight guard, woman," Volya continued. "I don't trust these southern scum as far as I can throw 'em."

"Of course I did, old man. There are no reports about any more Alyrion outposts this far north, but after what happened here in Draebard, I'd have to be a fool to take any chances. I think, if anything, *we're* going to be the ones at more risk." Magoldis curled her lip. "A meeting with most of the northern chiefs present is as much of an opportunity for the Empire as it is for us."

I shivered a bit at the implication.

"Then it will be good for us to stick together," Andoc said. "Strength in numbers."

"My thoughts exactly," said Leader Magoldis.

Over the following days, final arrangements were made for guarding the village in Volya's absence, and for the makeup of the Draebardi delegation. In addition to Andoc, Volya was taking Jacun, along with two younger warriors I didn't know well—Guldarok and Deven. Senovo was also attending, as, somewhat to my surprise, was I. As a final addition, Senovo had suggested that Favian join us, using the argument that his experience with horses would make him useful during the journey, and that he could act as a runner to take messages back and forth at the meetings in Rhyth.

I suspected there was something Senovo was not saying, but when I pressed him, he merely replied that he thought Favian's presence could be helpful to us.

Our departure fell one week before the meetings were due to begin. Ambassador Derenza had left detailed directions to the meeting site, along with a rectangular section of hide covered in odd markings and so thinly scraped that it was nearly transparent, which Volya was to present upon our arrival. Magoldis had received a similar object.

Senovo and Eiridan had studied the marked hides with fascination, theorizing that they were a method of communicating information—similar to the tally marks that I might use to keep track of supplies or mark out days, but more advanced somehow. I had taken a look out of curiosity. I could see that some of the markings might be construed to represent a human figure or a stylized building, but I confess I could make nothing of it beyond that.

As Horse Mistress, it fell to me to organize most of the logistics of our travel over such a long distance. After thinking on it and experimenting a bit with different pack configurations, I settled on traveling with a dozen horses—eight riding horses and four to carry supplies. A wagon would have been better, but consultation with Andoc made it clear that getting a wagon across the mountain pass would be impractical.

So it was that nineteen people—Draebardi and Mereni— rode out with the early morning sun rising off to our left, heading south down the road that led to the logging forests. The last time I had been this way, Senovo and I were attacked and kidnapped. I watched Senovo closely, feeling my own heart beating with irrational nervousness, but could see no indication that our surroundings caused him any concern.

I looked around at the warriors surrounding us—a well-armed, well-supplied contingent of fierce fighters who would guard us with their lives, if necessary—and told myself, very firmly, that this time things would be completely different.

FIVE

I had never traveled with such a large group before — well, not unless you counted the two-day trip back from the hill fort after our rescue, which I'd spent being mostly insensible in the back of a wagon. Other than that, I had only ever traveled with my father when I was a young child, by myself when I fled my village to eventually settle in Draebard, and with Andoc and Senovo on the journey to Meren.

It was slower this way, for one thing. The packhorses limited how fast we could move, and it seemed that someone was always needing to stop for a rest or some food or to take a leak. To make up for the relatively sluggish pace, Volya and Magoldis had us start early in the morning and ride until darkness made further travel unsafe.

Rhyth, I gathered, was six days' solid riding, and the meetings were seven days away when we left. I was caught between dread and excitement about the journey. I had always loved seeing new places and getting out into the wild parts of Eburos, but the thought of being in the place where Senovo had been sold and kept as a slave for almost half of his life made my gut churn.

For his part, the priest was quiet and tense, his interactions with our fellow travelers calm, but cloaked in the careful distance that meant he was walling himself off from the world as a means of self-protection. It hurt my chest to watch it.

Andoc was keeping a careful eye on Senovo as well, I knew, and I was not surprised when he suggested we share a tent with Senovo and Favian on the first night. Since Andoc and I were handfasted, Senovo was a eunuch and Favian, just a boy, no one objected or thought much of it. Even so, it was frustrating not to be able to wrap Senovo up in our arms and make him forget his worries.

The next morning, I woke to find that Andoc had rolled over in his sleep and flopped an arm against Senovo's chest during the night, while Favian had unconsciously scooted closer on his other side until he was pressed up against his mentor's shoulder. Senovo slept on, oblivious, but the pressure around my heart eased a bit.

The forested hills immediately south of Draebard gave way to dry, flat front-range on the morning of the second day, and we had our first clear view of the southern mountains. They ran right across the narrow section of Eburos that separated the north from the south. On both the eastern and western coasts, the range ended in cliffs overlooking the sea—a formidable barrier for anyone attempting to reach the island by ship.

We were heading for the western pass through the mountains, which was the closest route to Draebard. There was also a crossing further east, and those two trails marked the only easy way to travel from the north to the south.

And, of course, the term *easy* was relative. This stretch of the mountain range was not tall enough to rise much above the tree line, though we could see mightier peaks in the distance, snow-capped at the top, even though it was the height of summer. Still, the trail through the pass appeared steep and rocky from our vantage point, and as we approached the foothills I could see why Andoc had argued against bringing a wagon.

I wondered if anyone here besides Senovo had ever been this way before. Then I thought about Senovo—seventeen years old, injured, with no supplies of any kind—traveling on foot over the challenging trail ahead of us, and abruptly wished that I hadn't.

We were near the rear of the group, and I was startled from my somber thoughts by a gasp off to my right as we rounded a bend, the vista of steep slopes opening out in front of us. I looked around to find that Favian had reined his horse to a halt and was staring at the mountains with his mouth open. All the blood had drained from his face, leaving his complexion deathly gray.

"Favian?" I asked, turning Kekenu back to join him.

My voice got Andoc and Senovo's attention, along with Keenan and another Mereni warrior who was riding nearby. Favian did not respond, his attention still fixed on the landscape ahead of us. Andoc gave him one glance and whistled shrilly, gaining the attention of the rest of the group before they got too far ahead.

Favian wavered in the saddle, and before I could do more than grab for the boy's reins, Senovo was off his horse, rushing forward to steady him and ease him down from his mount's back. Favian's knees wobbled and failed to hold him for a moment. Senovo supported him with an arm around his shoulders as Andoc dismounted and joined them.

"Favian," Senovo said, and something in his tone raised the fine hairs on the back of my neck. "Tell us what is wrong."

My former apprentice looked from one to the other of us, his eyes wide with horror.

"Elder Brother," he said, finally fixing his frantic gaze on Senovo and clutching at his white robes, "it's the mountain. *It's the same mountain!*"

Senovo's expression was grim, but showed none of the same shock that I knew must be obvious in mine.

Andoc just looked confused. "What mountain is this you're talking about?"

I spoke up when Favian just shook his head. "Favian had a fever dream when he was ill, about a mountain range on fire and people dying in the flames."

"They were screaming," Favian whispered, his eyes once again locked on the slopes we were about to traverse.

Andoc's brows drew together. "And it was this mountain range? You're certain?"

"I've never been here before, but it's the very same," Favian said, looking as though he was near to tears. Around us, the others were returning, with various expressions of impatience and curiosity.

"What's all this?" Volya asked. "Something wrong with the boy?"

Senovo inhaled deeply, and I could almost see his mind turning the situation over. When he spoke, his voice was unruffled. "Favian was quite ill recently. I believe it's just a moment's weakness. Give us a minute or two and we'll be ready to continue."

The Chief frowned. "I seem to recall that bringing him along was your idea, High Priest. Perhaps you should have thought of that before dragging him halfway across the island with us."

"No doubt you are correct, Chief Volya," Senovo said easily. "We'll just get him back on his horse and be along in a moment."

Volya grumbled something uncomplimentary under his breath and reined his horse around, heading toward the mountains once more. The others followed, leaving Andoc, Senovo and I gathered around Favian.

"I'm sorry," Favian said in a small voice. "I didn't mean to cause trouble."

"There's no cause for concern, Little Brother," Senovo said, crouching down in front of Favian to search his face. "Now, quickly, tell me one thing. In your dream, you were not trapped in the fire yourself? You were watching it from some distance away?"

Favian swallowed hard. "Yes, Elder Brother. I was seeing it from right here, where we are now. But the flames were up on the slopes."

Senovo squeezed his arms briskly and stood. "Very well. There is nothing to fear, Favian, I promise you. Only let's get you mounted again and catch up with the others, shall we? I wouldn't want us to be left behind."

I swallowed the questions I wanted to ask, and held Favian's mount steady while Andoc helped the boy clamber up into the saddle in his awkward acolyte's robes. I did not miss the speaking look that Andoc gave Senovo afterward, or the small, negative shake of the head he received in return.

As the day wore on, the terrain grew more challenging. The air was thin and crisp as we climbed higher, but I grew increasingly tired even though I was not exerting myself to any great degree. In addition, my head was starting to pound. I thought at first it was just me, but others around me were flagging as well. The elders, in particular, seemed to struggle more the higher we rode.

Even so, the view when we finally reached the top of the pass was something I would never forget. Behind us, Draebard's lands lay spread out like a banquet—familiar landmarks seen from an unfamiliar perspective. Ahead of us, the mysterious lands of the Rhytheeri beckoned, strange and new.

We camped on the side of the mountain that night. The temperature dropped rapidly, shocking me with how cold it got considering the time of year. My ignorance of the mountain's conditions meant that I had not packed warm clothing or additional blankets, and there was a fair bit of grumbling as the riding party stoked the fires and split into groups to huddle together inside our tents.

"You weren't to know how cold it would be here," Andoc comforted. "I certainly didn't."

"It's my fault, really," Senovo added. "I've been across the mountains before. I should have mentioned the chilly nights."

Somehow I sincerely doubted that Senovo had carried warm furs along with him on his flight from the Rhytheeri, and thinking about him shivering his way through the night, alone and in pain, made me feel even worse. The only saving grace was that the four of us spent the night in a comfortable tangle, sharing body heat, though Favian's presence obviously prevented us from engaging in anything more intimate.

In the morning, the wind whistled sharply down from the peaks. Even so, once the sun came up, its rays warmed us quickly—Deresta's gift to her children. The older members of the party in particular moved slowly, but they still *moved*.

We descended carefully from the heights, letting the horses pick their way along the rocky trail at their own pace. As we reached the southern foothills and left the mountains behind, I could see Favian visibly relaxing. At the same time, whatever aspect of the upland air that had so drained us of energy began to lose its grip.

I looked around, trying to ignore what I knew of the people who lived in this part of the world and focus on the land itself. The south was considerably different than what I'd grown up with. Though the foothills here exhibited the same evidence of burgeoning drought as our northern lands, the view from the hill we were currently cresting showed a patchwork of green and gold around the twisting course of a large river. It was as if someone had planted giant garden plots the size of livestock pastures along the river's banks, each filled with only one kind of plant.

It seemed to me a rather odd thing to do, but from what I could see, the Rhytheeri had done it on an almost unimaginable scale. Had people really cleared that much land and painstakingly planted it with individual seeds? Were they actively going through and pulling up the other plants that tried to grow, to achieve the striking uniformity I saw before me? What was the point?

I wanted to ask Senovo, but Senovo had grown pale and withdrawn ever since we descended the southern slope of the mountain range. I did not think he would thank me right now for asking him to recall more about his childhood home.

That night, we camped in a patch of trees near an oxbow lake. By Ambassador Derenza's description, this marked the rough halfway point in our journey — three days' ride behind us and three days' ride ahead. Senovo picked at his food under Andoc's watchful gaze, and said little. The mild weather prompted our motley contingent to forego tents, and I chafed at the knowledge that sleeping in the open would make it impossible to offer Senovo any sort of comfort during the night.

I chafed, that is, until the priest looked up and caught Favian's eye.

"Little Brother," he said. "I feel the need to commune with the spirit of the wolf tonight. Will it frighten you if I take his form?"

Favian's eyes were wide and fascinated in the firelight. "Of course not, Elder Brother. I would be honored to spend time in the presence of the wolf. Is there anything I need to do, or..."

Senovo smiled — the first I had seen from him in some time. "No, Favian, you don't need to do a thing. Should you have need of anything, ask Andoc or Carivel, and they will help you."

Favian nodded, his head bobbing up and down almost comically. One corner of Senovo's lips was still upturned in amusement, but his eyes when he looked over at Andoc and myself were filled with pain. He dropped into a crouch, and a moment later the wolf shook off his white robes. Favian gasped sharply, but moved almost immediately to pick up the robes and fold them neatly over a fallen branch.

Silence fell around the campsite. When I glanced around, almost everyone was staring, though there was no hostility — only captivated interest. Senovo stared back with shining yellow-green eyes, and slunk around the fire to curl up at Andoc's feet.

"Well, well," said Leader Magoldis, who had paused in a discussion with Elder Briethe upon noticing Senovo's transformation.

A radiant smile brightened Briethe's wrinkled features. "The Old Magic walks among us tonight, my friends," she said, watching the wolf with shining eyes. "Truly, we are honored by the gods."

Several of the people here had seen the wolf before, but several others hadn't. Volya was watching Senovo with a speculative expression, and I could almost see him thinking of ways that he might best utilize his High Priest's gift to further his own power and influence. Most of the warriors appeared impressed, but not surprised or alarmed. Magoldis leaned back after a moment and sipped her wine, returning her attention to the silver-haired elder sitting next to her.

"You've met a shape-shifter once before, Briethe, have you not?" she asked.

Briethe's smile softened; became wistful. "I have. I met Lorish before she disappeared into the wildlands east of here."

"She's the one who could turn into a fox, right?" asked Keenan, who was lounging nearby.

Briethe nodded. "Little slip of a thing, she was. We were both young when I met her." The elder's expression turned troubled. "The Rhytheeri priests were trying to get her locked away, you see. They couldn't very well bring a girl into the priesthood, and I think they were afraid of having that kind of power running free, outside their control. So she fled. I've often wondered if she's still alive out there somewhere."

As Briethe spoke, Senovo crept forward along the ground until he could rest his muzzle across the toe of my boot while still leaning his haunches against Andoc's leg. I reached down and scratched his head absently.

"You've been to Rhyth before, then, Elder Briethe?" I asked.

"Oh, *yes*, dear." The old woman let out a rueful laugh. "I didn't tag along on this trip for my health, believe me."

"Briethe's father had quite an active trade partnership with some of the port masters along the southern coast," Leader Magoldis said. "Back when there was more commerce between the north and the south than there is today."

"My mother and I used to travel with him sometimes when he would go to negotiate new trade deals," Briethe said. "Though we tended to journey by water rather than by land. Much easier, in my opinion. Those mountains are positively brutal on old bones."

I rubbed one of Senovo's ears and thought idly about a woman living a lifetime in the wildlands as a vixen. There had been a time, before Andoc and Senovo, when I'd have jumped at the chance to become a horse, living free in a herd like Kekenu had been doing when I found him. Was Lorish lonely, though? Did she have other foxes for company, or did she still miss people?

Senovo whined and twisted his head to the side as my fingernails found exactly the right spot behind his ear. Gradually, everyone went back to what they'd been doing, sparing only the occasional glance in our direction. When the attention focused on him waned, the wolf relaxed a bit more and unglued himself from our sides.

Favian, who had been trying valiantly not to stare, offered Senovo a piece of dried meat from the rations he had been picking at earlier. His smile when the animal sniffed at him for a moment and delicately took the morsel from his hand rivaled the full moon in its glow. After that initial overture, the wolf seemed content to settle next to the boy and finish his meal, even going so far as to trot down to the edge of the lake alone and slake his thirst afterward.

While he was gone, Keenan sidled up to us. "I still can't quite get over that," she said.

"I'm with you there," I replied. "It really is something, isn't it?"

The wolf paused outside the circle of firelight, glowing eyes fixed on the new arrival.

"Should I leave?" Keenan asked.

Andoc shook his head. "No, Keenan, you're fine." He gestured to the wolf, stretching out a hand, palm up. "Come on, Fur Ball. Keenan's a friend, you know that."

Senovo sniffed the air for a moment and returned to us, slotting his body in between our legs as we sat propped against a downed log.

Keenan smiled at him, but made no move to get closer or touch him. "Looks like I finally get to meet you properly, eh?"

The wolf's tail thumped against Andoc's boot.

"You three are close," Keenan observed.

"Yes," I agreed. There was no point in denying it. Keenan had seen more than most, and as Andoc had said, she was a friend. She had been there when Andoc fell to his knees between us and kissed us during our reunion after the battle at the hill fort. She'd seen me delirious with pain and fever, calling Senovo's name, begging the Healer to help him. If she hadn't figured out the truth by now, she must have a pretty good idea at the very least.

"He's lucky to have you both," Keenan said softly.

"We're lucky to have him," Andoc replied without hesitation.

The following day was quiet as we rode through the fertile lowlands, detouring around boggy areas that persisted near the river despite the lack of rain. Again, Senovo changed into the wolf after we set up camp. He spent the night curled up at our feet, happily accepting handouts from Favian and allowing a fascinated Keenan to stroke the soft fur covering his forehead.

The day after that, we began to run into people as we entered the area of strange, patchwork crops that I'd seen from the foothills. The fields were dotted with little settlements—not even villages, just small collections of huts. It took me longer than it should have to realize that these small hovels housed the slaves that worked the cropland, each group managed by an overseer or two.

When I finally noticed the collars on the necks of the thin, stooped figures hoeing the dirt and pulling weeds amidst the amber grain, the bottom dropped out of my stomach. My eyes flew to Senovo, who was staring straight ahead, his expression as pale and still as polished marble. Beside me, Andoc's jaw was tight, a muscle working at one corner as he ground his teeth silently.

We rode on. Smaller rivers joined the one we were following, the resulting watercourse widening to the point that it was difficult to make out details on the other side. At the crossing of one such tributary, someone had built a bridge of huge planks, resting on piles of stone placed at regular intervals in the water. Our group halted and I eyed the odd construction nervously. I had never heard of trying to take horses across such a thing, and could only imagine the disaster that would occur should the planks give way when we were halfway across.

Briethe rode forward to the edge. "It's all right," she said. "These things are surprisingly sturdy. We should probably only cross one or two at a time, but it's quite a bit safer than trying to ford a river this deep on horseback."

"You heard the Elder," Magoldis said. Living up to her title of *Leader*, she eased her nervous mount past Briethe's and urged it onto the wood. The mare danced backward, but a solid kick had it leaping forward onto the bridge. It pranced sideways, trying to run as its hoof beats echoed strangely beneath it. Magoldis reined the mare in tightly, though, and they reached the other side without mishap.

"It's fine!" she called, waving a hand to beckon the rest of us to follow her.

Briethe went next, her phlegmatic old gelding stepping onto the planks with only minimal hesitation. Volya followed, and I had a quick look around to determine how best to get the packhorses across, pairing them with lighter riders like Favian and myself to minimize the amount of weight crossing at once.

With some of the animals balking at the unfamiliar footing, it took us a long time for everyone to get across. I was the last, with Kekenu lifting his feet comically high and setting them down daintily on the echoing wood, the last packhorse sticking close to his haunches and snorting nervously. It was nerve-wracking, but when we were all on the other side, our supplies were still dry, as were we—not something we would have been able to boast, had we been forced to swim the horses across.

On this side of the river, there were more people. The track became a road, and we met occasional travelers coming or going, though they gave our large, armed party a wide berth for the most part. The sun was hanging low on the horizon and our leaders were looking for a likely campsite for the night when we heard screaming.

Andoc, Senovo, and several of the warriors whirled their horses around, searching the field we'd just ridden past for the source of the cry. When Keenan spurred her horse forward into a gallop and plunged into the waist-high grain, Senovo, Andoc, and I followed her without a thought.

My heart was in my throat. Ahead of us, a large man with bulging muscles and fine clothing lifted a vicious-looking whip over his head, poised to bring it down across the back of a cowering girl not much older than Favian. Perhaps a dozen other slaves stood arrayed in a half-circle, some distance back from the overseer. Some of them clutched each other in fear, others looked on blankly with dead, sunken eyes in bony faces.

The man with the whip looked up at the sound of approaching hoof beats, a sneer still etched across his sun-lined face.

"Stop right there!" Keenan ordered, reining to a halt and nocking an arrow into her recurve bow as she steadied her mount with her knees. Andoc was only a moment behind, swinging down from the saddle and handing me his reins with a smooth movement. Andoc's sword scraped ominously as he drew it from his belt and stalked toward the overseer, careful to keep out of Keenan's line of fire.

"Back away from the girl," Andoc said.

The overseer lowered his whip and took a single step back. Beside me, Senovo dismounted, and I took his horse as well.

"What is the meaning of this?" the overseer demanded in the same heavy accent as Ambassador Derenza and the men who had abducted me and Senovo from the woods. "What business of yours is this? A barbarian, a woman, a priest, and a beardless boy?"

"I might be a barbarian," Andoc said, "but if you think I'm going to let you whip a little girl bloody, you're even stupider than you look."

"How dare you! These slaves are the property of Master Iaden of the Five Lakes! Set yourself against me, and you set yourself against him."

Keenan drew the arrow back another fraction and sighted down it. "Wow. That would probably sound really impressive if we had any idea whatsoever who this *Master* Iaden was," she said dryly, her aim never faltering.

The girl who had been cringing on the ground started to crawl away toward the other slaves, trying to put more distance between herself and her tormenter. With a cry of rage, the overseer lifted the whip again. Before it could fall, though, an angry wolf appeared between them, ears flat back against its head and lips curled in a dangerous snarl.

SIX

The pair of horses I was holding spooked and the man staggered back in shock, blood draining from his face. Several of the slaves cried out and pointed, talking excitedly among themselves.

"*Lupiandas! Lupiandas!*" I heard them saying.

The girl had fallen backwards onto the ground, her mouth open as she stared at the large animal standing protectively in front of her. She righted herself and crawled forward, wrapping her arms around the wolf's bristling shoulders fearlessly.

"*Lupi?*" she asked. "The gods have finally sent you for us, after so long?" Tears were spilling down her cheeks.

The wolf allowed the embrace, continuing to hold the overseer at bay with bared teeth and a sinister growl. Behind me, I heard the rest of our party approaching. In the chaos of approaching riders, one of the slaves darted forward and snatched the girl away from Senovo. Several of them ran, disappearing into the taller crops as they made for the woods at the edge of the field. A few stayed behind, looking lost and helpless.

Magoldis and Volya dismounted, striding forward side-by-side to confront the overseer. "What is going on here?" Volya demanded.

With the overseer's victim gone and enough people confronting him that he would not dare to attempt physical retaliation, Andoc sheathed his sword and stepped forward to place a hand on the nape of Senovo's neck. The wolf subsided with a final rumble of warning.

Keenan lowered her bow and arrow as she replied, "This man was whipping a child. We stopped him."

"I was *disciplining* a *slave*," the man said with a snarl.

Briethe rode forward, her spine straight in the saddle. "And does your employer know that you are starving and abusing his property?" she asked, as haughty as any ruler.

"My employer leaves all decisions about these slaves to *me*," he boasted. "He has no time for such details."

"And in doing so, he allows you to lose him money!" Briethe snapped. "Would he tolerate such treatment of his horses? His oxen?"

The overseer flushed red. "I will not take slander from the mouth of an old woman! You are the ones who have cost him money—his slaves have escaped thanks to you!"

Senovo growled again and strained against Andoc's grip. The overseer's eyes flickered back to the wolf. Nervous sweat beaded his brow.

"You," he said, "and this *unnatural animal*."

"So drag us before the magistrate, in that case," Briethe told him. "Good luck with that, by the way."

"Come," Magoldis said, gesturing imperiously for everyone to remount and make ready to leave. "We still have far to travel."

Andoc guided the wolf away with a firm hand. "Time to go, old friend. We're finished here."

We left the overseer cursing behind us and rode hard as the sun slipped beneath the horizon, wanting to put some space between our group and anyone the man might conceivably round up to come after us. The wolf loped along beside Kekenu. When we finally found a dense stand of trees where we could camp, it was nearly full dark, so we put up tents by the light of a fire kept small to avoid drawing unwanted attention.

As we were eating, Volya walked over and dropped a heavy hand on Andoc's shoulder. The wolf raised its head at his approach, abruptly watchful.

"You can't protect every slave in the southern lands, lad," Volya said, not unkindly. "Keep trying, and you're likely to get someone killed."

I swallowed. Andoc did not answer. Eventually, Volya shook his head and left us alone. A moment later, we heard him organizing a night watch to warn us should anyone approach.

"Favian," Andoc said, "could you give Carivel and me a bit of time alone in the tent with Senovo? Sometimes when the wolf is unsettled, it makes the transition back into his human form... difficult. I think he'd worry that seeing it firsthand would upset you."

Favian digested this for a moment, and nodded. "All right. Could you tell him for me that what he did — what you all did — made me proud to be Draebardi?"

The wolf was watching Favian with wide, amber eyes. Andoc reached forward and clasped the boy's shoulder briefly. "You just did, lad," he said.

I followed Andoc and Senovo into our tent silently, still deeply troubled by what we'd seen. Andoc drew me into an embrace. I let myself sag against him for a moment, glad that he did not seem to feel the need for words. The wolf crawled into our laps, nosing his way between us until our embrace encompassed him, too.

"I'm sorry, Senovo," I whispered. "I'm so sorry. You should never have had to come back here."

The wolf shuddered, and we were holding Senovo, naked and human. He gasped, clutching at our arms, trying to catch his breath. "They'll kill her," he rasped into Andoc's shoulder. "If they catch her — if they catch any of them — they're as good as dead."

"They didn't catch you," Andoc said, pressing both of us close.

Senovo's chest convulsed and began to hitch rhythmically under our hands — silently weeping.

"You did the best you could," I said, my own voice none too steady. "She has a chance now. They all have a chance. They didn't, before."

Senovo shook his head as if in negation, but the noiseless convulsions gradually slowed to a standstill. The three of us held each other for a long time. Eventually, I eased myself out of the embrace.

"Stay here," I ordered. "I'll get your robes and let Favian know it's all right to come to bed. Do either of you need anything? Food? Drink?"

"Thank you, *caradi*," Andoc said. "I think we're good now."

Fortunately, someone had bundled up Senovo's discarded clothing as we left the overseer's field. I left his boots and breeches where they were, grabbing the white robes and beckoning to Favian. Once Senovo was dressed, we all crawled inside.

"Are you all right, Elder Brother?" Favian asked in a small, tentative voice.

"Yes, Favian," Senovo answered, his own voice hoarse. "I was upset by what we saw, but I'm all right."

"This is a horrible place," said the boy. "I wish we didn't have to be here."

I heard Senovo's throat click as he swallowed. We were silent after Favian's youthful pronouncement, unable to argue the sentiment. The acolyte curled up on Senovo's far side, grasping his mentor's upper arm. I reached across and ruffled my hand through Favian's hair in wordless reassurance before settling on Senovo's other side. My hand came to rest on his chest, over his heart, as Andoc curled around me from behind.

Sleep was a long time coming.

⁂

We arrived in Rhyth the next day. I'd had no real sense or understanding of the scale of the place—where I had expected something on the order of Meren, or perhaps a bit bigger, there was in fact, a vast, sprawling collection of roads, houses, buildings made of stone and wood, pens of animals, market stalls, tents, lean-tos, and more people crowding the streets than I had seen in my entire life. The smell as we made our way deeper into the city was indescribable. It formed an impenetrable miasma of rancid body odor, human and animal waste, smoke, rot, and cooking food that seemed to cling to the skin.

I had absolutely nothing to compare it to.

My awe as I came to grasp the sheer size of the place quickly gave way to discomfort. Though I was traveling with a large group, I felt exposed. People stared at us as if we were some sort of exotic display, with our strange clothes and weapons. It was even worse when I first noticed the Alyrion soldiers walking through the crowds, patrolling the streets in twos and threes. Instantly, I was thrown back to the hill fort.

This is different, I reminded myself over and over. *This is different.*

I was with a large group. We'd been invited here, not captured. My lips moved as I murmured Utarr's prayer under my breath.

All who seek shelter shall find it.

All who grieve shall be comforted.

All the gods' children will receive solace.
Ask at the temple and gain the help you need.
All who seek shelter shall find it.
All who grieve shall be comforted...

The sights, sounds, and smells buffeted me, leaving me dizzy and nauseated. It was all I could do to follow the rider in front of me and keep the rope I was holding to lead the packhorse from slipping from my numb fingers. I had no conception of the passing of time.

A hand closed on my upper arm and I flinched, a gasp escaping my lips. It was Andoc, reaching across from his own horse and calling my name as if he'd been trying to get my attention for a while. I blinked back into awareness of my surroundings. We had arrived at a part of the city where the air was fresher. Trees, shrubs, and flowers grew in a vast courtyard, and ahead of us stood the largest manmade structure I had ever seen.

"Are you all right?" Andoc asked. "We're almost there."

I nodded, and stared at the massive stone building that rose before us. I had always considered the temple in Draebard to be an exceptionally large building, designed to house a score of priests as well as accommodating the religious and spiritual needs of the tribe. This was on a *completely* different scale. I simply could not conceive of quarrying so much stone and hauling it to one place, or stacking it so high without fearing that the whole thing would collapse in on itself from its own weight.

It was, in a word, astonishing.

"Have you ever seen anything like this before?" I asked Andoc after wetting my dry mouth enough to speak.

"Never," he said. "Kind of puts a whole new perspective on things, doesn't it?"

I could only shake my head, at a loss.

The wide, flagstone road leading up to the front gate was lined at intervals with pairs of guards—Eburosi, not Alyrion—who watched us pass with impassive eyes, their heavy staves held at their sides in readiness.

Volya and Magoldis, riding at the front, approached the massive wooden gates leading inside the building. The entrance was easily as wide and tall as the gates Senovo and I had been taken through at the... at the hill fort. I looked up and saw more guards patrolling back and forth along the tops of the wide stone walls, far above my head.

Our group reined to a halt, and a guard stepped forward to take the rectangular sections of marked hide from the two leaders. He examined them for a moment, nodded, and started shouting orders for the gate to be opened and attendants sent to assist us.

A faint shiver went down my spine as we rode through the gates, which closed behind us with an ominous *thud*. The building was laid out around a courtyard that was easily larger than Draebard's village green. It was mostly paved with stone, but scattered throughout the space were various fruiting and flowering trees, filling the air with perfumed scents. Entrances into the interior of the huge building dotted each of the four walls surrounding the courtyard, and arched windows were spaced at intervals, higher up. I could see people through them — apparently there were rooms built on top of other rooms, people going about their business while walking around above their neighbors' heads.

It was enough to make my own head spin.

An officious looking man approached, dressed in a flowing tunic edged with gold that draped unattractively over his round stomach.

"Greetings!" he said in a booming voice, and bowed graciously to Chief Volya. "The King of Rhyth welcomes the Chief of Draebard to his palace. And, of course, the Chief's lovely wife." He bowed to Magoldis, with a wink.

I felt my eyes grow wide, and risked a glance at Andoc, who also looked like a deer caught in the light of a hunter's torch.

The pudgy official continued, oblivious. "Now, I believe the Mereni Leader is also among your delegation…?"

I held my breath, waiting for the explosion. Magoldis, to my surprise, stayed silent, but I saw her turn her head to Chief Volya with an expression that clearly conveyed curiosity as to how he was going to handle this. The rest of the group appeared to be mired in various shades of mortification and foreboding.

Volya cleared his throat. "Yes. *She* is," he said, with poorly veiled irritation. "May I present Leader Magoldis of the Mereni?"

He gestured to his red-haired companion, and the official looked confused for a moment before recovering.

"Ah, yes, I, er, see," he said. "Please forgive me. I was not told to expect a, well, a *woman*. Welcome, Leader Magoldis, to the palace of Rhyth."

"Charmed, I'm sure," Magoldis said, and her voice could have peeled varnish from wood. I choked on a wholly inappropriate bubble of laughter and coughed to cover it. Around me, most of the Mereni were glaring at the little Rhytheeri man, and most of the Draebardi were looking deeply uncomfortable.

The official smoothed down his tunic. "Yes. Indeed. At any rate, allow us to see to your horses and take your supplies inside. We have rooms for you all."

"Where are the horses to be penned?" I asked. "They are my responsibility and I would like to be able to check on them later."

A lad standing nearby stepped forward. "They will be stabled behind the south wing," he said, and gestured toward a wall with an open doorway wide and tall enough for animals and wagons to pass through. "I will personally ensure that they are properly cooled out, fed, and watered."

I nodded, appeased, and dismounted, handing Kekenu and the packhorse over to the young man. Several other boys hurried forward to take the others' horses away as well.

"Now, if you will all follow me, I will show you to your rooms." The official smiled, his smarmy expression making my skin crawl. "I fear the rather large number of guests arriving means you will have to share, but the accommodations are spacious, so hopefully it will not be too much of a hardship."

We followed the man inside, where rich, woven tapestries hung on the walls. Smoky lamps in recessed sconces lit the areas that did not receive sufficient light from the windows. It was cool inside the thick stone walls, and again my memories drifted unbidden to the chilly larder in the hill fort. I rubbed my wrists, unconsciously chafing the places where iron shackles had rubbed the skin raw.

The official led us to a hall of rooms on the ground floor. There were ten doors, five on each side, so we split up into pairs. Senovo guided Favian toward the room next to the one

Andoc claimed for us, and I felt a tinge of disquiet at the idea of having him out of my sight.

Behind us, Briethe spoke up. "Excuse me, young man," she said to the official. "I'm sorry—I didn't catch your name. I don't suppose it would be possible to get a hot bath after our long journey. I'm afraid this old body isn't as resilient as it used to be."

The little man bowed. "Of course, Madam." He snapped his fingers, and a boy younger than Favian scrambled forward. A collar of leather and bronze circled his neck. "Boy, see to it that all of our guests have hot baths in their rooms this evening. Hop to it, now!"

The boy dipped his upper body in acknowledgement and scampered off. The feeling of suffocation returned, making me light-headed.

"We would appreciate having food and drink brought to our rooms as well," Magoldis said. "As Elder Briethe says, we have all had a long ride to get here."

The Rhytheeri man still looked uncomfortable in Magoldis' presence, but he bowed and said, "I will attend to it myself. Should you have need of anything, my name is Athodan. Ask any servant, and they will fetch me."

Scarcely had Athodan left to see to our supper when a line of young boys wearing collars trooped down the hallway, staggering a bit under the weight of the steaming buckets of water they carried. They were better fed than the slaves we'd seen working in the field, and I could see no sign of injury or bruising on any of them, but I was not surprised when Senovo said, "Come, Favian," and guided his acolyte into the room they had chosen, closing the door firmly behind him.

One of the boys fetched up at the closed doorway and bit his lip, looking worried. Andoc guided him to our door instead. "It's all right," he said. "You haven't done anything wrong. The High Priest doesn't want a hot bath right now, that's all. You can empty your bucket into our tub; you'll be done quicker that way."

The child nodded, relieved, and followed one of his compatriots into our room with his heavy burden. Andoc flopped back against the wall outside and ran a hand over his face. "Shit," he said, and I nodded.

"I need to get out of here," I told him. "I'm going to go check the horses."

"Do you want me to go with you?" he asked.

I shook my head. "No. I want you to make sure Senovo is all right. Or at least as all right as he can be, under the circumstances."

Andoc breathed out sharply through his nose and nodded. "Don't be too long," he said.

I stretched up to brush a kiss to his lips and headed back the way we came, stopping once to ask a servant for directions when I got turned around. The part of the building where the horses were kept was divided up into tiny individual pens, like a little room for each individual animal. It was, in my opinion, a horrible way to try and keep horses. Still, I supposed I could see the advantages in a situation like this where many unfamiliar animals were coming and going, including stallions and mares in heat.

It probably wouldn't do them any harm for the short period of time we would be here. I walked along the row of little pens, checking our animals over carefully. As the stable lad had promised, all had been rubbed down until they were clean and dry, with access to feed and a bucket of fresh water hanging at chest height from an iron ring in the corner. Kekenu looked up and tossed his head as I reached him, a half-chewed bunch of hay protruding from one side of his mouth.

"It's not for long," I promised him. "We'll go home soon."

On the way back, I met a group of guards coming from the other direction. One of them jostled his companions and pointed at me. "Look, it's another one. I'm starting to think the entirety of the northern hordes are coming over the mountains to Rhyth," he said. "Is that one a girl or a boy? I can't even tell."

His companions laughed and I gritted my teeth, keeping my eyes averted and skirting around them. "Not sure the northerners can tell the difference either," I heard another one say behind me as I picked up my pace. "Heard some godforsaken tribe wandered in here today with a bitch for a leader."

More laughter chased me back to the wing of rooms where Andoc and Senovo were waiting. The iron band around my ribcage—which had loosened briefly while I checked on the horses—was back, making it hard to breathe. When I opened the door to our room to find it empty except for a large metal tub full of steaming water, I felt a moment of panic before my wits returned.

Berating myself for my stupidity, I went next door to Senovo's room and found him seated at a table with Andoc and Favian, a sumptuous feast laid out before them. As my irrational bout of alarm faded, I took in for the first time the luxury of the rooms we had been given. In addition to the metal bathtubs—easily half again as big as the one in the temple in Draebard—there were also beds as large and fine as the one High Priest Rhystel had kept quietly hidden in his quarters. The hearth on the far side of the room was unlit at this time of year, but over it hung a metal hood to catch the smoke and direct it into a tube that appeared to lead outside through the wall. It was an ingenious way to prevent smoke from building up inside, since there was no opening in the ceilings of the ground floor.

More hides and tapestries hung over the cold stone walls, making the space seem cozier. The chairs were padded, with pillowed seats and backs. And the food—well, after six days of travel rations, the smell of roast meat, fresh bread, and steaming vegetables was enough to make my stomach grumble audibly.

"Join us," Andoc said, indicating a fourth chair.

I sat, and reached for food and wine. After I had sated my hunger, I slouched back into the comfortable chair. Across from me, Senovo's plate, while not exactly untouched, was still largely uneaten.

"I'm worried about you," I said, seeing no point in keeping it to myself.

"I am worried about all of us," Senovo countered. "You were very pale when you came in just now. Did something happen?"

I shook my head. "Nothing important. Apparently the Rhytheeri don't have a very good opinion of northerners, in general. Or of women."

"They think us barbarians," Senovo said. "Backwards and unintelligent. In addition, I'm sure Leader Magoldis's presence will raise eyebrows, at the very least."

"They keep slaves, and they consider *us* the barbarians?" Andoc's anger was controlled, but still obvious.

Senovo gestured to the spectacular building around us; the city beyond. "Slaves built all this. Without slave labor, Rhyth would not be so different from Meren, or Draebard, or any other place where people expect to make a livelihood with the labor of their hands."

Favian sat quietly, looking down at the table as we talked. I rested my forehead on my hand, digging my fingers into my temples to combat the headache I felt coming on.

"Go enjoy your bath, Carivel, if you are finished eating," Senovo said, his voice softening. "And, Andoc—go enjoy your bond-mate. After six days of abstinence, I imagine if I still had bollocks, they'd be aching right now just from being in the same room as the pair of you."

Favian made a faint, strangled noise of suppressed amusement—or possibly, horror—and I looked up at Senovo, searching. He was far too intelligent for his own good, and he had just neatly maneuvered us into leaving him alone for the night. Well—not *alone*, since Favian was here, but *away from us*. And, of course, he'd done so in such a way that we couldn't very well protest or talk to him about it in front of Favian.

Andoc was also staring at Senovo with drawn brows, and the silence stretched, tension growing in the room.

"Look," Favian said, after a long, uncomfortable moment, "I already know the three of you are sleeping together, all right?" When our eyes moved from Senovo to him, he blushed and looked down at the table again before adding under his breath, "It's not like you're all that subtle about it."

A matching blush crawled up my own neck, even though I'd had my suspicions that Favian saw more than most people did. Senovo recovered first. "Ah. Yes. Very well. In that case, I'll speak plainly. I am all right, but I would prefer to brood in relative solitude tonight. Please go have sex and get rid of the tension that has Carivel nearly crawling out of her own skin, and you ready to strangle the next person who looks at you sideways. I will join you another time if I can safely do so."

Andoc blew out a breath. "Fine, *amadi*, if you're sure. Though I hope we haven't just scarred your acolyte for life."

Favian scowled. "I am gonna be a priest someday, you know. Might not be old enough for that part of it yet, but I know about what people do together."

"And, on that note..." Senovo said, sounding tired.

I pushed my chair back from the table, not exactly happy about the situation, but more or less resigned. Andoc followed. We both stepped forward and kissed Senovo on the forehead, and I gave Favian's shoulder a squeeze for good measure. "You're going to be a great priest," I told him.

"Thanks," he said, still blushing.

We took our leave and went back out into the hallway. Several of the other doors were open, with the sounds of conversation or the splashing of bath water coming from within. When we entered our own room, steam was still rising gently from the tub in the corner. I stared at it, full of misgivings.

"Go on," Andoc said. "You weren't the one that asked for it, and using it doesn't mean that you support slavery. In fact, if you *don't* use it, the poor kids will have hauled all those buckets in here for nothing."

"Right. I suppose that's true," I said. Andoc's words made complete sense, though they did very little for the niggling sense of guilt lodged behind my breastbone.

I closed the door behind us and started stripping off. When large hands closed over mine, stilling them, the muscles of my shoulders and spine relaxed for the first time since we'd reached the city. A trickle of need slid into my belly and pooled there.

"Let me," Andoc said into my ear. "Senovo's a slippery bastard sometimes, but he also wasn't far wrong. After five nights lying tangled up with you in a tent and not able to touch either of you the way I wanted to, *I'm* the one in danger of crawling out of my skin."

SEVEN

$\mathscr{S}$uddenly desperate to feel Andoc's skin against mine, I twisted in his arms until I was facing him and could stretch up on tiptoes to capture his mouth. He grasped my hips and pulled me flush against him, letting me feel the hard length of his cock. The heat of his body was like a brand, even through our clothing. Needing more, I moaned into the kiss and pulled away.

"Off—get it all *off,*" I said, attacking his clothing since he wouldn't let me attack mine.

He laughed a bit and let me drag his summer tunic over his head, raising his arms to help. We fumbled the ties on each other's breeches and smallclothes, our tangled hands getting in the way as much as anything.

When the lacing finally gave way, we both stumbled around the room while trying to get our boots and trousers off without falling over. We probably looked like utter fools, but the important part was that we both ended up naked.

"Take me like you did at the handfasting," I begged, dragging him toward the ridiculously huge and ornate bed by one hand.

Andoc made a low, rumbling sound in his throat. "Thought you were going to have a bath," he said, even as he twisted me around and lifted me up to kneel on all fours at the edge of the mattress.

"I'll need it more in a few minutes," I said.

"That you will," he agreed. A large hand closed over the nape of my neck and pressed me down until my upper body was lying flush on the mattress, my arse in the air.

Andoc shoved my knees together, pressing my thighs tightly against each other so he'd have something to thrust into. Finally, he grabbed my right arm and shoved it between my legs. "Play with your cock," he ordered, "but don't come until I tell you to. Now, *stay.*"

I made an undignified whimpering noise and burrowed my fingers into my folds, seeking the small nub that was already swelling and peeking out of its hood. The warmth of Andoc's body left me, only to return a moment later. Fingers, slick with oil still warm from the lamp, delved into the space at the apex of my thighs from behind.

I steadied myself with my free arm, and moaned when Andoc grabbed my hips in both hands. His hard prick pressed into the space he had prepared, sliding along my inner lips, igniting fire in its wake. I rubbed the pads of my fingers over the head of my tiny female cock, slick now with oil and my own moisture. Pleasure flowed through my body, growing deeper and darker when one of Andoc's hands moved from my hip back to the nape of my neck, pinning me in place.

All that was missing was Senovo. I put the thought firmly aside—he was not rejecting us; he was entitled to a bit of space when he needed it. He wasn't even alone. Favian was with him, and he was right on the other side of the wall from us. He wanted us to have this.

Andoc's hips stilled, and the hand on my hip ran possessively up my side and over my breast. "It's all right, *caradi*. Just because this isn't what he wants from us tonight, he's not saying that he doesn't still need *us*," he said with eerie perception.

I rubbed my cheek against the soft furs on the bed and thrust back against him. "I know," I said. "I know."

He rolled his hips, pressing against me intimately. "Make yourself come, Carivel. Let me see you fall apart beneath me while I mark you."

I shivered and thrust back against him. The angle was awkward, but my fingers moved faster over my sensitive flesh, the forced abstinence of the last several days making my body eager and ready. Andoc pumped his hips in a lazy rhythm that sent sparks along my cunt. I burrowed my face into the bed, smelling the musk of the rich furs. It was almost a surprise when my release rose up and dragged me over the edge.

Andoc groaned and pulled out from between my thighs, his hand tightening over the back of my neck. Dimly, I was aware of the sound of flesh slapping against flesh, and a moment later, ropes of hot seed painted my back and buttocks. "*Fuck*," I gasped, the unexpected heat and delicious filth of it drawing another shuddering convulsion from my body.

My muscles gave up the fight to keep me upright, and I slithered down until my knees were hanging off the bed.

"Naloth's *balls*," Andoc said into the skin of my shoulder, half collapsing above me. One hand dragged through the mess cooling slowly on my back, spreading it around. "The things you do to me…"

My cunt clenched with a weak pulse of fresh desire, and I moaned into the bed. After resting against me for a moment, Andoc pushed upright and dragged me with him, ignoring my mumbled protest.

"Bath," he said firmly.

Right. Bath. I could do that.

We made our way somewhat unsteadily across the room, where I stepped into the tub and slid down into the water without grace. It was lovely—no longer hot, but a perfect, comfortable level of warmth for a summer evening. Eyes closed, I sank deeper, listening as Andoc dragged a heavy chair across to sit next to me.

"Good?" he asked.

"Mmhmm," I replied.

"Are you going to help me clean up as well?"

I cracked open one eye. "Get in, then. I think we'll both fit. It's even cool enough now that you won't parboil."

He smiled—sated, but with a hint of mischief. "Maybe in a bit, when I've had a few minutes to recover. For now, though, I had something else in mind."

My questioning noise was cut off when he brushed a finger—still sticky with his own release—over my lower lip. My breath caught, my sex immediately growing hot and heavy under the water. I licked the sticky smudge from my lip, rolling the bitter sea-salt taste around in my mouth. Andoc lifted his hand again, and I grasped his wrist, dragging it close so I could lick his palm and the base of his thumb, chasing more of the distinctive flavor.

He exhaled unsteadily. I hummed around his skin, laving at it with my tongue. When his palm was clean, I kissed my way up his index finger and sucked it into my mouth, fellating the digit like a cock. My body was warm—floating in the chest-high water, but still somehow weighted and sluggish with desire. It felt natural to sink deeper into the bath under the press and slide of a second finger into my mouth, so I did.

Water slid over my ears, cutting off everything except the sound of ripples against metal and my own heartbeat. My eyes were next, leaving me in pleasant, isolated darkness. A hand appeared under the back of my head an instant before I would have slipped under completely, supporting my nose and mouth above the water line. Tiny waves lapped at the edges of my lips, still wrapped around Andoc's fingers as I licked the release from them.

I was surrounded by the smell and taste of him, cut off from sight and sound. My sense of touch was concentrated on the rasp of callused skin against my tongue and lips, the strong hand cradling my head, the tickle of water rippling against the edges of my nostrils.

Every muscle in my body was relaxed. The outside world might as well have been a thousand leagues away. Nothing mattered but taste, touch, smell, and the exhilarating loss of control at being held like this, connected by a bare thread to air and light. It was intoxicating. *Freeing.* I wondered if Senovo would love it as much as I did.

I pictured it. We would open him up and press my curved wooden cock inside him to the hilt, leaving it to shift and rub against his sensitive flesh with every tiny movement. We'd put him in the tub and bind him wrist to ankle, leaving him helpless to lift himself out of the deep water. Andoc would support him exactly like this, cradling one hand under his head. With the other, he'd fist Senovo's hardening prick with slow, unhurried movements, driving him toward an inexorable, shattering release while I fed my other wooden cock — the one we used for sucking — past his lips, a fraction at a time, until he was taking it all.

A noise of wanting echoed around my secluded little world, and I realized it must have come from me. Andoc's fingers slid free of my mouth, but before I could mourn the loss, he replaced them with his lips. His hand slid down to play over my nipples as he kissed me at the boundary of water and air with slow, deep movements of his tongue. His hand moved lower, cupping my sex possessively and slipping a finger in to play over my inner lips. At almost the first touch, I moaned my second release into Andoc's mouth as it crested over me in a wave of profound relaxation and surrender.

Afterward, I sank deeper into the soft and protected places inside my mind. Andoc ended the kiss and lifted my upper body, propping me up and draping one of my arms over the edge of the tub so I wouldn't slide back down. I frowned at the sudden loss of his touch. A moment later, though, he was stepping into the bath with me, maneuvering me to one side so he could sit down and arrange me curled up against him, half in his lap with our legs tangled together. His added bulk raised the water level, some of it spilling noisily over the edge and onto the stone floor. Water lapped against my chin as I burrowed into him, pressing my face against the crook of his neck. His arms tightened, holding me securely.

"If I could keep both of you safe like this all the time," he said softly, "I would."

His voice echoed oddly through the water that was still blocking my ears. I didn't care. "We wouldn't want you to, though," I murmured into his skin. "Not really."

"I know," he said, and kissed the top of my head.

I let myself drift, safe in Andoc's arms. When the bathwater began to cool, I felt him drag a cloth over my body, scrubbing away the last of the travel grime. I must have fallen asleep at some point during the process, because the next thing I knew, I was opening my eyes to find myself in the large bed. It was morning. My head was pillowed on something soft, and fingers were stroking soothingly through my short hair. I blinked the blurriness from my vision, recognizing the white linen of Senovo's flowing robes under my cheek.

"Hmm?" I asked, still sleepy and disoriented.

"I fear the world has turned upside down," Senovo said. "The gods have truly forsaken us, and left us dwelling in a world of madness."

There was a hint of amusement in his voice at odds with the dire pronouncement, but all I could manage in response was, "Eh?"

"You appear to have slept on, oblivious, through whatever event it was that successfully woke Andoc this morning."

I craned around, looking at the empty expanse of mattress behind me. "Shit," I said conversationally. "Seriously?"

"Indeed. I'm afraid you may never live this down," Senovo confirmed. "He came and got me just before dawn. I don't think he wanted you to wake up alone."

I pondered that for a moment, the words pulling a warm woolen blanket over my mind once again. I nuzzled back into Senovo's lap and closed my eyes as his hand continued to play across my scalp, ruffling the hair with each pass.

"That's nice," I said.

"I can understand his concern, now that I've seen you. You're not really back yet, are you?"

"Jus' woke up," I said. "Gimme a minute, yeah?"

"Minutes—certainly," Senovo said, still stroking. "Hours—I'm afraid not, sadly. We'll be expected before too long."

Something inside my chest sank slowly. "Don't you ever find it difficult to come back from this feeling?" I asked.

"Frequently," Senovo replied.

I started the unpleasant process of rejoining a world where the people around us kept slaves and hurt Senovo and had disdain for all of us simply because we were northerners.

"Where did Andoc go so early?" I asked.

"Chief Volya called a private meeting with the warriors, I gather."

I drew in a deep lungful of air, and let it out slowly. Stretching, I glanced at the window again. The light looked *wrong*, somehow.

"Wait," I said, and straightened into a sitting position. "What time is it?"

"Mid-morning."

"What!" The little jolt of shock was infinitely more effective at bringing me to full awareness than Senovo's infernal slow stroking of my hair had been. "You should have said something!"

"I believe I just did." The amusement was back in Senovo's voice.

"I need to—" I faltered. Someone else was taking care of our horses. "I need to…"

"Yes?" Senovo prompted, his raised eyebrow communicating clearly that he was still laughing at me on the inside.

"There's nothing I need to do this morning, is there?" I finally said, resigned to being the butt of his amusement.

"Not quite yet, no," he confirmed. "Although you did miss breakfast."

"I'm still full from last night's supper."

"Well, then. No harm done, and I daresay you needed the rest." Senovo rose briskly from the bed, but I stopped him with a hand on his arm.

"What about you?" I asked. "Was your brooding productive?"

Senovo stilled, his head dipping. "Brooding is never productive. However, I am as well as might be expected while we are in this place, amongst these people. I will do my best to seek help should I need it—you have my word."

"All right, then," I said, and let his arm go. I rose and started dressing, blushing a bit when I had to go searching for various items around the room. "I'm not surprised I wasn't invited to Volya's meeting, but why weren't you? Seems like the High Priest should be there."

Senovo reached down and tugged one of my boots out from under the bed frame. "I don't believe our esteemed Chief has any more interest in my opinions regarding strategy than he does in yours," he said, tossing me my errant footwear.

I frowned. "Then why bring you along in the first place? High Priest Jyrrel didn't come with the Mereni contingent."

"My presence is an implicit threat, or at least, a demonstration of power, in Volya's mind. He is happy enough the lead the tribe boasting a shape-shifter as High Priest, though I imagine he wishes it was embodied in someone a bit more respectable than me."

"Someone more *tractable* than you, you mean," I said darkly.

"Rhystel knew how to play the games of leadership and politics," Senovo said. "I don't."

I scoffed and pulled on my other boot. "Horse shit. You may not *like* playing games of leadership and politics, but you sure seem to be doing all right so far."

"We shall have to agree to disagree, I think."

When I straightened, a question that had been percolating in the back of my mind came to the forefront. "Volya may have been smarter than I gave him credit for, bringing you here. The people in Rhyth know you." Senovo looked up sharply and I shook my head. "Not your face, I mean, but they know your story. The delegation that came to Draebard basically said as much. Those slaves, though… the ones in the field…"

I trailed off, troubled.

"What about them?" Senovo asked, though his expression had closed off as I spoke.

"They called you *lupiandas*. Wolf-patron. The little girl clutched you in her arms; she was completely unafraid. She asked if you'd finally come back for them. As if the slaves here have been expecting you."

EIGHT

The priest paled. "I... don't remember any of that."

"I had wondered," I said softly.

He fumbled for a chair and sat down. Part of me regretted bringing it up, but it would have been worse for him to discover that he'd become a sort of symbol to the slaves of Rhyth during the middle of a delicate negotiation or important meeting.

"If the southern slaves have put their faith in a desperate boy afflicted with a dangerous curse, I fear they will be deeply disappointed," he said in a hoarse voice, his eyes staring at nothing.

Senovo's hands were clenched into fists in his lap. I crossed to kneel in front of him and clasped one of his hands between mine until it relaxed, and he looked at me.

"You're not a desperate boy any more," I told him.

He raised a derisive eyebrow. "You think not? Perhaps Andoc is correct—you do not look deeply enough, Carivel."

"Actually, my eyes are just fine, thanks," I said. "And they see the High Priest of Draebard, one of the two bravest and kindest men I've ever met. They see the spirit of the wolf, who protects his pack from danger at all costs."

Senovo scoffed, an angry noise.

"Andoc would agree with me," I pressed.

"Andoc is hopelessly biased by sentiment," Senovo said. "And so are you."

I sat back on my heels, regarding him. "I've upset you. I'm sorry."

A muscle in Senovo's jaw ticked. "No. It was important that I know about this. You told me. Now, unfortunately, we are both expected at the King's meeting. We should go."

I sighed, knowing when I'd lost a battle, and rose to my feet. Senovo stood and ushered me out of the room, his impassive facade firmly in place. We picked up Favian from the room next door and headed toward the main wing of the palace. Senovo stopped the first servant we met and requested an escort to the site of the meeting. The boy bowed and hurried to direct us through the hallways to a different wing of the building, where the corridors were filled with unfamiliar men wearing northern dress. He indicated a grand entrance with people coming and going in a steady stream before leaving us to our own devices.

"I didn't expect so many people," I said, staring at the crowded corridor. Favian was looking on with wide eyes beside us.

"Most of the tribes will have sent someone," Senovo replied. "Ambassador Derenza was not exaggerating when he said that these meetings could decide the future of Eburos as a whole."

Not for the first time, I found myself overwhelmed by the scale of what was happening around me. How could it be that mere months ago, my biggest concerns were whether Jorun was happy with my work at the horse pens or not, and if someone would catch me crouching down to piss and realize I was female? Now, chieftains and warriors mingled around me, not giving me a second look in my nondescript breeches and man's jerkin. A shape-shifting High Priest walked with me side-by-side as we entered to meet with a king.

The meeting room was the single most impressive indoor space I'd ever seen. Where much of the palace consisted of two or even three stories of rooms stacked on top of each other, this chamber had nothing above it except for the distant ceiling. Five tall men standing on each other's shoulders could not have reached to touch it.

Stone columns like giant tree trunks dotted the room at regular intervals, the only thing that kept it all from collapsing down on our heads, I suspected. The floor was polished granite, slick as oil beneath the soles of my boots. One end of the room held a raised dais with an ornate chair sitting on it. The frame of the thing was covered in beaten gold, and the seat and back held cushions colored in a deep red. Ermine and fox fur draped over the arms.

The rest of the room was filled with numerous tables laid out in a grid so that people could easily pass between them. I gathered that each tribe would sit at a different table, while the leaders of Rhyth presided over the meeting from the raised dais. This was confirmed a moment later when Senovo touched my arm and gestured to a table near one corner, where Volya, Andoc, and the other Draebardi warriors sat.

The three of us crossed the crowded space to join them.

Volya was engaged in a spirited discussion with an old man I didn't know when we arrived. Even this close, I could not make out their words over the general hubbub of so many competing conversations. A shiver of claustrophobia overcame me for a moment despite the size of the room—to have this many people crowded together in such a way seemed unnatural, and I didn't like it at all. Particularly when many of these tribes had fought with each other in the past.

Andoc looked up at our approach, and I could not help my double take at his appearance. His expression was pinched and unhappy; his face, pale. I wondered with sudden trepidation what had happened during the early morning meeting that Senovo and I had missed. The other warriors looked grim, but I could gather nothing else from their faces. I shot Andoc a questioning look. He pressed his lips together and shook his head minutely.

Senovo's sharp eyes surveyed the scene and met mine. A brief flicker of one expressive eyebrow showed that he'd noted the same things I had. He seated himself directly across from the Chief, and motioned Favian to stand behind him, at his right shoulder. I took the empty chair on his left, somewhat unsure of the protocol in this situation. No one objected, though, so I settled back to wait and watch.

People continued to circulate around the room, speaking loudly to each other. Several of them stopped to talk to Volya, and I was able to make out enough to understand that the various tribes were attempting to feel out their neighbors' positions before the meeting officially started. This continued long enough that I found myself growing bored despite the novelty—at least, until a gray-haired priest in light dun-colored robes approached Senovo and dipped his head in greeting.

Senovo straightened in his chair beside me.

"Forgive me," said the newcomer. "You are the High Priest of Draebard, yes?"

Senovo's features could have been carved from marble. "I am."

Across the table, I felt Andoc's attention fall on us.

"I am Mabios, assistant to the High Priest of Venzor," said the old man. I looked at the priest with new interest—Venzor was where Andoc had been born.

"Mabios!" Andoc said, his worried expression from earlier lifting slightly. "I didn't expect to see you here."

Mabios smiled, his eyes crinkling. "Hello, Andoc. It appears that the years have been good to you."

Andoc leaned forward. "You as well, sir. How is Mother faring?"

"Ah—she caught a fever toward the end of the winter that was rather hard on her, but she has recovered for the most part," said Mabios. "She misses you."

Andoc's expression turned wistful. "I will try to get home for a visit before the weather turns," he said. "Please tell her that I think of her often, and give her my love. Tell her, too, that I was handfasted this spring."

My cheeks warmed.

"I would be pleased to do so, of course, Andoc," the old priest said. His expression sobered and he returned his attention to Senovo. "High Priest, I had hoped for a chance to speak with you. There are several... *stories*... that have been making their way from village to village in recent weeks, but I do not wish to presume..."

"The stories are true," Senovo said. "I am a shape-shifter."

His expression was still the distant, guarded one that I hated so much, but his eyes flashed gold for a moment, the wolf shining through.

Mabios' expression was that of a man who had never expected to be gifted with such a thing in his lifetime. "Extraordinary," he said on a low breath. "I am honored to make your acquaintance, Brother. You must forgive me for approaching you about such a thing when Eburos is embroiled in her own troubles, but this is a situation with which you would seem to be uniquely positioned to address."

Senovo frowned, confusion breaking through his facade as he looked up at the Venzori priest. "Of what situation do you speak?"

"There is a young man from a small village north of Venzor," said Mabios. "He, too, is a shape-shifter." I caught my breath in surprise. "His ability manifested only a few months ago, when bandits attacked his family on the road. His older sister survived the attack and brought him to the temple, but he is a very troubled boy. When it was suggested to him that it might be best for him to join the Priests' Guild, he ran away. Needless to say, his sister is very worried for him, as are we all."

There was a moment of shocked silence. *Another shape-shifter?* It was Favian who spoke first, his eyes wide and fascinated. "Excuse me, Elder Brother, but what form does he take?"

Mabios looked at the acolyte with a kind and tolerant expression. "He takes the form of a lion, Little Brother. That is part of the reason we in the temple are so concerned, both for his safety, and the safety of others."

Senovo's utter shock was hidden behind his customary impassive expression, but still visible to one who knew him well. "In... what way do you think I can help with this situation?" he asked carefully. "Particularly if no one knows where he is?"

Mabios made a small gesture of frustration. "We hope that he will return. Or, failing that, perhaps he will be located and brought back to Venzor by someone else. I wish only to get help for the lad, and get him to understand that he will be better off within the temple. You would seem to be the most qualified person to offer that help, assuming he reappears."

"And what makes you think that being in the Priests' Guild is best for this boy, if the mere prospect terrifies him so?" There was fire behind Senovo's eyes now.

The Venzori priest looked taken aback. "It has been the custom for many generations, High Priest. I would have thought you would agree that it is the best way for him."

I held my breath, exchanging a glance with Andoc.

"Would you?" Senovo said in a mild tone. He laced his fingers together on the table and examined them for a moment. "Well. As a priest, it is, of course, my duty and my desire to help all of the gods' children as I am able. If this boy surfaces and is willing to speak with me, I will certainly do so. You may assure him that I will listen to whatever he wishes to say without judgment or preconception."

The old Venzori priest looked at Senovo for a long moment, clearly hearing and understanding what was left unsaid. Eventually, he dipped his head in respect. "I thank you for hearing me out, High Priest Senovo. Andoc, I will deliver your message to your mother. May the gods look kindly upon you all during this time of strife."

"I do believe you've shocked him," Andoc said to Senovo once the old eunuch left to return to his tribesmen.

"I will not see anyone bullied into the priesthood," Senovo said. Anger was still simmering under his cool exterior.

"I would expect nothing less, my friend," replied Andoc. "Think, though—another shape-shifter on Eburos..."

"Another reason to make sure that the Empire never holds sway in the north," I added, grim. "They would see this boy burned at the stake. Senovo, too."

The Empire's religion dealt cruelly with anything that did not fit neatly within its framework, and magic was certainly one such thing. When we had been his prisoners at the hill fort, the Alyrion commander had taken great pains to describe to Senovo in detail what would happen to him if he were discovered to be a shape-shifter.

"They will not hold sway as long as the last northern warrior draws breath," Andoc vowed. His eyes moved to Volya, deep in conversation with another chieftain at the far end of the table and oblivious to our discussion. "I only hope it does not truly come down to that."

Again, I wondered what Senovo and I had missed this morning. Whatever it was, I got the impression that, once we found out, we wouldn't like it very much.

My thoughts were interrupted by the sound of a wooden staff striking stone, coming from the direction of the dais. The noise level dipped as people turned to look. At the front of the room, Rhytheeri officials were mounting the stone steps. Elsewhere in the room, people were returning to their tables as the meeting appeared ready to get underway. When the room had quieted for the most part, the sound of horns rang out from the entrance.

A tall, thin man wearing ridiculously ostentatious clothing entered, flanked by two burly warriors. This, I gathered, must be the King of Rhyth. He made his way down the central passage between the tables, strutting past as if he owned the place. Which, to be fair, I supposed he did. Like many of the Rhytheeri men I had seen, he shared Senovo's high cheekbones and dark hair, but unlike Senovo, his eyes were hard. Cruel. I disliked him immediately.

As he approached the ornate throne, the officials on the dais bowed almost to the floor while the northern guests looked on, unimpressed. If this was the man that the Emperor had installed as a figurehead, I couldn't help thinking that the Emperor could probably have chosen better. The King of Rhyth looked as though he would have a hard time even picking up a sword or an axe—much less wielding one. He had clearly never been a warrior, and I wondered what sort of background or quality of character had landed him in this position.

However he had achieved his exalted state, the Rhytheeri King clearly relished it. He looked down his nose at his fawning courtiers, letting them scrape before him for a long moment before seating himself on the throne so they could rise.

The official with the staff stepped forward. "His Eminence, King Flenaar of Rhyth!" he announced, to a chorus of low muttering around the room. I wondered if he had expected us to applaud, or what. When nothing else followed his pronouncement, the official cleared his throat nervously. "We are gathered here today under the King's auspices to discuss an overarching peace treaty with our neighbors to the south, the Empire of Alyrios!" More silence. "To, er... to that end, His Eminence wishes to speak to you all regarding the recent disturbing reports of unrest in northern Eburos."

The King did not rise, but merely waved the official back into the background. His voice, when he spoke, was surprisingly pleasant.

"Peoples of the north. For too long, Eburos has been divided by geography and by culture. The north and the south once traded freely by sea, but now, they might as well be separated by a mighty wall for all the contact between them. The Empire seeks to unify our island and elevate it to the status it deserves—"

"The Empire seeks to unify us under the heel of their boot!" someone called from the far side of the room, and several voices rose in support, including Volya's.

The King rose, and gestured around the cavernous room. "Look around you," he said. "Has Rhyth suffered for its commerce with the Empire? Have we been crushed?"

A priest in white robes rose at a table nearby. "Have you not?" he asked, his voice echoing around the large space. "Tell me then, why has the Temple of Utarr in front of the palace been replaced by a shrine to the false god of the Alyrions?"

"My friend," the King replied, and a chill slithered up my spine at the familiar address paired with those hard, cold eyes, "Eburos has long welcomed many gods into its pantheon. Deimok is but one more."

"The followers of Deimok would see all other religions destroyed!" said the priest. "Their adherents burned!"

"Fear-mongering and nonsense!" the King scoffed. "One may still find the priests of the Old Religion throughout Rhyth. Why should a single new temple mean the end of the old ways?"

Beside me, Senovo sat very still. He had no reason to think kindly of the Rhytheeri priests—yet, as a shape-shifter, the new followers of Deimok would see him dead in a heartbeat. I could only imagine the conflict he must be feeling.

"Word has it that the cult of Deimok is growing in Rhyth," the priest said. "Will what you say be true ten years from now, or twenty?"

"No one can see the future," said King Flenaar. Senovo tensed, and I glanced at him curiously as the King continued. "I submit that we Eburosi would do better to worry about the present than fret over something that might or might not happen a generation from now. The Empire is unimaginably powerful. Alyrios offers us wealth and progress the like of which Eburos has never seen before."

Another man stood—a grizzled warrior whose bearing marked him as a Chief. "Alyrios offers only subjugation! They seek our resources, nothing more. And in Rhyth, they have found a foothold. Without support from the southern tribes, the Emperor's ships could have been driven from our shores. If not for the beachhead they have here, how difficult would it have been for the Empire to bring across enough men and materiel for a sustained incursion? The Rhytheeri are spineless collaborators, nothing more! You seek to keep the yoke from your own shoulders by helping the Emperor throw it across ours!"

There was more noisy support for this sentiment from the crowd. The King allowed it to go on for a few moments before the staff striking the floor brought the meeting under control again.

"Whereas you," said the King, "risk bringing down a bloody and protracted war on all of us. Do you really think that a handful of northern tribes can prevail over an Empire that brings entire countries to their knees? Why risk that when the alternative is so much simpler?"

Volya shot to his feet, startling me. He pointed an accusing finger at the Rhytheeri ruler. "Maybe the north can't beat the Empire, but we can damn well descend on Rhyth and turn your precious city into a pile of smoldering ashes!" His voice rose to a shout. *"Who's with me?"*

My heart stuttered in shock, and across from me, all the blood drained from Andoc's face. Around the room, chaos erupted, the few cries of support overwhelmed by noises of shock and confusion. *Was the Chief of Draebard declaring war on the south of Eburos?*

Under the cover of the confusion, Andoc rose and crossed to Volya's side. Senovo followed, and so did I. Andoc took the Chief's arm, speaking low enough not to be overheard beyond our table.

"Chief," he said, his voice low and earnest, "we *can't* do this. Aside from the practical considerations, there's a huge difference between defending the north from invasion and starting a civil war on Eburos. We might as well send an open invitation for the Empire to come in and march right over the top of the survivors after our forces destroy each other."

The other warriors looked torn, their eyes flickering between their Chief and their First. Senovo stepped forward, adding his voice to Andoc's. "While it is true that matters of defense are the purview of the tribal chief and not the High Priest, to take such action without discussing it first is unacceptable. *You risk Draebard's future."*

"We did discuss this at length, only this morning," Volya retorted, his eyes snapping with anger that seemed almost manic.

"At a meeting to which I was pointedly not invited," Senovo said.

"As you said yourself, this is not a *religious matter*," Volya said. "Don't step beyond your remit, Senovo, or I'll slap you down so fast your head will spin."

I caught my breath, shock and anger coiling in my chest at Volya's audacity, coming on the heels of his own transparent attempts to usurp power from a young and untried High Priest when Senovo first ascended to the position. Andoc stepped closer, placing himself between them. His hand was still on Volya's upper arm, and his face expressed distress and betrayal.

"Chief," he said, "you agreed at the meeting to wait until we'd discussed this with Magoldis and some of the others before acting. We can't do something like this unilaterally!"

Volya jerked his arm free and rounded on Andoc. "I find it telling that you were the only person at the meeting who wishes me to seek a woman's permission for going to war. Am I a boy asking for my mother's consent before going on a hunt?"

"*You're our leader*," Andoc said. "You have a duty to your people not to place them in unnecessary peril! The Mereni are our allies! Our alliance with them was *your idea*."

Volya's demeanor went cold and furious. "I am disappointed in you, Andoc. You've changed, since this unnatural girl got her claws into you." My stomach swooped, even as my anger surged higher. "It grieves me that I can no longer trust you to support me as a First Warrior should support his chieftain. You give me no choice but to strip you of your position. Jacun, rise. You are now First Warrior of Draebard."

NINE

Andoc reeled back a step as if struck, his face going white as a ghost. Senovo grasped his elbow. At the table, Jacun looked like a startled rabbit, frozen motionless in surprise. His mouth hung open silently. I might as well have been carved from ice, for all the control I had over my own body.

Rallying, Andoc pulled away from Senovo. "That is, of course, your decision, Chief Volya," he said. "I have ever served at your pleasure. Nonetheless, you must not pursue this course of action. You will bring destruction down on all of us."

"That he will," said a new voice, and Leader Magoldis dragged Volya around to face her with a strong hand on his arm. "Do you always punish loyalty and good sense when it pricks your pride?"

The two of them glared at each other, Volya having to tip his head back slightly to look up at the Mereni Leader.

"This doesn't concern you, woman," Volya said, his voice a growl. "It's Draebardi business!"

Magoldis raised an eyebrow. "If you want to throw over your First Warrior for daring to have an opinion, that's your business, old man. But when you try to drag Meren into an ill-conceived war without even giving me the courtesy of a warning, *you'll answer to me.* I won't even get started on trying to drag other unaffiliated tribes along with you, without a formal agreement in place beforehand."

Volya's eyes narrowed. "So you're ready to roll over and let the Emperor jam his cock between your legs? Has the whole of Eburos gone soft? *They attacked my village! They killed my people!* I'll see the Alyrions *off* of this island if I have to kill every last Rhytheeri collaborator to do it!"

If Magoldis' expression had been chilly before, it was *glacial* now. "You risk our treaty with your posturing, Volya. Stop and think, before you risk all of Eburos as well."

With that, she turned, leaving Volya grinding his teeth behind her. Draebard's little drama was interrupted by the

Rhytheeri officials attempting to restore order again. Senovo urged Andoc back to his seat. The very fact that Andoc allowed himself to be led spoke to his continued shock. I followed, dropping into my own chair, unable to fully grasp what had just happened. The other warriors at the table looked down, unwilling to meet Andoc's eyes.

The treaty with the Mereni that Andoc, Senovo and I had worked so hard to forge — that had caused such upheaval in our own lives — was in tatters. I wasn't sure what I was supposed to feel about that. Unable to bear Andoc's glazed look of betrayal any longer, I looked to Senovo instead. The priest was stony-faced, his expression under perfect control, while beneath it simmered more anger than I had ever sensed from him since I'd known him. He met my eyes, and in that moment I knew that Senovo would stand toe to toe with Volya to protect Draebard, no matter what it took. With my own gaze, I tried to convey that he would not be alone.

Around us, the meeting devolved into angry debates and shouting matches for the rest of the day. A few tribes spoke up in support for Volya, while most berated him for warmongering. Not only was the entire thing completely unproductive, but the way the King simply sat back and let the northern leaders argue gave me chills. He was like a snake, his cold eyes watching hapless prey wander ever closer to its own destruction.

Almost, I thought, as if he knows that he can count on assistance from a powerful ally should the north decide to attack Rhyth.

I shivered.

As the sun slanted low through the arched windows in the far wall, the gathering gradually broke up, concluding with the same sense of chaos and uncertainty that had reigned since Volya's shocking outburst. We returned to our rooms, our group's progress slowed by the number of people waylaying us to either berate Volya or congratulate him. When we finally reached the familiar hallway, Volya entered his room without a word and slammed the door behind him. Jacun looked at Andoc for a moment as if he might say something, but then he seemed to deflate. He and the other warriors slunk away to their own rooms, leaving Andoc and me alone in the silent hallway with Senovo and Favian.

"Is there going to be a war now?" Favian asked in a small voice.

Andoc closed his eyes for a moment before reopening them. "I hope not, Favian," he said.

"Come, Little Brother," said Senovo. "It smells as though the servants have brought us food. We will have a light meal and go over some more of the religious histories afterward, to calm our minds." He met Andoc's eyes. "I will be along to join you later this evening, old friend."

Andoc nodded silently, still looking like he'd been punched in the gut, even hours after Volya's betrayal of his years of loyalty. Senovo's eyes slid to mine briefly—a promise of support—and I mouthed *thank you* in return.

The priest led Favian into their room with a protective hand clasped on his small shoulder, leaving the door open behind them. I did the same thing to Andoc, setting him down in a chair at the table and pressing a plate of food into his hands a moment later. The repast tonight was as sumptuous as it had been the previous evening, but it might as well have been chopped straw for all the notice I took of the taste. The two of us ate, heedless of what we were putting in our mouths. When our plates were empty, I pushed back from the table, unable to take the silence any longer.

"Talk to me, Andoc. Please," I said.

There was a momentary hesitation before Andoc shook his head slowly. "There's not much to say. I'm all right. But our Chief definitely isn't."

I ignored the blatant lie, understanding completely the need to appear strong and unaffected when at one's weakest.

"He doesn't have enough outside support to carry through with his threat," I said.

Andoc shook his head. "And while we all argue about it, the opportunity for a meaningful alliance against the Empire slips away."

He was right, and there wasn't really much to say to that. I got up and nudged Andoc until he scooted his chair back, so I could straddle his lap and hug him close. He sighed and brought his arms around me, tucking me under his chin. That was how Senovo found us some time later. He crossed from the door to stand at Andoc's back, one hand on his shoulder and the other hand on mine.

"How's Favian?" I asked without moving.

"Exhausted," said Senovo. "He will sleep now, despite his worries."

"Stay tonight, *amadi*," Andoc said, "please."

"Old friend, you do not even have to ask," the priest replied, his voice rich with feeling.

An idea slipped into my mind, and I raised my head enough to kiss Andoc briefly before disentangling. "Stay here, both of you," I said. "I'll be right back."

Andoc frowned. "Where are you going?"

"To arrange for our evening's distraction," I said.

Outside, I closed the door behind me and went looking for the nearest servant. It still made me uncomfortable to interact with them, but what I needed to ask for was innocuous enough.

"Excuse me," I said to a young man walking toward me with an empty wooden tray.

He stopped and dipped into a brief bow. "Yes, honored guest?" he asked.

"This is a slightly odd request," I warned him, "but I was wondering if you could bring me two wooden practice swords?"

If the question surprised him, he showed no sign. "Of course. Shall I bring them to you here?"

"Yes, that's fine," I said. "I'll wait."

The servant bowed again and hurried off. A few minutes later, he returned with a pair of blunt edged practice weapons and presented them to me. "Will these do, honored guest?"

"Yes," I said with a smile. "This is perfect. Thank you... I'm sorry, what was your name?"

The servant looked surprised for a moment, before a faint blush of pleasure crossed his features. "They call me Tiff," he said.

"Thank you, Tiff," I said. "I'll return them when we're done."

Tiff smiled and nodded, then went back to his duties. I carried my unwieldy prizes back to the room and let myself in, sidling through the doorway awkwardly with the long wooden swords held under one arm. Inside, Senovo looked up. The two of them hadn't moved much since I'd left; Senovo still stood behind Andoc's chair, but now his arms were wrapped around

Andoc's chest. Andoc's head leaned back to rest against Senovo's sternum, his eyes closed.

I whistled softly to get his attention.

When Andoc lifted his head and Senovo straightened away, I tossed one of the swords across the room in a graceful arc. With a warrior's reflexes, Andoc raised a hand to catch the hilt as it slapped against his palm.

He looked at the blunt weapon with a frown of confusion, and then looked at me. "Carivel… what are you doing?"

"Question," I said formulaically, lifting the other practice sword and using it to point at Andoc. "Is there anything that any of us can do tonight to influence this situation?"

Andoc seemed to deflate a bit in his chair, some of the tension draining out of him. Behind him, Senovo looked at me approvingly.

"No," said Andoc, "as you are perfectly well aware."

"I just wanted to make sure you were aware of it, too. So, there's no reason we can't distract each other from our troubles for a bit?"

"No, there isn't," Senovo said.

"While I appreciate the sentiment, I'm not entirely sure I'm distractible at the moment, *caradi*." Andoc was still seated in his chair, leaning forward a bit after reaching out to catch the practice sword, which hung limply from his hand.

Recognizing an opening when I saw one, I said, "I'm sorry to hear that," and charged forward across the room, my own dull blade outstretched. Surprise lit Andoc's face comically for a moment, and then his sword was up, somehow tangling with mine in an ever-widening spiral of movement that sent the sturdy hilt spinning out of my grip. The heavy length of wood went flying across the room to clatter against the wall and fall to the floor with a dull *thud*.

I stared after it stupidly as Andoc moved the tip of his blade to dimple the soft skin immediately under my ribcage. "Well, shit," I said. "That was a bit more humiliating than I expected, actually."

Andoc's features softened—not a smile, but a look of helpless affection. "So, not a draw this time, then?" he asked.

"We could have a do-over?" I offered hopefully.

"Perhaps not," Senovo said. "I'm not certain the furnishings would survive." He looked at Andoc, who was still uncharacteristically quiet and withdrawn. "Since Andoc already has much on his mind this evening, I believe I will decide the details of your forfeit tonight. Yes?"

"Thank you, *amadi*," Andoc said. "That would be much appreciated."

I nodded my own agreement, intrigued.

"Having been the beneficiary of your ever-increasing skills in fellatio recently, I believe it is time for you to progress to a slightly more advanced technique. Does that sound like a suitable penalty?"

"Only if you want to, Carivel," Andoc said. "Your cock-sucking technique isn't anywhere near as important to me as your enjoyment and your enthusiasm."

"I want to learn," I said with a smile. "But Senovo, just be aware I've got a long way to go before I'll be throating Andoc like you do. Unlike some people in this room, I actually have a normal gag reflex."

Senovo smirked at me, accepting the teasing with good humor. "Perhaps not quite *that* advanced, then. However, you may surprise yourself. Sometimes all that is needed is a little motivation. Tonight, I would like you to simply let Andoc rest against the back of your throat, and hold him there."

I swallowed, saliva flooding my mouth at the thought. "And my motivation?"

"I will be touching you while you practice, but I will only allow you to come once you succeed."

My nipples hardened. In front of me, Andoc let the tip of the practice sword drop away from my belly to rest on the ground as he stared at Senovo. "All right," he said. "I take it back. I'm distracted after all."

⤳ ♕ ⤶

Even after months of having him, I didn't think I would ever get enough of Andoc's cock. The way it smelled. The way it tasted. The way it filled my mouth completely, my lips stretching around it. Andoc's hand ruffled through the fine hair at the back of my neck, while Senovo's deft fingers played along the seam of my cunt, delving inside to spread the wetness he encountered there.

To lie naked like this, sucking and laving at salty flesh, sliding further down the shaft and back up again in an easy rhythm—I could happily do this for hours. Tonight, though, I had a different goal laid out before me. There were, I thought, some disadvantages to loving a priest. Namely, the fact that he knew my body better than I did, in many ways. Also, the fact that he was evil, and manipulative, and... and... *oh, gods* how could he keep me this close to coming for so long without *actually being able to come*?

I wriggled and groaned a bit around the cock in my mouth, dipping my head to take more until my throat closed and my stomach clenched, forcing me to back off. Senovo eased his ministrations enough so that I could think again, past the buzz of frustrated pleasure draped over my awareness. Andoc stroked my cheek in encouragement.

"Easy, *caradi*," he said. "You're doing so well. You already feel wonderful, just like this."

I hummed around him, the sound transforming into a mewl as another frisson of pleasure from Senovo's sure touch skittered up my spine. The cock in my mouth slipped a bit deeper.

Senovo inched me closer to the edge and backed me away, my climax still tantalizingly out of reach. "The secret to throating a cock," he said, "is not to be afraid of the feelings it produces within your body." His other hand slid over the globe of my arse, fingers trailing into the cleft to brush across my entrance. "It is messy at first—your eyes burn and your nose runs and you drool onto your lover's flesh. But you will not actually come to harm. You are not truly choking; it is only for a moment or two, and then you will pull away."

The soft pad of Senovo's finger pressed against the pucker of my arse. I immediately relaxed and pushed out against it. The finger slipped inside, sending new sparks through my body— the slight stretch and burn fading to unimportance next to the pleasure.

"Just as your body fought the intrusion of a finger at first," Senovo continued, "it fights this intrusion as well. And just as it came to accept the pleasure of penetration, it can come to accept this new surrender with pleasure."

"Though it doesn't have to be tonight, *caradi*," Andoc added. "We can stop any time you need to."

I made a noise of disagreement at the suggestion, and wriggled against the finger, seeking more friction. Andoc continued to caress my hair and face, dragging a finger over my wet, swollen lower lip. I looked up the length of his torso, meeting and holding his eyes even though my own were beginning to water. He exhaled shakily and his cock twitched in my mouth.

"Try again for us," Senovo said, as he pushed me closer to my release once more.

I closed my eyes, dizzy with what he was doing to me. Relaxing, I allowed the weight of my head to slide my lips further down Andoc's shaft until his tip brushed my throat and made me gag. This time, though, I just let myself go limp, trying to focus on Senovo's fingers rather than the jerking protest of my throat muscles. My stomach heaved alarmingly and subsided. Tears and snot flooded my face.

It doesn't matter, I thought, as Senovo's fingers continued to send sparks up and down my spine. Nobody in this room cared if my face was sticky and tear-stained.

I breathed in wetly, filling my lungs before pressing Andoc just a final bit deeper. Oddly, that seemed to make it easier—my throat muscles fluttered a couple more times and subsided. Andoc's flesh pressed intimately into mine, big and scary and perfect and overwhelming. My heart pounded. My body balanced on a knife's edge of pleasure under Senovo's touch.

"There, *caradi*," Andoc said, his voice hoarse with desire. "Senovo, let her come now."

Senovo dragged his fingers over the throbbing flesh at the apex of my cunt and I came, grunting around Andoc's cock as pleasure slammed through me. Red flashed behind my closed eyelids for the space of several heartbeats before dimming to gray. I was only distantly aware as Andoc lifted me away from his twitching cock with a groan.

"*Fuck*," he said. "Just so you know, *amadi*, it was basically torture not to move or come during that performance. You've been hiding a deeply sadistic streak all these years."

Andoc pulled me up his body by the shoulders until my head was pillowed on his chest. I opened my eyes, still dazed, to find Senovo crawling up between Andoc's legs. Andoc's cock was an angry red color—the head, almost purple. Veins stood out along its length.

"As distractions go, it was effective, was it not?" Senovo asked. "Besides, all things come to those with patience."

Andoc hissed as Senovo swallowed him down, bobbing his head a few times before taking him smoothly to the root. I watched, sated and heavy with accomplishment. One of my hands crept out, and I fondled my fingertips along Senovo's cheek... his jaw... down to where Andoc's length bulged against the muscles of his throat. I rubbed at the head of Andoc's cock through Senovo's tender skin. Senovo quivered under my touch, even as Andoc cried out and came, one arm clutching my shoulders to hold me to him, the other hand buried in Senovo's hair.

Senovo gasped as Andoc eventually eased him off, the movement drawing a final shuddering aftershock from the spent man. The eunuch's pupils were blown wide and dark. I craned forward and kissed him, but there was nothing to taste, so deeply had Andoc been buried when his release spurted down Senovo's throat. Though we were all shaky with reaction, I'd had a bit longer to recover, so I stumbled out of the bed on unsteady legs long enough to extinguish the lamps and run a damp rag over my sex and thighs.

"Love you both," Andoc murmured when I rejoined them in bed and curled up, putting Andoc in the middle. He sounded half asleep already, but I couldn't help the smile of affection that I pressed against his shoulder in the dark. Across from me, Senovo's hand inched forward until it covered mine. I turned my palm up and squeezed. Moments later, sleep claimed me.

Despite the upheaval of the day — or perhaps because of it — we slumbered peacefully through the night together. Morning light was just beginning to penetrate the room's darkness when all three of us were awakened by a scream from the room next door.

TEN

*F*avian. I bolted upright, my heart pounding. Next to me, Andoc jerked awake. Senovo was already out of the bed, grabbing his robes and flinging them around his shoulders as he rushed across the room and wrenched open the door. I followed, picking up Andoc's shirt and shrugging into it—covering myself to mid-thigh.

Outside, a few other people were sticking their heads out of their doors, emerging in various states of undress. Andoc emerged from our room in his smallclothes just as Senovo opened the door to the room he and his acolyte shared. I was too groggy and panicked to devote the proper amount of worry to what the other people in the hall made of the three of us coming out the same room first thing in the morning, barely dressed.

In the dim light beyond the doorway, Favian wrestled his bedclothes, crying out "No!" in a choked, high-pitched voice.

It was another nightmare, like the one he'd had in Draebard during his fever. Behind me, I felt Andoc relax marginally upon realizing there was no external threat. Senovo, on the other hand, looked as worried as ever.

"Favian!" he said sharply, fetching up against the edge of the bed. "*Wake up.*"

Favian moaned and flailed with one arm as if fighting to free himself from something, his other arm still trapped in the blankets. I leaned forward and caught his slender wrist as gently as I could, restraining him.

"Andoc," Senovo said in a low voice, "Get the others away from here. Tell them it's just a bad dream."

Andoc nodded, heading back to the door where Keenan and Jacun were both hovering, not sure if they should enter. "Just a nightmare," he said. "Nothing to worry about."

Favian was still fighting in the dream, jerking against my hold. I called his name, giving the wrist I held a sharp shake.

The boy's eyes flew open, his black pupils almost swallowing the thin blue rings of his irises.

"Little Brother," Senovo said, "you're safe. It was merely another dream. All is well."

I cautiously let him go.

"S-Senovo?" he asked, his gaze darting around the unfamiliar room.

"I am here. So are Andoc and Carivel. You're awake now; it's over. Can you tell me what you dreamed?"

Andoc rejoined us by the bed. Favian's panicked eyes flitted from one to the other of us as if searching. "Chief Volya... is he—?"

"Is he what?" Senovo prompted gently.

But Favian only shook his head, seeming to come back to himself somewhat. "Nothing," he whispered, even as tears began to squeeze from the corners of his eyes.

His body shook with the effort not to weep, and unsure what else to do, I pulled him against me in an embrace. Senovo rubbed a hand over his back in soothing circles.

"It's all right, Little Brother. Only a dream," he said again, but his eyes were clouded with worry.

When the boy sat back a few minutes later, it was with an embarrassed expression. Andoc had retreated to the doorway to keep any other people from sticking their noses in, but Senovo and I remained perched on the edge of the bed with him.

"Better now?" I asked, resisting the urge to thumb away the tear tracks on Favian's cheeks.

He nodded and wiped his face with his sleeve, not looking at me.

"Do you want to tell us about it?" I said.

He shook his head, still studying the dyed woolen blanket resting across his knees.

I sighed, and looked to Senovo, who still appeared troubled. When he saw me watching him, though, his expression smoothed and he slapped his palms down on his thighs, briskly. "Well, then," he said, "Since we're all awake, we might as well break our fast and find out what the day is to hold for us. Favian and I will meet you in your quarters shortly, Carivel."

"Sure," I said. "Give us a few minutes, though—we're not exactly dressed for the occasion.

Favian's eyes wandered from my bare legs to Andoc's bare chest, and he blushed. I chewed the inside of my cheek to maintain a neutral expression. I didn't want to embarrass him any further, but I could well sympathize with Favian's reaction to seeing Andoc in all—or at least, most of—his glory. I gave the boy's shoulder a quick squeeze and got to my feet.

Taking Andoc by the arm, I led him from the room. "Come on, you. I'm hungry. Aren't you supposed to keep me fed?"

Andoc scoffed at me, but I could see his worries closing in again like storm clouds crossing the sun. His broad shoulders almost seemed bowed under the weight of recent events. We dressed and breakfasted with the others before returning to the meeting room to see what was going on. The rest of the party from Draebard had not yet arrived, but Magoldis and her Second Warrior, Wynethal, were seated at their table, deep in discussion with Elder Briethe.

Wynethal's sharp eyes rested on us, and he drew the Leader's attention to our entrance. Magoldis stood and beckoned us over. I wasn't sure of the protocol of speaking with her like this, when she and Volya were in the middle of such contention. However, she was still the Leader of a powerful tribe, and we could hardly ignore her summons.

"Leader," Senovo greeted, taking the initiative as the highest-ranking member of our party.

"High Priest Senovo," Magoldis replied, with a tip of her head. "Horse Mistress. Andoc." I winced at the lack of a title. "You needn't look so worried. It's not my intention to place you in an awkward situation by attempting to discuss your Chief's recent decisions. I merely wish to extend an invitation. Should you have need of it, there is a place for all of you in Meren. I know how much you risked to forge the treaty between our tribes—yes, even you, Horse *Mistress*—and you have earned my respect for it."

The three of us shared a look, as Favian stood by nervously. Senovo cleared his throat. "We are honored by your words, Leader Magoldis, but I believe Draebard has more need of us now than ever before."

Magoldis nodded, as if she had expected such a response. "I think, High Priest Senovo, that you are absolutely correct in your assessment."

The Mereni Leader gave us another long look before returning to her seat at the table, and her earlier discussion. The four of us continued on to the table we had occupied the previous day. Andoc and I sat down to wait. Senovo went off with Favian in tow to speak with some of the other priests present at the meeting, in hopes of gaining more insight into the other tribes' intentions, as well as to get what information he could about the rumored rise of the cult of Deimok in and around Rhyth.

A little while later, Volya and the other warriors arrived. I wondered if he would ignore us completely, but after seating himself with a huff, the Chief turned to us and asked, "Is that boy of Senovo's all right now?" in a gruff tone.

"It was just a nightmare," I said coolly. "Nothing to worry about."

"Hmph. He seems a bit of a delicate lad. Not sure why Senovo brought him along in the first place."

The Chief's observation didn't seem like something that required a response, so I didn't give one. I wondered if Volya was already beginning to regret his decision to demote Andoc — as well he should.

My musing was interrupted by Senovo's return. Favian seemed to have recovered himself — his color had returned and his expression had smoothed out, though he flicked occasional nervous glances toward Volya when he thought no one was watching. Senovo sat down and laced his fingers together, reporting on what he'd discovered without any prompting.

"I have spoken to several of the visiting priests. There has been much discussion overnight of renewing the push for a defensive alliance among the northern tribes. A few have also gone out into the city to speak with the Rhytheeri priests about the new temple to Deimok behind the palace. They report that the Alyrion presence in Rhyth is far larger and more influential than is immediately apparent."

"There were Alyrion soldiers on the streets when we arrived," I said, remembering the way their presence had made my blood run cold.

"Indeed. Evidently they are engaged in organized patrols. In addition, some aspects of Alyrion law have been enacted in parts of the city. Limits on the private ownership of weapons; restrictions on the practice of some religious ceremonies."

Volya slammed a fist down on the table. "They're like a tumor growing on the island! This is *exactly* what I've been talking about."

"It seems likely," Senovo continued in an even tone, "that, given the degree of collusion between Rhyth and Alyrios, any attack on the Rhytheeri would garner a response from the Empire's troops—many of whom are already stationed here."

Volya glared at him. "Would you rather fight them here, or in the streets of Draebard?"

"I would rather not fight them at all. However, since peace does not appear to be an option, it seems more prudent to fight them somewhere we actually have a chance of beating them."

I could see Andoc visibly restraining himself from entering the conversation, and felt my own anger flare again. How foolish was Volya to silence his own best warrior when war was imminent?

Volya's response was interrupted by the crack of wood hitting stone on the dais. Horns sounded, announcing the arrival of the Rhytheeri ruler and his retinue. I looked around. The room seemed less tightly packed than it had yesterday. I wondered if some of the tribes had already left amidst yesterday's infighting.

Once King Flenaar was installed on his throne, the official who had called the meeting to order spoke. "Good people of the north," he said, "we have an honored guest today. Upon hearing of this meeting, the Emperor of Alyrios has sent his own representative to speak to you, that you may better understand the implications of any decisions made here."

The crowd muttered at the unexpected news, and I felt a tinge of unease. This was supposed to be a chance for *Eburosi* leaders to come together and discuss things. The main doors opened, and a wiry, silver-haired man with a patrician nose strode in. My breath caught, and Senovo's hand closed on my knee under the table to steady me. The Alyrion representative could have been the brother of the Field Marshall that had held and tortured us at the hill fort, so similar were they in appearance.

To make matters worse, he was followed into the meeting hall by fully two dozen armed Alyrion soldiers, who marched behind him and clattered to a halt as he stepped up onto the dais. The soldiers pivoted and positioned themselves at regular intervals along the main walkway leading from the door to the throne, looking out over the crowd as if on guard.

"What is the meaning of this?" someone cried. Several people stood up in shock or anger, including Volya. Andoc, Jacun, and the other warriors at the table tensed. Jacun's hand went for a sword that wasn't there.

My heart was pounding in my throat. Senovo still clasped my knee, motioning with his other hand for Favian to stand behind Andoc for protection. None of the visiting tribesmen were armed—it was part of the protocol for diplomatic talks that weapons be left behind so that everyone could speak freely, without fear. To bring armed soldiers into such a parlay was an outrage.

The Alyrion official turned and surveyed the scene from next to King Flenaar's throne, looking down his nose at the assembled crowd. "Calm yourselves, please," he said, his voice carrying through the echoing stone space. "These men are my personal guard, nothing more. Please, take your seats."

Volya did no such thing. Instead, he pointed accusingly. "You bring armed men to a parlay! I have long known that the Empire lacked honor, but this proves it yet again!"

A swell of supportive voices rose from the other tables.

The Alyrion raised an eyebrow. "A mere cultural misunderstanding, I assure you. There was some question of my personal safety at such a… *contentious* meeting. You are in no danger from my men. Let us move on to more important matters. I am here to discuss the Emperor's terms for peace. It is my understanding that Ambassador Derenza already communicated the details to many of you during his travels across the northlands."

Volya was still standing, as were several other people. "You can take your terms right back to the Emperor and tell him to stick them where the sun doesn't shine. The north will not pay tribute to a tin-pot dictator with delusions of godhood," he said. "Nor will we listen to this claptrap any longer. We are leaving."

With that, he pushed away from the table and gestured us to follow him. There was little choice but to do what he said. I held my breath as the Chief strode straight up to one of the guards and shouldered past him. The Alyrion's hand closed on the hilt of his sword and the sound of steel being drawn was unnaturally loud in the silent room.

"Stand down, soldier," said the Alyrion official from his position on the dais. "Everyone here is fully aware of the consequences of such defiance, once the Emperor hears of it."

The soldier slid his sword back into the scabbard, watching impassively as the rest of us walked past him and headed to the main doors. Behind us, I could hear other chairs scraping against the floor as if more people were rising and leaving, but I could not bring myself to look back. Being so close to armed and armored Alyrions was threatening to send my mind straight back to the room in the hill fort where I had been kept shackled in the cold and dark, convinced that Senovo and I would both be tortured to death before anyone came to rescue us. Only Senovo's hand clenched tight on my shoulder kept me upright and moving forward.

When my awareness next flickered back to the present, we were standing in front of our rooms, though I had absolutely no memory of getting there.

"Pack your things," Volya snapped. "We'll not spend another minute accepting the Rhytheeri's *hospitality.*"

Andoc looked from me to Volya's retreating back. "I *have* to try to talk to him," he said.

"Go," Senovo replied. "I've got her."

I couldn't really follow what they were talking about, but a moment later, Senovo was leading me into the room I'd been sharing with Andoc. "Favian, wait for me in our room, please. I'll be along as soon as I can. Start packing our saddlebags," he said.

When we were alone, he moved to stand in front of me, holding me firmly by the upper arms. "Look at me," he said. "I'm safe. We're both safe. Do you know where we are, Carivel?"

"Yes," I said, and burst into helpless tears, clutching at him. He pulled me close and held me through the short storm of weeping.

His soothing voice murmured against my ear. "*All who seek shelter shall find it. All who grieve shall be comforted. All the gods' children will receive solace. Ask at the temple and gain the help you need.* Breathe for me, now, Carivel. Just breathe."

I nodded and leaned against him for a few more moments before pushing away. "Sorry. *Sorry,*" I told him, swiping at my face with one hand. "I'm all right now."

He ducked a bit to get a better view of my face. Satisfied, he blew out a breath. "Well. This has certainly been a less than ideal development."

The door opened and closed, admitting Andoc. "Volya won't even speak with me," he said in a grim voice. "Carivel?"

I waved him off. "I'm fine. Sorry. Just had a bad moment when that soldier went for his sword."

Andoc drew me into a brief embrace and kissed the top of my head. "Don't worry about it. I've been having a series of bad moments pretty much since we got here."

"As have we all, I think. Since it appears that we are, in fact, leaving, I'll go help Favian get ready," said Senovo.

Andoc nodded.

"Thanks, Senovo," I said. The priest smiled, or tried to—a brief quirk of the lips that did not reach his eyes.

I slumped back against Andoc's steady strength. "This is really, really bad, isn't it?"

"We were going to end up fighting the Empire regardless. What terrifies me is the idea that we might just have lost our best chance of allying with the other tribes. I mean, we'll still be fighting the same enemy, but if we don't collaborate on strategy…"

He trailed off, but the meaning was clear. Unaffiliated tribes fighting as ragged individual bands of warriors had no chance against the full might of Alyrios.

"Come on," I told him, wiping at my face again. There was nothing else to say, really. "Let's get packed up. Volya would probably relish an excuse to leave the two of us behind."

We bundled up our meager belongings and headed out into the hall, joining the rest of our party. Magoldis and the Mereni contingent were just returning as we left. Volya shouldered past the redheaded Leader, ignoring her hiss of annoyance. She met my eyes as I followed meekly along in the others' wake. I got the impression she wanted to say something, but in the end, she just shook her head in irritation and continued toward her room.

⤙ ⚜ ⤚

Some time later, we were trotting on horseback through Rhyth's congested roadways with the pack animals in tow. The back of my neck prickled whenever an Alyrion soldier patrolling the city turned to watch us ride past. Volya was going on loudly and at length about the dishonor of the Empire and the spinelessness of the Rhytheeri, which did nothing for my nerves.

I had wondered during the previous day's meetings about the King's odd behavior. For such a proud man, he'd seemed content enough to let the tribal leaders argue back and forth about attacking the south without ever raising an objection. Now, it occurred to me that he had gotten exactly what he'd wanted — discord between the northern tribes and a lack of organized opposition to the Empire's advance into Eburosi territory.

Andoc and Senovo had probably already realized that. I wondered if Volya truly had no inkling, or if he was just too angry and prideful to care. Now, the Chief was telling Jacun that the Empire would never have time to organize an invasion into the northlands before winter set in, and bragging that by spring, he'd have an alliance of tribes ready to descend on Rhyth. Jacun nodded in agreement every once in a while, otherwise keeping silent — his face pale and set.

Again, I was struck by how enormous Rhyth really was, as we finally reached one of the openings in the wall that demarcated the outer boundaries of the city proper. Beyond, the houses and other structures thinned out. Even further away lay the strangely homogenous fields of grain, beans, and other food crops. Now, I had a better understanding of the logic behind such strange farming practices. A population the size of the one behind us could never live on hunting, herding, and the occasional garden plot. The slaves in the fields labored not to feed their families, or even their masters' families. They labored to feed the entire city of Rhyth.

I suddenly longed for the simple village I'd called home for the last three — almost four — years, with a depth of feeling I would never have expected, given my recent trials there. Draebard had not always been good to me, but it was my home now, and I desperately wanted to get back to it.

Unfortunately, there were still six solid days of riding between us and Draebard, all of it to be spent with a Chief who seemed, at times, to be losing touch with reason. I ached anew for Andoc, hurt deeply by his mentor's betrayal, though he fought not to show it. Andoc had always placed a huge amount of importance on his skill and position as a warrior, I knew. I vowed to make absolutely sure he was aware that I didn't care one whit whether he was First Warrior or a winemaker or someone who fired clay pots for a living, as long as he was ours. Mine, and Senovo's.

The houses around us gave way to a stretch of road leading north toward the fields and the river. There were few people out and about at this time of late morning—for the most part, everyone was busy doing whatever it was they normally did for the day. We rounded a bend, and finally the sights and sounds of the city were truly behind us. I took a deep breath and let it out, soaking in the sound of the wind rustling the leaves of the trees off to our left, and the grass turning from green to gold in the dry summer sun to our right.

Volya had finally gone silent, thank the gods. In fact, no one seemed to have much stomach for conversation. It was for that reason we were able to hear the distant pounding of hoof beats approaching from some distance behind us. Andoc reined his mount to a halt and turned to see what was happening, but the galloping riders were still hidden by the trees and the bend in the road.

"Someone's in a hurry," Jacun said with a frown, halting his own horse as well.

"We should get out of the road," said Andoc. "Let them past."

Volya motioned for us to do so, and we led the packhorses off the packed dirt and onto the grassy verge away from the trees. The same prickly feeling that had afflicted me in the city returned with a vengeance.

"Andoc, I don't like this," I said.

"Believe me, you're not the only one," he replied.

Volya and the warriors drew their swords, moving forward to face the curve where the approaching riders would appear while Favian, Senovo, and I held back. I glanced over at Favian, only to discover that he was deathly pale, his eyes full of terror. He opened his mouth as if to say something or shout a warning, but no sound came out.

"Favian?" I asked, only to whirl around as the galloping riders rounded the bend and charged toward us.

Before I could even blink, a javelin flew through the air and impaled itself in Volya's side, knocking him from his horse to lie in a heap on the ground.

"Carivel!" Andoc shouted. "Get the others into the trees! *Run!*"

ELEVEN

I was frozen for a bare instant before the command registered. "Come on!" I yelled, and grabbed Favian's reins since he still seemed to be mired in whatever horror had gripped him a moment ago. Kekenu and I charged toward the trees on the other side of the road, with Favian's and Senovo's horses flanking us. Senovo's longer-legged mare drew half a length ahead, only to fall as another javelin buried itself in her neck. Kekenu twisted under me, dodging around his injured herd mate.

"*No!*" I screamed, watching in horror as Senovo went down with the horse, only to roll free in the form of the wolf an instant later. The animal fought its way loose from Senovo's clothing and scrambled upright, unhurt. He snarled and bounded back the way we'd come, toward the fighting.

"Senovo, *don't!*" I cried, but it was too late. He was gone.

I dragged Favian's horse into the shelter of the trees, ducking and weaving to get deeper into the underbrush. We were not well hidden by any means, but at least in here a javelin would most likely hit a tree trunk before it could hit us.

"Oh, gods," Favian whimpered beside me, one hand covering his mouth, "oh, *gods*, it's my fault. My fault!"

I could spare no further thought for him, though, watching the vicious battle from between the gaps in the trees. *Please, Mighty Deresta*, I prayed with every fiber of my being, *let us get out of this and I swear I will learn archery properly and never go unarmed again. Please, please...*

Andoc charged his bay gelding directly at one of the attackers, sword raised in readiness. I had expected the riders to be Alyrion, but they wore Rhytheeri garb. The two opponents collided with a dull thud of horseflesh and went down. My stomach heaved as Andoc's gelding rolled once and staggered to its feet, leaving his rider on the ground. Andoc tried to rise and fell back with a cry, his leg twisting under him. His sword was still in his hand, though, and he crawled toward the motionless heap that was Volya.

The Rhytheeri horse flailed and, badly injured, could not rise. Its rider lay nearby, unmoving. At that moment, the wolf leapt into the fray, tearing at the hamstrings of one of the attackers who had been unhorsed during the initial clash of fighting. The Draebardi warriors were outnumbered, though — fighting back to back in a tight knot while Andoc sprawled across Volya, his sword at the ready to protect the fallen Chief.

"We have to go help!" Favian cried, trying to drag his horse's reins free from my grip.

I held on, feeling sick to my stomach as I said, "Favian, *no!* We'll just be a distraction to the others!"

With a cry of frustration, Favian flung himself out of the saddle. I followed, quick as a flash, and grabbed his arm to stop him. He struggled, yanking against my grip. "Let me go! I have to — it's *my fault!*"

I still couldn't spare the attention to try and make sense of his words. Beyond the trees, Jacun staggered with a cry as his opponent's sword found its mark, but righted himself and immediately resumed fighting. One of the other warriors fell — I couldn't make out who it was. The battle looked hopeless, and I blinked away the tears of horror that were threatening to blur my vision.

My mind was slow with fear. I had to figure out what to do — should we run or hide if the others fell? Would Favian fight against me? Give away our presence with his struggles? More hoof beats pounded toward the fight and I nearly shouted in relief as Magoldis and the rest of the Mereni galloped onto the scene as if from nowhere.

With my heart pounding, I crept closer to the edge of the trees to watch, still maintaining a tight grip on Favian's arm. The Mereni warriors descended like avenging spirits, their battle cries echoing through the trees. The tide turned swiftly — the Rhytheeri attackers now the ones outnumbered and already weary from fighting.

I tried to follow the chaotic battle, but dust had risen to obscure the twisting bodies of horses and humans as metal rang against metal. When things finally quieted, I grabbed Favian's hand and we charged forward to rejoin the others. Several

Mereni whirled toward us with raised weapons, only to relax upon recognizing us.

Most of those who were still on horseback dismounted now that the fighting was over, though a couple rode off to keep watch along the road for any more approaching riders. I skidded to a halt amidst the scene of devastation. The wolf appeared unhurt, crouched protectively next to Andoc. Andoc was conscious but pale, clutching at his right leg, which was twisted horribly above the ankle. The iron band around my lungs eased at seeing them both alive, even as my stomach rebelled at the unnatural, *wrong* angle of Andoc's broken limb.

I looked away, only to have my eyes fall on the dead bodies littering the area. Deven and Guldarok, the other two Draebardi warriors who had accompanied us, were obviously beyond help. A Mereni warrior who I didn't know by name lay nearby, his head nearly separated from his shoulders. The eight—no, *nine*—Rhytheeri attackers also lay dead. Jacun sat a slight distance away, holding his tunic up while Keenan and another Mereni warrior fussed over a deep slash running across his side.

Magoldis knelt next to a huddled form in the trampled grass near Andoc and the wolf. In a daze, I let go of Favian's hand and moved closer, dropping into a crouch next to Andoc. The Mereni Leader lifted Volya's upper body to settle him in her lap. Blood pulsed around the wooden shaft impaling the old man's side, in time with his still beating heart. His eyes were glazed, but he blinked up at the red-haired Leader with recognition.

"What are you doing here, woman?" he asked, his voice barely more than a hoarse whisper.

Magoldis' brows drew together, and her own voice was suspiciously unsteady. "I came after you to yell at you some more, you idiotic old man."

"Oh? Do I have to take your screeching into the afterlife with me as well, then, harridan?" asked Volya, no malice left behind the words.

The Mereni Leader was silent for a long moment. "You know, I might have married you if you hadn't been such a conceited prick about it," she said eventually.

The rusty sound that emerged from the Chief's throat could almost have been a laugh. "Eh. We'd have killed each other inside of a week." He tried to lift his head and look around, his expression clouding. "Where's Andoc? Is he — ?"

"He's alive," Magoldis said.

"Oh… good. *Good.* Tell him… sorry. He's a… brave lad. I shouldn't've…"

Volya trailed off. He coughed, and blood bubbled from his mouth. His eyes slipped closed as he fought for breath, the wet sound loud and horrible in the unnatural silence of the impromptu battlefield. We watched, unable to look away, as the old Chief's breathing grew more labored, and finally rumbled into silence on a final, shaky exhalation.

Magoldis looked at Andoc, weeping silently next to me, and back down at the dead Draebardi chieftain cradled in her arms. "He heard you, old man."

⚜

After allowing us a scant few moments to indulge our shocked grief, Magoldis urged us to get moving. "Carivel," she said, "go round up the horses. First, though — the wolf. Either get him back to human again or get him away from Andoc. We need to set the bones in that broken leg so we can splint it — and I'd rather not have my throat torn out for my troubles."

The wolf shook itself, and a moment later Senovo was steadying himself against Andoc's shoulder, breathing heavily.

"All right?" I asked, and he nodded, wrapping a protective arm around Andoc's upper body. With a final glance at Andoc — still clutching his injured leg, his face a portrait of misery — I got unsteadily to my feet and went to fetch Kekenu from the woods.

I was glad to be elsewhere a few minutes later, when Andoc's choked scream proclaimed that someone had realigned the bones in his leg… or at least, tried to. Queasiness warred with guilt at not being there for him, but I told myself that what I was doing was more important, and he wouldn't want an audience to his pain, regardless.

Kekenu nickered as I approached. I was pleased to see Favian's horse still hovering close by, though the reins had tangled around the animal's front legs, causing the leather to snap. I caught the chestnut gelding and knotted the reins back together so they were usable. After a quick check of Kekenu's girth, I mounted and led the other horse back out onto the road.

Favian was still standing exactly where I'd abandoned him earlier, as if unable to move or act on his own. I was worried about him, but frankly I was worried about a lot of things right now, and he was just going to have to wait until we were somewhere safe.

"Favian!" I called. He looked over at me slowly, still pale and gray-faced. I rode up and tossed him the reins to his horse. His hands came up to catch them reflexively. "Mount up," I ordered in my best Horse Mistress voice. "You're helping me round up the loose horses."

The boy looked at the reins in his hands as if he'd never seen them before. "I—I can't—"

"Yes, you gods-damn well can," I said, channeling Jorun. "Now, *mount. The fuck. Up.*"

A faint flush of pink colored Favian's pale cheeks, and he scrambled into the saddle. I stole a glance at the cluster of figures in the grass beside the road. Andoc was slumped in Senovo's embrace. At some point, someone had found the priest's robes and draped them over his shoulders. Magoldis and Briethe were crouched over Andoc's leg, working on splinting it.

I tore my gaze away. "Come on," I said, and led Favian out into the grassy field where several of the horses had run after they got loose.

It took quite some time to get all the animals rounded up and perform makeshift repairs on the broken tack. Magoldis ruthlessly quashed Keenan's suggestion of camping here by the road, to allow the injured to recover a bit before trying to travel.

"In case you hadn't noticed, the Draebardi are marked for death," she said plainly. "Chances are, so are we. We're going home. Load up our dead on some of the Rhytheeri horses. Leave the assassins behind for the carrion birds."

So it was that our ragged group made its way north through the fields of wheat, oats, and lentils, avoiding roads and settlements where possible. I'd put Andoc and Senovo together on Kekenu's broad back. I led them by the reins from Andoc's horse. The bay gelding had thankfully escaped serious injury—unlike his owner. Senovo sat behind Andoc, practically holding him up as the blinding pain of his broken leg threatened to send him into unconsciousness with every jounce or bump.

Jacun, with his midriff tightly bandaged to slow the bleeding from the sword wound in his side, rode by himself for a while, the reins clutched in one hand and his other arm wrapped around the injury. Before long, though, we were forced to stop so one of the Mereni men could hop up behind him to give him something to lean against, and to control the horse for him.

Favian, as a former apprentice at the horse pens, had been tasked with leading the string of nervous horses carrying the bodies of Volya and the dead warriors. Others led the packhorses, and the whole procession was so painfully slow that I dreaded to think how long it would take us even to get to the mountains—much less, home.

As the sun slipped low in the sky, we stopped at the edge of a small river, where the woods hid us from prying eyes. It took three Mereni warriors to get Andoc down safely to the ground from Kekenu's back, and even then, he cried out as his leg was jostled. Jacun was pale and feverish, the bandage wrapped around his torso stained with red.

I hurried around, helping set up camp and see to the horses as fast as I could manage. When I returned, Briethe was ordering two men to carry Andoc to the edge of the river and set him down so his leg was trailing in the gentle current, in hopes of bringing down the swelling. Someone had cut his boot off earlier and slit his breeches to the knee. Even in the fading light, I was shocked at how bad the leg looked—black and blue with bruising, and swollen to more than twice its normal size within the confines of the tightly bound splints.

Andoc groaned back into awareness at the first touch of cold water. Senovo and I immediately replaced the Mereni men, supporting Andoc between us at the edge of the river.

"How are you?" I asked, even though the question was beyond foolish.

Andoc only shook his head, and let it loll against Senovo's shoulder.

"Senovo?" I asked, letting it go for now. "What about you?"

"About the same as yourself, I would imagine."

That bad? I almost asked, but caught myself before the words came out. We sat there for some considerable time, with

Andoc swimming in and out of consciousness in our arms. Eventually, a rustle of movement caught my attention and I looked up to see Favian approaching with food and drink for us. The boy still looked like death.

"Sit, Favian," Senovo said. "I fear we have been neglecting you, Little Brother."

As if his words had opened the floodgates, Favian sank to the ground and broke down into hitching sobs. I was exhausted, not remotely up to dealing with yet another crisis, but once again, Senovo proved to have a nearly limitless well of patience and strength, at least for those he considered his charges.

"Come now," he said. "Set the food aside for the moment and just sit with us. It has been a terrible, trying day."

Favian set the food carefully to one side and curled up in a ball, just beyond Senovo's reach. "I have come to ask for forgiveness, Elder Brother. I'm s-so sorry. I didn't mean for this to happen!"

I remembered Favian's odd behavior during the battle, even as Senovo frowned in the gray light of dusk and spoke. "Little Brother, you have done nothing that requires absolution." His confusion came through clearly in his tone.

Favian shook his head almost violently, his arms still wrapped around his knees.

I spoke softly, recalling Favian's words. "During the attack, you kept saying it was your fault. It's not your fault, Favian. The Rhytheeri attacked us because Volya defied the Empire."

"You don't understand! I didn't warn you ahead of time, and I could have! I dreamed what happened, last night, but I was too scared to say anything! Now the Chief is dead, and Deven and Guldarok. Jacun and Andoc are injured, and I could have stopped it!"

TWELVE

Senovo breathed out, a long and controlled exhalation. "Little Brother," he said, "you had no way of knowing your dream would come to pass. How could you know? It has never happened to you before."

"I dreamed the mountain!" Favian retorted. "I've never *been* to the southern mountains before, but it was the same place!"

"You dreamed a mountain on fire, with people burning. That did not happen," said Senovo carefully. "There was no way of knowing about this dream, and even if you had, the attack was upon us so quickly that there was nothing you could have done to help."

"There should have been," Favian said through his tears.

"There wasn't," Andoc said weakly, evidently having awoken to hear Favian's declaration. "It's not your fault, Favian."

The boy buried his head in his knees to muffle his weeping. Senovo sighed and left Andoc leaning against me so he could cross the short distance and gather Favian into his arms. He scooted back, pulling the boy with him until we were all huddled together at the edge of the river.

"You are not to blame," he said with finality, tucking Favian under his chin and letting him cry himself out.

I hugged Andoc closer, taking in the implications of Favian's revelation. My former apprentice had the second sight. I remembered that Jyrrel, the Mereni High Priest, had a similar gift, and wondered at it. This must have been what Senovo was worried about, both after Favian's fever dream, and this morning when his screams woke us. He was right, though— even if Favian had warned us ahead of time, it was unlikely that Volya would have taken such a thing seriously enough to change his course of action. And, as Senovo said, the attack had been so sudden and violent that a few more seconds of warning would have done little to change the outcome.

I shivered, thinking about what it would be like to dream of horrific future events, never knowing until it was too late whether such a dream was a true vision, or simply a nightmare.

As often seemed to happen, Senovo's thoughts were running parallel to my own. "High Priest Jyrrel of the Mereni has a similar ability to your own, Favian. We will go and speak to him as soon as is practical, once we get home."

Home.

I refused to think about the possibility that we wouldn't be able to get back to Draebard safely. Yet it was there, lurking in the back of my mind. Jacun could still die of blood loss from his wound, and I could barely conceive of someone riding for five days with a broken leg as Andoc would now be forced to do—through the mountains, no less.

My unhappy thoughts were interrupted by Briethe's approach, and I looked up.

"Elder," I said, by way of greeting.

"A sad day," she said, easing herself down carefully to sit next to the wineskin and pile of traveling rations Favian had brought earlier. Briethe unwrapped the pemmican and handed a portion to Senovo, who passed it on to me when Andoc shook his head in weary negation. The rest of us ate slowly, knowing that we had to keep our strength up.

"I neglected to thank you earlier for assisting with Andoc's leg," Senovo said.

Briethe only shrugged. "I'm no healer, but you learn a thing or two by the time you reach my age. Glad I could be of some help. Now, though, it would be best if he could at least drink some watered wine. Or, better yet, un-watered wine, to help with the pain." She passed the wineskin, and I helped Andoc steady it and take a few sips. "That's better. I know it's an awkward spot here on the riverbank, but if you can, you should bed yourselves down right here so that leg can stay in the water overnight. Traveling will make the swelling much worse—we must combat it in any way we can."

"We'll figure something out, in that case," I said. "Thank you."

"A *sad* day," she said again, climbing stiffly to her feet and pausing to give my shoulder a gentle pat as she wandered off.

I left Andoc in Senovo's care so I could build a little fire near us and bring our bedrolls down. We plied Andoc with more wine, although I suspected that it wasn't going to be enough to even touch the pain of a shattered leg — not unless we got him so drunk he passed out. That would bring with it far more problems than it solved come the following morning, so we only urged him to drink enough to slake his thirst.

I set up the bedrolls so Andoc could lie back and keep his lower leg in the water, while Favian and I lay on either side of him, our heads even with his chest and our feet pointing away from the river. That way, he couldn't roll over in his sleep and hurt himself more, or end up in the waterway somehow.

When everyone else was settled, Senovo shed his robes and crouched down, shifting back into the form of the wolf. The big predator curled up in the space above Andoc's head, framed by my body and Favian's. He scooted down until Andoc took the hint and used his haunches as a furry pillow, before huffing out a little rumble of satisfaction and tucking his nose under his tail to sleep.

✵

The night was long and restless. I kept waking to the noise of Andoc groaning in discomfort, or carefully schooling his breathing to hide the strain he was feeling. I pressed my face into his upper arm, wishing there was *anything* I could do to help him.

The following morning, the swelling in Andoc's leg was somewhat reduced, and he gamely nibbled on a bit of dried fruit before letting himself be hoisted onto a different horse. Senovo — once again in human form — braced him from behind, same as yesterday. I was careful to put the two of them on a docile animal. I would have much preferred to keep them on Kekenu for the whole journey, but it was too much to ask of the little gelding. He was strong for his size, but not strong enough to carry two grown men almost half the length of Eburos.

So, today, I rode Kekenu instead, leading Andoc and Senovo on a bay mare that I knew to be even-tempered. Nonetheless, every time she took a misstep on the uneven ground or snorted at something off in the bushes, my jaw clenched a bit tighter.

We were forced to ride at a slow walk, stopping frequently, and I could already tell that we were progressing far more slowly than we had on the trip here. Jacun was weak enough that he, too, had to be held upright on his horse, though at least the bleeding from his wound had slowed to a trickle during the night. We still kept away from the main roads, but this forced us to take long detours whenever we came to a river too deep to cross with our injured, or terrain too rough to traverse.

We saw few people—only the occasional group of slaves working in the fields when we strayed close to cultivated land. They gave us a wide berth, looking on with dull eyes as we plodded along, some of our horses laden with blanket-wrapped dead bodies that were already starting to stink and attract flies as rot set in.

Every day, Jacun seemed to get a little better, while Andoc got a little worse. He was stoic, bearing the pain without complaint, but his leg grew more swollen every evening, and he frequently had trouble maintaining awareness long enough to carry on a conversation.

It took us five days to reach the mountains, and the ascent that had been difficult before was positively tortuous now. By day, Senovo rode behind Andoc, his arms wrapped tightly around the wounded man. By night, the wolf watched over him, curling up next to him to offer comfort and warmth. Senovo, too, grew more drawn and gaunt-looking with every endless day of riding. I'm sure I did as well. My shoulders were knotted with constant tension and worry; I had to force myself to eat and drink.

On the eighth day after our departure from Rhyth, we descended into the foothills on the northern side of the range. Magoldis and her advisors seemed to have concluded that we were now safe from pursuit, because we kept to the roads and tracks from that point on, rather than riding across country.

It should have taken us two more days to reach Draebard. Instead, though we were able to make better progress now that we had roads to follow, it took us three-and-a-half. During the last two, Andoc became delirious when he was aware at all, frequently struggling against Senovo's grip, begging us not to amputate his leg. It was a testament to both Andoc's weakness and Senovo's determination that the priest's hold never faltered, even as weariness and worry seemed to age him before my eyes.

When we finally—*finally*—reached the familiar roads running through the logging areas south of the village, we met

Jeppel and a couple of other men pulling felled logs back to Draebard with a team of horses.

"Jeppel!" I called as soon as we were within hailing distance.

The men looked up. When we got close enough, I dismounted from the horse I was riding that day.

"What happened?" Jeppel asked, eyeing the motley group with its bundled bodies, swarming with flies. "Where is the Chief?"

"Ride ahead to the village, as fast as you can," I told him, ignoring the questions. "Get Healer Sagdea. Tell her we have injured… and dead." Jeppel's mouth was hanging open, but to my relief, he climbed up on the horse I handed him and dug his heels into its sides, heading for Draebard at a gallop.

The other loggers stared at us in dismay as we trudged toward home, leaving them behind. Leading Kekenu and his precious cargo on foot brought every ache in my body into focus, but the constant movement also helped to keep the weariness at bay. None of us had been able to sleep properly. Senovo and I had hardly been able to sleep at all since Andoc's condition deteriorated into feverish incoherence.

Even now, he mumbled heartbreaking pleas not to cut him—not to take his leg. "Just let me die!" he slurred, pushing weakly at Senovo's supporting arm. Senovo's hand kept an iron grip on his tunic, grasping the linen fabric with claw-like fingers that refused to let go.

The familiar huts of Draebard appeared through gaps in the trees, and I don't think I'd ever been so relieved to see anything in my life. Jeppel had been good to his word, and people were hurrying out to meet us.

"The Healer is waiting in the temple," called one of them, and I recognized Favian's father, Renthro, carrying little Frella against one hip.

"Father!" Favian cried, and flung himself from his horse to run to his father's embrace.

"Thank the gods, Favian," Renthro said into Favian's hair. "When Jeppel came riding into town with the news, I feared the worst."

"I'm alright, Papa. But I—I have to go help at the temple now."

I felt a flash of pride as Favian straightened and went to take the rope connected to the horses carrying the dead bodies. Several other people stepped forward to take the packhorses away and unload them. I gestured to the man riding with Jacun to follow us and led Kekenu toward the temple, where Healer Sagdea was waiting for us.

"Where will I find the village elders?" Leader Magoldis called out.

Renthro answered. "Ask at the meeting house. Someone there will help you."

Magoldis nodded. She and Briethe peeled away to head for the meeting hall. Keenan trotted up next to me.

"Shall I go tell Dalon that you're back?" she asked.

"Yes, please," I said. "Let him know what has happened and that I'll be at the temple. I'll try to get to the pens before nightfall. Tell him to get a poultice on Andoc's gelding's hind leg. I don't like the way it's been swelling the past few days."

The group broke up on their various errands. A couple of the Mereni warriors followed me to help get Jacun and Andoc off their horses and inside the temple, for which I was grateful. As the familiar building came into view, Novice Feldes bustled out to meet us. His deep-set eyes ran over our little procession, taking everything in.

"Favian," he said, his voice admirably calm, "take the bodies to the area behind the temple, near the river. Eiridan and some of the acolytes will meet you there to deal with them. High Priest, are these two the only ones injured?"

"The only ones bad enough to require the Healer, yes," Senovo said, his voice rusty and exhausted.

Jacun roused himself to speak. "Help Andoc first. I'm all right. Just get me to a bed and I'll be fine."

"It's true that Andoc's condition is more serious," Senovo confirmed, "but they both need care."

Feldes nodded, and fussed around us as the uninjured helped the injured down from their horses and supported them inside. Senovo dismounted from Kekenu once Andoc was safely in the arms of the two burly Mereni men who had followed along to assist. He wavered a bit as his feet touched the ground, and I steadied him.

Reston emerged a moment later and came to take the horses. I handed over Kekenu's reins and thanked him. "Take them to the pens and have Dalon corral the Mereni horses separately," I told him.

The feeling of relief at having other people to rely on once again was intense, but it didn't eliminate my desperate worry for Andoc. Senovo and I hurried inside, following the sounds of movement and voices. Andoc and Jacun had been taken to two unused rooms in the temple barracks, side by side so the Healer could move from one to the other as efficiently as possible.

She was with Andoc when we arrived. "Out! Out! For the gods' sake, how do you expect me to work with you all hovering?" said the Healer. "Feldes, get me that sedating infusion I asked for. I don't have all day!"

Feldes and the Mereni men pushed past us in their haste to get out of the room, and away from her wrath. Senovo and I hovered in the doorway, watching as Sagdea muttered to herself and snapped directions to her apprentice, who was busy unwrapping the wooden splints around Andoc's hideously swollen leg.

Andoc cried out and flailed at the women, obviously with no understanding of where he was. The Healer cursed and wrestled his nearest wrist back to the bed. Her attention flickered to the two of us standing in the doorway.

"You two," she said. "Get in here and keep him calm while we work."

Senovo broke free from his immobility an instant before I did. We squeezed past the healers and seated ourselves on either side of the bed, each taking a hand. Andoc's weak, uncoordinated movements hit me someplace deep inside—it was wrong, for him of all people, to be so helpless. Andoc was the strong one. Andoc was the one who kept us all going when things were hard. I wasn't quite sure how to exist in a world where that was no longer the case, and it frightened me.

"When did this happen, exactly?" Sagdea asked.

I cast my mind back, trying to do the mental math, but Senovo beat me to it. "Eleven days ago," he said softly.

"And the delirium?"

"Two days," I replied. "Though he was in and out of awareness well before that."

Sagdea cursed again and went back to ignoring us. I stroked Andoc's forehead with my free hand, but he only jerked his head back and forth, trying to avoid the touch. "No..." he moaned. "Leave me 'lone... don't take my leg... *don't...*"

"No one's taking your leg," I said, a bit desperately, but Andoc did not register the words.

"Bit early to promise that," Sagdea said, her voice grim as she bent close to prod at the livid bruising.

Worry lodged in my throat, rendering me mute.

"He has clearly and repeatedly expressed his preference to keep the leg, no matter what," Senovo said, though I could see that it cost him to do so.

Sagdea shook her head, still not looking up from the injury. "It won't necessarily be up to him. Not if he was already delirious when he started saying that." Her eyes flicked up to meet mine for a fraction of an instant, and I felt the blood drain from my face.

"Such discussions can wait until you have had more of a chance to assess things, can they not?" Senovo asked.

"Hmm," Sagdea said in backhanded agreement, clearly paying more attention to Andoc's leg than to our discomfort with the conversation. When she spoke again, it was to her assistant. "Methea, go find something we can use to elevate the limb. Then return to my hut and get the lower leg splints and my leeches."

"Yes, Healer," Methea replied, and hurried from the room.

Feldes returned a minute later, with a cup of liquid in his hands.

"Get that into him," Sagdea ordered brusquely.

Feldes handed the cup to Senovo, who handed it to me while he rearranged himself against the headboard and lifted Andoc's upper body to rest against his. The smell from the rich liquid was sweet and slightly earthy—I recognized it as the same drink Senovo had prepared for me to help me sleep after our return from the hill fort.

I gave it back to him and gathered both of Andoc's hands in mine to keep him from moving. The day was warm and it had been hours since we'd gotten any liquid into him, so thankfully Andoc drank without fighting us once the pleasant mixture touched his lips. A few minutes later, his restless movements and disconnected mumbling trailed off, leaving him limp in Senovo's arms.

"That's better," the Healer said, finishing her palpation of the injured limb.

"How bad?" Senovo asked.

"Bad," said the old woman. "Whoever set it got the bones pretty well aligned, but the muscles are badly torn and this swelling—*ha*! I'll be wanting a word with whoever decided that sitting him on a horse for eleven days without getting him proper treatment first was a good idea."

"That would be me, as it happens," came a new voice from the door, and I looked up to find the Mereni Leader standing there.

Sagdea straightened. "Is that so? Well, you may have cost this young man his leg. What in the gods' names were you *thinking*, making him travel like that?"

Magoldis only raised an eyebrow. "I was thinking that we were in hostile territory full of people trying to kill us, and had better get out of there as soon as gods-damn well possible. How is the other one? Jacun?"

Sagdea huffed. "My assistant looked at him. He is a singularly lucky young man. The wound is not infected, and while he may lose some range of motion on that side, the placement means he should not be badly maimed."

"That's as well," Magoldis said, "seeing as how he is your new Chief."

The Healer stilled for a moment, her shoulders bowing. "It's true, then."

"Yes," Senovo said. "Volya is dead, as are Deven and Guldarok."

"I spoke to the village elders and informed them of Volya's decision to make Jacun his First Warrior," Magoldis said.

I thought I detected a note of apology in the Leader's voice, but that didn't stop my temper from flaring. "You heard as well as I did when Volya expressed his regret over that decision with his dying breath!"

"I did," Magoldis agreed. "However, he did not formally revoke his previous pronouncement. In addition, there are other considerations right now."

"What *other considerations*?" I snapped.

To my surprise, it was Senovo who answered. "Draebard needs a Chief, Carivel. Andoc is in no condition to lead the village, and Jacun is a good man who will do his best for the people in these dangerous times."

THIRTEEN

That he was right did not prevent the little prick of betrayal I felt at Senovo's words.

"Just so," said Magoldis. "If Andoc survives, he will no doubt play an important role in Draebard's future."

My heart stuttered in sudden fear. "Of course he'll survive!" Without any conscious decision to do so, I looked to Sagdea for reassurance.

"I will do all I can for him," she said. "We will see how the leg looks tomorrow, and discuss our options then."

By *options*, I gathered she meant *amputation*, and my stomach churned anew. Methea returned, carrying a bundle of supplies, and Magoldis stepped back to let her past.

"I will take my leave now," Magoldis said. "Healer, do I have your permission to speak to Jacun? There is much to discuss."

Sagdea waved a hand in Magoldis' general direction. "Yes, yes. Don't wear him out though. Most of the danger is past, but the elders may have to muddle along without him for a few days yet."

"As you say," Magoldis agreed, and left without another word.

My head was still spinning with equal measures of worry and outrage at the unfairness of it all. Methea crossed to the bed to help Healer Sagdea splint the leg again and elevate it on a rough wooden frame carefully padded with blankets. Even in his unconscious state, Andoc moaned in pain as the leg was manipulated. Senovo and I soothed him as best we could.

Finally, Sagdea attached the leeches at strategic points across the swollen flesh. "They will help the blood to flow around the injury as it should, if the gods are kind," she said. "Now, I must go see to Jacun, and make sure that Mereni woman hasn't upset him too much. I will return soon. Make certain Andoc is not left alone."

With that, she and Methea gathered up their supplies and bustled out. I sat for a moment, simply breathing, as Senovo eased Andoc's upper body down to rest on the pillows. I got up and walked around the bed to his side, feeling so disconnected that it was as if I was floating, my feet never touching the floor. Senovo stood to meet me and I more or less fell into his arms. I knew I was shaking, so it took a few minutes for me to realize that he was, too.

"I don't know how to do this," I said, looking down at our unconscious touchstone.

Senovo was silent for a beat. "One moment at a time, I suppose. There is no other way, Carivel."

"We're home, at least," I said. "We made it this far."

"We did, yes. I can stay with him for now, but I will have to speak to the elders this evening."

I nodded. "I'll go to the horse pens and check in with Dalon, in that case. I'll be back in a couple of hours."

With a final squeeze, I pushed away from Senovo's embrace and reached down to kiss Andoc's cheek. When I looked back from the doorway, it was to see the priest once again sitting propped on the edge of the bed, his head tilted back to rest against the headboard, his fingers stroking through Andoc's hair.

⁓⟋ ♛ ⟍⁓

The horse pens were buzzing with mid-afternoon activity when I arrived. Limdya was the first to notice me, looking up from where Tenibral was showing her how to check a horse's legs for heat.

"Carivel!" she exclaimed, and several other people in the area looked up as well.

"Where is Dalon?" I asked without preamble.

"He's in the far pen," said Tenibral. "One of the Mereni horses was acting colicky."

"There are all sorts of stories flying around," Limdya said. "What happened? Is the Chief really—"

"Chief Volya is dead," I said loud enough for all those nearby to hear. "As are Deven and Guldarok, and one of the Mereni men who came to our aid. We were attacked by Rhytheeri assassins as we left the city."

"So Andoc is Chief now?" Tenibral asked.

I swallowed. "Andoc is… badly hurt. Jacun was also injured, but not as seriously. He is Chief now."

Limdya was watching me with eyes that saw too much, so I cleared my throat. "Get back to work. I need to speak with Dalon, and he can fill you in on more of the details later."

I escaped before Limdya could say anything in response and went looking for Dalon. As Tenibral had said, he was with the Mereni horses, listening to the gut sounds of a large chestnut mare while Lundis held up her opposite hind leg to keep her from kicking at him. I let them finish, waiting quietly.

"I think she's all right now — it sounds like things are moving again. Keep walking her until she passes manure, though, and don't forget to offer her water." Dalon straightened away and waved Lundis off to keep the mare moving around.

As soon as he noticed me, he lifted a hand in greeting. "Still in one piece, then?" he asked as we crossed to meet each other.

"One of the lucky ones, yeah," I said grimly. "Favian's all right, too."

"That's good. You know, someone needs to stick a sword through every last one of those southern bastards, not to mention their Alyrion fuck-buddies," Dalon said with all of the tact and diplomacy I'd come to expect from him. Mind you, it wasn't as though I was in disagreement with him, precisely.

"Chief Volya expressed a similar sentiment, not long before the Rhytheeri King sent a group of assassins after him and put a javelin through his gut," I replied. "And… I'm sorry, but Deven was killed in the same battle. I know he and your cousin were close."

Dalon nodded. "They'd been talking about handfasting each other in the autumn. She'll be distraught. I heard they got Guldarok, too?"

"Yeah. And one of the Mereni."

"How's Andoc?"

I looked away. "Broken leg. I guess it's pretty serious."

"He's strong. I'm sure he'll… y'know. Pull through." Dalon took a breath as if to add something else, but stopped himself. I looked back up at him.

"What?" I asked.

Dalon looked distinctly uncomfortable. "Nothing. Just… well, there's been some talk. You should maybe know about it so it doesn't take you by surprise."

A slight sense of foreboding settled in my chest, though I'd have thought there was little else that could go wrong at this point. "Go ahead, then," I said, my weariness coming through in my voice.

"People… are saying that Volya demoted Andoc. Made Jacun his new First Warrior."

"That's true," I allowed. "Though Volya also said as he was dying that he regretted the decision."

Dalon shifted on his feet and cleared his throat. "They're also saying that… maybe Andoc didn't do as much as he could have to protect Volya during the attack, because he was pissed off at the Chief for making someone else First Warrior in his place."

I stared at him for a long moment, my fists clenching. "Tell me who said that. I'll bloody well kill them."

"I'm not naming any names, boss," Dalon said. "You know how gossip is around here. Like I said, I just thought you should know."

In fact, I was completely at a loss as to how gossip could have spread around the village so quickly… though I suppose I should have known better. Andoc was well liked, but he had also been in an enviable position within the village. If there was one thing I'd learned in recent months, it was that anyone with power was a target for those who wanted that power for themselves.

"Fine," I said, venom still audible in my tone. "The next one who opens their mouth to spout that kind of crap, tell them that Andoc crawled over with a *fucking broken leg* to protect Volya after a javelin struck him from out of the blue. And if they still want to make an issue of it, they can fucking well take it up with *me*."

"All right, boss," Dalon said, raising a hand as if I was a fractious horse that needed calming. "I'll tell 'em. Now take a breath, yeah? You look like you're about to burst something."

I took a breath. In fact, I took a few breaths. "I am beyond done with this shit for today," I said eventually. "Talk to me about the horses."

Dalon seemed to relax a bit and dutifully reported on what I'd missed. Once again, I was struck by how lucky I was that my one-time nemesis had ended up being such a staunch—if occasionally uncouth—ally.

"Still plotting to take my position for yourself, I see," I said without rancor, once I was up to date on the goings on at the pens.

"Nah," Dalon said. "I didn't touch the inventory on the tack or the other supplies. There's some stuff around here that you don't pay me enough to mess with."

"Nice to know I'm not completely surplus to requirements, I suppose," I said dryly. "I guess I'd better get started."

I spent a good part of the afternoon starting on the summer inventory, while keeping a weather eye on the activities of the day outside. When the sun grew low in the sky and it became obvious that things were well in hand for the evening, I headed back into the village to relieve Senovo.

When I arrived at Andoc's sick room, it was to find the wolf curled up on the bed next to Andoc's hip. Not terribly surprised by this development, I sat down next to him, careful not to jar Andoc's leg. Senovo nosed up to me, whining a greeting. I scratched him behind the ears, taking comfort from his warm, affectionate presence.

Andoc was still out cold after the sedating drink the Healer had ordered, so any attempt to feed him would have to wait for a bit. Sagdea had obviously been back since I had left, as the leg was now swathed in damp, cooling cloths.

"Come on," I told Senovo. Grabbing an extra blanket from the end of the bed, I placed it on the floor against the wall and sat down on it. Once I was comfortable, I beckoned the wolf to join me. Senovo climbed half onto my lap and licked at my jaw. "Best shift back now," I continued, not wanting him to accidentally jostle Andoc by transforming on the bed.

The wolf stared at me, the rich amber-green eyes unchanging as his body shifted around them. I steadied Senovo when he blinked in momentary dizziness, and leaned forward to kiss him while he was still soft and disoriented, his mind only partway back. He closed his eyes and kissed back, nuzzling against me for a precious, unguarded moment before we both had to face reality once more.

"How is he?" I asked, once we had parted. "And how are you?"

Senovo swallowed and tested his voice. "He... is unchanged. And I am better for curling up with him for a while. Though I may have given the Healer's apprentice a fright."

"You can't have been any more frightening than Sagdea," I said. "And the poor woman has to put up with her almost every day."

"A fair point," Senovo agreed.

"Why don't you go have a quick wash and get ready to speak with the elders?" I paused, my mood growing sour again. "Though you should probably know, there's a rumor going around the village that Andoc let Volya get killed because he was upset about the Chief making Jacun First Warrior."

Senovo sighed and leaned back against the wall, sitting shoulder to shoulder with me. "Such things are inevitable, though that makes them no less vexing. I imagine Magoldis will be happy to set the record straight, as will Jacun himself once he is strong enough."

It was true, and the thought made me feel a little bit better. Honestly, it would have been easier to stay angry about things if Jacun had been an arse. But he wasn't. He was an old friend of Andoc's, who had been kind and supportive toward me when few people in Draebard accepted me. He would probably make a perfectly decent Chief.

"You're right, of course," I said. "Go on then, off with you. I'll stay here and watch over Andoc. Though if you could wheedle some food out of Feldes for me on your way out, it would be much appreciated."

Senovo stretched, joints popping, and clambered to his feet with something less than his usual grace. He still looked haggard, and he'd lost weight during the journey, but watching him pad naked across the room to retrieve his robes was nonetheless the highlight of my admittedly awful day. After a final check of Andoc, he returned and leaned down to kiss my hair.

"I will step outside of my assigned role as resident ascetic long enough to make sure you have supper," he promised, "if you agree not to spend the entire evening worrying about things you cannot control."

"I'll try," I said, staring at Andoc's oblivious form on the bed. "No promises."

Senovo's fingers brushed my cheek, and then he was gone, leaving me to take care of the person who had always taken care of us. The bed looked more comfortable than the floor, so I grabbed the blanket I'd been using as a seat and arranged it against the headboard. Andoc mumbled a bit as the mattress dipped under my weight—the drink must have been starting to wear off.

There were candles scattered around the room, but with the cloths draping his broken leg, I couldn't get a good look at it. I was desperate to know if it was improving, but my fear of Healer Sagdea's wrath should I disarrange her handiwork was greater than my curiosity. Instead, I studied Andoc's face. Dark circles, almost like bruises, underlined his eyes. His skin was dry and warm—we had not been able to get nearly enough liquid into him over the past few days to combat the arid summer heat.

Mostly, though, it was his unnatural stillness that frightened me. Even in sleep, Andoc was usually bigger than life, snoring and sprawling across the available space as if sleeping was a pleasure he was determined to experience to the fullest. Now, he almost seemed… *small*. Docile.

It was silly, really—he was still the same large, muscular man as always, laid out beside me on the bed. But the spark— the spirit and cockiness that made Andoc, *Andoc*—was diminished somehow. Buried under weakness and days of unrelenting pain.

And now, the Healer was going to try to make me decide if he would keep his leg or lose it. Once again I railed at the unfairness of it. Andoc would apparently rather die than lose the limb—and suddenly, months after the fact, his discomfort around Ciero, the Mereni artist who'd lost a hand in battle, made *so* much more sense. I, on the other hand, just wanted Andoc to live. Was that selfish of me?

Ciero seemed content enough with his life; in fact, he was one of the happier people I knew. One could argue, though, that losing a leg was worse than losing a hand. Andoc would be unable to walk. He would never wield a sword again.

A fat teardrop plopped against Andoc's collarbone, and I realized I was crying. I dashed the tears away with an angry movement and tried to pull myself together. This was ridiculous. No one was getting out the bone saws yet. I was doing *exactly* what Senovo had warned me against, too.

When Favian knocked on the open door a few minutes later, I was more or less in control once again. Still, the distraction was a relief.

"Hi," said the boy in a shy voice. "Novice Feldes sent me here with food and drink."

With a final surreptitious swipe across my eyes, I rose from the bed and crossed to relieve him of some of his burden. "Hi, Favian. Come on in."

Favian followed me inside and put the remainder of the food down on the small table near the bed. "How is he?" he asked, looking at Andoc with worried blue eyes.

I busied myself with removing the stopper from the clay jar of stew and pouring some into a bowl. "Still asleep," I said, "though I think he'll wake soon."

Favian nodded.

"Have you eaten?" I asked.

"Yes," said the boy, still watching Andoc's still form. "Hey! Look — I think he just moved."

I immediately returned my attention to the bed, and sure enough, Andoc's head was turning restlessly back and forth against the pillow. I set the bowl down with a clatter, spilling broth over the rim, and sat down on the edge of the bed.

"Andoc?" I asked, praying that he would be lucid.

He blinked his eyes open, staring muzzily at the rafters. After a moment, he worked his dry tongue around his mouth, trying to speak. "Where — ?"

"We're in the temple. In Draebard. We got home around midday," I said eagerly. "Do you remember?"

Andoc frowned. "Brain feels… fuzzy."

"I just bet it does," I said, relief flooding me. I looked up at Favian. "Favian, go get the Healer!"

Favian nodded and rushed off to find Sagdea.

"Are you hungry? Thirsty?" I asked.

Andoc didn't answer in words, but his stomach rumbled audibly.

"Let's get you propped up," I said, and started grabbing extra pillows and furs to stuff behind his back. At the first movement, however, he let out a choked cry as his leg injury made itself known. "Sorry, I'm sorry," I babbled. "Here. Take it slow, try to breathe."

When I finally got his upper body situated against the pile of bedding, his skin was pale and he was sweating.

"Thought maybe… I dreamed…" he mumbled.

I hated to be the one to disillusion him. "I'm afraid not. It all really happened." I poured a bit of broth from the stew into a cup. "Try to drink this."

I had to hold the cup for him as his hands trembled, but he drank several sips. As I was setting it aside, the Healer arrived.

"He's awake," I said as she came through the door.

Sagdea raised a silver eyebrow at me. "I can see that, Carivel. Lucid?"

"Sort of," I answered. Andoc hadn't said much, but what he *had* said made sense. "He asked where he was and if he'd dreamed the battle."

"Hmm," said Sagdea, and turned her attention to her patient. "So, young man, are you back with us then?"

"Think so," Andoc said around a thick tongue. "Feel strange…"

"That will be the sedative, most likely. You remember what happened, though?"

Andoc swallowed again, and I held the broth up for him to take another sip. He cleared his throat, wincing when even that small movement jarred his injury. "Leg… Volya?"

"I'm afraid so," said the Healer. "Your leg is broken. Chief Volya is dead."

Andoc closed his eyes and let his head fall back.

Sagdea gently lifted the wet cloths draping Andoc's leg, and he hissed in pain. I paled—the limb remained grotesquely bruised and swollen. A few leeches still clung to it. The Healer plucked them off and returned them to a jar in her bag, only to replace them with new ones. After examining the leg from all angles, she straightened and addressed her words to both of us.

"There has been a tiny bit of improvement, but not as much as I would like," she said. "There is a real chance that the flesh below the break will begin to blacken and rot, which would inevitably spread beyond the leg and kill you. Though still risky, amputation offers a higher likelihood of survival at this point."

"No," Andoc said, without raising his head or opening his eyes.

"Carivel, as Andoc's bond-mate, you have a say in this as well."

"He said *no!*" I flared — unable, when push came to shove, to go against Andoc's will on this. "It's *his leg.*"

I could only hope that Senovo would agree with my decision, and once again I cursed the culture that viewed his relationship with Andoc as fundamentally less important than mine.

The Healer's lips twitched in a frown. "Very well. Should you change your mind, let me know immediately. It is not something that benefits from being postponed. In the meantime, we will continue with the current treatment, and hope that things do not deteriorate any further. Try to get a little more nourishment into him, Carivel, and I will send another sedating drink to help him rest through the night."

I nodded, not trusting myself to speak politely to her even though I knew that the Healer was only trying to save Andoc's life. Sagdea huffed and reapplied the wet cloths that had been draped over the injury before leaving us alone again.

Already, Andoc was fading, his words slurred. "Sorry… Car'vel. Didn't mean t'… let you down like this."

I picked up the cup of broth. "You haven't let anyone down, you great lout. Now get some more of this into you."

Andoc managed a few more swallows before his head lolled back and he fell once more into sleep, or possibly unconsciousness. I ate half of the remaining stew and left the other half for Senovo when he returned. The wine in the skin was rich and red. It was tempting to drown myself in it, but Andoc might need me. I wished that I'd thought to bring along some leatherwork to repair — anything to keep my hands busy.

As it was, I stared at Andoc's face and fretted as the sun outside the window sank, giving way to darkness. One of the acolytes that I didn't know well — a Mereni transplant — came by to drop off the sedative, not that it was much use when Andoc was already dead to the world. When Senovo arrived, late in the evening, it was a relief despite his drawn face and the exhausted slump of his shoulders.

"The elders have been made aware of everything that took place in Rhyth," he said. "Leader Magoldis is still here, and was quite helpful in that regard. I believe she and most of the Mereni contingent are planning on leaving in the morning, though Keenan and another archer are staying behind to continue working with you."

I remembered my vow, in the heat of the battle, to become proficient at archery so I would never again be a useless bystander during a fight. "Good."

"I will perform the funeral for our dead tomorrow," Senovo continued. "I can stay with Andoc for much of the day, if you can return by late afternoon to watch him. I... assume that missing the ceremony will not trouble you overmuch."

"It won't, no." I stroked a hand through Andoc's hair. "Senovo, Andoc woke while you were gone and seemed more lucid. The Healer came and he told her not to take the leg. I... I supported him, when she asked me to overrule his wishes and let her amputate."

Senovo swallowed. "It is his decision." His voice was a whisper. He cleared his throat. "Besides, such a procedure could well kill him anyway. Amputation above the ankle is a very serious matter."

"He won't die," I said, as if my certainty could somehow make it so.

"We'll all die someday, Carivel. But Andoc is strong, and he has much to live for."

⌒〰 ⚜ 〰⌒

Senovo and I took turns napping during the night while the other kept watch. Sometime after midnight, Andoc woke, once again delirious, and it took both of us to get the sedative down his throat.

The following day was gray and blustery, but only a spattering of rain hit the ground—doing little to relieve the nascent drought. The village was solemn, readying for the burial of its Chief of many years. I stayed with Andoc while Senovo eulogized the man who had made our lives so difficult these past months.

Senovo and I fell into a sort of pattern over the following few days. We traded off the duty of watching over our injured lover, and enlisted Favian or Eiridan on the rare occasions that we were both required elsewhere at the same time. Sagdea or her assistant visited several times a day, using so many leeches on the injured leg that it was amazing Andoc still had any blood left inside him at all.

By the third day, he was staying awake and aware for longer stretches at a time, and I felt hope begin to surge in my breast. On the evening of the fourth day, Senovo and I were both present when the Healer straightened from her careful inspection of his foot.

"I believe you will keep the leg, Andoc, though I doubt it will ever be quite right again," she said. "The blood is beginning to flow properly to your foot once more, at any rate. The flesh is not dying."

Andoc's listless response was in stark contrast to my own elation and Senovo's quiet but profound relief. "Thank you, Healer," Andoc said. "I know you worked hard to save it."

Sagdea looked down her beaky nose at him. "I worked hard to save *you*, Andoc," she said. "To do otherwise would have made me a mortal enemy of both Draebard's High Priest and Horse Mistress, after all. What you decide to do with that life now… well, that's up to you."

Andoc blanched, and I took Sagdea's words as confirmation that Andoc would never regain his place as a warrior. Senovo and I thanked her, and assured her that neither of us was foolish enough to make an enemy of the village Healer.

"Glad to hear it," she said, as she packed up her things and made ready to leave. She paused by the doorway, and looked back for a moment. "Perhaps I spoke hastily, before. It seems that what he chooses to do with his life may also be up to the two of you."

⤙ ⚜ ⤚

Though Andoc's body was finally mending, his spirit did not seem to be. I frequently caught Senovo's worried looks whenever Andoc failed to respond to a quip, or take any sort of interest or pleasure in what was around him. His easy affection with the two of us seemed noticeably absent, almost as if he were holding himself apart from us consciously. Only the wolf seemed able to worm past his strange defenses. It was not unusual as the days wore on to find the animal curled up on the bed with him, one of Andoc's hands gripping the shaggy fur as if it was the only thing keeping him tethered to the world.

Meanwhile, Jacun's wound improved rapidly, and the new Chief walked out of the temple under his own power just over a week after we'd returned to Draebard. Senovo attended the ceremony during which the elders formally elevated him to the position of tribal chieftain, though I pled off—not completely certain of my ability to contain my emotions.

Andoc was still not himself.

Things finally came to a head on the day that Sagdea proclaimed he could leave the temple and go home. He had already been hobbling around on wooden crutches for two days, though his ambition for getting anywhere more interesting than the chamber pot seemed strangely lacking for a man who had been cooped up in a tiny room under near-constant supervision for so long.

As I was packing up a small bag of Andoc's belongings that had accumulated during his recuperation, he cleared his throat. I looked up to where he was seated on the edge of the low bed.

"Now that I'm not a complete invalid anymore, we should probably talk," he said.

"Oh? Talk about what?" I asked with a frown.

Andoc appeared to find something deeply interesting about the seam of his loose trousers as he continued. "Senovo should be here, too. It concerns him as well."

The non-answer raised a specter of disquiet in my chest. "All right. Wait here—I'll just go and get him."

I returned with Senovo in tow a few minutes later. "He's about to say something stupid," I told the priest. "I can tell."

That Andoc did not rise to the bait was cause for concern in itself. He looked down again, not meeting our eyes. "First off, I wanted to thank both of you for playing nursemaid when I know you had more important things to do."

I drew in a breath to dispute the idea of anything being more important than caring for him when he was injured, but Senovo's hand on my forearm stopped me.

"Carivel," Andoc continued, "this is no longer the relationship you agreed to. I realize that. There's a big difference between being handfasted to a First Warrior and being handfasted to a crippled pauper with no title and no prospects."

I pulled away sharply from Senovo's grip so I could cross to stand in front of Andoc, who still sat on the edge of the bed, looking at the floor. "What are you trying to say to me, Andoc?" I asked, something harsh and ugly rising in my throat and making the words come out in a hoarse croak.

Andoc finally looked up at me, his brown eyes flat and lost-looking as they had been since the battle outside of Rhyth. "I can't be what you need anymore, Carivel. We can break the handfasting whenever it's convenient for you."

I stared at him for a long moment with my jaw hanging open before I hauled off and slapped him across the face as hard as I could.

FOURTEEN

Quick as a flash, Senovo's arms were around my chest, pulling me away.

"How dare you! How *dare* you!" I practically screamed, fighting against Senovo's hold even as tears rose up and tried to choke me. The shocked surprise breaking through Andoc's facade of listless apathy only served to make me angrier.

"I don't get the impression that Carivel has any interest in breaking the handfasting, old friend," Senovo said with enviable poise. "Your nose, perhaps. But not the handfasting."

"Senovo," Andoc said, one hand covering the cheekbone I'd struck. "I'm no good to either of you like this. Even before I was injured, you no longer needed me, *amadi*. Since you made peace with the wolf, you have strength of your own... strength beyond measure. You don't need mine. And Carivel, you are the Horse Mistress of the village. You don't want to be saddled with a used-up man who can barely walk. I'll only hold you back."

I sobbed, and tried half-heartedly to struggle out of Senovo's hold again.

"Perhaps you could let us decide that for ourselves, Andoc," the priest said mildly.

"I didn't expect to survive this," Andoc whispered, more lost than I'd ever seen him.

The defeat in his tone drained all the fight from me, and I sagged in Senovo's arms.

Senovo spoke, his voice sad and gentle with sudden understanding. "And ever since it became apparent that you would, you've been living with the expectation that we would both forsake you as soon as the chance arose."

He loosened his grip and I found myself staggering forward, falling to my knees before Andoc. Wrapping my arms around his waist and burying my face against his chest. Shaking.

Andoc's arms came up to hold me and he curled forward as if in pain. The bed shifted as Senovo settled beside him, half facing him, and drew both of us into an embrace. Andoc let himself be drawn; moments later I felt the shudder of his chest under my cheek as he began to weep.

"All will be well, old friend. You'll see," Senovo said, as we both leaned against his understated but resilient strength. "I'm sorry neither of us were able to predict the direction of your thoughts before they could take root and torment you so. Now, though, rest easy in the knowledge that no one is forsaking anyone, now or in the future. Isn't that right, Carivel?"

"*Never*," I croaked against the warmth of Andoc's chest. His arms tightened around me. "I will *never* let you go."

Andoc gulped in a breath of air. "I don't deserve you. Either of you."

"I believe all three of us have entertained that particular thought at one time or another," Senovo said. "And yet, here we all are."

And there we stayed, until my knees were aching from the unforgiving stone floor and my tears had dried, stiffening the material of Andoc's tunic under my cheek.

"I don't know what to do now," Andoc said.

Senovo eased him upright, and I sat back on my haunches, releasing my grip around his waist. "I would suggest a meal, followed by some much-needed rest."

"Rest?" Andoc said. "I've done little else, these past weeks."

Senovo smirked, an expression taken directly from Andoc's own arsenal. "I wasn't suggesting it for your benefit."

"Seconded," I said, my voice still rough from emotion. It was true. Senovo and I were both exhausted—worn down by worry over Andoc's lack of spirit and the distance he'd tried to put between us.

"Come to my rooms," said Senovo. "You can return to your hut tomorrow, if you wish it."

"Yes," Andoc said. "Tomorrow. I'm so sorry, both of you. I never meant for any of this to happen."

"I'm sorry I hit you," I put in. My voice was small.

Andoc reached down to pull me into another hug. "I'll just count myself lucky that you used an open hand, shall I?"

Senovo stood up and dusted himself off. "Come along, both of you. Andoc, you need to start eating better. You've lost weight."

I disentangled and climbed to my feet, joints creaking as I looked at Senovo critically. "You've got no room to talk. You're wasting away."

"Then it's as well we're going for a meal. We'll eat in the refectory, I believe. It's high time you spent some time in company other than the two of us and Healer Sagdea."

"Senovo, I look like some sort of wild mountain man. I probably smell to high heaven and my beard hasn't been trimmed in weeks."

"Vanity has no place in the temple," Senovo replied in a haughty tone, and I could not hold back the bubble of amusement and relief that rose in my chest.

"You're one to talk," said Andoc. "I love you, *amadi*, but you're the vainest priest I've ever met."

"I'm sure I have no idea what you mean."

The light exchange settled something in my chest that hadn't been sitting right for weeks now. "You're right, though," I told Andoc. "You do stink. And I say that as someone who shovels shit for a living."

"Yes, since you mention it, perhaps a wash before we put him in my bed might not go amiss," Senovo said. "Food first, though."

"All right. All right. I'll come quietly. Someone's going to have to carry my bag, though." Andoc lurched up unsteadily to balance on the wooden crutches Sagdea had provided. Despite his return to banter and good-natured grumbling, however, there was an aspect of vulnerability on his face that I had never seen before today. It tugged at something that lived deep inside my chest.

Rather than risk knocking him over by rushing into his arms yet again, I forced myself to pick up the packed bag, and went ahead to place it in the High Priest's quarters while Andoc and Senovo made their slow way to the refectory. They were just seating themselves when I rejoined them.

Most of the members of the temple were present, taking a meal of fish and roasted vegetables that Feldes served from large platters. Andoc replied politely to the greetings and well wishes of our fellow diners, though he still lacked his customary twinkle.

Eiridan immediately launched into an esoteric discussion with Senovo about some new insight he'd received from a visiting trader regarding the cryptic symbols that the Rhytheeri used to convey information. It was actually a rather fascinating subject, and also worked handily to divert attention away from Andoc and his injury.

I even joined in with them, speculating on how such a thing could simplify the kind of inventory that was currently taking up most of my time at the horse pens. Jorun had a complex system, honed over many years, of different-colored wooden chits and small, indoor sand pits full of temporary tally-marks, but the whole thing was still a nightmare, at least to someone of my temperament. We discussed how symbols marked on hides or tree bark might be useful with keeping track of various supplies throughout the year, and almost everyone had some idea to add at one point or another.

When the meal was finished, I felt relaxed and at ease in a way I had sorely missed since the journey to Rhyth. Andoc and I went ahead to wait for Senovo in his rooms while the High Priest completed his duties for the day. I deposited Andoc in one of the heavy chairs and laid his crutches on the floor nearby.

"I'm going to go grab a couple of buckets of water from the bathing area," I told him. "I imagine we could all do with a wash."

Andoc's hand grasped my arm as I started to turn away, halting me. I looked down, a question in my eyes.

"I really am sorry for what I said earlier," he said simply.

My expression softened, and I covered his hand with my own. "You know, I only realized after the fact that I did almost exactly the same thing to you, after the hill fort. I can't believe I forgot. Shall we just agree that we're both idiots, and call it even?"

Andoc closed his eyes. "Agreed. I'd forgotten, too. Or rather, I didn't put the two things together in my head. It just seemed like a completely different situation."

"I guess that's why we have Senovo," I said, and leaned down to kiss him before straightening again. "Now, stay here. I'm going to get those buckets, and maybe even liberate some soap while I'm at it. Back soon."

I wandered through the halls of the temple that had become more of a home to me than my own little hut at the edge of town, enjoying the feeling that things might actually be all right now, for a little while at least. The Empire hung poised above our heads like a woodsman's heavy axe, but for tonight, I could convince myself that Volya had been right, and they would not be able to organize an invasion before winter set in.

With a bucket of lukewarm water in each hand, some rags thrown over my shoulder, and a sliver of hard soap tucked under one arm, I made my way back to Senovo's rooms. When I arrived, it was to find that he had returned, and was helping Andoc out of his clothing. I put the buckets down and removed the cushions and furs from the sturdy wooden chair Andoc had been sitting on. With the chair's padding safely out of the way, he could sit while we washed him, and not have to balance on one leg.

Senovo and I washed first, helping scrub each other's backs. I might have been tempted to take advantage, but even after weeks without sex, my exhaustion outweighed my desire for anything more strenuous than sleep. When we were clean, we turned our attention to Andoc, who had been watching us with eyes made shiny by emotion.

He grew half-hard as we lathered soap over everything we could reach, but, like me, it seemed that Andoc's body craved rest and closeness more than sexual release. That didn't stop us from kissing and caressing whatever skin happened to be in reach as we scrubbed and rinsed, but the touch was almost chaste—more about giving reassurance than erotic pleasure.

By the time we'd supported Andoc carefully over the wet floor and across the room to lie on Rhystel's ridiculous feather bed, I was aching for the bliss of sleep—of being wrapped up safely in Andoc's and Senovo's arms. We put Andoc on the side next to the wall, so his left leg would be protected from jostling. I climbed in after him, while Senovo moved around the room, extinguishing the lamps. When he joined us and curled around my back, I couldn't help the gusty sigh of pleasure that escaped. Andoc wormed an arm under me to guide my head onto his shoulder, and within moments I was asleep.

When I awoke just before dawn, it was to find that I had moved during the night until I was wrapped around Andoc like an exceptionally friendly squid. A candle was burning nearby, and I gathered that Senovo had woken before me and was already up. Andoc, of course, slumbered on, a look of profound peace on his handsome features. Had he been anyone else, I would have worried about waking him as I disentangled my limbs and sat up. Since it was Andoc, though, I slid free and reached down to kiss his forehead. He hummed in his sleep and turned toward the warm spot I'd just vacated, bringing a heartfelt smile to my face.

"Even with the buckets right here to hand, cold water seems needlessly cruel this morning," said Senovo, coming up to lean on the footboard with both hands so he could watch us.

My smile widened. "Aww, look at that. You're going soft on him, Senovo. Who'd've thought?"

Senovo's eyes crinkled in the candlelight for a moment before he sobered. "Are you well this morning?"

"Much better for finally understanding what the problem was," I said truthfully. "I'll help Andoc get back to his hut—assuming he still wants to go—and then I intend to devote the morning to playing around with using those symbols we talked about for my inventory. I'm also supposed to meet with Keenan and Wendes later to work on archery."

"Good. I'm sure you understand, however, that this still won't be easy for him. Andoc was never able to picture himself as anything other than a warrior, even when he was a youth."

"I do understand." I looked down at Andoc, still sleeping on, oblivious. "But right now, he just needs to focus on healing. His options for the future will depend a great deal on how well the leg mends."

"True enough," Senovo said. "Why don't you get dressed? In the mean time, I'll try to get him up without resorting to anything overly drastic."

I shuffled to the edge of the large mattress. "You could always transform into the wolf and lick his ear again."

Andoc rooted into the pillow and let out a loud snore.

Senovo sighed. "It may come to that."

By the time I was dressed and ready, Senovo had succeeded in his quest by fair means or foul. Andoc still expressed a desire to go back to his hut for the day, so I shouldered his belongings and wandered along with him. This was a considerably more ambitious journey on crutches than anything he had attempted before. When I sensed him flagging as we crossed the green, I decided to stop at the cookhouse and get some breakfast for us. It was another warm, dry day, so I left him at one of the outside tables while I bought the food.

I was still something of a controversial figure among Gretya's older daughters. Inviting Limdya to apprentice at the horse pens had reduced the friction in some ways, but increased it in others—Limdya's new path as the only girl among a pack of rowdy boys was not an easy one.

Nonetheless, Charyal had taken her late mother's policy of turning no one away to heart, and a few minutes later I emerged with cold meat and salted porridge for the two of us. Andoc ate ravenously, his body finally recovered enough to demand fuel for further healing. My own appetite was also better for having the air clear between us.

I left Andoc in his hut, tamping down my slight sense of trepidation. I couldn't help but worry about what would happen with no one around if he fell or needed help. I knew, however, that treating him as though he were helpless would only make him feel worse about his current limitations. Senovo had promised to send Favian or one of the other boys to bring him food at lunchtime, I reminded myself, and that was only a handful of hours away. He would be fine.

"Don't get into trouble without me," I said, and pressed close to kiss him. It bothered me that he didn't grab my hips... pull me against him... make some quip about getting into trouble *with* me if he wasn't allowed to do it without me. Senovo was right—knowing that we would not leave him had helped, but it hadn't solved all of Andoc's problems.

"I suppose someone in this handfasting needs to go out and earn a living," he said, trying to make it a joke and falling short.

I kissed him again and left to see to my duties. The pens were just waking up for the day, tousled lads arriving sleepy-eyed from their beds. When everyone was present and accounted for, I called a meeting to discuss the new ideas for the summer inventory. Many of the apprentices looked blank, but a few grasped the potential immediately. I ended up sending everyone off to start the morning's chores except Dalon, Limdya, and Varin.

"I used to help Mother with inventory at the cookhouse," Limdya said, her eyes shining with interest. "This is a great idea. We could have everything hanging on a wall in one building, and use the squares of hide to keep track of supplies as we used them, instead of having to play things by ear and do a full count every season."

"It wouldn't be perfect," Dalon warned. "You know the lads. Some of them'll forget to mark things off, or do it wrong."

"It's still better than what we have now," said Varin. "I could take a few hours and try to come up with some symbols for all the various supplies."

"Good," I said. "Limdya, why don't you help him? And when you go to lunch, one of you can visit the tanner and explain to him what we need. The hides need to be really, really thin, and scraped completely smooth. I'll ask Eiridan if he knows what the Rhytheeri use for pigment. I imagine charcoal or grease paint would probably work."

The meeting broke up, and I went back to doing my inventory the way Jorun had taught me, not wanting to get any farther behind on it than I already was. I worked through lunch without realizing it, only looking up when Keenan poked her head into the storage building.

"We're here," she said unnecessarily. "Hey, I heard that your Healer let Andoc go home, finally. How's he doing?"

"Better," I said with a smile, since that much was true. While I liked Keenan quite a bit and considered her one of my few real friends, to say more about it right now seemed too much like a betrayal of confidence.

"That's good," she said. "Come on out when you're ready. Wendes wants to try a new style of arrow. He thinks it will fly farther than what we've been using."

"Is New Boy here today?" I asked.

Keenan grinned at my use of the nickname. "He is. He's tacking up some horses for us."

"It certainly didn't take you long to get him trained," I observed, amusement turning up one corner of my lips. "I'm impressed."

"Pups are easy to train," she said, still smiling. "I'll be fair, though. He's no great shakes with a dagger, but the kid is a talented archer."

"Good with the horses, too, which is exactly what we need. I probably shouldn't tease."

Keenan laughed aloud. "Oh, Carivel. Of *course* you should! Always tease the new boys. It's good for them."

The afternoon passed pleasantly enough, despite my occasional pauses to worry about how Andoc was getting on. I split my attention between archery and inventory, dispensing praise and suggestions for improvement to Limdya and Varin as they reported back on their progress with the new system.

Wendes' lighter arrows were an unqualified success. Everyone agreed they worked better with the short recurve bows than what we had been using before. Indeed, when my own turn came, I was able to hit the center of one of our painted straw targets from horseback for the first time ever. Of course, my next several shots went comically wide, but the brief taste of success still left me flushed with a sense of accomplishment.

So wrapped up had I been in the day's activities that it was almost a surprise when the boys rode in with the herd for the evening. I looked at the sun, shocked to see how low it had dipped. The archers put up their horses for the day, and I was just finishing a last count of the chariot harnesses, when Favian interrupted me.

Immediately, my heart rate sped up, thinking that something must have happened to Andoc.

"Horse Mistress?" he said formally. "I am to inform you that there is an important meeting taking place in the meeting hall, and your presence is requested."

I frowned. That was odd. "Really?" I asked. "Who requested me?"

"The High Priest thought that you would want to be present," Favian said. "He's the one who sent me."

Odd, indeed. "Very well," I told him. "I'll come right away. Would you mind checking on Andoc for me? I don't want him to wonder where I've gotten off to."

"Andoc is already on his way to the meeting, Horse Mistress."

"Oh," I said, taken aback. "Thank you. I'll head there now. If you're not needed back immediately, Favian, you should go visit the white colt. I'm sure he'd like to see you, as would your friends here."

Favian's face lit up, once again the excited, horse-loving boy I remembered rather than the serious temple acolyte. "Thank you, Ma'am. I will."

I gave his shoulder an affectionate squeeze and headed out to find Dalon. Once I was confident that everything was under control for the night, I hurried toward the meeting house, eager to find out what was going on. The village was still in some degree of upheaval, with Volya's death coming so close on the heels of the Alyrions' deadly attack and the massacre at the temple.

The meeting could be about anything, really—the Empire, the Rhytheeri, the other northern tribes. I felt a brief moment of nervousness that it was something to do with me, or my position, but frankly, Volya had been my harshest critic, and he was gone. Jacun harbored no ill feelings toward me, and had no reason to try to make an issue of my position in the village. At least, as far as I knew, he didn't.

There was little point in speculating. I was almost there. Torches burned inside the large hall, lighting it brightly even as the sun slipped beneath the horizon outside. I followed the sound of voices to the main chamber, which was filled nearly to bursting with townsfolk.

I was short enough that it took a fair amount of jostling and squeezing past broad shoulders before I could locate Andoc or Senovo. Both of them were seated near the head of the large table that dominated the room—Andoc frowning, and Senovo with an air of quiet satisfaction.

I made my way to stand behind Andoc's chair, feeling a protective streak come to the fore. As Horse Mistress, I had every right to be here, and I ignored the jaundiced looks that some of the seated elders gave me. That I was also Andoc's bond-mate was beside the point; if Leader Magoldis' presence had not succeeded in convincing some of these old men to move beyond their preconceptions, it wasn't my problem to deal with right now.

"What's going on?" I asked, pitching my voice for Andoc's ears alone.

His frown deepened. "I have absolutely no idea. Senovo is being tight-lipped about it, but he has a gleam in his eye that's making me nervous."

"What?" I said, feeling mild amusement at his obvious discomfiture. "Don't you trust him?"

"He's getting far too good at his job," said Andoc. "I always thought there was something about the office of High Priest that attracted devious men, but now I wonder if it's not the other way around. Something about becoming High Priest turns men devious."

I snorted. "Just be glad he's on our side."

"Oh, believe me, I am."

There was a rustle around the room as attention turned to the door. The crowd parted and Jacun entered in full regalia, his sword sheathed at his belt and colorful feathers braided through his dark hair. The new Chief still moved stiffly, though his injury was healing well by all accounts.

He crossed the room and moved toward the head of the table, the villagers giving way to let him past. I searched myself for any lingering resentment and found none; only a sense of regret at the way things had turned out after the final, turbulent days of Volya's rule. Jacun was a good man. He would be a good chieftain — better than Volya had been, I suspected.

When Chief Jacun reached his place of honor, rather than sit, he stood facing the rest of the room and placed his hands on the back of the chair.

"People of Draebard," he began when the room had quieted. "Respected elders. Thank you for coming here today. There is a matter of great importance which I must discuss with you — one that impacts Draebard's future, and possibly the future of Eburos as a whole."

I felt a surge of worry — had there been fresh news of the Alyrions?

Jacun continued. "Before his death, Chief Volya elevated me to the position of First Warrior, as you all know. What you don't know is *why*. The Chief's hatred of the Alyrion Empire after their unprovoked attack on our village was profound. And of course, he was not alone in that hatred.

"When we discovered the extent of the collaboration between the Empire and the Rhytheeri tribe, however, Volya's hatred grew to encompass them as well. And — again, as many of you already know—he acted on that hatred during the negotiations, by threatening to unite the northern tribes and invade Rhyth."

There was a bit of muttering around the room. While it was true that Senovo and Magoldis had reported the details of the talks to the village elders, not everyone present in the room today had known about Volya's bombastic threats.

Jacun cleared his throat. "One man dared to question the wisdom of Volya's unplanned ultimatum. He did so privately. Respectfully. And he continued to do so, even after Volya stripped him of his position in a fit of anger. The man was First Warrior Andoc."

Again, there was a murmur of conversation around the room. In front of me, Andoc sat very, very still.

"There have been a handful of rumors that, after losing his position, Andoc did not do all that he could have to protect his Chief," Jacun said. "I'm here to tell you that those rumors are scurrilous and completely without merit. I watched Andoc drag himself across the ground with a broken leg—sword clutched in his hand—to defend Volya after a javelin struck the Chief and felled him from his horse. Anyone who wishes to accuse Andoc of cowardice or dereliction will answer to *me*.

"However, there is someone present today who was guilty of cowardice in regards to our late Chief. I am that person. I agreed with Andoc's objections to Chief Volya's declaration of war against the south, but I said nothing."

My eyes flickered to Senovo. The look of carefully veiled satisfaction was still on his face.

At the head of the table, Jacun unsheathed his sword. "The Chief of Draebard should be someone brave enough to speak up for what's right, no matter the cost to himself. And everyone here knows that before his fit of temper, and indeed after, Chief Volya had long wished Andoc to be his replacement."

He lowered the sword to rest the flat of the blade across his open palms, and stepped around the table until he was standing next to Andoc's chair. I don't believe Andoc was even breathing.

"To that end," Jacun said, placing the sword ceremonially on the table in front of him, "I hereby resign my position as Chief of the tribe, and pledge my sword to Andoc, rightful First Warrior of Draebard, in front of all those present."

FIFTEEN

The silence was absolute. I could sense Andoc struggling for words, but dared not lay a hand on his shoulder or otherwise interfere.

"Jacun," he began haltingly. "*Chief* Jacun. We... have been friends—brothers in arms—since we were barely men. You do me an incredible honor with this gesture... but... I may never even be able to walk properly again, much less wield a sword or leap from a chariot to do battle. I cannot be a warrior any longer."

Jacun looked down at Andoc with an intense expression in his eyes. "Perhaps that is true, brother," he said. "Perhaps you cannot be a warrior. But you can be our Chief, and help guide us through a dangerous and uncertain future." Jacun straightened and looked to Senovo. "High Priest? Do you agree to this?"

Senovo smiled, a gentle and serene expression. "The whole of the village knows that Andoc and I have been close friends and companions for many years now. For that reason, I recuse myself from the discussion. Let the elders decide it as they may... but know that your words and actions tonight prove beyond doubt that you would, indeed, be a worthy Chief to the Draebardi, Jacun."

Elder Tolmac stood, his thin white hair reflecting the torchlight. "Jacun. Andoc. I must say, I have never seen or heard of anything like this before tonight. We will need to discuss it, but I personally see no reason to go against your wishes in the matter. I do have one question, though. War with the Empire must be Draebard's primary concern right now. Andoc, I realize that you have barely been released from your sickbed, but tell me this. Do you have a strategy in mind for dealing with this threat?"

Andoc drew breath to speak, but Jacun beat him to it. "I can answer that, Elder Tolmac. As soon as I heard that Andoc had been released from the temple today, I met with him to discuss the coming war. He does, indeed, have a strategy that may yet save us from destruction or enslavement."

Andoc cleared his throat. "I have been thinking about our situation quite a bit in recent weeks," he said. "I believe that we already have the answer we need, straight from the mouths of the gods, as it were. However, it will require cooperation with other tribes and a great deal of preparation if we are to be ready when the Empire strikes."

Several of the elders bent their heads together around the table, talking amongst themselves. Tolmac leaned down to confer with those closest to him.

"Very well," said the old man. "We will retire to another room to debate the matter. I do not expect it will take very long."

The elders rose and exited the hall, leaving excited chatter in their wake. Many people hurried out behind them, no doubt to spread the gossip far and wide before anyone else could steal their thunder. Andoc looked up at Jacun, who was still standing by his chair.

"Jacun," he said, "you know you don't have to do this."

"Andoc," Jacun said, "I'm a warrior, but I have *no idea* how to win a war against an Empire that rules entire continents. If Draebard is to survive, I assure you, I *do* have to do this."

Senovo had quietly risen and crossed to join us without me noticing. "It's in the elders' hands now," he said. "As it should be. I meant what I said, though—you are an honorable man, Jacun."

"And honorable man would have spoken up when Volya scuppered the talks in Rhyth, Senovo. But I'm trying to do better."

I finally found my voice. "Andoc, what did you mean when you said that the gods had told us how to win against the Empire?" I asked.

Andoc craned to look up at me, his face grim. "Exactly what I said, *caradi*. If I'm right, we will have the deities to thank for our defense."

Our conversation was interrupted by several merchants who came over to express their opinions on the night's events, and, it seemed, several other unrelated matters. I faded back and let Andoc and Jacun deal with them. I looked up a moment later to find Senovo at my side.

"You knew," I accused in quiet tones.

"I did," said Senovo, not bothering to deny it.

"Will the elders agree to it?"

Senovo shrugged. "I don't see why not. There is no benefit to keeping a Chief who does not want to be Chief. Not when there is a more qualified candidate waiting to take over."

I looked back to Andoc, who was skillfully fielding the merchants' opinions and complaints, the charm that I had occasionally seen him wield to such devastating effect in full force for the first time since the attack outside of Rhyth.

"He'll be all right now, won't he," I said, not even making it a question.

"I believe so, yes."

The elders returned barely twenty minutes later, trooping back to the table and seating themselves. Tolmac remained standing.

"After a brief discussion," he said, "we have decided to accept Jacun's proposal to make Andoc the chieftain of the Draebardi. Andoc, do you agree to this?"

Andoc pushed his chair back and rose awkwardly onto his good leg, balancing with a hand against the table. "Elder Tolmac… respected others… please understand that this has all been a complete surprise to me. That said, if the Draebardi wish me to lead them, I will do so to the best of my ability. I can only pray that your faith in me is not misplaced."

Tolmac smiled. "Andoc, the elders know well that chieftains are as human as the next man. The gods will is the gods' will, and all men can ask is that those who lead them do their best. Draebard is blessed to have not one, but two honorable leaders standing before them tonight."

Andoc and Jacun both looked humbled. Andoc spoke, his voice carrying over the hush of the room. "We are the ones honored, Elder. I realize that my position remains unofficial until such time as a formal ceremony can be arranged, but as my first act, I would like to make Jacun First Warrior of the Draebardi once more."

There was a smattering of spontaneous applause, people slapping their thighs in approval.

"It is more than I deserve, Andoc," Jacun said. "I accept the position, and vow before all those present to be a better counsel to you than I was to Chief Volya."

Andoc and Jacun grasped each other, forearm to forearm, even as Senovo and I shared a look of utter satisfaction.

That satisfaction was tempered quickly enough, as Andoc immediately threw himself into his new work to the detriment of his own recovery. The first few times Senovo or I had to go searching for him late at night, only to find him deep in consultation with the weapon makers, or the chariot makers, or the wizened little man who oversaw the village coffers, we put it down to his desire to become as familiar as possible with the particulars of his new position.

When the dark bags under his eyes grew so noticeable that other people started to comment on them, and when the weight loss associated with his injury continued even as his leg began to heal, I dragged him to Senovo's room, crutches and all, and practically shoved him down on the bed.

"Tell him," I ordered Senovo.

The priest sighed. "When have I ever been able to tell him anything, Carivel?"

Sensing that I wasn't going to get the support I wanted from that quarter, I laid into Andoc myself. "You're running yourself into the ground! You'll never heal properly if you don't eat and sleep!"

Andoc's sigh mirrored Senovo's, and made me want to punch him on the nose. He lifted one hand to his forehead, digging the fingers in as if battling a headache. If he was, I thought uncharitably, it served him right.

"*Caradi*," he said, "if it's a choice between my health and Draebard's survival, I think you already know which one I will choose."

"Don't you *caradi* me," I snapped. "If you collapse from a fever or otherwise end up bedridden, *then* what is Draebard supposed to do?"

"Perhaps a compromise," Senovo said, ever the voice of reason. "We understand the importance of your work to defend the village, but there is no reason why meetings with the swordsmith or the Keeper of Coin cannot be accompanied by a decent meal."

I crossed my arms and glared at Andoc, daring him to disagree.

Unexpectedly, he laughed, and lowered his hand from his sore temples to look up at Senovo. "*Amadi*, if you'd told me a year ago that you would ever be the one trying to force food on *me*..."

"So. Is that a *yes*?" I asked, still glaring.

"Look, you two. I'm not neglecting myself purposely. But it's hard to stomach food when I know how much needs to be done, and how quickly it has to happen. When I *know* what the consequences will be if I fail." Andoc rubbed at the muscles of his injured leg absently.

"Perhaps you should simply consider a basic level of self-care to be another task which requires your attention," Senovo offered.

"I'll try to do better," Andoc promised. "And, look, I know I've been neglecting both of you as well... I'm sorry."

My anger drained away on a slow breath. "Don't be stupid. We know it's not by choice. Besides, it isn't as if I haven't been working into the night trying to keep up with day-to-day things while also spending hours with the archers."

Andoc made a sort of vague, there-you-have-it gesture with one hand.

"But at least I eat," I added pointedly.

"All right, Carivel," Andoc said. "Message received. Really."

"Very well," said Senovo. "Enough nagging, in that case. Have your new spies sent any word from Rhyth yet?"

"Not yet," Andoc replied, sounding suddenly tired. "And at this rate, I'm going to bankrupt the tribe within the space of a few months, as much gold as they're costing me."

I dragged a chair over to listen intently, hypocrite that I was. I hadn't precisely lived a sheltered life up until this point, but I'd still had no idea of some of the things that went on between tribes. How many of the charming traders and traveling bards I'd casually spoken with over the years had actually been spies from other tribes, sent to gain information about the wealth or political might of a neighboring village?

"Espionage is an uncertain and capricious pastime," Senovo said. "Perhaps it has merely taken more time than anticipated to find a place from which to operate and get a message out."

"I hope you're right," said Andoc.

One of the first things Andoc had arranged after taking over the position of Chief was a small network of Rhytheeri spies to keep an eye on the Alyrion troops stationed there. A fast rider would be sent across the mountains to warn us, at the first sign they were gathering a force to head north. Elder Briethe had been invaluable in helping to contact southerners willing to spy on their brethren in exchange for gold, her old family links to Rhytheeri traders giving Andoc a form of access he would never have had otherwise.

Even so, spying was a dangerous business. Life threatening, even. The men who had agreed to do it expected compensation commensurate with the amount of risk they were taking on. And, of course, there was no way to guarantee that they would follow through on their part of the bargain rather than simply disappearing into the alleys of Rhyth with Draebard's gold, never to be heard from again.

It was a gamble. At best, Andoc figured that such a warning might give us four or five days' head start, given the realities of organizing and moving a large number of troops over long distances, along with the provisions needed to support them. But those few days could be critical.

Draebard was not a poor village, by any means. It boasted good horses, fine artisans, and several productive tin and copper mines within its tribal territory. And yet, part of the reason the coffers were well stocked with gold and silver was because Volya had been a notorious skinflint. Now, Andoc was spending that accumulated wealth like water to support the desperately important and time-sensitive projects needed for the tribe's defense, and I could tell it bothered him to go against his mentor's established preferences so radically.

"Gold and silver will do none of us any good if we're dead, or enslaved," I told him frankly. "Would you rather leave coin in the coffers for the Alyrions to take after they've razed Draebard to the ground?"

"Of course not," Andoc said, but I could see that hearing someone else say it aloud made him feel better about his decisions. "It's merely another thing to worry about. What if there isn't enough to fund everything that needs to be done?"

"Then you'll do something else," I said. "Put up land as collateral; put up one of the mines. We have other things of value besides money."

"Have the Mereni agreed to help set up camps in the foothills?" Senovo asked.

"They have," Andoc replied. "Fortunately, Magoldis seems willing to put the past behind us now that Volya has paid the price for his hubris. She says she's amenable to resuming the treaty between our tribes."

I nodded, unsurprised. "Well, for what it's worth, we have eight archers now who can shoot reliably from horseback. Keenan is planning on going back to Meren soon to start training more warriors there."

The corner of Andoc's lip quirked up. "And do you count yourself among those eight reliable archers, *caradi*?"

I lifted two fingers at him in a rude V-shape, making his smile widen for a moment. "Ha, bloody ha. Don't mock me. I can at least hit the target most of the time while standing on my own two feet, now. Let's leave it at that, shall we?"

Senovo raised an amused eyebrow. "Don't let him fool you, Carivel. I have reason enough to be thankful for Andoc's own lack of accuracy with a bow and arrow."

"It was *dark*," Andoc protested.

"Oh, so now you're offering excuses for *not* having successfully shot me?"

I'd heard this story before, but it didn't stop Andoc's defensiveness from being funny.

"*I didn't know you were a shape-shifter*, for Deresta's sake!" he said. "All I knew was that a huge wolf was stalking me in the forest. Am I *ever* going to live that down?"

"Not likely," I said, grinning.

"I have so few things to hold over you, my friend," Senovo said. "Allow me to keep the ones that I do have."

The tension was broken, and I stood up. "I'm going to the refectory to see if Feldes put any food aside. Senovo, take his crutches away so he can't make a run for it before I get back."

This late in the evening, the temple was largely quiet. However, as I had suspected, there was still a small pot of soup warming next to the cooking fire, and a few rounds of flatbread on a shelf nearby. I returned to the High Priest's quarters with my bounty, only to find Andoc already dozing against the headboard, with Senovo keeping watch.

"Nope," I said, poking Andoc repeatedly in the ribs until he snorted awake. "Not happening. Food first, then sleep."

Andoc grumbled and took the bowl I handed him, slurping at the soup and scooping meat and vegetables up with flatbread, until it was empty.

"Clothes," I ordered, and started disrobing by way of demonstration. "That way I can be sure you won't wake up in the middle of the night with your mind full of some new scheme that *has* to happen *right now*, and immediately sneak off to who-knows-where."

With a huff, Andoc undressed awkwardly, his leg still a noticeable hindrance. We were all bone-tired, but I exchanged a look with Senovo, and the two of us chivvied Andoc into the center of the bed. We slid down to take turns licking and sucking his half-hard prick, rolling and tickling his balls until he stiffened fully under our mouths. Our tongues tangled around his cock, and we paused at intervals to kiss each other, only to return our attentions once again to Draebard's overworked tribal chieftain.

Eventually, Andoc groaned and spilled, flooding my mouth with salty seed as I swallowed around him. Senovo's hand on my cheek pulled me away, into another kiss, and I shared the dregs with him, humming appreciatively as he licked into my mouth. I was too tired to chase my own pleasure—more interested in cuddling up against warm skin than finding release. Senovo, for his part, showed no inclination to do more than mirror me as I crawled up to mold myself against Andoc's side. Within moments, Andoc fell into an exhausted sleep, and I followed soon after, confident that he would now sleep through the night.

Weeks passed in a flurry of messengers, scouting parties, planning, and archery practice. Under our watchful eyes, Andoc made good on his promise to take better care of himself, though stress and worry had reduced his body to lean sinew and hollowed his face, adding years to his appearance.

Of the three of us, it was Senovo who was least affected by the ongoing planning and preparations. He was the one who badgered us to eat when we forgot, and utilized his heretofore unappreciated devious streak to arrange time for us to be together, though it was still by no means as much or as often as I might have wished. Draebard came first, and we all understood that.

Summer was giving way to autumn, though the seasonal north winds still brought no rain with them. The cooler temperatures were welcome, though. Again, I gave thanks for the wet spring that had allowed pastures and vegetable plots to flourish before the late drought set in. The rivers were low, but far from dry, and it was likely that the snows would arrive a few weeks hence. All in all, things could have been much worse, in so many ways.

Everyone was on edge, knowing that if the Alyrions were going to move before the weather turned, it would have to be soon. I poured my own worry into increased archery practice, and though Andoc still teased me at every opportunity, my hours of training were finally paying off. I was an average archer from the ground, but I now counted myself as competent from horseback—at least, I did when I was riding Kekenu.

Andoc's leg continued to improve, though it was obvious to everyone that Healer Sagdea's initial assessment had been correct. It would never again be normal. Nonetheless, Andoc was eventually able to go from using a pair of crutches to using one, and, from there, to discarding the crutches altogether in favor of a heavy walking stick.

His new limitations bothered him; that much was obvious. I frequently found myself silently thanking Jacun for his actions, since I suspect that without his responsibilities as chief of the village, Andoc would have been disconsolate. For his part, Jacun had returned to his old position as First Warrior with enviable grace. He was frequently absent, taking the lead role for now when it came to traveling from village to village, coordinating the plans on which our safety and security rested.

When he returned from a trip to Meren on a relatively warm autumn afternoon, I raised an eyebrow as he stepped down from his stocky mare and handed her off to me. "I should probably ask how the meeting with Magoldis and the elders went," I said in a wry tone, "But I'm actually much more interested in where you got those marks on your neck."

To my delight, Jacun blushed scarlet, a hand coming up to cover the livid love bites just visible above the collar of his loose linen shirt. He cleared his throat. "Ah… yes. Just—*ahem*—just a small accident."

Even his ears were red. Eventually, I had pity on him. "Of course," I said hiding my smile even as I wondered who the lucky woman was. "Clumsy of you. You, um, might want to put on a scarf or a neckerchief before you meet with Andoc, unless you want to be subjected to a detailed interrogation."

His smile was sheepish. "Good idea. Thanks, Carivel."

Of course, it still took less than a day for the gossip to start making the rounds—people whispering that Jacun was courting Magoldis' daughter, First Warrior Varanis. Jacun did not deny it, though I couldn't help thinking with a smirk that there was apparently a bit more going on than mere *courting*.

"A good match," Senovo opined over a late dinner the following day. "It seems likely that Magoldis will support them should they wish to make things official."

"Of course, if they do, it means either Draebard or Meren will lose their First Warrior," I said.

Andoc frowned. "I can't afford to lose my First Warrior right now." He paused for a moment, his expression lightening and growing speculative. "Though, mind you, I wouldn't say no to having Varanis join the Draebardi."

"How would you decide which one of them retained the position of First?" I asked, curious.

Andoc smirked. "Simple—throw 'em in a chalk ring together and see which one walked out at the end."

"And would you warn Jacun to wear a codpiece?" Senovo asked, referring to Varanis' rather memorable victory over Andoc that spring in Meren, when she had felled him with a well-aimed kick between the legs.

Andoc laughed aloud, a sound I didn't hear nearly often enough these days. "That would depend entirely on how well-disposed I was feeling toward him at the time. Though, honestly, I suspect that particular story has made the rounds of every warrior in the north by now."

"I'm sure the inevitable embellishments have made it into a truly epic tale as well," Senovo said, his own amusement understated but clearly present.

"I can only imagine," I told him. "You're right, though. It's a good match. I hope it works out."

By the time a lone Rhytheeri rider galloped into the village on his blowing, lathered mount, the chilly days were outnumbering the pleasant ones. As the weather had begun to turn, so had Andoc's mood. Every time the skies clouded, threatening rain or snow, he grew more nervous and agitated, watching the weather obsessively until it passed, usually leaving behind only a smattering of fat drops that barely settled the dust or a light flurry of dry snow that disappeared within hours.

Now, the outcry of excitement at the dramatic new arrival drew the attention of everyone inside Charyal's cookhouse, where Andoc and I had met for a brief meal before returning to our duties. Andoc's face paled, and he lurched upright, hobbling outside as fast as he could. I followed half a step behind.

Once outside, I hurried forward to take the horse's reins, steadying the exhausted animal as its rider stepped down.

"I have important news," said the man in a breathless voice.

Andoc beckoned a young girl over from where she had been watching the excitement. He quickly directed her to find the elders and send them to the meeting hall.

"I am Chief Andoc," he said, returning his full attention to the messenger. "What is your news?"

The man bent over to rest his hands on his knees as he regained his breath. After a moment, he shook his head, and straightened. "Coin first," said the man. "Message afterward."

I could see a muscle working in the corner of Andoc's jaw, but he controlled his impatience. "You'll get your coin, stranger. Come to the meeting house. I'll see that you receive food and wine, and I'll deliver your payment personally."

The man nodded, still breathing heavily after his hard ride. I looked from the meeting hall to the exhausted animal I was holding, and sighed. The horse was near collapse; I would hear the details of the man's report soon enough. Leading the gelding slowly toward the horse pens, I stopped the first lad I saw and sent him ahead to have Dalon ready a wool blanket and some warm water for the ill-used creature.

By the time I returned, the village was in an uproar. Depending on which excited conversation you listened to, the Empire was on its way by land or by sea, and it was either a few days away, or right on our doorstep. I ignored it all as best I could and made a beeline for the meeting house, pushing my way through the crowd inside until I recognized Eiridan's distinctive dun-robed figure in a corner.

"What's the word?" I asked as soon as I got close enough.

Eiridan looked grim. "The messenger reports that Alyrion troops were preparing to move when he left. It is only part of the troops stationed in Rhyth—no additional forces had arrived in the city recently—but they still number in the hundreds."

I let my breath out slowly, trying to calm the sudden unsteady trip of my heartbeat. "Andoc was right, then. Not a full-scale invasion of the north, but still more than enough to take Draebard. Where is he, do you know?"

The novice priest pointed to the far side of the room, and I had to hop a bit to see over the shoulders of the people around us. A tight knot of warriors and elders were conferring near the head of the large table used for meetings. "Right," I said. "I'd better go, then. Thanks, Eiridan."

"May the gods smile on your endeavors, Horse Mistress," he replied, the familiar words carrying new weight under the circumstances that now surrounded us.

When I finally managed to reach the others, it was to find an argument in progress.

"If you think I'm going to sit here twiddling my thumbs while Draebard's future hangs in the balance," Andoc was saying, "then you are sorely mistaken."

"Andoc," Elder Tolmac replied, "no one is doubting your dedication to Draebard's defense. But speed is of the essence. Given your injury—"

"*Damn* my injury!" Andoc flared. "It's not as if I'm planning on running to the mountains on foot! I can still sit on a horse as well as the next man."

"And if there is fighting?" Tolmac asked.

It was Jacun who answered. "If there is fighting, Elder, then it means we have already lost."

Knowing Andoc, there was only one way this was going to go, and we were wasting time. "Andoc resumed riding more than two weeks ago, Elder Tolmac," I said. "There is no reason why he should not join us."

Tolmac still seemed faintly surprised whenever I appeared in the meeting hall or, even more shockingly, actually *spoke up*, but he was not, in fact, a stupid man. He knew when he was outnumbered.

"Well, then, there's no point wasting time standing here, is there?" he said, waving a hand in irritation.

"Are we leaving now, in that case?" I asked, already guessing the answer.

"We are," Andoc said grimly. "Ready the supplies and the horses. There's no time to lose."

SIXTEEN

Everything had been in readiness for weeks now. It was only a matter of saddling the horses and fastening our packs and saddlebags into place. Eight of us would be riding to intercept the Alyrions, splitting into two groups as we approached the newly established camps in the foothills. We were not a fighting force—far from it. Our company consisted of four warriors—Jacun, Keenan, Balzoc, and Zolis—along with Andoc, Senovo, Favian, and myself.

It was late in the day, but we would ride through the night, stopping only to rest the horses occasionally. The journey to the mountains that had taken almost three days with the large, combined contingent of Mereni and Draebardi delegates that summer would take us less than a day riding flat out in a small group without pack animals.

Dusk was approaching when we mounted up and rode away from the village, heading for the southern logging roads. Cantering along the rutted tracks in the deepening dark brought back bad memories—of bringing Senovo here, the night after High Priest Rhystel died; of our capture by Rhytheeri bounty hunters. I focused on the feeling of Kekenu's powerful muscles bunching and releasing beneath me, my eyes on Andoc's broad back as he rode in front of me beneath the uncertain light of the moon.

Our plan was to put as much distance between us and Draebard as possible before the moon set. We would be forced to slow at that point, both to rest the horses and reduce the risk of a stumble or fall. I wasn't too worried, though—the horses would be able to see far better than we could in the black of night.

When Andoc finally raised a hand and reined his gelding down to a walk, the broken hills of Draebard's southern forest was giving way to open ground and the silver crescent of the moon was just disappearing behind the trees.

Once everyone had a few minutes to get their breath back, I called, "Eat, everyone. Jorun used to say that there's being tired, and there's being hungry, but being tired and hungry at the same time will have you nodding off before you know it."

There was a rumble of appreciative laughter from Balzoc and Jacun, both of whom had been around long enough to develop a good appreciation for Jorun's earthy wisdom over the years. We rummaged through our bags for dried meat and fruit, washing it down with watered wine from the skins hanging on our saddles. When the horses were cool enough, we stopped at the next stream we came across to water them, letting the animals' more acute senses hone in on a place where the water still pooled a few inches deep in the mostly dry creek bed.

The night was long and desolate, broken by the rattle of wind in dry leaves and the occasional cry of a wild animal. When a pack of wolves howled mournfully in the distance, I shivered in unconscious reaction.

By the time the false dawn began to lighten the eastern sky to our left, my mind was fuzzy with fatigue and my head was starting to pound. We trudged on, each wrapped in our own exhaustion and worry, barely speaking until the light of the sun's rays breached the horizon.

I took a moment to examine Senovo and Favian—both tired and pale, but sitting straight in their saddles with their heads held high. My attention moved to Andoc who, despite his insistence on being here, must have been in considerable pain. His leg was approaching the point of being as well healed as it was likely to get, but the muscles around the mended bone had been torn and twisted. His injured calf had wasted away until it was barely half the circumference of the healthy one, and I knew from having worked with him during his slow recovery that resting his foot in the stirrup became uncomfortable after a short period of time.

Indeed, when I looked, the leg was hanging loose, the toe twisted slightly to the outside. To compensate for the weakness, Andoc now used a stout, peeled branch about the length of his outstretched arm to tap the gelding's side and direct him, instead of using his heel. Andoc's face was haggard, but I knew he would not give up on our desperate, last-ditch defense as long as he still drew breath.

We stopped for a few minutes to relieve ourselves, and so I could check the horses over after riding through the night. Andoc's gelding had been prone to occasional puffiness in his right hind pastern ever since the fall that had broken his rider's leg. The joint was swelling a bit now, but although it was unsightly, it wasn't warm to the touch and he'd shown no signs of lameness. I wasn't worried.

Balzoc gave Andoc a leg up into his saddle once we were ready to proceed, and the rest of us clambered aboard with limbs made stiff and weak by fatigue. With the return of the light, we were able to pick up the pace once more, the brisk autumnal wind pressing at our backs.

Daylight and the relatively flat stretch of land between the forest and the southern mountains made our progress easier. The morning was chilly despite the sun. However, that actually helped the horses, which would have quickly become overheated had we tried to keep up such a pace in the height of summertime. As it was, we slowed at intervals to let the animals blow, but we were able to maintain a steady canter for long periods in between, eating up the distance as the impressive peaks in front of us grew closer, dwarfing everything else.

When the trail split at a collection of derelict stone structures that had once been a thriving trading post, we reined to a halt.

"This is it," Andoc said. "Jacun, take Balzoc, Zolis, and Senovo, and head for the eastern pass as fast as you can. Once you get there, you know what to do."

"We'll take care of things on the eastern side, Chief," Jacun said. "Don't you worry. Be safe, all of you. We'll see you again soon."

"That you will," Andoc agreed. "Take care of yourselves as well."

His eyes met each of theirs in turn, lingering for an extra moment on Senovo's. The priest nodded, his eyes moving from Andoc's to mine. I bit my lip, not wanting to let my misgivings show. Finally, Senovo looked to Favian.

"Be brave, Little Brother. The gods are with us; all will be well," he said.

Favian looked down, a flush staining his cheeks as he nodded. A moment later, the others wheeled their horses around and headed down the left-hand trail, toward the eastern camp of Mereni tribesmen huddled at the base of the mountains.

I continued to worry at the skin of my lip, trying to tamp down the irrational panic at the idea of Senovo being parted from us like this. It made sense—I knew it did. Under the circumstances, Andoc wanted someone from the temple at each of the two camps, and since Favian had to come with us, Senovo was the logical choice.

That didn't mean I had to like it, though.

I snuck a glance at Andoc, only to find him watching me in turn, complete understanding visible in his expression.

"Come on," he said to all of us. "We've still got a fair distance to go today."

We rode on. As we grew closer and closer to the mountains, Favian's trepidation grew visibly. Andoc was beginning to flag, riding hunched forward in the saddle with weariness and discomfort when he thought no one was looking. I was mired in worry for Senovo, for Andoc, for Draebard itself—my head pounding with fatigue in the bright afternoon sun. Only Keenan seemed her normal self, focused and alert, sitting easily on her tall gray mare.

A small track led off of the main trail, barely noticeable among the underbrush. Andoc turned onto it, leading us deep into the woods. The twisting path slowed our progress to a crawl. We rode for nearly an hour; the dappled light of the setting sun was giving way to gray dusk when the ramshackle camp finally came into view. It had taken us longer to get here than we had hoped, but as long as we arrived before the Alyrion forces did, we had succeeded in this part of our quest at least.

"Who's there?" called a voice as we trotted up to the little collection of tents and hastily constructed lean-tos hidden amongst the trees.

"It's Andoc," shouted Andoc in return.

Jeppel stepped forward from where he had been leaning against a gnarled old trunk, standing watch. "Oh, shit," he said, looking pale in the evening dimness. "Are they coming, then?"

"It sounds like they may be," Andoc said. "A messenger reached the village late yesterday afternoon, and said troops were on the move. Depending on how organized they are, I think we can expect them to reach the mountain pass within the next couple of days. Is everything ready here?"

Jeppel's mouth twitched into a frown. "I would have liked to get more done, but I think what we have will work. Guess it'll have to, eh?"

"I guess it will," Andoc agreed. He looked around at the other people sticking their heads out to see who had arrived. "Right. I think we can safely assume the Alyrions won't march through the night, so we're all right for now. First thing in the morning, though, we'll need to set a watch on the mountain and keep it rotating from then on."

Jeppel nodded. "It's too late to show you where we've got everything set up before we lose the light, but I can take you around in the morning, as soon as the sun's up."

"Thanks, Jeppel. For now, if you could help us get settled in and show us where the horses are penned, that would be great." Andoc swung his bad leg over the saddle and lowered himself to the ground very carefully, leaning against his horse's shoulder until he could un-sling his walking stick from his pack.

The rest of us dismounted as well. Favian and I each took two of the horses and followed Jeppel to get them unpacked and cooled out before it grew too dark to see. I was surprised that there were no fires lit in the camp, but after a moment's thought, I could see the sense of it. Even hidden in the deep woods, the smoke from cooking fires could be visible to Alyrion scouts ranging ahead of the main force as they descended the northern slopes.

Resigning myself to a restless, unpleasant night, I led Favian back to the collection of makeshift shelters once the animals were all cared for and secure. We found Keenan sharing out wine from our skins, talking cheerfully with the men of the camp. Now that the cover of darkness would hide any smoke, someone had lit a small fire and was spitting a brace of fat hares to roast over it.

Even though my stomach rumbled at the smell, I was honestly more tired than I was hungry. Fatigue was making it difficult for my body to combat the chill of the evening, especially when blasts of wind whistled through the gaps in the trees. I shivered.

"Favian?" I asked, looking down at the lad walking next to me. "How're you doing?"

"C-cold," he said, his arms wrapped around himself.

"Me, too," I said. "Come on. Sit by the fire for a while."

I put a hand on his shoulder and guided him around to where Andoc was sprawled near the crackling flames, his game leg stretched out in front of him. Without ceremony, I flopped down next to him and dragged Favian with me, pulling him into my arms even as I wormed my way under Andoc's shoulder, wedging both of us against his side.

Keenan appeared in my field of view a moment later and handed us a blanket, which I accepted gratefully.

"Are you doing all right?" I asked her.

She smiled. "I love the cold. Not like you soft Draebardi types."

I didn't have anything handy to chuck at her, so I had to be satisfied with sticking my tongue out and pulling a face. Keenan laughed. "You're punch-drunk, Carivel. Get some sleep. In fact, we should all try to get some sleep."

"Wise words," Andoc agreed. "Jeppel, I assume you've got a watch set for tonight? None of us are going to be much help after a night and a day in the saddle, I'm afraid."

"Yeah, we're good," said Jeppel. "Nothing more to be done until morning."

⁊⧫⁊

As I had suspected, the night was an uncomfortable one. Despite my exhaustion, I awoke repeatedly at the unfamiliar noises of the deep woods. Andoc, Favian, and I slept curled together, but it was still cold — the wind reducing the benefit of the modest fire considerably. I was worried for Favian, but he wasn't shivering and actually seemed to be sleeping more peacefully than I was. Andoc was restless as well, though I could tell he was trying to minimize his movements to avoid bothering us.

When enough sunlight started to filter through the trees that we could see, it was something of a relief. The camp was already waking up, someone moving to smother the fire while others went to care for the horses. I groaned and stretched aching joints that popped and crackled in protest.

Of the four of us, only Keenan seemed rested and alert. Andoc was grim; Favian was pale and frightened, while I was exhausted and sore. We tried to stay out of everyone's way as we grabbed a quick bite to eat and made ourselves as ready for what the day would bring as we could. Once we were organized, Jeppel reported that he'd sent a lookout on horseback to a point partway up the mountain where the top of the pass was visible, to keep watch for the approaching forces.

Then, he took the four of us through the woods to show us what the members of the camp had been working on for the past few weeks. I was impressed, to be honest. I'd never had much use for Jeppel, but he had done well here under harsh conditions with very little outside support. Andoc also seemed pleased, as did Keenan. Favian, on the other hand, looked vaguely ill.

We returned to the camp, and busied ourselves with the organization of the watches and signals that we would need to have in place at all times from now on. Andoc was still confident that the Alyrions would not march at night, particularly through the difficult terrain of the mountains. Keenan agreed. Their commander would be foolish to exhaust his men before they ever got close to the field of battle.

However, the possibility of scouts at night could not be completely discounted. For this reason, we decided to keep a night watch not only around the camp, but at the edge of the woods near the main trail, where a person might observe a scout riding past without being seen in turn.

With so many places that needed constant watching, the four of us quickly offered to join the rota. When everything else was in place, Favian handed Jeppel the heavy pouch he'd brought from the temple, still looking decidedly queasy. Jeppel took it away to start sharing out the contents among the people who would need it later.

After that, it was all a matter of waiting.

And waiting.

And *waiting*.

I rode along the shortcut that would take me out to the trail and up the side of the mountain to relieve the man who had been keeping watch over the mountain pass. Both he and his horse looked bored beyond measure, and I was caught between the hope that my own shift would be uneventful, and the desire for this whole thing to just be *over*.

The view from the rocky outcropping was astonishing, and I took a few minutes to appreciate it as I lounged on Kekenu's back, his breath making steamy clouds in the cold, thin air. I was well bundled up since my previous ignorance about the chill of the mountains had cost our party several cold, uncomfortable nights on the way to and from Rhyth. Even so, the air nipped at my nose and ears, and I frequently had to jam my mittened hands under my armpits for a few minutes to thaw them.

My gaze flickered back and forth from the empty pass above, to the undulating ocean of red, yellow, brown, and green treetops spread out around and below me. It was an amazing and humbling sight. I looked back the way I'd come, trying to see if the camp was visible at all from up here. It wasn't. With no smoke to give it away, tucked into the trees as it was, you would never guess that a band of people had labored there for weeks.

What was visible, though, were the series of irregular bare patches where they had cleared trees and underbrush in a wavering line along the base of the mountains. Whether someone who didn't know what to look for would notice it, and what—if anything—they would make of it if they did, I had no idea.

Hours passed, and I grew gradually colder and more bored in turn. I kept my eyes on the pass once the wonder of my surroundings wore off, but no soldiers appeared. Eventually, Keenan showed up to relieve me.

"I'll ask you if you still enjoy the cold when you get back later," I told her, adding, "Be safe," as I reined Kekenu around and headed back down the steep trail. I had a moment's worry that I would not be able to find the shortcut to the camp and would have to ride all the way back down to the point where we'd come in the previous evening. Fortunately, Kekenu's sense of direction was somewhat better developed than my own, and he turned into the inconspicuous trailhead half-hidden behind a pile of boulders.

The rest of the day passed in a kind of anxious crawl, with no news from either Keenan or Jeppel, who relieved her for the final watch since he was familiar enough with the trails to negotiate them after dark. When he finally returned with a shrug to indicate the lack of new information, and when the night watches were set, we settled in for a second miserable night.

The wind, if anything, was even worse than it had been previously, and it brought with it a scent of snow that had Andoc up and pacing worriedly around the fire with his walking stick, unable to settle.

Needless to say, no one slept well. The morning saw occasional dry snowflakes swirling among the trees, but there was nothing for it but to keep doing what we had been doing. So it was that I found myself shivering on an exposed ridge, my hands buried under Kekenu's mane to try and keep them warm, when a glint of silver caught an errant ray of morning sunshine at the top of the pass.

I caught my breath and held it, staring fixedly.

Movement. Men, and horses. Mere specks in the distance.

The Alyrions were coming, by the dozens. By the hundreds.

I whirled Kekenu around and charged back down the rocky, dangerous trail, trusting the little horse to keep his footing as I urged him faster. It was still almost a two-hour ride back to the camp, and both of us were sweating and panting for air when we arrived.

Andoc was coordinating things at the encampment when I arrived. He took one look at me and called, "Jeppel! They're coming! Send runners out to warn the others and get someone to the secondary lookout point!"

The camp burst into frantic activity, people running out on foot and hurrying to saddle fresh horses. Andoc turned his attention back to me, steadying me as I swung down to the ground on shaking legs. "How many?" he asked.

I could only shake my head, still trying to get my breath back. "Hundreds," I managed after a few moments. "I didn't stay to get a closer count."

Andoc blew out an explosive sigh. "It doesn't really matter. This will work, or it won't. If it doesn't, there's really no backup plan."

"It will work," I told him. "It has to work. Where's Favian?"

"He's stationed at the closest pile," Andoc said. "Keenan is at the next farthest one."

I nodded. "We need to get the camp packed up, yes?" I asked. "And I need to walk Kekenu for a few minutes— he's soaked with sweat."

A new swirl of snowflakes blew around us, and I saw Andoc flinch as several hit his cheek. "As long as he's the only thing that gets soaked," he said, his tone grim. "But, yes, there's time. In fact, there's going to be quite a bit of time yet."

The hours passed like cooling treacle. Those of us left at the camp bundled up the supplies that we would need to take with us once we fled the results of our handiwork. With the horses packed and a new rider sent to check that everyone was in place and ready, I helped Andoc climb onto his gelding from the top of a sturdy, downed tree trunk and followed him to the secondary lookout point to see how things were progressing.

Our timing was surprisingly good. When we arrived, Jeppel was watching the mountainside closely, a hand raised above his eyes to shield them from the occasional swirls of blowing snow.

"They're getting close to the halfway point," he greeted us. "What do you think, Andoc?"

Andoc examined the progress of the distant specks down the mountain trail. "Let's give them a bit more time. I don't want them to have even the slightest chance of getting back to the top of the pass."

Jeppel nodded. "Think this snow is going to hold off?"

"I think it had better."

Not too long after that, the snow started to come down faster, gathering in nooks and crannies as the stiff wind blew it around.

"We can't wait anymore," I said.

"No, you're right," Andoc agreed. "Jeppel, light it up."

Jeppel nodded. "Right you are. Might want to stand back a bit."

He moved to the huge pile of dead trees and branches lying nearby, going to the north side where twigs and leaves were set under the larger pieces of wood to act as kindling. The shattered remains of one of the barrels of pine tar Andoc had purchased from the eastern ship builders lay a bit further up the pile, its contents coating the wood beneath.

Jeppel carefully sprinkled some of the priests' fire-starting powder that Favian had brought for us onto the kindling, sheltering it from the wind with his body as he pulled out a flint striker and struck a spark. The result was startling.

He backed away quickly, joining us a safe distance away as the powder flashed brightly, catching the twigs and dry leaves. The wind licked at the flames, driving them up to the pitch-soaked branches and the remains of the wooden barrel, which flared to life seconds later. Jeppel hastily untied his nervous horse from a tree nearby and mounted, the three of us retreating back toward the camp as the whole pile began to go up, quickly catching some of the underbrush and shrubby trees nearby.

Andoc's plan was underway. It was very likely that the person manning the next nearest pile of fuel would be able to see the smoke and flames from this one, which was further up the side of the mountain and therefore fairly visible. That person would give us an hour or so to ride back down and join them before lighting the new pile. Once that one was burning, we would all move on to the next, and the next, gathering more people along the way until we ended up back at the camp and could head out together to the northern trail back toward Draebard.

Even though we would be heading deeper into the forest to get back to the camp, we would also be angling slightly north at the same time, while the autumnal wind would be driving the flames south, up the side of the mountain.

Toward the Alyrion troops, who were now many hours away from the summit, and safety. They would be trapped on the slope, unable to escape the approaching inferno in time — just as Favian had foreseen in his dream, months ago.

Andoc and Senovo had been fairly confident, based on Favian's vision, that the Alyrions would come across the western pass. It was, after all, the shortest route from Rhyth to Draebard. However, since there were only two good routes through the mountains, Andoc had decided to play things safe by establishing a second camp below the eastern pass to set up the exact same defense that Jeppel had arranged here at the western pass. That was where Jacun and Senovo had gone, just in case we had all guessed wrong.

If all went according to plan, we would ride back to the crossroads and join them to let them know that the Alyrions were defeated, before all going home together. First, though, we had to ensure that the scheme would work.

The ride down from the secondary lookout point was not as frantic as my flight down the mountain this morning had been. Time was still of the essence, but we also had to save the horses' strength for the long ride ahead. It took just slightly more than an hour to reach the next log pile, where we were greeted by a man named Penron, with pale, freckled skin and reddish-blonde hair.

"I was starting to wonder if I should light this up without waiting for you," he said. "Glad to see you made it back safe."

"Thanks, Pen," said Jeppel. "Go ahead and light 'er up right now."

The snow was still coming down steadily, but it didn't stop the pitch-stained pile of dry deadwood from flaring into life, licking at the branches of the surrounding trees within minutes.

"That's good enough," Andoc said, shading his eyes as he watched the fire spread. "Let's get moving."

We continued further into the woods along the base of the mountain, pausing at every pile to make sure it started burning well before moving on to the next, our ranks swelling at each stop. Keenan's pile was second to last. For the first time, though, the results were less than spectacular. The topography around us sheltered the area from the wind, and the snow had settled deeper here. The kindling and pine tar still burned, but it was a slow, smoky fire and did not immediately spread.

"Leave it," Jeppel said after a few minutes. "Move on to the next one."

We rode on to join Favian at the last woodpile before the camp. By this time, there was a strange, low crackling noise coming from the woods behind us. It was distant, and oddly distorted by the muffling influence of the trees. Still, something about it made the animal part of me sit up and take notice, the hair pricking on my neck.

Favian looked to be on the verge of fainting, so pale were his features, but he sprinkled his powder on the kindling and lit a spark with fumbling fingers. Unlike the last one, this pile burst into immediate life, lashing violently at its surroundings within minutes.

"It's done," said Andoc. "Let's get out of here."

We veered north, back toward the encampment where a handful of people were still waiting, ready to join us with the packed supplies. We would ride northwest along the trail that eventually rejoined the main road, where we could get a decent view of the fire's progress up the mountain.

Several of the horses spooked when a herd of deer burst across the trail in front of us, fleeing for their lives from the firestorm. Other wild animals followed in unnaturally large numbers, their usual shyness and solitary tendencies forgotten in the face of the all-consuming maelstrom behind them. I steadied Kekenu with a hand on his neck, and spared a solemn prayer for the uncounted small lives we had condemned to a fiery death this day.

The remaining men were ready for us when we reached the remains of the camp, now stripped of the hides and tent poles that we would need for our coming journey. Snow swirled around us as we headed out, retracing the route that Andoc, Favian, Keenan, and I had followed two days ago to get here. Though we were far from the real danger and could feel no trace of heat coming from behind us, my senses continued to tingle with the instinctive animal need to *run, flee, escape* or face certain death.

I spared a moment's thought for the Alyrion soldiers. Had they realized yet what was happening? Were they running? Were they scared? Did they know they were going to die?

Every instance of cruelty — small and large — that I had suffered at the hands of the Empire crashed over me at once in a wave of loathing and rage.

I hope so, I thought, practically shaking with the desire for bloody revenge.

We continued down the narrow trail that meandered through the foothills, taking care that no one fell behind. The light took on a strange, pinkish-orange cast, made more surreal by the continuing eddy of snowflakes across my vision. With the rhythmic jounce of Kekenu's stride carrying me forward, I had to fight occasional bouts of dizziness as my eyes struggled to focus past the swirl of white.

Eventually, the snow tailed off, much to everyone's relief. It was early in the season to receive much more than a dusting, but now, about an inch lay across the ground, blowing into small drifts here and there. A few minutes later and with little warning, the twisting trail through the woods disgorged us onto the main road leading from Draebard to the mountain pass.

Almost as one, we turned our horses to look at our handiwork. The foothills hid our view of the road that ran through the pass, but even from here we could see how the fires we'd set had grown and merged together, still climbing steadily up the steep slope of the mountain.

Andoc called out so everyone could hear. "Favian and I will have to go closer, to the bend in the road where we can see the pass clearly. None of the rest of you need to come with us if you don't want to, though."

Jeppel looked around at the men he'd been sharing a camp with the last few weeks. "Nah," he said. "We'd best see it through to the end. We'll just end up wondering, otherwise."

Andoc nodded. "Very well. Carivel? Keenan? What about you?"

"Try and stop us," Keenan said, beating me to it.

We rode on, deeper into the foothills, though some of the horses balked and fussed, instinctively resisting the idea of going back toward the flames. It was less than an hour's ride to the place where Favian had stopped in horror during our journey to Rhyth as he came face to face with the landscape from his dreams. Though I remembered that the place was just after a sharp curve in the trail, I didn't recognize it at first with the light covering of snow obscuring the surroundings.

Favian did.

He pulled his horse to an abrupt halt, staring ahead as if mesmerized. Indeed, once I followed his gaze, I remembered the way the vista had opened out, giving us a clear view of the trail over the mountain for the first time.

The view was not so clear now. Smoke hung in a pall over the glowing red and orange of burning trees. As predicted, the wind had driven the fire unerringly across the pass, and the entire side of the mountain was an inferno. We could not see the soldiers from this distance—not through the smoke and flame—but they had been marching down the slope for more than half a day when the fires were lit, and there was no earthly way for them to have made it back up the mountain in time.

Though the strange, crackling rumble of a mountain engulfed in flames was still audible over the howling wind, the screams of dying men were not—swallowed up by the power of nature gone mad. I had a sneaking suspicion, however, that Favian could hear them... at least in his mind.

At the reminder of my former apprentice, I tore my eyes away from the spectacle to check on him, only to find that while our attention was focused on the mountain, Favian had slid down from his horse and crumpled into a ball, sitting in the snow.

SEVENTEEN

"Favian," I cried, and leapt down from Kekenu so I could rush over to him.

Several other people turned, and Keenan immediately dismounted to join us. I knelt down next to the distraught boy. His body was like ice as I drew him into my arms.

"All those people. All those animals," he whispered.

Keenan pulled the blanket from her bedroll and brought it over to us, crouching to help me wrap it around Favian's shivering form. "There, now," she said, once Favian was tucked into the folds. "Look away, Favian. You don't need to watch."

But Favian only shook his head, his eyes fixed over my shoulder on the destruction we had wrought. "No. I have to see. If I don't see it, how could I have *Seen* it?"

Andoc had ridden over to join us as we fussed over the slender acolyte. "*Favian*," he said, looking down from his horse. "You've seen enough now. It's all right. Look at me." Reluctantly, Favian looked away from the glow of orange and red, though I suspected he was still seeing it regardless. Andoc nodded encouragement. "That's it. Now listen to me. *You saved Draebard*, Favian. *You've saved us all.*"

I felt Favian's chest hitch under my hands, and his head jerked back and forth in tiny, almost unconscious movements of negation.

"Come on," I told him, "you're half frozen. You can ride with me for a while."

"No," Andoc said from above us. "Set him up here. He can ride with me."

I nodded, and pulled Favian to unsteady feet. Keenan helped me lift him up into Andoc's strong grasp, and between us we settled him in front of Andoc in the saddle. Leaving the vividly imagined screams of dying soldiers behind us, we mounted up and headed for the derelict trading post at the fork in the road leading to the eastern pass.

The tumbledown stone walls of the old buildings made an effective windbreak, and helped contain the heat from our fires. With no more reason remaining to hide our presence, we gathered a generous amount of wood and built the fires up high enough to drive back the chill that had set in after the day's snow.

I would not be able to relax fully until we rejoined Senovo and the others and returned safely home. Still, it was good to be able to curl up someplace relatively warm and sheltered, without the unrelenting weight of worry bowing my back. We had done it. The gods had shown us, through the medium of Favian's vision, how to prevail over the Empire. It was too late in the season now for them to try again. We had dealt them a vicious blow, and Draebard was safe from the threat of invasion until spring.

Andoc, too, appeared as if a weight had been lifted from his shoulders, and the others were flush with the success of their labors, passing around wine and food as if it were a celebration. Only Favian seemed unaffected by our victory. Listless and pale, he stared at the flames of the campfire, and it was not difficult to guess where his thoughts lay. Not for the first time today, I heartily wished for Senovo's presence.

Eventually, exhausted by the day's exertions, we settled down in our bedrolls to sleep. Favian's skin was still chilly to the touch, and I pulled his unresisting form down to lie curled between my body and Andoc's, wrapping all three of our blankets around us.

Andoc gave off warmth like a banked hearth in the cozy space, and before too long, Favian dropped into a fitful sleep. "Do you think he'll be all right?" I asked quietly, once I was sure he would not hear us talking.

"I hope so," Andoc replied. "I hated dragging him back to see the fire, but he was right. How could he have *Seen* it, without seeing it?" He sighed. "The gods may have saved us, but they have a cruel streak sometimes."

I gently brushed the hair off Favian's forehead. "Senovo will know what to do," I said.

It was a bit more than a day's ride to get to the eastern pass. When we did, it was to find everything there quiet and calm. Zolis was on watch at the camp; he hurried forward as soon as he recognized our horses. "Did they come?" he asked breathlessly. "Did it work?"

"They came," Andoc said, "and they paid for it with their lives."

Zolis let out a whoop and ran to spread the word. A moment later, Senovo arrived, and the last of the tension that had been coiled in my chest started to loosen. After a brief once-over to determine that everyone was present and unhurt, however, Senovo's eyes were only for Favian.

"Little Brother," he said softly, and with no further prompting, Favian slid from his horse and stumbled into Senovo's arms.

Senovo merely held him for a long moment.

"They're all dead," Favian said, the words calm but faint. "Because of me."

Senovo stood in thoughtful silence, considering his words carefully.

"The gods' gifts may sometimes seem capricious. Even cruel. But they always—*always*—have a reason for their actions." He smoothed a hand over the back of Favian's head. "And they never give those gifts to someone who lacks the strength to carry them. The burden you now carry is the price of Draebard's survival. But you do not need to carry it alone. Do you understand?"

Favian nodded hesitantly against his shoulder, and I felt tears pricking at my own eyes. How long had it taken me to learn that lesson? Would I ever have learned it, without the two men here with me now? I hoped Favian would be a better student than I had been.

⤛ ⚜ ⤜

Our own reunion was somewhat more subdued, in the presence of so many onlookers.

"You did it, old friend," Senovo said, grasping Andoc forearm to forearm.

Andoc's smile was wan. "I only followed where I was led."

I darted in a moment later to press a chaste kiss on Senovo's cheek, and was rewarded with an arm settling briefly around my shoulders, holding me in place for an instant before letting go.

"So," Andoc said, looking around at the peaceful camp, "it looks like I dragged everyone out here for no reason."

"It was a reasonable precaution," said Senovo. "The Empire does not have a large naval contingent at Rhyth, so that really only left them two options for coming overland. It made sense to cover both, as far as possible."

"Well, I'm glad it ended up being unnecessary. I wouldn't like to make a habit of causing the kind of devastation we just left behind us."

Senovo's voice turned wry. "It will certainly serve as a memorable beginning to your reign as Chief."

"If you're not careful," I added, "you're going to get a reputation."

"As long as it's the kind of reputation that makes the Emperor think twice about sending more troops, I think I can live with it," Andoc said, though his expression remained grim. "Unfortunately, I suspect all we've done at this point is prick his pride."

Jacun had wandered up to join us during the exchange, and shook his head. "Maybe so," he said, "but it doesn't change the fact that he can't do much about it until next spring. You managed this in only a few weeks, Andoc. What will you come up with given six whole months? I'm not worried."

Andoc's expression softened, but his words were rueful. "You put too much faith in me, Jacun."

"Nonsense," I said. "He's just relieved he doesn't have to come up with something himself."

Jacun grinned at me. "You're not far wrong. Now come on… this should be a celebration. Let's go see how much wine is left."

⤳ ♕ ⤳

Normally, such a celebratory feast would have gone on long into the night. Since everyone was exhausted and homesick, however, it lasted until people started getting slightly drunk, at which point they tended to stumble into the nearest tent and fall asleep. With the greatest of enjoyment, I crawled into one such tent and curled up next to the warm, furry form of the wolf, already bracketed on the other side by Favian, fast asleep and dead to the world. Andoc eased himself carefully inside after me and tied the flap shut.

I slept better than I had in days, waking with a slight hangover that did nothing to dim my appreciation of finally feeling *rested*. Once everyone was up, we puttered around getting the second camp packed and then headed out at a leisurely pace toward Meren and Draebard.

"Are you going home now?" I asked Keenan as we trotted along under a blue sky, the snow melting quickly as the day warmed above freezing.

"Yes," she said, "though if the weather cooperates I'll try to visit Draebard at least once to let you know how the training with the Mereni archers goes. I think we've got almost two dozen who could become proficient on horseback over the course of the winter."

"Glad to hear it," I told her. "I'm sure Zolis would miss you if you were absent for too long."

"That's because you don't tease him enough," she retorted with a grin.

We continued in easy silence, stifling laughter when Zolis craned around to look at us as if he'd sensed us talking about him. I also tried to keep an eye on Favian, aware that Senovo was doing the same. The acolyte rode close to his mentor, not joining in the conversation that ebbed and flowed among the group, but at least he looked better than he had after the fire.

Late in the afternoon of the first day of travel, we reached the split between the road to Meren and the track that would lead us west to rejoin the road to Draebard. Keenan embraced me, squeezing hard, and whispered, "Look after your men, yeah? They're going to need it," into my ear.

I squeezed back, and said, "I will. You look after Ciero. Tell him I never did get a chance to see that carving of Nietre after it was finished."

We smiled at each other, and Keenan mounted up to join the other Mereni who had come to help at the logging camps. Once they had headed off down the road with a final wave, our group was diminished by nearly half.

Andoc looked after them for a moment, before turning to the rest of us. "Home," he said simply. "Let's go."

Home happened two-and-a-half days later, where we were greeted by cheers and shouts of relief. Under the circumstances, I could well understand the excitement and joy at our safe return, even if it made me want to hide behind the others, away from all the attention.

The villagers had been left with no way of getting news, trapped in a constant state of worry. Either *we* would appear, or hundreds of soldiers bent on Draebard's destruction would appear. The remaining Draebardi warriors would have defended the settlement with their lives, of course, but everyone knew that if Andoc's plan failed, Draebard was as good as lost.

Our return heralded safety for the village, through the winter at least. I looked around at the excited faces, immediately picking out Renthro and little Frella near the front. I watched with a heartfelt smile as Favian dismounted and ran to them, the little family coming together in a tangled embrace.

Nearby, Charyal stood, wrapped in a shawl against the cold, her lower lip caught in her teeth as she searched for Jeppel. The moment she saw him, her expression looked like the sun coming out from behind the clouds. For all that the two of them seemed to fight continuously, it was obvious that their feelings for each other were genuine.

Feldes and Eiridan were hovering at the edge of the group with several of the acolytes, and Senovo made his way over to reassure them and deliver a report that no doubt included warnings about the help Favian was likely to need in dealing with his gift. It made me feel better knowing that my former apprentice would have all the support he could ever hope for.

I was considerably surprised to discover that I had my own little welcoming committee waiting, as well.

"Welcome back, boss," Dalon said, stepping forward to take Kekenu's reins as I stepped down. He was joined by Limdya, Varin, and Tenibral. I smiled, unable to stop the little blush of surprised pleasure that rose to my cheeks.

"It's good to be back," I said, meaning every word.

I turned to smile at Andoc, still sitting on his gelding behind me, only to find him already deep in solemn conversation with a group of elders. Our Chief was not looking half as pleased or relieved as everyone else seemed to be.

It was late in the season for a festival, but that didn't stop a spontaneous celebration from springing up the following day. The herdsmen slaughtered a couple of fat steers, the vintners dragged out enough barrels and wineskins to have the entire village hung over for a week, and people braved the chill weather to eat, drink, laugh, dance, and fuck long into the night.

Still, Andoc spent most of his time closeted with Tolmac, the weapons makers, and the Keeper of Coin, only showing his face long enough to satisfy the crowd who wanted to cheer him for his victory. His preoccupation continued through the next day, and the days that followed. To be fair, I had little room to complain—I, too, was wrapped up in my duties, cursing again the circumstances that seemed to pull me away from Draebard nearly as much as I was present. As with previous trips both planned and unplanned, I found myself playing catch-up as I tried to stay on top of everything that needed attention.

For this reason, I let things go with Andoc for the better part of two weeks before finally deciding that enough was enough. After a quiet word with Senovo, who was busy with his own duties but not quite as overwhelmed as Andoc and I were, I took advantage of a sunny afternoon when the wind was not as sharp as usual to kidnap Andoc and drag him to the horse pens.

"Should I even ask?" he said. His tone was good-natured, even though I could practically see his thoughts turning back to whatever plan or scheme he'd been focused on before I arrived to interrupt.

I merely shushed him as I continued to lead the way toward the alley we had set up with archery targets.

The late summer drought had finally given way to cold rains and the occasional wet snow as autumn surrendered to winter. However, the alleys between the pens had been packed solid by the passage of countless hooves and feet over the years. They were covered in a bit of muddy slush, but not badly enough to impede Andoc's progress with his walking stick, or to prevent what I had planned for us.

Andoc raised an eyebrow when he noticed Senovo lounging near the closest fence, the cowl of his heavy winter robe pushed back to bare his handsome face to the winter sunshine.

"Why do I suddenly feel as though I'm the victim of an ambush?" Andoc asked in a wry tone. "What are you doing here, Senovo?"

"I've been instructed to act as an impartial adjudicator for the coming contest," Senovo said, his hands tucked neatly into his loose sleeves to keep them warm.

"Oh? And what contest would that be?" Andoc said.

I unslung the small recurve bow from over my shoulder and pulled out one of Wendes' lightweight arrows. "I believe it's called *archery*," I said, laying on the irony with a heavy touch. "I'm told it's some sort of martial pursuit."

Andoc stared at me for a beat, and burst out laughing. "So it is, *caradi*. So it is." He eyed the bow and arrow with amusement. "Though that bow looks like something I would have used when I was knee-high to a pony."

I passed over the weapons with careful dignity, not allowing my own grin to break through. "Well, if you'd been paying more attention to what we've been doing over here, Chief Andoc, you'd know that we decided on this style of bow weeks ago."

The twinkle did not fade from Andoc's expression. "Fair enough, *Horse Mistress Carivel*. I have obviously been remiss. I don't suppose you're going to give me a few practice shots first, to get the feel for a new weapon?"

"Why on earth would I want to do something like that?" I asked. "I don't recall getting any instruction in wrestling or swordplay before our previous contests."

"She does have a point there," Senovo said from his spot against the fence, his own amusement clear.

"Very well, then," said Andoc. "I know when I'm beaten. Do I at least get to brace my hip against the fence, to compensate for my bad leg?"

I gestured grandly toward a sturdy post opposite the nearest target. "Be my guest."

Andoc shook his head and snorted, but hobbled over to the fence without complaint, the bow and arrow held in one hand. He made a show of leaning his walking stick against the lowest rail and set himself up, drawing the bowstring back a few times without nocking the arrow to get a feel for the unfamiliar weapon.

I went to stand against the post next to Senovo, shamelessly enjoying the view. Andoc had at least been taking his promise to look after himself more seriously, now that the immediate crisis was past. While not yet back to his previous weight, his gaunt frame had filled in somewhat, and even in winter clothing his broad shoulders and narrow hips drew the eye. Intent focus sharpened his handsome features as he set himself for the shot. Bracing the bow with his left arm, he drew back the arrow, holding the tip between the knuckles of his second and third fingers. He stood poised, his form perfect despite his weak leg, and sighted down the length of the shaft to the target.

A moment later, he let fly, and the point of the arrow embedded itself on the edge of the ring that formed the bull's eye.

I groaned. "All that fussing about *unfamiliar weapons*, and you nearly hit the center with your first shot. Typical!"

He grinned, but there was a faintly sheepish cast to it. "Sorry, *caradi*, but you have to remember that I lived and breathed this stuff for a good portion of my life before, well…" He trailed off and gestured down at his leg.

"That's it," I told him. "You're joining the mounted archery team. I just need to get you riding with your knees instead of your hands and your heels."

Andoc looked surprised, and it took me a moment to realize why.

Senovo tipped his chin up. "She's right, you know. The damage to your leg may make swordsmanship impractical, but there is no reason why it would be a hindrance to using a bow and arrow from horseback."

"I… honestly hadn't thought about that," he said, still looking taken aback. "It will have to come second to my duties as Chief, but… thank you, *caradi*."

I smiled, pleased to have given him back something he'd thought was lost. "Don't mention it," I said. "Now, give me that bow, and let's see if I can humiliate myself to a lesser degree than during our previous contests."

Both men wisely kept their mouths shut, and I drew another arrow from the quiver resting across my shoulder blades. I took up Andoc's position by the fence, and breathed in slowly through my nose as I lined up the shot. Remembering all of Keenan's patient tuition, I exhaled through my lips, my body going still and focused.

The arrow hurtled away, and struck the target dead center.

"Yes!" I crowed, hopping up and down, dignity completely forgotten in the moment. Several apprentices stopped what they were doing to stare at me, no doubt feeling smug at having their suspicions about my sanity — or lack thereof — publicly confirmed.

Andoc groaned, even as Senovo said, "I believe you have been beaten fair and square, my friend. Allow me to offer my quarters as the venue for a celebratory dinner this evening, to mark Carivel's victory."

"*Dinner*?" Andoc quoted wryly. "Is that what we're calling it these days?"

"Yes, it bloody well is," I said, still flush with my accomplishment. I pointed a finger right in Andoc's face. "And no trying to wriggle out of it, either."

Andoc swept a hand up to rest over his heart as if wounded. "Could you really think such a thing of me, *caradi*?" he asked, and my chest swelled at the glimpse of the old, playful Andoc, unbowed by the weight of his new responsibilities. "I'm *hurt*."

My grin was probably ridiculous by that point, and I didn't care. "You'll get over it. So. Dusk. Senovo's rooms. Bring wine. In fact, bring *lots* of wine."

"Your wish is my command, O Mighty Victor. I have a feeling I'm going to need it."

⚜

We did, in fact, get Andoc more than a little drunk that evening. He seemed to find the whole seduction vaguely hilarious, as I plied him with rich food and strong drink, even going so far as to sit on his lap and feed him tidbits of sweet fruit when the bulk of the meal was finished. His eyes were laughing at me as he sucked each one from my fingertips, and I relished being able to drive the darkness from his expression for a few hours, at least.

Senovo watched us with a tolerant smile from his chair nearby, twirling the stem of his goblet idly between his fingers. "You'd better stop feeding him soon," he said in an amused voice, "or he'll be too stuffed to fit anything else inside."

Andoc choked on a snort of laughter. "Have you been a bad influence on him, Carivel? Or have I?" he asked me.

"It must have been you," I said. "He's been coming up with stuff like that out of the blue since shortly after I started sleeping with you both. It shocked me pretty badly the first time, I can tell you."

Senovo did not break expression, though a faint blush rose to his cheeks. "Why do you assume I needed to be corrupted? It should be pointed out that I seduced Andoc originally, not the other way around."

"*Amadi*, you and I appear to have slightly different recollections of the event," Andoc said. "Still, that tragically beautiful face of yours could have seduced a wooden post, or a chunk of stone on the ground. You can hardly hold it against me if I succumbed."

"I never said I held it against you," Senovo said, and rose to stand next to us, leaning down until he could kiss Andoc, one long-fingered hand cradling his cheek.

I managed to stifle the embarrassing noise of affection that wanted to escape as I watched the two of them teasing each other. Andoc, for his part, did make a noise—a low sound of pleasure—and his cock twitched beneath me, obviously unfazed by all the wine he'd drunk.

"Clothes," I said, putting the last piece of fruit aside, suddenly unwilling to wait a moment longer. "Both of you. Naked. Bed. Now."

EIGHTEEN

Senovo pulled away with a smile before dropping a brief kiss onto my lips as well.

"Bossy, isn't she?" Andoc asked, still faintly flushed from the combination of wine and Senovo.

"She did beat you today," Senovo reminded him. "I believe she is entitled at this point."

I yelped as Andoc spilled me off his lap, grinning at me. "I have to wonder if she's got the balls to back it up, though."

I steadied myself against the table, and grinned right back at him. "I might not have the balls, but I've got the cock to back it up. In fact, it's sitting right on that shelf over there." I tipped my chin to indicate the curved wooden cock and intricate leather harness sitting in pride of place near the bed.

"Ah, but it's not only what you've got," he shot back. "It's what you can do with it."

"Not to worry, I know *exactly* what I'm going to do with it," I said, and started unlacing Andoc's breeches even as he loosened the ties on his jerkin. "I've been planning *extensively*."

"Have you, indeed?" Andoc asked, even as he shrugged out of the leather jerkin and dragged his linen shirt over his head. "Now I'm *really* worried."

Senovo ran a hand over the newly exposed skin of Andoc's shoulder and upper arm. "Surely there is nothing a slip of a Horse Mistress and a eunuch can dish out that the Chief of the village is incapable of withstanding."

I urged Andoc to lift his hips so I could drag his trousers and smalls down. Boots and stockings came next—my movements careful as I eased the right boot off of his injured leg. Finally I was able to pull everything down and off, leaving Andoc sprawled naked in the chair. I pressed a few kisses along the tight twist of scarred muscle around the place where the break had been, watching with interest as a faint blush colored his chest and neck.

Senovo kissed him again a moment later, masterful in a way I had never observed before. Andoc noticed, too, if his muffled noise of interest was any indication. When Senovo let him up for air, he met the eunuch's eyes and asked, "Well, now... am I to play host to more than one stiff cock tonight, *amadi?*"

"Only if you desire it," Senovo said.

Andoc smiled. "I desire you in all ways, old friend... I would hope that you know that by now. As I told you once before, you only ever had to ask."

I forced down the lump rising in my throat. "Unless you two want me to start sniffling into my sleeve like a little girl, shut up right now and get on the bed. Senovo. *Clothes.* You're wearing too many of them."

Andoc shared another look with Senovo, and heaved a long-suffering sigh. "Like I said. Bossy."

Senovo shrugged and stepped back to let Andoc rise unsteadily to his feet. The priest's hands moved to untie the fastenings of his robes without complaint. Meanwhile, I clambered to my own feet and offered Andoc an arm to help him across the room, leaving his walking stick propped in a corner.

Rhystel's ridiculous feather bed was piled invitingly with furs, blankets, and down-stuffed pillows. I still got the occasional urge to giggle when I saw it, thinking of the straw-stuffed leather pad on the dirt floor in my own sad excuse for a hut at the far end of the village. That rather pathetic mattress wouldn't have done at *all* for what I had planned. Rhystel had loved Senovo like the son he'd never had, and as bequests went, there were far worse ones than this bed.

Andoc flopped down on the bed in question dramatically — playing the part of the condemned man to the hilt for a moment before he broke expression and leered at me. "You still seem overdressed, *caradi.*"

I kissed him, and started removing clothing, making a show of it. I still had no clue what either of them saw in my unexceptional body, but they apparently saw something. For that reason alone, I was more than willing to indulge Andoc.

"Much better," he said, once the last scrap of linen had joined the pile of clothing on the floor.

"I like a man who's easily pleased," I told him, and climbed on top of him to kiss him and rub our bodies together.

Senovo joined us a moment later, a coil of rope in one hand and a pot of grease in the other. I slid my hands along the hard muscle and sinew of Andoc's arms, drawing his hands over his head and holding him there. I was on sufferance and I knew it—bad leg or no, Andoc could have flipped me over and pinned me in the space of a single breath. That didn't prevent my pleasure at play-acting the conqueror, however. My sex was already heavy and wet as I pressed Andoc into the bed and ground against him.

That pleasure was only increased when Senovo slipped onto the bed, graceful as a dancer, and looped the rope around Andoc's trapped wrists. He wove it into a simple and beautiful tie that I knew from experience to be completely inescapable, and used the free ends to bind Andoc to the sturdy rail running across the headboard of the heavy bed frame.

I straightened up to get a better view, straddling Andoc's hips, and caught my breath. He was laid out beneath me, arms stretched above him and showing off every taught line of muscle through his shoulders, chest and stomach. He let me look, one corner of his mouth tilting up in the cocky smirk that I hardly ever got to see these days.

"So," he asked, his eyes flicking lazily from one of us to the other. "Now that you've caught me, whatever are you going to do with me?"

I stared at him for a long moment, my mouth watering. "Everything. We're going to do everything to you."

Andoc's cock stirred, and I rolled my hips in response.

"Senovo," I said, "I want you to open him up. You've had more practice than me, and I want this to be good for him."

I leaned down to kiss the sensual smirk from Andoc's lips and dismounted so Senovo would have room to work while I watched and played with Andoc's cock. We urged our captive to lift his hips up so we could stuff a couple of pillows beneath him, exposing the tight pucker of his arse. "All right?" Senovo asked after arranging his legs.

"I'll squeal if something isn't all right, *amadi*. I promise," Andoc said, still sounding more amused than anything else. "I'm not made of clay, you two. I won't shatter."

I scooped a bit of grease from Senovo's pot and gave the half-hard prick in front of me a leisurely stroke up and down. "Really?" I said "And here I was rather looking forward to taking you to pieces."

Andoc laughed, and thrust up into my hand. "Big words. We'll see if you can live up to them."

I grinned, and settled down to watch Senovo as I absently tugged and stroked at Andoc's cock. For his part, the priest had made himself comfortable in the cradle of Andoc's spread legs and was mouthing at his balls, tickling the sensitive skin with the tip of his tongue, only to suck first one, and then the other of the heavy stones into his mouth. Andoc hummed in appreciation, his cock stiffening in time with the deep suction.

After a few minutes of this treatment, Senovo let his sac slide free, glistening and wet. I ran my thumb over the head of Andoc's cock, spreading the dribble of seed I found there. As Senovo scooped up a generous portion of grease with his fingertips, I tightened my grip and started a steady rhythm, up and down with a twist of my wrist on every stroke.

Senovo slid greasy fingers over Andoc's tightly clenched opening and began to massage it with slow, easy movements. "I'd like you to come before we get too far into this," he said. "It will help you stay relaxed."

"That's probably a good idea," Andoc said, already sounding pretty thoroughly relaxed to my ear.

A sudden flash of inspiration struck, and I crawled around until I could straddle Andoc's head while facing his feet, lowering my sex to his lips even as I stretched forward to lick and kiss at his cock. He groaned and buried himself in my folds, sending a delicious jolt of pleasure through me. I ground against him, not being gentle about it, and whimpered as he thrust up into my mouth in retaliation. Meanwhile, Senovo continued to slide slippery fingers around and over his opening, describing decreasing circles until the very tip of one finger slipped inside, only to spiral out again, stretching and massaging the rim.

I arched my hips, using Andoc's mouth as I wished, putting him wherever felt best at the moment. It didn't take long until we were both close, my blood tingling as it rushed under my skin. Andoc swelled in my mouth, the veins on his cock standing out as my tongue curled around him. When I felt him tense, ready to explode, I pulled off and sat up, pumping with my fist until he arched and came, splattering ropes of come across his own belly and chest.

The sight of him beneath me, messy and defiled from his own release, pushed me over a small peak as well. He moaned and licked at me as I pulsed into his mouth. Once I'd had a moment to recover, I slid off his body and kissed him, tasting myself where my own wetness had coated his lips and chin. Suddenly remembering a certain bath I'd shared with him in Rhyth, I dragged a finger through the mess on his belly and touched it against his lips until he opened for me. Senovo had apparently been splitting his attention between us, because he mirrored my movements, finally pressing a finger smoothly into Andoc's arse as I pressed into his mouth, feeding him his own release.

Andoc's eyes were closed, his brow slightly furrowed as he accepted the dual intrusions. I lifted my other hand to stroke over his forehead until he opened them again, meeting my gaze.

"Still all right?" I asked, and he rolled his eyes a little.

I let him spit out my finger so he could speak. "Of course I'm all right. Though I must say, you have a *filthy* mind, *caradi*. I approve, by the way."

"I learned from the best," I told him with a smile, and gave him another kiss before moving to settle down where I could get a better view of what Senovo was doing.

Apparently, what Senovo was doing was having his finger squeezed really, really hard.

"Looks like he's as strong there as he is everywhere else," I observed, draping myself partly across Senovo so I could peer over his shoulder.

"Indeed. I'm beginning to fear for my poor eunuch's prick," Senovo said wryly, "such as it is."

I kissed the side of his neck. "Your prick is beautiful," I told him. "I *love* your prick. That said, I see your point. Do you want me to go first?"

"No, no," Senovo replied in an absent tone, working patiently at the firm flesh until it began to flutter and ease. "It's a risk I'm willing to take."

"Is anyone going to ask my opinion on the matter?" Andoc asked.

"Nope," I told him cheerfully, and reached forward to roll his balls in my palm—a gentle movement. His cock twitched in response.

I resettled myself with an arm wrapped around Senovo, rubbing over his chest and stroking his flat brown nipples as he patiently eased the way past Andoc's tight opening.

"Push against me," Senovo ordered, and slid two fingers in when Andoc complied.

"*Gods*," Andoc said. "I know it's been awhile, but I don't recall it being this much of a struggle."

Senovo snorted. "You were younger then. And probably hornier."

"Is that even possible?" I asked, unable to resist.

"Have I mentioned lately how funny you two are?" Andoc wriggled a little, trying to ease the strain.

Senovo pressed deeper, searching, and crooked his wrist. "How's that?" he asked.

Andoc unclenched a bit more, releasing a slow breath. "Yeah, that's it I think. 'S good. Still jealous that I don't seem to feel it like you do, though."

Indeed, such stimulation was usually enough to bring Senovo to full hardness within moments. Possibly it was because he had only recently climaxed, but Andoc's prick remained stubbornly limp, only giving the occasional small jerk now and then. Even so, I could see that the slow stroking was helping him relax, his muscles easing around Senovo's questing fingers. After a few minutes, Senovo added more grease and pressed three digits inside.

"That feels all right," Andoc said. "I think it's probably good enough, don't you?"

"I'd say so," Senovo agreed.

I kissed Senovo's neck again, and Andoc's hip, then scooted down until I could stand up to get my harness and the soft leather thong coiled up next to it. When I returned to the bed, Senovo had moved to straddle Andoc's chest, stretching forward until Andoc could kiss and lave at his small, limp prick.

I put everything but the grease and the thong aside. Coating my fingers, I trailed them down the enticing crease between Senovo's buttocks, and was gratified to see his prick start to stiffen. Andoc made a low noise of appreciation, and wrapped his lips around Senovo's half-hard cock. He slid up and down with evident enjoyment, and I caught my breath.

"How is it I've never seen this before?" I asked. "Senovo, is this the first time he's sucked your cock?"

Senovo huffed out a breath of amusement. "No, of course not," he said.

Andoc pulled off with a light pop. "What kind of lover do you take me for, *caradi*?"

"I suppose we've just been distracted by other possibilities lately," Senovo said, only to grunt in appreciation when Andoc took him right to the root.

"Well, it's amazing," I said, mesmerized. I shook myself free from the intriguing slide of Senovo's flesh past Andoc's lips, and focused on the soft pucker of skin under my fingers. Senovo's body, unlike Andoc's, was immediately welcoming. It accepted my first finger almost greedily, igniting a new tingle of desire in my belly.

I prepared him just as he had prepared Andoc, until I could slide three fingers into him without resistance. Because I could, I added a fourth, and was rewarded with a shudder and a hissed breath of surprise.

"I'm ready," he said on a slight waver. "Bind me now."

Since I had first been introduced to the concept, I'd watched Andoc bind Senovo's cock once, and done it myself once, under Andoc's close supervision.

"Suck him hard for me," I told Andoc as I slipped my fingers out and cleaned my hand on a damp rag. The thong was made of soft suede, pliable and not too thin. Andoc slid back until he was sucking only the head of Senovo's prick, and I tied a simple loop around the base. When it was snug, but not *too* snug, I added several smooth loops going perhaps a quarter of the way up the shaft to keep him stiff without constant stimulation. Once the free end was tucked neatly under the final loop to keep it in place, I backed away to examine my handiwork.

"Does that feel right?"

"Yes," Senovo gasped. He pulled away from Andoc's mouth—binding him always made the head of his prick exceptionally sensitive—and took a couple of deep, controlled breaths.

Andoc smiled up from where he lay, still tied to the bed frame. "I'm all ready for you, *amadi*. Let me feel you now."

I saw Senovo shiver, and took a moment to smear more grease over Andoc's opening, pressing my fingers inside to make sure he really was still ready. Finally, I ran a greasy hand over Senovo's cock, drawing a strangled sound from him that went straight to my own cunt.

"Take him, Senovo," I said. "He's all yours."

Senovo positioned himself between Andoc's legs as Andoc arched his hips to give him better access.

"Bear down," I reminded him as the blunt head of Senovo's prick pressed at his entrance.

Senovo sank inside a moment later, all of the breath leaving his lungs at once. He braced himself above Andoc, and I ran a soothing hand over his back as his chin dipped and his muscles began to tremble.

"Carivel," Andoc said, a sudden urgency coloring his voice, "my arms. Untie me."

Without stopping to ask questions, I hurriedly untied the slipknot binding Andoc's wrists to the bed, and loosened the simple weave binding his hands together.

"*Amadi*, come here," Andoc said, immediately bringing his arms up to draw Senovo down into an embrace. "I've got you."

Senovo surrendered with a choked noise, curling against Andoc's chest.

"That's it. You feel wonderful inside me, beloved. Just rest here a moment."

Senovo was still shaking, little bursts of shuddering movement that grew shorter and farther apart as I watched. I resumed rubbing a hand over his back and flanks, trusting Andoc to know if anything were truly wrong. Senovo's eyes were tightly closed, but the look on his face appeared to be something like bliss.

When he was resting quietly, Andoc kissed his temple. "There, now. That's better. If you're ready, Carivel has her harness. She'll fuck you until you come inside of me. I want that, don't you?"

"Yes," Senovo said, his voice barely a whisper. "I do want that."

At that particular moment, I mostly wanted to cry at how beautiful they were together. At how Andoc could take effortless control the very moment that one of our sharp edges came unexpectedly to the fore—even while he was tied to a bed, being fucked. My memories of the other time Senovo had fucked someone were tangled up in the messy maelstrom of emotion that had occurred during my breakdown in the weeks after our capture by the Alyrions. I still remembered, though, that he had been quite deeply affected. At the time, however, he'd been focused on me. Now, he had nothing to focus on except his own feelings.

"I can give you that, Senovo," I told him, pressing kisses down his spine. "Just stay right there for a minute."

I slid off the bed and stepped into the leather harness, buckling it snugly so that the curved wooden cock attached to the ring at the center bobbed out in front of me, emerging from the thatch of curls between my legs as if it belonged there.

I wasted no time in greasing it up and crawling back onto the bed. I hitched one of Senovo's legs to the side to expose his slick, loose hole, as Andoc raised his own leg to accommodate the movement. The easy slide as my carved cock breached Senovo drew a shudder of pleasure from both of us. I pressed in steadily, not stopping until our hips were molded tightly together. Senovo cried out as the unyielding tip slid across his sweet spot. His hips snapped forward instinctively, burying him deeper in Andoc, whose arms tightened around him to steady him.

"That's it," Andoc said. "I want you to have this, beloved. I'm so glad I can give this to you. I just wish you'd told me sooner that you needed it."

Senovo made another bereft noise and fucked himself back on my cock, then forward into Andoc.

"Here. Let me," I said, and grasped his hip. After a bit of experimentation, I set up a rhythm, fucking into Senovo and pressing him deep inside Andoc in turn, only to pull both of us back and do it again. Within minutes, he was panting against Andoc's neck, moaning or whimpering with every stroke. "Up," I ordered, feeling powerful and strong as I guided Senovo's upper body out of Andoc's arms and into my own.

With one arm around his chest to help him stay upright, I eased his hips back just enough that I could reach down with my other hand and free the end of the thong, unbinding his prick and tossing the bit of leather to one side. Senovo groaned deeply as I pressed him back into Andoc.

"Come for us, *amadi*," Andoc said, rolling his hips even as I bit down on the graceful line of Senovo's shoulder and sucked hard.

Every muscle in Senovo's body locked solid, and he quivered through a powerful climax, caught between us as his cock pulsed inside Andoc's tight passage and his arse clenched around the wood impaling him.

I worried at the bite mark, close to the edge myself after feeling Senovo come apart under my hands and cock.

"Gods above," said Andoc, looking up at us. "It may not do much for me physically, but that is a thing of beauty to watch. Senovo, love, come down here."

Senovo had already softened after his release, and he slipped out of Andoc's body. I eased out of Senovo in turn and helped him down to curl up against Andoc's side before sitting back on my haunches.

"I'm not quite finished with you, you know," I told Andoc once they were comfortably settled together. "I still haven't come."

Andoc smirked at me, even as he tucked Senovo a bit closer against him. "Liar. You came all over my face earlier. There's still some of it drying in my beard."

"I haven't come from *fucking*," I clarified.

Andoc's grin was wider now. "Well, if you're planning on doing something about it instead of just complaining, you'd better come here and get some while the getting is good."

"Oh, I intend to." I loosened the harness just enough to twist the curved cock around in its ring so it was pointing up, perfect for fucking face to face. I slathered it with more grease, and slathered Andoc's opening with more grease as well, intending to make him feel this but not wanting to hurt him accidentally. "Are you ready?"

Andoc was still smirking, all cocky challenge. "Show me what you've got," he said.

I knelt at his entrance and hooked his good leg over my elbow—my own grin predatory. Andoc was still loose and open from Senovo's cock, but my wooden prick was bigger. His smile faded to a look of concentration as he focused on staying relaxed; letting me in. The head popped past the outer ring, and we both caught our breath.

Senovo opened lazy eyes, running a smooth hand over Andoc's chest and twisting a nipple between his fingers. Andoc breathed out in surprise, and I slipped inside fully. I paused for a moment to let him adjust, feeling the base of the carved cock move against my mons as his muscles pulsed around the shaft. When he was ready, I pressed deeper, hitching his leg up a bit higher.

Just before I bottomed out, Andoc jerked under me, his eyes opening wide but staring at nothing.

"Oh," he said, as if surprised.

I blinked. "*Oh?*" I echoed, and pulled back an inch or two so I could thrust back in, a little harder than before. My eyes tracked down from Andoc's face to his cock, which twitched and started to fill. My eyebrow rose. "Well, well. Now isn't *that* interesting…"

Andoc had nothing to add, so I pulled back and did it again. And again. Senovo roused himself enough to look on with interest, one hand still twisting and rolling a pebbled nipple. Andoc clenched a handful of blanket with the hand that was not wrapped around Senovo's shoulders. A strange noise slipped past his control, and my grin widened.

"Senovo," I said, "I do believe our Andoc is having some sort of an epiphany."

"Try thrusting harder," Senovo advised, pinching a nipple sharply as I thrust into Andoc with real intent.

"*Fuck*," Andoc gasped. "Yes, keep—*ah*! Keep doing that."

"Oh, I am *happy* to keep doing this," I said with glee, suiting word to deed. My voice turned singsong. "You're going to come on my cock tonight… this is *brilliant*."

Senovo cut off any commentary that Andoc might have cared to add at that point by the simple but effective expedient of sticking his tongue down Andoc's throat. I enjoyed the view and fucked into Andoc with everything I had, feeling my own climax grow closer with every grind of the wooden cock's base against my swollen sex.

When Andoc's muffled noises grew desperate and I could no longer put off my own release, I reached down and fisted his rock-hard prick up and down in time with my thrusts. In no time, he arched off the bed, coming all over himself in messy spurts as Senovo swallowed his frantic cries.

The sight and sound was enough to push me over the edge as well, my cunt pulsing as waves of pleasure slammed into me, leaving me dizzy as they slowly subsided.

"Oh, gods," I moaned. "That was… that was…"

Senovo pulled back to let Andoc get his breath. "That was… something," Andoc managed, his voice hoarse. He cleared his throat. "Is everyone good, then?"

The little pieces of my scattered wits were slowly reassembling into something approaching coherence. I pulled out of Andoc carefully, aware of how sore he was likely to be in the morning. "I feel like I should be the one asking that question," I said wryly.

"I may not be walking properly tomorrow, but at least I have a ready-made excuse for it," Andoc said, the humor returning to his own voice. "Seriously, though, Senovo—I get it now."

"It's nice, isn't it," Senovo said, still floating a little on his own happy cloud, if I was any judge.

Andoc burst out laughing. "Not the word I would have chosen, but then, you've always been a master of understatement."

As the least fucked-out of the three of us, I roused myself enough to get some rags and clean up. "Well, I'm glad that my prowess with a bow and arrow ended up leading to an enjoyable experience for everyone."

"Your prowess is not in any doubt, *caradi*," Andoc said as I settled down and tucked blankets and furs around us. I couldn't help the little flush of pleasure that lightened my chest at the words. With a smile, I curled up across from Senovo, on Andoc's left side, humming happily when he wrapped an arm around me and began stroking my shoulder.

I lay in pleasant post-coital lassitude for some time. Gradually, Andoc's fingers slowed their gentle back-and-forth rhythm against my skin. I glanced up at his face in the light from the merrily crackling hearth fire, expecting to find that he'd fallen asleep. Instead I found him staring into the middle distance, a frown marring his strong features.

I rolled up on an elbow and brushed a fingertip over the wrinkle between his brows. "I'd hoped to distract you for the night, but it's only been a few minutes and I've already lost you to your worries again."

Andoc's smile was rueful when he met my eyes. "Sorry. They're big worries, and I'm afraid I don't know how to set them aside completely."

I was frowning now as well. "We have time, Andoc. Jacun was right. Think what you did in only a few weeks. Now, we have months."

"But we can't do anything until I have a strategy, *caradi*... and I don't have a strategy. I don't even have the *inkling* of a strategy. How can a few scattered tribes fight off an Empire?"

"Mmm," said Senovo from Andoc's other side, not even bothering to open his eyes. "I've had a thought about that. Need s'more time to think about the details..."

"There you go," I said. "You told me a long time ago—way back in Meren—that if Senovo says he has an idea, you can be sure it's a good one."

"No, it's actually a really crazy one," Senovo said, still sounding half asleep. "Sorry."

Andoc laughed softly. "*Amadi*, you should know by now that the crazy ideas are by far my favorite kind."

"I would never have guessed," I said, completely deadpan.

Andoc sighed. "Yes, very funny. You set fire to *one* mountain..."

"Just so you realize that this isn't all on you," I told him, sobering. "Draebard's future rests on all of our shoulders, not only on its Chief's."

"What she said," Senovo murmured with something less than his usual eloquence, the words slightly muffled against the skin at the juncture of Andoc's neck and shoulder.

"See? *You're not alone*," I said, looking into Andoc's warm brown eyes. "We're in this together. Promise us you won't forget that."

Andoc reached up a hand to draw me back down into his embrace. "As if I could, *caradi*. As if I could."

end of Book 3

THE HORSE MISTRESS:
BOOK 4

ONE

"I have to admit, I'm not thrilled with this plan, Senovo," said Andoc.

Andoc, Senovo, and I were sharing a quiet meal in Senovo's rooms after a long day of work. Indeed, this particular day had seemed even longer than usual with the howling wind driving blasts of icy sleet through the village. Here in the temple, though, it was warm and snug. Sitting around a table eating hot food and drinking good wine with the two people who meant most to me in all the world should have been a perfect way to spend an evening. However, like Andoc, I was not at all pleased after Senovo informed us — out of nowhere — that he intended to venture into the forest overnight in the form of the wolf.

"Why now?" I asked him.

Senovo leaned back in his chair and regarded us, the picture of serenity. "Two weeks ago, I told you both that I had an idea regarding the north's defense against the Empire."

Andoc nodded, still looking unhappy. "A crazy idea, you said."

A faint flash of self-deprecating humor crossed Senovo's features and was gone in an instant. "Yes, quite. I've been thinking about the specifics since then, but — truly — the only way to learn what I need to know is to go out and investigate it for myself."

"Alone," I said flatly. "In the wildlands. In the middle of winter."

"The wolf is not hindered by cold and snow, Carivel," said Senovo. "Quite the opposite. I would find it much more arduous to do such a thing in the height of summer, to be honest."

Andoc took a deep breath and leaned forward, placing his elbows on the table. "I have more reason than most to appreciate the wolf's survival skills during the depths of winter, *amadi*. But I would still like to understand what *exactly* it is that you're hoping to accomplish here."

"This is about what happened on the night of High Priest Rhystel's death, isn't it?" I interrupted, before Senovo could answer. "When the wild wolves came down from the hills to grieve with you."

Senovo remained unruffled. He leaned forward, mirroring Andoc's position with his own. "It is. Strange wolves have approached me before over the years, during those occasions when I could no longer hold back the change. I always ran from them. I thought they were seeking to defend their territory, and would attack me."

"But the wolves we met that night showed no signs of attacking." I said with a frown, my memories drawn immediately back to the strangeness of the whole experience. "The lower ranking wolves submitted to you as if seeking your approval, and the pack leaders treated you as an equal. They appeared almost protective of you."

"I'm afraid I remember few details of what happened, beyond the overwhelming feelings of loss and mourning," Senovo admitted, his voice growing quiet.

Andoc looked at him intently. "It was your anguish that called them. You howled it out to the forest as if your heart was breaking... and they came. They added their voices to yours."

"So you both described to me, afterward," said Senovo. "However, I have no true memory of it. That is why I must go and find out for myself what connection I have with... others of my kind. I feel very strongly that it is important for me to do so."

"I'll go with you," I said quickly, irrational fear overtaking me at the thought of Senovo alone in the wilderness. Vulnerable.

"No, Carivel." His voice was kind, but firm. "This is something I must do by myself. Besides, while winter may not be a hindrance to the wolf, I would not see *you* battling the cold and sleet when it is not necessary for you to do so."

Andoc looked down at his hands, drawing my attention. "We're agreed on that part, at least. I've sent far too many people out lately to do exactly that."

Senovo's eyes moved to Andoc as well. After the collapse of the meetings in Rhyth between the leaders of the northern tribes, Andoc had been forced to send volunteers from Draebard to visit any villages with whom they might have ties of blood or friendship, in hopes of forging some kind of useful alliance before Alyrion troops descended on Eburos in the spring. Asking his people to take such risks by traveling in winter weighed heavily on him, I knew.

Senovo knew it as well, and his expression grew pained. "My words were not meant as a criticism of your actions, old friend. You have done only what was necessary. And when our turn comes to reach out to potential allies, I will willingly accompany you on four legs or two. You know that."

"As will I," I added. "But I'm still not happy about you going out alone, Senovo. The people who are traveling are at least doing so in groups. What if something happens?"

Senovo's gaze bore into mine for a moment. As ever, his eyes saw too much. "There are no Rhytheeri bounty hunters lying in wait in the woods, Carivel. Not now, in the depths of winter. And even if there were, how would they tell one wolf from any other? I will be in no more danger than any of the other dozens of times I have changed over the years, since I first escaped from the men who owned me."

Thinking about Senovo's flight from his southern masters—alone, injured, without resources of any kind—*really* didn't help me feel any better. In fact, such images were the stuff of my nightmares, more often than I cared to admit. Something of this must have showed on my face, because Senovo rose from his chair and crossed to mine, extending a hand for me to take. I allowed myself to be pulled to my feet and into his arms, where I burrowed against him gratefully.

I wasn't surprised to hear Andoc's chair scraping a moment later as he pushed it back, followed by his halting footsteps as he limped over to us and embraced Senovo from behind.

"You must do as you think best, *amadi*," he said. "Not that either of us could stop you even if we wished to. After all, you outrank our Carivel, here, and while you don't *quite* outrank me, I'm reliably informed that religious matters are outside the Chief's purview."

Senovo huffed in quiet amusement.

"So they are. Good of you to remember," he said, a hint of humor audible in his voice.

Of the three of us, only Andoc had ever expected to gain significant power and influence within the tribe during his lifetime. Senovo and I were the outcasts—the black sheep in the flock. That we had risen to the heights we had — High Priest and Horse Mistress of the village — would have been deeply funny had it not come about in response to so much death and tragedy. Even so, the surreal nature of our current circumstances occasionally caught one or the other of us by surprise, as it had Senovo just now.

"Promise you'll be careful, at least," I said into the soft folds of white cloth under my cheek.

Senovo eased me away until he could meet my eyes. "I give you my word. I'll even make a point of avoiding the area around the horse pens, since I've no desire to be pelted with rocks again." I couldn't help it — even in the depths of worry, I smiled a bit at the memory. "Now, though… the evening is still young, and I don't believe Andoc is expected at the meeting house for another hour or so. Come. Why don't you both remind me of what it is I'll be returning to?"

Powerless to stop myself, I surged up and kissed him, pouring all of my love and concern into the press and slide of our lips. Behind him, Andoc stretched forward until his mouth was next to Senovo's ear.

"*Amadi*, I'm *shocked*. Are you trying to distract us with sex?" he asked, amusement coloring his tone despite his earlier dark mood. "What sort of behavior is that for a High Priest?"

Senovo pulled back enough to answer, his breath puffing intimately across my lips. "Me? Would I ever do such a thing?"

"Yes, you bloody would," I growled, pressing against him from chest to knee. "Because you are secretly evil and you know perfectly well that neither of us can resist you."

Before Senovo could reply, Andoc swept the collar of his robes to one side and bit down on the juncture of his neck and shoulder. Senovo stiffened, a faint tremor running through his body where it pressed against mine. His eyes fluttered closed, the expressive arch of his brows drawing together to form a faint furrow as he focused inward, surrendering to the sharp sensation.

I groaned at the sight and latched onto the nearest bit of exposed skin I could reach — a tempting jut of collarbone. When Andoc and I finally drew back, two new red marks marred Senovo's perfect skin, and he was breathing in short pants.

"You need a reminder of where you belong, *amadi*, is that it?" Andoc's low, controlled tones made both of us shiver. His hands slid forward, playing with the ties of Senovo's robes. "Something to take with you... to help you remember?"

Senovo's reply was a sharp exhalation. The fastenings came loose under Andoc's sure touch and the robes gaped, revealing a new stretch of skin. When Andoc tangled one hand in the heavy plait of hair favored by members of the priesthood and used it to pull Senovo's head back, I pounced on the exposed arch of his neck, trailing biting kisses up the length of the taught tendon.

Senovo gradually went slack between us, eyes still closed, mouth falling open. I traced his lower lip with the pad of my thumb. "I want that mouth on my cock tonight," I said breathlessly, already picturing his lips sliding down the length of carved wood. I met Andoc's burning gaze over Senovo's shoulder. "And I want to suck you."

Andoc's rumble of approval inspired another quiver of reaction in Senovo. "Bring both of your cocks," Andoc said, referring to the pair of wooden phalluses Senovo had gifted me after my handfasting to Andoc last summer. "I've got a use in mind for the curved one as well. Oh, and throw some furs down on the floor near the hearth. We'll have more space to work, and it will be warmer."

I gave Senovo a final kiss, nipping at his swollen lower lip as I pulled away, and crossed to the bed. The feather-stuffed monstrosity was always piled with a rather ridiculous number of blankets, furs, and pillows, so there were plenty of options for putting together a comfortable nest close to the fire for the three of us. When I was satisfied with the result—and in real danger of being hopelessly distracted by the sight of Andoc peeling the clothing from Senovo's unresisting form before starting on his own—I made myself turn away to gather the rest of the supplies we'd need.

A moment later, I returned with grease, the two polished wooden cocks, and my harness. Senovo was not quite as far gone as I'd assumed, because he looked up at me from where he was curled naked in the middle of the pile of furs and cushions. "You're overdressed," he said in that mild priest's voice, which he occasionally used to hide his truly wicked sense of humor.

"Blame Andoc," I said, my lips twitching as I tried not to smile. "He's the one who's got me fetching and carrying like the lowliest apprentice."

"Hey, now—what do you expect? Look at me, I can barely walk," Andoc defended. "Besides, being Chief of the village ought to come with *some* benefits."

This time, I didn't even try to stop my snort of amusement. I was really rather relieved that Andoc could finally begin to make light of the terrible injury that had ended his career as a warrior, though I knew his limitations still troubled him.

"Of course, O Mighty Chief," I said, and began to unfasten my heavy winter jerkin. "As always, your lowliest wish is my greatest command."

Andoc's own grin crinkled the skin around his eyes in a most appealing manner as he closed the distance between us. "*Finally*, some respect."

As ever, it was a huge relief to put aside our wider troubles for a little while and lose ourselves in the easy love and pleasure of our relationship. Worry for Senovo and his self-imposed quest still nagged at me, but right here, right now, we would take him at his word. We would remind him of why he must always, *always* return to us—because we were not complete without him, and he was not complete without us. Only together would the three of us be strong enough to face the uncertain future that awaited.

I smirked up at Andoc. "My respect for you knows no bounds, *Chief Andoc*. Well, except when it comes to horseback riding. You're actually fairly shite at that."

Andoc might have had a bad leg, but I was still tackled to the floor and pinned beneath him in the soft mass of furs before I could so much as take a breath. Desire surged, and I writhed against the hard body above me, loving every second of it.

"Still reasonably proficient at wrestling, though," Senovo put in from his spot nearby.

"Very," I squeaked, as Andoc's cock slid intimately against me. He laughed at me, and gave another little thrust.

"Count yourself lucky that my attention will be mostly on Senovo tonight," he said, before rolling off and turning his focus to getting my clothes off. I grinned and added my fingers to the task of untying laces and pushing garments down and off.

When all of us were naked, Senovo stretched across to get my harness and the straight wooden phallus we used for fellatio. His movements as he crawled over to me and settled himself between my legs were graceful... almost sinuous. I lifted my hips to help him put the harness on, struck yet again by his ethereal beauty in the firelight.

"Don't you just want to ravish him sometimes?" Andoc asked, propped on one arm to watch. His other hand fisted slowly around his large cock, sliding up and down in an easy rhythm.

"Frequently," I managed, my mouth going briefly dry as I looked back and forth between the two of them.

Senovo looked up from his task, a faint flush of pleasure or embarrassment staining his cheeks. His eyes were dark, the pupils blown wide. "As it happens, I believe you're in luck tonight," he said.

He tightened the last buckle around the top of my thighs. The carved cock jutted out, thick and shiny, from the thatch of wiry hair growing between my legs. As always, I felt a delicious surge of power — of *rightness* — when I looked down and saw it there. Senovo licked his lips, and moisture immediately flooded my cunt.

Meanwhile, Andoc had grabbed the grease and the second wooden shaft while we were distracted. This phallus was gently curved, designed to give a man pleasure by pressing against the place inside where he was most sensitive.

"On your side, I think, *amadi*," Andoc directed, and Senovo sprawled across the furs to give him access, his top leg hitched forward, out of the way.

I held my breath watching avidly as Senovo began to kiss his way up the crease of my thigh and along the shaft of my cock, while Andoc opened him with strong, thick fingers. Senovo made a low noise in his throat as he was breached, and kissed his way back down the wooden cock, his tongue darting out to play along the seam of my inner lips below the base.

He continued to tease, blowing air across my dripping flesh and brushing butterfly touches of his lips and tongue here and there. Occasionally, he went very still and gave a low whine when Andoc twisted his wrist or added another finger. Before long, Andoc slid his fingers free and reached for the second wooden phallus. He greased it generously and met my eyes, raising an eyebrow.

I grinned, recognizing a cue when I saw one. As Andoc positioned the cock at Senovo's entrance, I guided him up with a hand cradling his head and placed the tip of the cock I was wearing against his lips. He stared up the length of my body, gaze locked on mine through dark eyelashes, and slid his lips over the flared head, taking it into his mouth at the same time Andoc pressed the other toy into his arse.

I couldn't help the little groan of appreciation that the sight pulled from me… not that I tried very hard. Senovo trembled in silent reaction when the tip of the curved cock dragged across his sweet spot. I watched with pleasure as his small eunuch's prick twitched in reaction and started to fill.

So much had been stolen from Senovo when his owners had castrated him against his will. I found a kind of deep comfort in being able to bring him the kind of pleasure that the men who owned him would have seen him denied for the rest of his life. I suspected Andoc felt the same way.

Perhaps it was some sort of subtle, private revenge against those who had mutilated him, but Senovo was without a doubt the most sensual person I knew. He did not feel sexual lust like I did, or like Andoc did, but his surrender to the pleasure we could provide him was profound and complete. Watching him sink into it brought every protective instinct I possessed to the fore.

Of course, it also brought every ounce of raw, animal *need* to the fore. My cock might have been wood and not flesh, but I swear I could feel Senovo's movements as if it were. He bobbed shallowly along the length as Andoc fucked him with the curved cock, bringing him slowly to full hardness. When Senovo's prick was stiff and twitching, Andoc turned to me.

"I'm going to lie down as well, so we can all suck each other," he said. "Don't bring me off yet, though. I'm enjoying this far too much."

I managed a moan of acknowledgement as Senovo dragged his fingers along my soaked folds, lighting new sparks in their wake. Andoc hitched himself around to lie on his side, our torsos forming a triangle in the nest of furs as we lay, head to groin. His cock was already red and leaking. I fisted it, rubbing the dribble of seed over the crown with my thumb and reaching forward for a taste. Andoc grunted and thrust into the circle of my hand.

"*Fuck*, that's good," he said, and manhandled Senovo into position so he could swallow his prick.

Senovo *keened* around the thick shaft of wood in his mouth, and I let go of Andoc's cock in favor of reaching down to slide my palm over the priest's cheek, steadying him as he panted rapidly through his nose.

"Gods, you two," I said, pleasure coiling in my belly like a serpent ready to strike, "I don't know which of you I want to watch more. You both look amazing."

It was true. Ever since I'd first seen Andoc sucking Senovo, I couldn't seem to get enough of it. Nor could I get enough of watching — and feeling — Senovo swallowing my own cock. As if to make my decision easier, Senovo began to work his way farther down the unforgiving length of wood — a trick I had originally seen him perform on Andoc's generous prick the very first night we slept together, and one of which I was still envious.

"That's it," I whispered. "Let us fill you up until you overflow and spill for us…"

Senovo moaned and redoubled his efforts, stretching to get a better angle. His hips circled restlessly, no doubt grinding the tip of the phallus buried inside him against the place where he needed it most, even as Andoc laved and sucked at his modest shaft. When he was positioned the way he wanted, I moved my hand to the back of his head, guiding him down the final few inches. The feeling as he yielded and my cock slid home past the ring of his throat sent me over a small peak, beads of sweat popping out across my face and chest. I trembled with the unexpected release, holding my hips very still.

Senovo followed me into release a moment later, his climax silent but powerful. My hand trailed down to stroke the distended skin of his throat as he jerked and spent in Andoc's mouth. Eventually, he pulled back from my wooden cock with a gasp, still wracked by weak spasms of pleasure. Andoc pulled off a moment later with a wet noise that was positively obscene.

"All right, *caradi*," he said in a hoarse, slightly breathless voice, "*now* you can make me come."

I fell forward, desperate to get at his cock with hands and mouth.

"Not — *ah!*" He broke off as I swallowed him down. "Not that it's likely to take much…"

I hummed around him and sucked my cheeks in, overcome by the smell of sweat and musk. Meanwhile, Senovo roused himself enough to nuzzle past my cock and harness until he could lap at my folds, dipping his tongue a bit deeper with each pass and flicking it lightly across my oversensitive nub. Every so often he would give a little shudder. Knowing Andoc's deliciously sadistic streak, I suspected it was in response to the curved wooden cock sliding unerringly back and forth across the delicate place inside him.

The combination of that knowledge and Senovo's clever tongue had me on the verge of a second release within minutes. I stretched my tongue forward and flattened it as Senovo had taught me, relaxing my jaw so I could at least take Andoc into the back of my throat, even if I couldn't swallow him all the way yet. Ignoring the urge to gag, I wrapped a hand around his base and pressed him in a bit deeper, the feeling of being perfectly filled more important than the brief, uncomfortable clench of my throat muscles.

Andoc's hips flexed instinctively, and I followed the movement, tracing a thumb over his balls as they drew up close to his body. His cock swelled and throbbed, heavy on my tongue, and then he was coming in great, choking spurts—drowning me in his release even as Senovo's clever mouth pushed me over the edge after him.

Things went a little wobbly for a bit—in the best possible way—as my body struggled to make sense of the overwhelming sensations crashing through it. When I came back to full awareness, Andoc's cock was softening in my mouth, and Senovo's warm breath was tickling my inner thigh. I swallowed reflexively a couple of times, drawing a final shudder from Andoc as he slipped free from my lips.

We lay there for a bit, totally spent. Eventually, I scooted around so I could crawl up into the space between Andoc and Senovo. The priest was still lying with his head pointed toward our feet. My own head was about even with his hips, so I amused myself for a while by palming the base of the wooden cock still buried inside him, moving it in slow circles. He retaliated by dragging a finger through the slick mess of my release and playing with the rim of my own puckered opening. Meanwhile, Andoc threw an arm over my torso and pinched a nipple between his thumb and forefinger, rolling it back and forth with slow, tortuous movements.

We lay together for some time, trading teasing touches with no urgency behind them. Eventually, Andoc rolled onto his back with a sigh.

"You have to go," I guessed.

"I'm afraid so. Wouldn't do to keep the elders waiting."

I stifled inappropriate laughter at the idea of the elders coming to look for him and finding the three of us like this. The expressions on their faces would be priceless, I was sure. With a final tap on the base of the toy to get his attention, I asked, "Senovo, are you all right? Do you want this out now?"

Senovo stretched, catlike. "Not particularly, but I suppose I should go as well. I do, however, consider myself *thoroughly* reminded of my place, so thank you both."

My mood sank at the idea of Senovo leaving for the wildlands, but as Andoc had said, it was his choice and we couldn't exactly stop him. A brief image of Senovo bound to the bed, our helpless captive, as we fed him by hand and pleasured him until he completely forgot about his dangerous quest flashed across my mind's eye. I tamped it down ruthlessly.

Instead, I pressed a kiss to the smooth skin of his hip and eased the cock out of him, putting it aside to be cleaned. He sighed at the loss, flopping onto his back for a moment before rolling into a crouch. A moment later, the wolf shook itself, sending fur flying. It was a blatant strategy to prevent me from making any more efforts to stop him leaving, but I still couldn't bring myself to be irritated at him.

I waved my hand back and forth in front of my face, clearing the air. "Senovo, I love you dearly, but why in the gods' names are you shedding *in the middle of winter?*"

The wolf whined and crept forward to lick at my face and jaw. I wrapped my arms around him and buried my face in his ruff, more hair getting in my eyes and nose.

"Be careful, you hear me?" I said.

The only answer was the sound of happy panting.

Andoc squeezed my shoulder and stroked the animal behind the ears. "He's always careful, *caradi*. He's practically made being careful his life's work... except when it really counts."

I remembered a tense standoff with Volya across the length of a table. An Alyrion prison cell. "Yes," I said on a sigh. "I know."

Eventually, I let go of Senovo and brushed the fur off of my face. Andoc and I cleaned everything up and dressed, after which the three of us prepared to part. With Senovo leaving for the night, I decided to go to Andoc's hut to sleep rather than stay at the temple. Andoc was meeting with the elders to discuss the latest intelligence from Rhyth and the progress of the first groups to travel to other tribes in hopes of forging new alliances.

As for Senovo... well. He trotted along beside us as we made our way out of the temple, promptly disappearing into the cold, windy night like a spirit dissipating into mist.

TWO

I shivered, not only because of the sharp sleet stinging my face and neck.

Andoc leaned down and gave me a kiss. "Try not to worry," he said.

I frowned. "Tell you what. I'll worry about him exactly as much as you will."

There was no humor in Andoc's breath of laughter. "Fair enough, I suppose. I'll be back as soon as I can."

I nodded. "See you soon. I need to go back to Senovo's room; I forgot my satchel." I forced an insincere smile. "Give the elders my love."

He snorted. "I should, just to see their looks of disapproval."

After a final quick embrace, I turned back to the temple and left him making his way toward the meeting house, leaning heavily on his walking stick as he went.

The satchel—which contained some leatherwork that needed repair—was still hanging from the back of my chair. Since I was here anyway and not in any particular hurry, I decided to take the dishes from supper back to the refectory and clean them, to avoid becoming a target of Feldes' mild irritation.

The temple was quiet tonight, most people preferring to huddle at home rather than venture abroad in the blustery sleet. I was not particularly surprised to see lamplight coming from the refectory, nor to hear the low sound of voices within—the acolytes often gathered there to chat and pass the time once their duties for the day were finished.

I *was* surprised, however, to discover that one of the voices belonged to Limdya, who was seated at a table, deep in discussion with Favian, the youngest temple acolyte.

"Hello," I said, curious as to what had drawn my newest apprentice from the warm hut she shared with her sisters to speak with my former apprentice. Both of them looked up in surprise, evidently not having heard me come in. "Sorry," I continued, "I didn't mean to interrupt you. I was just returning some dishes, in hopes of heading off a lecture from Novice Feldes about the importance of tidiness."

Favian's lips twitched in a brief smile before he sobered, once again becoming the picture of a serious, dedicated religious student. "Good evening, Horse Mistress. It's no problem; we were just talking."

"Is everything all right, Limdya?" I asked.

On the one hand, whatever they were talking about was probably none of my business. On the other hand, though, I was the one who had invited Limdya to work at the horse pens, making her the only female apprentice and the first openly female individual ever to tend the animals. Though she had agreed to it freely, it still wasn't an easy position for her, and I felt a degree of responsibility for any problems she might be facing because of it.

Limdya blushed and looked away. Her relationship with me was a rather complicated one. Before the secret of my birth sex had become publicly known, she'd had a serious—and completely unrequited—romantic crush on me. Though I had appeared to be a beardless boy, I was in fact several years older than her. I had tried very hard never to lead her on, but she was still understandably furious when she found out what I had been hiding.

And now, she worked for me. To say it was still somewhat awkward was an understatement, the likes of which would have impressed even Senovo.

"It's all right, Limdya," Favian said. "You don't have to say anything if you don't want to. Carivel will understand."

Limdya chewed her lower lip for a moment. "No," she said. "It's fine. I started talking to Favian a few weeks ago. He's been helping me learn more about horses so I don't feel utterly useless at my job."

I went still, turning Limdya's words over. This was serious, and it was something I should have noticed without being told. For about the hundredth time, I wondered if I would *ever* become a worthy successor to Jorun, the previous Horse Master. I set the satchel and dishes down so I could pull out a chair across from the pair.

"You're not useless at your job, Limdya," I told her seriously. "I have absolutely no complaints about your work since you became an apprentice. You're picking everything up really fast."

"Told you," Favian muttered under his breath.

Limdya shook her head. "You don't understand. I'd barely ever touched a horse before last summer—just a few stolen pats here and there when I was riding in a wagon with mother or Charyal, getting supplies for the cookhouse. All of the others grew up with horses. They know what to do when a colt acts up. They can take one look at a horse and know if something's wrong with it. And my riding! I feel like an idiot bouncing around up there, barely able to hold on and hoping the horse doesn't spook or run off with me. I know that's why I always get the simple jobs, like taking manure to the vegetable gardens and cleaning the saddles."

I laced my fingers together and rested them on the table. "Honestly, Limdya, you get those sorts of jobs because you're the newest apprentice. And the fact that you do them well, without complaint, puts you ahead of many of the new apprentices I've seen since I started working for Jorun four years ago."

Limdya shrugged, clearly unconvinced.

"Have the others been giving you a hard time?" I asked, and she laughed a bit.

"The only girl at the pens?" She blushed and glanced at me before correcting herself. "Well... sort of the only girl. You know what I mean. But, yeah, of course they have. That's not the problem, though—it's nothing I can't handle. And anyway, it's only a few of them. Dalon's all right, and Lundis has been trying to help me when he can."

"You'll tell someone if it gets too bad," I said, not phrasing it as a question. "Me, or Dalon, or even Favian."

Limdya waved the words away. "I don't need *protecting,* Horse Mistress. I told you, that's not the problem."

I leaned back in my chair, studying her. "I don't quite know what to tell you, Limdya. The only way to get experience with anything is to do it, and keep doing it until you get good at it. No one at the pens was born being good with horses. They all learned. Some, more than others," I finished dryly.

"I know that. Honestly, I do," said Limdya. "It's just frustrating. Everyone is so busy all the time that I don't want to ask for more help, so I figured I'd come here and talk to Favian instead."

Favian grinned. "I'm glad you did. I don't regret joining the temple, but I do miss the horses. It's nice to talk about them, at least."

I turned to my former apprentice. "As far as I'm concerned, you can do more than talk. Whenever your duties permit, you're welcome to come out to the pens and give Limdya some pointers. I can speak to Senovo about it, if you'd like." *Assuming he returns safely*, my inner voice added, helpfully shifting my attention straight back to my worries.

"That's all right. I'll ask him," Favian said. "I don't think he'd mind."

"Would you do that, Favian?" Limdya asked, her eyes shining. "Really?"

Favian blushed a bit. "Why not? I told you, I still miss the horses."

I watched the exchange with interest. Hopefully Limdya wasn't about to replace one impossible crush with another — not only was Favian promised to the temple, slated to become a eunuch upon his ascension from acolyte to novice priest... but he also preferred other boys. Still, Limdya's personal life really *was* none of my business, and her excitement did seem to be more about getting help with the horses than about Favian himself. She could do far worse when it came to both friends and tutors, so I resolved to stay out of it.

"That's settled, then. Good. I look forward to seeing you at the pens more often, Favian. The white colt still misses you."

Actually, I supposed I was going to have to talk to Andoc about Volya's horses soon. The former Chief had no heirs, so by rights, the buckskin mare he'd prized so highly, along with her two creamy white colts, were Andoc's now. I wondered how he would feel about that, given his rather tempestuous relationship with Volya in the days before the old man's death.

Favian, on the other hand, was thinking about none of this. "I look forward to seeing the colt again. Does he have a name yet?"

I shook my head. "Not yet. Chief Volya wanted to wait and see if the colts would make a chariot team before naming either of them. I suppose it will fall to Andoc now. Which is sort of amusing, since his own gelding doesn't even have a name."

The acolyte's face fell at the mention of the dead Chief, and I berated myself for bringing him up. Favian had started having prophetic dreams the previous summer, and despite all evidence and reassurance to the contrary, he still blamed himself for not warning anyone when he'd had a nightmare about Volya's death that later came true.

Limdya salvaged the mood before I could apologize. "That's not true at all," she said. "I've heard Chief Andoc call that poor gelding any number of interesting names over the past few weeks. Usually when he was trying to get him to stand next to a fence or a tree stump so he could mount."

I couldn't help it—I burst into laughter. Even Favian hid a smile behind his hand. "I'll tell him you said so, shall I?" I managed, once I had myself mostly under control again.

Limdya looked horrified, her face going beet red. "Oh, please don't, Carivel! I'd never be able to look him in the eye again."

"Fine, I'll just tell him it was one of the apprentices—I won't say who," I promised. "Sorry, Limdya… it's just too funny to pass up. I've been on him about his horsemanship skills for ages now."

"Fine, all right then," she said, the humor of the situation clearly overcoming her embarrassment. After a moment, her face grew thoughtful. "Do you ever stop and think about how much everything is changing?"

"Yes," Favian and I said, practically in unison.

"Pretty much every single day," I added.

"Sometimes I don't feel like I can keep up with it all," said Limdya.

I was saved from having to come up with something comforting or profound by Favian, who I still maintained was going to make a damned good priest once he got a bit older.

"High Priest Senovo says that sometimes all you can do is take one step at a time. Keep moving forward, and let the things you can't control take care of themselves."

"Wise words," I said, "though not always the easiest advice to follow."

"Yeah," Limdya agreed quietly. I wondered if she was thinking of her mother, murdered by Alyrion soldiers, or perhaps of Draebard's future.

I pushed away from the table and stood up. "I'll leave you to your discussion now. Sorry to have intruded, both of you. Just know that no matter how busy I am, you can always come to me for help if you need it. That goes for you, too, Favian. Understood?"

"Yes, Horse Mistress," Limdya said, while Favian smiled faintly and nodded.

"I'll try to get out to the pens soon," he promised. "Right now I'm helping Father's neighbors take care of Frella."

I frowned. "Did Renthro join one of the groups traveling to other villages?" I asked, surprised that I hadn't heard about it, if so.

Favian nodded. "He was born in Teth, and he still has family there. It's too bad it's winter—I imagine they would have loved to meet Frella, but taking her would have been too dangerous. He went with two other people on a big loop through several villages to the west."

"It was good of him to volunteer," I said. "When is he due back?"

Favian looked suddenly uncomfortable, and it was Limdya who answered. "They were due two days ago. But they probably just stopped somewhere to wait out the snow and sleet," she added quickly.

"I'm sure he's fine," Favian said, sounding anything but. "He'll be back soon. Maybe tomorrow."

"No doubt you're right," I said, keeping my voice calm and full of certainty. "Well, have a pleasant evening, you two. Remember, come to me if you need anything."

They both nodded, and I took my leave, dropping the dirty dishes off in the kitchen and giving them a quick scrub. The conditions outside were even more unpleasant than they had been when I'd gone out with Andoc earlier. The sleet had been joined by flakes of dry snow, swirling along the roads and through the gaps between buildings. I huddled against the stiff wind, wishing I'd thought to bring along a winter cloak, and hurried toward Andoc's hut.

Despite my extended conversation with Favian and Limdya, I'd still arrived before Andoc—not surprising, given how fond most of the elders seemed to be of their own voices. I let myself in and went about lighting a fire in the hearth, relieved when the crackling flames began to beat back the cold and dark. After warming myself in front of the merry blaze for a few minutes, I stripped off my outer layers and lit a couple of candles so I could see the leatherwork I'd brought along properly.

I'd always had a deft hand for braiding the fine leather thongs used to make whips and bridles, so it was relaxing to curl up on the floor with my back braced against the bed, a heavy fur draped over my shoulders while I unpicked the torn section of the decorative headstall and set about repairing it.

Even so, my mind wandered against my will, returning continually to my worries. Was Senovo all right? Was he cold? Had he found other wolves, and would he be safe with them?

If they accepted him as part of the pack, would he want to come back afterward?

I shook my head to dislodge that unwelcome thought. Months ago, I had confronted Senovo about his aversion to shifting. Eventually, he had admitted his fear that the wolf would somehow take over, swallowing his humanity and making him disappear as a person. I had argued passionately that *he was the wolf*, and that by fighting the change, he was fighting himself.

I swallowed a bitter laugh. Really, if we somehow managed to lose Senovo now, I had only myself to blame. I was the one who had convinced him to accept—and even embrace—his gift.

Andoc entered the hut as I was finishing up the final splices on the repaired bridle. He limped over to the hearth and held out his hands to warm them, with his walking stick tucked under one arm.

"Hey," I greeted. "How did the meeting go?"

His face was strained, but he tried to smile. "Long. As usual. And, as usual, there's not much news, but what there is, is bad."

"I'm sorry to hear that." I tucked the end of the final thong under the braid and set the headstall aside. "I talked to Favian when I went back to the temple to get my bag. He and Limdya were chatting about horses. I think they're forging a friendship."

Andoc's expression fell at the mention of Senovo's acolyte.

"He mentioned that his father had gone with one of the delegations traveling west of here," I continued. "I gather they're overdue to return."

"Yes," Andoc said.

"It's probably just the weather," I offered. "The snow has really been piling up these last few days. Maybe they decided to wait it out."

"Maybe. I should have tried to talk Renthro out of it," Andoc said. "He has a little girl to look after."

"It was his decision," I told him seriously. "You didn't ask him to do it, much less force him to do it."

Andoc blew out a long breath and came over to sit on the bed. I leaned against his good leg, resting my head on his thigh. "I asked everyone in the village to do it," he said.

"You asked them to *volunteer*. You gave them a choice. They know as well as you do that without alliances among the northern tribes, we stand no chance against the Empire."

Andoc leaned forward, an elbow resting on his knee. He rubbed his hand over his face as if trying to remove cobwebs. "Even so."

"*Even so*, nothing," I said. "There's no easy way to put this, but they'll be *dead* if Alyrion soldiers overrun the village. We all will be—dead, or enslaved. Even little Frella."

He flinched at the words, still hiding his face behind his hand. "Gods, Carivel, how did I ever end up in this position? What if I can't protect them?"

I wished suddenly, desperately, for Senovo's presence. But Senovo wasn't here. He was pursuing his own rather desperate bid to help save us. It was left to me to give Andoc the support he so badly needed. I took a deep breath. Let it out. Looked up at him.

"Then you will die knowing that you did the very best you could, and if the gods are just, we will meet again in the next life. I have faith in you, Andoc. Draebard has faith in you. Not because we think you are infallible, but because we know you will give your all."

Andoc was quiet for a long moment. "I don't deserve you," he said eventually. "You, or Senovo. Come here, *caradi*."

I allowed him to guide me up onto the bed and into his arms. He held me tightly to his chest, and I lay there in silence, half on top of him, for quite some time.

"Senovo will be back in the morning," I said, hoping that if I sounded sure enough, it would be true. "And Renthro's group will return soon."

Andoc said nothing, but continued to hold me close through the night.

As it happened, Senovo did not return in the morning. However, when Renthro's group returned at mid-day—one member short—there was a wolf trotting along beside them.

THREE

Iwas having a quick lunch at the cookhouse when the cry went up outside on the green. I hurried out, and the initial rush of relief at seeing Senovo—apparently unharmed—gave way to a sinking feeling as people excitedly milled around the horses. *Two* horses, not three. Neither one of which was carrying Renthro.

I stopped a girl who had wandered up, presumably eager to see what all the fuss was about.

"Go to the temple," I told her. "Find Novice Eiridan or Novice Feldes and tell them that something has happened to Renthro. Have them bring along a set of robes for the High Priest."

The girl nodded, wide-eyed, and ran off, the hood of her fur parka flopping down around her shoulders as she bounded through the snow. It was a bit warmer today, but I was still wearing a cloak, for which I was thankful. I unfastened the clasp and swept it off, shivering a bit as the winter air nipped at me.

Senovo had slipped off to the side, out of the way. The villagers were becoming more accustomed to seeing the big wolf from time to time, but many still gave him a wide berth. Now, though, his presence was largely ignored in favor of questioning the returning travelers about what had happened. Everyone was talking at once, and I couldn't make out much of what was being said.

I crossed to the animal, who perked up and trotted over to meet me as soon as he noticed me. The wolf shook himself, and an instant later, Senovo straightened, naked and barefoot in the trampled snow. I steadied him and threw the heavy cloak over his shoulders.

"What happened?" I asked, once he seemed to have regained his equilibrium.

"I don't know," he replied. "I was on my way back to the village when I heard and smelled two familiar riders on the road. I could tell something was wrong. They were upset."

The travelers were still surrounded by a small mob of worried townsfolk. Senovo straightened away from my grip on his shoulder and stepped forward.

"Make way," he said in a voice that effortlessly cut through the excited chatter. "Let Ladira and Chanthi past. We must go to the meeting hall and speak with Andoc."

The group quieted, and a couple of people steadied the horses so the two could dismount.

"Take the horses to the pens," I called.

A moment later, Eiridan came hurrying across the green, scanning the crowd until he saw us. His gaze was worried, and he held a set of robes draped over one arm and a pair of boots in his hand.

"High Priest," he greeted, handing the clothing to Senovo. "Horse Mistress. Novice Feldes will bring Favian along in a moment. What has happened?"

Senovo quickly donned the clothing while I told Eiridan what little we knew. "Renthro did not return with the rest of the group. We're going to the meeting house to find Andoc and get the details of the story."

The novice priest's expression was grim. "I'll stay here and direct Feldes and Favian to the meeting hall when they arrive."

"Thank you, Eiridan," Senovo said. "I fear our youngest brother may soon need our support more than ever."

Eiridan closed his eyes for a moment as if in weariness. "*All who grieve shall be comforted,*" he quoted. "*All the gods' children will receive solace.* Favian will have whatever help he needs, High Priest."

Senovo clasped Eiridan's shoulder briefly before throwing me a glance. "Come, Carivel. Let's find some answers."

Chanthi and Ladira were hovering nervously inside the door leading into the meeting house when we arrived.

"Don't worry. Follow us," Senovo said, indicating that they should come with us, down the hallway to the main room, where low voices could be heard in solemn conversation.

Inside, the elders were once again in discussion with Andoc, apparently oblivious to the recent excitement on the green. Several of them looked up in surprise when Senovo knocked on the frame of the door and cleared his throat.

Andoc smiled as Ladira and Chanthi appeared in the doorway. "Ah, you're back! That's good news." I could see the moment he registered Renthro's absence. His expression fell. "Where's Renthro?"

Chanthi—a tall lad a few years younger than I was—looked away, his face twisting with strong emotion. Ladira, a middle-aged merchant with a thick gray beard, spoke for both of them, a faint tremor in his voice.

"Renthro is dead, Chief Andoc."

I had suspected as much ever since the pair had arrived without him, but my stomach still churned upon hearing the stark confirmation of our worst fears.

Andoc's expression closed, the mask of *leader* falling firmly into place. There was neither grief nor condemnation in his voice when he quietly asked, "What happened?"

Ladira shook his head, as if still trying to make sense of things. "The winds north of Teth were brutal, driving the snow and sleet into heavy drifts. We had talked about hunkering down and waiting it out. But Renthro was eager to get back to his daughter. He argued that we should keep going."

Andoc nodded his understanding.

"The land is full of crags and broken hills in that area," Ladira continued. "We were trying to be careful, but the visibility was poor. Renthro's horse slipped and fell into a narrow crevasse. We think he must have been killed instantly."

There was a sharp gasp from the doorway behind me, and I whirled, a sinking feeling in my chest. As I had feared, Favian stood frozen just outside the room, all of the blood draining from his face as I watched. A moment later, Novice Feldes came hurrying up as fast as his large bulk would allow.

"Favian!" he said between puffing breaths. "I told you to wait for me!"

But it was too late. Senovo closed his eyes for an instant and took a centering breath. "We grieve with you, Little Brother. Tell us what you need right now."

I wasn't at all sure Favian even registered the words. He was still staring at Ladira, his face pale and gray-tinged. The merchant looked devastated.

"Where is he?" Favian asked in a quavering voice. "*I need to see him!*"

Ladira opened his mouth and hesitated. "I'm so sorry, Favian. We tried to get him out. We spent more than a day trying, but we couldn't reach his body."

Favian wavered as if he might collapse, but jerked free when Feldes moved to support him. A thin noise of pain emerged from his throat, tearing at my heart. Without a body, there could be no funeral. Renthro's spirit would not rise on the smoke; his ashes would not feed the soil of the village.

The grief stricken acolyte raised a trembling hand, one finger outstretched, though it wasn't clear if he was pointing at Andoc, Renthro's surviving companions, or everyone in the room. "This is your fault! If it weren't for you, *my father would still be alive!*" He stumbled and half-collapsed, catching himself against the heavy timber of the door frame. "Oh, gods. *Frella.* I... I have to..."

"Frella is fine right now. She is safe with your father's neighbors," Senovo said. "Come and sit down for a moment, and then we'll go talk to them." He moved forward to take Favian's arm, but the boy knocked his hand away and staggered upright.

"*Leave me alone!*" he shouted, and fled the room.

Senovo sighed.

"He'll go to his sister," Feldes said.

"Yes," Senovo agreed, his voice heavy with weariness, before addressing the room at large. "I'll go after him. The rest of you still have much to discuss."

"I'll come with you," I said quietly.

"Thank you," Andoc said, his mask barely covering the dismay at having sent Renthro to his death. "Ladira, Chanthi, none of this was your fault. Please... as painful as it is, we should move on to the results of your discussions with the other villages..."

⚜

During the brief period of time while we were in the meeting house, the weak sun that had brightened the sky throughout the morning disappeared behind a new bank of slate gray clouds, perfectly reflecting my mood. Senovo and I trudged in silence along the slushy road, heading toward Renthro's neighbors' home.

I'd had a passing acquaintance with Favian's father, and knew him as a hard-working widower who was passionately devoted to both his children and his adopted village. After his wife Favaela died giving birth to Frella, he could have moved back to Teth, where he had relatives to support him. But he had made a life in Draebard, and he chose to stay even though it left him essentially on his own with the heavy responsibility of two young children.

Favian was nearly a decade older than his baby sister. The boy had apprenticed himself to Horse Master Jorun at an unusually young age to free up more resources for the small family. Renthro had once confessed to me that he felt guilty for having left Favian so much to his own devices when Frella was a baby, but it was obvious that he had still been a loving and supportive father. Favian had adored him.

Money was tight, but Renthro managed to scrape together enough to pay his neighbors to watch Frella when he could not, rather than leaving her unattended or relying on charity. If only his sense of duty had not extended to volunteering for such a hazardous winter journey.

When Senovo and I reached the modest hut next door to Renthro's near the edge of the settlement, we could hear young children crying within. We exchanged a look, and Senovo stepped up to knock on the door.

A plump, harried looking woman with brownish-gray hair escaping a messy bun opened it a moment later. "Oh, thank the gods!" she said immediately. "Have you come about Favian? He's gone half-mad! He barged into the house and grabbed Frella, and he won't talk to me or let me within an arm's length of either of them!"

"Favian has had a serious shock," I said, speaking over the clamor of frightened children. "He just learned that his father was killed in an accident while traveling."

The woman went pale. "Oh, *no*. Not Renthro!" she said. "The poor boy!"

"May we come in, Bellea?" Senovo asked, breaking the woman out of her startled reverie.

"Yes," she said hastily, as if suddenly becoming aware that we were standing in the open door, letting the cold in. "Yes, of course."

The little hut was crowded and chaotic, made more so by the squalling of three of Bellea's four children, obviously upset by Favian's strange behavior. Senovo's acolyte was huddled against the wall with his four-year-old sister held tightly in his arms—probably *too* tightly, since she was also crying.

"*Go away*," Favian rasped in a hoarse voice as we crossed the cluttered floor and crouched in front of him. His face was twisted in anger and pain.

"No," Senovo said simply. Gently. He eased himself around until he was sitting against the wall next to Favian, their shoulders just brushing. I mirrored him, sitting on Favian's other side.

From this position, I found that I was looking directly down at Frella's face. Her eyes—the same summer-sky shade as her brother's—were flooded with tears that tracked down her chubby, reddened cheeks, joining a small river of snot that had formed under the force of her crying. I felt the same sense of extreme discomfort that I always did around very small children—especially ones who were upset—and tried to put it aside.

Now, I could feel Favian's body starting to hitch and shake next to me, as his emotions finally caught up with him. Indeed, my own eyes were burning and suspiciously wet as I contemplated the scope of the boy's loss. Only Senovo seemed his usual imperturbable self, offering silent support and strength to his bereaved acolyte, as Favian succumbed to his grief.

We sat like that for some time, until Favian's breathing evened out and Frella subsided into wet sniffles. The little girl still had no idea what was going on, I suspected; she only knew that her brother was upset and it frightened her. Bellea had herded her own brood to the cooking area on the far side of the structure, trying to give us as much room as possible.

I had no idea how to help Favian, who had now lost two father figures in the space of a year— first Jorun, who had been a mentor to both of us, and now, Renthro. I could only follow Senovo's lead, saying nothing, but trying my best to offer a calm, supportive presence. Eventually, Senovo's quiet patience paid off.

"I'll have to leave the temple," Favian whispered, sounding utterly lost.

"No," Senovo replied, "you will not. Not unless you wish to."

"I will, though," Favian insisted. "With Father gone, I can't afford to pay for someone to take care of Frella."

Frella frowned and wriggled around until she could look up at her brother's face. "Where's Papa gone?" she asked plaintively, and Favian descended into helpless tears again.

Senovo smoothed a strand of damp, light brown hair away from Frella's cheek before letting the hand fall to rest on Favian's shoulder. "Your Father has gone on a very important journey to visit the gods, Frella. He thought he would be able to come back to you, but the gods needed his help so badly that they called him away. He loves you very much, and wants you to know that Favian will look after you and take good care of you."

It was too much—now I was crying as well, though at least I had a lifetime of practice at doing so silently.

"When can he come back?" Frella bleated, her face crumpling again.

"I'm so sorry, child," Senovo said. "He won't be coming back."

Frella *wailed*, and something about the noise seemed to draw Favian out of himself. He straightened his spine and tucked Frella closer against himself, his embrace becoming less desperate and more protective. "Shh, Baby Sister," he said, "I'm here. I won't leave you. *Shh.* I promise, Frella. I won't leave you alone."

Frella let herself be comforted and rocked in her brother's arms, gradually crying herself out until she fell into a restless sleep, exhausted by her tears.

When she was finally quiet, except for the soft, wet noises as she breathed through her congested nose, Favian turned to Senovo, something like panic in his eyes. "What do I do now? What do I *do*?"

"We will go next door to your father's house," Senovo said with complete equanimity. "Frella will benefit from a nap in familiar surroundings, and you will benefit from some more time to think, and to grieve. I promise you—just as you will not leave Frella alone, I will not leave you alone, either, Little Brother."

Favian nodded slowly, still looking very lost. He climbed onto unsteady feet, cradling Frella against his hip as she slumbered on, oblivious.

"I have to go back to the pens and let them know what's happening," I told Senovo quietly. "Will you be all right for a while?"

"Of course," he replied. "While you're out, pick up some food and supplies for us, please—enough for a couple of days. I don't know what Renthro will have kept on hand."

"Right," I said, and gave Frella a slightly nervous look. "Um… what does she eat?"

Senovo's expression was patient, but vaguely pitying. "She's four, Carivel. She eats the same thing as you or I."

"Oh," I said, feeling stupid. "Yes. Sorry. I'll be back in an hour or two, then."

Senovo located Frella's tiny winter cloak and helped Favian wrap it around her. I gave Favian my own cloak to cover his acolyte's robe, and hovered uselessly as Senovo guided him outside with a protective arm around his narrow shoulders. Bellea stopped me with a hand on my forearm as I made to follow them. Her eyes were slightly red and puffy as, I'm sure, were mine.

"Look," she said, "I feel awful about this, but Favian's right. I can't keep caring for Frella if there's no money. My husband and I barely have enough as it is. I'm not even sure what we'll do for our own four, now that Renthro won't be paying me any more. I mean, if it's an emergency I'll try to help, but… I just thought you should know."

"I understand," I said, too overwhelmed by the day's events to have much thought to spare for Bellea's predicament. "I'm sure we'll figure out something. Sorry to cause such a disruption for you this afternoon."

"Don't be silly," she said, and her face fell again. "Poor Renthro…"

I nodded vague agreement and made my escape, secretly thinking that Bellea's pity would be more use to Favian and Frella than it was to Renthro, who was now forever beyond such things. I stopped by the meeting hall to give Andoc a quick report and let him know that Favian and Frella were safe in Senovo's care, and that I would be spending the night with them.

"Good, *caradi*. That's good," he said, and kissed my forehead briefly. "I'll leave you to it. I don't think Favian particularly wants to see me right now."

I wished I had words to reassure him, but he was probably right and we both knew it. From the meeting hall, I went to the horse pens.

"Hey, boss," Dalon greeted. "I was about to send out a search party. Couple of boys brought two horses back a while ago. Pretty sure we sent three out originally."

His expression was grim, and I nodded. "Renthro's dead. His horse slipped on the ice and fell into hidden crevasse."

"Aw, *shit*. Poor Favian. Kid can't seem to catch a break. He all right? And his little sister?"

"Not really," I said. "Senovo's looking after them."

Dalon shook his head in dismay. "That really sucks. Look, there's not much going on this afternoon. If you need to leave, you can—I'll get everything finished and closed up before dark."

"Thanks," I said gratefully. "I should go lay in some supplies so Favian won't have to worry about it for a few days. I owe you one."

"I'll add it to all the others you owe me, then, shall I?" Dalon said, with a quick, sad smile to let me know he was teasing.

"You do that. Who knows, someday it might even be worth something."

Dalon snorted. "Tell the kid I'm real sorry about what happened, will you? I'll come by and visit when he's had a little time to deal with things."

"I will. See you in the morning, Dalon."

I made a quick round of the pens to make sure that no one else needed me for anything, before heading off to pick up enough food and drink for the next couple of days. When I knocked on the door, Senovo answered with a finger raised to his lips, which I took to mean that both of the siblings were asleep. He took the food as I nodded in understanding, pointing to the hearth, myself, and then outside to indicate that I would go check the supply of firewood.

There was a good-sized pile of logs near the house, but not much chopped firewood left. I thought with a pang that Renthro must have been planning to chop more once he got home. Frankly, I was relieved to have something to do that didn't involve being around Frella while she was so upset. Even in my own head, that sounded awful, and I prodded at the knot of feelings as I set the first log down and picked up Renthro's ancient, well-used axe.

Thunk!

Ever since I could remember, I'd been uncomfortable around babies and small children.

Thunk!

I'd always sort of assumed it was because I had no siblings of my own, and had been a shy child with no real friends growing up.

Thunk!

With all of the hours I'd spent talking to Eiridan after my capture and imprisonment at the hill fort, though, I was gaining a better picture of just how badly my mother had damaged me with her beatings and hateful words. Now, I suddenly wondered if I had her to blame for *this* bit of madness as well.

Thunk!

Frella was an innocent little girl who needed all of the support she could get, my own included. She had never done anything that should make me want to stay away from her. So why did I have such a strong reaction to being around her?

I chopped several more logs without coming up with an answer. Resolving to act like a normal human being around the poor kid regardless of how screwed up I was inside, I bundled up the freshly chopped firewood and heaved it onto my shoulder. Inside, Senovo was seated quietly near the hearth, watching the flames with faraway eyes. He looked up at my approach.

Favian and Frella were huddled on the palliasse in the far corner, still wrapped around each other and fast asleep. I lowered the bundle of wood to the dirt floor as silently as I could and stacked it piece by piece in the rack near the fireplace. When I was done and there was no more busywork to distract me from the small tragedy playing out around us, I settled next to Senovo, my shoulder pressing against his.

With a final glance to confirm that Favian truly was asleep, I asked, "*Will* Favian have to leave the priesthood? Someone really does have to look after Frella, after all."

"No acolyte of mine will be turned out of the temple unless he truly wishes to leave," Senovo said. He threw me a look. "I have heard you recite Utarr's prayer of solace many times, Carivel. I'm sure you realize that it is not merely a pretty verse."

Even had Eiridan not recounted part of the prayer today upon learning of Favian and Frella's bitter loss, the words would have come to my mind effortlessly. They had worn tracks through my memory over the last several months, so often had I relied on them for balance and comfort.

All who seek shelter shall find it.
All who grieve shall be comforted.
All the gods' children will receive solace.
Ask at the temple and gain the help you need.

The goddess's promise to her children gained new poignancy under the circumstances, but I still could not understand what, precisely, Senovo was proposing.

"But... how?" I asked. "Frella can't exactly live at the temple."

"Can she not?" asked Senovo, in that particularly mild voice which I had come to recognize as masking the High Priest's rare bouts of passion.

I blinked. "She's a girl, Senovo," I said carefully.

Senovo's gaze flashed gold in the firelight. A frisson passed across the back of my neck. Not fear—never fear—but still a visceral reaction to the formidable power and force of will that Senovo had always possessed, but so rarely drew upon.

"She is a *child*," he said, his voice still even. "And while she may no longer have parents, she does not merely have one older brother to protect and care for her—she has many."

A sudden wave of chagrin hit me, as I truly stopped to think about the hypocrisy involved in *me*, of all people, arguing that Frella should not stay at the temple because she was female. After another quick look to ensure that Favian and Frella still slept, I turned to Senovo and wrapped my arms around him, burying my face in his shoulder.

"I love you very much," I told him, "and I don't know what I did to deserve not just one truly good person in my life, but two."

I had surprised him, apparently, because he sat frozen for a moment before his arm came up to wrap around my shoulders in return.

"I'm... not sure it's a matter of being deserving," he said after a pause. "I think perhaps the gods place others in our paths who can help us grow, and achieve all of which we are capable. That certainly seems to have been the case for me."

I hugged him tighter for a few moments before pulling back.

"Papa?" came a small voice from the bed.

Favian snorted awake a moment later and sat up, disoriented.

"Favian," I said, not wanting our presence in the house to startle him. "Senovo and I are here. Do you need anything?"

"I want Papa," Frella said plaintively.

There was an uncomfortable pause. "Papa's gone, Frella," Favian said, his voice sounding scraped raw.

"Oh," Frella answered, her face falling. "I'm hungry. Can we have fish tonight?"

Favian looked lost for a moment, as if the practical considerations of everyday life were beyond him at the moment.

"I didn't get any fish," I said, "but I brought some rabbit meat and turnips, and an onion. I happen to know that High Priest Senovo makes a pretty mean stew, and we have some flatbread to go with it." In truth, I also happened to know that Senovo disliked cooking, a fact confirmed by the faintly dirty look he shot me. "What?" I added under my breath. "You've eaten my cooking a few times, and I *know* you don't want to subject the poor kids to *that*."

He sighed. "A fair point, well argued. Come, Frella. You can help me pick out which turnips to use. Carivel and Favian can chop them up for us."

Frella wiped at her puffy face and crawled out of bed. "I'll show you where Papa keeps the things for cooking," she said in a slightly shy voice.

While Senovo and Frella puttered around, I crossed and sat down by the edge of the straw palliasse. Favian was still tangled in his father's blankets, his arms wrapped around himself as if he didn't know what to do with them now that he wasn't holding his sister.

"How are we going to live?" Favian asked, though I got the sense he wasn't directing the question to me, so much as pouring out some of the fears that had been circling around his mind like carrion birds since he learned of Renthro's death. "I can't get work without finding someone to look after Frella, and I can't pay anyone to look after her unless I get work. We'll end up begging for alms outside the door to the meeting house."

I wanted to hug him, but I could tell he was still too raw to accept it. Instead, I ducked my head until he finally had to meet my eyes. "You've made a mistake," I told him. "You discounted something Senovo tried to tell you earlier."

"What?" Favian looked confused, and I was struck again by just how much he was struggling to take everything in right now.

"When you said you'd have to leave the temple, and he told you that you wouldn't. You didn't believe him."

"I can't be an acolyte and still take care of my sister," he said dismissively, almost angrily.

I propped myself on one hand, regarding him steadily. "You can if Frella lives at the temple with you, and has a whole big extended family of uncles and brothers to help you."

Favian gasped as if I'd punched him and I tensed, concerned. He clutched at his chest with one hand. "Th-the High Priest wouldn't... he couldn't..."

"The High Priest can and he will," said a voice behind me, and I craned up to see Senovo looking down at both of us, his arms crossed. "Now come here, both of you, and chop these turnips."

I urged Favian to his feet and guided him over to the rough table where Senovo had the ingredients for the stew laid out. The boy was dazed enough that I kept a close eye on him as Senovo handed him a knife and set him to chopping, but he applied himself to the mindless work without mishap. I followed suit, watching Frella watch me from her perch on the chair next to the table as she snacked on a bit of bread, swinging her lower legs back and forth through the air.

When the iron pot full of stew was safely hanging from a sturdy metal tripod over the fire, Senovo took Favian aside and sat him down. To my dismay, Frella immediately came over to my chair and lifted her arms to be picked up. I fought down a ridiculous wash of panic.

She's a child. She only wants attention and comfort. Why should that be so upsetting?

With a deep breath to calm the pounding of my heart, I helped her crawl up into my lap, where she settled against me, feeling small and heavy and strange.

"Favian," Senovo was saying, "the brotherhood of those who serve the temple is not an abstract concept. You are my family, and you are in need. I have the ability to help you, and I will."

Favian was still badly off balance. "I don't know what to say. I don't know how we'll be able to repay you."

Senovo only raised an expressive eyebrow. "Does the wolf ask for recompense when it protects its pack? Let us hear no more talk of *debts* and *repayment.*"

"Wh-what about Father's hut?" Favian's eyes darted around the homey structure, no doubt thinking of all the memories he must have of this place.

Senovo sat back, considering. "It is your hut now. Yours and Frella's. While there are no formal restrictions on members of the priesthood maintaining possessions, it is true that most do not keep a home outside of the temple. You have a few different options that I can see. You can sell it and use the money as a form of security for Frella's future. You can keep it for her to live in when she is older. If you do that, you might consider letting it out in exchange for money in the mean time, either to someone who wants to live in it or someone who wants to use it for a business."

Favian looked even more dazed than he had before. "I don't know how to make that kind of decision."

"I would not suggest making any decisions right now," Senovo continued. "Why don't you stay here with Frella for a few days? You can bring her for visits to the temple during the daytime to help her become comfortable there. I see no reason for sudden upheaval."

Favian nodded, overwhelmed. Frella sat curled in my lap, watching the proceedings with wide-eyed interest. We were silent for a while as Favian digested what Senovo had told him.

"I have to go apologize to Chief Andoc and the elders. Also to Chanthi, and Ladira," he said some minutes later.

"I'm certain it would make Chanthi and Ladira, in particular, feel better to know that you do not truly blame them," Senovo said. "Now, though, it is cold outside and the wind has picked up again. Perhaps tomorrow."

Favian hugged himself, and even from across the room I could see that he was starting to tremble. "I... feel strange. I don't—"

"I know. Come here," said Senovo. He stood, guiding Favian up and into his arms, holding him close until the boy's tears spilled over and he began to weep once more. Frella wriggled free of my grip, running over to wrap her small arms around her brother's legs and press her face against his hip. I followed her and embraced Favian from behind, relieved to finally be able to offer comfort to the boy who had suffered so much recently.

"It's all right, Favian," Frella said in her high, clear little voice. "I won't leave you alone either."
Favian only buried a hand in Frella's tangled honey-brown hair and cried harder.

FOUR

The night was long and bleak, with the wind whistling past the eaves and sending little gusts through the cracks around the shutters and door. Senovo and I did not precisely *keep watch*, but we did pass the hours of darkness in a state of semi-awareness, ready to wake at the slightest sign of distress from either of our charges.

It was nearly morning when Favian started to toss and moan, only to jerk awake a few moments later.

"Favian?" Senovo asked softly. The boy was breathing heavily, and looked around as if unsure where he was for a moment until his eyes fell on Frella, still asleep on the other side of the straw mattress.

"I dreamed," Favian said, his voice little more than a whisper. "I saw Father's funeral."

I crouched down next to Senovo by the bed. "Favian, there's no body," I reminded him.

He frowned, the expression barely visible in the light from the embers of the banked fire. "I know, but it felt like a true dream." Favian shook his head, his features twisting into anger. "What use is this stupid gift if I couldn't even use it to save Father?"

"Your gift saved all of us from the Alyrions," Senovo said, "your father included."

Favian made a curt, dismissive gesture. "Only for him to die a couple of months later. Why didn't I foresee *that*?"

"I don't know the answer to that, Little Brother. Perhaps the knowledge could not have been used to save him, in any case. If so, such a vision would only have caused you more pain."

Favian's prophetic dreams were a complete mystery to me. They had started when he was sick with a fever, and I was still strongly of the opinion that foreseeing terrible events—never knowing until it was too late whether they would come to pass or were merely nightmares—sounded more like a curse than a blessing. At least dreaming of his father's funeral did not foretell additional death and destruction. Indeed, given Favian's grief and the lack of a body, it sounded more like a bereaved son's wishful fantasy than second sight.

The boy ran a hand over his face and let the subject go. "Is it morning?" he asked.

"Almost," I said. "Not worth trying to go back to sleep, at any rate."

Senovo rose and stretched. "Favian, why don't you see to the fire? We'll let Frella sleep a little longer. There is bread and stew left over from last night if either of you are hungry."

"I should stop in and speak with Andoc," I said. "Then I'd better get to the horse pens unless you need me for something."

"No," Senovo said. "We will stay here for a little while. It's likely that well-wishers will start arriving this morning to pay their respects. We'll go to the temple around mid-day."

The lost look Favian had worn yesterday returned. "I don't want to have to talk to people. Not yet."

"They won't expect you to carry on a scintillating conversation," I told him, remembering the days following my father's death when I was a child. "They just want to stop by and let you know they feel bad for your loss."

"I know that," he snapped. "I remember. I lost my mother a few years ago."

At the time, I imagine Renthro had fielded the condolences and polite small talk. I was confident, though, that Senovo would not allow Favian to be overwhelmed, and I suspected that dealing with the distraction of friends and neighbors descending on the little hut with armloads of food and sympathy would provide something of a distraction from Favian's bitter, circling thoughts.

"Just take the free food and say *thank you* a lot," I advised. "Leave the rest of it to Senovo. I'll come by the temple around lunchtime to look in on you, all right?"

Favian nodded mutely, not meeting my eyes. I shared a look with Senovo and went to splash some water on my face. By the time I had bundled my cloak around me and headed out into the bitter morning cold, Frella was stirring and the sky was lightening in the east.

I'd come up with an idea as I was lying half-awake during the night, and I needed to talk to Andoc. It was a rather large and intimidating idea, actually. I was fairly sure it was the right thing to do, but the thought of it also made me somewhat queasy. I honestly had no idea what Andoc was likely to make of it.

Andoc's hut—*our* hut— was quiet and dark when I let myself in. The banked fire had done a decent job of keeping the cold at bay, and I took my outer layers off before crossing to the bed.

"Hello, *caradi*," Andoc said. I could just make out the reflection of his eyes in the orange light from the embers.

Andoc's sleeping patterns had always been a fairly good indicator of how serious a given situation was. When there was no immediate threat, he slept like the dead—Senovo and I joked with each other about various extreme methods for waking him, and teased him mercilessly about his habit of sleeping until mid-morning.

However, when there was danger, or when his protective instincts were roused, Andoc had a warrior's ingrained habit of sleeping with one eye open. Since his injury at the hands of Rhytheeri assassins and subsequent rise to the chieftaincy, he had also shown signs of occasional insomnia when he could not let go of whatever problem or crisis currently plagued his thoughts.

I hoped Renthro's death had not kept him awake all night.

"Hey," I replied, and indulged myself by ducking under the covers with him. He pulled me in for a deep kiss. When we parted a few moments later, I stroked chilly fingertips over his cheek.

"How are they doing?" Andoc asked.

"They're grieving. Senovo is with them; he won't leave them alone. I almost think Frella is taking it better than Favian. Or maybe she just doesn't understand. She's so young."

I had been two years older than Frella when my own father died of an unknown sickness that filled the lungs with fluid until the victim couldn't breathe anymore. Several in our village had succumbed to the illness that year. I remembered parts of what had happened with startling clarity, while other parts were hazy and indistinct.

"Children are more resilient than people think," Andoc said. I thought of the welts and bruises that had frequently decorated my back as a child, and could not disagree. At least Frella knew only kind words and gentle, protective hands.

"I need to talk to you," I said, before I could start second guessing myself too badly.

Andoc made a questioning noise and rolled up on an elbow.

"Senovo is going to take Frella into the temple, so that Favian can care for her there with the help of the others and still remain an acolyte," I began.

Enough light was coming through the east-facing window now to illuminate Andoc's look of helpless affection. "Of course he is," he whispered. "The old softie."

"I've been thinking, though. Renthro didn't have much. Only his hut, really, and Favian is obviously overwhelmed by the idea of selling or renting it. Senovo will look after him and Frella, but I thought... maybe you and I should take guardianship of them. I mean," I hurried on, "You and I and Senovo are as good as handfasted, at least as far as the three of us are concerned. And if Senovo is taking formal responsibility for them, well, maybe you and I should, too."

I trailed off under the look Andoc was giving me, unable to read his thoughts behind the odd expression. A moment later, he shook his head as if to clear it and pulled me into his arms.

"Yes," he said. "We should. Assuming Favian agrees, of course. He's young, but he's not too young to be the head of his own household if he'd rather be. It's largely up to him, and he has no reason to look kindly on me at the moment."

I hugged Andoc in return. "He was angry yesterday. Upset. He's already talking about making a formal apology."

"Oh, *gods* no. If he's willing to speak with Chanthi and Ladira, it would probably be good for all of them, but he doesn't owe me or the elders anything." He shuddered a bit under my hands at the thought.

"Well, you can tell him that personally whenever he comes to talk with you. We probably need to have a word with Senovo before either of us says anything to Favian, though. I can't imagine he'd object, but even so—" I shrugged. "I feel like I should give someone the opportunity to save Frella from being stuck with me as a guardian."

Andoc regarded me strangely. "I'd hardly consider that to be something she'd need saving from."

I waved the words away with an awkward laugh. Of course Andoc would have no way of knowing about the special brand of madness that sent me into a near panic at the thought of merely holding the poor little girl in my lap for a few minutes. Besides, I was picturing guardianship more as a way to secure Favian and Frella's future than anything else—with luck, Senovo would have most of the day-to-day necessities under control already.

To change the subject, I asked, "Were the negotiations with the other villages successful, I hope?"

Fortunately, Andoc let my obvious ploy to divert his attention pass. "Sort of. Teth and Gebrall are with us, but they're both fairly small tribes. None of the others were willing to commit to anything solid without knowing more details about the northern alliance and our strategy. Of course, it's pretty fucking difficult to offer more details when almost no one will give me a commitment. And to top it all off, we still have no idea how the Empire plans to attack."

I propped my back against the headboard. "If they try to come over the mountains again after what you did to them last time, I'll eat my boots."

Andoc sighed. "I agree that an invasion by sea is more likely, but having an opinion is different from *knowing*."

Setting an entire mountain on fire to trap and kill the legion of Alyrion troops marching across it had been a bold move on Andoc's part, but also a desperate one. Had Favian not foreseen the resulting firestorm and the screams of dying men in a dream, I don't think any of us would have ever come up with such an idea. Now—in the absence of any more helpful visions from the gods—Andoc had to devise some sort of plan to counter a much larger attack. *Orders of magnitude* larger.

He was doing everything he possibly could, but so far no useful information had come through the network of spies that he and Leader Magoldis of the Mereni had put in place. Attempts to forge a last minute alliance of the northern tribes during the depths of winter were proceeding far too slowly, and now, those attempts had cost Draebard its first life.

Outside, the sun was peeking over the horizon, promising a small respite from the blustery storms that had plagued us for much of the winter. I shared a quick breakfast with Andoc and arranged to meet him at the temple at midday to speak with Senovo. When I arrived at the pens a short time later, the apprentices were just starting to trail in for the day.

Limdya caught my eye and came over, her expression pale and troubled. "I heard about Renthro," she said. "How is Favian?"

"Senovo is looking after him and Frella," I told her, "but he's about like you'd expect, I imagine. He's pretty raw right now, but I think he'd appreciate a friendly face. I'm going to look in on him at lunchtime if you'd like to come."

"Yes, I'll come," Limdya said. "I know exactly what he's going through."

I nodded, overcoming my awkwardness with my newest apprentice long enough to clasp her shoulder for a brief moment. Limdya and her sisters had been orphaned during the Alyrion attack on Draebard the previous spring. Worse, the girls had been the ones to find their mother's body after she'd been stabbed through the heart. I felt a familiar pang of bitter hatred toward the Empire that had caused so much grief in our village.

"Once Favian has had a few days to get things sorted, try to get him out here to the pens," I said. "Frella, too, if you like — though someone will have to watch her carefully. I think it would help him."

"I'll see what I can do," Limdya said, before turning her attention to more immediate matters. "In the mean time, if you've got a few minutes, I have some new ideas for organizing the inventory. I also have a question about choosing the right bits for different horses. I asked three people yesterday and got three different answers."

I snorted in mild amusement at her expression of irritation, and led her to the storage building to see what she'd been working on.

The morning passed pleasantly enough, made a bit more bearable by the bright sunshine and relatively calm wind. At lunch, Limdya and I walked to the temple. We found Favian in the altar room, kneeling in contemplation before the large stone slab while Frella played with a small bronze statue of a lion nearby. Eiridan leaned unobtrusively near the entrance, splitting his attention between the two siblings.

He dipped his head in silent acknowledgment as we came in, then made himself scarce to give us some privacy.

"Oh, Favian," Limdya said, and crossed to kneel next to him so she could fling her arms around him.

"Hi," Favian said in a small voice, and hid his face against her shoulder.

"I'm so sorry," said Limdya. "Any time you need to talk, I'm here."

"Thanks," Favian said, still into Limdya's shoulder. "I just… haven't really gotten my head around it yet, you know?"

Limdya nodded and gave him a final squeeze before letting him go. "I do." She looked over at Favian's little sister, who had paused in her play to stare at us. "Can I say hello to Frella?"

Favian nodded. "Of course you can."

Limdya smiled and crawled over to where the little girl sat, bronze lion still in hand. "Hi, Sweetheart. How are you?"

I watched in mild awe as Frella climbed into Limdya's lap to be hugged, as if she did so every day. "Papa's gone," said the little girl mournfully.

"I know, Frella. I'm so sorry that happened. How are you feeling?" Limdya asked.

"Sad."

I had expected her to say *frightened,* and I had to take a moment before I realized it was because when my own father had died, I'd been terrified at the prospect of being all alone with my mother.

"I was sad when my mother died, too," Limdya was saying. "Having my sisters there helped, though. We were all sad together, and that made it a bit easier. I'm glad you've got Favian to be sad with."

"Me, too," Frella said, still clinging to Limdya like a limpet.

She's going to make an amazing mother someday, I thought.

Realizing that I was standing frozen near the doorway like a useless hunk of stone, I broke free of my thoughts and went to join Favian at the altar.

"Frella likes it here," he said as I sat down beside him, cross-legged.

"I'm glad."

"I think maybe this could work after all."

I smiled. "Someone told me a long time ago that when our esteemed High Priest tells you he has a plan, you can be fairly certain it's a good one."

"It certainly took you long enough to believe me," said a new voice from the doorway.

Favian scrambled to his feet. "Chief Andoc!" he said in surprise.

"I'm sorry, Favian, I didn't mean to startle you," Andoc said.

"No, I'm the one who's sorry," Favian said, his face going a bit pale. "I had no right to speak to you and the elders the way I did yesterday."

Andoc raised a quelling hand. "Whoa, now. Just stop. You had every right, and no one is upset. I'm certainly not, and, frankly, the elders yell at each other so often and so loudly that I don't think most of them even registered it."

Favian looked almost faint with relief. "Oh. Thank you. That's very kind of you to say. I apologized to Chanthi and Ladira earlier this morning. I'm… glad no one took offense."

Limdya clambered to her feet with Frella still cradled against her. "Of course no one took offense, you silly boy. Hello, Chief."

"Hello, Limdya. I see you've made a new friend." Andoc smiled at Frella, who had a thumb stuck firmly in her mouth, though his eyes remained sad. "Hello, Frella."

The little girl hid her face, suddenly shy.

"I'm afraid I've come to steal the Horse Mistress away for a few minutes," Andoc said. "Carivel, Senovo is waiting for us."

I was fairly relieved to be *stolen*, truth be told, as pretty much all I'd managed since arriving was to hover around feeling awkward. I followed Andoc out to where Senovo was waiting for us in one of the quiet rooms used for counseling.

"Carivel has an idea," Andoc began without preamble, as soon as the door closed behind us.

Senovo looked up, one eyebrow raised. "Oh, yes? How worried should I be?"

"I think Andoc and I should take formal guardianship of Favian and Frella," I blurted, too nervous to properly take umbrage at the teasing.

The other eyebrow quirked up for a moment before Senovo consciously smoothed his expression. "Indeed? That would be a very kind gesture, assuming Favian is open to the idea."

I took a centering breath. "Well, you've basically done the same thing already, and since Andoc and I consider ourselves bonded to you in all but name, it only makes sense. The gods know I wouldn't wish myself on anyone as a parent, but Andoc and I both have status now, and that might provide them with a bit of security. Assuming, of course, that the Alyrions don't show up in a few months and raze the entire village to the ground."

"Security is something of a relative concept these days, to be sure," Senovo agreed with a wry twist of his lips. "I would be happy to speak to Favian and Frella about your offer—I suspect the conversation will be less uncomfortable that way. I assume we are discussing inheritance and patronage more than actual parenting?"

"As far as I'm concerned," said Andoc, "the pair of them are welcome to make themselves at home in my hut to whatever degree they wish. I doubt Favian is looking for a replacement for Renthro, though—and besides, when it comes to a mentor and father figure, I can't think of a better one than you, *amadi*."

There was a beat of silence. "If you'd said those words to me a year ago, I would have laughed in your face—you do realize that," Senovo said.

"He's right, though," I said. Senovo had taken to caring for his little brood of acolytes and novices like one born to it. It was amazing to think that he, like me, had known such neglect and cruelty as a child. Unlike me, however, he'd overcome it.

"A lot has changed in a year," Andoc said. "Not all of it has been for the worse."

How true that was. A year ago, both Senovo and I had been hiding, trying to keep to the shadows in hopes that no one would discover our secrets. Andoc had been a successful young warrior with full use of both his legs. And no one in Draebard ever went to bed wondering if enemy soldiers would come during the night to kill them.

I had also been alone.

Now, we were the three most powerful people in the village, though that concept still sat rather awkwardly on my shoulders. Our mentors were dead, and somehow—gods help us—we had been thrust into the roles of mentors ourselves. Most importantly, the three of us had found love and acceptance with each other. Though we might all die at the end of a sword before the trees finished flowering this spring, I could not even conceive of returning to a time *before*.

"No," Senovo agreed after a moment of silent contemplation. "Not all of it has been for the worse."

The next morning, Favian accompanied Senovo to meet with us. He shyly agreed to the guardianship, going to great lengths to clarify that it was mostly for Frella, and that he did not expect any special treatment or coddling.

"I will gladly step aside as soon as you have a legitimate heir, sir," he told Andoc. "I would only ask that Frella receive some modest support until she is married."

"There aren't likely to be any *legitimate heirs*, as you put it," Andoc said seriously. "And I could not be more proud to name you as my heir, Favian."

I struggled with the queasy knot of discomfort that always followed on the heels of any discussion about having children, even as Favian flushed.

"I'm only a temple acolyte, sir," he said. "It's not exactly the most prestigious position for a Chief's heir."

Andoc only smiled. "Favian. I'll have you know that some of my closest friends started out as temple acolytes."

Favian's eyes flicked to Senovo, and he flushed deeper.

"If you're saying you want to come back to the horse pens, though…" I began, in hopes of breaking the tension.

Favian's eyes never left the High Priest. "No," he said softly. "No, I'm not."

The following days passed in relative peace. Andoc continued to devise possible plans for Draebard's defense. Senovo resumed his nighttime excursions in the form of the wolf, though he was careful to always be back within a few hours. I split my time between the horses, training Draebard's contingent of mounted archers, and our new family members, spending several nights in Renthro's hut until Favian finally moved Frella into the temple with him. My feeling of complete emotional incompetence persisted through Frella's unpredictable bouts of weeping and childish, plaintive questions about the nature of death.

Fortunately, both Andoc and Senovo were better at dealing with a grieving little girl than I was. Additionally, Limdya made frequent appearances when her duties allowed, adding weight to my speculation that she and Favian were developing a strong friendship.

I was a bit more use to Favian, whose grief was more adult in nature. Once Frella was safely installed with her new band of guardians at the temple, I more or less dragged him out to the horse pens and threw him into a corral with the white colt he'd loved so much when he was apprenticed to work there. The colt was nearly a yearling now, and going through an awkward gangly stage that promised a huge growth spurt at the first sign of spring grass.

I dropped a tangle of equipment at Favian's feet. "Don't come out until you can ground drive him at the walk, turn him in both directions, and back him up three steps," I said, before leaving him to it.

The colt wandered up to sniff at Favian's hair, then reached down and picked up the leather training surcingle in his teeth, shaking it up and down playfully. An involuntary smile crossed my features, and I headed off to catch up on my own work. Two hours later, Favian proudly guided the young horse through the alleys to where I was working with a group of mounted archers and brought him to a smooth halt. His smile was the first I'd seen from him since Renthro's death.

⚜

The following day, Dalon came back from his lunch break in a hurry, his breath puffing in steamy clouds around his face. "There's a messenger from Rhyth at the meeting hall," he said. "You'd better get over there — it sounds important."

I jogged all the way to the village green, the cold air burning my lungs. The messenger was already gone, however, and instead I found Senovo, Andoc, First Warrior Jacun, Balzoc, and a gaggle of elders deep in conversation.

Andoc looked up at my entrance, his expression grim but focused. "Good, you're here. Sit down, Carivel — we've had some news."

I dragged a chair back and sat. "Dalon said there was a rider from Rhyth?"

"That's right," said Andoc. "One of the spies. He didn't stop long — he's already headed on to Meren."

"What did he say?" I asked, feeling my heart pick up speed.

Jacun answered. "There is word from the mainland that the Emperor is readying for a large-scale naval assault. The spring invasion will come by sea, not land."

It was as we had suspected, but the independent confirmation freed Andoc to make some firmer plans.

"Do we know where?" I asked. Northern Eburos was a somewhat challenging place to reach by water. The coastline was rocky and largely impenetrable. I had grown up near the water myself, but in an area with no port or sea trade. Aside from a few hardy souls who collected mussels and urchins from the base of the cliffs, no one really braved the ocean. The nearest port was a day's ride to the south—a much larger town built on the cliffs over a protected bay.

One of the white-haired elders replied. "The western seas are too stormy to make for good passage in the springtime. They'll probably attempt to take one of the three eastern ports big enough to moor an armada."

Andoc nodded. "At least we have a plan of action now. We need to get the tribes who control those three ports allied. Then we'll divide all the forces from the landlocked tribes evenly among them."

"Meren has ties with Erylaan," Jacun said. "I could go there with Varanis, and maybe a couple of the Mereni elders if they're willing."

"My grandfather had family in Dellwyn," Balzoc said. "I'll volunteer to lead a party there and talk to them."

"Very well," Andoc said. "I was planning to go to Venzor and talk with them personally, so I'll make a loop along the coastline and stop at Llanmeer on my way north. There are a few other small villages between the two where I can stop as well."

I pictured the route in my head, and my stomach churned. "I—" My voice caught, and I had to pause to clear my throat. "I should probably go with you, in that case. I was born in one of those villages. Actually… my mother still lives there."

FIVE

I could feel both Andoc's and Senovo's eyes on me, but I didn't dare look at them.

"I'm from Keld," I clarified. "I... can't guarantee that my presence will hold much sway with the leaders, but I do know the people there."

And they knew me. They knew me as an awkward, skinny girl who refused to fit in and claimed to have the spirit of a boy. They knew me as the child who often held herself stiffly, as if in pain, a bruise peeking out here and there from the edge of a sleeve or neckline. Possibly, they knew me as a thief who had stolen boy's clothing from a washing line and run away. The more I thought about it, the more it seemed like Andoc might be better off taking a complete stranger with him to negotiate in Keld.

Fuck.

"All right," Andoc said, after a nearly imperceptible pause. To my immense relief, he moved on without further comment. "High Priest Senovo will join us as well, since he has traveled with me to Venzor before. Jacun, Balzoc—I don't want anyone traveling in parties smaller than three. Find some volunteers to go with you. Not warriors, though. Even though we're confident the attack won't take place for a couple of months, I don't want to draw too heavily on Draebard's defenses."

The meeting broke up soon afterward and I slipped out before anyone could catch me. As I returned to the horse pens, I was in a daze. I had never expected to return to Keld during my lifetime. What in the gods' names had I been thinking?

Burying myself in my work, I resolutely did not think about the conversation I would need to have with Andoc and Senovo. Perhaps I should just tell Andoc that it had been a mistake, and I would only hinder any potential alliance with my home village. I paused in my inventory of the grain stores, chewing my lip.

On the other hand, after Renthro's death, was I really ready to send Andoc and Senovo into the snow-covered landscape without me? No. No, I wasn't. I would have to downplay my discomfort at returning home, and divert any questions they might have about my past. They knew it had been unhappy. There was no reason to dredge up the details.

With that in mind, I pasted on a pleasant expression and returned to the temple at the end of the day, ready to turn aside any attempts at interrogation. I stopped first at the old storage area Senovo had converted into a room for Favian and Frella upon deciding that Favian's tiny sleeping cell was inadequate for two people.

It was empty, so I followed the sound of voices to the refectory, where I found what seemed like the entire temple talking and eating together.

Feldes noticed me first. "Ah! Hello, Horse Mistress. Can I interest you in some supper? We have preserved greens and stewed pork with mayapples."

I forced a smile. "Sounds lovely, thanks," I said, even though my stomach quailed at the thought of food.

He served up a generous plate and handed it to me. Since it would have been suspicious for me to try to avoid him, I sat down across from Senovo, in the seat next to Favian.

Favian looked at me with an expression of combined worry and excitement. "Senovo says you're all going north in a couple of days."

I tamped down the small flash of panic that we were to leave so soon. "That's the plan, certainly."

"I've always wanted to visit Llanmeer," he said. "They say there's a stairway carved right into the cliff, and it leads down to a beach covered in white sand. The water is supposed to be so clear you can see straight down to the bottom, and all the fish swimming around."

"Yes, that's right," I replied.

"You've been there?" Favian asked, only to be distracted when Frella poked him in the arm and asked for more mayapples.

"Once," I told him, "when I was very small. I went with my father to meet someone he was doing business with. I do remember how clear and blue the sea was."

Just like that, I was transported back to that wonderful trip. My father had been a kind and loving parent, if a somewhat indulgent one. Looking back, I wondered if he was trying to make up for his wife's bitterness and quick temper. They had both been unusually old when they'd had me. I think my father was so relieved to have a child at all that he was willing to turn a blind eye to my frequent misbehavior and odd ideas.

I had only gone on a handful of trips with him, but each one had been an amazing adventure... not to mention a wonderful few days of freedom from my mother. I drew myself back to the present with difficulty and smiled at Favian and Frella. "I'll bring you both back some seashells."

"What's a seashell?" Frella asked.

Senovo, who had been watching the exchange quietly until now, spoke up. "The old High Priest had a modest collection of shells, Frella. Small animals in the ocean live inside them for protection, like natural armor. I will show you later."

Frella nodded, wide-eyed.

"Have you ever been to Llanmeer, Elder Brother?" Favian asked.

"I have not," said Senovo.

"But you've been to Venzor before?" I said, remembering Andoc's words.

"Twice, in fact—with Andoc. The first time was not so terribly long after we met. Rhystel was rather insistent, as I recall."

I hid a smile. High Priest Rhystel had been a hopeless meddler. He had apparently decided early on that Andoc would be good for his angry young novice. The old man had been ruthless when it came to pushing the two of them together. "And the second?" I asked.

"It was not long after Chief Volya's son died. He and Andoc were close friends. I believe Andoc was forcibly reminded about the importance of family, and he—understandably—wished to see his mother. He was upset enough that I did not want him to travel alone." Senovo turned his attention to Favian, whose expression had fallen. "Andoc's father also died in an accident when he was about your age."

Favian looked surprised. "I didn't know that."

"It's true," I said. "He fell off a roof while trying to repair a leak during a thunderstorm. Speaking of which, where is Andoc this evening? More meetings?"

"Just so," Senovo said. "Now that there is solid information, the warriors are planning strategy."

It went unsaid that Senovo or I might need to drag Andoc away and spike his wine with sleeping draught, to get him to rest ahead of what was likely to be an arduous journey across the wildlands to Llanmeer. To my relief, the conversation soon turned to other topics. Eiridan had somehow managed to obtain another couple of examples of the cryptic symbols that the Alyrions and their Rhytheeri allies used to transmit information without the use of a verbal message. He invited me to examine them, and in return, I explained the new ideas Limdya had come up with for recording our supply tallies.

When the meal was finished, I excused myself to start packing for the journey. It was something of a thin excuse, but Senovo let it pass—for which I was grateful. I puttered around my hut until nearly midnight before wrapping a cloak around my shoulders and heading out to see if torches were still burning at the meeting house. They were, so I showed myself in and discovered Andoc, Jacun, Balzoc, and several of the other warriors gathered around the table, looking exhausted.

"You'll all come up with better plans after a few hours' sleep," I said to the table at large.

"She's right," Balzoc said to Andoc, scrubbing a hand over his eyes.

There was a muttering of scattered agreement around the table, and everyone got up to go home. I shoved Andoc's walking stick into his hand and chivvied him out the door behind the others.

"Are you really all right with going back to your village?" he asked as we made our slow way toward the temple. "I don't get the impression you have happy memories of the place."

"Of course I'm all right with it," I lied. "Besides, how could I pass up an opportunity to meet your mother?"

The ploy worked. Andoc smiled ruefully in the silver moonlight. "She's one of a kind, that's for certain."

The temple was silent when we arrived. Crenelo was taking the night watch, and he smiled at us and waved us inside. A single candle burned low on the table in Senovo's room, welcoming us even though the room's owner was missing.

"He's gone out again, hasn't he?" I asked in a tone of resignation.

"I guess so," Andoc said, and settled on the edge of the bed with a sigh.

Senovo had paused his forays into the woods while he was looking after Favian and Frella, but once they were settled into the temple, he had started slipping out again. When pressed, he could not explain exactly what it was he hoped to learn from communing with the wild wolves, but he was adamant that there was something important he needed to find out.

"Did you eat?" I asked, diverting my attention back to things I could actually control.

"Yes, I did. I've told you before—you don't stick a bunch of warriors together in a meeting room for hours at a time without providing plenty of food."

I snorted, pleased Andoc was apparently still taking his promise to look after himself seriously. "Good. Come on, in that case. I'm about to fall asleep with my eyes open, and you can't be much better off."

It was the truth—we were both so exhausted that we dropped off in the middle of a quick fumble, Andoc's hand cupping my breast and mine resting intimately over his semi-erect cock. I had half-expected nightmares, but I slept straight through until a chilly, wet nose wormed under the covers next to me, followed by a cold, furry body that quickly warmed in the cozy space. I threw an arm around Senovo and went right back to sleep.

The sun was already up when I blinked awake to find him once again human. Oversleeping provided me with the perfect excuse to hurry out to the horse pens without much conversation. I was starting to feel vaguely guilty about my secrecy regarding my childhood, but I simply couldn't face talking about it right now—not even to them. Soon enough, I thought grimly, we would have *days* of travel with no distractions to be found. Let them try to pry it out of me then.

The final day before we left was a flurry of activity. The trip to Llanmeer, up the coast and then back inland to Venzor, would be almost as long as our journey to Rhyth had been. I decided to bring along a pack horse, which would not only allow us to carry extra supplies, but would also offer us an alternate mount in emergencies, should something happen to one of the other horses.

Andoc's bay gelding had never been quite the same after the terrible fall that had shattered his rider's leg, so I had recently replaced the animal with a Mereni mare I'd traded for last autumn. By Mereni standards, she was rather phlegmatic, though she shared her long legs and astounding turn of speed with the rest of her eastern kin. I'd gotten a good deal on her because she had failed to become pregnant the previous spring despite being bred several times. I had hopes that a different stallion would succeed where the first had failed, but if not, she would still make an exceptional riding horse.

To my pleasant surprise, Andoc seemed to get along better with her than he ever had with the long-suffering bay gelding. The only drawback was her height, but since he now needed assistance to mount even a short horse, it probably didn't make much difference in the grand scheme of things. I was trying to convince him to let me teach her to go down on one knee for mounting, but for now he was still clinging to the possibility that his leg would improve enough to mount normally... unlikely though that was.

I toyed with the idea of riding Nietre, but after Renthro's accident, I eventually decided that I would rather trust myself to Kekenu's steady reliability and familiarity with rough terrain. For Senovo, I chose the same gray mare that he'd ridden to Meren the previous spring.

Once again, Dalon proved his value as my unlikely ally and second in command, as we carefully went over everything that needed doing while I was likely to be gone. The position of Horse Master had always involved as much time spent dealing with village matters as with the horses, and I was still in awe of how effortless my old mentor Jorun had made it appear. By contrast, I felt as though I was forever playing catch-up. I consoled myself with the thought that Jorun had never had to deal with circumstances quite as dire or extraordinary as those Draebard now faced.

With horses and provisions organized for each of the three groups that would head out in the morning, I went to the meeting house, not terribly surprised to find both Andoc and Senovo there with the elders and the others traveling to talk with the tribes controlling the ports. I sat quietly off to the side and listened, trying to take in all the advice the elders were dispensing for conducting successful negotiations.

I had really only been involved in a single treaty negotiation before—the one with the Mereni the previous spring. I had learned quickly, though, that Andoc and Senovo both had a surprisingly adept hand at such things. I was confident that everything would go as well as it could.

To my relief, the elders shooed everyone away to get a good night's sleep before setting out at first light. Senovo seemed distracted as we walked back to the temple, looking out into the winter gloom of evening beyond the edge of the village.

"Are you going out tonight?" I asked, struggling to keep any hint of disapproval or worry from my tone.

"What?" Senovo asked, and forcibly dragged his attention back to me. "Oh. No. Perhaps not. We should all be well-rested for the journey."

Relief made my shoulders slump, and I nodded agreement. I could not explain the sense of unknown peril that increasingly overcame me whenever Senovo left us to join the wild wolves, any more than he could explain what he hoped to learn. It was different from the reactive panic I'd initially felt at the thought of him being alone in the wildlands. That had been an irrational fear for his safety caused by our experience at the hands of the Rhytheeri bounty hunters. This was a fear of… something else. Something that threatened Senovo from within rather than without.

I could not tell for certain if Andoc shared my concerns. He hadn't been much happier about the idea in the beginning than I had. But Andoc had known Senovo longer, and he was also filled with single-minded determination to defend Eburos against the Alyrions at any cost. If Senovo could offer any hint of an advantage in the coming struggle, Andoc would take whatever risk was necessary to grasp it.

As it tended to do at odd moments, the sense of teetering on the edge of something huge and unstoppable washed over me, making me shiver. Andoc wrapped his free arm around my shoulders, and I huddled against him as we continued our slow progress.

The temple was warm and bright. I would need to stop by my hut in the morning to get my saddlebags, but for tonight, there was nothing to draw me away. Frella must have been waiting for us to return, because she ran forward with a childish squeal of excitement as we rounded the corner of the hallway that led to the refectory.

My predictable but inexplicable surge of discomfort as she approached brought me to a standstill in the middle of the hall. As if sensing it, Frella slid to a stop as well, staring at me for a moment before diverting to Andoc and Senovo.

"I made this!" she said with a proud grin, and thrust a vaguely animal-shaped lump of clay up at them. "It's a wolf!"

Andoc took it and made a show of examining it. "Well, now. I think she's captured your likeness quite skillfully, Senovo. Don't you?"

A smile crinkled Senovo's eyes for a moment before he sobered. He took the rough sculpture and crouched down to the little girl's eye level. "Indeed you have, Frella. If the weather is fair tomorrow, Favian can take you to the potter to fire it. Brother Eiridan has some pigments you can use to paint it afterward. I will look forward to seeing it when we get back from our journey."

"I wish you didn't have to go," she said, her face falling. "What if the gods call you away like they did Papa?"

"We will try very hard not to let that happen," said Senovo. "And in the mean time, you will have Favian and all of the others here with you."

Frella appeared to think this over for a minute before nodding, though the frown lines still marred her chubby face. She reached out to reclaim her clay wolf. "I'm going to tell Favian we're visiting the potter tomorrow!" she declared, and ran off in the direction she had come.

Senovo straightened, only for Andoc to reel him in and brush a kiss to his forehead.

"Fatherhood suits you," he explained when Senovo glanced at him, startled.

A faint blush stained the priest's cheeks. "Hardly fatherhood," he demurred.

I wondered for the first time whether parenthood was something Senovo had aspired to, before the choice was forever taken from him at the age of seventeen. The thought jarred, until I reminded myself that just because the idea of having children horrified me, it didn't mean other people wouldn't long for children of their own.

Something settled within my perception—a new facet of the man I loved coming to light before my eyes. Andoc had made it clear on a couple of occasions that he was not averse to having children, though I had never sensed it was a driving desire for him—which was certainly a relief for me, as his bondmate.

But Senovo—upon High Priest Rhystel's death, Senovo had immediately gathered the two surviving acolytes under his wing. And in the months since, his little brood had grown to encompass the transplanted Mereni novices and acolytes, Favian, and more recently, Frella. Now that I thought about it, it was actually surprising that I hadn't put the pieces together before now. Senovo had been denied a family of blood, so he had made his own family of choice.

Unable to help myself, I followed Andoc's example and pulled Senovo into my arms so I could stretch up to place my own kiss on his cheek, making his blush deepen.

"Come on, you two," Andoc said. "We need to rest. And if you keep that up, *rest* is going to be the last thing on my mind."

In truth, we were all tired enough that rest was not a hardship—though we did end up lying in a delicious tangle with Senovo pinned so tightly between us on the bed that he had to wriggle a bit until he could breathe properly—all without a whisper of complaint on his part, of course.

The morning came, as it always did, with little care as to whether I was ready for it or not. The wind was blustery; the temperature, bitter. The sky was clear, however, and promised a day fit for travel, much to everyone's relief. We said our goodbyes at the temple, bundled up, and wandered, bleary-eyed, to the horse pens, where we were joined soon afterward by Jacun, Balzoc, and their traveling companions.

"Say hello to Varanis for us," I teased Jacun. "Oh, and everyone else in Meren, of course."

"Yes, it may be quite cold on the eastern plains," Andoc added helpfully. "I do hope you won't be forced to huddle together in a tent overnight."

"Likewise," Jacun retorted with the hint of a smirk.

Andoc looked around, including everyone in his gaze. "I'm sure I don't have to tell you all to be careful. Watch out for each other, and don't take any unnecessary risks. If you have a bad feeling about something, don't do it."

The others nodded solemnly. Limdya and the boys had been readying our horses as we talked. As she handed Kekenu off to me, I placed a hand on her arm. She looked up, her expression surprised.

"Do me a favor and check in on Favian and Frella when you can," I said. Her face cleared in understanding.

"I will," she promised. "Come back safe."

With a final nod to Dalon, quietly overseeing everything from the background, I mounted up and took the lead rope attached to the pack horse's halter. When everyone was ready, Andoc gestured for us to move out. Kekenu tossed his head and champed at the bit, frisky in the cold. The others followed us. While Jacun and his party soon peeled off to follow the trail leading east toward Meren, Balzoc and the others stayed with us for a good part of the first day before we parted ways.

We were following the track that led north toward the summer pastures, and I was suddenly reminded of that horrible day last spring, after the attack on Draebard, when I had ridden out along this track with most of the surviving apprentices in tow, to find the herd after I stampeded them away from the village in the middle of the night to protect them from the Alyrion soldiers.

That had been the day when everything began to change. Some things for the better, some things for the worse... but all told, very little remained the same.

I shook my head to dislodge that line of thought. The wind tugged at my scarf and the hood of my winter cloak. I hoped the sun would warm things as midday approached, but this was going to be a grueling journey regardless, for horses and humans alike. I had packed as much feed for the animals as it was reasonable for us to carry, but they would have to find most of their fodder by pawing through the snow and ice whenever we stopped and made camp.

I'd also brought along quite a bit more food for the humans than I would have during the warmer parts of the year. Not only was it quite possible that we would be delayed by weather and trapped somewhere far from the nearest village, but we would also require extra food simply to keep ourselves warm.

I tried to keep an eye on the others as we rode. So far, no one appeared to be more than vaguely uncomfortable. It would be all too easy for the cold to take hold in one of us, though, slowly draining the strength from his spirit before anyone noticed. When the flat pastureland gave way to rolling hills that intermittently protected us from the wind, I gave a sigh of relief as the sun finally began to warm my shoulders and face.

We stopped briefly to let the horses break through the ice on a stream and drink, while we ate fatty pemmican and drank from the wineskins we had kept warm against our bodies, under our cloaks. The afternoon passed in a slightly more pleasant fashion than the morning, and before the sun had traveled halfway to the western horizon, we arrived at the fork in the track that would lead Balzoc's group north to the port of Dellwyn, and us northeast to Llanmeer.

Andoc turned his mare to face the others. "Safe journey and good fortune," he told them. "And remember, no unnecessary risks."

Balzoc flashed a quick, tight smile. "The same to you, Chief. I, for one, have no intention of joining the gods before I have a chance at those tin-plated cowards who think they can crush us under their heels like so much garbage."

The others nodded, determination hardening their features. After a final round of goodbyes, Senovo, Andoc and I headed down the trail toward Llanmeer, intent on gaining more distance before the short winter day forced us to stop and make camp. I led the way on Kekenu, who had grown up in a wild herd and had more experience with the poor footing.

The snow here in the hills had blown into drifts, with some places nearly bare and others almost deep enough for the little horse to flounder. After the first unexpected deep spot, he slowed of his own accord, stepping tentatively whenever the snow grew deep. I let the pack horse I was leading have plenty of play in the rope, and the others followed in our footsteps.

Riding over such uneven footing was surprisingly hard work, and by the time the sun had dropped low in the sky, I'd gone from being cold to being hot under my heavy clothing.

"Is anyone else sweating?" I called to the others.

"Yeah, a bit," Andoc replied. "We need to get camp set up and a fire going before the temperature starts to fall after dark."

We immediately started looking for a wooded spot to stop for the night. There were patches of trees in the hills, but it took us longer than we would have liked to find a grove large enough to provide deadfall for a fire and a decent windbreak. I was shivering again by the time Senovo got the fire going. I had to pause and warm myself in front of the flames before I could finish untacking the horses and get them all picketed, where they could forage under the snow in a wide circle around the trees to which they were tethered.

It was not ideal, since someone would have to keep an ear peeled throughout the night in case any of them became entangled in the ropes. But hobbling them would prevent them from pawing the snow away to expose the dead grass underneath, and I didn't dare leave them loose. Kekenu would *probably* stay nearby, and the others would *probably* stay with him, but I wasn't willing to risk our lives on the strength of *probably*.

Finally, with the dark of evening barely held at bay by the flickering blaze of the campfire, the three of us wrestled the double-walled hide tent over a convenient, low-hanging branch and staked it into place as best we could with the ground frozen solid.

"Food," Andoc decreed. "Lots of it. Preferably hot."

We warmed pemmican by the fire, and melted snow in a metal pot until it was nearly boiling. We poured half of this into cups to steep dried herbs and conifer needles for tea. The rest we used to boil dried meat for a weak soup.

With the fire baking my front and the winter night nipping at my back as I ate and drank my fill, I was not precisely *comfortable*, but I was not miserable either. The others also seemed to have weathered the first day of travel without too much difficulty, though I imagined that Andoc's leg must have been aching something fierce.

Senovo appeared increasingly withdrawn, until Andoc finally stretched out and nudged him with a foot. "Still with us, *amadi?*"

Senovo started faintly, and refocused on his surroundings with a blink. "Yes. Forgive me. I was just thinking that perhaps I should venture out tonight while you two are sleeping. There may be different packs of wolves this far from the village."

I swallowed a surge of disquiet. Andoc frowned as he mulled the statement over.

"While I cannot stop you, and would not presume to try, I... would rather you didn't," he said carefully, and I held my breath, waiting for Senovo's response.

The priest's gaze turned inward for a moment, a furrow forming between his brows only to smooth over a few heartbeats later. "Very well," he said, and I breathed again. He glanced at both of us before continuing, "I am aware that it disturbs you both, and for that, I am sorry. However, I must ask for your trust. I can only tell you that this is important. Something... compels me to pursue it. I cannot tell you why."

"It's the *compulsion* part that bothers me," I said quietly.

"Agreed," said Andoc.

Senovo smiled, though it did not reach his eyes in the orange firelight. "It is not an irresistible compulsion. Not like the compulsion to change when I have fought the wolf for too long. More of a conviction that to do nothing is a mistake."

I chewed on my lip for a moment, debating. "Perhaps... you could change during the day, and travel with us as the wolf. Then you would be able to hear or smell if we came near any new wolves during the journey."

Andoc's jaw worked back and forth as he considered it, but Senovo nodded, looking thoughtful. "Perhaps," he said. "Wolves are nocturnal hunters for the most part, but I would be able to scent their dens and territorial marks if we came close enough." He quirked an eyebrow. "It would probably be more comfortable to travel on four legs as well."

Andoc looked at him frankly. "I still don't like the idea of us being separated in unfamiliar surroundings."

"As the wolf, I can track you easily enough." Senovo paused in thought for a moment. "But perhaps we could agree that I would inform you before straying too far afield."

"That seems like a reasonable compromise," Andoc said after a short pause. He smiled, but it was forced. "Though I suspect you of merely looking for an excuse to wear your fur coat while we shiver in the cold."

"Merely a happy side effect, I assure you," said Senovo wryly. "Now, however, rather than be cold, let us warm each other up, inside the tent."

Andoc gaze turned smoldering. "Yes. Let's do."

SIX

Despite the harsh conditions and my worries over Senovo's proposed wanderings, desire trickled through my belly. My voice turned low and hoarse as I said, "Someone needs to keep an ear open for the horses to make sure none of them get tangled up."

Andoc smirked at me. "Then I suppose we'll have to make sure you stay quiet."

The desire pooled, growing warm and heavy even as I protested. "Hey! You two are every bit as loud as I am."

He leaned on an elbow against his log and raised an eyebrow, still watching me with a gaze almost as hot as the fire. "Maybe I just like picturing you with your mouth full."

Across from us, Senovo made a small noise, even as a pulse of wetness threatened to soak my smallclothes. "*Tent*," I said, rising and heading there myself. I did not need to look behind me to know that the other two were following.

The tent was snug for three people, which suited me perfectly at the moment. The two heavy hides forming the walls trapped an airspace in between, keeping the inside warm and preventing condensation from forming on the inner wall once our bodies heated the small space. We had dragged in conifer boughs to insulate ourselves from the cold ground, and blankets lay piled in a heap, ready to form a cozy nest for the three of us.

I crawled inside and dragged off my boots, breeches, and smalls, leaving everything above the waist on. The cold immediately bit into my exposed flesh, and I shivered. The others followed—Andoc somewhat awkwardly, with his bad leg. He closed the flap behind us, plunging us into darkness. It felt protected inside. Private, almost den-like. I wondered if Senovo appreciated that quality.

Before I could decide whether to ask him, Andoc was manhandling me to lie between the two of them, but with my head facing their feet. Senovo busied himself wrapping and draping coverings around and over us until everyone was swaddled from head to toe. I was completely muffled under the heavy furs, warming quickly with the heat thrown off by three bodies. My head rested on Andoc's upper thigh, my arm thrown across Senovo's hips a few inches away, and I moaned as the possibilities became apparent.

A thought intruded. "The horses?" I asked.

Andoc's reply was muted, and I realized his head must still be uncovered. "I'll listen," he said, "and we'll check them when we're done."

His callused hand slid over my lower back and buttocks, and just like that I was gone. He urged me to lift one leg and straddle Senovo's face. Senovo helped position me where he wanted me and rearranged the blankets so I was still covered — trapped with him under the heavy folds. The tip of his tongue played along the edges of my cunt, a touch so light it seemed barely there.

My breath escaped into the stifling blackness under the blankets, and I scrabbled at the ties of his breeches and undergarments. Beside us, Andoc's hand left my arse and I could feel the movement as he worked on his own fastenings. As soon as I could yank Senovo's clothing open and out of the way enough so that I could get to his limp, moleskin-soft prick, I wormed one hand over to Andoc's body and was rewarded when my fingers encountered his own thick shaft, hard and pulsing under my touch.

My mouth watered at the feast set before me, even while a quiver ran up my spine as Senovo lazily explored between my legs. With a hand on his hip, I urged Andoc to scoot up a little bit further. He did, and molded himself to Senovo's side, leaving both cocks within easy reach of my hands and mouth.

The smell of sex grew thick and heady inside our little cocoon, making me feel as drunk as if I'd consumed an entire wineskin on my own. I fell on Senovo's prick, licking and nuzzling, while simultaneously pumping Andoc's throbbing length in my hand.

Senovo slowly began to stiffen under my lips and tongue, until I could wrap my other hand around his base, teasing and stroking with a gentler touch than I was using on Andoc. When he was hard enough, I took him into my mouth and sucked — rewarded by the gasp of pleasure that puffed against my own wet, sensitive flesh. His tongue returned a moment later, sliding deeper to part my inner lips and tease at my pulsing nub. I moaned around him.

I fell headfirst into the dizzy, weightless feeling of being muffled beneath the heavy blankets. Senovo slowly drove me mad with his clever tongue, even as I tried to return the favor with mine. Andoc was a hot, thick weight in my other hand, his shaft growing slick under my fingers as seed dribbled slowly from his slit.

As soon as Senovo was completely hard, I shifted so I could swallow the head of Andoc's cock instead, pumping Senovo in my hand while chasing the salty taste of Andoc's excitement.

When Andoc's fingers tangled in my short hair and urged me down so the head of his cock pressed at the entrance to my throat, I shuddered and nearly came all over Senovo's face. Andoc's strong hand guided me along the length of his shaft with slow, unrelenting movements, while I echoed his rhythm on Senovo's prick with my own hand. Senovo's tongue circled my engorged flesh, and I whined around the thick cock stretching my lips wide.

Andoc pressed deeply again. I struggled to take him, loving the feeling of powerlessness—of being filled and used while Senovo pleasured me at the same time. I gasped in disappointment when Andoc pulled me up and off, but it was short-lived. The guiding hand eased me back over to Senovo, and pressed me down onto his less generously endowed prick until I was taking him all the way, my nose brushing the downy thatch of soft pubic hair at the base.

Senovo hummed in appreciation, and rewarded me with a slow lick over my throbbing nub with the flat of his tongue. My release rose once again, only to subside, hovering just out of reach. I went pliant, letting Andoc guide me back and forth between the two of them, filling my mouth with first one stiff cock, and then the other. A study in opposites, Senovo's body grew soft and relaxed under me, while Andoc's muscles corded with tension as his climax approached. When he was close, the fingers of Andoc's free hand returned to my lower back, only to trail down the crease of my buttocks and toy with my puckered opening.

Andoc's other hand urged me down his shaft until I was taking him deeper than I'd ever managed before. I came explosively, followed an instant later by Andoc, who spurted down my throat with a rough groan. I swallowed around him again and again, shuddering as Senovo lapped up my release. His gentle licking and nibbling drew a final few twitches from my spent sex.

Andoc eased me off of his softening prick. I fumbled around with heavy limbs that didn't want to work properly, until I could get at Senovo's again. He was still half-hard, and we nuzzled each other lazily for a while, enjoying the warmth and coziness of our protected little nest as Andoc stroked whatever parts of us he could reach.

Eventually, Senovo's movements tailed off into the deep, rhythmic breathing that signified peaceful sleep, and I was right on the edge of dozing myself. I could have happily fallen asleep right there, with my head pillowed in the crease of Senovo's thigh, but once again strong hands grasped my shoulders and guided me up until I was pointing the right way.

Senovo mumbled a protest, but fell right back asleep once I was settled next to him. My hair was sticking out in every direction as my head emerged from the blankets.

"Horses," I murmured, trying to muster the energy to get up and pull my breeches and boots back on so I could check them.

"I'll go," Andoc said quietly, pressing a kiss to my neck.

I drifted into slumber barely a moment later. When I awoke, it was almost morning, and Senovo lay awake next to us, watching the two of us sleep.

"One of you should have woken me for a watch," I said through a yawn. Beside me, Andoc slept on, oblivious.

"We will tonight," he promised.

"Everything all right?" I asked.

"All quiet. Though it smells like there may be more snow blowing in."

"Ugh," I complained. "I guess it shouldn't come as a surprise."

"I can lead the way if it starts to get bad. The wolf can find a safe path, even in poor conditions."

"That's a good idea." I stretched, trying not to jostle the others in the confined space of the tent. "You'd better wait to change until we have the horses tacked up and ready to go, though. Kekenu and the gray mare have seen you before, but I don't want the other two to spook and snap the picket ropes."

"Very well."

I stretched and went rummaging for my discarded clothes and boots so I could get dressed under the covers. When the commotion failed to wake our fearless leader, I yanked the blankets off of him and opened the tent flap to let the gray morning light—and, more to the point, the frigid air—inside. Andoc jerked awake with a mumbled curse, and I exchanged a sly grin with Senovo.

"You're learning," said the priest.

Once Andoc was more or less coherent, we explained the plan to him. He ran a hand over his face to clear the cobwebs and nodded, probably as relieved as I was that the weather conditions would keep Senovo close to us today.

We readied ourselves as best we could and ate a large breakfast. It was, perhaps, not quite as cold as it had been the previous morning when we left Draebard, but Senovo was right about the sharp tang of snow carried on the blustery wind. Scarcely had we left the campsite with the wolf trotting happily ahead of us on broad, snowshoe-like paws, when the first flakes started to fall.

Settling in for an unpleasant day, we huddled in our saddles and followed doggedly behind. I led the way on Kekenu, ponying the gray mare beside me, while Andoc hung back a bit with his Mereni mare and the packhorse. Both horses watched the strange predator nervously for quite a while before finally settling down. We stopped for a midday meal in the lee of an eroded hillside, feeding scraps of dried meat and pemmican to the wolf as the three of us huddled together for warmth.

True to his word, Senovo led us unerringly through the blowing snow when the storm picked up in the afternoon. It was a relief when, late in the day, patches of blue sky appeared in the northwest, heralding the return of calmer weather. Unfortunately, the back edge of the storm brought with it a bone-chilling cold. The weak sun had not yet touched the western horizon when Andoc called a halt.

"We need a fire," he called from behind me, and gestured at a relatively protected copse of trees off to our left when I turned to look at him.

I nodded agreement and whistled. The wolf stopped, sniffing the air for a moment before trotting back to join us. We made our way carefully down the side of the hill to the campsite. Once under the protection of the branches, Senovo shook the clinging snow from his heavy coat and plopped down on his haunches.

"Do you get the impression that we're on our own when it comes to setting up camp?" Andoc asked dryly.

I snorted in amusement despite my numb fingers and toes. "I think he's just waiting for someone to get him some clothes, actually."

"Maybe so," Andoc agreed, amused as well. "Still, I at least want to get the fire going before he changes back."

"Agreed," I said. "We can tie the horses up for a few minutes. I'll gather the wood, you get the kindling ready."

Between us, we got a decent fire going using deadfall and a pinch of Senovo's fire-starting powder. I dragged Senovo's clothing and boots out of his saddlebag and held them out near the flames to warm them. Sure enough, as soon as he had something to wear close at hand, the wolf padded over to the fire and shifted.

Senovo wavered at the shock of fresh snow against his bare skin, but caught himself on one hand and one knee. I quickly threw his robes over his shoulders and steadied him while Andoc handed him stockings and boots. "Thank you," he said hoarsely. "Well. That was certainly not the most enjoyable experience I've ever had."

"Just like old times, huh," Andoc said, as he steadied him from the other side, bracing himself with his walking stick.

"I'll put a blanket or something down next time," I promised. "Or you can just wait to shift until we have the tent up."

Senovo shivered and allowed us to help him down onto a fallen log, where he quickly pulled on breeches, stockings, and heavy boots. Once I laid his winter cloak across his shoulders, he sighed in relief. "That's better. Forgive me, it's only a momentary discomfort. No cause for concern. Now, let me help you get set up for the night."

We finished making camp with frequent breaks to hold our hands in front of the crackling flames. The temperature continued to plummet, and it took far longer to warm ourselves up under the blankets inside the tent than it had the night before. True to his word, Senovo woke me in the middle of the night to take the final shift watching over the horses. We were a slightly dispirited crew when we emerged into the bitter morning light, facing, as we did, at least two and possibly three more days of steady travel to reach Llanmeer.

The third day was clear but cold, and by the time the sun had reached its zenith, we entered an area that had seen far less snowfall. With the way relatively clear, the wolf began to wander, darting off onto side trails only to reappear a few minutes later. At first, my heart pounded every time I lost sight of him, and Kekenu flicked his ears back in confusion as my muscles tensed unconsciously. About the fifth or sixth time, though, I felt Andoc's eyes on me and turned to meet his gaze.

"Trust him, *caradi*," said Andoc. "He gave us his word he wouldn't go far."

I nodded hesitantly and took a deep breath of icy air, letting it out slowly. Senovo had promised. I trusted him. It was the middle of winter, and we were the only ones foolish enough to be out traveling. There were no bounty hunters hiding in the woods. I tried to let the tension flow out of my body and focus on the trail ahead.

True to his word, Senovo did not wander terribly far, and checked back in with us every so often. Though Andoc and I were exhausted and chilled by the end of the day, we had also made good progress toward our destination. The hills had leveled out onto a flat plain over the course of the afternoon, allowing us to quicken the pace, since there was only a shallow covering of snow on the trail.

I was secretly relieved, because this open plain was not good wolf habitat. As the country grew flatter, Senovo's side trips ended. He loped along next to us, stopping only to dig into the burrow of an occasional unfortunate rodent. On the negative side, there was no shelter to be had for our camp that night, and only scrubby brush to burn. In the absence of any convenient tree branches, we jammed tent poles in whatever crevices we could find and braced them with piles of rocks around the bases. We made Senovo wait to shift back to human form until we were all inside, but even with the three of us huddled under the blankets, it was cold. Little blasts of icy air wormed past the flaps of the tent opening and under the walls every time the wind shifted.

I was also nervous about the horses, tied as they were to shrubs that would not withstand a sudden jerk from a large animal. I would have felt better if we could watch them constantly, but we'd quickly run out of fuel for the fire, and trying to stay outside all night without heat would be the height of foolishness. The result was that I slept poorly even when one of the others was on watch, jerking awake at the slightest noise.

Indeed, my fears came to pass as morning approached. I was abruptly wide awake at the first sound of pounding hooves and startled snorts, even before Andoc grabbed my shoulder.

"Senovo," I said sharply. "Get up! Something's wrong outside!"

Senovo blinked into awareness almost immediately, and the three of us crawled out into the bitter darkness. An indigo wash of false dawn painted the eastern sky, and there was just enough starlight to see by. Kekenu's irregular white patches caught my eye first, still safely tied to his picket. The gray mare was a ghostly form nearby, and after a moment I made out the darker shadow that was the pack horse. All three were on full alert, heads up and staring into the distance.

I pointed to the place where Andoc's mare had been. The shrub was gone. "The Mereni mare took off," I said. "She's probably dragging her tether behind her. *Shit.* Right—I need you both to stay calm and quiet. Andoc, go catch the pack horse and hold onto him. Senovo, take the gray mare. Don't let either of them get loose, whatever happens."

Andoc grabbed up his walking stick and immediately hobbled toward the pack horse, as Senovo crossed to his mare. My heart was pounding, but I crossed to Kekenu with a confident stride and scratched his forehead as he crowded up to me.

"Easy there, old friend. Let's see if she'll come back to us on her own in a minute. If not, I might need your help." After a few moments of listening, I heard the distant sound of approaching hoof beats. "Hold on!" I called to the others. "Do *not* let those horses get away from you!"

The chestnut mare came tearing out of the darkness, her picket rope flopping and jerking behind her, the scrub bush bouncing along at its end. In her mind, the broken shrub was chasing her, occasionally bumping her hind legs and haunches, terrifying her further. The other horses danced around and jerked against their handlers, the instinct to flee after their frightened herd mate a strong one. To my relief, the mare did not charge right through our midst, but circled the edge of the camp instead.

Unfortunately, she showed no sign of slowing down or stopping. I gritted my teeth and led Kekenu over to his own bush so I could unfasten the tether. Then, I quickly looped the picket rope around his neck and tied it into a pair of reins. After stuffing the free end of the long rope under my belt to keep it from flopping or dragging on the ground, I grabbed a hank of Kekenu's generous mane and vaulted onto his broad back.

"Hold those horses, both of you!" I repeated, and sent off a quick prayer that Andoc with his bad leg and Senovo with his relative lack of horse experience would be up to the task.

Kekenu half-reared and I gripped with my knees, gathering the reins in hands already going numb from the cold. I urged him around, setting off after the chestnut mare. I suspected the frantic horse would continue to gallop in wide circles around the camp, her instinct to flee from the thing chasing her at odds with her instinct to stay near the other horses. As long as we could keep them from getting loose and joining her in headlong flight, we still had a chance to salvage the situation.

With this in mind, I circled closer around the camp, trying to catch the sound of the mare's hooves over Kekenu's steady hoof beats and rhythmic breathing. Eventually, I heard her coming our way again and craned around until I saw her silhouetted against the light cover of snow. I guided Kekenu to run parallel to her, gradually edging closer. Normally, the stocky pinto horse would not have had a prayer of keeping pace with her, but the mare had been running flat out for several minutes now and was beginning to tire.

I urged Kekenu on, hoping desperately that the footing held no surprises for us. I just needed to get close to her long enough to reach over and grab the dragging picket rope. As it happened, the mare's herding instinct soon had her crowding in next to us, and Kekenu snorted as the bouncing, tumbling brush threatened his own legs and haunches.

"I'll fix it, Kekenu, I promise," I said, leaning over precariously to grab for the rope hanging from the mare's halter. "Just trust me for another few seconds…"

My fingers were stiff and numb, but after a bit of fumbling they closed around the heavy length of cord almost by chance. I straightened on Kekenu's back, tether in hand. Now came the tricky part—the mare was in a complete frenzy, all of her training forgotten, and as soon as I slowed Kekenu, the broken shrub would be bouncing around practically under his legs. I had no saddle or stirrups to brace against if he panicked as well, or if the mare fought against the rope and tried to break free.

With a deep breath, I sat up straight and deepened my seat, slowing Kekenu to a less frantic pace. At the same time, I tugged the mare's head toward us with little jerks, trying to shift her balance and disengage her hindquarters. To my relief, her haunches swung away, forcing her pace to slow as she scrambled sideways, still trying to escape the bush.

"*Whoa*," I said softly, and Kekenu slid to an abrupt halt. I felt him shudder and jump in place as the brush hit his hindquarters, but I was already leaping from his back. I let the mare's rope slide through my hands until I could set myself, knees bent and feet spaced widely, one in front of the other. I tightened my grip just as I ran out of rope, and the sudden pressure on the halter jerked the mare's head around.

The mass of scrubby wood hit my back and I stumbled forward a step, but the mare had already whirled to face me. Seeing the dreaded shrub, she immediately began to scramble backward and I followed her, letting her move but not allowing her to turn around so she could run again. Kekenu trailed behind us, the end of his rope still tucked loosely in my belt. After the mare had dragged me maybe thirty paces, she finally came to a stop, nostrils flaring with every breath. Sweat dripped from her heavy coat.

"Are we done now?" I asked, a bit out of breath myself. Behind me, Kekenu snorted and sidled up to nudge at my shoulder. "Brave boy," I praised.

The mare was still shaking, steam rising from her body as the first light of dawn crept across the snow-covered plain. I fumbled in my boot for a knife, keeping a close eye on her. As quickly as I could, I sawed through the tether and let the shrub fall to the ground behind me. Kekenu immediately reached down and shoved the offending piece of scrub with his nose, rolling it across the snowy ground. At the end of the rope, the mare spooked and danced backward another couple of steps.

"Very helpful, Kekenu," I groused, and moved hand over hand up the rope until I could get to the mare's head. "Right. Let me rephrase this for you, mare. *We are done now*. Come on."

I gestured Kekenu forward and pulled his rope free from my belt, so I could lead one horse in each hand. It was light enough now for me to look around and locate our sad little camp, a surprising distance away. I sighed, and trudged off to rejoin the others.

It took long enough to get back that the sun was already peeking over the horizon when I was close enough to hail them.

"Well, that was fun," I called. "We should start every morning like this!"

Andoc and Senovo were both dutifully holding onto their respective horses. With the excitement over, Andoc left the pack horse and hobbled toward me, his brow thunderous. "*What in the gods' names were you thinking?*" he demanded.

SEVEN

My temper flared. "I was thinking that it would be good if I could stop your mare from running herself to the point of collapse and dying of exhaustion in the cold. What did you think I was thinking? Now go get a blanket for her before she catches a chill."

"You could have been killed!" Andoc snapped.

I glared at him. "Says the man who fought people with swords for a living, up until recently. We are in the middle of nowhere in the middle of winter, in case you hadn't noticed. We can't exactly afford to lose a horse!"

"We have an extra horse!" Andoc was nearly in my face now.

"We have a *pack horse*! Which would you prefer to leave behind, the food, or the blankets and tent hides?" I made no attempt to hide my sarcasm.

"We could have made it to Llanmeer just fine, and gotten another horse there!"

I growled in frustration. "Or we could try *not losing the horses we already have*!"

Senovo cleared his throat, and we both turned to look at him, suddenly realizing that we were essentially shouting in each other's faces. "I think perhaps the cold and lack of rest is contributing to this argument," he said in a level voice. "Andoc, Carivel trusts us to do our jobs as we see fit. It behooves us to trust her to do hers." His eyes settled on me. "Carivel, from our vantage point, what you just did appeared a rather risky undertaking. I would urge you to remember that if I travel as the wolf, I do not need a horse, and therefore we do, in fact, have an extra one."

My jaw worked, a thread of embarrassment weaving through my haze of righteous indignation. I glanced quickly at Andoc to see how he was reacting. He coughed, and looked to the side.

"When you galloped off into the dark, we couldn't see what was happening. I was frightened for your safety, *caradi*," he said quietly.

I swallowed, and looked away as well. "The mare would have run until she collapsed. She's a good horse; I didn't want to lose her. I didn't really think, beyond that."

Senovo looked between us and nodded. "Very well, both of you. No harm is done. Perhaps, in the future, a bit more communication will be warranted during any unexpected crises. For now, though, I'll just go and get you that blanket."

I met Andoc's eyes warily. "I need to walk these horses. Are we… all right?"

Andoc stepped forward and pulled me in for a deep kiss. When we parted, he stared down at me with searching eyes. "I couldn't bear to lose you, Carivel. You should know that, if you don't already."

I swallowed the lump in my throat and nodded, thinking of the handful of times when I had feared I would lose him, or Senovo. "I understand. I'll try to weigh the risks more carefully from now on."

Senovo returned with a heavy woolen blanket, which I threw over the sweaty mare's back and neck. "Do you need any help?" he asked.

I shook my head. "No, I'll see to them. Assuming you're traveling as the wolf again today, Andoc should ride the gray mare. This one's already exhausted, and the sun's barely up."

"All right. We'll take care of the camp," Andoc said. "What about you? Are you warm enough?"

My smile was wan. "Nothing like a nice stupid argument to get the blood flowing first thing in the morning. I'm fine. And good job on keeping the other horses from running off, by the way. Otherwise we really *would* have been in a mess."

Andoc shuddered at the thought. "That we would. You'd better get those animals moving now, I suppose. We'll bring you some food in a few minutes."

⤙⚜⤚

The runaway and its aftermath delayed us quite a bit that morning. We also had to maintain a slow pace thanks to the exhausted mare. It was early afternoon on the following day when the port town of Llanmeer finally appeared in the distance, huddled near the edge of the rocky cliffs overlooking a large, protected cove on Eburos' eastern coast.

Llanmeer had been one of the largest settlements on the island a generation ago, but the dearth of trade between the north and the south in recent years had undercut its prosperity. I still had fond memories of journeying here as a very young child with my father—some of them crystal clear, some clouded by the passage of time until they were more feelings than true recollections.

"I didn't ever really expect to see this place again," I said, as we joined the main road leading into the center of town. "Have either of you been here before?"

"No, this is my first time," Senovo said, having changed back to human form at midday in anticipation of our arrival.

"I've visited twice as part of Volya's contingent," said Andoc. "It's been a few years, though."

"More than a few for me," I admitted. "I was a very small child at the time."

Ahead of us, people were taking notice of our arrival. It was a fine, clear day, and several folks were out and about on various errands as we rode into the main part of the settlement.

"Hello, strangers!" hailed an older man, straightening from a workbench where he had been splitting a log into fence rails. "Bit of an odd time of year to be traveling, isn't it? What's your business in Llanmeer?"

The three of us rode up and stopped, allowing Andoc to take the lead. "Hello there. I am Andoc, Chief of Draebard. This is our High Priest, Senovo, and our Horse Mistress, Carivel. We have come here to meet with the leaders of Llanmeer about an imminent threat from the Alyrion Empire."

The man examined us for a long moment. His eyes raked over my body in that searching way I'd come to hate so much over the past few months, ever since my birth sex had been revealed. "Chief of Draebard, eh?" he asked, returning his attention to Andoc. "And a woman in charge of the horses? What happened to Volya? And old Jorun?"

My heart clenched at the unexpected mention of my dead mentor, and I had a sudden flash of worry that we would be turned away, unable to convince the Llanmeeri that we were who we said we were.

Andoc shook his head, his expression grim. "Horse Master Jorun was killed during the Alyrion attack on Draebard last spring. Chief Volya was murdered by Rhytheeri assassins after we left the meeting of the northern tribes in Rhyth a few months ago."

The man's eyebrow rose. "Is that right?" he asked. "Well, then. I suppose you'd better talk to my brother. He's the Chief of Llanmeer. I expect you'll be needing a place to stay, as well."

"That would be appreciated," said Senovo.

Our new acquaintance's attention moved to the priest, and his expression grew speculative. "And you're Draebard's High Priest? The one they say is a shape-shifter?"

"I am."

"Huh. Well, it's an honor to meet you. I guess you must have something pretty serious to talk about, at that, since you were willing to travel all this way in the dead of winter. Let me call my wife to show you the way to the inn, while I go track down my brother and the rest of the council. I'm Reardon, by the way. Pleasure to make your acquaintance."

"Thank you, Reardon," I said. "Our horses have had a hard journey. Are there pens at the inn, or should we take them to your Horse Master for keeping?"

"You can keep them at the inn if you prefer," Reardon said, still looking slightly askance at me. "Dereen will take you there." I nodded, and Reardon stuck his head inside the wooden structure behind him. "Dereen! Come out here for a minute, woman."

A few moments later, a round-faced woman emerged, drying her hands on a linen apron before tucking them under her arms. "What is it, Reardon? You're letting the cold in." Her bright eyes flickered to the collection of strangers on her doorstep. "Oh! Hello."

Reardon cleared his throat. "We have important visitors from Draebard, Dereen. Get your cloak and show them to the inn while I find Brinn. They can come to the meeting hall once they're settled."

"Yes, of course," Dereen told us with a pleasant smile. "Let me just take the soup off the fire and I'll be right back."

Once she returned, Reardon went off to find the town's leaders, and we followed the cheerful, gray-haired woman to a large building two streets over. We thanked her and got directions to the central square and the meeting hall before sending her back to her neglected soup. Looking at the bright red painted double doors of the rooming house, I realized with a jolt that this was the very same inn where I had stayed with my father. I could not specifically remember the stoop-shouldered man who greeted us, but he was certainly old enough to have been the proprietor at that time.

The realization sent a very strange and confusing flood of feelings running through me. To distract myself, I tried to focus on practicalities. Andoc and Senovo took our saddlebags, while I accompanied the boy to the pens behind the building with our horses. It would be a relief to get a night or two of decent rest without having to worry about the animals' safety — and no doubt they would appreciate a day or two of good feed that they didn't have to paw out from under a layer of snow and ice.

"See that you keep a close eye on the chestnut mare," I told the boy, who nodded, wide-eyed. "She's had a rough time of it on this trip. And don't let the pinto hog the others' feed."

Once I was satisfied with the horses' care, I headed into the inn. It was blissfully warm inside. I sighed in relief as I drew my hood back and opened the fastenings on my cloak. The proprietor waved me toward a room at the back, where I found Andoc and Senovo stowing our belongings.

Andoc looked up at my approach. "Horses all settled? If so, we should probably head for the meeting house. It wouldn't do to keep Chief Brinn and his council waiting."

We bundled up again and made our way to the center of town, though we ended up being the ones forced to wait. Still, before too much time had passed, Reardon returned with a slightly older, slightly shorter man who was obviously his brother, the Llanmeeri Chieftain.

"Chief Brinn," Andoc said. He braced himself with his walking stick so he could bow, maintaining eye contact with the older man. Senovo and I followed suit.

Brinn dipped his head in acknowledgement, and examined Andoc closely. "I remember you," he said. "You came with old Volya a couple of times for trade negotiations." He gestured to Andoc's leg. "Looks like you've had some hard fortune since then."

Senovo spoke up smoothly. "Andoc was injured while trying to protect our late Chief, during an attack by assassins on the road home from the meetings in Rhyth last summer. Unfortunately, several people were killed in the battle, including the Chief himself."

"And the assassins, too, I assume?" Brinn asked.

"Yes," I said, "thanks to some timely help from members of another tribe who came upon the battle by chance."

It was simpler not to mention that it had been the Mereni, whose acceptance of women in positions of power tended not to sit well with more traditional tribes. Senovo flicked a nearly imperceptible expression of approval in my direction, and I lifted an eyebrow in return. I'd spent too much time with him this past year not to have *some* of his devious nature rub off on me.

"Fortunate," Chief Brinn observed. "Of course, I was at that meeting as well. I'm afraid those of us who stayed after Volya stormed out did not hear any reports about the attack on your contingent, or his death. I must say, though, that your Chief did not win himself many friends in Rhyth."

Andoc nodded. "Volya felt very… passionately… about the situation with Alyrios. That passion extended to the southern tribes who have allied with them. Now, however, I am more concerned about the direct threat from the Empire than I am about Rhyth."

"You have news," Brinn said, not phrasing it as a question. "The elders will be along shortly. Come, let us go inside and make ourselves comfortable."

Brinn hesitated when his eyes reached me, and I felt the familiar flush of irritation at people who could not simply accept me for what I was and move on. No doubt Brinn was debating whether to allow a *female* into the meeting hall. I met his eyes with a level gaze of my own, waiting to see if he would make an issue of it openly.

Senovo's sharp eyes took in the moment's pause. "Horse Mistress Carivel is a respected member of Draebard's leadership, Chief Brinn," he said. "Incidentally, she is also Chief Andoc's bondmate."

I could see Brinn weighing the new information—see the moment he decided it was not worth pressing the matter. My gratitude to Senovo for smoothing over the awkwardness warred with renewed annoyance at the fact that I was only here on sufferance, now that Brinn saw me as Andoc's *woman*. I clenched my jaw to keep from grinding my teeth and pasted on a neutral expression.

We went into the building, where we were joined before long by a group of old men, who greeted us with varying degrees of warmth and arrayed themselves around the heavy, rectangular table dominating the main hall. To my surprise, at the last minute, a blond-haired man in High Priest's robes hurried in. While he was not as young as Senovo, he was considerably younger than any other High Priest I had ever met or heard of. His eyes were very blue and very clear. Something about his gaze, when it landed on me, made me feel as if I had been laid bare.

"Elders," Chief Brinn intoned. "High Priest Thadrik. Thank you for coming on such short notice. Our guests have traveled from Draebard with important news of the Empire."

Andoc stood. "I appreciate your willingness to meet with us today. I am Chief Andoc, former First Warrior of Chief Volya of Draebard. I have come with High Priest Senovo and Horse Mistress Carivel to warn you of an impending naval attack on one of Eburos's northeastern ports by the Alyrion Empire. According to my spies, the Emperor has commanded his ships to sail for either Dellwyn, Llanmeer, or Erylaan as soon as the winter storms subside in the Eastern Sea."

There was a round of surprised muttering as the elders reacted. Meanwhile, the Llanmeeri High Priest stared fixedly at Andoc, sending a new frisson of disquiet up my spine.

Brinn raised an eyebrow. "It seems you did not exaggerate the importance of your message. Thadrik?" He turned to the priest.

Thadrik tore his eyes away from Andoc and nodded. "He is telling the truth. They are who they claim to be, and he believes what he is saying wholeheartedly."

I glanced at Senovo, who was leaning back in his chair with one dark eyebrow raised. My gaze flicked between the Llanmeeri Chief and his High Priest in confusion.

"Forgive me," said Chief Brinn. "Our High Priest has the ability to sense duplicity in others. It is a very valuable skill in situations such as this one, as you can imagine. No offense was meant, but you can understand my reasons for having him here."

Without meaning to, I mentally reviewed everything we had said since arriving, and suddenly remembered —

Thadrik's icy eyes were on me. "The man-girl is hiding something, however."

My heart thudded in a moment of irrational panic before I calmed. There was nothing for it, unless I wanted to sow doubt over Andoc's mission. "It's nothing to do with the Empire, or the invasion," I said. "Andoc and I are not actually handfasted. We underwent the ceremony, but I consider myself more male than female. We did not consummate. It was easier to maintain the fiction, since my connection to Andoc eased people's perception of my... unusual situation."

Brinn stared at me for a long moment, and nodded. "Personal scandal does not interest me when we are talking about an invasion. Particularly an invasion right on my doorstep." He turned back to Andoc. "Chief Andoc. You have stated that you maintain a network of spies in the south. What other steps have you taken since Volya's death?"

Andoc cleared his throat. "The north *must* have an alliance, Chief Brinn. We missed our greatest opportunity at the meeting in Rhyth, and the loss of that opportunity was mostly Draebard's fault. I have been sending delegations out all winter to parlay with other tribes. We have some agreements for troops and support in place, but not enough. Most tribes have been unwilling to commit without knowing more details about the threat, and those details only came to light in the past few days."

Brinn sat back in his chair, his hands folded over his stomach. "And you plan on leading this proposed alliance, do you, Andoc of Draebard? You are a young man, and an untried Chief."

Andoc leaned forward, intent. "I plan on forging this alliance, yes. And I plan on doing whatever is necessary to protect our way of life."

Senovo wove his fingers together and met Chief Brinn's eyes over the top of them. "Chief Andoc has also neglected to mention that he was the organizing force behind the defense at the western pass last autumn."

There were several gasps around the table.

"*You* burned the southern mountains?" asked one of the elders.

"I did," Andoc replied, his voice grim.

Brinn glanced at High Priest Thadrik, who nodded confirmation. "Well," the Chief said. "You are obviously not exaggerating when you say you will do whatever is necessary. You have a strategy in mind for the coming attack as well?"

"Not as much of one as I would like, though we are pursuing some possibilities. I think it's clear, though, that we need troops and supplies on the coast, and we need lots of them." Andoc settled back in his seat. "I have groups meeting with all three of the towns located at potential invasion sites. We will also be meeting with the largest inland tribes now that we have more reliable information. We seek commitments of both warriors and gold. Meren is already with us, as are a number of smaller tribes and unaffiliated villages."

Brinn nodded thoughtfully. "I cannot fault your passion, or your initiative, Chief Andoc. I must discuss details with the council, but it's clear that it would be foolish for Llanmeer to ignore your warning, or your request."

I let out a slow breath, tension draining from my chest along with the air. It was true that it would have been imprudent for Brinn to have turned us away, knowing that his town was at risk, but that hadn't stopped me worrying. I looked around, only to find High Priest Thadrik's piercing eyes on me once again. I shivered, even though I had nothing further to hide.

"We will discuss this immediately," Brinn was saying. "In the mean time, please enjoy Llanmeer's hospitality. Draebard is many days' ride from here; I'm sure your party could use a few hours of rest."

"Indeed," Andoc said. "We cannot tarry here long, but a warm fire and something to eat beside traveling rations would be most welcome while you and your council meet privately."

"In that case, I will send a messenger to the inn as soon as we can come to an agreement." Brinn rose, and everyone else followed suit.

We bowed, and made our way from the hall. Outside, I took a huge, cleansing breath, the smell of the sea tingling in my nostrils despite the cold.

"Well," Andoc said, "I think that went about as smoothly as we could have hoped."

"Have you ever heard of anyone with an ability like High Priest Thadrik's before?" I asked.

"Never," Senovo said. "It's really rather extraordinary. If time permits, I would like a chance to speak with him in more depth."

"He makes me uncomfortable," I said.

"If he can't prevent it from happening, I'd think the ability would become incredibly wearing in a very short time," Andoc observed. "It's a useful skill, to be sure—but I certainly don't envy him."

"No doubt you're right," I allowed, "but I still have no desire to spend more time in his presence than I have to." Another whiff of the sea breeze teased my senses. "Can we go down to the beach before we head back to the inn? I want to see it while I'm here."

Andoc smiled fondly. "And here I thought you'd be clamoring to get back to a warm fire at the first opportunity."

"I grew up by the sea, you know," I said wistfully. I didn't add that this trip might be my last chance to enjoy it, depending on what happened to us in the spring.

"I grew up near the water as well," Senovo put in, "though it was a different sea. Come. You promised Frella seashells, after all."

My smile was sad as I turned and led the way, following the smell of salt. Llanmeer was built at the edge of cliffs overlooking the sea. They were much lower here than they were at many points along the coast, which, combined with the natural harbor beyond the bay, had made it an obvious place to put a port. Still, the cliffs meant that moving goods from ship to shore was not a simple undertaking. In addition to a series of large baskets and platforms that could be raised and lowered using a system of pulleys, there was also a wide trail of stone steps carved out of the living rock, wending down to the beach.

It was to this manmade path that I led the others. Andoc blew out his breath when he got a good look at it, but followed gamely enough, accepting a shoulder for support from Senovo and using his walking stick to help keep his footing.

Someone had carefully swept the snow and ice from the rocky steps, and though our progress was slow, we made it down to the sandy, gently sloped beach with no problems. I wandered to the boundary of land and water, where angry waves slapped against the white sand and tried to drag it back to the depths. The others came up to flank me, and I stared for a long time at the mesmerizing vista. After the retreat of a particularly large wave, Andoc stretched forward to poke at something in the sand with his stick.

I darted forward after the next swell came and pulled a conch shell free, holding the perfect spiral cradled in my hand.

We returned to the inn for a meal, and were relaxing near the fire when the promised messenger arrived.

"Chief Brinn and the elders wish you to know that they have accepted your proposal of an alliance, and wish to speak with you about the details in the morning," said the lad.

"Thank you," said Andoc. "We will join them in the meeting hall first thing."

Once he had gone, Senovo raised the cup of wine he was nursing in a small salute. "Congratulations, old friend. Another step forward."

"I only hope Jacun and Balzoc are having as much luck."

I spoke up. "The port towns will understand the risk they face. Brinn was right—they would be foolish to discount the offer of help."

"Just so," Senovo agreed. "It is always easier to convince someone to act in their own interest than to act to help others. The challenge will be to convince the tribes elsewhere on the island that the Empire's planned invasion is real and threatens them directly. That said, the three of us have already brokered a successful treaty between a notoriously prideful man and the woman who publicly spurned him. A trial by fire if there ever was one."

Andoc snorted at the reminder, his mood lightening—as Senovo had no doubt intended. "A fair point, *amadi*," he said. "I consider myself reassured—thank you."

Senovo smiled, the expression softening his perfectly sculpted features in the firelight. He rose, and pressed a kiss first to Andoc's forehead, and then to mine. I closed my eyes, soaking up the feeling of warmth and belonging. He straightened away, and addressed both of us. "Now, if you've no need of me for a bit, I believe I will pay a visit to the temple before it gets too late. I really do want to have a conversation with Thadrik, and I assume we will be leaving for Keld in the morning as soon as we have met with the council."

I froze in my seat, taken unaware by the strange wave of panic that flooded me at Senovo's innocent words.

EIGHT

Andoc nodded, unaware of my sudden shift of mood. "Yes. We do need to keep moving. There's a lot of territory to cover before we head home."

Keld. I had been largely successful at shoving my awareness of our upcoming trip to my childhood village into the back of my mind and hiding it there. Now, though, there was no avoiding the fact that we would arrive in Keld *tomorrow*, and it was as if all of the emotions I'd been holding at bay hit me at once.

I kept very quiet and still as Senovo headed out to meet with Llanmeer's disconcerting High Priest, old instincts driving me not to draw attention to myself when I was vulnerable. Once Senovo was gone, Andoc turned to me with a smile that was more of a leer.

"Well, *caradi,*" he said with good humor, "it appears we've been abandoned. Whatever shall we do with ourselves to pass the time until our roaming wolf returns to us?"

At any other time, I would have had a witty quip to hand, and been sitting in Andoc's lap with my tongue down his throat before the echoes of our voices faded. As it was, I forced an unconvincing smile and said, "Actually, I'm completely exhausted. All I can really focus on right now is sleep."

Well... sleep, and the way my heart was suddenly pounding so hard that it was difficult to breathe. But still, I was proud of the way my voice sounded almost normal. That didn't stop Andoc's brows from drawing together in worry as he studied me.

"You do look pale all of the sudden. Are you feeling all right?"

I tamped down the rather hysterical bubble of laughter that wanted to break free. "Yes, fine. Just tired." *Liar, liar, liar,* chanted the little voice in the back of my head. "I know it's early, but if it's all the same to you, I think I'll go on to bed."

Andoc nodded, still looking worried. "You want company?"

"No, why don't you wait up for Senovo. I'll probably fall asleep as soon as my head hits the pillow." *Ha.*

"All right. Sleep well, then." Andoc was still watching me closely, so I molded my expression into an agreeable smile and escaped to the little alcove with the bed in the corner of the room.

I wanted to curl up with my clothes and boots still on—ready to flee at a moment's notice—but that would be too suspicious. Instead, I made myself strip down to my linens and lie calmly under the covers. I lay on my side with my back to the room, resisting the urge to curl up in a defensive ball. With all of my focus on mimicking the even breathing of sleep, I tried very hard not to think of either the past or tomorrow's destination, and failed miserably.

Time passed like mud drying in a puddle. The silence was broken only by my too-even breathing, and an occasional creak or clink as Andoc shifted in his chair near the fire and poured himself more wine.

A small eternity later, the door to the room creaked on its hinges, heralding Senovo's return.

"Glad you're back, *amadi*," Andoc said. "Something's wrong with our Horse Mistress. I thought it would be best to wait for you before I bearded her in her den."

I could picture Senovo's eyes flicking over to my huddled form with perfect clarity, though my back was to the room. I kept very still, the wounded child that still lived inside of me insisting that if I didn't move or make a sound, I might be left alone. It was irrational, nonsensical. It had never worked—even back then—and the adult part of me knew it would not work now. Yet I had no control over my body to move or speak. Nor could I control the way my breathing sped up as twin weights settled on the bed on either side of me, or the fine tremor of dread that ran through my muscles.

My heart was thudding like a drum when a soft hand rested on my head in a gentle caress, even as my instincts insisted I should expect anger and harsh blows. A second hand, strong and callused, pressed between my shoulder blades and stayed there.

"Can you talk to us, beloved?" Senovo asked.

I shook my head, burying my face in the pillow. I could no more have formed words at that moment than I could fly. It was all I could do to drag air into my lungs.

"Very well. We are here, and we will watch over you. You are safe with us. Let yourself feel whatever it is you need to feel right now. You don't have to fight it." Senovo's voice was calm and soothing. I tried to latch onto it, but that calm was far beyond my reach.

My breathing grew increasingly ragged until it felt like my chest must burst from the pressure. The hands never left me, two points of sanity in my descent into madness. My arms and legs ached and tingled. To faint would have been a relief, but of course I didn't. The panic seemed to last forever—I had no conception of time passing.

Finally, my body called a halt to the fit of madness, possibly due to pure exhaustion. My breathing slowed; my heart no longer threatened to escape the cage of my ribs. Everything *hurt*—the pain of muscle and sinew pushed to their limits. I wanted desperately to release the tension by weeping or perhaps vomiting, but I didn't even have the energy for that much.

My silent companions continued to stroke my skin and hair with small, rhythmic movements, making no other demands. Embarrassment began to war with all the other emotions clamoring for my attention, until I finally cracked open an eye and rasped, "Sorry. I'm all right."

Andoc blew out a soft breath behind me. "I've seen *all right*, Carivel, and I'm reasonably sure this isn't it."

"Is this related to our upcoming visit to Keld?" Senovo asked.

Of course—what else? I almost said, before realizing that I had never actually told either of them about my childhood, beyond a vague indication that it had been unhappy. I stilled in shock. How could it be that I hadn't told them?

"My mother," I said instead, my voice little more than a whisper.

"She still lives there?" Senovo asked patiently, as if he wasn't having to drag information out of me like a healer digging out the root of an infected tooth.

I nodded, and then added, "As far as I know." The others waited for me to continue, but instead of providing any more useful information, I blurted out, "I don't think I can do this."

"Can you tell us a bit more about it?" Senovo prompted.

It took several moments before I could get the words out.

"She... beat me. When I was small. Called me horrible names. Accused me of terrible things." I swallowed hard. "She blamed me for my father's death."

Senovo's hand never faltered, but I felt Andoc tense behind me and cringed away from his silent expression of anger, hating myself for my involuntary response. I hadn't reacted this badly for more than two years now — I'd thought I was past it.

"And how old were you when your father died?" Senovo asked, redirecting my attention. "You were quite young, were you not?"

"I was six," I said, my voice breaking a bit over the simple words.

Senovo's hand moved from my head, trailing down my arm to take one of my own hands in a gentle grip. He lifted it to his lips, kissing the knuckles before lowering it. "You understand that as a six-year-old child, you could not have been responsible for your father's death?"

"Yes!" I said, almost angrily. "I'm not stupid!"

"No," he agreed, "you aren't. But you *are* aware of the bonds in which the past may hold us without our knowledge."

He was referring to a discussion we'd had months ago, about the way our pasts could affect us in the present. I immediately slid from anger back to childish uncertainty. "Do you think I should see her? Talk to her?"

It was Andoc who answered. "I think we have to stop in Keld and try to arrange a treaty. But that doesn't necessarily mean you have to see her."

"People will talk if I don't."

There was a slight pause.

"If you're not used to people talking by now, I don't quite know what to tell you, *caradi*," Andoc said.

"What is it you fear, exactly?" asked Senovo. "Or perhaps I should say, what is it *in the present* that you fear? Not fears from the past."

I tried to think, silently cursing the pounding headache that was following hard on the heels of my earlier fit. "She's an old woman now," I said slowly. "Part of the reason I ran away when I did was because I couldn't trust myself anymore not to hit back. I'm an adult. She can't hurt me now."

Senovo's eyes were sad. "On the contrary, beloved, I suspect she can still hurt you quite badly. With words... with disappointment that she has not magically started to love you as a mother should, during the time that has passed since you saw her last."

Tears rose up without warning and choked me. I experienced a moment of fresh panic before remembering that, almost a score of years after my mother had screamed abuse and slapped me across the face for weeping during my father's funeral, it was finally safe to cry again.

I buried my face in the pillow and sobbed, each convulsion stabbing a new flash of pain through my aching head. I was dimly aware of Andoc settling down to spoon up behind me on the bed, one arm thrown over my waist. Senovo remained sitting in front of me, still holding my fingers entwined with his.

When I finally cried myself out, I felt utterly wretched. I had been exhausted to start with after our difficult journey, and now I doubt I could have walked the length of the room without collapsing. My head threatened to split open like a ripe melon.

"Ow," I said faintly. "*Ow.* I thought that was supposed to help, but everything hurts." My voice was wet and nasal, my nose completely clogged. Somewhat sheepishly, I struggled into a more upright position. Andoc let me go immediately and sat up as well, while Senovo rose and returned a moment later with a cloth dipped in cool water.

I took it and tried to clean up my face. Without meeting their eyes, I said, "I need to see her. I need her to know that she didn't break me."

"Very well," Senovo said. "It is entirely your choice, Carivel."

"We'll be right there with you, though. I won't allow you to be alone with her," Andoc added.

I felt as though the declaration should have angered me, but in truth, it was a relief. I nodded.

"Can you rest now?" Senovo asked. "I could probably beg a sleeping draught from the temple if you need one."

The truth was, I could barely keep my eyes open despite my pounding head. "No. My head just aches, that's all. I'll sleep, only..."

"Yes?" Andoc prompted.

"Stay with me," I said softly.

Rather than answer in words, Andoc drew me back down onto the straw tick mattress. Senovo got up again, and I heard the sound of the rag being rinsed and wrung out. When he settled down and draped the cool cloth over my aching forehead and eyes, a different kind of tears threatened — tears of gratitude. I let them wrap me up between them and gave into my exhaustion with a deep sigh.

I awoke to quiet voices the next morning. Fingers brushed softly over my temple in a slow, soothing rhythm.

"I'm not used to having to fight the urge to hit an old woman." That was Andoc, using the low tone of voice one employed when trying not to wake someone nearby.

Senovo spoke softly in reply. "People who hurt others are often sick or hurt themselves. We do not know if she suffers from a derangement of the mind, or if she herself was treated in such a manner early in life, and merely repeated the pattern."

"*That's not an excuse.*" Anger now, though still delivered in a quiet voice.

"No. It is not. Such circumstances may explain cruelty. They do not excuse it."

I stretched, feeling my muscles pull and ache. My head still throbbed — a dull echo of my heartbeat. Today was going to be a very long day.

"Can't we just stay here in Llanmeer for a bit?" I asked, only half joking. My voice was raspy with sleep, and I yawned. "They used to have a wonderful bath house behind the inn. That sounds really good, doesn't it?"

"I'm sorry, *caradi*," said Andoc, and he really did sound regretful. "Unfortunately, we need to keep moving. Unless you're truly unwell — how do you feel this morning?"

I sighed. "Tired and sore. Nothing serious," I assured him.

"I have some willow bark tea steeping," Senovo said. "I'm afraid I didn't bring anything stronger. Also, you'll have to forgive us for talking about you while you slept."

I shrugged a shoulder and shook my head. "I don't mind. It was a lot to put on you both, and frankly, it's nice to have people who care enough to be upset on my behalf."

Andoc leaned down to press his lips to mine, and I closed my eyes, sinking into it. Why would anyone choose to be horrible to other people when they could share love instead? I would never understand it. When Andoc broke away, I immediately reached for Senovo, who surrendered easily for his own kiss.

"Is it time to go back to the meeting house?" I asked when we parted, not thrilled about the idea, but resigned to its inevitability.

"Almost," Andoc said. "We wanted to let you sleep as long as we could first."

"Thanks—I definitely needed it," I said. "When we get back to Draebard, I'm going to sleep for a week."

"I'll be sure to warn Dalon," Andoc teased gently.

Senovo handed me a cup of willow tea, and I shuffled into a sitting position so I could drink the bitter brew. The change in elevation and the hot liquid did at least cause my clogged nose to drain, which immediately eased my headache.

"Oh, that's better," I said in relief. I craned around to look out the window. "How's the weather today? Any oncoming blizzards I can use as a delaying tactic?"

"Sadly not," Senovo replied. "It appears to be cold, but clear."

"It was worth a try," I muttered, and nudged Andoc with my foot. "Come on, then, let me up. You're sitting on top of the blankets, and I want to check the horses before we meet with Chief Brinn."

Andoc let me get out of bed and stumble around on weak legs, getting dressed and trying to wash the last traces of the night's tears from my face. I was strangely ravenous, so he went to fetch food from the inn's kitchen while I braved the morning cold to make sure that the boy who worked for the innkeeper had fed the horses properly and broken the ice on their water trough.

By the time we arrived at the meeting hall to meet with the Chief and the council, I was feeling nearly human, so I was at least able to follow what was going on and answer questions about the logistics of moving horses and supplies overland to the port town in the spring. The three of us left a couple of hours later with a provisional plan in place for Llanmeer's defense, and an agreement to send regular messengers back and forth with news.

It was difficult not to drag my feet when it came time to pack up and leave, but I managed. Senovo opted to travel on horseback with us rather than shifting—quite possibly because he wanted to keep an eye on me—and I couldn't deny I was grateful for the gesture. I spent the day focusing on Kekenu's reassuring presence under me, on Andoc and Senovo, steadfast at my side, and on the beautiful blue sky overhead.

It worked up to a point, at least until the once-familiar glow of Keld's hearth fires appeared in the deepening gray of dusk. One of those fires was my mother's.

Maybe she's dead, I thought, and immediately felt horrible for thinking it. Still, it *had* been more than four years. *What kind of daughter goes four years without checking on her mother?*

The kind whose mother beat her black and blue, and called her a twisted freak of nature, I thought angrily, only to shake my head when I realized I was silently arguing with the specter of my mother inside my own head. *Gods.* I must truly be losing my reason.

"All right?" Andoc asked from my left, evidently sensing my gradual descent into madness.

"Nope," I answered. "Not remotely, but thanks for asking."

"Does Keld have an inn or a way-house?" Senovo asked.

"It didn't when I left. We never really got many visitors." *Shit.* We would have to stay with my mother. I felt my stomach drop.

But Senovo only nodded. "In that case, we will sleep at the temple," he said without missing a beat.

Ask at the temple, and gain the help you need. The words filtered into my mind without conscious thought—part of Utarr's prayer of solace. The priests in Keld had not been friends to me as a child, but today I was traveling with the High Priest of a powerful tribe. The temple would not dare turn us away. Relief washed over me.

"Yes," I said. "Of course."

"Who is the Chief in Keld?" Andoc asked.

"It was Yaris when I left, but he was a very old man. I've no idea if he'll still be in charge or not. And I should warn you, Keld was never a military power. I don't know how much they'll even be able to help."

"We need more than warriors, *caradi*," said Andoc. "Any assistance that Keld is willing to offer with food, coin, or other supplies would be helpful."

We rode quietly into town. The main road was deserted on the cold winter evening, so I led the way to the temple, battling the surreal feeling of traveling the familiar path as an adult. The last time I had done so had been for yet another in a long series of consultations with the priests about my dogged insistence that my spirit was male. On that particular occasion, the Horse Master's apprentice had found me sneaking around behind the pens, trying to watch one of the boys starting a colt in harness.

I shook my head. I was Horse Mistress in my own right, now. What would my old village make of that?

The temple loomed ahead of us, a much smaller structure than the one in Draebard. Keld had only ever had a handful of priests and acolytes. Torches on either side of the door threw out a welcoming light. Senovo dismounted and handed me his reins, before stepping forward to knock.

A few moments later, the door creaked open to reveal a young man in acolyte's garb. He took one look at Senovo's white robes of office and bowed hastily. "The temple of Keld welcomes you, Elder Brother. How may we serve?"

"Good evening, Little Brother," Senovo replied. "My companions and I have traveled from Draebard to meet with Keld's leaders. We require a bed for the night."

"Of course. Please allow me to call someone to take your horses," the acolyte said immediately. I peered at his face, trying to see if I recognized him. Judging by his age now, he would have been barely out of childhood when I left. He looked vaguely familiar, but I couldn't place his name.

Senovo nodded and the lad hurried off, returning a few minutes later with a second acolyte. I kept my face in the shadows as the newcomer took the horses away to be cared for at the pens, wanting to postpone the inevitable reaction to my reappearance as long as possible.

"Come," said the first acolyte. "I will take you to the High Priest and see about readying rooms for you."

Andoc thanked the young man, and we followed him inside with our saddlebags thrown over our shoulders. He led us to the lamp-lit altar room where I had received so many lectures while looking up at the shrine to Deresta that dominated the back wall of the large space.

"High Priest Aejor," called the acolyte, "we have visitors from Draebard."

My heart jolted at the name. Aejor had been a middle-aged priest when I left—I remembered him as a pale and somewhat timid figure in the background during my lectures from the old High Priest, Uldus.

Movement caught my eye as Aejor looked up from his task in one of the shadowed corners of the room. He was still a thin, nondescript figure with light brown eyes and sandy hair going gray. In fact, he had changed very little in the last four years, except for the white robes he now wore. When he spoke, his voice was still tentative. Diffident. A striking contrast to every other High Priest I had ever met.

"Hello? Yes?" he asked, coming forward to meet us. "This is quite a surprise, I must say! Welcome, welcome…"

Senovo and Andoc stepped forward to greet the man, while I hung back.

"Greetings, Brother," Senovo said, his rich, sonorous voice a striking counterpoint to Aejor's vague, befuddled tones. "I am Senovo, High Priest of Draebard, and this is Draebard's Chief, Andoc."

He hesitated, his eyes flickering in my direction, and I stepped forward reluctantly into the light of the burning lamps.

"Hello, High Priest Aejor," I said quietly.

Aejor turned in surprise at the sound of my voice and stared at me for a long moment.

"Cara?" he asked. "Child, can it really be you?"

An unexpected lump rose in my throat, rendering me mute.

"Indeed," Senovo answered for me. "Though she goes by Carivel, now. Our companion is the esteemed Horse Mistress of Draebard, who graciously agreed to join us on our journey, since she is familiar with Keld."

Aejor's eyes never left me while Senovo spoke, and he slowly walked toward me as if drawn by a length of cord. When he was close enough, he lifted his hands to cradle my face. "Oh, my child. It *is* you. I never thought to see you again. The temple of Keld failed you badly, Cara. *Carivel. I* failed you. After you left, I feared you lost. I cannot tell you what it means to me that the gods have finally given me a chance to atone."

The lump grew in size until it choked me, the sound like a sob. "My mother—?" I whispered past the heavy obstruction.

Aejor's sandy brows drew together, accentuating the worry lines that marked his thin face. "She still lives. She is… much the same as ever, I fear. I do my best to ensure her needs are met, but her spirit remains… troubled."

I nodded, and stepped back, needing space. Aejor let his hands drop. "Forgive me," he said. "I should not speak of such personal matters in front of guests."

Both Andoc and Senovo had remained silently in the background as Aejor and I spoke, but I turned burning eyes to them now. "It's all right, High Priest. Senovo and Andoc are privy to all of my secrets. In many ways, they know me better than I know myself."

Aejor's expression softened. "All of us should be lucky enough to have friends like that. I welcome you back to Keld, Carivel, and apologize humbly that I did not protect you as I should have, when you were younger. It could not have been easy for you to return… but I suppose you never lacked for bravery, did you?"

I could only shake my head with a small, helpless movement, once more stuck for words.

"That she didn't," Andoc said, stepping forward to rejoin the conversation.

"Yes. You will have to excuse my reaction, Chief Andoc, High Priest Senovo. I'm sure you didn't travel all the way from Draebard in the middle of winter merely to return my lost lamb to the flock—though I must thank you for it nonetheless." Aejor took a deep, centering breath, and I did the same. "Allow me to secure you rooms for the night, and then I will inform Chief Yaris of your arrival personally. Would you prefer three separate rooms?"

"A single room would be preferable," Andoc said without missing a beat, and I loved him dearly for it.

Aejor looked surprised for a moment, but smoothly let it pass. "Of course. It is best to keep our loved ones close when they may have need of us. Carivel… shall I inform Sabrael that you are here?"

I chewed the inside of my cheek for a long moment. Could I put off seeing my mother until tomorrow? "No," I said eventually. "I'll go now, and see her myself."

"We'll go together," Andoc said firmly. "High Priest, could I prevail on you to postpone our meeting with the council until tomorrow morning?"

Aejor nodded, a knowing look in his eye. "Of course. It is growing late, and I'm sure your journey must have been exhausting."

"Thank you," Andoc said.

Aejor showed us to a room with a bed large enough for three people to use if they didn't mind being very friendly, and we stowed our bags. He offered food, but I was fairly sure anything I tried to eat would just come right back up. Finally, there were no more excuses to put off the short journey to the modest hut where I had been born.

I led the way, ridiculously thankful that Andoc's bad leg slowed our progress. He flanked me on the right, and Senovo flanked me on the left, making me feel, if not *safe*, at least supported. My stomach churned, and several times I thought I actually would throw up before we got there. Humiliation at the very idea won out, however, and I took slow, deep breaths as we approached the familiar door.

Any hesitation at this point would probably have been enough to send me running right back to the temple, so I stepped up to knock on the chipped and pitted door without pausing to think. The wait was agonizing, but eventually the handle rattled and the door cracked open.

"What do you want at this hour of the night?" demanded a shrill voice, and the door opened to reveal a wizened, hunched old woman. I had to look down to meet her gaze.

My mother stared at us with rheumy eyes, examining us for several beats in the light from the hearth fire. She sucked in a sharp breath as her gaze locked on mine, her expression running through a complex series of emotions before finally settling on a fascinating combination of anger and pathos. I had no idea what my own face must look like.

"Hello, Mother," I said.

NINE

"Cara?" whined the woman who had given birth to me. "Good gods. I thought you must be dead."

Thought, or hoped? I wondered.

"Why else would you abandon your own mother for four long years?" she continued, bracing a hand against the doorframe as if it was all that was keeping her from collapse.

"Not dead. Obviously," I said, feeling strangely detached as I looked at the rather pathetic figure in front of me. "And if it really needs saying, I abandoned you because you beat me and said hateful things to me for most of my life. I figured that part was fairly self-evident, to be honest."

Hurt flooded my mother's face, and she looked with horror at the two men arrayed on either side of me. "Cara! Why would you tell such terrible stories in front of strangers! I can see you haven't changed since you were a willful little girl."

I was still watching the conversation as if from an outsider's perspective, my mind safely sheltered from the madness I'd grown up with. "They're not strangers, and I tell these *stories* because they're true. Sabrael of Keld, meet High Priest Senovo and Chief Andoc, both of Draebard. Chief Andoc and I were handfasted last spring," I added, with a moment's vicious satisfaction when my mother's mouth opened and stayed that way. "Perhaps you could invite us in, rather than keeping us standing here in the cold?"

The old crone looked from Andoc to Senovo and back again. She... *simpered*, the display sickening to someone who knew her history of cruelty. "Of course... come in, come in! To think, a Chief and a High Priest on my doorstep!"

We followed her inside. I could feel the stony disapproval coming from Andoc on my right, but Senovo stepped forward to fill the awkward silence. "Thank you, Sabrael," he said. "Your daughter goes by the name Carivel now, and you should know that she has achieved great things. She is the first female

Horse Mistress Draebard has ever had, and has garnered a great deal of respect for her expertise with the animals."

To my not-very-great surprise, my mother ignored his words to focus on the only thing she truly cared about. "Wife to a tribal chieftain," she gushed to the room at large. "I *knew* I could fix her!" Her attention centered on Andoc, and she tapped a wrinkled finger against her temple. "She was such an odd child, you know. Sick, in the head. I told her over and over that if she ever wanted to find a bondmate, she had to pretend to be normal. But would she listen?" Her expression fell. "You have to be careful, though—I think she's cursed by the gods. They punished me for bearing her by taking my husband away."

I watched with distant fascination, the words slipping past me harmlessly. Andoc was not faring quite so well—anger was beginning to bleed through, in the form of tension in his jaw and the cords of his neck. He still had not said a word, I noticed, which was unusual for such a normally charming, loquacious man.

"I assure you, Carivel has been nothing but a blessing to Draebard, and to us, Sabrael," Senovo said. He glanced from Andoc to me and back again before returning his attention to the shriveled old woman who had made my childhood such a nightmare. "Now, though, we thank you for your hospitality, but I fear Andoc has important business with the Chief of Keld, and of course he will want his beloved wife nearby. Unfortunately, we must take our leave of you."

I marveled at Senovo's deft handling of the impossible woman, whose expression immediately melted back into smug happiness. "Yes, yes, of course. Imagine—my little Cara, the wife of a Chief!"

A small wave of disgust mixed with pity washed over me as I looked at her, and truly *saw* her, perhaps for the first time in my life. Sabrael of Keld had only a passing acquaintance with reality. While having sole responsibility for a child who was... *unusual*... probably hadn't helped the situation, I realized now that my presence, and my unique set of issues, had never been the source of my mother's problems.

I wondered for the thousandth time what my father had ever seen in her.

Senovo exchanged a bit more banal and disjointed small talk with her, and the three of us escaped the claustrophobic, cluttered little hut. I took a deep, cleansing breath of cold air and let it out slowly. Somewhat to my surprise, Andoc immediately wrapped me in his arms, right there in the middle of the street.

"It's all lies," he said into my ear. "All of it. You understand that? Please tell me you do."

I nodded slowly, feeling oddly strong — almost invincible. "I do, Andoc, I promise. If I was truly as bad as all that, surely the gods would not have blessed me by bringing you and Senovo into my life."

Andoc let me go long enough for me to wrap my arms around Senovo as well, gripping him tightly even though I was shaking a bit. He held me for a long moment. Afterwards, we made our slow way back to the temple with Andoc's arm a warm weight across my shoulders, and Senovo a steadfast presence at my side.

✲⋙✲

That evening, the three of us made love despite our exhaustion, trading kisses deep into the night. The following morning, we met with Yaris and Keld's small council. I was shocked at the warmth of the welcome I received, and we left the meeting hall with the promise of livestock, fodder, and wagons to transport it in the spring, along with whatever warriors Keld could spare.

We rode out an hour or so later. High Priest Aejor embraced me and offered the three of us his blessing for our endeavors, growing slightly teary-eyed when I forgave him for whatever perceived failing he felt he had perpetrated in the past.

"I do have one request, though," I told him. "Make sure she's taken care of, so that I never have to see her again."

"I would have done that anyway, child," said the High Priest.

When Senovo shifted into the shape of the wolf in preparation for our departure, Aejor's brilliant smile of wonder transformed his plain, thin face. I would remember that smile for the rest of my life, I was absolutely sure.

There were a handful of other small villages between Keld and Venzor, and we stopped at all of them. Most were easily convinced that it was in their best interest to ally with larger tribes like Draebard, who might protect them in the coming war. While we did not gain many additional warriors, we did start to form a useful supply chain for the goods and coin that would be so crucial in supporting the large troop numbers necessary to defend the coast.

Some five days later, we finally arrived at Venzor. As the country became more heavily wooded, the wolf had been wandering farther afield. Senovo shared with us that he had come across the dens of several packs of wolves, but it was obvious that he was becoming increasingly frustrated with his inability to elucidate what exactly he hoped to achieve.

I suspected that Senovo had never spent such a large amount of time in animal form since his initial escape from the Rhytheeri priests. I wasn't at all fond of the way he seemed distant even when he was human now, as if he was always awaiting his next chance to disappear into the forest. Andoc also seemed worried, but, when pressed, he would only reiterate that Senovo deserved our trust and support in his strange, self-appointed quest.

Still, it was a relief to arrive at Andoc's old home. His mood lightened as soon as the large village appeared in the sheltered valley below us, and lifted further when the wolf reappeared from a side trail, his tongue lolling and a few burrs twisted into the fur at his flank.

I dismounted and rummaged in the gray mare's saddlebags for clothing and a spare blanket, which I put down on the snowy ground. Senovo settled on the insulating square of woven wool and changed, brushing the offending burrs out of the way when they fell away from his now hairless side. He shivered as the cold air hit his bare skin, and took his clothing eagerly.

"Almost there, *amadi*," Andoc observed, one corner of his lips turned up in a half-smile.

"So I see, old friend," Senovo replied, shrugging into his robes and fastening them. "Carivel, I feel I should warn you that you may find Andoc's mother somewhat... overwhelming... given your own previous experience in that regard."

I raised an eyebrow, not quite sure what to make of the cryptic statement. "Oh? Should I be worried that I won't come up to scratch as his bondmate?"

Andoc laughed — a sound I didn't hear nearly enough these days. "Hardly. Just that you may be about to get mothered to within an inch of your life."

"Ah." It was a sad commentary on my childhood that I couldn't really picture what that might mean, so I shrugged. "Bring it on, in that case. I'm probably overdue at this point."

I had a vague idea that normal mothers made regular meals for their children, purchased or created toys for them, and tried to protect them from things that might hurt them. The memory of Gretya's kind face and gap-toothed smile floated momentarily across my mind's eye. I also had a suspicion that whatever motherhood was supposed to entail among normal people, Andoc's mother must have been particularly good at it to produce a son so selfless and protective of those he loved. A little tingle of nervous excitement shivered through me at the realization that I was about to find out firsthand.

When Senovo was ready, we mounted up and headed down the winding trail toward Venzor. Andoc's home appeared to be on roughly the same scale as Draebard, or perhaps a bit larger. In addition to the personal aspects of the visit, this would also be a chance to add significantly to the troop strength of the northern defense. Since in my experience, pretty much everyone who knew Andoc liked him, I felt good about our chances.

"Someone please remind me that I have responsibilities now, and can't rush straight down to Mother's house," said Andoc.

"I suspect you would be forgiven for doing so," Senovo offered with a half-smile, "but perhaps it would be more politic to stop in at the meeting hall first and announce our arrival."

"It will probably take some time for them to call a proper meeting once they know we're here, won't it?" I asked. "No one will blame you for visiting her while we wait."

Andoc's smile lit his face. "Yes — you're right."

I tried to think of the last time I'd been that excited to see anyone besides the two of them. It was probably when I was a child, and my father returned from a long trip. My heart did something complicated as I watched the years fall away from Andoc's face, leaving behind a young man about to be reunited with a distant loved one.

"Come on!" he called, and urged his mare into a canter.

The winding trail widened out into a proper road, and before I knew it we were entering the outskirts of the large village. There was little doubt that Venzor saw more visitors coming through than Keld, and it didn't take long for our arrival to garner attention. It was just past midday, and though a light snow was beginning to fall, many people were out and about, taking care of the day's business.

"Andoc, is that you?" called a middle-aged woman, drawing the hood of her cloak back to see more clearly. "Gods above—it is! Whatever are you and your friends doing, traveling at this time of year?"

Andoc pulled up near the woman, beaming. "Merine! It's good to see you! Unfortunately, this isn't only a social call—I need to speak with Chief Ranulth and the elders as soon as possible."

Merine nodded. "I figured it must be something serious to have you braving the weather. Shall I let Iseboa know you're here?"

The way Andoc's features softened told me that Iseboa must be his mother. "That would be wonderful, Merine. I plan on going straight there once we've let someone at the meeting hall know we're in town. I'm sure she'd appreciate a bit of warning before I show up on her doorstep."

Merine laughed. "Probably, though I predict she's going to box your ears either way, for staying away so long. I'll go there now and tell her to expect you."

"She probably will, and I'll probably deserve it," Andoc admitted, still grinning. "Tell her Senovo is with me—and that I've brought someone new for her to meet."

Andoc threw me a wink and I blushed, even as Merine's attention shifted to the two of us. "Of course," she said warmly. "And welcome, both of you."

"Thank you, Merine," Senovo said. "It is always good to be back in Venzor, whatever the reason."

After Merine hurried off to speak with Andoc's mother, and after Senovo looked in at the meeting house to announce our arrival—sparing Andoc the necessity of dismounting and remounting with his bad leg—the three of us rode across town to a cheerful, generously sized hut with brightly painted shutters and a tangle of ivy growing over the walls.

The door burst open before we'd even turned onto the cobbled walkway, and a short figure wearing a gray dress and a white shawl hurried out, heedless of the cold, or the snowflakes dusting her dark hair.

TEN

"*A*ndoc," the woman exclaimed, and her son was off his horse and hobbling to meet her faster than I would have given him credit for with his damaged ankle.

"Mother!" The two of them came together in a heartfelt embrace — Andoc's mother weeping tears of joy as she wrapped her arms around her son and squeezed tight.

I dismounted quietly and caught up Andoc's mare's reins, where he'd left them dangling in his haste. I was aware of Senovo stepping down from his own horse behind me.

Iseboa eased free after a few moments so she could get a better look at Andoc. "Oh, my dear — your leg!"

Andoc flushed and looked away for a moment, still self-conscious about the ugly injury that had ended his career as a warrior. "I broke it last summer," he admitted. "It's fairly well healed now — no cause for worry."

His mother pulled him down to kiss his forehead, her eyes still bright with tears. "As long as you're all right, that's the only thing that matters," she said firmly. "Just promise me that there were no ladders or roofs involved."

That startled a choked laugh from Andoc. According to the story he'd told me, his father had died after falling from their roof while trying to patch a leak during a storm. I was a bit shocked that the two of them could joke about such a thing.

"No ladders," he confirmed, sobering. "I'd like to think I did at least manage to learn *that* lesson during my misspent youth. In fact, this happened during a battle."

"One in which he acted with predictable heroism, I should add," Senovo added, moving forward now that the initial reunion had concluded.

"Senovo!" Iseboa said, and embraced him as well. "Where are my manners? Oh my goodness-it's so good to see you!"

Senovo leaned down and returned the hug with every evidence of affection, burying his face in Iseboa's soft woven shawl. Whatever extraordinary maternal talents Andoc's mother possessed, it was evident that Senovo had also succumbed to them without much of a fight. Even watching them from a distance made tears start to prickle unexpectedly behind my eyes.

It wasn't long before Iseboa's attention naturally turned to me. Andoc saw, and stepped in before my nervousness could take too strong of a hold.

"Mother, this is Carivel, Horse Mistress of Draebard. She and I are handfasted, after a fashion," he said.

Iseboa did not immediately try to embrace me, as I had half expected. Instead, she stepped forward to clasp my free hand in both of hers. "Greetings, Carivel, and welcome to my home. I cannot tell you how pleased I am to meet you." Her eyes crinkled into a smile. "Your unusual title tells me you must be quite an extraordinary person—" She looked between the three of us, raising an eyebrow. "—and I'll admit I can hardly wait to hear how someone becomes *handfasted, after a fashion*. Now, though, there's a hitching post by the side of the house, if your horses will be all right there for a little while so you can come in and warm up."

"That will be fine, thank you," I said, battling sudden shyness. Of all the people I'd met during recent months, none outside of the Mereni—with their female leaders and warriors— had reacted to my title of Horse Mistress with such honest interest and grace. I couldn't help wondering what Andoc's mother made of me... this plain-looking person in boy's clothing who had somehow become handfasted—sort of—to her son.

Senovo and I tied up the four horses, leaving them saddled. Andoc and Iseboa helped us carry the saddlebags inside, since it was fairly evident that we would be staying the night with her. I would have to make proper arrangements for the animals before then, but we had watered them at a stream shortly before we arrived and they would be fine for now.

The large hut where Andoc had grown up was warm and welcoming inside. Brightly colored woven blankets decorated the wooden furniture, and the large weaving frame resting in the corner gave a strong clue as to where they had come from.

"Come in!" Iseboa said brightly. "Make yourselves right at home, and pardon the mess."

She bustled around, tidying away a distaff and spindle full of woolen yarn, and moving odds and ends off the chairs near the hearth so we could sit. Andoc and Senovo immediately did so, completely comfortable in the homey surroundings. I followed suit, not wanting to appear as awkward as I felt.

We accepted the hot, spiced mead she offered us, and I took a long draught, appreciating the way it warmed my chilled body. Finally content with her hospitality, Iseboa dropped into a chair and leaned forward, hands clasped and elbows on knees as she regarded us keenly.

I took a quick moment to study her. At a guess, she could count forty years, or perhaps forty-five. My own mother had been almost past childbearing age when she finally had me, and was now an old woman. Iseboa, by contrast, was bright and lively, with only a few streaks of gray in her hair and a hint of crow's feet proclaiming her age. Short and slightly plump as she was, it was difficult to believe that she was mother to such a tall, muscular man… at least until you noticed twinkling brown eyes nearly identical to Andoc's looking out of her soft face, and the same glint of slightly devilish good humor around both their mouths.

"Now," she said firmly, "tell me all the news. And don't think I haven't noticed those white robes, Senovo."

Andoc blew out a breath. "That will make for a longer story than you might think, I'm afraid." He paused, visibly gathering his thoughts. "I suppose it all started last spring when Volya got a message from an Alyrion commander whose troops were occupying the old hill fort south of Draebard, demanding a parlay…"

Andoc told the bulk of our story. He didn't hold anything back, only glossing over a few of the more harrowing parts. Senovo added a few words here and there, and I hesitantly spoke up in a couple of places, when Andoc made it clear that it was up to me how much of my personal story I wanted to tell.

It struck me for the first time, hearing it all laid out in this way, what an extraordinary tale it actually was. I could only imagine how difficult it must be for Iseboa to take it all in. To my surprise, when we were finished, instead of focusing immediately on Andoc's rise to the chieftaincy as my own mother would have done, she leaned forward and took Senovo's hands in hers, though her gaze included all of us.

"Thank goodness the three of you have worked out a way to be together," she said. "I can't tell you how relieved I am, Senovo. When I got word from Mabios last fall that Andoc was handfasted, I didn't honestly know what to think." She met my eyes and held them. "Carivel, please believe me when I say that I would have welcomed you with open arms, regardless. But it would have broken my heart to think of Senovo being cast aside, when I know how much he and my son love each other." Her gaze moved to Andoc, and a small smile played around her lips. "I realize now that I shouldn't have worried."

Senovo looked down at their joined hands. "I... would have stepped aside," he said quietly. "A relationship between a man and a eunuch—"

"*Is just as important as any other relationship,*" I interrupted hotly. My heart broke to think that even after everything we had gone through, Senovo still thought his place with Andoc somehow less worthy or less secure than mine, and I could not hold my tongue. "If Andoc had been capable of such cruelty, I would never have loved him in the first place!"

"And rightly so," Iseboa said with finality. "Fortunately, Andoc's heart has always been too big for him. I suppose it's only right that it should beat for two other people rather than one."

"*Mother...*" Andoc said, and I was somewhat amazed to find that we'd *embarrassed* him—a feat I had not previously been convinced was even possible. He shook his head with a small laugh at himself, before turning and placing his own hand on top of his mother's and Senovo's. "I thought you might be upset that I'd faked a handfasting, to be honest. Even though it was the only solution I could see at the time."

Iseboa gave Senovo's hands a final squeeze and sat back, regarding her son. "I'd have been more upset if you'd made Senovo perform an actual handfasting for you. Though you did put him in something of an awkward position, regardless."

Senovo raised his eyes to look at her. "As I assured Andoc and Carivel at the time, I am something of an expert when it comes to lies of omission, Iseboa."

She lifted an eyebrow. "Yes, and that's a whole different issue. A *shape-shifter*, Senovo—*really?*"

It was fascinating to watch Senovo squirm like a guilty first-year apprentice. "Yes... well. I... considered telling you during my last visit, but I was ashamed. In those days, I had little control over the wolf. It was a part of myself that I found painful to acknowledge. For many years, your son was the only person alive who knew."

"Oh, Senovo," Iseboa said with a sigh. She rose and crossed to Senovo's chair so she could draw him into another embrace. Once again, the powerful High Priest disappeared in an instant, replaced by a young man who desperately craved acceptance and love despite his painful past. A small ache took up residence in my chest, and I swallowed against it.

"Carivel," she said, meeting my eyes, "you may have chosen an unconventional path to walk, but I'm here to tell you that you could not have found two better men to walk it with."

"I know," I replied softly. "I couldn't agree more."

⟡

The small reunion was interrupted a short time later by the arrival of Venzor's Chief himself. Ranulth was a hulking, middle-aged man, taller than Andoc by perhaps half a head, and bulging with muscle. Laugh lines were etched into his weathered face.

"Andoc, by all the gods! Come here, lad," he said in a booming voice. Andoc rose with a grin to meet him, and they exchanged a hearty embrace. "Sorry to show up unannounced like this, Iseboa, but I could hardly credit what Elder Lerand told me. Had to come and see for myself."

Ranulth gave Andoc a vigorous pat on the shoulder and accepted the cup of mead Iseboa pressed on him.

"You might as well join us for a bit, Chief," she said, "unless you need to drag them away to the meeting hall already, of course."

"No, Iseboa—I won't steal your son away just yet. I told everyone to assemble after sunset. Wanted a few words in private first, as it happens." The Chief's jovial demeanor sobered. "There have been all sorts of wild stories making the rounds these last months, Andoc. I see now with hindsight that I should have attended the meetings in Rhyth myself, instead of merely sending an envoy. At the risk of being indelicate, lad, it sounds like your late Chief lost touch with his reason well before he parted ways with his life."

"The attack on Draebard last spring changed him, Ranulth," Andoc said. "He was drawn away from the village on a ruse, along with many of the tribe's warriors—myself included. The Alyrions descended on the village in the middle of the night while we were gone. They massacred the priests in the temple barracks... killed women and children."

I shivered. Though my grief had faded with time, the horror of the attack remained, an indelible mark on all our memories. That horror was not lost on Ranulth, I could see.

"That would be enough change a man, all right," he said. "So, if old Volya died after the summer meeting, then I suppose the brilliant maniac who set fire to the southern mountains was—"

"Er... yes. That was me," said Andoc. "Although you could just as easily say it was the will of the gods."

"One of the acolytes at Draebard's temple has the second sight," Senovo explained. "He foresaw Alyrion soldiers dying on a fiery mountainside months earlier."

Ranulth sat back in the chair Iseboa had offered him. "That may be so, High Priest... but it still took a leader to actually make it happen, I'll wager."

I spoke up for the first time. "I was keeping watch at the mountains when the Alyrion troops crested the pass. There were hundreds of them. If not for Favian's vision and Chief Andoc's leadership, Draebard would have been overrun. Destroyed. And who knows if they would have stopped there?"

Ranulth nodded, then looked at me curiously. "We've not met," he said.

"I'm Carivel."

"Carivel is the Horse Mistress of Draebard," Andoc said unapologetically, "and, more recently, my bondmate."

Ranulth's eyebrows drew together as he studied me. "Really? I took you for a lad," he said. "A Horse Mistress, eh? Sounds like the Mereni's way of thinking must be gaining a foothold in your part of the world."

I wasn't sure what to say to that, but Senovo rescued me. "One cannot argue with results. Despite old superstitions, Draebard's herd is thriving under Carivel's care... just as Meren is thriving under Magoldis's leadership."

"I met her once, you know," said Ranulth. "Magoldis, that is. She seemed like quite a woman. I suppose Meren could do worse for itself."

As reactions went, Ranulth's was a tame one, and I relaxed a bit. Except for Keld, I had tried to keep mostly to the background in the places where we'd stopped to negotiate. It was a relief to know that I would apparently not end up tarnishing Andoc's reputation in his home village.

"Ranulth," said Andoc, "the Alyrions are coming, whether we like it or not. I've got a small network of spies running in Rhyth, and word is, the Emperor is invading the north by sea in the spring."

Ranulth's expression turned very serious. "You *have* been busy, lad. So, you think they'll land at one of the eastern ports, then?"

"I think they'll have to. The weather is too unpredictable on the Western Sea in the spring. I won't mince words, Ranulth. I need your help. Badly. Volya scuppered the talks in Rhyth with his warmongering. We lost our best chance for a solid alliance. I've spent the winter trying to coordinate some sort of unified defense, but time is running out. I've lost people to the winter weather — good people — and I've almost nothing to show for it. You're a respected leader in the north. I need your voice behind me."

Ranulth studied Andoc closely for a long moment, and set his cup aside. He stood up and clasped a strong hand on Andoc's upper arm. "You'll have it, lad. I won't see a son of Venzor try to carry the entire future of Eburos on his shoulders with no support. We're with you."

I could see the effort it cost Andoc not to sag visibly in relief, and was forcibly reminded of the pressure he'd been under for such a long time now. It was all too easy to forget sometimes, because he normally carried it with such grace. I vowed to do better at reminding him that he was not, in fact, alone in this.

"Thank you, Chief," was all he said, but his tone conveyed the depth of his feelings.

Ranulth let him go with a half-smile that faded quickly. "You must know, however, that even if we could muster every warrior on the island, there's no guarantee we can stand before the forces of the Emperor. If you want my opinion on the matter, that's why the other tribes are dragging their heels—it looks too much like a hopeless fight to them."

"I'm well aware, believe me," Andoc said, grim.

Ranulth raised an eyebrow. "Unless your acolyte has had any more helpful visions?"

"Sadly not," said Senovo.

"Though we are pursuing some novel possibilities for the island's defense," Andoc added, his eyes straying briefly to Senovo. "Nothing solid yet, unfortunately."

"Well, I suppose that still means more coming from you than it would from most men," said the Venzori Chief, "though I'll remind you politely that you can't burn the sea."

"More's the pity," Andoc agreed.

"I'll leave you to your mother for a bit, lad. Come to the meeting hall later and we'll talk with the elders." The Chief tipped his head to Senovo and me. "High Priest. Horse Mistress."

"We'll be there," Andoc said. Once Iseboa had shown Ranulth out and closed the door behind him, he half-sat and half-fell into his chair, sagging in a way he hadn't let himself earlier.

"Are you well, old friend?" Senovo asked, concerned.

Andoc nodded, waving us off. "Much better than I was this time yesterday, *amadi*. It's just relief—don't fuss."

"Don't you tell me not to fuss," scolded Iseboa. "I'm your mother." She bent down to place a kiss on Andoc's head, and he blushed faintly. "Now, stop fretting for a few minutes and just relax here with Senovo, while Carivel and I go see about some food."

I looked up, surprised, in time to see Senovo raise an eyebrow.

"*Don't* let her cook," he said.

"Hey!" I retorted, even though my cooking skills were, in fact, largely indefensible. Andoc snorted in faint amusement, as Senovo had probably intended.

Iseboa rolled her eyes at both of them. "Carivel is my guest, you clods. I'm not *actually* going to make her cook. I'm trying to get her alone so we can talk about you in private. *Obviously.*"

"Well, yes. Obviously," Andoc said, still amused. "*Caradi*, don't say anything I'll have cause to make you regret later."

"No promises," I told him, and placed my own kiss on his cheek, following it up with a good-natured glare at Senovo.

I should have been nervous at the prospect of being alone with Andoc's mother, but something about her simply made it impossible. I followed her meekly into the kitchen, where she gestured for me to sit on a padded stool and set herself to peeling vegetables.

"How is he, really?" she asked, glancing up to meet my eyes. "He looks like he's aged ten years since I saw him last."

I chewed my lip, but I could only tell her the truth. "Senovo and I were really worried about him after his injury, Iseboa. We didn't know how to help him. Becoming Chief gave him a new reason to live, but the position brings its own host of problems, as you've seen."

"He always did take on more than his fair share. Even as a boy."

I smiled, not surprised by the revelation. "I think both Senovo and I have plenty of cause to be thankful for that trait."

Iseboa's expression softened. "Yes... well. Believe me when I tell you, I'm happy he has you both. I can't imagine him going through all of this alone."

A small chuckle escaped my lips. "Neither can I—mostly because all he'd have to do is flash those dimples and he'd have admirers falling all over him. He's... not exactly cut out for the life of a hermit."

Iseboa's answering laugh was clear and light. "No, I suppose not." She looked at me, sobering. "There's a difference, though, between having admirers and having a family."

I felt the small ache behind my sternum return. "You're right, of course. It's funny—Senovo is a eunuch, and your son handfasted someone who doesn't want to make a family for him, so the two of them just went off and made their own. Senovo was like a mother bear with a pair of cubs when Favian and Frella were orphaned. Andoc was right there to support him in it, too. I... really respect that about them, Iseboa."

Iseboa was looking at me curiously. "You're part of that family as well, Carivel."

My eyes dropped to my lap as if of their own accord, and I felt a flush rise up my neck. "Well, in a manner of speaking, I suppose I am. I wouldn't wish myself on anyone as a parent, though—surrogate or otherwise."

From the corner of my eye, I saw Iseboa put the knife aside, giving me her full attention. "Now, why ever would you say that?" she asked, sounding genuinely mystified. "From what I've heard and seen today, any child would be lucky to have you in their life."

I looked up in surprise. "I'm a pariah, Iseboa. A woman who dresses as a man."

"No," Iseboa said. "You're a man who was born in a woman's body. It happens sometimes, even if people don't like to talk about it."

I stared at her in shock. It was the first time in my life that I had ever heard anyone speak of other people like me.

"I was born in a small village on the western coastline," Iseboa continued. "There was a pair of sisters living there, except they weren't actually sisters. They weren't related at all — they were lovers. One of them was a eunuch who had run away from the temple in a town further up the coast. He dressed and acted like a woman. I only found out about it by accident. I don't think anyone else in the village even knew." She shrugged. "They were nice people. I really liked them. And what was the harm in it?"

I continued to gape at her for a long moment before I could drag my voice back under my command. Even then, it was hoarse. "I thought I was the only one."

"Oh, goodness — I shouldn't think so, Carivel. Just because people try to ignore something when they don't understand it or it makes them uncomfortable, doesn't mean it's not real. And I should add, the eunuch's companion was a widow with two small children. They seemed perfectly content with their odd little family, so I hardly think that being as you are disqualifies you as a parent."

A wave of shakiness passed over me and I gripped the edges of the stool. "It's not... just that, though." I swallowed hard. The words kept flowing, without any conscious decision on my part. "I have no idea how to be a parent. My father died, and my mother was..." I trailed off. "Well. She wasn't a good mother. We visited her on the way here. I hadn't seen her since I... ran away. But she hasn't changed. She still hates me, and I... and I think I hate her, too."

There was something simultaneously terrible and wonderful about admitting it out loud. I glanced up quickly, looking for censure, but Iseboa was listening intently, no judgment in her expression.

"And I can hardly even bear to be in the same room as a young child, much less touch them or speak with them," I continued in a rush. "So you see, I'm quite serious when I say that I have no business with children. I tried, with little Frella — I really did… but I can't. What if I—?" I cut myself off and swallowed convulsively.

Iseboa let the silence stretch for a few moments while I wrestled with my thoughts, before gently prompting, "What if you… what? Carivel?"

"Hurt her?" I whispered eventually, the words dragged from the depths of my being. The truth of them echoed even as I said them — a revelation.

"Is that something you feel inclined to do?" Iseboa's voice was merely curious — still utterly devoid of anger or disgust.

I forced a couple of deep breaths to combat the dizziness I felt. "No, but… children misbehave. They make mistakes. They act willfully. What if I—?"

"Respond the way your own mother used to, when you misbehaved?" Iseboa supplied. "Can you picture that, Carivel? *Really* picture it in your mind, I mean?"

The dizziness was getting worse, but I tried my best to imagine myself yelling abuse at Frella. Hitting her. Putting marks on her tender skin. My gorge rose and I clutched at the tabletop, jarring it and making a couple of onions roll away from the pile of vegetables. "Oh, gods…"

Suddenly, Iseboa was there. "Hey — easy there, sweetheart. Easy now — I'm sorry. Just breathe." She placed her hands on my shoulders and when I didn't flinch away, drew me into her arms. Her body was soft and yielding, but her arms were strong. I had never been held in quite this way before. Something inside me seemed to unfurl from a place where it had lain for years, hidden in the shadows. Iseboa held tight as she continued. "Carivel, I know I've only just met you, but you could no more hurt a child than you could fly. I bet you've never so much as raised your hand to a horse in anger, have you?"

"No." I shook my head, but a moment later another truth spilled out. "But… I've killed people."

"So has my son," Iseboa replied without hesitation. "But he would never harm an innocent, and neither would you. Now, do you want me to call him in for you, or maybe Senovo? I'm so sorry, dear heart—I never meant to upset you so."

Quickly, I shook my head again. "No, they'll just worry." The fit was passing—I could breathe properly now, and my vision steadied. Somewhat sheepishly, I eased back and swiped the back of my hand across my face.

"Knowing those two, they'll do that regardless," Iseboa said, peering at me closely and nodding with satisfaction as I straightened away from her support. "There now—you look a little steadier, I think."

"Yes—sorry. I'm all right. I think everything is just closer to the surface so soon after seeing my mother again." I gave my eyes a final swipe, even though I hadn't truly been crying. "But I still have no idea how to be a parent to Frella."

Iseboa settled back on her own stool and regarded me. "Then don't be. Be a mentor. Be a role model. Be a teacher, or a friend. Please don't ever tell him I said this, but I have a sneaking suspicion that Senovo is already mothering the poor child half to death."

The laugh that was startled out of me was wet and congested, but welcome nonetheless. "However did you guess?" I asked.

Iseboa chuckled as well. "It actually makes a lot of sense, now that I know about the wolf. He wants his pack around him."

That was exactly it, wasn't it? I met Iseboa's eyes, their deep brown so very similar to Andoc's. "You're right, of course. And it isn't lost on me how lucky I am to be included in that. I haven't been part of a family since my father died."

Iseboa's gaze softened. "Well... it's probably somewhat presumptuous of me. But you *are* handfasted to my son now." She smiled. "*After a fashion*, at any rate. In my eyes, that makes me your mother—should you have either the need or the desire for such a thing, of course."

"Thank you," I whispered, tears threatening yet again.

She smiled, winked at me, and slid a knife and a whole onion toward me. "Here," she said. "I lied earlier about making you help with the meal. Now peel that and chop it up, so you'll have an excuse for your red eyes when the others inevitably get bored and come in here to bother us."

I couldn't stop the smile that bloomed across my face.

The meeting with the elders that evening was everything that we could have hoped for and more. Ranulth was true to his word, and leapt wholeheartedly into plans for strategy and support in the spring. The council of elders made several suggestions for the most efficient means of conveying news and disseminating information to Venzor's allies in the region, until Andoc's vision for the island's defense finally began to look less like a desperate gamble, and more like a workable plan.

When we eventually collapsed into the pile of furs and blankets that Iseboa set out for us near the hearth that night, we were completely exhausted. I fully expected to be insensible until morning, so it was a considerable surprise when Senovo suddenly sat bolt upright next to me, hours later. The movement was so abrupt that it even succeeded in waking Andoc—normally a rather monumental undertaking when we were somewhere safe and warm with no crisis threatening.

"Whu—?" Andoc said, looking around as he tried to get his bearings.

"Senovo?" I asked, wondering if he'd had a nightmare or something. The priest was practically vibrating with tension next to me—breathing deeply, almost as if scenting the air. His eyes were wide in the orange glow of the banked hearth fire, the pupils large and black. I placed a hand on his arm, trying to ground him.

"I have to go," he said, as if the words were being torn from his throat.

My heart jolted with sudden fear, and started thudding rapidly. "Go? Go where? Senovo, it's the middle of the night!"

"I know. I… I'm sorry. There's something. I need to—" His words were oddly disjointed, which did nothing whatsoever to reassure me.

Andoc's hand closed over his other arm, clearly restraining rather than supporting. "Senovo. You're not going anywhere until you tell us what's happening."

Senovo looked jittery, as if he were contemplating trying to break free and make a run for it. It was so different from his usual response to Andoc that my fear ratcheted higher. "Talk to us," I begged.

His mouth worked for a moment before he finally spoke. "There is… something outside. It calls to the wolf. Please—let me go. You *must* let me go immediately."

Andoc looked torn, and was quite possibly as afraid as I was. But it was clear to me that Senovo *would* go unless we physically restrained him somehow, and I was not at all sure he wouldn't fight us even if we did—either as the wolf or as himself. Though it seemed to take an immense effort on my part, I removed my hand from the corded muscles of his forearm.

"Promise us you will come back by morning," I said, a slight quaver in my voice. "Senovo. *Promise.*"

Senovo dragged wild eyes back to look at first me, then Andoc, seeming to note our agitation for the first time. "Yes, I promise," he said. "Only you *must* let me leave now."

Andoc appeared to loosen his grip with some difficulty, and as soon as he was free, Senovo practically bolted for the doorway. A moment later, the wolf was running off into the night.

ELEVEN

Andoc rose slowly and hobbled to the door, which was still hanging open on its hinges. He closed it reluctantly.

At the same instant, Iseboa emerged from the bedroom, a candle held in one hand and a sleeping robe wrapped tightly around her body. "What's happened? Is something wrong?" She looked around. "Where is Senovo?"

Andoc continued to stare at the inside of the front door. "I have absolutely no idea," he said.

The rest of the night passed miserably, not to mention *slowly*. Iseboa heated some water for tea, and we sat by the window, cracking open one shutter so we could keep watch through the gap. We were huddled in blankets against the cold air coming in from outside, hoping for a glimpse of gray fur and yellow eyes. No one managed more than a light doze, and I barely even managed that. My mind turned in circles that grew tighter and tighter as the time slid by. *Had we lost him? Should we have tried harder to keep him from leaving?*

"He'll come back," Andoc said, after catching me chewing on a ragged fingernail.

I admired the certainty carried in his voice and wondered if it was feigned or not. We were meant to leave for Draebard this morning. What if he *didn't* come back?

"I won't leave him behind," I said. "And I won't let you leave him behind either."

"No one is leaving anyone behind, *caradi*," Andoc said, and drew me against his side with an arm around my shoulders. I came willingly, though the tension did not leave my neck and jaw.

"Whatever could have caused him to act in such a way?" Iseboa asked. "You say he's never done this before?"

"Never," Andoc said, "and I really wish I knew."

The first shafts of sunlight were just beginning to filter between the walls of the huts nearby when two figures stumbled out of the shadows. Senovo was leading a slender adolescent boy on unsteady legs. Both were naked in the bitter morning chill.

"*Gods!*" Andoc cursed, bolting to his feet so fast he sent a clay cup tumbling to the floor, where it shattered, spattering cold tea everywhere. Iseboa had been dozing in her chair, and jerked awake at the noise, even as I scrambled to retrieve a couple of blankets from the floor and charge outside to meet them.

Senovo's teeth were set against the cold, and he helped me wrap the first blanket around the boy's shoulders before taking his own. The lad's ribs stood out starkly and he was covered with old scrapes and bruises. He cringed from my touch, but I ignored it in favor of wrapping Senovo up and half-dragging them both into the hut.

Andoc and Iseboa were already stirring up the fire and adding more wood, coaxing it into a blaze. Senovo led the shivering boy to the hearth and deposited him on the nest of furs still piled there.

"Food," he said hoarsely. "He needs food."

Iseboa hurried to the kitchen to fetch something left over from last night. Meanwhile, I went to get Senovo's clothing, as well as something from my own bag for the boy to wear. When I turned back, the blanket had slipped from one of Senovo's shoulders, revealing four bloody scratches slightly longer than the span of my hand. I froze, hissing in reaction.

Andoc followed my gaze and frowned. He grasped Senovo's uninjured shoulder and faced him. "Talk to us," he said, and it was not a request.

"I didn't mean to do it," muttered the boy, still huddled in his blanket.

"There was a small misunderstanding," Senovo said, his voice still a bit raspy. "It's of no import."

My mind was worrying at this strange series of events, trying to drag them into a pattern that made sense. "Is this the boy that the priest from Venzor told us about, when he spoke to us in Rhyth?" I asked. Andoc drew in a sharp breath.

Iseboa returned carrying two bowls of stew. The boy inhaled the smell of meat and vegetables as he peered up at her with cautious eyes through a tangled mane of russet hair. She stopped short, staring at his face, her mouth hanging open.

"Ithric?" she asked. "Merciful gods. Does your sister know you're back?"

The boy shook his head. "I was coming back to see her, but I was afraid to come into the village. Then I felt a strange wolf nearby…" He looked at Senovo mistrustfully, and averted his face again.

"I sensed another shape-shifter somewhere outside the town last night," Senovo said, the tense lines of his body beginning to relax as the fire warmed him. "Or, rather, the wolf did. It was a rather extraordinary sensation, I must say."

"Apparently so, judging by the way you hared off with no explanation," Andoc said, and let his hand drop from Senovo's shoulder. His brow was still drawn into a sharp frown.

"Yes. I apologize for that. The wolf grew very strong, very quickly. It was difficult to think about the situation as a human thinks. It wasn't my intention to scare you."

Iseboa straightened from handing Ithric his bowl and moved to give Senovo his. "You did scare them, though. You scared all of us." She sighed. "But you're back now. And so is Ithric."

I studied the lad more closely, as much as I could while he was huddled in a shapeless blanket and shoveling food into his mouth. This was apparently the boy who had manifested shape-shifting abilities when his family was attacked by bandits on the road. His parents had been killed, but he and his sister survived. The Venzori priest who spoke to us in Rhyth—Mabios, his name had been—told Senovo that Ithric had run away when it was suggested that he should join the temple.

When Favian had asked what form he took, Mabios said he changed into a lion. I stared at the claw marks on Senovo's shoulder, unable to suppress a faint shudder.

"I won't join the temple," Ithric mumbled between shoveling spoonfuls of stew into his mouth. "I just want to see Alyndra."

"I'm sure she'll want to see you, as well," Iseboa said. "We'll go as soon as you've had a chance to warm up and rest a bit."

Ithric nodded, still looking a bit overwhelmed at the attention he was receiving. I wondered if he had been living as a lion all these months. Either way, he'd obviously had a rough time of things, judging by his gaunt, undernourished frame and the smattering of old injuries marring his skin.

When his bowl of stew was empty, he peered at Senovo again. "Who are you? You're not from Venzor."

"I am Senovo of Draebard." Senovo gestured to Andoc and me. "This is Iseboa's son, Andoc, and this is Carivel, Andoc's bondmate."

Light brown eyes flecked with gold raked over me, taking in my close-cropped hair and male clothing before returning to Senovo. "You're a eunuch. Are you a priest?"

"I am, though I assure you I have no intention of dragging you to the temple."

Ithric's eyes narrowed. "Why should I trust you?"

"Because I myself was initiated into the priesthood against my will when I was not much older than you. I will not see anyone else treated that way."

The boy studied Senovo for a bit longer, and nodded. "How long have you been a shape-shifter?"

"Since I was seventeen. Like you, I shifted unexpectedly during a traumatic event." Senovo did not offer more. He had made his peace with the wolf for the most part, but I knew that particular memory was still a painful one.

Ithric nodded again, drawn back into his own memories by the look of it.

"Priest Mabios approached me last autumn about you," Senovo continued. "He is worried, as are others in Venzor who care about you. If you are amenable, I have agreed to help you as best I can, based on my own experiences, with the understanding that I will not attempt to influence you into joining the priesthood."

The boy's face twisted into a frown. "What makes you think I need your help?"

Senovo raised an eyebrow. "Well—you're starving, for one thing."

The frown deepened. "The north's not good for lions. Maybe I'll go south. Find a pride to live with."

I joined the conversation. "The Alyrion Empire is taking over in the south. They burn shape-shifters at the stake."

"They'd have to catch me first," Ithric replied with a stubborn tilt to his chin.

I thought of the cats that patrolled the storage buildings around the horse pens in Draebard, and how impossible it was to get them to do anything they didn't want to.

"Very well, Ithric," Senovo said. "As it happens, Draebard is several days south of here. You are welcome to accompany us there as the first leg of your journey."

Ithric eyed him uncertainly for a moment, as if trying to figure out a way to argue against the very thing he'd said he wanted. I had to suppress a smile—attempting to match wits with Senovo was a thankless pursuit at the best of times.

"Fine," the boy said eventually.

"What about Alyndra?" Iseboa asked. "Would you truly leave her again so soon?"

Ithric ducked his head to hide his expression once more. "She doesn't need me. She'll probably get married soon to the miller's son just like Pa and Ma always planned."

Iseboa looked unhappy, but didn't press the issue. "Why don't you get dressed, and we'll go talk to her? Carivel brought you some clothes you can borrow, and I think I have an old pair of Andoc's boots somewhere that might fit you."

The five of us shuffled around the hut, getting ready for the day after a night of too little sleep and too much worry. Andoc and Iseboa ganged up on Senovo to put salve on the claw marks across his shoulder and bandage them, while I continued to watch Ithric as unobtrusively as I could.

My clothes were a bit big on him, but not ridiculously so. When he stood, however, his jutting ribs and collarbones were even more noticeable until he laced up the shirt. I tried to picture him as a lanky, adolescent lion, attempting to find and kill prey in the middle of winter with no hunting experience and no pride of other lions to support him. The boy was lucky that he hadn't starved to death in the months since he'd run away.

I turned to Andoc. "Do you still want to leave this morning?"

Andoc considered for a moment before making a decision. "No. We all need a few more hours of proper rest first. We'll also have to decide how to pack the horses with the addition of a fourth person."

We had left the horses in the care of Venzor's Horse Master the previous evening, and they would be fine there until we were ready to leave. Fortunately, we were on the final leg of our journey, and had already used many of our supplies, leaving less to carry with us. Of course, we would now have another person to feed on the way back home.

"I think we can redistribute what supplies we need evenly among all four horses. We may have to keep a slower pace so as not to overtax them, but frankly the conditions will probably slow us down regardless," I said.

"I'll take Ithric to see Alyndra now and leave the three of you to rest, in that case," Iseboa said.

"Someone should inform Priest Mabios that he has returned," suggested Senovo.

"*No*," Ithric said. "I don't want people to know I'm back."

"Then tell your sister to let them know you're all right after we leave," Andoc said, exhaustion making him curt. "I'm not kidnapping you and taking you to Draebard in secret."

Ithric nodded reluctantly, and accepted the cloak Iseboa gave him. Iseboa crossed to wrap her arms around Andoc and drag him down so she could kiss his cheek. When she pulled back, her smile was wan. "This isn't quite the visit you'd pictured, I'll wager," she said. "I'll be back as soon as I can. Get some sleep, all of you." Her gaze flickered over the three of us and she ushered Ithric out the door.

When it closed behind them, Andoc let out a gusty breath. "Food and rest, in that order. I'd still like to get a few leagues of travel under our belts this afternoon."

I felt sorry for Andoc, who would no doubt have preferred to spend a relaxing few days with his mother before braving the unforgiving winter conditions once more. Time was a constant press on his mind, however, and he was already worrying about the seemingly endless series of difficult tasks that would need to be completed before spring if we were to have any chance of survival... much less of victory.

I took a moment to wonder how Jacun, Balzoc, Varanis, and the others were faring—hopefully they had enjoyed the same success we had on our journey so far.

Andoc and I ate some of Iseboa's excellent stew before the three of us settled back down before the hearth to try and rest, at least until the others returned. If Andoc and I wrapped Senovo up a little tighter between us than was perhaps warranted in the warm hut, he made no mention of it.

"What do you think it means that you could sense Ithric's presence from a distance?" I asked.

"I do not know," Senovo replied, "though it is apparent to me now that the shape-shifters of Eburos share some sort of connection."

I was too tired to expend much effort on trying to figure out how that fact might tie into Senovo's insistence that his ability would be somehow important in the coming struggle. There would be plenty of time on the bleak journey home for that.

⚜

We dozed together through the morning. Senovo and I awoke when Iseboa and Ithric returned shortly before midday. Ithric looked both sad and angry, but did not offer any insights about his conversation with his sister. I figured it was none of my business anyway, and devoted myself to shaking Andoc awake so we could make our farewells and get on the road.

Iseboa insisted on feeding us again before we left, not that any of us were inclined to argue with her. When we were done, Andoc looked up, a complicated mix of emotion on his handsome face.

"I know I ask you this every single time I come home and the answer is always the same, but... you could come with us?"

Iseboa smiled, even as she wiped a tear from the corner of her eye. "My life is in Venzor, Andoc. Maybe when I'm old and helpless, I'll let you cart me to Draebard in the back of a wagon, and the three of you can wait on me hand and foot in my twilight years." She laughed softly, and another tear spilled over. "*Mother of the Chief.* I can see it now—I'd spend my days sitting on a great big padded chair, telling stories about the trouble you used to get into as a boy."

A great well of affection for this woman I'd only met yesterday rose up inside me, and I stepped forward to hug her. "I'd be curled up at your feet listening intently to those stories, in between bringing you sweetmeats and spiced wine," I said.

Iseboa hugged back. "I look forward to it, in that case. I'm so glad you came, Carivel. Remember—family is important, but nothing says you can't make your own if you need to. I am pleased and honored to call you part of my family."

I swallowed the surge of nervousness that sped my pulse, and said very deliberately, "As I am pleased and honored to call you *Mother*." My voice only quavered a tiny bit, despite the strange feelings coursing through me.

Iseboa huffed out a pleased little noise and squeezed tighter. "Be safe, Carivel. And don't be a stranger."

I nodded and reluctantly let go, only to be replaced by Senovo. "I apologize for bringing such unforeseen excitement to your doorstep last night," he said, "but I am deeply grateful for the chance to see you again. Thank you for your continued kindness and generosity. And thank you for raising Andoc to be who he is."

"You are every bit as much my son as he is, Senovo," said Iseboa. "And you are welcome here any time—on four legs or two."

Finally, Andoc stepped forward to envelop his mother in an embrace. "Goodbye, Mother. I'm sorry we can't stay longer. Perhaps when the battle is done…"

"I'll hold you to that," Iseboa said, her own voice growing unsteady. "I love you very much, Andoc. Promise me you'll remember that other people love you as well, and that you'll let them help you and support you."

"I promise. I've learned that lesson well in the past year," he said. "I won't forget."

They parted reluctantly, and Iseboa gave Ithric a watery smile. "Be well, Ithric. Remember that Alyndra loves you, even if she is hurt and angry right now."

Ithric didn't look up to meet her eyes, but he did nod, and I wondered what had passed between him and his sister.

We were a subdued group as we headed out to pack up the horses and depart Venzor. I was a bit surprised that Senovo had not offered to travel as the wolf, freeing another horse to carry the supplies. That wasn't to say I was displeased, though—quite the opposite. I had no desire to let him out of my sight after the previous night. And, indeed, he may well have been resisting the desire to go searching for other wolves at least in part as a tacit apology for frightening us so badly.

I was intrigued to discover that the horses were unaccountably nervous around Ithric. "Have you much riding experience?" I asked.

"A bit. Not much," he said, eyeing the gelding we'd been using as a packhorse warily as it snorted and tried to back away from him. "Never had this problem, though. What's wrong with these horses?"

I quirked a wry eyebrow. "I think they're a bit reluctant to let a lion jump on one of their backs. Here. You'll have to ride Kekenu."

Kekenu was nervous as well, but he trusted me enough to submit to the lion-boy with only a bit of snorting and head-shaking.

"Keep your body relaxed and don't grip with your legs," I ordered. "Sit up straight; don't hunch forward."

To be safe, I put a lead rope on Kekenu and ponied him from the gelding I was riding until I was sure he would be all right carrying Ithric. It was fascinating to ponder, even if it was also another thing to worry about as we traveled. Though horses were always frightened of Senovo at first when he was in the form of the wolf, I'd never seen him have problems with them while in human form. I wondered if it had something to do with the fact that Ithric had been living largely in animal form for such a long time now. Did a shape-shifter's inner animal truly begin to take over when given free rein for too long, as Senovo had originally feared?

Whatever the case, horses were nothing if not adaptable. After a few hours of travel, they calmed down around the skinny boy. This was a relief, since travel conditions had certainly not improved since we'd arrived in Venzor. More snow had fallen, and while it was not deep enough to hinder our progress, it still meant that we had to be vigilant or risk the same fate that had befallen poor Renthro.

When we finally made camp for the night, Ithric eyed the tent with misgivings. I couldn't really blame him—I wasn't too thrilled about sharing such close quarters with a stranger either. The four of us would have to be practically on top of each other to fit.

"I could shift and spend the night as the lion," Ithric said, still looking uncomfortable.

"Absolutely not," I replied immediately. "You'll scare the horses off and then where will we be?"

"I will change," Senovo said. "The horses already know the wolf, and it's no hardship. In fact, there's probably room for me at your feet, so I won't even have to be outside."

Andoc nodded. "All right. That's what we'll do, then."

It wasn't too bad in the end. I curled up next to Andoc, while Ithric lay on his other side. Senovo was a warm, familiar weight at our feet, near the tent opening. We trusted him with the watch — we were all exhausted, but the wolf would awaken at the first hint of a disturbance. His nose and ears were far more sensitive than a human's.

The pattern repeated over the following days, though Senovo did return to traveling as the wolf on the third day. While this had the benefit of freeing up his horse to carry our remaining supplies, it also put me on edge. For the final part of the journey, it seemed that we barely saw him in human form at all.

Meanwhile, Ithric grew increasingly withdrawn and agitated as we approached the more familiar lands around Draebard. I realized with a flash of insight that the lion must be getting restless after being contained for so long. Finally, on the last evening before we were due to arrive home, I took him aside.

"You need to change before we arrive in Draebard. I can see the signs. Ride out with me on Kekenu. We'll go away from the camp so you can shift and let the lion run for a bit. You have to promise me that you've got enough control to leave the horses alone, though."

Ithric scowled at me. "Of course I do. I'm not stupid."

I nodded. "Fine. Let's tell the others and go before it gets too much colder."

Andoc was not thrilled, but saw the sense of it. Senovo, who had changed back to human form and was huddled next to the fire, nodded sagely.

"Would you like me to come along, Carivel?" he asked.

"No, it's fine," I said.

Andoc shot a look at Ithric that said it had damned well better be fine, and the boy flushed. I suddenly remembered the half-healed claw marks on Senovo's shoulder and shivered a bit, but I would have Kekenu with me, and I was pretty confident we could outrun an undernourished, adolescent lion if we really had to.

"Keep a close eye on the other horses just in case they get nervous," I added. "We'll go back along the trail at that open field we passed on the way here, but even the smell of lion might be enough to set them off."

"We will," Andoc promised. "Don't be too long."

With Ithric riding behind me, I headed back to the stretch of open grass. Ithric dismounted and unfastened his cloak, though he left it draped over his shoulders as a nod to both warmth and privacy as he undressed beneath it and handed his clothes up to me. I rode a little way away and turned Kekenu back to face him, prepared for the gelding's startled jump backwards when Ithric shifted and bounded away.

"Whoa, boy," I said, studying the tawny cat in fascination even as I steadied the little horse.

Ithric's gangly feline form promised impressive size when he was fully grown, though his pelt was dull and rough right now, and his ribs and hipbones stood out every bit as much as when he was human. The first hint of a russet mane was just beginning to show along his neck in the gray evening light.

When I was confident he was not going to turn on us unexpectedly, I rode back to where his discarded cloak lay on the ground and dismounted to retrieve it. Kekenu was staring fixedly in the direction the lion had disappeared, but did not seem overtly panicked as I stepped up into the saddle once more and laid Ithric's clothing across his neck and shoulders to keep it warm.

We waited until dusk gave way to full dark. The moon rising in the east cast a ghostly silver glow across the snow-covered landscape, and I was just beginning to worry that Ithric had decided to make a run for it and leave us behind when Kekenu tensed and lifted his head, ears pricked sharply.

A few minutes later, movement caught my eye, and the big cat slunk toward us on silent paws. Clouds of steam rose in rhythmic bursts from its nose and mouth, making it seem like some magical creature in the moonlight.

Though of course, it *was* a magical creature, I reminded myself as it halted perhaps thirty paces away and sat down, tail curling around its legs. Kekenu was tense and ready to bolt, only his trust in our years of partnership keeping him in place beneath me. Taking a leap of faith, I stepped down and lifted the clothes from the horse's back, holding the reins tightly in one hand.

I walked forward, the little gelding following me with considerable reluctance, until I could proffer the clothing. "Come on, Ithric," I said. "Let's head back to the others so we can warm up at the fire."

The lion shook itself, and suddenly a human boy was crouched in the snow. Ithric shivered and reached for the clothes.

Our final day of travel dawned snowy, and by the time we straggled into Draebard, we were battling a full-blown blizzard. The wolf led us unerringly through the swirling white, or else we would have been forced to hunker down and wait it out, stranded only a league or two from the safety of home. As it was, the townsfolk were all inside with their shutters drawn tight, and our return went unremarked until Andoc dismounted and hobbled up to the entrance of the temple to pound on it.

Favian opened the door, his face lighting up as he recognized the man and wolf standing outside. "You're back!" he exclaimed, peering through the snow to confirm that I was also present and accounted for. The gesture sent a small surge of warmth through my chilled body.

Behind me, Ithric balked. "I won't stay in the temple," he said, and Favian peered at the newcomer curiously.

"Fine," I said, my patience worn somewhat thin after a day riding in the brutal conditions. "In that case, you can help me take the horses to the pens and get them unsaddled and fed."

"Will you be all right?" Andoc asked.

"It's not exactly the first time I've gone to and from the pens during a blizzard, Andoc," I reassured him. "I'll follow the fences and walls. We'll be fine."

I knew Andoc would not relax until I was back safely, but he nodded and forced a smile. I took two horses and Ithric took the other two as we headed back to the edge of the village. As I had expected, the lads were huddled inside the largest storage building, and Varin replied to my knock in moments.

"Horse Mistress!" he said, and the others immediately crowded forward to see.

Dalon pushed through the crowd to meet us. "Welcome back, boss," he said. "You picked a hell of a day for it, didn't you? We were just warming up for a bit before trying to get feed out for the herd."

"It's good to be back, Dalon. This is Ithric, by the way — he joined us on the trip from Venzor. Let's get these horses untacked and put up for the night. They've had quite a tiring journey."

In seconds, we were swarmed as the boys efficiently stripped the four horses of their saddles and packs and rubbed them down in the shelter of the large building. When they were dry and had been offered fresh water, we put them out with the herd. I helped the boys lay out feed for the night while Ithric sheltered inside, out from under foot. We all made our way back to town, hanging onto each other's cloaks and sleeves, dropping people off along the way.

"If you're dead set on avoiding the temple," I called to Ithric against the wind, "you can stay in my hut tonight. Of course, that would make you an idiot, because the temple has food and warm fires, while my hut does not."

Ithric hesitated for only a moment before the mention of food swayed him, as I had hoped it would. "Fine, let's go then," he said. "I'm only agreeing to stay there because of the storm, though."

"Whatever you say," I agreed readily, since my only interest at this point was to get back to Andoc, Senovo, and the others.

At the temple, Favian was waiting for us, ready to open the door and let us inside, out of the blustery snow. Unlike the unheated storage building at the horse pens, it was blissfully warm inside. Somewhat to my surprise, Favian darted forward and hugged me, ignoring the snow clinging to my clothing.

"Hi," he said, somewhat sheepishly.

I smiled, happier than I could express to be back home. "Hi, yourself. Staying out of trouble, I trust?"

He blushed a bit. "Trying to. Although Frella did get into some ochre paste and used it to paint pictures on the back wall of the altar room."

I laughed aloud. "Who knows? It could well be an improvement. That wall was pretty boring before."

I saw the moment Favian really looked at Ithric for the first time. Ithric, who had been doing his best to fade into the background, glanced up at the same time. Their eyes caught and held. I watched as Favian's pupils dilated, his lips parting slightly.

Oh, boy, I thought, and cleared my throat.

TWELVE

The two boys jerked their gazes away from each other at the noise.

"Favian," I introduced, "this is Ithric of Venzor. Ithric is the shape-shifter that Priest Mabios told us about when we were in Rhyth." Favian's eyes grew wide, and darted back to the other boy as I continued. "Ithric, this is Favian. Favian and his sister Frella are under Andoc's guardianship. And, well, mine too, of course. Favian is one of High Priest Senovo's acolytes, as you may have gathered."

"Hello," Favian offered, somewhat tentatively.

Ithric only nodded once in acknowledgment, a sharp gesture.

I sighed and took off my cloak, which was heavy with melting snow. Favian shook his head as if to clear it and said, "Sorry—let me take your things. The others are in the refectory."

He hurried off with the wet cloaks a moment later, as if eager to escape from Ithric's presence. I led Ithric through the familiar halls until the sound of voices heralded the small reunion taking place in the room beyond.

"Horse Mistress Carivel!" greeted Novice Feldes. "Do come in and join us! You too, Ithric—pleased to meet you."

Ithric looked as if he would much rather flee the room full of priests and acolytes, but I was fairly confident that the blizzard outside would deter him from any rash action. I was also tired, cold, damp, and hungry, so I ignored his discomfiture in favor of flopping down at the table with the others.

"It's good to be here, Novice Feldes," I said with complete sincerity. "Hello, everyone. Now, if you'll excuse my horrible manners, I'm dying for some of whatever's in that pot."

Feldes grinned and served me soup, bread, and spiced vegetables, following it with another large serving for Ithric. I barely remembered to bless myself, touching my fingertips to my forehead, lips, and heart before falling on the meal like a starving man. Beside me, Ithric — who certainly had a more legitimate claim to that description than I — did much the same. Senovo entered a moment later, restored to human form, and sat down beside me, our shoulders brushing. Andoc smiled at us, the lines at the corners of his eyes crinkling, and I winked in return, relieved beyond measure to be exactly where I was.

Ithric reluctantly stayed at the temple until the storm cleared, at which point I gave him the use of my tiny, ramshackle hut, since I rarely used it myself these days. As Senovo had no doubt expected, despite the boy's original declaration that he would continue south to live as a lion, the lure of plentiful food and a warm bed held him captive far more effectively than any physical restraints we could have devised.

To my delight, two days later, First Warrior Jacun returned from his journey to Meren and Erylaan with my friend Keenan in tow in addition to his original companions. After our initial exuberant embrace, she drew me aside.

"I have almost two dozen mounted archers ready to fight, Carivel," she said seriously. "And I need to talk with Andoc and your elders about an idea that one of the weapons makers in Meren came up with. Can we meet with them tonight?"

The meeting house was bustling that evening as Jacun reported on the response from the council at the port of Erylaan. While more skeptical than the rulers of Llanmeer had been, they were open to allying with other tribes in the north to aid in their defense should the Alyrions attempt to attack their town. However, the port master was firmly of the opinion that Erylaan was the least likely landing point for the naval invasion, because of the difficulty in getting large ships moored close enough to send out smaller landing boats during the spring riptides.

Andoc listened intently to Keenan as she described the Mereni weapons maker's idea, nodding with a thoughtful frown as she explained how it might be utilized in conjunction with the archers we'd been training for the past several months.

When Andoc asked if Senovo had anything to add, the priest only shook his head, though his excursions into the wilds since we had returned had continued nightly.

Keenan stayed on for a couple of weeks, joining me to work with the other Draebardi archers whenever conditions permitted. Meanwhile, Ithric began to accompany Senovo on some nights, though I wasn't sure if he was helping Senovo or merely using the excuse to shift often enough to keep his inner lion content.

When not roaming, the Venzori boy could often be found flustering poor Favian. The two of them seemed constitutionally incapable of leaving each other alone, even though they rubbed each other the wrong way whenever they were in the same room for more than a handful of minutes. On a few occasions, I caught Andoc and Senovo exchanging rueful looks, and I wondered if they were remembering themselves at a younger age.

Senovo, though… Senovo worried me. Whatever he was trying to learn from the wild wolves, he was obviously not succeeding. More concerning, though, was the way in which that failure was affecting him. In all the time I had known him, I had *never* seen him chronically short-tempered and snappish. And while he could occasionally be distant when other things were on his mind, it seemed now as if he was actively pulling away from the two of us. It left me wrong-footed and anxious. I could also see it eating at Andoc—just at the time when he most needed his focus for the coming battle.

Finally, I couldn't keep my peace any longer.

"We're losing him," I fretted, on yet another evening when Andoc and I lay in Senovo's bed, in hopes that Senovo himself would grace us with his human presence sometime before morning.

"And what would you suggest I do about it?" Andoc flared, only to run a frustrated hand over his face an instant later. "Sorry. *Sorry, caradi.* Gods, this is getting to me. You're right, of course, but we can't *force* him not to pull away from us."

I wrapped my arms around him and laid my head on his chest. "I know we can't. I have no idea what to do either."

⤛ ⚜ ⤜

The days slipped by in a flurry of messengers, meetings, and worry. As the winter began to ease, Andoc and Jacun joined

Keenan in preparation for one last trip to Meren, where they planned to finalize everything with Magoldis. The general consensus seemed to be that the north had mustered a much stronger defense than anyone could have expected after the disastrous meetings last summer, but it still wasn't going to be enough against an Empire that controlled entire continents.

I saw the travelers off, clasping Jacun's hand and giving Keenan an affectionate hug before sharing a heartfelt kiss with Andoc. Senovo had not yet returned from his nightly wanderings, and his absence was like a physical ache.

The priest was apologetic at missing Andoc's departure when he finally did show up, but he was still distant. My temper snapped, after days of my having emotions drawn tighter than a bowstring.

"And if he dies like Renthro did, on the journey? If we never see him again?" I clenched my fists and glared at him. "What's the last thing you said to him? *Do you even remember?*"

Senovo appeared taken aback. "I asked him to speak with Elder Briethe in Meren, to see if she could tell him any more details about the southern shape-shifter she met when she was young... Lorish, the one who changed into a fox."

"Well, I'm sure that will be a huge comfort to him if anything bad happens!" I flared.

Senovo's brows drew together. "We may all be dead come springtime, if I can't learn what I need to know. Is that preferable?"

"You can't even explain to anyone what it is that you're trying to do!"

Senovo's face could have been carved from stone as he answered. "No. I can't," he said, and walked away, leaving me alone.

The ache in my chest grew so sharp that it threatened to send me to my knees. I gathered anger around me like a cloak to combat it, with limited success. Thankfully, with the weather easing, there were a number of tasks at the horse pens that needed to be addressed after having been left undone while the conditions outside were too harsh. I threw myself into my work, more than content to fix fences, shovel manure, and haul loads of fodder back and forth until my back was aching and I was exhausted enough to fall into a restless sleep... alone. My anger with Senovo was so great that I retired to Andoc's hut rather than stay at the temple. I would have retreated completely, back to my own sad little hovel, only I'd let Ithric stay there and the last thing I needed was to be stuck in a cramped room with the odd, prickly boy.

On the third night after Andoc's departure, not even my exhausted muscles were enough to drag me down into slumber, so I was wide awake and staring at the rafters above the simple pallet-bed when I heard scratching at the door. I'd been lying there long enough that it was closer to morning than not, I was fairly certain. The sound came again and I sat up, listening—it was far too deliberate to be some small animal scrabbling randomly around the walls.

With a decent amount of confidence about what I would find, I rose and opened the front door a crack. The wolf looked up at me with glowing yellow-green eyes and whined. Complex emotions battled inside my breast, but there was never any question that I would open the door. The instant I did, the animal slunk inside and flopped onto the floor, staring at me hopefully.

I closed the door with careful deliberation and crossed to sit down on the bed, trying to swallow past the heavy lump that had lodged itself in my throat. The wolf belly-crawled across the distance separating us, whimpering as it approached. A wet nose pressed against my leg, nuzzling, and the first tears of frustration and fear shook themselves free as I clapped a hand over my mouth to try to stifle them.

A moment later, I had a lap full of wolf, and I gave in, clutching Senovo to me and weeping into the heavy fur at his neck. He was far too much of a canny bastard to shift into human form so I could lay into him properly, of course. Part of me resented him for it, while another part was unspeakably grateful just to have him in my arms and not have to fight with him.

Before long, I cried myself out and fell into a deep sleep of total exhaustion, still wrapped around the furry, comforting form. It seemed only a moment later that a broad tongue swiped across my cheek, dragging me into wakefulness to see the first rays of sunlight peeking through the chinks in the shutters. New tears tried to rise up, but I forced them down. There was no further time for such things now.

I grabbed the fur at the wolf's cheeks, framing the animal's face. "I *know* you love us, Senovo," I told him. "It's killing us to watch you pull away. This only works with all three of us."

The wolf whined and wriggled forward to lick my face again. I shook my head, trying to armor my heart against the guileless beast.

"I have to go. I'm late to the pens already," I said.

I paused a moment, wondering if Senovo would shift back, but he didn't. Even so, it was beyond me to be truly angry at the wolf. How could I be? If anything, I felt a little bit better after the reassurance that Senovo still cared enough to come and comfort me, whatever his form. Apparently, for now, that would have to suffice.

The animal appeared at Andoc's door on the next four nights as well, though Senovo was a master at evading me in his human form during the daylight hours. Finally, a week after they had left and just as I was starting to worry seriously about their safety, Andoc's party returned late in the afternoon, with two new additions in tow. I met Andoc with a tight embrace and a kiss as he dismounted from his mare, relief coursing through me at having him back.

"Hello, Carivel, dear," Elder Briethe greeted from the back of her ancient gelding. "It's good to see you again! I don't suppose you could do me a favor and get someone at the temple to arrange for a—"

"Hot bath?" I suggested, a smile pulling at the corners of my mouth.

Briethe laughed merrily. "Ah! Already, Draebard's Horse Mistress knows me too well." The short, silver-haired woman dismounted carefully, stretching her back with a series of audible pops before turning to the other unfamiliar figure.

I studied the second woman with interest. She was hovering at the back of the small group of horses, her body language shy and focused inward. I estimated that she was roughly the same age as Briethe, but where the Mereni elder was plump and outgoing, the newcomer was sharp-featured and wary—a tiny slip of a woman without an ounce of fat on her, all muscle and hard sinew.

Briethe followed my gaze. "Horse Mistress Carivel, may I present Lorish of Rhyth... a friend from long ago."

Surprise jolted through me. Lorish, the *shape-shifter*? My eyes flew to Andoc, who returned my look with a meaningful one of his own. Remembering myself, I turned back to Lorish and offered a slight bow.

"Greetings, Lorish," I said. "Welcome to Draebard. We're honored to have you here."

Lorish dipped her head in a quick nod of acknowledgment, still looking like she was poised for a quick getaway. Her eyes held the same strange distance that I had seen so often in Senovo's of late, and I felt a faint chill of inexplicable foreboding.

"Indeed we are," Andoc echoed, handing off his horse to Tenibral as several of the boys moved forward to care for the animals. Andoc's gaze flicked to me, still weighty with hidden meaning. "*Caradi*, it's very good to be home. To say this was an eventful trip would be putting it mildly. We have much to discuss with the council, but I also need to speak with you privately as soon as possible."

I nodded. "Of course."

We were interrupted by Lorish's sharp, indrawn breath. A moment later, Ithric came running up, looking around somewhat wildly until his eyes fell on the Rhytheeri woman. Several of the horses spooked at the boy's sudden arrival, and I gestured for the lads to get them under control and take them away.

"Ithric?" Andoc asked. The boy's eyes never wavered from Lorish, who looked back in similar fascination.

"I felt—" Ithric began, only to turn as Senovo also arrived, slightly out of breath.

"There is another shape-shifter nearby," he said urgently, his eyes casting around until he, too, focused on Lorish.

"There is indeed," Briethe said, obviously fascinated. "High Priest Senovo, may I present Lorish? And I assume you must be Ithric, young man—Andoc told me all about you. It's a pleasure to meet you."

Ithric only nodded, still staring.

"Well," Andoc said. "I think it's clear we all need to talk. Jacun, could you round up the council and ask them to assemble as soon as possible? I'll get our guests some hot food and we'll meet you at the hall."

"Of course," Jacun agreed, and the others headed off to warm up and get something to eat, leaving Andoc and me alone with Briethe and three wary shape-shifters. Senovo blinked and seemed to come back to himself.

"You must forgive my surprise, Respected Elders," he said, addressing both Briethe and Lorish. "I was not expecting anything like this. Andoc, welcome back, old friend. I am pleased that everyone has returned safely." His attention returned to Lorish. "It would be my honor to offer you the hospitality of the temple. If… you are comfortable with that?"

I remembered that the Rhytheeri priests had tried to make Lorish a virtual prisoner when she was a young woman, rather than have a female shape-shifter at large, outside of the control of the temple.

Lorish, who had still not spoken a word, moved closer to Briethe and looked at her uncertainly. Briethe gave her a reassuring smile and took the other woman's hand in a loose grip. "I have some acquaintance with Draebard's young High Priest, my friend," she said. "I am confident that he has no designs on your freedom."

Ithric looked between the two of them. "If it helps," the boy said haltingly, "he promised when we met that he wouldn't try to force me into the priesthood. I've been here for weeks now, and so far he hasn't."

It was perhaps not the most ringing of endorsements, but Lorish seemed to take it at face value. "Very well," she said, her voice rusty with disuse and tinged with a heavy Rhytheeri accent.

Andoc smiled, and he, Senovo, and I led the way to the temple.

"How are you, my friend?" Andoc asked Senovo in a low voice as we walked.

Senovo shrugged one shoulder almost imperceptibly. "Carivel will no doubt tell you that I am not at my best."

Andoc glanced at me and I gave a tiny shake of my head, unwilling to get into it right now. Again, I got the sense that Andoc was nearly bubbling over with some news that he had not yet shared.

"With any luck," he said, still for our ears alone, "I have a couple of things to help with that."

Once we arrived at the temple, I took Favian aside and asked him to get some buckets of water heating so our visitors could have a soak later in the evening. The Mereni novices, Eiridan and Feldes, greeted Elder Briethe warmly. Upon being introduced to Lorish, they both bowed low.

"It is a true pleasure, Madam," Feldes said. "We are at your disposal."

"That makes a change," Lorish said in her soft, slightly raspy voice.

"The offer is sincere, Respected Elder," Eiridan replied, no hint of offense in his tone. "Draebard is not Rhyth. No one north of the mountains need ever fear a priest."

To my surprise, Lorish blinked as her eyes grew wet with tears. Briethe, who was watching her closely, immediately stroked a soothing hand over her back.

"Thank you," Lorish said.

I continued to watch the strange old woman as unobtrusively as I could. Feldes herded us into the refectory for food and wine, which Andoc and Briethe accepted with gusto after their two-day journey. Meanwhile, Lorish ate with her fingers, picking bits of meat out of her bowl and ignoring the rest. She sniffed the contents of her wine goblet warily and set it aside with a brief curl of her lip.

Conversation was surprisingly sporadic at first, with everyone curious about Lorish but also aware of her obvious discomfiture. Finally, Briethe took pity on us.

"Lorish showed up in Meren a couple of weeks ago, asking for me," she said. "You could have knocked me over with a feather — we were barely more than girls when we met the first time."

"If I may ask, what brought you to the north, Madam?" Feldes asked.

Lorish's eyes darted around, never meeting anyone's gaze directly except Briethe's. "Bad things in the south. Since the mountains burned. *Bad* things."

Briethe took up the thread again. "As near as I can determine from speaking with Lorish, there are mobs roaming the lands around Rhyth, taking anyone who is even suspected of having magic and burning them alive, or drowning them."

"Gods above," I breathed in horror.

"I told all the foxes to leave," Lorish muttered. "Go north. I went, too. Had to tell Briethe. Briethe can help." She glanced up at us for an instant before her eyes darted away again.

"I'm so glad you did come, my friend," Briethe said.

When I looked over to gauge Andoc and Senovo's reactions, it was to find Senovo pale as a wraith. I stared at him, worry flooding my stomach.

"You *told the foxes to leave*," the priest said, his voice strange and frightening.

"Yes, wolf-patron," Lorish said, and Senovo sucked in a sharp breath at the title. "It's a bad place. I told them to go."

"You told them to go… and they did?" Senovo's eyes were like burning coals, though Lorish seemed unconcerned.

Ithric looked back and forth between the two of them. "Why wouldn't they?" he asked, sounding confused.

Senovo's astonished gaze turned to the boy.

Andoc cleared his throat. "Why indeed?" He looked at Senovo with a complex mix of emotion in his expression. "I realized, after talking to Lorish and Briethe in Meren, what it must be that you've been seeking to accomplish these past weeks, Senovo. You've been trying to bring me an army of wolves, haven't you?"

THIRTEEN

I could count the number of times I had seen Senovo truly lost for words on the fingers of one hand. He looked from Lorish to Ithric and back again, his mouth slightly open. His face remained more or less the same color as his white robes of office.

"I can't get them to listen," he said eventually. "The wolves will come, and they accept me, but I cannot communicate complex ideas to them."

"You are still rooted in the world of men, priest," Lorish said. "You think like they do."

I thought of Ithric living as a lion for months. Of Lorish, living as a vixen for years… for *decades*. Both of them gave off a sort of vague sense of not being at home in their own skins, as if their clothing was some strange encumbrance and the culture around them a complete mystery. Then, I thought of Senovo. Suave, self-possessed Senovo, of the silver tongue and the deliciously devious wit. What use would wolves have for such things?

All his life, Senovo had fought the wolf inside him, fearing and hating that part of himself, innocent though it was in reality. A wolf was unvarnished animal truth—love, hate, fear, anger, hunger, affection. Yet even as a wolf, Senovo was still tied to the human world… tied to *us*. How many wild wolves would have scratched at Andoc's door, begging to be let in so they could comfort me when I was upset? How many would curl up at the foot of a tent when the thrill of a hunt in the moonlight beckoned just outside the flap?

Precisely none, of course. *None* of them would.

To raise an army of wolves against the Empire that wanted to destroy us, Senovo would have to forsake his ties to humanity. To *us*. Had Andoc realized any of this?

Senovo had, that much was certain—probably at the same moment I had done so. The realization was stark in his expression. His gaze sought mine, for… what? Confirmation?

Reassurance? To my eternal shame, I looked away, unable to meet his eyes.

"Makes you think, doesn't it?" Briethe interjected, cutting through the sudden tension.

"You need an army of animals?" Ithric asked. "To stop the people who want to kill everyone who has magic?"

"Let's just say that at this point, it really wouldn't hurt," Andoc said.

"It's still just human things, lion-boy," Lorish said dismissively. "Animals don't care about man's stupid wars."

"Lions fight for territory," Ithric said. "They *like* to fight. Just because a fox would rather run away, doesn't mean a lion or a wolf would."

Lorish snarled low in her throat before seeming to remember herself and hunching back in her seat again. "It's your hide, boy. No business of mine," she said, directing the words at her picked-over bowl of stew.

Ithric curled a lip in response and returned his attention to Andoc. "I know other shifters we could ask."

Andoc stared at him. "You… what?"

"I found some people living in the northern mountains who can turn into bears," he said matter-of-factly. "I stayed with them for a while last summer. They could maybe help you."

Senovo was once again beyond speech, and I wasn't faring much better. Eiridan touched his forehead and heart, muttering, "*Merciful Utarr…*"

"Perhaps the Old Magic is not so old and rare as we have come to believe," said Briethe philosophically. "Chief Andoc, I think at this point we should adjourn to your meeting hall and speak with the rest of the council."

Andoc shook himself free of his surprise and nodded. "Yes, you're absolutely right."

We rose and donned our cloaks—all except Lorish, who shook her head, dismissing the meeting as *men's concerns* and indicating that she would stay in the temple.

The elders were assembling as we arrived, and to call the meeting *lively* once Andoc and Briethe had presented their information to the council was a considerable understatement.

"This may be the most ludicrous idea for a defensive tactic I've ever heard in my life," Elder Tolmac said, after Andoc had laid everything out.

"We've already gathered just about as many troops as we're likely to get, Elder," Andoc said. "And it's not going to be enough."

"Do not misunderstand. My observation wasn't necessarily meant as a criticism, Chief Andoc," Tolmac replied. "Particularly given that I'm talking to a man who set an entire mountain on fire."

Andoc colored a bit, even though we'd warned him long ago that he was never likely to live that particular maneuver down.

Tolmac turned to Ithric. "What about it, lad? You're really willing to do this? Travel north to the mountains to speak with the people you met there, and then all the way south again?"

"I'll help, yeah. I was planning on going south anyway, where there's more lions, but I wouldn't mind talking with the bears again first." He grinned. "They were great at catching fish."

The elder looked at Ithric oddly, but merely nodded and turned his attention to Senovo. "High Priest? What are your thoughts on this matter?"

Senovo shook his head slowly back and forth. "Elders, I have been... unable... to achieve the same sort of communication with animals that Lorish and Ithric describe. I... I am unsure if I can succeed."

"You have a better idea of the problem now, though," Andoc said gently, and part of me wanted to jump up and shake him for continuing to encourage Senovo, given what his *success* was likely to mean for the three of us.

"I... am unsure," Senovo repeated.

"Well," said Tolmac, "I think I speak for the council when I say that we have every faith in you, Senovo. You'll just have to keep trying."

Senovo nodded, still looking as stunned and overwhelmed as he had since the moment Lorish first mentioned commanding the other foxes. The meeting droned on for a little longer, and I sat, impatient, waiting for a chance to pounce on Senovo once it was over and hopefully force him to actually talk to us.

When the strategy session finally broke up, however, Andoc placed a hand on my arm as I was leaving the meeting hall, following Senovo's fast-moving white robes a short way ahead. I looked up at him to see what he wanted, and when I glanced back, Senovo was already gone.

"*Fuck*," I cursed. "Andoc, we'll lose him! He'll run off into the woods and disappear again."

"And you think you'd be able to stop him, short of locking him in a room with the shutters barred? He'll come back in the morning, if not sooner. Now, though, I need to talk to you alone, Carivel. It's important."

"Don't you understand what this means, Andoc? Why are you not more upset about this?" I snapped, feeling as if everything was falling apart around me.

"Because of what I'm about to tell you. Come to my hut," Andoc said, sounding very serious.

I looked in the direction Senovo had gone one more time, but there was nothing for it. I followed Andoc to his hut, waiting impatiently as he closed the door and laid a fire in the hearth to drive back the late winter chill. When he was done, he guided me into a chair and crouched in front of me, taking my hands in his.

I blinked, taken aback and suddenly more worried than ever. "Andoc… what is it? What's wrong?"

Andoc took a deep, centering breath. "Lorish wasn't the only unexpected revelation I stumbled across on this trip, *caradi*. While we were there, High Priest Jyrrel sent a message asking to meet with me privately."

"Jyrrel?" I echoed, remembering the powerful Mereni priest who had accidentally revealed Senovo's secret to the world. "What did he want?"

Andoc looked up at me earnestly with his brown eyes. "He wanted to share a vision that he'd recently experienced. A powerful vision that he said he couldn't ignore."

Jyrrel had the second sight—the same gift as young Favian. A new wave of worry washed through me, and I shuddered at the thought of all the terrible things the old priest might have foreseen. "What—? Tell me, what did he dream?"

When he spoke, it was as if Andoc couldn't believe the words, even as he was speaking them. "*Caradi*, he foresaw himself presiding at a handfasting. A *three-way handfasting*, between a chieftain, a eunuch, and a man with a woman's body."

My heart stuttered, skipping a beat, and I suddenly couldn't breathe. "He didn't—he couldn't have—"

"He did. He said he prayed long and hard before deciding to share it with anyone, because of what it would mean. But he is convinced it's a true vision. He will have to see it happen now… or how could he have *Seen* it?"

"Oh dear gods," I said. "Dear gods above." I pushed forward and practically fell out of the chair, into Andoc's arms. As we clutched each other, a new thought assailed me. "Senovo won't believe it. Or he'll—I don't know—convince himself that he's unworthy, or something. Andoc, you haven't been here. You don't know how bad things have gotten with him."

"They've been bad for a while now, beloved," Andoc said. "And I finally understand why, I think. He's stretched between two different worlds, unwilling to fully commit to either one. It hasn't occurred to him yet that he can choose one now, and another later."

I held Andoc even tighter. "But how do we convince him? He'll barely even speak to us!"

Andoc eased me back until we could see each other properly. His eyes were dark and grim with promise. "Oh, I have *just* the thing for that, believe me."

The following morning, I led Nietre, the black Mereni stallion, and the tall chestnut mare that Andoc favored to the temple, both saddled and loaded with supplies for fast travel. It was all I could do to keep my swirling nerves at bay, but I knew from long experience that to be anything less than centered and collected around Nietre was to risk a sudden attack of teeth and hooves. We would need the stallion's strength and speed over the coming days, so I was forced to set my misgivings aside as I readied him.

Once the horses were safely tied outside the temple, however, everything came crashing back. What Andoc proposed had the potential to miscarry in a spectacular manner, given Senovo's recent behavior. Our future hinged on the next few minutes—assuming Senovo was even back, and human, and that we could successfully run him to ground.

Andoc was waiting for me when I arrived. We both wore comfortable traveling clothes. "Ready?" he asked, and I nodded, not letting my misgivings show.

Inside, we found Eiridan keeping watch.

"Is Senovo here?" I asked.

Eiridan looked, if anything, somewhat relieved to have us there. "He is. We are… concerned about him. You will find him in the altar room."

"On four legs or two?" Andoc asked.

"He is in human form." Eiridan swallowed. "I believe he is… praying. He has been for hours now."

My heart ached for our tortured shape-shifter. "Thank you," I whispered to Eiridan, who dipped his head in acknowledgment.

"Eiridan," Andoc said, "would you mind gathering the priests and acolytes in the refectory? We may have an important announcement to make shortly."

The novice priest's face betrayed curiosity, but he merely nodded. "Of course, Chief Andoc. I will see to it."

We left Eiridan and walked down the familiar hallway, where we found Senovo just as he had described, kneeling at the altar to the gods Utarr and Naloth, his forehead and clasped hands resting on the unforgiving stone. His back was bowed in obvious misery.

"*Amadi*," Andoc said in a quiet voice. The single word carried through the echoing space, rich with feeling, and Senovo's spine tensed visibly.

A moment later, he dragged himself to his feet, looking pale and unhappy in the flickering light of the torches. "I cannot speak to you now. Not until I've made a decision about what to do."

We crossed the empty space, coming to flank him on either side.

"That's fine," Andoc said. "You don't need to talk."

Without pausing or making a fuss of it, he took Senovo's hands into one of his and wrapped a length of soft rope around his wrists, binding them together as Senovo stared down in blank shock.

"What… are you doing?" Senovo asked, bewildered.

"I'm tying your hands, so that Carivel and I can abduct you and take you to Meren. The three of us have an appointment there with High Priest Jyrrel in a couple of days, at an altar not much different than this one," said Andoc conversationally. "Normally, of course, I'd have to ask your father for permission first, but under the circumstances, I think we can dispense with the form of the thing. As far as I'm concerned, your father lost the right to any consideration from me on the day he and your mother sold you to slavers."

Andoc tied off the ropes with a gentle tug, and Senovo gaped at him, completely incapable of speech. *Twice in two days,* I thought. *Amazing.* Finally, Senovo appeared to realize what he must look like and snapped his jaw shut. There was another long pause as he stared from one of us to the other.

"Are you… *bride-napping* me?" he said eventually, and his shocked, *indignant* tone was so different from the cool distance I'd grown used to of late that a faint flush of relief bloomed in my chest.

"As it happens, we are," I told him. "Though we'll have to ask you not to cheat and slip out of the ropes by shifting. That would just be embarrassing after all the trouble we've gone to in setting this up."

He stared some more, and his breath began to hitch in what I eventually recognized as slightly hysterical, wheezing laughter—the first laughter I had ever heard from him in the entire length of our acquaintance. His knees buckled a moment later, and he sat down hard on the edge of the altar.

"There's no such thing as a three-way handfasting," he choked out, once he'd regained a thread of control over his voice.

"Tell that to High Priest Jyrrel," Andoc said. "He's the one who contacted me and told me it had to happen. Not that either Carivel or I are in any way averse to the idea, mind you."

"But… but that's—" Senovo cut himself off and swallowed, hard. "How would that even *work*?"

"You'll have to ask him," I told him. "He's already seen it in a vision, apparently, so I assume he'll have the details figured out by the time we get there."

Senovo's chest began to hitch again, but this time he shut his eyes tightly after a few moments, and tears began to leak down his face. I *itched* to hold him, but both Andoc and I understood that he would have to work through this revelation on his own.

"I can't do this," he said. "I can't—not now."

Andoc knelt in front of him and took Senovo's face tenderly in his hands, angling it until Senovo met his gaze. "Yes, you can," he said. "You didn't choose a life of service to the gods, Senovo—and yet, they could have no more dedicated servant than you. Is it such a surprise that they have finally chosen to repay you for all of your sacrifices in some small way?"

Tears were still spilling down Senovo's cheeks. "I was repaid on the day that High Priest Rhystel pushed you into my life, old friend. And when the two of us found Carivel, I was repaid twice over."

I sat down on the altar next to him, and stroked my thumb over the wetness staining his cheek. "Come with us, Senovo. Please say you will. It's all we've ever wanted from this life."

Senovo closed his eyes for another few heartbeats, his body shaking between us. When he was able to take an unhindered breath again, he opened them and looked at us. A bare hint of his old wry humor appeared as he lifted his bound wrists. "Beloved," he said, "how can I refuse?"

An unexpected sob jerked through my own chest, and I wrapped my arms around him, holding tight. Andoc lifted Senovo's hands to his lips and kissed them.

"*Amadi*," he said. "My heart. Thank you."

Senovo leaned forward until his forehead was resting at the juncture of Andoc's neck and shoulder, breathing deeply. One of Andoc's hands came up to cradle the back of his head; the other closed around my shoulders. We rested there for a few minutes until everyone was steady enough to rise.

"Come on, you two," Andoc said, urging us up. "We'll leave shortly, Senovo, but there is one thing we need to do before we go."

Eiridan had been good to his word, and everyone from the temple was gathered in the refectory, talking in low voices. They looked up as we entered, taking in their High Priest, flanked on either side with his hands bound in front of him.

"High Priest...?" Feldes asked somewhat nervously.

It was Andoc who spoke. "Thank you all for coming. As most of you are no doubt aware, High Priest Senovo, Horse Mistress Carivel, and I are lovers. Recently High Priest Jyrrel of Meren shared with me that he had dreamed a true vision, in which he presided over our handfasting." There was a sharp gasp from Favian. "I'm pleased to inform you that Carivel and I will now be taking Senovo to Meren, to ensure that the prophecy is fulfilled as the gods intended. We are aware, of course, of the controversial nature of this undertaking, but the three of us would appreciate your blessings nonetheless."

I looked around the large table, full of excitement and nervousness at finally—*finally*—being able to admit the truth publicly. Feldes appeared dumbfounded at the announcement, and several of the transplanted Mereni acolytes were eyeing each other uncertainly as if they didn't know how to react. Crenelo and Reston looked amazed, slow smiles lighting up their faces. Meanwhile, Favian leapt up from the bench and hurried forward, wrapping his arms around Senovo, who hastily lifted his bound arms out of the way.

"Congratulations, Elder Brother," he said. "Blessings be upon you."

Senovo awkwardly rested a hand on top of the boy's head for a moment. "And to think you didn't believe me when I told you all those months ago that even a eunuch priest could find happiness," he murmured, for the boy's ears alone. Favian huffed out a laugh and moved to embrace first Andoc, and then me as well.

Eiridan also rose and came forward. "If it is my blessing you desire, then you shall have it freely, Elder Brother. May Utarr and Naloth smile on your extraordinary union." He lifted his fingers to each of our foreheads. "Safe journey to you. We will await your return eagerly."

"Thank you, Eiridan," I said, and he quirked a smile at me, his pleasant features crinkling into laugh lines.

"Perhaps *this* ceremony will not require sedating tea," he said, referring to his self-appointed fictional errand during my disastrous handfasting ceremony with Andoc the previous spring.

I couldn't help it—I laughed aloud as happiness flooded me. "I can almost guarantee that it won't," I assured him. "Well… not unless High Priest Jyrrel needs some, anyway."

Eiridan's answering laughter was silent, but his shoulders shook with it nonetheless. "It sounds like he will have only himself to blame if he does, Horse Mistress. Please give him our regards when you see him."

"We will," I said, still flooded with exhilaration at the sudden turn our lives had taken.

Andoc was grinning as well. "Feel free to spread the gossip far and wide, by the way. *After* we've left the village, if you don't mind."

My heart swelled even further at the words, though Senovo still appeared overwhelmed at the idea of having our relationship thrown into the public eye. I shook my head—I had already been the butt of widespread public disapproval for having had the temerity to be born into a female body. I was confident that Draebard would not truly forsake its High Priest, its Horse Mistress, and its much-loved young Chief in the weeks before an unthinkable war. The villagers' disapproval and whispers of scandal held no more fear for me now.

After taking our leave to a chorus of well-wishes ranging from uncertain to heartfelt, we led Senovo to his rooms to dress for winter travel and pack a final few supplies. Senovo himself still seemed terribly fragile as we helped him into thick breeches and warm boots. With a cloak draped over his shoulders and mittens covering his bound hands, we ushered our captive out to where the horses were waiting.

Bride-napping was an ancient practice, the serious application of which had been banned by the priesthood countless generations ago. Once, women really were dragged from their families during raids and forcibly abducted to neighboring villages to be wed to their captors.

In more recent times, however, it had become an entirely symbolic gesture, and was considered hopelessly romantic by many. A man who wished to wed a woman from a different village would seek her acceptance and then ask permission from her father or other male guardian to abduct her by horseback for the ceremony in his home village. In addition to the secret thrill of the forbidden and the romantic nature of the play-acting, I gathered the practice also had implications for the negotiation of a bride price or dowry. Thankfully, however, none of the three of us needed to concern ourselves with such things.

Our abduction of Senovo was something entirely different. It was our promise to him that we wanted him of our own free will. That we considered him valuable—a prize to be taken and protected. Cherished.

I could tell that he was still struggling in the aftermath of being informed out of the blue that he was going to get the thing he longed for with so much passion—the thing that he had never even dared to acknowledge as a possibility. He was dazed; brief expressions of radiant happiness and terrible fear chasing each other across his pale face.

Outside, I untied Nietre and mounted. Between us, Andoc and I helped Senovo up to sit behind me. I guided him to lift his arms and place them around me, his bound wrists resting on my stomach.

"If I fall, I'll take you with me," he whispered.

"Senovo, I believe you've just described the two of us in a nutshell," I observed, pausing for a moment before adding, "but, yeah, if you could *not* fall, that would probably be for the best."

He chuckled, that strange hitch of breath that seemed to straddle the divide between laughter and tears, and his arms tightened around me for a long moment. Andoc untied his mare and led her slowly to a conveniently placed section of low wall at the edge of the courtyard. He stowed his walking stick behind the saddle and climbed carefully onto the wall so he could mount. When he was settled, he turned to us.

"Are we ready?" he asked.

My smile seemed to have etched itself into my features permanently. "I've been ready for this since that first night we spent together in Meren," I said. "Senovo?"

Senovo nodded, his forehead resting against the nape of my neck. "Hold on, then," I warned him, and wheeled Nietre around to head out on the eastern road toward Meren, and our future.

FOURTEEN

We rode steadily until midday, after first letting the fractious horses have their heads for a league or so to take the edge off. Senovo clung to me as Nietre's hooves ate up the ground beneath us with powerful strides. He had never ridden one of the tall, long-legged Mereni horses before, and I could feel his heart pounding and his breath coming fast in response to the stallion's stunning turn of speed.

"You understand now why I love it so?" I asked, once we had slowed to a steady, rocking canter.

"Perhaps," he murmured into my ear.

I could certainly think of few other things as intoxicating as riding a fine horse under the late winter sun, with Senovo's warm body pressed against my back and his familiar arms wrapped around me. Andoc was a solid presence at my side, his chestnut mare blowing out in steady snorts that matched the rhythm of her footfalls.

He caught me staring at his handsome profile and grinned, eyes soft. His gaze rested on both of us for a long moment, possessive and loving. The combination of feelings flowing through me slowly unknotted the tension that had been coiled around my spine for weeks now, and I felt a trickle of liquid warmth in my belly for the first time in longer than I cared to remember.

"Time to stop for a bit?" he asked, when the sun reached its zenith.

"We should let the horses walk for a while to cool off first," I agreed, "but then we can find someplace to rest and eat, yes."

"Thinking about food and rest in the middle of the day, Horse Mistress?" Andoc teased. "My, my! Apparently I have trained you well… even if it did turn out to be a rather lengthy and arduous process."

"I suppose it was inevitable that you would eventually rub off on one of us," Senovo offered, and my chest swelled further at the return of the old, familiar banter.

"I just figured we'd all need to keep our strength up for the next few days," I said with a cheeky grin. "If we're to take *proper* advantage, I mean."

Andoc laughed, a sound I dearly loved. "I always did like the way you think, *caradi*."

We let the horses rest and blow, ambling along until we came across a sheltered glade beside the trail. Was it the same one where we had stopped on our way to negotiate with the Mereni last spring, exhausted by fresh grief and lack of sleep after the attack on Draebard? With the trees bare and patches of snow lingering on the ground, I couldn't tell.

There was a small, trickling brook nearby, carrying melt-water away as the daytime temperature started creeping above freezing. We let the horses drink, after which Andoc dismounted and draped his mare's reins over a low-hanging branch so he could limp over to Nietre's side and help Senovo down.

I followed and tied the stallion to a sturdy tree of his own. With an armful of blankets clutched to my chest, I joined the others by the bole of an elderly tree and helped them set up a dry place for the three of us to curl up and eat. Andoc deposited travel rations and a promising looking wineskin on the ground cloth, then drew Senovo down to sit between us.

"Can I safely assume that you're not planning on making a run for it at this point?" he asked, even as he pulled off Senovo's mittens and untied his wrists.

"I wouldn't dare, with such attentive captors watching over me."

Senovo flexed his fingers, and I snuggled up next to him so I could throw a heavy blanket across our shoulders. Andoc passed the wineskin, and I was unsurprised to discover that the contents were, in fact, up to his usual excellent standards. When I was done, I handed it to Senovo and attacked my portion of pemmican. It seemed that all of my physical urges were reawakening at once—the simple fare melted on my tongue like the finest festival cuisine, and my skin felt flushed and sensitive where I pressed against Senovo through two sets of heavy clothing.

"You've been very quiet since we left Draebard, Senovo," I said. "We want you to be as happy about this as we are."

Senovo did not look up. "I... am afraid."

"Afraid of what?" Andoc asked.

"The warriors pledged by the other tribes will not be enough to defend the north," said Senovo. "You *know* this to be true, Andoc. If Ithric and I cannot succeed, it is very likely that both you and Carivel will die, since I have no doubt that both of you will end up in the front ranks during the invasion, riding side by side."

"If the north falls, I consider death in battle preferable to life under the Empire's boot, *amadi*," said Andoc.

"I agree," I said.

Senovo shook his head. "Whereas I would much prefer to live in a world that still has the two of you in it. I am afraid that by bonding with you — tying myself so inextricably to the human world — I will lose my chance to bring you the army you need to survive. So you see my dilemma. If I give myself to you, I may lose you both forever."

Andoc set aside his food and took Senovo's hands in his. "I submit to you that it's a false dilemma, old friend." Senovo's sculpted brows drew together in a question. Andoc shook his head and continued, "Right now, you cannot connect with the wolves because you insist on keeping one foot in the human world. *Our* world. But as Carivel would no doubt be happy to tell you, lately you haven't been able to connect properly with us either, because you also insist on keeping one foot in the wolf's world."

"It's true," I said. "Even when you're here, you're not really *here*."

"I propose that you commit yourself fully to the human world for a few days," Andoc continued. "Be here, with us. Become our bondmate. Give yourself over to us — to our love for you. Come back to Draebard afterward and say your farewells to everyone there who cares for you. And then, commit yourself fully to the wolves. Do what you must do for the coming battle. Knowing that we love you and accept your choice, freely and with grateful hearts."

Emotion clogged my throat at the prospect of letting Senovo go, once the ceremony was over and we had returned home. "But promise us," I whispered, "that when the battle is done, you'll come back to us."

"You say it as if such a thing is simple," Senovo said.

Andoc smiled, but there was a sadness to it. "I have a feeling, *amadi,* that it will be just as simple—or as difficult—as you decide to make it. In my experience, most things in life are."

There was a long pause.

"I... will try," Senovo said softly, as if the words were being pulled from him. "You have always had more faith in me than I have in myself. Both of you have."

"And we've always been right," I said, nudging his shoulder with mine.

"Just so," Andoc agreed. "Now, *eat.* Carivel wasn't joking when she said you were going to need your strength for what we have planned for you."

Senovo swallowed, visibly trying to pull himself back from the raw, painful topic under discussion. "I shudder to think," he managed, with the barest hint of his old dry humor.

⚜

As it happened, the topic of what was to come was much on my mind through the afternoon, once we resumed our journey. Senovo—hands still unbound—was now riding behind Andoc on the chestnut mare, to give Nietre a rest from carrying two people. His arms were wrapped tightly around Andoc's middle, one hand resting over his heart and the other, low on his belly. Periodically, Senovo would bury his face in the space between Andoc's shoulders, as if overcome by a new wave of emotion.

I kept throwing lingering glances at them, so painfully beautiful together in their perfect blend of strength and softness.

What *would* a three-way handfasting ceremony entail? Senovo had asked exactly that question in his initial moment of shocked reaction. In many ways, I didn't even care, so long as we came out of it as bondmates. But as the horses carried us across the upland plateaus that marked the rough halfway point of our journey, I found myself speculating on the possible details. By the time we finally stopped to pitch camp for the night, I had come to two very important conclusions, though I resolved to keep them both to myself until we could all speak with High Priest Jyrrel tomorrow.

We were warming ourselves in front of the fire, bellies full and sleep threatening to overcome us when we heard wolves in the distance. Senovo's eyes were immediately drawn to the impenetrable darkness beyond the fire, his gaze growing far away. His spine stiffened, as if he might rise. A flood of disquiet churned through my gut.

Andoc's hand fell on the nape of Senovo's neck. "Stop," he said. "Stay with us, or go to them. But not this in-between. It serves no one."

I placed my own hand on the priest's knee, and silently begged him to stay. Maybe he saw the plea in my eyes when he looked at me, because he sank back and closed his own eyes tightly for a moment. When he opened them again, they were wet. "Forgive me, both of you. The compulsion—it pulls at my spirit, even now."

"There's nothing to forgive, *amadi*," Andoc said, and pulled him forward to press a brief kiss to his forehead. "I was merely reminding you. Come. We're all tired, and tomorrow will be a long day."

We retired to the tent, wrapping Senovo up between us. Andoc's hand wormed its way under my tunic until he could stroke a thumb back and forth over my nipple, sending a thread of hot pleasure to my sex with every lazy movement. I stretched my own hand out to rest on his hip, my legs tangled with Senovo's and his lips pressed to the side of my neck. We fell asleep that way within minutes.

⤚⚜⤙

The swift Mereni horses had gotten us much farther on the first day of travel than Draebard's short, native horses would have done. As the rugged plateaus gave way to sweeping valleys, my excitement and nervousness grew. Senovo was once again at my back, his long-fingered hands resting firmly over my stomach to keep himself anchored. I could feel his intermittent trembling where he pressed against me from hip to shoulder.

"Are you cold?" I asked, the first time it happened.

"No," he said, and his arms tightened around me. I covered them with one of my own.

The soft curls of smoke in the distance, rising from Meren's hearth fires, were our first warning that we had arrived at our destination. A few minutes later, we crested a small rise, and there lay the town, spread out before us. My heart began to beat faster with anticipation, even though I knew that there were still several things to be done before the ceremony itself.

"Straight to the temple?" I asked Andoc. "Or do you need to talk to Leader Magoldis first?"

"This isn't a formal visit, *caradi*," he said. "We dealt with most of the official business when I was here a few days ago, though I should have a quick word with her before we leave about Ithric and the shape-shifters in the northern mountains. For now, though, we have other concerns. The temple, I think."

"Actually," I said, "let's stop at the horse pens first and see if Previn is around. He can ride with you to the temple and take the horses back to be cared for—save us a walk. I trust him to deal with Nietre, for one thing."

"I think you mean, to save *me* a walk," Andoc said ruefully, gesturing down at his bad leg, "but I appreciate it nonetheless. Let's go, in that case."

We did, in fact, find Previn, who appeared to be in danger of bursting out of his own skin with excitement upon seeing Nietre standing there calm and attentive with his neck arched gracefully, carrying two people upon his back.

"Just look at him!" the boy exclaimed. "Horse Mistress, it's like a miracle!"

I smiled fondly and directed Previn to swing up behind Andoc in the saddle. The four of us rode to the temple and dismounted. Andoc and I removed the saddlebags full of our belongings so Previn could lead the two animals away to be cared for. The three of us walked to the entrance and bowed to the gods. Taking a deep breath, I stepped forward and knocked on the door.

A middle-aged priest I did not recognize opened it a moment later. "Good day, travelers," he said. "You are welcome at the temple of Meren. Elder Brother, our place is yours. Come in, please, and tell me how I may assist you."

Andoc and I bowed to the kindly priest, and Senovo dipped his head in acknowledgment as we entered and allowed him to close the door behind us.

Andoc cleared his throat. "We are here to see High Priest Jyrrel. Would you mind telling him that Andoc and his party have arrived from Draebard? He will be expecting us."

"Of course, Honored Guests," the priest agreed. "I will show you to a room where you may wait and refresh yourselves."

We followed our host to a room off the large space housing the altar, warmed by a cozy fire, with several comfortable seats scattered around. A low table held bread, cheese, dried fruit, and wine. Once the priest had gone, Andoc gestured us to sit together on a wooden settle padded with cushions while he poured us drinks and brought us food.

Senovo and I barely nibbled at the bread and cheese, but the wine was certainly welcome. Only Andoc seemed completely at ease as we waited. Not for the first time, I envied him the simplicity of his outlook. Almost as if sensing my thoughts, he aimed a tiny smirk in my direction. I rolled my eyes at him and wondered how much of a diplomatic incident it would cause if I was falling-down drunk for the upcoming conversation.

Fortunately for my sanity and the temple's supply of wine, Jyrrel did not leave us waiting long. I took several deep breaths as the corpulent High Priest entered and closed the door quietly behind him. All three of us rose to meet him.

"Good afternoon, my friends," Jyrrel said in his deep, booming voice. "Please be seated. The four of us have much to discuss. Brother Senovo, Horse Mistress Carivel—I hope this visit finds you both well after such an eventful winter. Chief Andoc, thank you for returning so promptly after our discussion a few days ago. I know you are all terribly busy just now."

"Never too busy for this," Andoc said sincerely, as we reseated ourselves.

"Indeed," replied Jyrrel. "I must say, when I first dreamed these events, I could hardly credit them. Only when I thought back to your first visit and the obvious bond that the three of you shared, did I realize that this might, in fact, be something that you would desire."

"I can think of nothing that I desire more," I said, meeting Jyrrel's eyes squarely. "And for that reason, High Priest Jyrrel, I would like for our handfasting ceremony to be public."

The other two looked at me in surprise. Jyrrel nodded and turned to them. "I see. Andoc, Senovo... what are your thoughts on this proposal?"

Andoc answered first. "While I admit I wasn't expecting it, I've no objections. Senovo?"

Senovo spoke slowly, as if feeling out the words. "It is likely... that not everyone in Meren will approve of such a joining. I... will admit that I understand the appeal of standing up in front of all and sundry to proclaim our... our *union*. But I want to be sure that you and Carivel realize that the attention may not be positive."

"Well stated, Brother Senovo," Jyrrel said.

"Attention has never bothered me, *amadi*, you know that," said Andoc. "I couldn't care less if some people are offended by what they see. If the gods were not in favor of this, they would never have given High Priest Jyrrel such a vision in the first place."

"I've been the butt of people's disapproval before, Senovo," I added. "I've let it bother me sometimes, too. That's a mistake I don't intend to make again in the future."

"You are all agreed, then?" Jyrrel asked.

Andoc met both of our gazes, searching, and looked back at the Mereni High Priest. "We are."

"There's something else," I added, before I could lose my nerve. Even so, I had to take a couple of deep breaths when the others looked at me, before I could continue. "High Priest Jyrrel, most people assume that Andoc and I are handfasted, but our union was never consummated. I have never been taken like a woman. In that sense, I am still a virgin."

Jyrrel raised his eyebrows in surprise. The others looked at me sharply.

I swallowed against the twist of nervousness in my stomach. I had thought about this long and hard today, but that didn't seem to make it any easier to spit the words out. "Senovo, I think you should take me... *that way*. During the ceremony."

Senovo studied me closely for a long moment before gathering my hands into his and raising them to his lips. He kissed first one, then the other, before lowering them again and speaking. "No. But I am honored that you would offer, beloved. If it is truly something you wish to explore, we will do so in private, afterward. But not during a public handfasting."

"It's not. I just want this ceremony to be right. To be *real*," I whispered. Tears threatened to rise, partly in relief at Senovo's immediate refusal, and partly in worry that this handfasting, too, would be a mere sham.

"Carivel," Senovo said, still holding my hands, "even if you wished for it to happen, new life could not grow from the fertile fields of our love. But you do not desire to bear children, and I am a castrate—I cannot sire children. Given those two facts, there is no point to such a union within the context of the ceremony. This handfasting is something new. Something different. Its value must come from that, or it has no value at all."

Meren's High Priest watched the exchange with interest. "Again, Senovo speaks wisely, Horse Mistress Carivel. There has never been a handfasting like this one before. I admit, I am as much at sea as anyone, but the gods never appreciate dishonesty. They want only the truth of your union."

A huge weight seemed to lift from my back. Could it really be the case that none of us would have to hide and compromise ourselves any longer?

"Thank you," I breathed.

Andoc had settled himself on Senovo's other side earlier, but now he stretched across the eunuch to press a kiss to my lips. "I've only ever wanted either of you as who you really are—not who other people think you ought to be," he said.

"That's why we love you," I said, meaning every word.

"Indeed," Senovo echoed.

Andoc quirked a smile, though his eyes were soft. "And here I thought it was my rugged good looks and my excellent taste in wine."

"Those don't hurt, either," said Senovo.

Jyrrel sat back, his fingers laced across his generous stomach. "Well. I do not presume to counsel the three of you as I might normally counsel a couple before their handfasting. I can't honestly think of any couples I've joined who had already weathered so much strife or proven themselves so steadfast before the ceremony ever occurred. So, I will merely ask you if you wish to speak of anything else, or if you are content with the decisions you have already discussed."

Senovo cleared his throat. "Brother Jyrrel, I confess I am still at something of a loss as to precisely how such a ceremony will proceed. Perhaps, since you have already foreseen it, a better question would be — is there anything *you* would like to tell *us*?"

Jyrrel let loose with a low rumble of laughter. "Ah, Senovo. I believe I shall trust to your instincts, and the gods' plans. Already, you have come to your own decision to make the ceremony a public one... as it appeared to be within my vision. Which, I might add, has saved me from being in a rather awkward position. As your priest, I could hardly attempt to pressure you into such a thing, if it were not what you truly desired. Fortunately, I didn't have to. I am confident that all will unfold as it should, without my interference."

"In that case," said Andoc, "I believe we are ready to proceed."

I nodded my agreement.

"Very well, my children." Jyrrel heaved his great bulk from his chair, and we rose as well. "I have arranged for a bath to be drawn, so that you may purify yourselves. I also spoke to Leader Magoldis about the possibility of this ceremony shortly after you left, Andoc. I'll send her a message to announce that it will take place this evening. No doubt word will spread quickly, but perhaps the short notice will not leave enough time for people to become overly upset about the idea, eh?"

We thanked Jyrrel for his counsel and allowed him to lead us through the temple until we came upon a novice, who was immediately tasked with showing us to the bathing room and assisting us in our preparations.

Already, my heart was beginning to pound with anticipation. I watched the others closely — Andoc appeared the picture of confidence, a faint smile relaxing his features. He caught me looking, and his eyes crinkled at the corners. Senovo was still pale and shaky, for all that he had maintained his composure during our interview with Jyrrel. I laid a hand on his shoulder from behind and he flinched, only to catch himself and give me a sheepish, half-hearted smile when he realized it was me.

The novice directed us to a steamy bathing room not too dissimilar from the one in the temple at Draebard. Once there, he instructed us to bathe one at a time, even as he shot nervous, awe-filled glances at Senovo, whose reputation as a shape-shifter was already long-established here in Meren.

"You two go first," Andoc said. "You know how I feel about parboiling myself."

"You could always go roll around in a snow bank outside, instead," I suggested sweetly.

"Or you could simply add a bucket or two of cold water to the tub until it better suited your tastes," Senovo offered, somewhat more practically.

I had gathered already that the ritual bathing was not meant to be used as an excuse to get one's hands on one's intended mates, so I contented myself with watching as Senovo stripped, his hands noticeably trembling with the ties of his robes and the lacing of his breeches and smallclothes.

I wished we could settle his mind somehow, but perhaps it wasn't surprising that he was all but overwhelmed, standing here on the cusp of something he'd never even allowed himself to believe he might be able to have.

Naked at last, he raised his fingers to the tight plait of thick black hair at the back of his head. The novice murmured something and moved forward, freeing the braid and letting Senovo's hair fall in loose waves. I tried not to be jealous. Honestly, I couldn't abide dealing with long hair—I just wasn't terribly thrilled about someone *else* handling this *particular* long hair. Or at least, someone else who wasn't Andoc. Still, as eager as I might be to get my hands on Senovo, it was also nice just to stand here and enjoy the view.

Andoc sidled up to me while the novice's attention was on Senovo. "Doing all right, *caradi*?" he asked, for my ears alone.

"Never better," I said truthfully, matching his low tones. "I'm still worried about Senovo, though. Do you think he'll be all right?"

"I think he still hasn't let himself truly accept what's happening. It shouldn't be a surprise, I suppose. This does mark something of a fundamental shift for him, after all."

We watched as the novice efficiently bathed Senovo and oiled his hair. When the young man started to plait it back into its tight queue, however, Senovo raised a hand to stop him. The novice nodded, and left it hanging loose as he gathered up a towel to dry off his charge. Finally, he slipped a clean, heavy robe over Senovo's slender frame to ward off the chill.

I was next, and submitted to being bathed with only a faint sense of embarrassment and discomfort. The novice was thorough but detached, and it was not as odd as I might have expected to let him run the rough cloth over my body, scrubbing away the travel grime. As he was rinsing me off, however, I made the mistake of glancing over at Andoc. His burning, possessive gaze sent a sudden jolt of lust through my belly. My eyes flew to Senovo, who was staring at me as one might stare at water in the desert.

Suddenly, I felt light-headed, and had to accept the support of the novice's arm as he helped me out of the copper tub. When I was wrapped in a soft robe of my own, the novice beckoned Andoc forward before I could forget decorum and do something thoroughly untoward. Despite his earlier grumbling, Andoc submitted to the ritual purification with good grace, while Senovo and I stood side by side, drinking in his beautiful body as it glistened with water and soap.

The novice helped Andoc carefully out of the bath, mindful of his twisted leg, and he braced himself against the rim as he was dried and dressed. Finally, the young initiate handed him his walking stick, and we were ready.

A window in the far wall showed that the sun had disappeared as we bathed, leaving the small patch of sky stained orange and indigo.

"The ceremony will commence at full dark," said the novice. "May I bring you food and drink first?"

"No," Senovo and I said in unison.

"Yes," Andoc said firmly. He turned a stern eye on both of us, and growled, "Trust me. You're both going to need it."

The way Senovo and I shivered in unison should probably have been embarrassing. "Food it is," I agreed weakly.

We were shown to another quiet, out of the way room. I could hear the sound of voices and movement coming from the central part of the large structure.

"It sounds like the crowd is already gathering," Senovo said, tension audible in his voice.

"Let them come," Andoc said. "Nothing matters tonight but us, *amadi*."

The novice returned with sweet mead and a selection of cold meats. Under Andoc's watchful eye, we ate sparingly and drank somewhat less sparingly. Outside, the growing rumble of assembled people suggested quite a large crowd, especially given the lack of notice ahead of time.

It was odd. I might reasonably have expected for my stomach to be churning with nervousness at this point, but it wasn't. True, my blood was rushing with anticipation—the same sort of sensation I encountered when throwing my leg over an untried colt for the first time, or while galloping Nietre flat out. But my only fear was for Senovo, whose tension seemed to rise even higher as the ceremony grew imminent. Surely he would not balk at the final moment—not when he was so close to getting his heart's desire.

FIFTEEN

"It is time," said the novice, as the sound of drums echoed through the temple. Normally, the signal that the ceremony was about to start would quiet the assembled crowd; however, I could not help but notice that, if anything, the rumble of voices grew even louder.

A moment later, several more priests and acolytes arrived at the entrance to the room — perhaps half a dozen in total.

"My brothers and I will accompany you to the altar room," said the one who had been attending us. "If you are ready, please remove your robes."

I took a deep breath and looked at Andoc for reassurance. He smiled, though there was a certain tightness in his expression. Senovo, for his part, was still pale and distant, the mask he often used to hide himself from others firmly in place. I clenched my jaw, vowing then and there that I would see that mask crumble tonight, for better or worse.

Andoc was the first to slip off his robe, followed closely by Senovo, and finally, me. For the second time in my life, I walked naked toward the altar, but this time, I was flanked on both sides by the men with whom I intended to join.

The others surrounded us like an honor guard... or a bodyguard. I wondered with a hint of trepidation what exactly it was that High Priest Jyrrel feared, for him to protect us in such a way. The noise swelled as we rounded the last corner before the altar room. Most of the voices were raised in confusion or excitement, but here and there I could pick out sounds of anger as well. Andoc obviously heard the same thing, from the way he pressed a bit closer to us and lifted his head to scan the crowd with watchful eyes.

There was a cry as the first people at the back of the mob sighted us, and instantly, we were the center of attention. People began to mill around us, trying to see past the tight circle of priests and acolytes. I felt Senovo cringe, and my hand sought his instinctively. His own was clammy, and trembled faintly in my grip.

Suddenly, a booming voice cut through the confusion.

"*Make. Way,*" High Priest Jyrrel ordered, the words echoing around the large space.

The noise and confusion gradually subsided into low muttering as the press of the crowd eased, allowing our escort to breach the mass of people and lead us toward the altar. I was short enough that I couldn't see much of anything except the backs of the novices in front of me.

When we finally reached the front, where Jyrrel was standing on the plinth overlooking the crowd with his head held high, I was shocked to find a line of warriors arrayed between the altar and the onlookers. The novices disgorged the three of us behind the safety of the grim-faced figures, and my wide eyes fell on Varanis as I walked past. She quirked an eyebrow in return, her face impassive. Beyond her, Keenan caught my eye and offered me a brief, strained smile.

Jyrrel ushered us to stand beside the altar with a sweeping gesture of his hand, and I was surprised yet again when Leader Magoldis of the Mereni stepped up to stand next to her High Priest, dressed in full ceremonial regalia.

"Peace!" she called, her voice rolling around the room with as much force as Jyrrel's had a few moments earlier. Finally, the crowd quieted. "You are in a temple, not attending a street festival! Your High Priest has an announcement to make — give him the respect that is his due!"

Jyrrel straightened and addressed the restless crowd. "Tonight, we are gathered to witness the handfasting of Chief Andoc of Draebard, Horse Mistress Carivel... and High Priest Senovo."

The crowd erupted again upon hearing confirmation of what had probably seemed to be a wild rumor. Jyrrel let it run for the span of several heartbeats before continuing.

"Nearly four weeks ago," he said over the noise, "the gods sent me a vision of this ceremony, which takes place now at their own behest. Those who wish to attend the handfasting with open hearts and open minds are welcome. Those with closed hearts and minds, leave now or face the gods' wrath."

"A eunuch cannot enter into a handfasting!" called a voice from the back somewhere. "It's outrageous!"

"Would you deny handfasting to a barren woman?" Jyrrel demanded, his voice rising. "Would you deny it to a widower too old to sire children? It is not for you to decide who may partake of Naloth and Utarr's gifts. Either demonstrate humility before the gods' will or begone from the temple!"

I watched with wide eyes as Magoldis and Jyrrel stood shoulder to shoulder, a solid bulwark between us and the crowd, fortified by the line of warriors arrayed around them. Senovo's hand in mine was freezing cold. I was almost afraid to look at his face, for fear of what I might find there. Andoc was a stalwart presence at my other shoulder.

"That was not a suggestion," Magoldis said over the people's muttering. "Either behave like civilized Eburosi, or go."

There was a momentary pause, and some people began to filter out beneath a nearly palpable cloud of their own outrage, thinning the crowd first in a trickle, and then a stream. When things finally settled down, fewer than half remained, and those that did were quiet. At Magoldis' sharp nod, Varanis and her fellow warriors stepped down from the edge of the raised plinth that held the altar and took places at the front of the crowd as spectators.

"You have my deepest apologies for my people's behavior," Magoldis said, addressing us directly. "I offer my blessings for your unusual union. May the gods smile upon your endeavors."

"It is only to be expected, Leader," Andoc said, standing tall and unconcerned in his nakedness. "No harm is done, and we humbly accept your blessing."

With Senovo standing seemingly frozen next to me, I wasn't entirely sure that no harm had been done. His breathing was shallow and fast—when I squeezed his fingers, there was no response. Worry rose in my chest.

"Then I will leave you in Jyrrel's capable hands, Chief Andoc. High Priest Senovo. Horse Mistress Carivel." The Leader nodded to us, and went to join the rest of the onlookers, standing beside her daughter.

"Before we begin, there is a final matter to be addressed," said Jyrrel. "Novice Adlan, please present the bindings from Chief Andoc and Horse Mistress Carivel's previous handfasting."

I looked with some surprise at Andoc. He must have brought the thong that Senovo had used to bind us along with him, and given it to the novice when I wasn't paying attention. Adlan removed the familiar length of soft leather from his wide sleeve and held it taut before the High Priest. Jyrrel removed a tiny ceremonial blade from his belt and nicked the center with a careful movement, weakening the leather without breaking it.

"Andoc. Carivel. Present your hands," he said.

We stepped forward and lifted our hands. The novice wrapped the thong around them, leaving the partially cut section midway between us.

"Circumstances may weaken a handfasting bond," Jyrrel continued, "but it is up to the participants to break it, if that is what they truly desire. Do you truly wish to sever the previous bond between you?"

Part of me was surprised that Jyrrel was allowing us the dignity of a formal annulment, given what I had told him about our previous ceremony. Still, I mused, perhaps he had foreseen this part as well.

"We do," Andoc said, and I echoed him an instant later.

"Then you may break the cord," said the High Priest.

Andoc and I jerked our hands back at the same instant, and the thong snapped in two with a dull twang. I stared at the broken binding for a long moment, thinking, *gods above, this is really happening now.*

"Your old union is broken," Jyrrel proclaimed. "Andoc. Senovo. Carivel. Tonight you tie your destinies together under the gods' watchful gaze. To symbolize this union, Novice Adlan will bind your hands, teaching you to work together as one, relying on each other as you have previously relied only on yourselves. Do all three of you agree to this public handfasting, freely and joyfully?"

My eyes slid to Andoc, standing tall and confident, and then to Senovo, still hanging back a pace, where I had left him when Andoc and I stepped forward to break the thong. My heart gave a lurch at the expression of near panic on his bloodless face.

"Wait... *stop,*" I said.

Andoc followed my gaze, and we were both at Senovo's side in an instant.

"Senovo," I urged, "say something, please. What is it, what's wrong? *Talk to us.*"

Andoc ignored words in favor of cupping Senovo's cheek in his hand. The priest's eyes snapped back from the unfocused middle distance, and he met Andoc's gaze with a sharp gasp.

"We need a minute," I told High Priest Jyrrel, as if the man couldn't have figured that out for himself.

"Sorry," Senovo whispered hoarsely, seeming to come back to the present and his surroundings. "No, I'm sorry—forgive me…"

Andoc was still watching Senovo carefully. "There is nothing to forgive, *amadi*. We'll wait as long as we need to." A sudden frown of worry creased his features. "Unless… you *do* still want this?"

"*Yes!*" Senovo gasped, before I could properly begin to panic. His own expression was horrified. "Of course I do!"

"What, then?" I asked, my own hand lifting to rest on the swell of Senovo's naked shoulder.

There was a pregnant pause. "What if—" Senovo broke off and had to swallow hard before he continued. "What if I'm not strong enough to leave you afterward?"

"Oh, *Senovo.*" Andoc drew the eunuch forward until their foreheads rested against each other. "If you only realized how strong you truly are."

I squeezed the shoulder under my fingers, drawing his attention. "Do you trust us, Senovo?" I asked.

"You know I do," Senovo said without hesitation, though his expression was still tortured, eyes tightly closed.

"Then *trust us now,*" Andoc said, in a voice that gave no quarter.

Senovo's face twisted in pain for a moment… and then cleared. He wavered a bit on his feet as the unremitting tension that had plagued him for hours, if not days, seemed to drain from his body in the space of a heartbeat, and half fell into our arms. Andoc, with his bad leg, staggered a bit until he could get his balance back, then immediately wrapped us both in a tight embrace.

"I trust you," Senovo said again, into the space between Andoc's chest, where his head was resting, and my cheek, pressed against his. For the first time in many weeks, I felt that he was truly *here* with us, body and soul, and the strength of my relief nearly brought tears to my eyes.

"We're ready now," I told Jyrrel, without moving from the tangle of arms and bodies.

The old priest smiled. "So I see. In that case, I ask you again—do you agree to this public handfasting, freely and joyfully?"

"We do," the three of us said in unison.

With some reluctance, we parted so we could stand side by side. Andoc stood on Senovo's left so that Senovo could help brace his injured right leg during the period of the handfasting. I flanked Senovo's other side, placing him between us— *protected*. Each of us took one of his hands in ours.

Novice Adlan came forward holding two thongs. One at a time, he bound us to Senovo with the intricate weave that would last a night and a day, leaving us completely reliant on each other until they were untied. Senovo's hand grasped mine with a desperate grip, as if worried that I would somehow slip free before the knot was tied. I clung back just as hard, projecting every ounce of reassurance I could muster.

Moments later, it was done.

"You are now joined—one heart, one soul," the High Priest intoned. "Celebrate your union before the gods and the people of Meren. Find your joy within each other, that new acceptance may grow from the fertile field of your love."

There was a brief pause. "Ever shall it be so," called Keenan from her place in the front row. She was echoed moments later by more people in a ragged, disjointed chant. The noise of the crowd might as well have been the buzzing of distant insects, so little did I care for it.

Without warning, Senovo tugged me toward him by our bound hands and kissed me like a drowning man seeking air. Everything else fell away as desire and jubilation crashed through me. Behind him, Andoc dragged Senovo's other arm across his back and pinned it between their bodies. Senovo moaned into the kiss, and I pulled away far enough to watch Andoc suck a line of red marks down the side of his neck, where they would be easily visible above the neckline of his robes— never to be hidden away again.

Senovo's small cock twitched hard against the crease of my hip. I looked around wildly to get my bearings and pulled the other two along with me as I backed to the edge of the altar. A soft pad of quilted woven cloth covered it, and I spared a momentary thought as I settled onto it that my idle musings during Keenan and Ciero's handfasting last spring had been correct — the padded covering was, in fact, far more comfortable than the simple animal hides used for handfastings in Draebard.

Senovo was still reeling, and half fell on top of me, kissing his way down my throat and over my breasts. "Please," he begged in a fractured voice, between kisses and bites. "Please..."

Andoc sat on the edge of the stone block. His free hand came down over the nape of Senovo's neck, and the eunuch shuddered. "Easy, *amadi*. It's all right now. Everything is all right. We'll open our new bondmate up together, so you can take her while I take you."

"*Oh, gods...*" I cursed, heedless of the fact that I was lying on the temple altar with two High Priests and dozens of other people witnessing my mild blasphemy.

For his part, Senovo *whined* and practically dove between my legs, nuzzling into my folds and lapping up the moisture that he found there. Lust draped a thin red fog over my vision, and I clamped my eyes shut as my body sang with the unexpected rush of pleasure. Our bound hands tugged at each other as he moved even lower, his tongue dragging over my clean, freshly washed skin.

What — ? I thought in surprise, an instant before its tip prodded at my puckered opening and my release crashed over me with no warning. I cried out at the feeling of Senovo's tongue circling my fluttering rim, and jerked helplessly beneath him.

"Well... I suppose that's one way to do it," Andoc said, sounding a bit breathless. "Perhaps some oil or grease, though?"

The last was directed at someone else, and I was vaguely aware of Novice Adlan stepping forward long enough to deposit a small stone bowl of tallow near the edge of the altar before fading back into the shadows. Andoc used his and Senovo's joined hands to scoop some up and warm it. I whimpered, deliciously oversensitive as a tangle of fingers slid along the crease of my buttocks, pressing and massaging.

Two fingers breached me, one elegant and soft, one strong and callused. I moaned at the familiar burn and tried to fuck myself onto them shamelessly. Andoc growled, his low rumble of desire doing all sorts of interesting things to my insides.

My body gradually grew heavy and boneless as they stretched me open, until I was merely lying there, completely relaxed and pliant after my climax. I gazed into Senovo's eyes, darkened and desperate with want. Another finger slipped inside me, and my lips parted with a breathy gasp.

Andoc leaned close until his lips were nearly touching Senovo's ear. "I think she's ready for you, *amadi*. Now, why don't we get *you* ready for *me*."

I whined in discontent as the fingers slid free from my body, hating the feeling of emptiness as my body tried to clutch at nothing. Senovo pressed an open-mouthed kiss to my hipbone, my thatch of wiry hair, and finally, my sex. I wrapped the fingers of my free hand into his long hair and held him there.

"Greedy," Andoc chastened, though I could hear the smile behind the words. "Let him up, *caradi*. I've no desire to kneel on the hard floor with a bad leg so I can get at him."

Knowing that the faster I obeyed, the faster I could have Senovo inside me, I used my grip to pull him up the length of my body so I could kiss him and taste myself on his tongue. He followed the tug with uncharacteristic awkwardness, hindered by his bindings, but fell into the kiss with abandon the instant our lips touched. Senovo dragged our hands up until they were pressed into the soft padding next to my head and held himself above me, leaving me thoroughly—and blissfully—trapped beneath him.

In my peripheral vision, I saw Andoc brace himself on his free arm next to us, and a moment later, Senovo gasped into the kiss and arched above me. My stomach fluttered as I realized that Andoc must be making him open himself up with their joined hands. I *attacked* his lips, thrusting my tongue into his mouth to mirror what Andoc was doing to him behind. Senovo's breath huffed out in a stutter of air, and he melted against me, much as I had done earlier under the combined assault of those same fingers.

Finally, Andoc was ready, it seemed. "No bindings for your cock tonight, *amadi*," he said into the shell of Senovo's ear. "You just let yourself go and enjoy it. I've a feeling that Carivel and I won't be far behind."

"Please, Senovo," I whispered into his other ear. *"Please. I need you inside me right now."*

Senovo shivered between us and closed his lips around the pulse at my neck. I melted a bit further into the altar for a moment, before lifting my right leg and holding the knee against my chest with my free hand, exposing myself to them. Andoc helped Senovo line up his hips with mine. His eunuch's erection was already fading without something to bind it, but then Andoc pressed his own hips against Senovo from behind and took him with a single unforgiving stroke.

Senovo cried out, and his prick surged back to full hardness. I wriggled my hips to put him where I needed him, letting Andoc press him slowly into my body. Every last lingering bit of tension flowed out of me as he shunted home, held tightly between us. In some ways, the whole thing was terribly awkward, with our hands bound and the edge of the altar digging into the top of my buttocks. And yet... it was still *so very good.*

I moaned my approval and pulled Senovo in for another kiss with my free hand. He seemed nearly lost from the sensations, jerking forward and back to bury himself inside me and Andoc, inside him. Before terribly long, his movements grew erratic and he *keened*, jerking out his release.

That was too much for Andoc, who followed a moment later with a groan, hips flexing. Senovo shuddered, trapped between us. The angle wasn't quite right for me to be able to come a second time, but that was perfectly fine with me. My blood was already singing with elation, and I held Senovo tight against me, pressing my lips to every bit of skin within reach as Andoc half collapsed on us.

We lay in an awkward tangle for a few moments before Senovo reluctantly lifted his weight off of me, bracing against our bound hands. The green-gold eyes I had fallen in love with so many months ago blinked open, staring down at me with a look of wonder.

"Love you," I said, looking past him to meet Andoc's gaze as well. "Love you both, so much..."

Senovo fell on me once again, his lips seeking mine. A strong hand stroked down the length of my flank — Andoc.

"I couldn't love the two of you any more if I tried," he said.

Senovo pulled away slowly, and several acolytes stepped forward to assist us to unsteady feet. The room was silent except for the occasional cough or shuffling of feet, and I suddenly remembered the presence of the crowd. They still didn't matter, though—not when we were about to be led away to a warm, private room where we would have no distractions but each other for one wonderful, perfect day.

Our plan to put Senovo at Andoc's right side to help him walk without his walking stick hit a bit of a snag when we realized how badly Senovo himself was reeling. Still we managed an ungainly stagger out of the back of the altar room and down a quiet hallway to the bedroom we would be sharing for the remainder of the handfasting. With only an occasional supporting hand from one of the slightly overawed acolytes, we arrived safely at our destination.

Andoc—ever the picture of charm—thanked the boys for their assistance. When the door closed behind them, leaving us alone in the well-appointed room, Senovo wavered, his knees threatening to buckle. Taken by surprise, I set my feet and braced him as best I could while Andoc did the same from the other side.

"I—I need to… sit down…" he said.

Andoc did a quick survey of our surroundings and gestured to the edge of the bed. We stumbled the last few steps and shuffled around each other until we could lower Senovo to sit between us. With his free hand, Andoc reached up and urged him to lean forward, cupping a steadying palm across the back of his neck.

"Breathe, *amadi,*" he said. "It's all right. It really happened. You're ours now."

Senovo's breath hitched for a moment before he shook his head and slowly straightened. "I was already yours."

I smiled, and reached over to stroke his long hair back and hook it over his ear. "Of course you were. But now, everyone knows it. We'll never have to hide again."

It was obvious that Senovo was still struggling to wrap his mind around this idea, but the look of dawning wonder on his face was absolutely beautiful to see.

"What do you need now, *amadi*?" Andoc asked. "For the next night and day, we wish only to care for you."

Senovo swallowed. "I want… so many things. But I'm very tired right now."

"Then we'll sleep until you aren't," said Andoc.

"It's no wonder you're exhausted," I added. "You've been spending so much time as the wolf that you've barely slept for weeks now."

Andoc looked around the room. "Our hosts have left us water and soap, I see," he observed. "A quick wash, and then we'll rest."

Senovo nodded, soft and trusting as Andoc cleaned the grease from their hands and pricks, before gently running a cloth between first Senovo's legs, and then mine. Desire flared weakly in my belly and I smiled. There would be time for all that once we'd slept.

I was as captivated as ever by the way Senovo relaxed into Andoc's care. It had been far too long since he had surrendered to us in such a way, and it was as if all of the pent up need to let himself sink into that safe, protected place was hitting at once, now that the ceremony had actually taken place. He slumped against me, nuzzling into my neck as Andoc finished up and set the rag and the bowl of water aside.

I gave Senovo a little nudge, charmed by the sleepy groan of complaint I received in return. "Come on, you," I prompted. "Let us get you arranged so we can wrap you up and get some rest."

After a moment's consideration, I got up and ducked under Andoc's shoulder, switching places with him so that we would all be more comfortable when our bound wrists were thrown across Senovo's body. Between us, we shuffled him into the middle of the bed—generously sized, though not quite as generous as the one in the High Priest's quarters in Draebard. Once we were as comfortable as we could be with our wrists tied together, I rolled up on an elbow and stroked the knuckles on my free hand over Senovo's temple in a soothing rhythm.

"Sleep now. We're not going anywhere," I said, and gave our bound wrists a little tug to demonstrate.

Senovo made an impressive attempt at relaxing straight down into the mattress, his breath sighing out in a soft puff that tickled my collarbone. Within moments, he was out like a snuffed candle.

"I was worried we'd broken him, there for a minute," I said softly, meeting Andoc's deep brown eyes across our new bondmate's slumbering form.

Andoc shook his head ruefully. "I think he's been carrying a lot of things inside him for a very long time. Now, he's having to let go of them all at once."

"If only we had longer," I said, aching at the thought of returning to Draebard. Of saying goodbye.

Andoc's expression grew pained, and I realized he was feeling guilty about dragging us back. Perhaps also about throwing Senovo to the wolves... so to speak.

"Hey," I said. "Stop. Don't look like that. We'll get through it, and then afterward, we'll have all the time we could ever wish for."

"If we all live," Andoc whispered. "If he comes back."

It was the first time he had expressed his fears about the coming battle so openly. "We will," I said, as irrational as it was to state such a thing as fact. "*He* will. And... if I'm wrong..." I paused. Swallowed. "Andoc, you two have given me so much more already than I ever expected to get out of this life. I thought I was doomed to always be alone."

Andoc closed his eyes tightly for a moment. When he opened them again, they were wet. "Never, *caradi*. Never again, if I can help it."

My own breathing went a bit wobbly, and my voice was hoarse when I nodded and said, "I know. Come on now. *Sleep.* You're not much better off right now than he is."

I could tell that only the desire not to wake Senovo kept Andoc from stretching over to kiss me, and I smiled at him. *Later.* It was true that the future still loomed over us. But right now? We had a night and a day all to ourselves.

SIXTEEN

Hunger—and Senovo's lips pressing a series of butterfly kisses against my collarbone—woke me some unknown amount of time later. It was dark. The fire was burning low but not yet reduced to embers, so I guessed it still must be well before dawn. I hummed and stretched, pulling Senovo's arm with me before I remembered the bindings.

"Hello, you," I said in a low, sleep-roughened voice, and rolled my head to give Senovo better access to my neck. "I'm hungry. How about you? Are you hungry? Thirsty?"

"A little thirsty, perhaps," he said against my skin, the vibration sending a frisson down my spine.

I wriggled around until I could catch his lips with mine and kiss him, slow and languid. When we were both breathless, I pulled away and looked around. The tall candles scattered around the room were designed to burn all night without having to be relit, and their light combined with the light from the hearth fire was enough for me to see the various items of food and drink that had been left on the table next to my side of the bed.

Scooting up into a kneeling position, I reached across for a flagon of wine and worked the cork free one-handed. There was a goblet standing nearby, but in the absence of polite company I saw no need to bother with it. Instead, I turned around so I could lean against the sturdy headboard and urge Senovo up to recline against my chest. To no one's surprise, Andoc slept on, even as his arm was jerked around during the change in position.

We rested against each other and took turns with the wine, which I held carefully to Senovo's lips with my free hand so he could drink. When he nodded to indicate that his thirst was sated, I set the flagon aside and took great pleasure in licking away the trickle that had spilled down his chin and into the hollow of his throat.

A further examination of the table showed a selection of fruit, salted meat, and cheese, all cut into manageable bites. I hooked the nearest platter a bit closer and alternated feeding myself and feeding Senovo, taking a secret delight in the small, surprisingly intimate act of care as he nibbled food from my fingers. When we'd both had enough and washed it down with a final draught of wine, I looked curiously at a small bowl of greenish brown powder nestled among the platters.

"What's this?" I asked, stretching enough that I could pick it up and look more closely.

Senovo peered at the bowl for a moment and sniffed the contents before letting his head loll back. "Not sure. Let me taste a little."

I wet one finger and used it to pick up a few grains. Senovo smiled and made a production of sucking the digit into his mouth and laving the pad, causing a lazy swell of lust to curl through me. He pulled back after a moment and chuckled, the low, pleasant sound still coming as a mild shock to me.

"Heslip powder," he said, still sounding amused. "You should try some once Andoc wakes up. The effects don't last very long, but they can be quite... *singular*, particularly in the right company."

I laughed. "Ooh... mind-altering substances, eh? I bet the Mereni are a lot of fun at parties."

"One suspects so, yes."

"Sleep some more first?" I suggested.

"Mmm," Senovo agreed.

The next time I regained awareness, both Andoc and Senovo were already awake, and I *really* needed to use the chamber pot. Morning light streamed through the gaps in the shutters, illuminating the room in dusty, irregular chinks.

"I was about to wake you," Andoc said. "I don't know about you, but I could very much use a piss at this point."

"Still the romantic," I replied, amused.

Our shuffling dance to relieve everyone's bladders was the same combination of awkward and funny that I remembered from my previous handfasting with Andoc. While we were up, Andoc put more wood on the fire from the pile resting thoughtfully near the hearth. As we ate and drank our fill, Senovo's method of taking food from our hands grew ever more suggestive until Andoc finally laughed.

"I believe our bondmate is attempting to communicate something, *caradi*. What do you think?"

By now, Senovo was shamelessly fellating my fingers, so I couldn't exactly disagree. "I think we should give him some of this... what was it? Horslip powder? And see what happens."

Senovo let my fingers slip free with a faint pop. "Heslip powder," he corrected. "And only if you take some, too."

"Oh, now this I *have* to see," Andoc said. "High Priest Jyrrel is spoiling us."

"How do you take it?" I asked, grabbing the tiny bowl.

"Just put a pinch under your tongue and let it dissolve there," Andoc said.

I shrugged and gave Senovo a pinch. "Do you want some?" I asked Andoc.

He laughed. "Probably best if at least one of us isn't completely off our asses. Besides, I wasn't joking when I said I wanted to watch this."

Beside me, Senovo shifted restlessly and nuzzled into Andoc. Not wanting to be left behind in the race to altered consciousness, I picked up a small amount and placed it under my tongue. The bitter taste was unpleasant, but before long an interesting tingle took up residence somewhere between my ears, and my scalp prickled as if all my hair was standing on end.

I swallowed to clear the unpleasant taste, and I was just opening my mouth to comment that I didn't really see the appeal of taking something just to make my head feel itchy when a flush of heat traveled down the length of my body. A moan emerged instead of words.

"And away we go," Andoc said, a smile curling his lips and making his eyes twinkle.

Drawn by my breathy groan, Senovo rolled over and licked a stripe up my breast, drawing a line of fire with his tongue.

"Deresta's *tits*," I gasped, and plastered myself to him from chest to ankle.

The effect was hard to describe... not that I was devoting terribly much attention to trying at that particular moment. It wasn't *precisely* sexual, in and of itself. More... *sensual*. If you'd asked me to recall one single fear or worry and focus on it, I wouldn't have been able to. Because who cared about all that, when pressing myself against Senovo felt so *good*?

"I really, really like this," I said, the filter between my mind and my mouth falling away with all the other unimportant things. "I like this *a lot*."

Andoc chuckled, and leaned across to kiss my temple. "Glad to hear it," he said.

I made a pleased humming noise and pried myself away from Senovo so that I could run our joined hands up and down his torso. Even the sensation coming from my fingertips as he writhed like a cat beneath my touch was enough to make me moan in appreciation. His skin was warm and silky, and the way he threw his head back, as if transported into bliss by the slow stroking, sent little tremors of happiness through my body.

I remembered the way Senovo's tongue had felt on my breast and wondered if I could make things even better for him. The idea sent a deep curl of heat through me, so I leaned over and returned the favor, licking across his flat, brown nipple and pulling it between my lips to suckle when it drew into a pebbled point. The noise that emerged from Senovo's throat went straight to my heart, making it swell impossibly further.

When Andoc moved his and Senovo's joined hands down to fondle the eunuch's velvety prick, I thought it might burst completely.

"Try touching yourself, *caradi*," Andoc suggested. "I'd offer to do it for you, but I can't really get a good angle from over here."

Watching Senovo arch and moan wantonly, I decided that this suggestion was an *amazing* idea. "*Yes*," I moaned, utterly shameless, and wriggled around until I could watch Andoc gently teasing Senovo's cock while also worming my free hand between my own legs to play with my sensitive nub.

During sex, there was a certain point, usually short-lived, where my release was inevitable, even though it was not truly upon me yet. Senovo—evil bastard of a priest that he was—had a surprising talent for pushing me *almost* to that place and pulling me back, over and over. Now, though, the slide of my own fingers brought me there within moments... and kept me hovering there effortlessly.

It wasn't release… not quite. In fact, I don't think I could have reached release if I tried while the powder still held me in its mellow thrall. Instead, it was the certain knowledge that nothing else I could have been doing would possibly give me any more pleasure than what I was feeling right now.

"Oh, gods," I breathed, and rubbed my cheek against Senovo's smooth chest, new tendrils of warmth spreading outward from the contact.

Senovo trembled beneath me. "S-so good," he said. "Love you both."

"We love you, too, *amadi*," Andoc said. "You deserve every moment of this happiness."

"I… I need…" The words tailed off into a whine.

"What do you need, beloved?" Andoc asked. My fingers slowed of their own volition while I awaited Senovo's answer, which seemed suddenly very important.

He swallowed hard and arched against the bedclothes. "I… want you to touch my sac. Both of you. I need… *please*. Please touch me there."

Andoc went very still, and I frowned. There was… some reason why we weren't ever supposed to do that, I was sure of it. But Senovo said he wanted us to. What should we do? I tried to reason it out, but I couldn't think properly. At a loss, I looked to Andoc. Surely he would know?

Andoc was staring down at Senovo with a frown of his own. He was silent for a moment or two before replying. "*Amadi*, I swear to you that we will give you whatever you need, but we'll have to wait until the heslip wears off first. We need to talk about it a little more before we do that."

I sighed, relieved that we both had Andoc here to make the decision.

Senovo looked up at him from the bed with pupils blown wide and dark. His face looked heartbreakingly young. "I don't know if I can," he said.

"We'll help you," Andoc said. "The three of us will figure it out together, I promise."

There was a long pause.

"It's starting to wear off already," Senovo said, and indeed, he was sounding slightly more like himself now.

When I focused inward, I could tell that the effects were fading for me, too, the buzz of pleasure giving way to a mild, nagging headache. "It is fading," I agreed. "How long should we wait?"

"Let's give it half an hour or so." Andoc smoothed his free hand over Senovo's temple, and resumed his slow stroking over the eunuch's half-hard shaft. Though no longer lost in drugged pleasure, he nuzzled into Andoc's side and went lax.

My own desire had subsided as my mind grew more connected and the truth of what Senovo was asking for began to sink in. Rather than continue to touch myself, I molded my body against his and pressed kisses to his shoulder and neck.

The very first time we'd lain together, Andoc had quietly warned me against handling Senovo's sac, which had been crushed years earlier during his forced castration. Not only did the empty flap of skin still pain him physically sometimes—usually during abrupt weather changes and cold, damp conditions—but Senovo's own early attempts to touch himself there had triggered something inside his mind, dragging him back to that cold table where he'd been held down, a leather strap forced into his mouth to keep him from biting through his own tongue. Little surprise that after a couple such attempts, he'd stopped trying out of fear.

For him to ask us now was...

I swallowed. What if it went horribly wrong, and we sent him back to relive the worst moments of his life? Why would he even want to risk that?

Time crawled by with agonizing slowness. Without quite being certain of how it happened, I found that the three of us had scooted even closer to each other until we were wrapped together in a tangled heap.

"I'm fine now," Senovo said from where he lay half-smothered between us.

"Carivel?" Andoc asked. "Have the effects worn off for you, too?"

"Yes," I said, and jammed up a fraction tighter against the others. "I can think clearly again, at any rate. Senovo, I don't want to do anything that might hurt you."

There was a stretch of silence.

"*Amadi?*" Andoc prompted. "Can you talk to us about this?"

I felt Senovo's ribcage expand and contract against us as he took a deep, centering breath. "I need... to let go of this final piece of myself. Of my past."

More silence.

"And you think this will help you do that?" Andoc asked.

Senovo's brow furrowed for a moment, and smoothed. "You already have every other part of me. This is the one thing I have held back, and I have only done so out of fear. I no longer wish for fear to keep me from freely offering my whole self to both of you. I wish you to know all of me."

A lump rose in my throat. "What if it goes wrong?" I whispered.

He thought for a long moment before answering. "Then I will be with the two people I trust most in all the world to bring me back from the past. Will you do this for me?"

Andoc and I looked at each other. My jaw worked as I thought about the depth of responsibility we would be taking, but this was not some grand, self-sacrificing gesture Senovo was making for us. This was something he was asking us to do *for him*. I took a deep breath and nodded. Andoc nodded back.

"Very well, *amadi*. As long as this is something you wish for yourself, and not something you merely think we desire from you, we agree," Andoc said, neatly echoing my own sentiments.

"It is," Senovo said, sounding almost... *relieved*. "I have lived with the past for a very long time, old friend. It is finally time to release it and look to the future, I think."

I swallowed against the obstruction threatening to steal my voice, until I could speak again. "How do you want to do this? Do you only want Andoc to touch you? Or both of us?"

"Both of you," Senovo said very quietly. "But... perhaps it would be best if you went first, so Andoc can focus on keeping me tethered to the present."

I nodded and made myself take deep, slow breaths. "Of course," I said. "Lie back, then, and let us take care of you. I'll warn you before I touch you there, but you can stop me whenever you need to." I met Andoc's serious gaze. "Andoc, you'll let me know, as well, if I need to stop?"

Senovo let out a little huff that might have been amusement under different circumstances. "It seems we've taught you well."

"You're good teachers," I said, and kissed him.

I didn't let him up until I felt him begin to relax beneath me, his lips becoming warm and pliant under mine.

"I *love* kissing you," I told him, the first hint of an idea coming to mind. "I remember thinking during our very first kiss that I could do it for hours."

Senovo looked up at me from where he lay half in Andoc's arms. A small smile quirked at one corner of his lips. "Flattery will get you nowhere, beloved. At least, nowhere that you could not get as easily without it."

"Hush, you," I said, mock severely. "Andoc, isn't he just the best kisser?"

Andoc hitched the priest a little more firmly into his arms and played along. "You'll get no disagreement from me. You know that little noise he makes when you tug on his lower lip?"

"I do indeed. It's almost as good as the noise he makes when you do this—" With no warning, I bit down on the muscle running from Senovo's neck to his shoulder and sucked hard, raising a mark that would partially overlap one that Andoc made earlier, during the ceremony. Senovo drew in a sharp, surprised breath—a gasp in reverse.

"Oh, yes. That one's good, too," Andoc said.

"H-honestly, you two, there's no need for a seduction," Senovo managed.

Andoc wrapped his free arm around so that he could slip his hand around Senovo's throat—not squeezing, just holding. The priest let his head fall back against Andoc's shoulder, arching into the loose grip as his eyes glazed over.

"Come now, *amadi*. I believe our Horse Mistress told you to hush," Andoc said.

"And then, there's that," I said, watching avidly. "I *really* love that."

"There *is* something about knowing that he'll submit to anything you want to do to him, and love every minute of it," Andoc agreed, his words tickling the shell of Senovo's ear. He stretched forward another inch and bit down on the eunuch's earlobe. Senovo shuddered and went pliant.

I balanced on my knees so I could run my free hand over Senovo's chest, down his stomach and around to his sensitive flank. "His skin is so soft. Softer than mine, by far."

"It's the temple life," Andoc said. "No calluses from hard labor. Lots of time spent inside, out of the sun and wind."

"A lot of priests are pale, but his skin is golden even without the sun." I leaned down and kissed Senovo's belly, then the top of his thigh.

"You know where his skin is the softest, though?" Andoc asked.

"Hmm," I said, considering. Senovo's legs had fallen open as he succumbed to our words and touches. I brushed fingertips over his puckered opening, the barest of touches. "You mean here?" My hand moved to cup his limp cock. "Or here?"

Senovo moaned softly, and I heard the click of his throat as he swallowed against the weight of Andoc's hand.

"I meant inside, actually. It's like being wrapped in warm moleskin."

"You're right," I said. "There's still one place we haven't touched, though, even though I've wanted to do it so badly sometimes. A place that someone hurt. I wanted so much to replace that hurt with love and care. To replace the memory of pain with the memory of pleasure. May I touch you there, Senovo?"

"Please," Senovo breathed, the shape of a word more than anything else.

Holding my breath, I slowly eased the palm of my hand along Senovo's inner thigh, until I was cupping the flap of impossibly soft wrinkled skin in my palm as one might cup a newly fledged chick. A shiver wracked Senovo's body and he clenched his eyes shut.

"*Amadi,*" Andoc said in a firm tone. "Open your eyes and look at me."

I remained absolutely motionless. I'm not sure my heart was even beating. Senovo's eyes flew open, panic lurking behind them.

"*Look at me,*" Andoc insisted.

The trapped breath left Senovo's chest in a great gasp. I suddenly realized that I wasn't helping matters with my own anxiety, and forced myself to breath as well. Made myself relax my locked muscles, and let the tension in my body drain away. Projected love, not fear.

"We have you," said Andoc with absolute certainty. "You're with us, in Meren, and I would die before I let anyone hurt you again. Now tell me, my heart. Where are you?"

The shivering grew worse as Senovo tried to answer, and failed.

"It's only me touching you," I said, unable to completely keep the quaver out of my voice. "Only us. Please stay here with us. Don't go back to that terrible place again."

"She's right, beloved," Andoc said. "You can *choose* never to go back there. Tell me now, where are you?"

There was a terrible beat of silence.

"With you," Senovo whispered, and the pounding of my pulse eased a bit.

"Does it hurt at all?" I asked, ready to pull away at the first indication that I was causing pain.

"Only on the inside," Senovo said, still shaking under our hands. "Don't stop, please. Not now, not like this."

I nodded, only to realize a moment later that he could not see the movement, his eyes still locked with Andoc's. "You are the bravest person I've ever known," I told him, "and I love you so much it aches."

"It's time to let go, *amadi*," Andoc said, desperately tender. "You've given this to us, now let us carry it for you."

Senovo made an awful, choked noise. Shuddered, and went limp. "Please," he said. "I need—" He looked at Andoc with pleading eyes.

Andoc nodded. "I know, old friend. *Caradi*, would you come up here and take him?"

I nodded, and carefully slid my hand away, drawing a new shudder from our charge. As quickly as I could, I scooted back up so I could draw Senovo into my arms. Andoc reached around awkwardly for the pot of grease sitting on the table by his side of the bed. A moment later, he moved to arrange himself on his belly between Senovo's legs.

"Love and shared pleasure has always been the greatest revenge you could have against the bastards who would pervert our religion by causing pain to the innocent," Andoc said. "They may have done their black-hearted best, but they couldn't take either of those things away from you."

I held Senovo tight, and he nodded against my shoulder—a jerky, disjointed movement.

Andoc scooped up grease and stroked over Senovo's cock before moving to tease him open with first one finger, then two. Senovo moaned against my skin as Andoc stroked inside him.

His shaft twitched and gradually filled, until I could position our joined hands around its stiff length, pumping slowly up and down. We pleasured him with lazy, unhurried movements, never letting up. Eventually, his breath grew ragged as he approached his crisis point.

"Touch me," he said. "Please, do it now!"

Andoc stretched forward to kiss and lick at the damaged flesh between Senovo's legs. He mouthed at the wrinkled flap, drawing it between his lips to suck and lave with gentle movements. Senovo cried out sharply, as if in surprise, and sobbed his release, his cock jerking in the warm space between our joined hands. He continued to weep even after the spasms ceased, burying his face in my neck. I held him close with my free arm, a few tears of my own escaping to slide down my cheeks and into his hair. A moment later, Andoc was behind him, rearranging their arms so he, too could embrace Senovo as he at last grieved openly for what he'd lost, so many years ago.

"I wanted them all dead," he choked out. "As they were dragging me into the chamber, I vowed to see every single one of them torn limb from limb. And then the wolf came, and did exactly that. It killed them. I *killed* them."

"You were mad with fear and pain, *amadi*. The wolf did what was necessary to get free from them and escape. There is nothing more natural than a wounded animal defending itself. I will be forever grateful to that part of you. It saved you, and brought you to us," Andoc said, as we had both said so many times before. Perhaps, I thought with a surge of hope, this would be the time that Senovo finally believed us.

"The wolf has saved all of us at one time or another," I added. "Without it, none of us would be here in this bed tonight."

Senovo's weeping was all the more heartrending for being completely silent, in spite of the violence of his shaking. Finally, he dragged in a ragged breath, like a drowning man surfacing from the depths. When he spoke, his voice was as hoarse as if he'd been shouting.

"When we return to Draebard, I will give myself over to the wolf. I will trust him to save us one more time, because the alternative is to see you both killed in battle. I couldn't bear that. I couldn't survive it."

My arms clenched around him involuntarily. "And afterward, you'll come back to us?" I could not keep the desperation from my voice.

"I don't wish to be parted from either of you," said Senovo, and it was almost an answer.

"You've always had difficulty trusting yourself, Senovo," Andoc said seriously. "But now, you'll find out what we've always known. We freely trust you with our lives, on four legs or two."

Senovo nodded slowly. "Please," he said, sounding completely wrung out. "I need you now. I need both of you inside me. Please make me feel it. Use me. Mark me. Let me go away for a little while."

I gave a little sob of my own and clung tighter. Andoc smoothed Senovo's hair out of the way and pressed a biting kiss to the side of his neck.

"Anything," he said. "Anything you wish."

Our saddlebags were propped against a corner of the bed, my harness and curved wooden cock nestled inside. Buckling it on was a challenge with only one hand, but Andoc helped. He and I took turns lazily fucking Senovo into insensibility as the day slipped slowly by in a haze of pleasure-drugged emotion. In between, we fed him choice tidbits of food, gave him sips of wine transferred from our own lips to his, and ran clean, damp cloths over him to wash away the sweat and the spend—only for someone to press into him once again and drive him toward another helpless release.

Though I could not yet bring myself to do so, Andoc brushed occasional stray touches over Senovo's damaged sac, treating it as simply another part of him to love. Senovo merely lay back, his eyes wide and dark with pleasure, sometimes giving a small shiver in response, but no longer tense and frightened by the contact.

At odd moments, I found myself crying, and one or both of my mates would pull me into an embrace. At odd moments, I found Senovo crying, as well, tears slipping down his face in a steady trickle without marring his perfect stillness and relaxation.

When Andoc gathered us both in his arms as best he could with the bindings connecting our wrists, and trembled silently against us for long minutes, I came back to myself enough to realize that the world outside the window was growing dark. A night had passed… and a day. I reached around until I could stroke my fingers through his tousled brown hair, a faint sense of numbness washing over me.

"It's over," I told him, "but it's not really *over*. Not yet. Not until we get back to Draebard."

I felt him take a deep breath and release it slowly. "Yes. Yes, of course. You're right. Come here, *caradi*."

I melted into the penetrating kiss, my lips swollen and tender from all the other kisses the three of us had enjoyed over the course of the day. When Andoc had kissed Senovo as well, and I had followed suit, we set about bringing our thoroughly debauched lover up from the depths with gentle words and touches.

When Senovo looked up at us with trusting eyes and suggested we find High Priest Jyrrel so he could finish the ceremony, I was rather surprised at the depth of tranquility that still seemed to cling to him, even though he had obviously returned to us from his place of respite. I had fully expected to have to essentially drag him from the bed, but he was nearly as steady on his feet as I was, and helped Andoc brace himself on his bad leg until the tight muscles eased after so much time lying down. If Senovo winced a little as we began to walk, throwing me a brief, rueful glance, that was perhaps unsurprising given what we'd spent the last several hours doing to him.

We entered the altar room to find a silent crowd gathered, not as large as last night's, but significant, nonetheless. Unlike the previous evening, those present parted for us without prompting, clearing a path to the altar, where the Mereni High Priest stood with his hands folded into the sleeves of his white robes.

"Chief Andoc," he boomed. "High Priest Senovo. Horse Mistress Carivel. The three of you have been bound for a night and a day, as the Ancestors prescribe. It is now my honor to enact the final part of your handfasting ceremony. Kneel before the altar, please."

Senovo helped Andoc down to the hard flagstone floor, his bad leg held awkwardly to the side. I followed, feeling the stone dig mercilessly into my knees. We raised our bound hands for Jyrrel's inspection, and he nodded. With deft movements of his pudgy fingers, he unwrapped first the thong binding me to Senovo, and then the one binding Senovo to Andoc.

"The bindings are whole and unbroken," he told the crowd, lifting the intact thongs so those nearest could see the truth of the words. "The ceremony is complete. Andoc, Senovo, and Carivel are now bondmates before the gods."

SEVENTEEN

Silence reigned for a long moment, only to be broken by a rather familiar whoop and the sound of someone applauding loudly. After a few more beats, others joined in, slapping their thighs. I rose and made to turn around, only to be nearly bowled over by Keenan's enthusiastic embrace.

"Congratulations!" she said, and moved to throw her arms around Senovo and Andoc, in turn, heedless of their nakedness. "I'm so happy for the three of you!" She looked back at the front of the crowd. "Ciero's here as well. He has a gift for you, Carivel."

Indeed, Keenan's husband was also mounting the plinth to join us, a leather bag slung over his shoulder. "Congratulations," he said. "It might have lacked a bit of the excitement that followed our own handfasting, but that was a good ceremony. Sorry some of the townsfolk are idiots."

Andoc huffed a breath of laughter at Ciero's blunt assessment. "No harm done."

Ciero smiled, his broad face dimpling as he rummaged one-handed in the bag. "Carivel, I want you to have this. I remembered that you seemed to like it while I was working on it in Draebard, and it only seems right."

He pulled out the ebony carving of Nietre, and I gasped at the beauty of the finished piece. "Ciero! It's *gorgeous*. I don't know what to say —"

Keenan hugged me again. "Say *thank you for the gift, Ciero,* unless you want us to be here all night," she teased.

"Thank you for the gift, Ciero," I said obediently, and accepted the small rearing horse with a hand still crisscrossed by marks from the thongs that had bound us. "The likeness is uncanny."

That was apparently all the payment Ciero required — his grin grew broader and a pleased flush colored his cheeks. "You're welcome, Horse Mistress. Mind that the real Nietre goes lightly on the way back to Draebard. The carving's front legs are a bit delicate where the wood grain changes direction."

"I'll be careful," I promised.

A tall figure appeared at Andoc's shoulder a moment later — Varanis. "If you three are ready to put some clothes on again," she said, "my mother would like to speak with you before you leave in the morning."

"Or, as we used to say, *congratulations on your handfasting*," Keenan chimed in.

Varanis raised an unimpressed eyebrow. "The war comes first, Third Warrior. Chief Andoc understands that."

"I do indeed," Andoc said, and only someone who really knew him would have detected the strain in his face. "We'll come to the meeting hall as soon as we've dressed."

"Very well," Varanis replied. "Magoldis is waiting for you. There have been some new developments with the design of the small trebuchets that our weapons makers have been working on."

All at once, Andoc's gaze sharpened, and I could see the moment when Andoc-the-lover once again became Andoc-the-warrior. My eyes met Senovo's and we exchanged a look.

"We'll come there at once," said Chief Andoc of the Draebardi.

⫷⫸

The meeting with Leader Magoldis and the Mereni council dragged long into the night. Andoc explained about Ithric and the northern shape-shifters, and how he hoped to be able to provide an army of bears to defend the northernmost port of Dellwyn, an army of wolves to defend Llanmeer, and an army of lions to defend Erylaan. Between the emotion of the day and the exhausting strategy sessions for the war, the three of us fell into bed afterward and almost immediately succumbed to sleep.

The following morning, we left for Draebard. I was somewhat surprised when, rather than shifting into the wolf to travel, Senovo climbed up behind me on Nietre and cinched his arms around my torso with a firm grip. I was hardly going to question it, though, so I only pressed one of my hands over his and reined the black stallion around, heading west with Andoc on his rangy mare at our side.

The day was relatively warm, and we made good progress before stopping for the night. Senovo was, unsurprisingly, still rather sore after what we'd subjected him to the previous day, topped off by long hours spent in the saddle. Rather than join in directly, he curled next to us in the tent and fondled my breasts and the crease of my arse as I lay on top of Andoc, positioned head to cock. I let his thick shaft press ever deeper into my throat as he pleasured me with his mouth, until we both came with a shudder and gushed our release over each other's tongues.

Afterward, I should have slept, but an idea that had come to me during the day continued to prod at me until I couldn't ignore it any more. Senovo was still awake as well, running his hand slowly up and down my back as Andoc snored beside us.

"Do you know where Andoc put the handfasting thongs?" I asked in a low voice.

Senovo's hand paused in its wanderings. "I believe they are in his left saddlebag, near the front. Why?"

"I want to try making something with them, but it's a surprise." The saddlebags were at our feet inside the tent, where animals would not be tempted by the food in them. I opened the flap to let light from the fire inside so I could rummage through the pack. "I can't sleep anyway, and I think it's warm enough outside by the fire, so I'll go keep watch and see if what I want to do will work."

"Very well," Senovo said, his curiosity evident but contained. "Take one of the blankets with you to throw over your shoulders."

I kissed him and tugged one of the blankets free. Andoc snorted and rolled over without waking.

Outside, the night was clear and chilly. The fire was still burning, but I put more scrub wood on it to build it up until it beat back the nighttime cold. When I was more or less comfortable, leaning back against Andoc's saddle with the blanket tucked around me, I selected a stick of the appropriate size from the pile of kindling. I looped both thongs around it so that I could grasp all four ends. Bracing the stick between my clamped knees to keep it steady, I began to braid.

The following afternoon, the three of us trotted into Draebard. Honestly, I had half expected pandemonium upon our arrival, since no doubt the news of our controversial handfasting would have reached the ears of every man, woman, and child by now. Instead, the mood seemed restrained... almost somber.

The weather was still pleasant for late winter, so I motioned for us to ride back to the horse pens, where I could be reasonably certain of finding a friendly face or two to explain what was going on.

"Hey, boss," Dalon greeted us, upon recognizing our distinctive mounts. "You really can't go a single season without ending up in the middle of some sort of scandal, can you? No offense, Chief Andoc. High Priest Senovo."

Andoc only lifted his eyebrows. "None taken, Dalon. Who are we to argue with the gods' will?" he said. "Nothing good ever comes of that."

"I s'pose not," Dalon said, sounding unconvinced but resigned. "High Priest, I don't know if anyone has told you yet, but Chanthi and Ladira took some other people with them on their last visit to Gebrall and Teth. They, um — they managed to get poor Renthro's body out of that crevasse where he fell. What was left of it, anyhow. They brought him home."

Fresh grief on Favian's behalf hit me in the chest with unexpected strength. "The dream," I said, suddenly remembering Favian waking from a dream of attending his father's funeral — something that had seemed impossible at the time.

Dalon frowned. "What dream?"

It was Senovo who answered, once Andoc had handed him down from the back of the tall chestnut mare. "Favian had a dream of the funeral ceremony shortly after his father's death. It appears that it was a true vision after all."

Dalon touched his head and heart in a brief, superstitious gesture. "And to think we used to have him mucking out horse pens."

"Nothing wrong with mucking out horse pens," I said. "It's a very meditative pastime."

My second-in-command shook his head. "Speak for yourself. Anyway, let me take your horses. I imagine you'll need to get back so you can deal with Renthro and all that."

"I assume we're not in danger of getting stoned by an angry mob for blasphemy?" I couldn't help asking.

"Honestly, boss, I think you've pretty much got them trained to expect the unexpected at this point. Plus, I don't think Draebard is stupid enough to disown its Chief, High Priest, and Horse Mistress a few weeks before an invasion."

"I suppose that's reassuring," Senovo said.

We returned to the temple with our saddlebags thrown over our shoulders, walking slowly in deference to Andoc's leg, which had been bothering him more than usual after a day of inactivity followed by two days' hard riding. Along the way, a few people stopped to greet us, while several others stared at us like we were something strange and frightening. No one offered congratulations or even mentioned the handfasting, so I gathered that the villagers' strategy was going to be to ignore the whole thing as much as humanly possible.

Tempting though it was to drag Senovo into a passionate kiss in the middle of the green just to drive the point home, I managed to restrain myself on the grounds that as reactions went, we could have received worse.

The air of careful, willful ignorance evaporated once Eiridan opened the temple door to greet us, however. His eyes roved over the three of us, taking in our appearance and demeanor. "Is it done?" he asked.

"It is," Senovo answered, a faint sense of wonder still coloring his tone.

Eiridan's smile bloomed, lighting up his pleasant features. "Well, then—congratulations to all three of you." He sobered after a moment. "I'm sorry to bear somber news during what should be a happy occasion, but—"

"Dalon told us about Renthro's body," I interrupted.

"Indeed," Eiridan said. "Well… come in. My apologies for detaining you in the temple doorway."

"How are Favian and Frella doing?" Andoc asked.

"It is difficult for them both," said Eiridan, "but in some ways it is also a relief, at least for Favian. High Priest, he wished to wait for your return so that you might officiate at the funeral."

"Of course," Senovo said. "If everything is prepared, we can perform the ceremony this very evening. I daresay Renthro has already waited long enough for his rest."

Eiridan breathed out softly. "Things are in readiness, yes. Novice Feldes and I consecrated the... remains... upon their return yesterday. Some of the townsfolk should be working on a pyre as we speak."

Senovo clasped Eiridan's shoulder briefly. "Thank you, Brother. The ceremony tonight will be two-fold. We will commend Renthro's spirit to the gods, and then I shall raise you and Feldes to the position of full priests. I wish to place you jointly in charge of the temple of Draebard before my... departure."

Just like that, the dread I had been pushing to the back of my mind slammed into me. *Senovo was leaving us.* My heart pounded with sudden panic, like the hoof beats of a galloping horse, and dizziness threatened to send me reeling. I reached out a surreptitious hand to steady myself against the wall.

"You are leaving to join the wolves?" Eiridan asked carefully.

"I am," Senovo said with absolute certainty, and the strength of will behind those two simple words made me want to weep. "I trust you and our brother Feldes to look after things in my absence and, just perhaps, to keep these two from doing anything too ridiculously foolhardy while I'm parted from them."

His eyes rested first on Andoc, and then on me, glinting gold-green. Eiridan followed his gaze.

"I'm afraid I wouldn't know where to start, Elder Brother," he said. "Though I'm certain the prospect of being reunited with you after the battle will provide a degree of motivation to remain safe and whole."

The ensuing silence ached in my chest like a wound. Beside me, Andoc's face was stricken as he, too, came to terms with the fact that we would soon have to say goodbye.

"Come," Senovo said. "Let us greet the others and see what comfort we can provide to our grieving children."

Andoc nodded, and I swallowed hard. We followed the elegant sweep of Senovo's robes as he led the way deeper into the temple to stow our belongings and reunite with the people who had become our unlikely family.

When we found them, Favian was pale and haggard, holding himself carefully straight. Frella gasped at the sight of us and ran forward into Senovo's arms. He crouched to meet her and swept her up against his shoulder.

"They brought Papa back, but he's only bones now!" she nearly wailed, as if bewildered by the terrible unfairness of it all.

Senovo hefted her up with him as he stood. Andoc immediately came over to wrap an arm around both of them and kiss the top of her head. "I'm so sorry for you, sweetheart," he said. "But now, Senovo can help your Papa's spirit say goodbye to you and Favian, and all his friends, so he can go up to join the gods."

"I hate the gods!" Frella declared. "I just want Papa back!"

For the first time, I saw Frella without the haze of my own troubled past obscuring her, twisting her form into something threatening and unsettling. Without conscious thought, I walked forward and placed a hand on her head, stroking her honey-colored hair out of her face.

"Sometimes I hate the gods, too," I told her. "I think everyone does, at one time or another. All you can do is cling to the people you still have around you, and try to remember that even when the gods' will seems cruel, they always have a reason for what they do."

My eyes slid to Senovo's face almost against my own volition, and the ache in my chest sharpened. To distract myself, I turned to Favian. He was still hanging back, maintaining his tenuous hold on dispassion as he watched Senovo and Andoc comforting his sister. I gave Frella's hair a final stroke and moved to stand next to him.

"How are you doing?" I asked.

He shrugged one shoulder, a gesture he had picked up from Senovo. "You were there when I had the dream," he said. "I already knew this was going to happen."

"Yes," I replied, "but that doesn't really answer my question."

Favian took a deep breath. "I think it would have been harder if the others had been able to bring Father's body home right away. In some ways, I've already grieved him. It's almost a relief now, because we'll have closure and know that he's with the gods. It's difficult for Frella, though."

"She's still got you," I told him.

He nodded, and looked up at me shrewdly. "Senovo's leaving us, isn't he." It wasn't even a question.

I wanted to weep. To rage. To curse the unfairness of it as Frella had cursed the gods moments before. But I couldn't.

"Yes," I said. "He'll come back, though. Even if he couldn't do it for Andoc and me, he doesn't have it in him to leave you and Frella behind, or your brothers in the temple. We are his family now."

Even as I said the words, the truth of them took hold somewhere deep inside me, and sent out weak tendrils of hope.

"Yes," Favian agreed, and the tender shoots unfurled a little more. "You're right."

He reached out and drew me into a hug. We were both shaking.

⚜

The ceremony was starkly beautiful. A late season snow shower sent a flurry of puffy white flakes dancing around the village green in the torchlight. Senovo stood tall and serene, wrapped in a new aura of power and tranquility as he eulogized the life that was finally returning to the gods that evening.

We did that for him, I thought with no small amount of wonder, as the High Priest's kohl-lined eyes traveled over the villagers, turned out in cloaks and furs against the late winter cold snap.

Normally, several acolytes would have lit the funeral pyre from all sides at once. Tonight, though, Favian stepped forward with a single torch, Frella held securely against his hip. He was pale but composed as he stepped around the pile of wood, lighting it at intervals until flames licked around the small shroud covering bare, chewed bones. Frella wept quietly, staring with wide-eyed fascination into the firelight.

Afterward, Senovo called Eiridan and Feldes forward.

"Last spring," he began, "a terrible tragedy befell Draebard. In addition to all of the other suffering and loss of life, the temple denizens were massacred and the High Priest was gravely wounded. Thanks to our friends in Meren, who were willing to look past the enmity between our peoples and envision a better future, today the temple is strong and whole once more.

"Novice Feldes and Novice Eiridan agreed to leave the village they called home. They came to Draebard and aided in the village's recovery under the most difficult of conditions. Tonight, I elevate them both to the position of full priest, that they may more easily assume joint control of the temple over the coming weeks."

There was a murmur of disquiet as the crowd digested Senovo's statement. He let it subside, and continued. "Feldes. Eiridan. Kneel before the gods, and the people of Draebard." The two lowered themselves to the ground, now dusted white with new snow. "You knelt as novices, but you rise as joint heads of the temple of Draebard in my absence. Please accept my deepest gratitude for all you've done. Not only for the village, but for me personally. The gods blessed Draebard richly on the day you both arrived."

The two priests rose — Feldes, somewhat awkwardly given his expansive girth. Senovo kissed each of them on the cheek, and turned to the crowd.

"As you may have guessed," he said, his clear, beautiful voice ringing around the open space, "I will be leaving — this very night, in fact — in hopes of utilizing my own gift from the gods to further the defense of Eburos against those who would see us dead or enslaved. Though I was not born here, know that I consider myself lucky indeed to be counted among the tribe of the Draebardi. You accepted an angry young shape-shifter into your midst without question or judgment, and I love you for it with my whole heart."

"No!" Frella shouted, and my eyes flew to where she was pummeling her small fists against Favian, fighting free from his hold and running to Senovo. "No! Don't leave! *You can't!*"

The air around me was suddenly too thick to breathe and I choked on it, until Andoc put his arm around me and pulled me against his side. Heedless of the huge crowd surrounding us, I began to cry quietly, unable to hold the tears at bay.

Senovo couched down and allowed Frella to fling her arms around his neck, clinging for all she was worth. "I must, Frella, I'm sorry. Dry your tears, now. It will be no different than the previous times I have traveled with Andoc and Carivel. The others will care for you until I return."

Frella pulled back until she could see his face. "You'll come back? You promise? You won't let the gods call you away like Papa?"

Senovo framed Frella's face in his hands to kiss her forehead, and my heart shattered. "I vow to you, Frella, before the gods and the people of Draebard. I will always return to my family, no matter what."

Favian came up to ease Frella away, so Senovo could stand. When he did, the boy stepped forward into his arms. Soon they were surrounded by Reston, Crenelo, and the other acolytes, hugging Senovo and extracting further promises that he would come back. When they finally retreated, Andoc led me forward to the space in front of the burning pyre. As we got closer, I could see that Senovo's eyes were as wet as my own.

Andoc raised a callused hand to Senovo's face in full view of the crowd, which had devolved into excited conversation after the unexpected announcement. "Come, old friend. I will not have us say our goodbyes in the middle of the green, in front of a funeral fire."

Senovo nodded and ducked his head as the reality of our parting finally overcame his composure. We let Andoc lead us to his hut, where it was quiet and we were unlikely to be disturbed. The instant the door was closed, I turned and half-fell into Senovo's arms.

"Did you mean it?" I asked. "What you told Frella—were you telling the truth?"

"Unless death prevents it, I vow that I will return to you both," he said into my hair. "Only I cannot promise that I won't be changed. That I will still be the same person I am now."

Relief flooded me, though it did nothing to ease the heartbreak. "Of course you will," I said. "I've told you before. You and the wolf are the same. It's a part of you."

Senovo's huff of breath was half laugh, half tears. "So you have, beloved." He rested our foreheads together for a moment before pulling back. "Andoc?"

Andoc was there in an instant. "Yes, *amadi*," he said, though his voice was suspiciously hoarse.

"You must promise me that you will both look after each other. If I were to return only to find that something had happened to either of you, I—" His voice broke. "I couldn't bear it."

Andoc pulled him into a penetrating kiss. Senovo made a small, broken noise against his lips. His eyes slipped closed, a tear sliding down his cheek. When they parted, Andoc pulled him into a tight embrace. "I promise we'll look after each other," he said. "But I can't promise that the worst won't happen anyway."

Senovo nodded against his shoulder. "I should go. While I still have the strength to do so."

"Wait!" I gasped, suddenly terrified that he would change into the wolf on the spot and run off. "Wait, please. I... I have something for you."

Senovo looked at me, pain in his eyes. "Beloved, I can't take anything with me. Not in the form of the wolf."

I took a deep breath, trying to keep my emotions from overwhelming me. "You can take this." I rummaged in the pocket of my breeches and pulled out the necklet I had braided the previous night. Senovo looked surprised, while Andoc craned forward to examine the length of leather.

"You made that?" he asked, fingering the round, braided button that would slip through the loop on the other end to hold it closed.

I nodded. "Using our handfasting thongs, yes. Senovo, will you wear it?"

Senovo ran his fingers along the supple length. The two thongs had been cut from different hides and were different shades of brown. The type of braid I'd used caused the contrasting colors to spiral around each other along the length of the necklet, while the braided button exhibited a regular zigzag pattern around the edge.

"It's beautiful," he whispered. "I would be honored... but what if it's damaged, or lost? The wolf will not understand the value of such a thing."

I covered Senovo's hand with my own. "It's only leather, Senovo. If it's lost, it's lost. It would just make me feel better to know that I'd given it to you, is all. To think that you had something of us with you in the wildlands."

Senovo leaned forward and kissed me, a lingering press of lips. "Then I accept."

Andoc took the necklet from our grasp and stepped behind Senovo, who bared his throat trustingly to his longtime love as he had done so many times before. I pressed my lips together tightly to hold the tears at bay as the band of leather settled around the base of his neck, as if it belonged there. When Andoc closed the fastening and slid Senovo's heavy plait of hair back into place with a final caress, the priest turned and took a step back.

"I love you both," he said, staring at us as if to memorize this moment and hold it against the coming weeks.

"We love you, too," I managed somehow… the gods alone knew how.

"Be safe, *amadi*," Andoc said. "Be strong. Soon all this will be behind us."

Senovo nodded. "Yes," he said, and unfastened his robes. A moment later, the wolf stood before us—a braided necklet nestled into the fur of its ruff and kohl lining its eyes, ending in a striking stylized curl at the corners.

Moving as if he were an old man, Andoc crossed to the front door and opened it. The wolf gave us each a last long look, and disappeared into the darkness.

Andoc held me close as I wept long into the night.

EIGHTEEN

CAIUS OPPITA OF ALYRIOS had always hated boats. Ships, too, like the huge battleship that had brought him and his fellow soldiers from the coastal capital city of Amarius to this godforsaken island. Boats were worse, though—less iron and wood between you and the water.

He could swim, after a fashion—but he harbored no illusions that he would be able to stay afloat in the ocean while wearing full metal battle armor. Mind you, fighting barbarian hordes while wearing a bathing costume would probably be an even worse plan, so he could understand his commander's dilemma, given the situation.

At least the sea was calm today—choppy waters would have made the whole thing completely intolerable. In fact, it was a perfectly pleasant spring morning. The waves lapped gently at the hulls of the landing craft within this protected cove, which lay beyond the beach of whatever barbarian port town they were about to invade. Some of his fellows had even gone so far as to lean over the edge of their sleek rowboats and exclaim over the clear water, with colorful fish and waving fronds of seaweed visible in its depths.

The only time Caius leaned over the edge of a boat was when he needed to puke. Which was, unfortunately, not that unusual an occurrence. Looking down at the water made things worse, in his experience. Much better to keep one's attention on some steady, far-distant point and try to ignore the disconcerting movement caused by the waves as much as humanly possible.

Had he been facing forward, he might have used their island destination as his visual anchor. As it was, he had to snatch glances over his shoulder from time to time to gauge their progress. This particular barbarian town was built on top of low cliffs that overlooked a gently sloping sandy beach. The cliffs in question would have made a pleasantly solid and reliable place to focus his attention as the narrow boat sculled through the gentle waves, if he hadn't been too busy rowing.

At least Caius had a simple job to keep him occupied. He didn't envy the longbowman positioned at the front of the sleek craft; poised and ready to rain death onto any barbarians who might take exception to the Emperor's finest warriors making landfall at their port. As he glanced over his shoulder again and got a better look at the tactical situation, Caius thought that it would actually be quite difficult to make a decent shot all the way up to the top of the cliff. At least, not until they were very close to the shore indeed.

In the end, it hardly mattered. Everyone knew that the northern Eburosi barbarians were barely even proper humans. They would have no way of knowing that an attack was coming. The cluster of buildings at the top of the cliff might appear to be a decent-sized village, but a few score of painted savages wielding clubs and soft bronze swords would never be able to stop the combined might of more than five thousand trained and armored Alyrion soldiers.

Once they made landfall, Caius and his fellows would fight their way up the wide stone steps carved into the cliff face. They would sack the town before the villagers had time to do more than curse their fate and beg mercy from their ancient pagan gods.

Caius glanced around, taking comfort in the imposing armada of streamlined landing craft arrayed around him. His boat was roughly in the middle of the group, though there were perhaps a few more ranks in front of him than behind him. It was an impressive sight to see the entire cove filled with identical landing vessels, each one manned by oarsmen and archers with their steel armor glinting in the sun.

Yes, this would be a good battle. At least, he assumed it would be. As a freshly commissioned eighteen-year-old soldier with no fighting experience, Caius had merely been told to row the damned boat and kill as many barbarians as he could skewer on the end of his sword once they reached the beach.

As tactics went, it sounded straightforward enough.

According to the more experienced soldiers, once they'd completed the initial assault, they'd have a nice beachhead from which to organize the incursion into the rest of this cursed and backward island. While there probably wouldn't be much in the way of spoils from this particular village, the interior was practically bursting with mines, according to the gossip among the troops. Silver, gems... maybe even gold. There would be wealth aplenty for the Emperor's faithful soldiers—as much as they could carry.

Another look over his shoulder proved that the leading boats were getting close to shore. Landfall couldn't come soon enough, as far as Caius was concerned—it would be a huge relief to be back on solid ground for the first time in almost three days.

"Oi!" called one of the other longbowmen from a nearby boat. "What's that?"

Caius turned at the noise, fighting a wave of vertigo as the boat swayed beneath the force of the other oarsmen doing the same thing. He followed the man's pointing finger back to the top of the cliff. They were close enough now for him to make out movement around several narrow wooden structures arrayed there.

Those were definitely people moving around. It looked like they wouldn't be landing completely unopposed after all. But that was all right. Any defenders would be overwhelmed by sheer force of Alyrion numbers, and Caius was positioned far enough back that he wasn't worried about becoming an early casualty. The foremost boats would be close enough to fire arrows within moments, and the rout would begin.

Several of the wooden structures moved unexpectedly—long arms springing up and flopping down again. Caius squinted against the bright morning sunlight, trying to row and watch what was happening at the same time. Were those trebuchets? *Seriously*? Did the barbarians think they could stop five hundred boats and thousands of men by throwing a few rocks at them?

More figures appeared at the edge of the cliff. Caius could make out tiny points of light, like distant sparks. The figures leaned back in unison, and even at this distance, he recognized the stance of archers drawing their bows. Flaming arrows shot through the air, arcing toward the first rank of boats.

What were they trying to accomplish? Even with the pitch painted over the wooden craft to keep them watertight, a flaming arrow would only cause a nasty burn to a single soldier, at best, before someone stamped it out or grabbed it and threw it overboard. Perhaps the display was meant to frighten them, but the Empire's trained soldiers had far more discipline than that.

A moment later, a handful of the leading boats burst into flames.

"What the fuck?" cried one of the men in a boat off to Caius' left.

Oarsmen in several nearby craft craned around to look, disrupting their rhythm of rowing. The boats nearby slewed, only to be quickly corrected as the coxswains' voices cracked out like whips, calling the rowers back to order. Caius whipped his head around and applied himself to his oars, but the back of his neck prickled.

What had he just seen?

"It's happening again!" called a longbowman in another boat.

This time, Caius could make out an audible *whoosh*, along with the screams of the soldiers caught in the swelling flames as several more boats caught fire.

"*Forward!*" roared the nearest field marshal, the cry taken up by the other commanders. "*Forward! Push through! Take the beach!*"

Cold sweat popped out on Caius' brow, but he and his fellow oarsmen redoubled their efforts. The sleek boats surged forward, passing the burning remains of other landing craft as they sank into the sea. His breathing grew uneven as he took in the horribly burned forms of soldiers going down with the wreckage.

The surviving boats at the front of the attack force would be landing by now—running aground on the sandy beach, with soldiers spilling out into the knee-deep water and charging toward the carved path to the top of the cliff. Longbowmen would be setting up on the beach, returning fire at the enemy archers above them. Whatever strange weapon the barbarians were using, it wouldn't be enough.

The coxswain in the back of Caius' boat gasped. "By the One God! There's hundreds of the bastards up there on the cliffs! What the *hell*? This was supposed to be a surprise attack!"

Caius chanced another look, taking advantage of the man's distraction. Wild figures with painted faces and leather armor swarmed around the first Alyrions to reach the top of the cliff, cutting them down even as some of their own fell in return.

The boat Caius was in was getting close to shore now. Movement caught his eye and he jerked around just as something small and round flashed by, hitting one of the oarsmen in the boat on his immediate right. Whatever the thing was, it burst on impact and sent a cloud of light powder flying around the boat. The unlucky oarsman coughed and waved a hand, trying to clear it.

At nearly the same instant, an identical missile glanced against Caius' arm, nearly spilling him out of the boat as he flinched and jerked away from the impact in surprise. The object flopped into the foot well next to his left boot. When his heart stopped pounding quite so hard, he stretched down and picked it up, steadying the oar one-handed.

It was a pouch made of the same sort of fragile, loose woven cloth that his mother used to hang cheese curds while the whey drained out. The thing was tied closed at the top with a bit of twine. He bounced it in his hand, judging the weight. It was heavy at the bottom, as though it had rocks in it. This pouch hadn't burst open on impact, but when he shook it, a bit of the same fine, grayish-brown powder that had coated the boat beside him filtered out.

"*Row*, damn you!" called the coxswain.

Caught out, Caius tossed the cloth bag overboard and grabbed his oar two-handed, putting his back into it.

Several men cried out a warning. A new round of flaming arrows rained down, and this time Caius' boat was within range. A few arm-lengths away, one of the fiery missiles fell on the powder-coated boat next to him. Caius flinched and ducked as its stern burst into an orange fireball, enveloping the unlucky coxswain and two of the oarsmen. Several others jumped overboard to escape the flames as Caius' boat swept onward. He watched in horror as the men disappeared into the unnaturally clear water, pulled into the depths by the weight of their metal armor.

Heart pounding, Caius turned back to gauge the state of the battle on the beach. His boat had almost reached the shore now. After a final few oar strokes, the keel scraped against the sand of the beach. They'd landed.

"Out! Out!" The coxswain rose, unsheathing his sword and using it to point at the beach and the cliffs beyond. "Join the battle!"

Arrows rained down from above, even as the Alyrion archers set up on the beach, ready to return the favor. Caius stowed his oar and drew steel, his hands shaking as men around him fell, pierced by lucky shots that missed their armor and hit flesh.

He pressed onward with his fellow soldiers, looking up at the source of the attack from the cliff top. This close, he could make out individual figures arrayed there. A loud whistle drew his attention to a slender boy sitting astride a short black and white pinto horse. The boy was gesturing behind himself, as though beckoning others forward. A muscular man with swirls of ochre paste on his face, mounted on a tall chestnut, also appeared to be directing other fighters into position. Both of them held short recurve bows.

A longbowman standing next to Caius drew a steel-tipped arrow from his quiver and nocked it, aiming for the barbarians' leaders. Caius held his breath, knowing such a shot would be difficult from this angle. But if he succeeded...

The man drew back, tension coiling through his shoulders. His entire focus was on the barbarian with the painted face, even as the Eburosi leader aimed his own bow and arrow.

Caius blinked as realization struck him. *The horse wasn't wearing a bridle.* The longbowmen's shot missed, clattering harmlessly off the rocks at the edge of the cliff. The barbarian's shot flew true, and Caius flinched away as the arrow pierced the longbowman through the neck. The man fell to the sand, choking on blood.

"*Forward!*" someone shouted, and Caius stumbled after the other soldiers heading for the narrow path up the cliffs.

His eyes darted back to the boy on the black and white horse. That animal wasn't wearing a bridle either. Two dozen more horses carrying archers cantered up and slid to a neat stop at the edge of the drop off, arrayed along the cliff top.

None of them were wearing bridles.

A shiver of deep foreboding ran down Caius' spine. Surely, this was the Old Magic. In Alyrios, pagan sorcery was feared, and its practitioners hunted down without mercy. Tales of the wild folk who bent animals' will to their own—making them into evil familiars to aid in their witchcraft—had been a staple of his childhood. They weren't merely made-up stories meant to frighten youngsters into their beds. Caius' own father, a respected guardsman, had been killed by a rogue pagan shapeshifter who could take the form of a stag.

He shook his head violently to clear it. He was a grown man now. A soldier in the Emperor's elite army. The more experienced fighters had regaled him with tales of pagan Eburosi sorcerers who could control the spirits of animals with magic. He'd laughed them off with the rest of the soldiers, pretending with a young man's bravado that they didn't chill him to his marrow... that they didn't fling his mind back to his childhood and a dead stag surrounded by the corpses of fallen guardsmen.

Around him, more soldiers were falling under the hail of arrows, but it was not enough to stop the press of numbers as the steel-armored troops ahead of him gallantly fought their way up the cliff path. Bodies tumbled free from the center of the battle, cartwheeling down the rocky escarpment to land in a broken pile below.

A haunting, unearthly noise rose over the clang of metal, the shout of orders and the screams of wounded and dying men. It wavered in an ululating howl, making all of the hair on the back of Caius' neck stand up.

"What was that?" someone cried. Several of the men around Caius halted, looking around for the source.

The sound rose again. Louder. Closer. More complex. Many voices raised as one. *Hundreds* of voices.

It was the sound of howling wolves. Scores of them, all at once.

Dread, bone-deep and instinctive, slammed into Caius like an arrow through the heart. Every tale he had ever heard of wolves at the door, ready to attack the weak and eat them, was suddenly at the forefront of his mind, impossible to ignore.

Who *were* these people? These *barbarians*? They weren't supposed to know about the attack... but they had. They could set boats on fire with magic powder, and control horses with the power of their minds. And now—

A sea of brown and gray fur and glowing yellow eyes erupted over the edge of the cliff and onto the wide stone stairway. The unnatural creatures slipped around and through the defending barbarian warriors like ghosts, only to tear into the attacking Alyrions, ripping at arms and legs and bellies.

Screams erupted—not only from the injured, but also from terrified oarsmen and soldiers on the beach and in the boats. Another hail of arrows fell from the cliff top, sending more men to the ground, clutching at thin wooden shafts that protruded obscenely from their bodies.

"*Hold. Your. Ground!*" screamed one of the Marshals, trying desperately but ineffectually to stop the foot soldiers who were turning back from the cliff path, fleeing the oncoming army of wolves. He continued to scream orders until three wolves converged on him, dragging him to the ground and ripping his throat out.

Within moments, the Alyrion forces were running for the boats in full retreat. Caius stood frozen for a single instant before he broke and ran with the rest of them. He was certain he could hear panting breaths and paws against sand converging on him from behind. His heavy armor slowed his footsteps until it felt as though he were slogging through treacle.

A coxswain was standing in knee-deep water by one of the landing craft as Caius staggered up to it. "Holy fuck," the man said, his eyes on the carnage behind them. "Holy *fuck*! Get back in the boat!" They both scrambled in, along with several other retreating soldiers. "Push off, you fools! Hurry!"

Caius and the others grabbed oars. They didn't need to be told twice. The boat bottom scraped along the fine sand until they were floating free, while all around them, other crews did the same as the attacking force fled under a new rain of arrows.

The boat slewed around in the shallows, knocking against its neighbors as they all tried to get away at once. Caius was trembling like a leaf in the wind as he dragged his eyes away from the snarling mass of wolves now spreading out over the beach—shaking the limp bodies of downed men like rag dolls—and looked up to the cliff top, seeking the barbarian leader and his bridleless chestnut mount.

The man still sat on his bewitched horse, next to the boy mounted on the short pinto. As he watched, a large wolf padded up to stand between the two of them. The horses didn't so much as toss their heads in alarm at the predator's approach, proving beyond a doubt that powerful magic must be involved.

Far from being alarmed by the wolf's appearance, the two barbarians immediately dismounted and made as if to greet the animal. There was a strange twisting movement that Caius' eyes couldn't quite follow, and suddenly a man crouched where the wolf had been. He straightened with help from the others, his body naked and dirt streaked.

The boy threw himself into the shapeshifter's arms, and the warrior gathered both of them into an embrace, no longer paying the slightest notice to the mass retreat taking place below.

"Holy *God*," Caius whispered. "Great God above. What *is* this place?"

Above him, the three barbarians clung together, becoming smaller and less defined as Caius' boat raced for safety, until they appeared to be a single figure disappearing slowly into the distance.

Epilogue: One Month Later

Favian tossed and turned, his head moving restlessly from side to side as strange images played out behind his eyelids. The blankets twisted around his arms and legs, and he muttered in low tones, distressed.

In his dream, he was lying in the same bed. His mind spun in lazy, drugged circles that were only partially effective as a distraction from the deep ache between his legs where his balls had previously hung. Senovo — *the High Priest*, he chastened himself firmly, only to giggle a moment later as his mind suddenly insisted that the whole thing was terribly funny — had talked Favian into putting off his initiation into the priesthood far longer than most acolytes did. Finally, shortly after his nineteenth birthday, he'd put his foot down and insisted that Senovo would either have to castrate him and make him a novitiate, or throw him out of the temple completely.

Andoc and Carivel had both been present for the confrontation. Andoc had rolled his eyes and said, "It's not as if you haven't tried every trick in the book to talk him out of it already, *amadi*. He wants to be a priest, and he wants to be a eunuch. It's a completely different situation from the one you suffered."

Carivel ran a hand through her close-cropped hair, ruffling it. "There's nothing that says you have to do it personally, is there? The castration, I mean," she asked with a frown.

Indeed, there was not, and it was Healer Sagdea who did the deed in the end, with the assistance of Priest Eiridan, while Favian snored and drooled under the influence of a powerful sleeping draught. Or so Reston and Crenelo had cheerfully informed him afterward, during one of the woozy stretches when he could actually stay awake and aware enough to understand speech.

Gods, his sac *really hurt*. He stared up at the rafters, trying to focus on the way they moved in slow, surreal waves when he was fairly sure they were supposed to stay still and support the thatched roof. Why had he woken up in the first place? Things had been fine when he was asleep. Maybe it was Frella who had disturbed him? But that couldn't be right. Senovo had taken his little sister to stay in his quarters while Favian recovered. So if it hadn't been Frella, then what had awakened him?

Oh, yes.

The girl. That was it. He looked back to the doorway to see if he'd imagined her. Which, apparently, he hadn't. Or at least, if so, he hadn't *stopped* imagining her yet, because she was definitely still there.

He didn't think she was supposed to be in his room, hovering inside the door while he lay naked under the light woven blanket, drugged out of his mind and barely able to string together a coherent sentence.

"Whu—?" he asked, his tongue feeling thick and dry.

He stared at her profile as she peered into the hallway— dark-haired, golden-skinned, fine-boned. Pretty, if one happened to be interested in such things. Which Favian hadn't been, particularly—not even *before* his balls had been cut off. At the sound of his voice, she whirled to look at him, and a tendril of shock wormed its way past the fluffy layer of wool inside his head.

The other half of her face was horribly scarred, the flesh looking nearly melted in places. Her eye on that side was wide open and milky.

"Shh!" she said sharply.

The world went gray at the edges for a moment. When it came back, she was standing next to the bed, and there was a wicked little blade pressed under Favian's chin. He snapped his jaw shut reflexively.

"This is Draebard, yes?" she asked, and Favian would have nodded, only the knife was really jabbing *quite* hard at the flesh of his neck now. She seemed to take his silence for assent, because she said, "Good. Now, priest-boy, unless you want me to open up your guts like a fish, take me to the shape-shifter called Senovo. I have unfinished business with him."

Favian's eyes flew open as he jerked awake from the vision with a gasp.

end of Book 4

RETURN OF THE
WOLF

ONE

The wolf had always loved the rhythmic feeling of paws loping along packed dirt. The steady *thud-thud-thud* of a fast-beating heart. The whisper of air filling lungs, sending strength through rangy muscle and sinew. Now, the tang of the sea teased at his nose from up ahead, twined among the rich, interwoven tapestry of other smells.

Some of those smells were bad. Dangerous. Metal and blood. Vomit and excrement. The smell of fear, the smell of rage. The smell of *human*. Ahead, the humans were killing each other at the edge of the water.

Stupid to run toward danger instead of away. This, from the scarred old alpha wolf running at Senovo's left shoulder. *Stupid strange wolf, not to know that.*

The shiny two-legs are coming to destroy the dens, he reminded his companion. *They will kill the cubs. We must attack first. Stop them. Protect the young.*

The old wolf loped along silently for a moment, digesting this. *Yes. Protect the cubs.*

The pack is strong, Senovo offered, hearing the rustling and panting of hundreds of furry bodies behind them. *We will drive them off.*

The smell of human became stronger as the mass of wolves approached the edge of the settlement. Senovo slowed in response to the nearly palpable aura of discontent and nervousness behind him.

Bad place, the old wolf beside him opined, a low growl rumbling in his throat.

This is our pack-brothers' den, he insisted. *They are defending it.*

Around him, wolves sniffed the air, taking in the scents of frightened females and their offspring huddled inside. Nursing mothers, clutching their mewling two-legged pups, sour with the smell of milk.

Yes, the scarred pack leader agreed, and followed Senovo along the strange-familiar dirt paths between the two-legs' odd dens.

The horde of wolves moved through the town in eerie silence, ignoring frightened eyes peering out through holes in the unnatural wooden den-structures. Ahead lay the sea, and the fighting. The clang of metal and the ear splitting screams of injured and dying warriors once again caused the mass of wolves to pause and mill about, uncertain.

At that precise moment, a tangle of two scents that Senovo knew better than he knew his own tickled at his nostrils, barely discernible beneath the overwhelming stench of humans attacking each other. He hesitated, his attention drawn by the distraction. The abrupt flip-flop that heralded the change in control within his lupine body assaulted him with no warning, like being bowled over and pinned on his back by a pack mate.

Many times he had played these dominance games with the foolish two-leg who shared his dichotomous existence, but now the nervous wolves were balking, already contemplating flight without his steady reassurance and leadership.

This was not the time.

In an instant, the wolf wrested control of his mind back with a warning snarl at the weak and needy part of himself that would place reuniting with his mates ahead of protecting their den.

Enough! Defend the cubs — drive off the intruders! Confident that the other wolves would follow him, Senovo ran forward and darted into the fray without hesitation.

It was a bloodbath.

Most of that blood belonged to the two-legs. The ones with shiny carapaces began to flee in terror within moments of the pack's attack, though all of them that could be caught were chased down ruthlessly on the beach and torn to pieces. Finally, when the last of the survivors had staggered back into the water and climbed into their hollow floating logs to escape, the wolf relaxed his hold on the internal presence battering away at his control.

Seldom before had his foolish human half shown such strength and determination when attempting to take over. It was sheer luck that the distraction caused by the internal struggle hadn't allowed a lucky blow from a weapon to pierce his flesh during the battle, but fortunately his thick pelt and quick reflexes had protected him from all but a few scrapes and bruises.

For the last few seasons, Senovo-the-wolf and Senovo-the-human had reached a sort of peace, after years of bitter struggle. It was only during the previous two moons, though, after Senovo-the-human had taken leave from his mates and subsumed himself completely within the wolf's mind, that the animal had truly been given free rein for the first time. Without the complicated and confusing morass of human emotion, human fears and human expectations, it was easy to return to the wild wolves and live among them.

Wolves were simple. Wolves cared only for the things related to the pack's survival. As long as Senovo presented his ideas in a way that fit within this framework, his fellows were content to follow his bidding. They would interact with him, as well — brushing shoulders, nuzzling at him, lapping at his face. But he was still an outsider. A castrated male with no blood ties and no hope of gaining any mating ties.

He was not truly pack. And it ached.

Now, Senovo-the-human pummeled at the wolf's constraint, even as the familiar tangle of dual scents once again teased his sensitive nose, bringing thoughts of *home, acceptance, belonging.*

Please, begged his human half. *Please! You must let me — we* must *go to them now!*

It would mean a return to the complexities of the human world, the wolf knew. But even the wolf could remember and appreciate the sense of loyalty. Protection. Devotion. With a sharp shake of his furry body, he peeled away from the mob of wolves still snarling and tearing at downed men, trotting back up the stone path to the top of the low cliffs.

Without fuss, the wolf padded up between two humans mounted on familiar friend-horses. *Not-prey,* the wolf remembered, and kept his body language calm and unthreatening despite the blood still dripping from his muzzle. As soon as he approached, the beloved human scents spiked with excitement and desperate hope. Both of them were sliding off the not-prey horses and hurrying toward him before he'd even come to a stop by the cliff edge.

"Oh, gods," choked Carivel, and that was too much for Senovo-the-human.

Before the wolf could even react, the jolting, wrenching change was upon him. His two-legged body sank to one knee, disoriented after so many weeks of being in animal form.

Senovo reeled and braced himself on his hands, overwhelmed by the taste of Alyrion blood coating his tongue... the stiff sea breeze against his suddenly naked flesh... the sharp sting of gravel against his palms and knee where he crouched on the ground, shivering. A familiar sense of horror at the violence he had just wrought assailed him, and his stomach heaved.

"Amadi!"

The beloved voice that Senovo had feared he would never hear again was hoarse; scraped raw. Then Andoc was kneeling at his right side, heedless of his bad leg, and Carivel was at his left. Strong hands closed around his upper arms and hauled him upright, steadying him as he wavered.

A choked noise broke free from Senovo's throat, and suddenly Carivel was in his arms, clinging to him with fingers made almost claw-like in her desperation to pull him close. She was weeping, hot tears mixing with the blood on his cheek and jaw as she pressed the side of her face against his. An instant later, Andoc's hard-muscled arms closed around both of them, crushing them to his chest.

"Thank the gods. Thank the gods," he breathed, over and over like a prayer.

Senovo shivered and gasped between them, unable to form words. Feeling simultaneously out of place within his own skin, and like a man coming home after years of absence.

"You did it, Senovo," Carivel said between sobs. "We did it. They're leaving. They're running away!"

Andoc held them even tighter. "It's finally over, *amadi*. We won. You can let go now."

As if all that had been required was permission from that familiar, much-loved voice, the tension flowed out of Senovo's aching muscles like the tide retreating in the harbor below. He sagged, kept upright by his bondmates' strength alone. Gray and red mist swirled behind his tightly closed eyes as he tried to take in both the words and the press of bodies against his. As he tried to make it all *real*.

"Please," he whispered. "I'm so tired…"

Andoc pressed a kiss to his disheveled tangle of dirty hair. "I know. It's all right. We can finally rest now, my heart."

Senovo nodded, relief crashing over him even as awareness fled and darkness overtook him.

When he awoke later, he was in a large tent, and Carivel was holding his hand. A smear of dried blood still marred her cheek from where she had pressed her face against his. The patter of light spring rain against the stretched hide of the shelter above them was a soothing rhythm.

It was a bit of a shock to find that he had not reverted to animal form as he slept, but the wolf was unexpectedly quiet and meek in the background. Perhaps it, too, needed a break from the constant demands of leadership and responsibility. He swallowed, feeling the braided leather necklet that had nestled—largely unnoticed—in the fur of his ruff these past weeks brushing now against the bare, sensitive skin of his throat.

"The other wolves?" he asked, his voice a rough croak.

Carivel helped him sit up and drink from a clay cup before she answered. The tang of wine was surprising after weeks of lapping up water from streams and puddles. He coughed as it burned its way down his throat.

"Gone, as far as we can tell," she said. "After you changed, they just sort of disappeared."

Senovo nodded and cleared his throat, setting the cup aside. Lifting fingertips to the side of his jaw, he encountered only clean skin. Someone had washed the blood from his face while he was insensible, though bits of gristle still stuck between his teeth.

"Andoc?" he asked, sounding slightly more like himself.

"He wanted to stay, but he had to make an appearance in the village and check on the wounded. How are you feeling now?"

After a moment's thought, he said, "Strange." He looked down, somewhat startled to find that he was still naked. He hadn't noticed.

Carivel followed his gaze. "Do you want some clothing? We thought it might bother you at first, after wearing nothing but fur for so long."

He nodded slowly. "In a moment, perhaps." In fact, he was still feeling quite awkward in his own skin. Overwhelmed, as the world of human rules and human expectations settled around him like a heavy cloak. He frowned. "I should… go and speak to the people as well. Should I not?"

"There's no hurry," said Carivel. "High Priest Thadrik and the other Llanmeeri priests have matters in hand, I'm sure."

He almost missed the slight quaver in his bondmate's voice, with all the other thoughts and feelings swirling around him.

Almost.

"Beloved," he said, and held out his arms. Everything fell away as the realization that they had survived—that they were *together*—truly penetrated for the first time.

Carivel dove into his embrace with the same air of desperation that she had displayed earlier on the cliff top. She was shaking. "I still can't believe it. I can't believe we made it. We're alive." Her chest hitched a few times. "*You came back.*"

The past and the present were gradually knitting themselves back into something resembling a coherent whole within his mind. "I did promise you, didn't I?" he said.

She nodded against his neck, her short-cropped hair tickling his ear. A moment later, she was straddling his lap, his face cradled between her hands as she kissed him. He braced himself with one hand against the bedroll and steadied her with the other cupping the nape of her neck, aching a bit at the knowledge his absence was responsible for her distress.

Andoc found them still pressed together a few moments later, when he ducked under the open tent flap, smelling of sweat and warm rain. "Well," he said, stopping just inside to watch. "Isn't that a sight for sore eyes?"

Carivel made a noise against Senovo's lips that was somewhere between a laugh and a sob, before pulling away a fraction.

"I do hope you've left some for me, *caradi*," Andoc continued, his voice hopelessly fond as he came further inside and dropped into a clumsy sprawl beside them, hitching his twisted right leg out of the way.

In response, Carivel directed Senovo toward him with a touch on the cheek. Senovo sank into Andoc's commanding kiss, feeling something that had been off kilter inside him slowly begin to settle. Andoc pulled away, only to press his lips to Carivel's as well. "Oh, that's better," he said afterward, sounding unaccountably relieved.

"I regret that I hurt you both with my absence," Senovo said softly.

"Don't," Andoc replied. "Because you also saved us with your absence. We've had lookouts posted since the end of the battle, but the Alyrions show no inclination to return for a rematch. The port master sent out a fast boat to make sure that they've truly gone for good, but I'll wager they have."

"Just so they haven't gone to see if the other port towns would make easier pickings," Carivel said, having more or less regained her composure.

"If they go north to Dellwyn, they'll find an army of bears waiting, and if they go south to Erylaan, they'll find an army of lions... assuming their boats survive the spring riptides." Andoc's voice was grim, but with an undertone of satisfaction. "The Empire fears and hates magic. I think we saw today just how deep that fear runs."

Senovo steeled himself. "The battle. How many dead? How many wounded?"

"Dozens," Andoc replied. "And perhaps one hundred and fifty dead on their side, many of them drowned. Remind me to thank the Mereni weapon maker who came up with the idea of lobbing fire-starting powder at their boats and igniting it with flaming arrows. It might not have been enough by itself, but it ensured they were already good and spooked by the time you arrived with our four-legged allies, Senovo."

"The warriors from Llanmeer insisted on leading the defense at the cliff path," Carivel said. "Most of the casualties were theirs, not Draebard's."

"The Llanmeeri fought bravely, and well," said Andoc. "Once we're absolutely certain that the Emperor's forces won't return, we'll withdraw back to Draebard. I've sent riders to find out what—if anything—happened at Dellwyn and Erylaan. We need to decamp soon—having an army this size concentrated in one place for any real length of time would be too hard for Llanmeer to support, even with the supplies coming in from other small villages in the area."

"It will be good to go home," Carivel said.

Honestly, the thought of returning to the intricate day-to-day management of the temple and the responsibilities of his position as High Priest in Draebard sounded utterly overwhelming to Senovo at that moment, but he merely nodded, unwilling to make an issue of it.

"How are you, Senovo?" Andoc asked. "Truly?"

Senovo hesitated, before answering honestly. "Still not quite myself, I fear. At least, not quite my *human* self."

Andoc nodded. "We all saw how Ithric was in the weeks after we first found him. Lorish, too, before she ran off again to rejoin the foxes."

At this, Carivel's arms tightened, as if in reflexive worry that Senovo would change and sneak back to the wilderness the moment she let him out of her sight. Given his behavior over the past several months, he supposed he couldn't really blame her.

"I don't think anyone expects you to be unaffected by your experience, *amadi*. That said, if you're well enough, I suspect it would be good for morale if you could make at least a short public appearance," Andoc continued.

Senovo tried to think through the steps that would be required for even a brief return to the wider human world. It was harder than it should have been. Clothes. Footwear. He lifted a hand to his head, feeling the nest of tangles and the two-month growth of tousled hair at the front, where it would normally be close-shaved. Andoc and Carivel had affectionately accused him of being vain on several occasions, and, in their defense, the small thread of mortification at the thought of what he must look like right now did nothing to counter their claims.

Carivel's lips quirked, though she tried to hide it. "Yes, you do, in fact, look like you've been pulled through a hedge backward—just in case you're wondering." She reached out and tugged something free from his hair. It was a bramble. "I pulled a few of these out while you were sleeping, but as you know, I've no real patience for long hair."

"We could just take a knife to it," Andoc suggested. "Cut it all off and be done."

Senovo's horror must have showed in his expression, because Andoc's hold on a straight face faltered, and Carivel dissolved into laughter.

"Your face," she said, struggling to regain control of her mirth.

"I'm joking, *amadi*," Andoc assured. "Mostly."

Carivel waved him off. "Don't worry. I have a better idea, assuming Andoc doesn't mind taking advantage of his status as a newly fledged war hero."

Now it was Andoc's turn to look appalled. "I'm not a *war hero*, Carivel!"

She just shook her head, catching Senovo's gaze long enough to roll her eyes at him. "Fine, then. Your status as a *visiting Chieftain*, in that case."

"… I suppose I can manage that," Andoc said after a slight hesitation, though he still looked taken aback.

Carivel nodded. "In that case, stay here for a few minutes, both of you. I'll be back in a bit."

⊱ ⚜ ⊰

Before the late afternoon gave way fully to evening, Senovo found himself being wrapped in a simple robe and quietly chivvied to the bath house behind Llanmeer's inn. The aftermath of battle had made it a sought-after destination for filthy, exhausted warriors, but Carivel had somehow bribed or threatened her way into procuring a private alcove in the back for them, with a tub full of hot water.

"You two and your baths," Andoc groused fondly.

Carivel only raised an eyebrow. "Have you looked at yourself? Don't think you're getting out of here without a scrub. Not if you plan on sharing a bed with us."

Having been painfully aware of the state of his own cleanliness ever since Carivel had brought it to his attention in the tent, Senovo had eyes only for the copper bath and the tantalizing wisps of steam rising from it.

"Fine. Go on, then," Andoc said, a smile tugging at the edge of his lips.

Carivel moved to stand in front of Senovo, so she could untie the fastenings of his simple clothing and remove the necklet she had braided using their handfasting thongs from around his throat. She set it aside carefully.

As Senovo dropped his robe, stepped into the bath, and sank into the warm depths with a moan of pleasure, humanity suddenly didn't seem quite such a daunting prospect. With a single soft inhalation, he slipped under the surface and curled up to rest on the bottom, blinking his eyes open against the sting of water to stare up at the reflection of torchlight dancing across the ripples above him. The rush of blood and his own heartbeat filled his ears, drowning out everything else as his muscles began to unknot and his pulse slowed.

A moment later, a strong, callused hand followed him down. Andoc cupped his cheek—sliding down until his fingertips could brush over the seam of Senovo's lips, lighting every nerve. Senovo closed his eyes as a second, smaller hand brushed across his chest to rest over his heart, soaking in the sensation of skin against skin. His air trickled away in a lazy stream of bubbles until his lungs were empty, and he pressed a final kiss to Andoc's fingertips before surfacing reluctantly.

Carivel was already shaking water from her wet hand and pulling off clothing by the time he blinked the water from his eyes. "Budge up. Don't think I'm bathing in your dirty scum—we'll leave that privilege for Andoc."

"As long as that gives it time to cool off first," Andoc said with good humor.

"Of course it will," Carivel replied. "You see? I'm just looking out for your interests. Soap!"

Andoc handed her the soap—a soft concoction mixed with fragrant herbs—before reaching for a jar of hair oil and tipping the contents over Senovo's scalp. Carivel lowered herself into the water to straddle his lap, and Senovo let himself drift, allowing the two of them to manipulate him as they wished, scrubbing and picking out tangles.

After he had returned the favor by running a rag over Carivel's body and face, carefully erasing the smear of rusty blood from her cheek, they rinsed each other off. Andoc guided

Senovo to lean back against the edge of the metal tub, his hair hanging in a loose, dripping mass over the edge.

He smoothed the ragged growth of hair back from Senovo's forehead. "It's been a while, but I'm pretty sure I remember this part," he said, a smile audible in his voice.

Senovo relaxed back as a sharp blade scraped along his scalp, shaving the hair from the front half of his head as required for a proper priest's queue. Each careful pass raised gooseflesh across his arms and chest despite the warm water. His soft prick twitched faintly against Carivel's sex where she still straddled him, watching the ritual in apparent fascination.

When Andoc was done, she stretched forward to claim another kiss from Senovo, who smiled a bit against her lips.

"It looks right to me," she said upon pulling back.

"Well *of course* it looks right," Andoc said in mock offense, and Senovo's smile grew a fraction wider. "It's not as though I've never done this before, you know."

He drew up a pitcher of water and poured it over the newly shaved expanse, washing away stray hairs. Senovo was completely unsurprised to find that there was not a single blade-nick marring his skin. After a final application of scented oil, Andoc twisted the long hair that remained between his hands to wring out the excess water. The pull on his scalp sent another flush of blood rising up Senovo's chest—sense memory recalling to mind other occasions when Andoc had controlled him with a commanding hand wrapped in his hair.

It would have been all too easy to tumble straight down to a place where he did not have to think, or worry, or do anything at all except let himself be used and pleasured by his mates, but Andoc was already drying his hair with one of the rough towels hanging from pegs along the wall. A few moments later, surprisingly deft fingers were plaiting the thick strands into a solid braid with only an occasional hesitation here or there when a hank failed to cooperate.

"Back to normal," Carivel observed, though her voice still contained a hint of uncertainty.

"Not *quite* that simple a process, I fear," said Senovo.

"But a step in the right direction, nonetheless," Andoc said firmly. "Come on—up, both of you. Let me get this over with, and we'll be off."

Once they had vacated the washtub, he stripped and scrubbed himself with a soldier's efficiency. A few minutes later, the three of them dressed. Andoc fastened the braided leather cord safely back around Senovo's neck, and they left the bathhouse behind, the water in the tub now a cloudy, unappealing gray.

"The worst of the wounded were taken to the temple," Andoc said. "The others are being cared for by locals in the village. We lost four men from Draebard—Juri, Roban, Beliac, and Ghel. We'll take the bodies home with us so their loved ones can attend the funeral. I believe High Priest Thadrik intends to perform a ceremony for the dead from Llanmeer tomorrow evening."

What does it matter, though? Senovo almost asked. *They're dead.* He caught himself just in time and blinked, human ideas and wolf ideas fighting for precedence in a confusing swirl within his mind.

His hesitation must have been obvious, because Andoc looked at him for a moment and said, "We can talk about that later, *amadi*. Right now, it would just be good if the people in our camp could see that you're back safe."

"Of course," he replied, still adrift.

Carivel linked an arm through his. "I'll stay right here next to you. It will be fine, and then we'll go hole up in a tent for the night. No more demands, just three pack mates curled up together in a den. All right?"

Senovo nodded, wanting that very badly.

"Something to look forward to," Andoc agreed.

TWO

The Draebardi camp along the cliff tops south of Llanmeer was lit with bonfires and torches. Warriors celebrated the victory with wine and ale despite their exhaustion. A fat pig turned slowly on a spit in the central meeting area, splatters of grease flaring as they dripped into the fire.

A ragged cheer rose as they were recognized, the sound moving across the length of the camp in an uneven wave. Andoc raised one hand with a smile.

"Our wandering wolf has returned to us, my friends!" he called, and Senovo flushed as the cheer rose in volume, becoming a roar.

It was perhaps a fortunate thing that, due to both the dignity of his position as High Priest and his own reputation for natural reserve, a mere dip of the head in a shallow bow was enough to placate the crowd, who raised flagons and goblets in salute. Even so, to call it an uncomfortable experience was putting things mildly.

Senovo had long desired to remain in the shadows, unremarked. When that had become impossible after the Alyrion attack on Draebard and the death of the previous High Priest, he had stepped into the role of public figure reluctantly, but effectively. Though he was often, by necessity, the center of attention during religious ceremonies, that attention had largely been on his position as High Priest rather than on *him* as an individual.

Now, though, the attention was very much on Senovo the shape-shifting eunuch from Rhyth, who had entered into a controversial three-way handfasting and then gone on to rally an army of wolves to defeat the invasion of an Empire. Just thinking about it made him feel somewhat faint, and he was pathetically grateful both for Carivel's arm in his, and the hand that Andoc rested on the small of his back to guide him through the various knots of celebrating warriors.

Much of the interaction that followed slid across Senovo's awareness without sticking. He was attuned enough to his bondmates, however, to realize that Carivel was only slightly less ill-at-ease than he was, and that Andoc was employing his natural charm and charisma to deflect as much of the attention as possible onto himself.

It took far, far longer than it should have for the words of a simple blessing to spring to Senovo's mind, so that he would have something to say when someone addressed him directly.

The gods' blessings be upon you might not have been the most inspiring response one could receive from a priest on the eve after battle, but it was something, at least. Something *human*.

As the humid spring evening marched toward night, Senovo gradually became aware of the broader goings-on around them. Little knots of giggling Llanmeeri maids were making the rounds of the camp, as were a few sloe-eyed young acolytes and novices from the local temple. The crowd was thinning somewhat as people began to disappear into tents in twos and, occasionally, threes or fours.

As soon as Andoc felt that it would not cause too much comment, he led Senovo and Carivel to the tent where Senovo had awoken earlier. The tent flap faced a large bonfire in the center of an open area, where a handful of people still sat, passing around a wineskin. It was a considerably roomier structure than the simple traveling tent they'd shared on their journey that winter. Light from the fire illuminated the interior in flickering stripes through the gaps around the hanging flap, but it still felt far more safe and protected than the camp beyond, or even the private alcove in the bathhouse.

Den, the wolf proclaimed quietly from the background, and settled. Senovo couldn't help his audible breath of relief.

"Get comfortable," Andoc said. "I'll bring food."

Carivel let out a contented sigh of her own and flopped down on the generous bedroll, more or less dragging Senovo down with her. He came willingly. "Get these off," she said, tugging at the plain set of robes he was wearing. "I can see they're bothering you."

Just about *everything* had been bothering him since he awoke, but he shrugged out of the itchy clothing without comment. She tossed it aside carelessly. "That's better," she said, before shedding her own jerkin and breeches. "And that's better still."

Andoc's hum of approval when he returned a few minutes later indicated his agreement with the sentiment. "Eat," he said, and pushed skewers of meat into their hands.

Senovo's stomach rumbled at the smell of pork. Though he had seen a few larger kills taken down by the packs he'd been staying with, his own diet had tended much more toward mice, frogs, grasshoppers, and the occasional cluster of low-hanging berries. His mind drifted unbidden to the last flesh that had passed the wolf's lips, and he shut down that trail of thought abruptly.

They ate in silence, though Senovo could feel the growing tension as Carivel tried to decide whether or not to speak about something that was obviously bothering her. Andoc passed him a wineskin, and the rich liquid went down easier this time than it had earlier in the afternoon.

"... what was it like?" Carivel asked eventually, hesitation clear in her tone.

Senovo set aside the wine and tried to frame an answer.

"It was... both incredibly simple, and the most difficult thing I have ever done," he said. "Wolves will follow a shape-shifter as long as the task makes sense to them. But leading wolves requires one to project an air of leadership *constantly*. At the first hint of distraction or uncertainty, I would immediately begin to lose them."

"It sounds exhausting," she said. "Not to mention terrifying, given what was at stake. How did you even sleep?"

"Infrequently, and with one eye open," Senovo said, a hint of wryness creeping into his tone.

"It's as well that you're one of the most effective natural leaders I know, in that case," said Andoc.

Though it did not seem to be meant as a joke, Senovo couldn't help his self-deprecating snort. "My friend, you have actually *met* me, yes?"

Andoc reached forward and took the empty skewer from his hand, setting it safely out of the way.

"Met the man who stared down Chief Volya and sent him creeping away with his tail between his legs, all without even raising his voice, you mean? As it happens, I've had the pleasure, yes." Andoc leaned into Senovo's space, and the wolf whimpered in the background, baring its neck and belly. Once again, Senovo found himself hanging by a thread, longing to sink down under the weight of the others' care and go away for a while.

"We both have, actually." Carivel sounded faintly breathless.

Senovo's throat was dry despite the wine he'd just drunk. "In my experience, *natural leaders* do not long to surrender themselves… to be used and taken until no thoughts remain in their heads beyond blissful submission to the will of another." He paused, drawing in a breath as his eyes slipped closed. "As I long to surrender myself to both of you now."

Andoc's hand came up to cup his cheek, and Senovo pressed into it, a desperate neediness overtaking him.

Carivel immediately pressed herself along his back, and he could feel the vibrations against his bare skin as she spoke. "I don't see that the two things have much to do with each other, honestly. I lead people as well—I'm the Horse Mistress, after all—and yet, I, too, understand the appeal of setting everything aside for a bit."

"Just so," Andoc agreed. "After weeks of having to be almost constantly vigilant, I'd think anyone would be ready for a break."

Andoc's hand trailed down until he could hook a finger under Senovo's leather necklet and use it to draw him forward, into a kiss. Just like that, Senovo was plunging into the warm depths—gone between one breath and the next. He groaned into Andoc's mouth, the noise swallowed as if it had never been.

A smaller finger replaced Andoc's under the necklet and tugged him away, guiding him around until Carivel's lips covered his. He gave himself over to them, letting them move him to and fro, never giving him a chance to get his breath back between deep, biting kisses. Eventually, Andoc's hand closed around his nape, bearing him down to the soft furs of the bedroll until he was sprawled on his stomach, a weak and shivering mass of *need*.

"We have you now, *amadi*. You can let go," Andoc said, with a final reassuring squeeze before his fingers trailed over the first few knobs of Senovo's spine and disappeared.

Before he could mourn the loss, Carivel's hip settled in his field of vision, cut across by a thin slash of firelight filtering in from outside. Her hand settled over the side of his head, thumb pressing slow circles into his temple and drawing a shuddering sigh from him.

"No need to think tonight," she said. "No need to worry. Now that we have you back, we will *never* let you go again."

Senovo nodded against her hip, trusting to their words. He didn't even attempt to fight the relieved tears that rose up to squeeze from the corners of his closed eyes without warning. There would be no more fighting tonight.

Andoc returned, and a trail of warm oil drizzled over his spine, sliding down to pool in the small of his back. Strong hands followed, kneading into muscles still drawn tight with the tension of weeks—*months*—of uncertainty and fear. Andoc pressed deep, and the noise that was torn from Senovo's lips sounded like a rusty gate hinge.

Carivel moved his plait of dark hair to the side and gathered up some of the oil on her own fingertips, then began a slow massage of the tight cords in his neck and shoulders. Her fingers dragged over the braided necklet, sometimes pressing it into his skin, sometimes sliding underneath it—always keeping him aware of its presence, and its significance.

After weeks of being exposed to the elements, the dry leather would soak up the oil even faster than his skin would, he thought idly, eyes sliding closed again under the dual assault.

Andoc was unrelenting, and Senovo's knotted muscles were no match for him. The sharp ache of probing fingers gave way to a trembling release of tension that made his head swim, as knot after knot surrendered and loosened. Carivel pressed gently into the delicate muscles behind the hinge of his jaw, and his body seemed to go warm and heavy all at once as everything melted into relaxation.

His soft moan was, in all probability, utterly obscene.

Senovo floated, safe and protected, while hands delved into the lax muscles of his arms and legs, still slick with oil as they pressed deep, leaving a tingling rush of blood in their wake. His body buzzed pleasantly, warm and *alive*.

Andoc's thumbs kneaded his instep—the soles of his feet were hard-callused now from weeks of running over dirt and stone. An oiled palm slid up his calf and guided his left leg up and out to the side, leaving him spread open. Oil dribbled into the exposed crease of his buttocks, and fingers followed, lighting sparks under his skin even as his limp form sank a fraction deeper into the bedroll.

Senovo was beyond everything — anticipation included. He lay in utter contentment, the muscles ringing his passage giving no more resistance at this point than any of the other muscles in his body. Andoc circled endlessly with two blunt fingers until the tips slid past the softened pucker as if of their own volition. A new haze of animal pleasure flooded Senovo's quiescent mind, soaking in and settling.

It grew deeper when Carivel rubbed the pad of her thumb over his lips and pressed inside, the weight heavy and grounding on his tongue. He suckled lazily; remembering the feeling of serenity at lying beneath the clear, warm water of the bath, looking up at the shining ripples above.

Andoc stretched him open slowly, pressing deeper until each movement brushed against the place inside him that set his mind flying. Senovo inhaled through his nose, smelling the clean, briny musk of Carivel's desire, and opened unfocused eyes. She was staring down at him with an expression of love so deep that it resembled pain, unshed tears shining in her eyes. Her right hand still cupped his chin, her thumb stroking inside his mouth. Her left delved between her own legs, playing across the sensitive flesh of her sex.

Another finger pressed into him from behind, and a frisson raced down Senovo's spine from the base of his neck to the place where he was being breached. His eyes rolled back, and he let them slide closed, attuned now to the small sounds indicating that both of his lovers were pleasuring themselves even as they slowly shattered him. The contents of his soul spilled out like oil from a cracked jar, only to be caught and held safely by the two people who would never, ever allow him to come to harm.

Another finger slipped inside him, his flesh giving way effortlessly to the stretch. Andoc pressed in further than he ever had before, his broad knuckles slipping inside Senovo's body, sliding deeper until his whole hand was enveloped except for his thumb.

Senovo trembled and keened around Carivel's flesh in his mouth as a strange, boneless climax crashed over him. A moment later, Andoc gasped, and ropes of hot spend branded Senovo's flank and buttocks. Next to him, Carivel sobbed and came, her hips nearly arching off the bedroll. Their hands on Senovo stayed still and gentle, however, never jostling him as they shuddered through their releases.

They cosseted him afterward like a newborn babe, and maybe he *was* new-born in a way, back into the world of men. Or maybe he wasn't—it hardly mattered. All that mattered now was bodies pressed against his among piles of warm fur and soft blankets, the dark and the quiet, and blessedly dreamless sleep.

✨ 👑 ✨

A night of surrender and release was, sadly, not a panacea, though part of him did seem to breathe easier for being properly reunited with his bondmates. The return to Draebard was just about as strange an experience as he'd expected it to be, and it was decidedly tempting to slip quietly into animal form for the journey rather than deal with the realities of *horses* and *wagons* and *belongings* and *people*.

Indeed, on the second night of travel, Senovo awoke between the others with a wide-jawed yawn and stretched luxuriously. He only realized when his front claws snagged in the blanket that he had shifted in his sleep, all unknowing. Carivel was propped on one elbow beside him, stroking a hand over the fur of his back.

Panic overtook him at the thought of having lost himself without even noticing, and he wrenched control of his body back with unwonted violence, gasping and choking in reaction as the wolf growled its discontent in the background.

Andoc startled awake on his other side, even as Carivel grabbed his shoulders to steady him.

"I'm sorry," he babbled, "I'm sorry, I didn't mean to—"

"What?" Andoc asked, still only half-awake. "*Amadi*? What's wrong?"

"He changed in his sleep, that's all," said Carivel, as if it was *nothing*, as if he hadn't just—

"Oh," Andoc said, relaxing back. He pulled Senovo down to rest against his chest and held him there while he tried to get his lungs back under control. "I suppose that's to be expected after everything."

Carivel curled around him from behind, throwing an arm over him so her hand rested on Andoc's stomach. "It's all right, Senovo. We've missed the wolf, too, you know. He's *you*, after all."

"Well... unless you're shedding," Andoc added, sleep already overtaking him. "In which case, I could live without loose fur in the bedroll..."

Senovo blinked, and shuddered, and tried to focus on breathing.

⚜

When the village of Draebard appeared in the distance, it stirred something deep in the human part of him. *Home.* The place that had taken him in. The people who had given him a reason to continue after he'd thought his life all but destroyed at the tender age of seventeen.

The reality, unfortunately, was overwhelming. If he'd thought the warriors' celebration the evening after the battle had been raucous, it was *nothing* compared to the jubilation of an entire village that had just heard of their success against the Empire. He thought that Andoc and Carivel tried to shield him from the press of excited humanity as best they could, but it was an impossible task. The villagers knew what Senovo had done, and now that it was apparent he had succeeded, he was assailed on all sides by people hugging him, kissing his cheek, slapping his back—

If he hadn't been so completely overtaken, he might have utilized some of the aura of authority Andoc had accused him of having—raised his voice, brought them to order. As it was, though, it was Andoc who bellowed, "Enough! He's been living in the wildlands as a wolf for months, people—let the poor man have some air!"

The mob receded somewhat, and Senovo tried to draw his dignity around him like a cloak. Too bad it felt more like a pair of torn and threadbare smallclothes.

"The gods' blessings be upon you," he managed, since that had seemed to work—more or less—during the celebration in the camp. Apparently, it would suffice for now as well, since the crowd erupted into cheers and whistles.

"Get him to the temple as quickly as you can," Andoc said under his breath to Carivel, who nodded and hustled him away.

It was probably vaguely ridiculous for the High Priest and the Horse Mistress to be darting behind buildings and through alleyways during a triumphant homecoming after the most significant military victory on the island of Eburos in living memory. Well… not *probably*. It was *certainly* ridiculous.

All that mattered to Senovo, though, was that the familiar sanctuary of the temple soon came within view, though there was a small crowd massed in the courtyard here, as well. But… this crowd wore robes of brown and light dun, and awaited his approach with calm serenity, not raucous excitement. Rather than cringe away, his inner wolf strained forward, eager to get to them. Feeling the change in him, Carivel let go of her grip on his arm.

Eiridan stepped forward and met him halfway, drawing him into an embrace. "Elder Brother," he said warmly, leaning back until he could examine Senovo and determine his state of wellbeing. "We have awaited your return."

Feldes joined them and clasped Senovo's hand. "High Priest. Welcome back."

The acolytes came forward hesitantly, and greeted Senovo one by one. As Crenelo excitedly reported on his upcoming ascension from acolyte to novice priest, there was a disturbance from inside the temple—running footsteps. Favian appeared at the door with Frella's hand clasped in his. The boy was wide-eyed and pale.

The air exited Senovo's lungs as if he'd been punched. *The cubs.* No, not cubs—the *children*. His family. The embodiment of what he'd sworn to protect, when he left his home and his humanity behind. Everything came crashing back in an avalanche of memory and comprehension when the two ran forward, and Senovo fell to his knees. The others made space for them as Favian and Frella flung themselves into his arms.

"Elder brother," Favian choked, burying his face against Senovo's shoulder. "Thank the gods."

"I missed you!" piped Frella. "I made another clay wolf for you while you were gone!"

Two more hands rested on Senovo's back. He glanced up to find that Andoc had somehow caught up with them, and now flanked him on his right side, while Carivel stood at his left.

Senovo gathered Favian and Frella closer. Tears of joy and relief slid down his face, unchecked. "I'm here," he said. "I'm *here*. It's all right now. I've come back to you."

finis

The Eburosi Chronicles continue in *The Lion Mistress*.

Curious about Andoc and Senovo's first meeting? Sign up at http://www.rasteffan.com/tec/ and get the free e-book prequel to the series delivered directly to your email inbox.

www.ingramcontent.com/pod-product-compliance
Lightning Source LLC
Chambersburg PA
CBHW060740210726
48292CB00012B/14